WITH BLOOD UPON THE SAND

THE

UPON

Also by Bradley P. Beaulieu:

The Song of the Shattered Sands

TWELVE KINGS IN SHARAKHAI
WITH BLOOD UPON THE SAND

*   *   *

OF SAND AND MALICE MADE

BRADLEY P. BEAULIEU

WITH BLOOD UPON THE SAND

Book Two of

The Song of the Shattered Sands

DAW BOOKS, INC.

DONALD A. WOLLHEIM, FOUNDER

375 Hudson Street, New York, NY 10014

ELIZABETH R. WOLLHEIM

SHEILA E. GILBERT

PUBLISHERS

www.dawbooks.com

This one's for Peter and Kathie Korth.
Thank you for all your support along the way.

The Great
SHANGAZI DESERT

THE GREA

Qarthüm

Ganahil

Samandar

THE THOUSAND TERRITORIES OF KUNDHUN

Çalabin

Baük

Sharakhai

Mazand

2016

N
W   E
S

0   100   200   300   400   500   600
Scale in leagues

◉ City   ⊙ Caravanserai   ···· Caravan Route

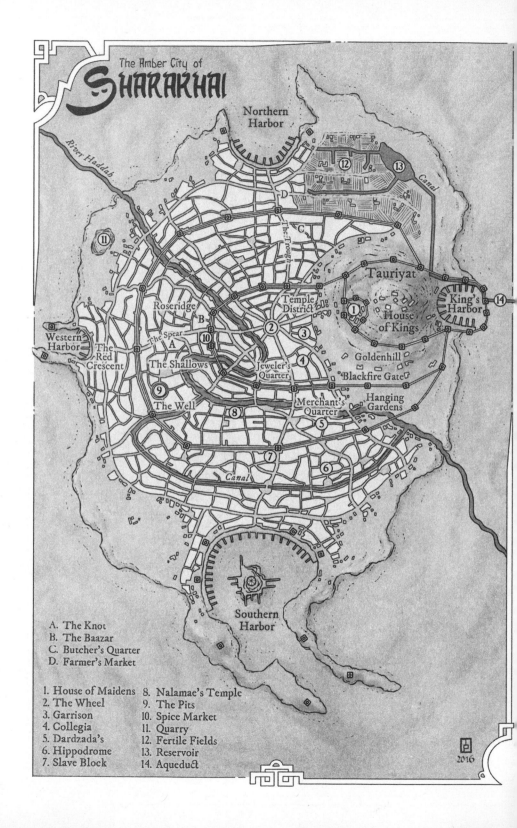

The Amber City of

SHARAKHAI

Northern Harbor

River Haddah

The Trough

D

C

Tauriyat

Temple District

King's Harbor

House of Kings

Roseridge

B

Goldenhill

Western Harbor

The Spear

A

Blackfire Gate

The Red Crescent

The Shallows

Jeweler's Quarter

Hanging Gardens

The Well

Merchant's Quarter

Canal

Canal

Southern Harbor

A. The Knot
B. The Baazar
C. Butcher's Quarter
D. Farmer's Market

1. House of Maidens
2. The Wheel
3. Garrison
4. Collegia
5. Dardzada's
6. Hippodrome
7. Slave Block
8. Nalamae's Temple
9. The Pits
10. Spice Market
11. Quarry
12. Fertile Fields
13. Reservoir
14. Aqueduct

2016

Chapter 1

CEDA CROUCHED, cradled in the branches of a well-tended fig tree, study-ing the movements of the Kings' soldiers, the Silver Spears, along the palace wall above. Staring up through the leaves, she measured their pace as they marched from tower to tower, noted how long and at which locations they tarried. She gave special attention to the changing of the guard, and was relieved that the same guards had been posted as on the other nights she'd hidden here. Most important, though, was their mood. She weighed it—as well as she could from a hundred feet below—and to her great relief, found them attentive, but no more than usual. Had they seemed more prepared, on edge in some way, she knew she would have been forced to abandon her plan to kill the King of Kings.

This great palace that sat atop Mount Tauriyat was named Eventide, and it was the home of Kiral, the King of Kings. Not only was it the highest and largest of Sharakhai's palaces, it was the most difficult to penetrate. Its walls stood higher than any other palace. Its western side was built atop a sheer rock face, making it near impossible for any sizable force to approach from that angle. Watch towers stood like sentinels every fifty paces, and the winding road leading up to it had a gorge spanned by a drawbridge that, unlike many of the other palaces on Tauriyat, was often raised.

Not that the palace had never been breached. With enough preparation, training, and, not least of all, patience, a woman or man could pierce any wall, gain any fortress. There were stories of the Moonless Host having done so many years ago. Whether or not they'd grown in the telling was anyone's guess, but one thing was certain: gaining the walls was only the first of their difficulties. There were the Silver Spears to contend with. There were the elite Blade Maidens, who protected the King. And there was the King himself who, even after four hundred years walking the sands of the desert, was still one of the Shangazi's most feared fighters.

Careful not to rock the leafy branches, Çeda leaned to one side to get a better look at a tall soldier marching along the parapet. A second Spear followed several paces behind, his helm and the tip of his tall spear glinting gold from the remains of the dying sun. From their high vantage, the two soldiers studied the vertical drop below them. Their gazes roamed the dry slope of the mountain. They stared out past the walls circumnavigating the whole of Tauriyat, to the sprawl of the Amber City. Çeda could see the city as well, an expanse of choked streets and mismatched buildings, of grand temples and leaning hovels. Some were old, some were new, some large, some small, some rich, some so decrepit they looked as if they'd crumble the moment the next sandstorm hit.

Çeda's heart drummed as a hot breeze picked up and wind tossed the leaves. One of the guards was staring right at her. The tree, one of dozens in a grove below Eventide, did much to hide her, as did her supple leather armor, which was dyed a mottled color that matched both the fig tree's bark and the rocky soil. She'd made the armor with padding that rounded her stomach, chest, and arms, making her appear bigger than she was. She'd bound her breasts and stuffed boots too large for her feet to make anyone who spotted her think she was a man. She was not only prepared to be seen before the night was done; she counted on it. Only, it wasn't supposed to happen *now*.

She stared at the guard, breathless, certain he'd spotted her, but a moment later he spat over the wall, said something to his comrade, and moved on, the two of them laughing with the sort of ease that was common to the shisha dens sprinkled all across the Amber City. Indeed, as if the thought had summoned the city awake, drums and music lifted into the warm evening air, some celebration now underway.

The Spears were soon lost from sight, swallowed by the gaping entrance of the next tower, and finally Çeda relaxed. Still, her confidence was beginning to erode. Where were the other Kings? They should have been here by now. The urge to abandon this plan as too bold and return to the House of Maidens was growing, but a night like tonight wasn't going to come again. She'd known weeks ago that she would come; it was practically a directive from the gods themselves, or if not the gods, then surely the fates.

When the sun set and the air began to cool, Çeda worried the moment had come and gone. Perhaps King Yusam's diary had been wrong. Or in her haste she'd noted the wrong date. But just then the sound of galloping horses drew her attention to King's Road, the paved road of endless switchbacks that wound its way like a serpent up the slopes of Tauriyat to each of the Kings' palaces. Twelve other palaces graced the mountain, but it was from Husamettín's, the King of Swords, palace that an honor guard of ten Blade Maidens and a large black wagon emerged.

A cavalcade of moths began to flutter in the space between Çeda's ribs as the wagon wended its way higher along the palace road. Eyes fixed on the wagon like an archer taking aim, Çeda pulled the teardrop necklace from inside her armor, took a white-and-blue adichara petal from within, and placed it under her tongue. She'd no sooner clipped the locket closed than her awareness began to expand.

Like the perfect unfurling of a freshly cut rose, more of the world became known to her. The conversations of the men and women preparing for the arrival of the other Kings—conversations hidden from her only moments ago—now drifted down from Eventide. The smell of roast meat filled the air, as did a savory mix of garlic, onion, and the sharp scents of lemon and coriander and sage. A thrill ran through her. Her physical form became vibrant, white hot. She *itched* to use it.

The most subtle effect, and the most dangerous on this particular night, was her awareness of the blooming fields. These were the groves of twisted trees, the vast ring around Sharakhai where the asirim slept. Like torches in the night, they brightened in her mind. Ever since she was young, when her mother had begun feeding her bits of pressed petals on holy days or during other rites of passage, she had been bonded to the adichara. She hadn't known their nature then, but she did now. She could feel the asirim in their slumber, could sense their tortured dreams.

She could call to them if she wished—they'd granted her that power—but that wasn't what she needed tonight. Like the guards above, it was imperative they remain unaware of her. After all, were the Jackal King to sense her presence here, all would be lost. So instead of calling to them, she distanced herself, becoming something ephemeral, spindrift lifting then lost.

The distant thump of horse hooves came louder as the wagon team and the Maidens' horses approached the entrance to Eventide. When they were lost from view and the clatter of the entrance bridge being lowered filled the cool night air, Çeda stared up at the palace wall and saw a lone guard standing at attention along the western side, facing inward.

Bless you, Nalamae.

Low and fast, she raced to the rock face. Upon reaching it she climbed, using the path she'd mapped for herself while waiting for the sun to set. Up she went, quickly, quietly, her body tight to the stone, arms and legs moving smoothly. She was a good climber without the power of the petals driving her, but with it, she reached the lower stone blocks of Eventide's walls in as little time as it took a man to piss. She moved slower then, careful to find space for the tips of her fingers to grip, for the edges of her boots to find purchase.

From within the walls, echoing up into a sky bursting with stars, came the sound of pounding hooves, of iron-rimmed wagon wheels rattling over stone. She approached the top of the wall and slowly raised herself until she could see the Silver Spear. With care, she drew a pre-knotted rope from around her waist and slipped one end over the merlon directly above her. The other end, wound into a noose, she held at the ready. She made a ticking sound and waited, controlling her breath, controlling her emotions. When the Spear remained standing at the ready, she made the sound again. This time he looked out over the wall, then down.

She was already swinging the rope up. It caught him neatly around the neck. Immediately she dropped, and the guard dropped with her. The noose cinched tight and he slipped over the side, arms scrabbling for purchase. His spear spun end over end toward the fig trees below. The rope went taut, and he swung like a headman's axe toward the wall. Çeda slid along the rope so that his weight struck her instead of crashing noisily against stone. Something along his belt bit into her stomach, but he made blessedly little sound as he slammed into her. A cough escaped her, loud enough that she might have been heard. She switched her grip from the rope to the collar of his hauberk. All her weight was on him now, the noose drawing even tighter. He tried to free himself, tried to draw the knife at his belt, but it was a simple matter to snatch his wrist. The noose was so tight he didn't so much as gurgle. She heard a popping sound, though, and then another. A moment later, his whole body went slack.

Like an ungainly ladder, she climbed his meaty frame until she was able to grab the rope, stand on his shoulders, and ascend once more. She prayed no cries of alarm would be raised as she slipped through the crenel and belly-crawled into the nearby tower.

Hearing none, she rose up until she could view the courtyard through the loophole in the tower. She watched as the wagon lurched to a stop. The team of horses at the lead shook their manes as four Blade Maidens dismounted and moved to stand beside the wagon. A footman in King Kiral's blue livery opened the wagon doors, and three men stepped out, the Maidens and the footman bowing their heads to each. The first was the tall form of Husamettín, King of Swords. Next came Mesut, the Jackal King, lord of the asirim. And lastly, Cahil, the Confessor King. Mesut and Cahil wore the fine clothes of the Kings of Sharakhai: khalats of vibrant cloth and thread of gold with turbans to match. In contrast, Husamettín wore simpler clothes—the utilitarian sort a desert shaikh might wear—but he had a most impressive sword at his side. Night's Kiss, the two-handed shamshir granted him by Goezhen himself.

Only when they had all exited the wagon did a fourth King appear. He came from the palace with three Blade Maidens waking in unison behind him. He was a tall, clean-shaven man. Even from this distance Çeda could see the pockmarks on his skin, evidence of some childhood disease that had struck well over four hundred years ago. This was Kiral himself, the one all the other Kings deferred to—or so Çeda had thought before entering the House of Maidens. She'd heard rumors of various rifts between the Kings since entering the House four months earlier. None of the other Kings would challenge his authority outright, but some would shed no tears were the Dawn King to topple from his lofty perch.

For a time the four Kings spoke, their conversation lost in the clop of hooves as the Maidens' horses were led away. The wagon, however, remained.

"Let's begin," Kiral said as the noise dwindled.

Çeda pulled the short bow from her shoulder as King Mesut nodded to the interior of the wagon. At this, a Silver Spear exited, holding a chain in one hand. When he drew on the chain, it clinked, and a woman stumbled into view. As she took the steps, her miserable state was revealed. The chain was affixed to a leather collar around her neck. She was gagged. Her hands were bound behind her, and her breath came jackal-quick. She was trembling, and yet she stood tall before King Kiral; she stared defiantly into his eyes.

Çeda had been pulling one of the four poison-tipped arrows from the quiver on her back, but she halted at this strange occurrence. Two months ago she'd stolen into King Yusam's private offices and read through his journal, the one he used to record the visions from the magical pool secreted away in his palace, his mere. The entries were snippets mostly, the most memorable bits and pieces he used to remind him of the things he'd seen. This meeting, on this particular day, had been mentioned several times. He had not, however, mentioned this woman, which meant either that he'd not seen it or had chosen to withhold it; she had no idea which it might be.

"Where shall we begin?" Mesut asked.

Çeda knew the answer even before Kiral waved to the patch of gravel situated between the greenhouse and the tower where she hid. The greenhouse had been mentioned in the journal.

Indeed, they moved to that exact location, four calm Kings and the terrified woman. "Kneel," Mesut said. When the woman didn't, Cahil kicked the backs of her legs out from under her so she fell to her knees. As he moved behind her and sliced through her bonds to free her hands, Çeda placed the arrow across her bow and nocked it. She held it at the ready, staring through the loophole in sick fascination. She thought of releasing the arrow now but, Nalamae forgive her, this was too important. She had to know more. The mere wouldn't have shown it to Yusam if it wasn't vital to him or the Kings or Sharakhai itself. If she revealed herself to soon, they would only perform this strange ritual another time, and she'd be none the wiser. So she waited as Cahil unstoppered a glass flask filled with a brown, muddy liquid. Waited as Mesut untied the gag and wrenched her head back. When they began pouring it down her throat, however, Çeda lifted the bow and drew the arrow back.

Finally, the flask was drained. Cahil stepped back, and Mesut let the woman go. She fell slowly to the ground, gripped in pain. She balled her hands into fists, struck them against the ground, as if waging a terrible battle within. But this was a battle already lost. Before Çeda's eyes, the woman's skin shriveled. Her cheeks grew sunken. Her hands became skeletal.

By Bakhi's bright hammer, what did Cahil give her?

Her own breath coming faster, Çeda sighted down the arrow, aiming for Kiral. She could kill him, here and now, assuming the wound from a single arrow and the poison on its tip would do their work against a man the gods themselves had seen fit to protect. She might take another of the Kings as well, maybe even three of them if the gods were kind.

Or she might put this woman out of her misery.

I should, she thought. And yet the arrow held steady, its point aimed squarely for Kiral's chest, indecision staying her hand.

Mesut stood beside the writhing woman. One of his sleeves was pulled back, revealing a bracelet of gold with a large black gem on it. The courtyard was deep in shadow, lit only by the braziers spaced throughout the grand courtyard, which was why Çeda was able to see the thin white cloud lifting from the gemstone.

It made the hair on her arms stand tall, made her insides twist. She wasn't even sure why, not until more of the stuff floated free and began to take form. It was a wight, she realized. She'd never seen one before. Not really. Only a glimpse in a boneyard when she was young. At the time she'd thought it her fear of that massive boneyard manifesting, the stories she, Emre, Tariq, and Hamid had told one another before going there with bravery in their hearts and a skin of wine to hand. The moment they'd seen a ghostly form floating above the grave marker, though, all the bravery the wine had lent them vanished like summer rain, and they'd fled. It had been a harmless day, even a fun day.

Here, in the courtyard of Eventide, it was anything but.

The wight drifted forward, guided by Mesut's outstretched hand. The woman stared at its approach, her screams maniacal now. At a wave from Mesut—a thing so akin to a pleasant introduction it made Çeda sick—the wight touched her. Immediately, the woman went silent, rigid as stone. With a measured pace not unlike a bone crusher ripping meat off one of its kills until it was sated, the wight slipped inside her. Then it dissipated and was gone.

For long seconds, all was silence. But then, as if she were rotting from the inside out, the woman's skin began to darken. Like a dirty wet rag left to dry in the sun, her already-tight skin drew in further, until she looked almost indistinguishable from the asirim, the sad creatures that lived beneath the groves of adichara trees far out in the desert. Çeda had been purposely masking her presence from the asirim, but she could hardly ignore the woman below, who shone like a beacon in her mind, shedding darkness instead of light. The woman was one of them now, and they were calling to her: a paean to her pain, but also a welcome to their clan.

Breath of the desert, the Kings had *created* an asir. What Cahil had given her, what the true nature of Mesut's golden band was, she didn't know, but she was certain they'd taken a living woman and re-created the spell the gods had placed on the asirim four hundred years ago on Beht Ihman.

Without knowing why, she realized her awareness of the asirim was strengthening. She tried to suppress it, fearing that Mesut, lord of the asirim, would sense her, but in the end it wasn't the Jackal King who found her, but the woman. She lifted her head and stared directly at the loophole through which Çeda was watching this grisly scene. The doomed woman lifted her skeletal hand and pointed. The moment she did, Çeda aimed and released her arrow.

The arrow flew true, directly for Kiral's chest, but Mesut stepped in front of him and snatched the arrow from the air, spinning in a blur as he did so. Another arrow was already on its way. This one caught Cahil across one cheek. The third arrow flew toward Husamettín, but he was already drawing Night's Kiss. He swept it in a broad arc, slicing the arrow in two as he dodged fluidly to one side.

She couldn't afford to shoot the fourth arrow. Mesut was already running toward the tower. The Maidens were charging as well. A dozen Silver Spears were converging along the curtain walls from the other towers.

Çeda turned and took two long strides from the tower to throw herself over the merlon where her rope was tied. Grabbing the near lip of the stone, she controlled her motion and dropped straight down, then grabbed the rope and slipped along its length. She slid until she reached the Silver Spear's lifeless form, at which point she climbed down his body, held on to his booted ankles, and dropped. She flattened herself against the steeply sloping stone and was able to slow her descent somewhat. Her light armor scraped with a sizzling sound. Something burned bright along her right shin as the leather tore through, but she reached level ground a moment later.

Taking a bag from her shoulder, she unfastened the tie and quickly began spreading the contents: dozens and dozens of caltrops. She scattered them generously along the ground in the most likely places for the Maidens or the Kings to drop down.

Above, she saw silhouettes—a trio of Blade Maidens—just as a bell began to ring from within the palace walls. She'd hoped to have more time before the whole of Tauriyat woke, but there was nothing for it now.

She turned and sprinted through the trees. Whether the Maidens were caught by the caltrops she didn't know. She heard no cry of alarm, but once or twice she heard running along the dry slope behind her. They were swift, even in the darkness, likely having taken petals of their own by now, but Çeda was well ahead, and she'd plotted her course carefully over the past several weeks, ever since reading Yusam's journal.

Her own petal powered her on, also granting her the sharp vision she needed to run full speed and avoid tripping over the stones that littered the landscape.

As she knew they would, other bells began to ring, more palaces picking up the alarm. *"Lai, lai, lai!"* she heard from behind, a demand for her to stop. But she could tell it was also a feint. There were other Maidens closer, hoping to catch her unaware.

She approached the walls around Tauriyat. She could see, faintly, several more Maidens running along the tops of the walls to intercept her. This had always been the weakest part of her plan. She couldn't predict how many

Maidens might be waiting along the walls. One Maiden was standing directly ahead, Çeda saw now. Without breaking stride, she drew her bow, nocked the last arrow, and released on the run. It struck the Blade Maiden through the neck. She fell backward off the wall, a short cry of surprise and pain going with her.

Çeda's lungs burned, but she pushed harder, soon reaching the stone where she'd secreted a rope and grapnel. She swung it through the air in widening circles as she neared the wall. Slowing only for a moment, she put her whole body into an almighty launch of the hook. The rope snaked through the moonlit night, and the hook caught on the far battlements with a clank. Then she was pulling herself up along the inside of the wall. After gaining the walk, she launched herself over the battlements and into Sharakhai proper.

She stood along the eastern edge of the city, near the temple district. Ahead was the old city—a maze of ancient buildings and drunken streets, built as they were for a city from a different age. She'd no more made it to a bend in the street than she heard behind her the thud of booted feet against stone, the pounding of swift strides.

Ahead, more bells rang, this time from the garrison, the largest and oldest of the Silver Spears' holdings. She ran toward those bells, a thing most would think terribly foolish, but she'd carefully chosen her exit along the wall so that the Spears might be drawn into the search as well. It would, she hoped, only add to the confusion and mask what she was about to do.

She sprinted along a short, dark street that led to an intersection of three others. Halfway down the street, a rope hung from a stone signpost advertising a Mirean leechman. When she came near, she leapt and seized the rope with both hands. Though her momentum sent her to swinging like a pendulum, legs dangling like a wooden doll's, she climbed as quick as she could and clambered onto the beam. After coiling the rope on top of the beam, she slipped over the edge of the roof.

Lying flat, she controlled her breathing and prayed that none of her pursuers would spot the rope, nor see the sign swaying, as she'd knocked it with her leg on the way up. Staring at the sky, she heard bootsteps along the street below. In moments they'd reached the intersection of streets. One hushed conversation later, they resumed, and soon had faded altogether. All around, sounds were waking the city that had been settling for slumber. The clatter of metal. Horse hooves ringing over stone. Soldiers mobilizing. The sharp orders from men and women alike.

At the corner of the darkened roof, Çeda unwrapped a bundle she'd hidden a week earlier. She pulled out her Blade Maiden's uniform: a black battle dress, a turban, leather boots, and her shamshir, River's Daughter. She stripped off her leather armor, shed the padding and the binding around her chest, and pulled on the clothes she'd been wearing nearly every day these past four months. She was a Blade Maiden once more. The leather armor, the bow, and the quiver she rolled tightly together and stuffed into a clay downspout on the outside of the building. The padding and cloth binding she took to the far side of the roof and dropped into the trash bin of a tailor's shop. The clothes might be found and they might not. If they were, the Maidens would likely assume one of the Moonless Host had tried to assassinate the Kings, and with any luck they'd think it was a *man* who'd changed garb in order to melt into the city. And if the clothes remained unfound, well, all the better.

As she lay there, staring at the moonless sky, any relief she felt at still being alive was soured by the realization of how badly she'd failed. Kiral. By the gods, she'd wanted Kiral. His death would have sent every court on Tauriyat into chaos. It would have lain to rest the notion, even more so than King Külaşan's death, that the Kings were immortal. Husamettín would have been nearly as good, since he and his Blade Maidens had been the cause of so much pain in Sharakhai and the desert beyond. She'd failed to deliver a killing strike against Cahil, but at least the arrow had nicked him. The poison she'd used paralyzed in seconds, killed within minutes. Surely not even a King could stand against it.

She had to admit, though, however short of reaching her goals she might have fallen, the night hadn't been a complete loss. She knew more about the Kings than she had that morning. She knew how utterly fast they were. She'd seen how they reacted. She had underestimated them, but she wouldn't do so again.

The sound of boots approached once more. A hand of Maidens moved like ghosts beneath her. When they reached the same crossing, they took the left fork. The moment they were out of sight, Çeda slipped over the edge of the roof, dropped to the street, and sprinted after the Maidens. She caught up to them just as they were meeting a contingent of ten Silver Spears. Çeda whistled, a request to be apprised of the situation, an implied request for orders from the commanding officer, in this case a tall warden of the Blade Maidens. Two more Maidens arrived behind her, one giving the same whistle.

The warden, who'd been speaking to the captain of the Spears, turned to them. "You three," she barked to Çeda and the new arrivals, "follow the Raven Road, then swing down along the Trough. Question anyone you find in the streets. We're searching for a man, short, wearing light leather, possibly armed with a bow, so take care. We'll meet at the Wheel after a sweep of our own."

Çeda and the other two Maidens nodded, and then they were off, running back the way they'd come toward the road that wound through the temple district. As they did, Çeda began to breathe easier. They would search the city—likely they would search the whole night through—but they'd not find the assassin. Not this night.

Chapter 2

Ramahd Amansir swam along the shore of the Austral Sea. The sea rolled beneath him, the swell rhythmic, calm as a baby's cradle, though darkness brewed to the south. Ramahd turned his back to the gathering storm and swam for the black sandy beach and the gray cliffs of his estate, Viaroza, that dominated the distant horizon. Between that beach and Ramahd sprawled a swath of sea so blue it made his heart ache just to see it. How he'd missed the calm of a simple swim, the way the water chilled him even as his muscles warmed to the effort. His body felt perfectly in tune with the waves, the cadence of his strokes playing against the swells' broader rhythms. The smell of the salty sea was sublime—the call of the white gulls, the chill of the water, so very different from the Great Shangazi.

How exotic those days seemed now. How mundane they'd become back then. The months he'd spent chasing his wife and child's killer had made the city of Sharakhai feel like a ship adrift, his purpose there a current carrying him farther and farther from his homeland. As much as it had pained him to admit, his life in Qaimir, one of the four kingdoms surrounding the Shangazi Desert, had become little more than a rapidly dimming memory in the face of that bleak, sun-blinding place. Strangely, though, after taking their prize near King Külaşan's hidden desert palace—Külaşan's own son, the blood mage, Hamzakiir—and returning home with Princess Meryam, his world had suddenly felt whole again, as if he'd never left Qaimir's mountains, her green foothills, the shore of the Austral Sea. The endless desert days, the heartache for his wife and child, the hunt for Macide, the unforgiving, unrelenting heat—he'd shaken it all off like sand from a cloak upon reaching Qaimir's capital, Almadan, and by the time he'd reached Viaroza on the edge of the Endless Sea, his sense of home had returned and it was the *desert* that had become the stuff of dreams.

There was one notable exception. Hamzakiir. He was a constant reminder of Sharakhai. Of the Kings. Of the fact that they were playing with fire by keeping him alive. Meryam's plan had always been to use Hamzakiir. It had been why they'd gone to the desert to make their bargain with the ehrekh, Guhldrathen; why they'd gone to King Külaşan's desert palace to wrest control of him from the Moonless Host; why Meryam had been trying to dominate his mind from the moment they'd crossed the border into Qaimir. He would be a powerful tool indeed, full of ancient knowledge the King of Qaimir could use to protect their homeland, or unleash against Sharakhai should they threaten Qaimir, or, as Ramahd suspected Meryam preferred, launch an assault against the Kings of Sharakhai for control of the desert. Meryam had claimed Hamzakiir would weaken quickly, that she would have him in no time at all, but Hamzakiir had resisted all attempts to dominate him, then and now.

Ramahd shook his head as memories came unbidden. The look of grim defiance on Hamzakiir's face as Meryam tried to tear down the walls within him. The shaking of his weak and wasted frame. The growing cries of pain. They were memories that haunted Ramahd's dreams, made his waking hours a chore. A constant reminder of all they'd abandoned in the desert so Meryam could play god. It was why Ramahd came to the sea to swim, as he'd done when he was young. To forget. To wrap himself in something other than pain and regret and sheer, unyielding will. But lately, even this, the steadfast refuge of the sea, was slowly being eroded by thoughts of those interminable sessions in the dungeon of Viaroza, and he hated Hamzakiir all the more for it.

Mighty Alu, how was it that Hamzakiir could still resist? Ramahd himself felt such a tattered remnant when Meryam finished her interrogations, and if *he* felt so, how could Hamzakiir stand against her day after day?

"It cannot last," Meryam told him only a week ago.

Ramahd had laughed bitterly. "The question has never been whether it can last, Meryam, but who will break first."

Meryam stared deeply into his eyes, and for a moment she'd seemed so much larger than the shivering, skeletal form he saw before him. "I will never break."

Ramahd had said nothing. Those four simple words were a talisman against the task before her, but they'd both heard the desperation in her voice. Years ago he would never have doubted Meryam's resolve, nor her abilities, but Hamzakiir was much stronger than either of them had guessed, and Meryam was weakening. How pitiful she looked, lying in bed wearing a sweat-stained nightdress, how battered. He thought surely she would crumble under the weight on her shoulders, and yet each time he carried her down to the dungeon, she pushed herself ever harder.

He didn't doubt her desire—that was strong as ever, perhaps more so now that she was close to breaking him—but her body was failing her. One day soon it would break, and then where would they be? Likely Ramahd would end up having to draw a knife across Hamzakiir's throat for the danger he represented, but that would leave the grim pact Meryam had made in the desert with the ehrekh, Guhldrathen, unfulfilled. She'd promised to deliver Hamzakiir to that infernal creature. She'd promised her own life as forfeit if she failed. Would the creature accept a dead body, its lifeblood drained? Likely not, and the gods only knew what it would do then. It might demand Ramahd's life as well, or even King Aldouan's, in recompense for the one he'd lost. There was no telling with such creatures.

Over Ramahd's shoulder, the dark clouds advanced like infantry. The wind drove harder, sending salty spray into the air. White froth now tipped the deep blue waves. Having no wish to be caught in a squall, he made for shore with longer strokes, with stronger kicks. He swore in those moments he could hear Hamzakiir's cries of anguish mixing with the dull roar of the surf around him. *A trick of the wind, those dark hours haunting me even here.*

And yet, not three breaths later, he spotted a man with dark hair and a billowing white shirt climbing down the stairs carved into the black rock of the cliff face. It was his first mate, Dana'il, and he was moving with haste. Ramahd swam harder, fear for Meryam chilling him more than the sea ever could. By the time he reached shore, the waves were thick with foam. Salt spray crashed high in the air. After climbing from the water to reach a stone jetty where a yacht and three smaller fishing ships were moored, Ramahd took the folded cotton towel from atop his pile of clothes and began drying his naked form.

By then Dana'il was sprinting along the jetty. "My lord, it's Meryam," he said as he came near. "She woke this morning and . . . She asked that I stand in for you today."

Ramahd tied his trousers, pulled his shirt quickly over his head. "After I ordered you not to?"

"Forgive me, my lord, yes." He rushed his words, clearly chagrined. "She insisted. She told me she'd choose someone else if I wouldn't join her. And . . ." He was staring at Ramahd with pity in his eyes.

"What is it?" Ramahd asked.

"I . . . I only thought to spare you from—"

Ramahd waved him into motion. "What's done is done." Together they walked side by side toward the cliffs. "Tell me what happened."

"Of course, my lord. It was"—Dana'il's soft features contorted into a haunted grimace—"difficult. For her, I mean, not me. She told me after I'd carried her back upstairs that she'd made a breakthrough. She'd wore him down, more than ever before. I thought surely she would sleep, but she grabbed my wrist, holding me there, and told me she needed urgently to speak with you. I tell you, I've never seen anything like it. She was in a fey mood, and the desperation in her eyes . . . She had that look of hers, the one that makes you feel mortal. I feared for her life even as she lay there safely in bed. I feared for yours as well."

"But why the urgency, Dana'il? She can't possibly mean to try again now."

"My lord, she *does* mean to. Something new, she told me."

This didn't feel right. It didn't feel right at all. "Give me her exact words."

"She said to fetch you, to say it was time for you to pull the rope as well."

He rolled his eyes, then fixed his gaze on the castle above. "How many times have I offered?" he said under his breath.

"I'm sorry, my lord?"

"Never mind."

The wind driving them, they made their way toward the cliff while, out to sea, the clouds gathered their might.

The wind, Ramahd thought. *How the wind will howl tonight.*

Meryam detested it when Ramahd helped her eat or drink, but he couldn't watch her struggle any longer. Sitting by her bedside, he cradled the back of her head while pressing a glass of honeyed goat's milk to her lips. She sipped, nostrils flaring, eyes staring fixedly at the painting of a mountain fastness on the wall. *Gaunt,* was all he could think while watching her drink. *So very gaunt.* He'd thought of leaving and forcing her to sleep until she'd regained her strength, but he'd decided on the climb up that he'd listen before making his decision.

When she finished the milk, she licked her lips and patted Ramahd's hand. "Well enough," she said, and he lowered her gently back down. Her eyelids were heavy. She wouldn't remain awake much longer. Despite the urgency she'd shown to Dana'il, she now seemed calm, perhaps appeased now that Ramahd had arrived.

"Tell me why you've summoned me here," Ramahd said.

"Because I need your help."

"You know you have but to ask."

Meryam chuckled, a tumble of stones. It became a wracking cough, but thankfully it was soon over. Her sunken eyes turned wicked. "Be careful what you offer, dear brother. You mightn't like what comes of it."

Brother, she often called him, though they weren't related. It was one small remnant of the days when Ramahd had been married to Meryam's sister, Yasmine. He'd called *her* sister as well. He'd liked their little ritual then, the two of them giving sly smiles to Yasmine, who was endlessly annoyed by it, but now it only served to remind Ramahd of the wife he'd lost in the desert, the daughter who had followed her mere days later.

"I'm well aware of the dangers, *sister.* What is it you wish? Shall we take up your father, the king's, offer? Bring others from Almadan to assist?"

Meryam waved at the air as if the suggestion were an annoyance akin to a buzzing insect. "No. What I need is your mind. Your will."

"Mine?" Ramahd crossed his arms over his chest, the chair creaking beneath him. "What can *I* do where you have failed?"

"And here we arrive at the difficulty. Hamzakiir was buried half dead and left for decades beneath Külaşan's palace. When he was raised by Macide and his men, he hungered for blood. He *still* hungers. I thought I could use that to my advantage. I've been pressing him each time we wage battle, but he's wary, Ramahd. And wily. A dozen times I thought I had him, but each time he retreats into his mind, and today he nearly turned the tables on me."

"Then we should wait. Give you time to regain your strength while we starve him."

Meryam scowled. "No. He is weak from my efforts. If we give him time to rest, *he* will regain strength as well. How he lives without sustenance, I do not know. Likely it was part of the bargain he made with Guhldrathen, and surely it's the very thing that kept him alive for so many years in the catacombs. I would give him no respite."

"Then what can I do?"

"I need bait, Ramahd."

Ramahd was not entirely surprised by the response, but the way she'd said *bait*, like *she* hungered for it as well, made him wonder how close to the end of her energies she really was. "You want me to draw him out."

Meryam nodded. "To draw him out, and in so doing leave him vulnerable."

"How?"

"With blood, dear brother. Yours."

"You wish me to give my own blood to a man who could kill us the moment he frees himself?"

"It's that or kill him and be done with it."

"Exactly what I've been saying since we took him in the desert. Let's return there and throw him at Guhldrathen's feet, then hunt for Macide as we've promised to do."

Meryam was already shaking her head, her body quivering terribly. "Even if I wished it, and I don't, my father would not allow it. Hamzakiir is a valuable piece on the aban board. The king will not throw him away so easily."

"Guhldrathen is a threat that grows every day, endangering us all."

"So dramatic. *I* may be threatened by the ehrekh. You may be. But he hardly threatens *us all*."

Ramahd took a deep breath. He wasn't going to argue again. Meryam wouldn't change her mind, and neither would her father. "When?"

Meryam smiled, nodding at him as if he were some prized nephew who had just taken a splendid turn at archery. "I would begin now."

Ramahd had thought Dana'il foolish for thinking so. Even now he thought Meryam was making light, but when she didn't return his smile, he knew she was sincere. "You can't be ready so soon."

"He is particularly weak."

"*You* are particularly weak."

"I don't wish to delay. I know I look frail, brother, but I am more ready than I have ever been. Together, you and I will break him."

He was ready to deny her out of hand. She normally took days to recover, and even then it felt as if she were pushing herself to the point of recklessness. "Why is it so important to do this now?"

"Because I nearly have him."

He tried to measure her words and her will, but he knew little of the red ways. Meryam must see some particular weakness in Hamzakiir she wished to exploit. Weak she may be, but Hamzakiir may be even weaker. Had they not been starving him all this time? And surely Meryam's dogged determination to break him had chipped away at Hamzakiir's defenses.

"Very well," Ramahd said at last. "If you think it's best."

"Oh, I do," she said, her dark eyes twinkling. "I do indeed."

In one corner of a cell beneath Black Swan Tower, the burning coals of a brazier cast a deep red light against the ceiling and walls. The air smelled of dampness and mildew. The contrast of the cold from the sea to the chill found here in the dungeon was stark. His swims were invigorating. His time spent here in the dungeon of Viaroza, however, never failed to cut him to the bone, as if the men and women and children who'd died in this place were still hanging on, refusing to go to the farther fields, preferring instead to reach for the hearts of living men with their spectral hands.

At the center of the cell Meryam leaned into a large padded chair. Dana'il stood by her side, ready to support her should she begin to fail. Facing her was a monstrosity of a chair, a veritable throne with dark leather straps, its wood stained indelibly by the blood of those who'd fallen into its unforgiving embrace, and within it sat Hamzakiir, the straps and their buckles holding him tight. Ramahd stood before this strange tableau—a healthy man, a broken woman, and an undying prisoner—wondering again if he'd made the right choice. It wasn't too late to change his mind. He could deny Meryam. He could lift the razor he held loosely in one hand and slit Hamzakiir's throat. And yet he remained silent, hoping desperately that this would all be over today.

Hamzakiir's head lolled forward, his lank hair hanging down to cover his face. He was so still many would think him dead, but Ramahd knew the signs: the sluggish movements of his eyes, the glacial expansion of his chest. His pulse could only be felt in the large veins along his neck, and even then seemed far too slow, far too weak to keep a man alive. He was like the golems the holy men of Malasan were said to create. And yet Ramahd knew he was anything but weak. For all Meryam had done to him, he was still a keenly dangerous man. *We play with fire*, Ramahd thought, *me and Meryam and her father, the King of Qaimir*. But what was there to do now but harness it lest it burn down everything around them?

"Come closer," Meryam said, flicking her fingers.

Ramahd complied. His gut churned at being so close to this broken remnant of a man. It was the same reaction he had to the asirim of Sharakhai, but somehow Hamzakiir felt more threatening. The asirim were simple creatures of rage, while Hamzakiir, if the stories of him were true, was filled with calculation, ambition, even hubris, qualities infinitely more dangerous.

When Dana'il held out a glazed bowl, roughly equidistant between Meryam and Hamzakiir, Meryam pointed a crooked finger to Ramahd. "Now . . ."

Ramahd stepped forward and held his right arm over the bowl. He lifted the razor and pressed its edge against his skin. Not twenty minutes ago, he'd used it to lay a wound across his left arm so that Meryam might drink of his blood in preparation for this, the second part of their ritual. He drew the razor back, creating a twin to the other wound. An intense burn came a moment later. Blood flowed. It pooled at the bowl's center, pattered against the cerulean glaze.

"Enough," Meryam said after a time.

Ramahd took the fresh bandage over his right arm and wrapped the wound, quickly and efficiently.

"Now lift his head."

Ramahd did, and Dana'il lifted the bowl with Ramahd's blood to Hamzakiir's lips. Hamzakiir was unresponsive for a time. His eyes were closed. A long, stained beard hung from his chin and his long, gaunt cheeks. But then his throat worked. His mouth parted.

"Be ready," Meryam said. "I will help, but you must hold him at bay for as long as you're able."

Ramahd's heart beat madly. Give him a sword. Give him a place to meet his enemy on the field of battle. As common as the *arcanos di crimson* was in Qaimir, he'd never been completely comfortable with it, even with Meryam, a woman he mostly trusted. It was far worse to be entwining his soul with a man like Hamzakiir, no matter that Meryam was here to protect him.

Dana'il stood across from Ramahd, holding the bowl steady, his eyes darting between Ramahd, Meryam, and Hamzakiir. There was fear in his eyes, and in the way he stood stock-still, tight as a bowstring, ready for whatever might come. The two of them had agreed beforehand that if things grew out of hand, he'd be given leave to plunge a knife into Hamzakiir's chest. Ramahd gave him a quick nod, and Dana'il nodded back. Ever stout was Dana'il, ever faithful.

Hamzakiir lifted his head, the chair's leather straps creaking as he strained against them. Eyes still closed, his head craned forward, as if it were a reaction he had no control over. Dana'il tilted the bowl up, a determined look on his face. Hamzakiir drank of the blood, tentatively at first. He swallowed, once, twice. The fresh wound along Ramahd's right arm flared to life, then immediately began to feel cool, then cold. Soon it was as though his right arm had been plunged into a cask of ice water.

Her eyes still fixed on Hamzakiir, Meryam said, "Sit down, Ramahd."

There was another chair in the corner, but Ramahd refused to move. "I will stand for this, Meryam."

She shrugged. "As you will."

Hamzakiir swallowed more blood. His eyes twitched beneath their lids. Ramahd felt his fingers going numb. The deep chill traveled up his right shoulder, across his chest, and down his left arm—the connection being formed between these two with him as the crude conduit.

Meryam had prepared him, but to feel it . . . The clawing cold spread to his chest, his torso, his legs and feet. Only when the cold ran through every part of him did a growing presence make itself known. At first it was nothing he could pinpoint, but rather a thing that encompassed the room, filled the darkness within it. It was a primal thing, a thing every man feared whether he wished to admit it or not. It was vast, this presence. Powerful. Undeniable, like the moons as they rose from the horizon in the dead of night.

Years ago, Ramahd had been dumped from a ship near the cold southern islands of the Austral Sea. Those desolate places were rimed with ice, scoured by the unforgiving wind. It had taken him long minutes to swim back to the ship, and by the time he'd regained the deck, his body had ceased shivering, which the ship's physic had said was a terrible sign. They'd taken him below-decks to dry him off and warm him. His movements, no matter how small, had felt like ice picks being driven through chinks in his frozen skin, fracturing him bit by bit.

The experience was not so different from what he felt in that cell below Viaroza, only it was much worse, for while he felt the same sort of physical pain, he also felt torn between two wills, Meryam's and Hamzakiir's. They were powerful in ways he hadn't fully comprehended, as if they'd been slumbering beasts, aeons lost, and now had risen and were girding for battle.

Meryam's breath came sharp and quick. "Have you returned to us?"

Her voice was calm, but Ramahd knew how hard she was fighting—he could feel the battle raging within him. Hamzakiir's strength was terrible, and it made Ramahd wonder at the sort of horror he might become if given the chance to heal. Ramahd had no hope of stopping such a thing; he prayed to Alu that Meryam did.

Indeed, her presence strengthened, a bastion against the coming storm. Dana'il's right hand now rested along the handle of his fishing knife. His look questioned Ramahd, but it was not yet time. Ramahd shook his head. Dana'il swallowed, eyes flitting like a cornered fox, first to Hamzakiir, then to Meryam. He motioned to Ramahd's right hand. The white bandage had somehow come loose. Blood trickled down Ramahd's fingers to tap against the grimy stone floor. Only then did he feel the warmth of it, a failing brand against a growing winter storm.

Hamzakiir slowly lifted his head. His pepper-gray hair hung around his face. His eyes seemed to have difficulty focusing, but then they came to rest on Meryam, and hardened. "Well, well," he said, his voice a bitter groan from long disuse. "The child from Qaimir."

"I found you for a reason, Hamzakiir. Do you not wish to know it?"

"I'll not speak to my captors as though they were equals. Release me, Meryam shan Aldouan, and we may talk. Do not, and I will free myself."

"Listen to me now," Meryam said, ignoring his words. "Listen . . ."

And Meryam spoke, though what she might have said, Ramahd couldn't say. He was feeling light-headed, and was having a difficult enough time simply keeping his feet under him. He breathed more deeply, feeling the bond running through him from Meryam to Hamzakiir. The two were fully linked now, though whether Meryam was getting what she desired from it, he couldn't say. What kept scratching away at his mind, however, was how she'd pressed, how she'd changed her own pattern after weeks of effort plodding in the same dogged fashion. Meryam, always so persistent. And that gleam in her eye when Ramahd had finally assented, as if she were pleased but didn't wish him to know it.

Eyelids impossibly heavy, Ramahd swung his head toward Hamzakiir, who looked stronger now, more able to sit his chair. Meryam was no longer speaking. It was Hamzakiir who spoke, whispering while Meryam listened, rapt. Dana'il had an expression of naked worry. He'd drawn his knife. He gripped it tightly in his right hand, holding it as if ready to drive it into Hamzakiir's chest but for whatever reason had decided against it. He caught Ramahd looking at him, eyes pleading for Ramahd to do something, to understand the danger they were all in.

But Ramahd didn't. Not until Hamzakiir looked up and asked Ramahd to unbuckle his straps. Only when Ramahd complied, his mind going through motions he knew to be very, very wrong, did he begin to understand what was happening, but there was a veil over his mind and his thoughts, preventing him from doing anything about it. Hamzakiir gave more commands, though what they might have been Ramahd had no idea. He saw himself helping Hamzakiir out of the chair, walking him slowly out of the room, up the stairs, and into the castle proper. He led Hamzakiir to the Lord's chambers, *his* own bedroom. And there he pulled back the bedcovers, helped Hamzakiir into the bed, and settled the blankets over him as if Hamzakiir were Ramahd's own grandfather who'd taken sick.

"Go now," Hamzakiir said easily, "I need my rest, but wake me on the morrow. There's much to do before we leave for the desert. And return for your sister. She'll be cold, I expect." He smiled absently and patted Ramahd's sticky, blood-covered hand. "We wouldn't wish her to catch cold."

Ramahd nodded, bowing his way out of the room. He returned to the dungeon beneath the tower. Meryam was as she'd been, sitting and staring at the empty chair across from her. Hadn't someone been sitting there? He was distracted by the form of a man lying on the floor. Ramahd stared at those lifeless eyes, the knife held loosely in one hand. A wide, gaping wound ran across his abdomen. His entrails lay spilled across the floor like coils of bloody rope.

How odd, Ramahd thought, for a man to do such a thing. Who the man might be Ramahd had no idea. He looked familiar, but Ramahd couldn't place him. Some thief, no doubt, given the punishment he deserved.

Ramahd turned to Meryam, who studied the empty chair, eyes agape. "What have I done?" she voiced in a breathy, quavering whisper.

"What did you say?" Ramahd asked.

She looked up to him, a hard sort of understanding forming in her eyes, but then the look faded. "I'm so very cold, Ramahd. Take me upstairs, won't you?"

"Of course," Ramahd said, and lifted her from her chair.

Chapter 3

A BROAD BLUE SKY HUNG over Sharakhai as Çeda headed down along
King's Road toward the House of Maidens. She rode her mare, Brightlock, a beautiful akhala with a copper coat and a tail and mane of sanded
brass.

Nearly three weeks had passed since her failed assassination attempt, and
the days that followed had unfolded in a strangely surreal manner. The Matrons had questioned her about her involvement that night, but seemed satisfied with the story she gave them: that she'd been out for a walk, that she'd
heard the bells, that she'd come running as fast as she could to join the hunt.
Dozens of other Blade Maidens were questioned, but what might have come
of them, Çeda never learned. Life seemed to go on as if little had changed.
The Maiden who'd died had been given a night of honor, one in which those
who knew her had sung songs, had told stories around a fire, but few others
would have guessed a Maiden had been killed. Even in the city, where the
Spears were searching for clues, Çeda heard rumor that it was not as exhaus-
tive or cruel as it might have been.

Çeda could think of only two reasons the Kings would suppress the
knowledge that an assassin had gained the walls of Eventide. The first and

most obvious was that several of the Kings had nearly been killed; surely they had no desire, so soon after King Külaşan's assassination, to reveal weakness of any sort. Could it be, then? Had Cahil lost his battle against the poison? She regretted the deaths of the Silver Spear and the Blade Maiden, but if Cahil had died then it would have been worth it.

The only other possible reason for their uncharacteristic ease was that they wanted no scrutiny brought on the grizzly ritual they'd performed. All in Sharakhai knew of the asirim, but precious few knew much beyond the story the Kings had fed them: that they were holy defenders of Sharakhai, that they'd sacrificed themselves on the night of Beht Ihman to save the city from the might of the desert tribes. Certainly they wished for secrecy. They'd sacrificed a woman. Created an asir in the bargain. Çeda had wondered often who that woman had been, and the only reasonable explanation was that she'd been a daughter of the thirteenth tribe. They'd taken someone with the blood of the lost tribe and used her to create another asir, a slave, a weapon to wield in their war against the Moonless Host. It made some sense in the context of the poem Çeda had discovered in her mother's book, which she had little doubt referred to King Mesut:

> *The King of Smiles,*
> *from verdant isles,*
> *the gleam in moonlit eye;*
> *with soft caress,*
> *at death's redress,*
> *his wish, lost soul will cry.*
>
> *Yerinde grants,*
> *a golden band,*
> *with eye of glittering jet;*
> *should King divide,*
> *from Love's sweet pride,*
> *dark souls collect their debt.*

The golden band on Mesut's wrist. He'd somehow summoned one of the *dark souls* with that bracelet. Or released it after it had been trapped within.

Gemstones could be used to trap souls. Everyone in the desert knew that. Could Mesut not have been given one such on Beht Ihman? Perhaps. But there would be precious few ways for her to learn the truth of it for the time being.

All too soon the machine that was the House of Maidens had returned to normality. Maidens patrolled the city or guarded the Kings. Others, Çeda among them, were sent on specific missions for their King or for the wardens who guided them. King Yusam had called Çeda to his palace several times for new tasks, and never had he or anyone else mentioned that four of the Kings had been in danger.

Still, Çeda knew better than most how quickly things might turn. King Yusam might see something in his mere that would implicate her. King Zeheb might hear whispers that would put him on her trail. They might find the disguise she'd used and find *something* she'd missed that might lead them to her. So Çeda watched everyone and everything warily. She'd been sleeping only a few hours each night, wondering when they'd wake her and drag her before the Confessor King, Cahil, for questioning.

Reaching level ground at last, she headed west toward the House of Maidens. As they did most days, the keep's inner gates stood open. She waved to the Maidens atop the wall as she neared. Shortly after, a young girl, a page, blew a whistle, and those traveling through the gates and into the House of Kings proper made way for her.

She rode to the stables, prepared to find her sword master, Sayabim, for more training, but the stable girl, a thin wisp of a girl, had a surprise for her. "The First Warden wishes to see you, Maiden Çeda," she said as Çeda slipped down from Brightlock's saddle.

As Çeda handed the reins over, the girl assiduously avoided Çeda's gaze. "Why?" Çeda asked.

"I couldn't say." The girl paused, then leaned in conspiratorially. "She's in the barracks courtyard. There's someone she wishes you to *meet*. Someone to"—her voice dropped to a whisper—"*properly fill out your hand.*"

"I thought you couldn't say," Çeda said, smiling.

The girl's face reddened.

Çeda laughed, but inside, she was taken aback. She'd been asking Sümeya about this for weeks. First Warden Sümeya's hand stood at four Maidens:

Sümeya herself, Kameyl, Melis, and Çeda. The opening left by Jalize, the Blade Maiden Çeda had killed in Külaşan's palace, had remained vacant in the months following her death. Çeda had been secretly relieved that no one new had come to fill it, for in that lay uncertainty she didn't need, but she'd known it would eventually be filled. The sort of woman Jalize's replacement might be, Çeda had no idea, but if she was like most of the Kings' daughters, Çeda would have to tread carefully around her. Very carefully.

"Well, who is it?" Çeda asked.

The girl shook her head. "I'm not to say."

"Well, I dare say you weren't supposed to tell me the rest, either!"

"I'm sorry, Maiden." Her gaze dropped to the straw-covered ground, her ears now burning bright as her cheeks. "I've said too much."

With a rough of the girl's hair, Çeda sent her away, then left the stables as a strange alchemycal brew of eagerness and unease began to stir inside her. Passing through the spartan buildings of the House of Maidens, she came to the barracks and its courtyard, where several dozen Maidens practiced sword-play with bamboo shinai. More sparred with padded spears or sent arrows biting into targets with quick, rhythmic pulls from their short bows.

Sümeya, First Warden of the Maidens and the leader of Çeda's hand, stood on the far side of the courtyard beside one of the sparring circles, watching two Maidens trade blows with naked steel. One of the Maidens was easy to recognize—Kameyl, a tall, imposing woman, the fiercest of all the Maidens, a wizard with blade in hand. The other was a young woman Çeda had never seen before. She had honey-blond hair bound into a long braid. She was seventeen, perhaps, and pretty in a composed sort of way, as if she might stop a fight to fix her hair.

"You wished to see me, First Warden," Çeda said.

Sümeya glanced her way. "Çeda," she said by way of greeting, then re-sumed her study of Kameyl and the Maiden-in-waiting. As well she might. She was likely judging the young, prospective Maiden's preparedness for her initiation ritual, which involved the *tahl selheshal*, the dance she and Kameyl were performing now. Sümeya motioned to the young woman. "Meet Yndris Cahil'ava, your new sister."

Çeda caught the note of displeasure in her voice, which made Çeda wonder how much say Sümeya had in taking Yndris into her hand. She'd had little enough in Çeda's case. Had it been up to her, she would have seen Çeda dead before allowing her to take up a blade and fight beside her, but Husamettín, her father, the King of Swords and Lord of the Blade Maidens, had demanded it. Had a similar demand been made here?

As Kameyl and Yndris continued through the prescribed steps of the dance, Çeda watched more closely. This, the song of blades, was the ritual battle an aspirant would wage before the Kings in the Sun Palace before she was allowed to enter the ranks of the Blade Maidens. They were a study in contrasts, these two. Kameyl was tall and powerful, Yndris short and sinuous. Kameyl was as stoic as she was efficient in her swordplay. Yndris would occasionally give herself over to wild flurries of attacks—an attempt to impress, perhaps. Kameyl fought with Brushing Wing, her ebon sword, while Yndris fought with a blade of mundane steel that Çeda doubted had ever been drawn in battle. Yndris was not a poor fighter, but she was undisciplined. Even in these few minutes of sparring, Çeda caught Yndris glancing over at them, and each time she did Kameyl punished her for it, snaking in one slash, then another, each of them biting into the light leather armor of her fighting dress.

As much as Çeda enjoyed watching Kameyl's form, she had trouble concentrating. A trio of Matrons in white dresses stood in a cluster on the far side of courtyard. They'd watched Çeda's approach and were now talking in low tones. She tried to convince herself it was nothing, but she couldn't help but think it was something to do with the assassination attempt.

Sümeya noticed, looking Çeda up and down before resuming her study of the swordplay. "You look as though someone's kicked your dog."

Çeda faked a smile as the Matrons, thanks be to Nalamae, strode together through a scalloped archway and into one of the barracks. "Dogs smell. And they sniff your crotch."

Sümeya gave Çeda that wry smile of hers, the one she reserved for her closest friends. "Is there someone else you'd like to have sniff your crotch then?"

Now Çeda's smile turned real. *Emre would do. Or Ramahd. Even Osman, if he'd have me.* "There might be one or two," she finally said.

"Tell me their names. I'll have both sent to your room tonight."

Çeda couldn't help it. She laughed. "When I want a man, First Warden, I'll knock him senseless and drag him there myself."

"Charming. I'm sure the men of Roseridge were throwing themselves at your feet."

The two of them chuckled for a moment. It was a strangely intimate thing amidst the clash of steel and the shouts of sparring playing out all around them. They both returned their attention to swordplay, but Çeda's mind had now drifted to Roseridge. Only that morning, a mission for King Yusam had brought her there. The mission itself had been simple. As simple as they could get.

"Go to the city quarry," he'd told her yesterday. "Reach it as the sun rises and study it until high sun."

"Nothing more?"

"Nothing more. Study it carefully and tell me what you find."

She'd seen little more than the backbreaking business of pounding and cutting stone and hauling it on mule trains up from that great pit. But before she'd returned to the House of Kings, she'd taken the chance to ride through Roseridge, going to the very street where she used to live. Her stomach had twisted in knots as she reined her horse before a door, its paint faded and cracked with age. She'd knocked, and footsteps had shuffled behind it, Old Yanca coming closer. The wizened woman soon appeared, squinting at the sun. She raised her hand to shade her eyes and fixed her gaze on Çeda. When recognition came, she pursed her lips and shook her head, her regret clear.

The knots in Çeda's stomach had all unwound in an instant, making her feel lost and alone and angry. Yanca was her sole contact with Dardzada the apothecary. She'd been waiting for months to hear some news, *any* news, of Emre. That quick shake of Yanca's head meant she'd heard nothing. The very notion made her sick with worry, as it had every time she'd thought of him since abandoning him in the crypts beneath Külaşan's palace.

Seeing Çeda's reaction, Yanca took her hand and patted it. "Word will come, my darling child. See if it doesn't."

"Of course," Çeda said, though she was beginning to doubt it. Her mind was telling her to be patient, but her heart wanted to scream. Dardzada had had more than enough time to send out queries to the Host, but she supposed it would be difficult getting word to the right people. The entire desert, for five hundred leagues around Sharakhai, was under siege after all. Ships of war still departed daily from King's Harbor, laden with Maidens and Silver Spears to hunt the Moonless Host and their sympathizers.

"Is it bothering you again?" Sümeya asked, snapping Çeda back to the barracks courtyard.

Çeda realized she'd been rubbing the puckered scar on the meat of her right thumb. It was a constant reminder of when she'd gone to the blooming fields to poison herself, to prove that she was a daughter of one of the twelve Kings. She'd later been saved when Dardzada, disguised as a foreign priest, had delivered her to the House of Maidens and Matron Zaïde had applied tattoos around the wound to control the poison. But just as Zaïde had said it would, there were times she hardly knew it was there and others when it ached horribly. Today, at least, it was only a minor irritation. "It's nothing."

Sümeya didn't seem convinced but made no further mention of it. "And our King? Was he pleased by your travels?"

Sümeya had never approved of her hand's missions for Yusam, but she had little choice in the matter, even as First Warden. In times of relative peace the Maidens often served at the whims of the Kings. It was a fluid thing, meant to protect the Kings' interest, but more often than not it seemed to create a nightmare for Sümeya as she tried to keep up with it all. In the months since Çeda's induction into the Maidens, Sümeya herself had been called away twice, Kameyl three times, and Melis over a dozen. Melis, in fact, had yet to return from her latest mission, the exact nature of which Çeda hadn't been told.

"I can never tell if he's pleased or not," Çeda said, referring to King Yusam. She'd told him what she'd seen in the quarry. When she'd finished, he'd narrowed in on the comings and goings of the pit foreman at the base of the elevator that brought workers up and down the eastern edge of the quarry. It seemed little enough, and indeed Yusam had simply nodded, taking it all in as if it meant something to him, and then dismissed her.

"He is difficult to read," Sümeya replied, "but he is also as straightforward a man as you'll find among our Lord Kings." Sümeya studied the sparring for a time. "Has he any further need of you?"

"He said only to return and prepare for Yndris's ceremony."

"Good." Çeda couldn't tell if she was pleased or not, though, not only from the indifference in her voice, but also the way she was frowning at Kameyl and Yndris.

"You were speaking of kicked dogs earlier . . ." Çeda said, referring to how distant she'd suddenly become.

Sümeya looked at Çeda with those intense brown eyes of hers, confused for a moment, but then understanding came. "It's only, there's always so much to do." She waved to Kameyl and Yndris. "There's peace to be found in the simple trading of blows."

Çeda couldn't disagree. She could be angry or worried or fearful while living her many lies in the service of the Kings, but when she sparred with Kameyl or Melis or, rarely, Sümeya herself, those emotions faded. The blows of her sword felt like a smithy's hammer, shaping her anew. "If it's swords you wish," Çeda said, placing her hand on the pommel of River's Daughter, letting that movement finish her sentence.

Çeda could see the eagerness in her, the wish to draw her sword and dance the dance of blades, but a moment later the look was gone. "Another time, young dove. Enough!" she roared when Yndris's motions became wild enough to be dangerous.

Yndris, however, fought even more recklessly, a thing Kameyl did not forgive. Kameyl blocked her blows with an effortless ease that Çeda had come to expect but was still impressed by. She stepped inside Yndris's guard with a blurring advance, snapping a kick into Yndris's chest. "Your warden said *enough*, girl."

Yndris tried to recover, but stumbled and fell. Kameyl stood over her, sword at the ready should Yndris be foolish enough to strike again. Yndris coughed, grimacing as she rubbed one hand against her chest. As she did, she looked not at Kameyl, nor Sümeya, but at Çeda. As if *Çeda* were the cause of her pain. She stood, sending an embarrassed glance Kameyl's way, then came to stand before Sümeya. She bowed, pointedly not looking Çeda's way.

"Yndris, meet Çeda, the fifth member of your hand. Çeda, Yndris Cahil'ava."

Çeda bowed her head, while Yndris merely stared, as if annoyed she'd been forced to acknowledge Çeda's presence, or was waiting for Çeda to address her as Your Grace. *A wonderful addition to our hand,* Çeda thought, *the daughter of Cahil the Confessor, a young woman no doubt as like to use a whip as her words.*

"What were you trying to prove?" Sümeya asked.

Yndris pointed to the sparring circle with the tip of her blade. "I was dancing, siyaf, nothing more."

"I am not your siyaf. And you have much to prove tonight."

Yndris bowed. "Of course," she said, though in a way that made it clear she felt entitled to the ebon sword that would be granted to her at the ceremony that evening.

Sümeya seemed displeased, but made no further mention of it. She beckoned Çeda closer. "Since the two of you are so eager for swordplay, why don't you spar awhile? I've things to discuss with Kameyl."

Kameyl sheathed Brushing Wing and picked up two shinai. "Go easy on her, Çeda." She tossed one shinai each to Çeda and Yndris, then followed Sümeya, the two of them wending through the sparring circles. She called over her shoulder, loudly enough for the entire courtyard to hear, "I can't have a dove with a broken wing if I'm to embarrass her in front of her father this evening."

Yndris stared at Kameyl's retreating form until she and Sümeya were lost behind a gathering of Matrons in white abayas.

Çeda stepped into the ring. "Come," she said to Yndris, but Yndris threw her shinai into the dirt and began walking away.

"We were told to spar," Çeda called.

Yndris stopped and turned. "With a mongrel like you? I think not."

Chapter 4

THAT NIGHT, a host of memories flooded through Çeda's mind as she
stepped into the Sun Palace's grand central hall. Not so long ago,
she'd been brought here herself as an aspirant and paraded before the Kings.
A feast had been provided. Çeda had danced with Ihsan the Honey-tongued
King. She'd been granted her ebon blade, River's Daughter, and she'd fought
Kameyl in what should have been a mock battle but which had nearly cost
Çeda her life. Kameyl had hoped to slice Çeda's neck and make it look like
an accident, and Çeda, not yet having earned trust from the Kings or the
Maidens or anyone else on Tauriyat, had been forced to defend herself, not
just from the attempt on her life but from Kameyl's accusations that she was
woefully unprepared to become a Blade Maiden. To her surprise, Husamettín,
the King of Swords, had stepped in and took Çeda's side against one of the
most storied women in the Maidens' long history. It had been a night of
roiling emotions, but in the end the Kings had approved her entry to the
House of Maidens.

And now Yndris's turn had come. Many had gathered for a feast to honor
her and to watch her perform in a mock battle of her own. No one who'd
been to both, however, could fail to notice the striking differences. All twelve

Kings had come to witness Çeda's ceremony. How many would come this night? Since the night she'd stolen into Eventide, she'd seen only King Yusam and Husamettín. She'd heard no word of Cahil the Confessor King, whom she'd nicked with one of her poisoned arrows, but she'd been petrified to ask for fear they would suspect her involvement. Surely she would have her answer soon.

As it turned out, she didn't have long to wait. Husamettín was already in attendance when she arrived. Cahil came shortly after with Yndris at his side. Çeda was practically holding her breath as he walked in, but the moment she spotted him, her disappointment came out in one long sigh. In her heart she'd known he survived—the Kings would have given *some* sort of response if he hadn't—but she'd thought surely the poison would have debilitated him. It was said to leave those who survived it unable to use their bodies as they once had. They shook horribly. They walked, if they could walk at all, weak-kneed, drunken, often needing help to go the smallest distances from their sickbeds. And yet here was Cahil, walking tall, looking for all the world like a man Çeda's own age. He was *smiling*, beaming with pride over his daughter's being granted her blade.

Çeda thought surely she'd been mistaken, that she hadn't caught him with the arrow after all, but when she came closer, she saw the light scar. Even knowing where to look it was difficult to see. How? How could he have survived with but a scratch to show for it?

Yndris caught Çeda watching her father. She stopped her conversation with a bent old woman and stared until Çeda finally looked away.

Curse the gods, Çeda thought. They were to blame for this. They'd extended their protection to the Kings, granting them long life, vigor, and even the ability to resist poison, it seemed. It was the only explanation that made sense.

She stifled her feelings of despair, hiding them behind a mask of pleasantry. The last thing she needed was for anyone to think her particularly interested in Cahil's presence, least of all Cahil himself.

Only two more Kings came to the ceremony—King Ihsan and the stocky Zeheb, King of Whispers. Husamettín was honor-bound to attend, and of course Cahil would come to see his own daughter granted her Maiden's blade. But to have so few attend was surely a grave insult. Making things worse, remarkably few others had come to fill this cavernous room. It had been brimming with guests on the night of Çeda's induction, whereas tonight a hundred at best had come, and surely most of them were Yndris's relations. It seemed a slight of some sort, but if that were so, Çeda had no idea what might have caused it.

As the feast wound down, a beam of sunlight shone brightly from a device built high into the dome above. The crowd formed a border around the sunlight, creating a makeshift arena, Yndris strode across the floor in her bright yellow dress. She came to a stop before Husamettín, pulling the cloth-of-gold veil across her face. Husamettín pulled an ebon sword from its lacquered wooden sheath and shared the design etched into the blade with Yndris and others gathered near.

Zaïde, the old matron who had saved Çeda's life by corralling the poison in Çeda's right arm, came to stand by Çeda's side. "She asked to fight as you fought," she said, nodding to Yndris and the King of Swords.

"And was her request granted?" Çeda replied.

"Should it have been?"

Çeda wondered how forthright she ought to be, but reckoned there was no point in hiding Yndris's brashness when it was so plain to see. "No."

"Why?"

"Because she'll likely embarrass herself and our House."

"Likely you're right, though you have to admit the urge to push herself comes from a place of loyalty."

Çeda turned to look at Zaïde. "What do you mean?"

Zaïde's brows pinched, distorting the worry lines and crescent moon tattoo on her forehead. "Did Sümeya not tell you how Yndris came to the Maidens?"

"No."

"You no doubt heard of the fire in the spice merchant's fort last year?"

She'd been there, seen it with her own eyes. She'd been trapped there with everyone else until the Silver Spears had freed them. "I heard."

"The Maiden burned that day was Veliri Cahil'ava."

The image of the old fort's interior bursting into flame suddenly returned to Çeda so vividly she flinched. Veliri had died while saving King Külaşan. The intensity she'd shown, breaking through the fort's wall, had been almost inhuman.

"Yndris," Zaïde went on, "is Veliri's sister. She may be young and she may be overly bold, but one can outgrow these things. The memory of her sister, however, casts a long and haunting shadow, and I wonder whether Yndris will ever fully step out from under it. Veliri was well-loved and died bravely. Now comes her younger sibling, a girl who never thought she'd be allowed to wear the Maidens' black, hoping to take up her sister's sword and continue her tale."

Hiding a grimace, Çeda hid her right hand behind her back and gripped it several times, trying to work away the pain that had suddenly returned. "Why choose her at all then?"

"It is a point of honor to offer a blade to a family that has lost a Maiden. But beyond that, the Kings value many things in an aspirant. The will to strike, with revenge driving the sword, is one of the foremost."

"Do you agree with them?"

By asking the question, Çeda had walked onto slightly dangerous ground—she still didn't understand Zaïde's place in this grand struggle for control over Sharakhai—but Zaïde merely tipped her head and gave Çeda an impotent shrug of her shoulders. "Who am I to agree or disagree?"

Husamettín was holding Yndris's blade, completing its story, which included, as Çeda suspected it would, Veliri's *valiant fight* against the Moonless Host. Çeda wondered at the wisdom in it. Her sister had held this very blade. It made some sense that it would pass to Yndris, but how much weight would Yndris now feel when she swung it? How hard would she push to eclipse her sister's deeds?

Having completed his tale, Husamettín sheathed the blade and handed it to Yndris. Yndris drew it, admired its keen edge against the sunlight shining down from the center of the dome above, staring at it as if there were no higher honor. A moment ago Çeda might have laughed, thinking it an act, a preening display for the benefit of her father, who watched near Husamettín with little more than forbearance. But now that she knew more of Yndris, Çeda realized how sad it was. She had no idea the sort of woman Veliri had been in life—whether she'd been honorable or not. Maybe she'd deserved to die a fiery death at the hands of the Moonless Host, the Al'afwa Khadar, and maybe she hadn't. What Çeda *did* know was that dozens of innocents had been condemned to die that day, not only those in the fire, but also the girls the Kings had rounded up in retribution; girls who were then hung from the walls of Hallowsgate.

It was a seemingly endless cycle of violence: the Kings against the Host, the Host against the Kings, each response emboldening the enemy, making them more desperate to even the scales. Sometimes Çeda thought both sides would only be happy when Sharakhai had been laid to waste. *Even then . . . Sharakhai could be a city of the dead and still they would battle over hills of bones.*

As Yndris sheathed the blade and took her place in the mock arena, the crowd's whispering fell silent. Not far from where Çeda and Zaïde stood, Kameyl stepped through the crowd and took her place at one end of the oval where she and Yndris would cross blades. Even here, in a mock ceremony that meant little in the grand scheme of things, Kameyl was intense. A desert asp, both deadly and graceful.

They took their positions, equidistant from the mosaic design on the floor: twin moons split by a spear head. Yndris held her blade high while Kameyl held hers crosswise, symbolically barring Yndris's path to the House of Maidens. In that moment, when all was still, the column of sunlight made the air between them glow, lending an ethereal quality to the ritual. Soon the two of them began the dance of blades. Their swords rang. Some would say they *sang*, the very reason they referred to it as a song instead of a dance. It was a fine show. Kameyl's form was perfect, and though Çeda could see Yndris's minor missteps—small misplacements of sword or scabbard, the tightness in Yndris's frame—few others would recognize them.

King Cahil watched with little outward show of emotion, but there was a sense of pride in the way he studied Yndris's every move, while others— King Ihsan and a good many of the courtiers near him—seemed to watch the crowd more than the ceremony itself. Indeed, when Ihsan saw Çeda watching, he smiled a handsome smile and bowed his head. Çeda looked away, but her eyes were soon drawn back, and Ihsan was still watching. He laughed, and Cahil noticed, regarding Ihsan crossly and then following his gaze to Çeda. In that moment, as Cahil's eyes met Çeda's, he seemed to weigh her. There was so much innocence in his features—in all but his eyes, which regarded her as a thing to be used and tossed aside. It sent chills along her skin, but she refused to look away. She didn't want him to think she felt guilty, so she held his stare until he returned his gaze to his daughter.

When the dance reached the point where the two of them would improvise, they did for a time, Yndris continuing to move with some skill if not grace, and when it finally came time for the end of the ceremony, the drawing of blood, Yndris held out her right wrist, and Kameyl drew a shallow cut along her forearm. Yndris did the same to Kameyl, and then the crowd clapped and whooped and stomped their feet.

As the crowd closed in around Yndris, congratulating her, Çeda said to Zaïde, "Could we speak a moment, Matron."

Zaïde paused, but then nodded. "Very well." She motioned Çeda toward one of the balconies that overlooked Sharakhai. The vast amber cityscape lay sprawled out before them with the desert laying claim to the expanse beyond. To their left, the horizon was lit a violent crimson.

The two of them had spent very little time together since Külaşan's death. That distance between them was the reason Çeda had taken things into her own hands the night she went to kill Kiral. Çeda was sure Zaïde's silence was purposeful—it was risky, even dangerous, to speak—but they might not see one another for weeks or even months. And yet, for all her eagerness, it was Zaïde who spoke first. "You've come a long way with the blade since you entered our care."

"I've never felt clumsier."

The amused twinkle in Zaïde's eyes hinted at how well she was able to read Çeda. "Sayabim is a harsh mistress. Believe me, I know. She was the warden of my hand for three years before she took the Matron's white. But it takes steady effort on the part of teacher *and* student to unlearn bad habits. Better to do it now, for all else will build on that foundation."

Sayabim was constantly telling Çeda about her *foundation* while using her thin stick to adjust Çeda's foot placement, her stance, her posture. *You'll never build a temple without it.* Çeda believed those words—she'd said similar things to her own students in the pits—but there were times when Çeda wanted to snatch that thrice-damned stick from Sayabim's hands and snap it in half.

"Don't forget, child, the others in your hand are some our most gifted Maidens. You cannot expect to learn all that they were taught in four months. Your bladecraft was bound to grow worse before it grew better." She paused. "The rest of your studies. How fare you in those?"

"Sayabim has been teaching me hand signs," Çeda said, "and Kameyl has been guiding me on close-quarter tactics."

"Sümeya has informed you of your bonding?"

Çeda nodded. It was something she'd been dreading for weeks. She'd been accepted by the asirim on the night she'd been taken to the blooming fields. They had come to her. They had communed. She'd learned many things that night, chief among them that the asirim were no holy warriors, as the Kings professed, but the remnants of the thirteenth tribe that had been sacrificed on the night of Beht Ihman. It had been that very sacrifice by the Kings that had secured them the favor of the desert gods. But the ceremony to which Zaïde was referring was something entirely different. She would soon be taken out to the desert, where one or more asir would be chained to her will—*brought to heel*, as Sümeya had put it. Knowing that the asirim were what remained of the thirteenth tribe, forced into service of the Kings by the gods themselves, it made her stomach turn.

"When will it begin?" she asked.

"Soon, I think. King Mesut is eager to see you bonded, to weigh your abilities."

"And this?" Çeda showed Zaïde her poisoned hand. "You said you would teach me how to fight it."

Zaïde took Çeda's hand in hers, looked more closely at the scar. Deep pain ran along Çeda's arm as she did so. Zaïde pressed the scar on the meat of Çeda's thumb, then along the words Zaïde herself had tattooed there. *Bane of the unrighteous,* and *The lost are now found.* Those tattoos, not only the two phrases but the elegant symbols and traceries on her palm and the back of her hand, had effectively hemmed the poison in, rendering it something Çeda could manage if not master. "Does it bother you often?"

Çeda had been about to ask the questions burning inside her. *Do you know Dardzada? Did you know my mother?* She wanted to confess her mission to Eventide, her attempt to kill the King of Kings, her utter failure to cripple even one of them. She wanted to tell her about the woman she'd seen in the courtyard that night. *How could they have done such a thing?*

The roar of laughter filtered out from within the palace, a reminder that this was neither the place nor the time. How could she speak of things with the Kings so near, especially Zeheb, the King of Whispers? "There are days when I hardly feel it," she finally said, "others when it aches terribly, but it's grown worse in the months since you gave me the tattoo."

The Matron nodded. "I'm sorry for the pain, but there is time yet. Come to me for herbs if you have need, but for now, continue to work with Sayabim. We can speak again on the way back from your sister Maiden's vigil."

Yndris's vigil. The very thought of seeing the asirim's plight firsthand somehow made Çeda's thumb flare even worse. But it also emboldened her, reminded her that while she waited and plotted, the asirim suffered.

"Matron?" Çeda's gut was turning somersaults.

Zaïde's brow knitted, perhaps sensing something in her voice.

Çeda grit her jaw, willed herself to speak the words—*Do you know Dardzada? Is he your ally?*—but before she could force the words out, she noticed someone walking onto the balcony, a tall man with bone-white skin and ivory hair. He held two narrow flutes filled with golden wine, one in each hand. He came to a stop, bowed to Zaïde, and spoke with a soft Mirean accent. "Forgive my interruption, Matron, but your good King Ihsan has need of you."

Zaïde tilted her head in assent. "Well then, since you've come only to send me away, perhaps you'd be so kind as to occupy our young Maiden." She motioned to Çeda. "Juvaan Xin-Lei, I'm pleased to introduce one of our most promising Maidens, Çedamihn Ahyanesh'ala."

Juvaan faced Çeda with a mischievous smile and bowed his head, a practiced, elegant gesture. "We've met."

The surprise that touched Zaïde's features was quickly hidden. "Well, then," she squeezed Çeda's arm, "I leave you in good hands." And with that she strode back into the palace, leaving Çeda alone with Queen Alansal of Mirea's chief ambassador in Sharakhai.

Juvaan held out a glass of wine. She accepted it with a smile and sipped, the sparkling wine bubbling along her throat as she swallowed. Notes of plum and pear and jasmine underscored a bitter mineral taste.

"A new import from the Austral Sea," Juvaan said, leaning against the marble balustrade. "It's rather taken the city by storm." When Çeda laughed, Juvaan went on, "You don't agree?"

"I rather doubt that any new fashion in liquor has swept through more than the House of Kings. The oud parlors will still sell araq. The tea houses will still sell their tea."

"I rather think the taverns and shisha dens along the Trough more forward thinking than that."

"Yes, but the ones that can afford this"—she lifted her glass—"serve clientele from the palaces and the Hill and the dandies who have come to taste the riches of Sharakhai."

Juvaan's smile widened, revealing perfect teeth. "Am I a dandy, then, Çedamihn?"

"You're no dandy, but I hardly think you venture into the hidden byways of Sharakhai."

"You might be surprised." He sipped from his glass. "In any case, what do you think?"

"Not altogether unpleasant," Çeda said, "but in truth I'd prefer a stiff shot of araq."

Juvaan shrugged. "Me as well, but I'm always eager to try something new, aren't you?"

"Yes."

"Perhaps you'll visit Mirea one day. I have a collection of rice wine I'd be happy to share with you."

"I doubt that I'll ever leave the desert."

"Oh? And why is that?"

"I have all I need here. What is there to find that I can't find in Sharakhai?"

"Why, the entire world, oh Çedamihn the White Wolf."

Çeda glanced over his shoulder to the massive room beyond the sculpted archway. "The White Wolf is dead. And to some, Sharakhai *is* the world."

Juvaan looked out over the city, the fading sunset washing his white skin a strange orange hue. "Is this your entire world then? Sharakhai?"

"And the desert beyond."

"You've no wish to visit the green valleys of Mirea?"

Çeda shrugged. "A visit, perhaps, but I suspect a land of constant rain would drive me mad."

A chuckle. "It isn't so bad as that. The patter of rain on the forest leaves can be a wondrous thing, the fragrant smell as it first begins to fall, especially in the deep green valleys beyond the capital."

"Said the man who's fled his country for the shores of Sharakhai."

Juvaan laughed. He looked handsome like that. "Fled, is it?"

"So my sources tell me."

She'd made a point of looking into his past. He came from a family of fifteen brothers and sisters. Most had taken up small land holdings or married into other families. A few ran the caravan route his family had owned for generations. Juvaan had captained a ship for a few years, but had decided to remain in Sharakhai, acting as the caravan's primary agent, brokering lucrative trade deals for when their ships returned. His knowledge of the flow of trade from all five kingdoms was unparalleled, and eventually Mirea's queen had noticed. As young as Juvaan was—he'd seen fewer than thirty summers, Çeda reckoned—he became one of the queen's trusted advisors. A scant year later, he'd risen to the rank of Queen's ambassador.

"Well, I wouldn't say 'fled,'" Juvaan said, "but there's no doubt I've come to love what the desert has to offer." He was looking at her with a hopeful expression; nothing more than that. He was a Mirean nobleman, after all, not some piece of Malasani caravan trash who whistled at the passing women. He was an attractive man, Çeda had to admit, tall and regal, like the snow leopards she'd seen in paintings from the northern kingdom. But for all that he was still a pawn of Queen Alansal, who was pulling many strings in the desert, and Çeda refused to get any closer to him than she needed to.

A lie, she said to herself. *Or at least, not the entire truth.* When she thought of Juvaan she couldn't help but think of another man: Ramahd, the ambassador to Qaimir. As charming as Juvaan may be, she wished she were standing beside Ramahd, not his counterpart from Mirea.

When Çeda said nothing in return, Juvaan downed the last of his sparkling wine. "It's fortunate our paths have crossed again."

"And why is that?"

"Because I have a proposition. You once said I could rely upon you."

"I did," Çeda said. It was an offer she'd made when she'd last come to the Sun Palace for her own feast. She'd begun to wonder if he would ever take her up on it. "What is it you wish?"

"Little enough. A bit of news here and there."

"News of what sort?"

"If I'm not mistaken, your hand now reports to the Jade-eyed King. I have heard word of several of you being sent on very specific missions."

She gave no reply, unsure where he was headed.

Juvaan's brow furrowed. "The mere is a wondrous device but also, as I understand it, imperfect. It tells him nothing on its own. It's up to Yusam to interpret what the mere shows, to piece together a puzzle that may be years in the making. My head swims when I think of all that he sees, the various threads he must follow. I'd like to know where he sends you and your fellow Maidens, and what you find."

"But as you say, the picture the mere paints is complex. What good will that do you?"

"Can you not see? Yusam will do the hard work for me. By seeing where he's sending you, and knowing the outcomes, I'll learn what he's most interested in. I don't need to know what the mere showed him, only the conclusions he's drawn from it."

"And my stories alone will give you that?"

"You are not my sole source of information from the House of Kings."

Çeda considered that. "And what would I get in return?"

"What do you want?"

This meeting had come as a surprise, but she had no difficulty answering Juvaan's question. "I want to know the movements of the Al'afwa Khadar." She needed to know what the Moonless Host were doing. Dardzada wasn't going to give her enough information—he almost certainly considered it too risky, especially with her living in the House of Maidens—and this wasn't something she could learn on her own.

"And how would I know that?" Juvaan asked.

From somewhere inside the grand hall, a woman shouted. A split-second later, a group of men roared in laughter. Çeda lowered her voice. "Because you supply them with funds, Juvaan. You supply them with intelligence."

He was unfazed by the accusation. "Supposing for a moment that's true, what makes you think I'm privy to the information you want?"

"*Make* yourself privy to it. I'll be risking my life by feeding you what I know."

"As will I."

Çeda gave him a flat stare. "My good lord, if you don't consider what I'm providing valuable enough to find the information I require, then tell me now and we can stop wasting one another's time."

"I've no way of knowing if what you can provide me is valuable."

He let the implication sit between them, an invitation for her to prove to him that she would be worthwhile as a spy within the House of Kings. She didn't like being manipulated like this, but then again, what she knew of Yusam's intentions was cloudy at best.

"Very well," she said, and she told him of the missions King Yusam had sent her on since entering his service. She finished with one that had taken her to a Kundhunese ship for a ledger Yusam wanted. It had contained little more than the captain's ramblings. A diary of sorts, filled with small tales, poems, sketches of his travels. What the King had hoped to find within those pages she had no idea, but when he'd finished examining it, she'd asked him something she'd been saving since her return from the ship.

"Did the mere tell you that the men on that ship treated with Ihsan's vizir?" she asked.

His head jerked back and his mouth had opened like a west end boy meeting the cruel realities of the Amber City for the first time. "Repeat for me what you just said."

"The captain and his first mate, I believe it was, were arguing, and they said, '*Tolovan ad jondu gonfahla.*' It means—"

"He will be the death of us," Yusam supplied.

Çeda had nodded, but Yusam was already ignoring her. He was staring at the book in wonder. Suddenly a chill ran along her skin. She tried to relax the sudden knot in her throat, swallowing over and over, trying to clear it and failing miserably.

This was it, she realized. This was the reason the mere had given him the vision: not to get the book, but so that Çeda would be sent to that ship, hear that lone phrase, and speak it before the King. He had just been given one of the many pieces of the puzzle he was trying to piece together. But what did it mean? Tolovan was King Ihsan's vizir, which meant that in all likelihood the Honey-tongued King was involved with the Kundhunese captain. What she didn't know was *why*, or how it related to Yusam and the mere's revelations.

Yusam recovered himself, set the book on his desk with great care, and said, "That will be all."

Juvaan took her stories in, nodding occasionally, his gray eyes sharp. When she was done, he gave her a practiced smile, the sort one would give to a servant who'd offered another flute of sparkling wine.

Then he said, "Do you remember the name of the ship?"

"The *Adzambe*. It means *gazelle* in Kundhunese."

"I know it." He meant the ship, not the word. His distant look convinced her he knew more than he was letting on.

"Do you know their business here in Sharakhai?" she asked.

Juvaan frowned. "I was under the impression you wanted information about the *Host*."

"Allies can share a bit of inconsequential information, can they not?"

"Let's call ourselves business associates."

"Then you're satisfied?" she asked, suddenly feeling as though this night wasn't going to be a complete waste after all.

Juvaan considered, his face a study in calm reflection, then he stepped back and, while holding her gaze, gave her a half-bow—a very Mirean gesture indeed. "I'll arrange a method for the two of us to speak." He raised his glass to his proposal. "Well enough?"

After a moment, Çeda nodded and clinked her glass to his, a crystal clear note that for one brief moment rose above the din of conversation filtering out from the hall.

Chapter 5

OVER THE SHALLOW DUNES, two leagues out from Sharakhai, Çeda rode at the end of a line of six horses. Zaïde led the way, with Yndris coming behind, then Sümeya, Kameyl, Melis, and finally Çeda. The twin moons were nearing their apex, the two nearly in line with one another, creating a ghostly landscape over the amber sands. Ahead, a dark line marked the edge of the blooming fields, beyond which lay a thousand pinpoints of light, the blooms of the adichara opening to the sister moons Rhia and Tulathan, basking in their heavenly glow. As they came closer, Çeda saw pollen drifting on the wind, glowing like some otherworldly mist that might whisk them away to the farther fields were they foolish enough to enter it.

As Çeda reined Brightlock over to follow the others up a shallow rise, she winced at the pain in her right hand. She switched and used her left to guide the horse, albeit clumsily. A week had passed since the feast held in Yndris's honor, and every day had seen Çeda's old wound grow progressively worse. At first it had been little more than an ache. But the ache had deepened; then it had felt like a fresh wound, tender to the touch. Now it felt as though the poison were spreading through her arm all over again, ready to sweep through her and take her life once and for all. She should have gone to Zaïde, but she hadn't wished to go crawling for aid when she knew this was something she needed to fight on her own. *There will be times when it will threaten you,* Zaïde had told her when she'd revealed the tattoo she'd made to protect Çeda. She'd tapped the images around the wound. *These will not protect you. You will need to fight it here instead.* She'd touched Çeda's heart, and Çeda had known it would be a battle she could never truly win.

It was becoming so painful she was tempted to tell Zaïde, but this wasn't Çeda's night. It was Yndris's, so she resolved to bite her tongue and tell the Matron in the morning.

When they neared the adichara, they slipped down from their horses to the sandy stone and gathered in a circle. They were so close to the adichara Çeda could feel them, not just the ones nearby, but those farther and farther away as they ringed the city. She'd had this sort of awareness before, but always after taking a petal. This was different. She could feel the swaying trees through the pain in her hand, a sense that the adichara were alive in a way she'd never quite understood, as if all the hatred burning within the asirim, held in check for centuries by the power of the desert gods, was now radiating from the trees that fed on the blood of the innocent.

A long, low wail fell over the desert. Çeda could hear the lament in that call, but she also felt it in her hand, in her arm. It deepened the ache, like roots reaching into the earth. It felt as if the asirim, all of them, had been given voice through this one wailing asir. In that moment, it was a creature of pure hatred, the embodiment of a people that craved vengeance above all else.

"Çeda?"

She turned, realizing Zaïde had been speaking for some time.

"She said kneel." This came from Yndris, standing while Melis, Kameyl, Sümeya, and Zaïde all knelt on the ground, waiting for Çeda to comply.

"Of course," Çeda said. "My apologies."

With Yndris waiting impatiently and Zaïde watching carefully, Çeda kneeled. She tried to compose herself, but it was difficult. The smallest movement of her right hand brought with it a burning pain that was difficult to manage.

Yndris knelt across from Zaïde. The ritual was now properly underway. Zaïde picked up a handful of sand and whispered a prayer to Tulathan. What she said Çeda couldn't tell, for her ears had started ringing, a sound that seemed to mingle with the wails of the asir, which were coming closer and closer. Couldn't the others hear it? Didn't they realize the asir was coming for them?

The others whispered their own prayers to different gods, and soon it was Çeda's turn. She hastily picked up a fistful of sand with her good hand and whispered as it sifted between her fingers. "Thaash feed your anger that you might take retribution against the enemies of Sharakhai."

The night was becoming dreamlike, and a terrible rage was boiling up inside her. It had little direction at first, but as she stared at Yndris, kneeling on the ground by Kameyl's side, she knew it was because of this girl, this whelp come to the Maidens, fresh from her entitled upbringing, a life that had been built on the graves of the unfortunate, on the lies the Kings had been feeding to Sharakhai for four hundred years.

Çeda blinked. Tried to quell the sudden hatred inside her. Beyond Yndris, she saw something dark moving among the adichara. The branches spread, creating a tunnel of sorts. It was the asir, once a man, now a blackened, shriveled thing. It wailed no longer, but stood at a half-crouch, the black pits of its eyes trained on the youngest of the Maidens, the one with her back turned. Its intent burned brightly in Çeda's mind. It would break the Maiden's frail form, drag her dying body into the adichara before the others could react. That, at least, would be some small recompense for all that had happened in the endless years since the gods had transformed him into this *thing*, this perversion of man. It plodded forward, but paused, sensing one of the Maidens watching, the one that had been kissed by Sehid-Alaz, its King.

Çeda sensed its unquenchable anger sweeping her up like a storm until she shared in it. Feeding it. *Thaash, Lord of War, let me join your servant. Let me be the one to take Yndris's foul head from her shoulders.*

Very well, came the asir's terrible voice from within her mind.

Before she knew what she was doing, she was standing with River's Daughter held inexplicably in her right hand. She stared down at Yndris, and the girl stared back, shocked and angry.

Sümeya, sitting to Yndris's left, was up in a flash, blade drawn in a glorious arc of shadowed steel. "What do you think you're doing, sister?"

Çeda blinked. Saw through her own eyes once more. The asir came forward over the ground in an animalistic lope. *Run*, Çeda called to the asir. *Run!* And then she pointed toward it. "There!" *Please run!*

Sümeya spun. The others stood and drew their shamshirs as the asir bounded over the rocky ground, heading straight for Yndris.

Çeda grimaced as the scar on her thumb grew hot. A rumbling shook the earth. As it ran, the asir ducked its head low and then craned it upward. The rumbling built into a bellow. It filled the air, rattled Çeda's bones. Ahead of the asir, sand and bits of stone lifted in a fan. It struck Çeda like a terrible storm, pitching her back, sand flaying her skin where it was exposed. Barely discernible in the deafening roar was Zaïde's voice. "Cease!" she called. "By Tulathan, I call on you to cease!"

But the storm raged on, and something happened that shook Çeda even amidst the madness. Just as her heart had fallen into sync with King Külaşan in the moments before she drove her sword through his chest, so it did now with the asir. The beat was a dirge, a lament for a love too early lost. It wasn't merely that she could *feel* the anguish in this creature; she *was* its anger. She was its endless well of hatred. She was its vengeance.

She could feel its burning desire to kill. To rend. She fanned the flames higher. Somehow unshackled from the gods' restraints, it raced to take revenge on the Kings for all they'd done. And what example could be more perfect than Yndris? Young. Bold. Generous with her contempt for all save the Kings and the grand house they'd built on the backs of the thirteenth tribe.

Çeda knew she was being carried on the asir's rage. From this creature, this *man*, who'd lived to see as many summers as the Kings, she felt not only anger, but his life, his story. She saw his hands test the grain of freshly sawn wood, saw him brush away the sawdust. Using that same wood, he erected a lintel for a home in a growing neighborhood that would one day be known as the Shallows. She saw a clear night with the twin moons high, a goddess with bright silver skin walking among the streets, her sister with golden hair at her side. She saw his brother fall to the ground and claw at the dirt before curling into a tight ball, wailing from the pain.

Then he was struck as well, by a dark suffering that smothered his senses. His will bent to another power, and then a dictate was laid upon his soul—a desire for blood, a will to harm those who stood against the Kings. He knew even then it was a hunger that would never be sated.

On gangly limbs he'd risen and loped toward the edge of the young city. He and dozens, hundreds, of others were being funneled through the city's gates. Given free rein, this unfettered race felt joyous. He howled. He called to his brothers and sisters, the young and the old, ready to feed on those who stood in the desert with swords in hand.

Innumerable spears lay pitched against their charge, but already he could feel his enemies' fear. He fed upon it. Beyond this night the enemies of Shara-khai would stand no longer. The very notion of a desert ruled solely by the rightful Kings of Sharakhai filled him with golden light, a pervading glee that eclipsed any petty concerns he may have had before.

Had he worried? Had he feared? It seemed not. The very notion felt like an insect boring its way deeper beneath the skin. It enraged him.

On he ran, the urge to feed building. But the memories began to fade, to darken. The shrieking wind, so loud only moments ago, dwindled, until all that could be heard was sand falling to the desert floor, a sound like rain against the river.

Çeda stood three paces away from the asir. He had been charging toward Yndris, but now he stood stock-still, his eyes meeting Çeda's. In that moment he looked like any mortal man might. One with brothers and sisters. One with a mother and father and a family, his roots embedded in the past, his once-vibrant hopes reaching like shriveled branches toward the future.

The truth was in his eyes. He was trapped within this pitiful form, en-slaved, lost, but through his eyes she could see his soul.

I am undone, she said to him.

His blackened lips pulled back in a grimace. A smile. An expression of joy, here at the end. *Long years I've prayed for this day.*

He turned to his right, eyes calm, accepting, and Çeda saw too late Yndris flying over the desert toward him. "Don't!" Çeda cried, running to intercept, but she was too late.

The asir stared up, not at the twin moons, but at the glittering firmament beyond, and in that moment Yndris swept her blade across his undefended throat. As his head toppled from his neck, his body crumpled to the stone.

All was silent save for the still-falling rain of sand. Yndris stared down at the blood pooling around the rag-doll form with a righteousness that sickened Çeda.

And then Çeda was charging toward her, sword held high, a cry of impotent rage bursting from her. Yndris met her blade with surprise in her eyes. She blocked one stroke hastily, then another. Çeda blocked a clumsy counter and stepped in while spinning, sending an elbow crashing into Yndris's jaw.

Yndris fell, but before Çeda could do anything else, Sümeya bowled into her from behind. She tried to roll away, to regain her feet, but Kameyl had now joined Sümeya.

Melis had her arms around Yndris, but Yndris managed to free herself, ebon blade still in hand. "Enough!" Melis called, but Yndris was already charging forward. Çeda was defenseless, held down by the two Maidens as she was. There was nothing to stop Yndris from cleaving Çeda's head from her shoulders just as she had the asir.

But then a white blur drove in from Çeda's left. Zaïde. She was running forward, moving faster than she had any right to. Yndris tried to snake past her, but Zaïde imposed herself along Yndris's path. Zaïde was like a blade herself, a weapon poised, quick and ready to defend.

Yndris tried bulling her way past, but Zaïde had her by the sleeve of her sword arm and was drawing her arm sharply down. Yndris was thrown, but she rolled along the ground, then advanced on Zaïde. Zaïde, however, had used that moment to step inside Yndris's guard; she sent a series of blinding, two-fingered strikes into Yndris's neck and armpits, more against her wrists and elbows. Yndris's head lolled. Her arms went slack. A strange moan escaped her as her eyes rolled up into her head. As she collapsed altogether, Zaïde swooped in to lower her gently to the ground.

The hiss of falling sand had stopped, but the clack of the nearby adichara had replaced it. Their branches swayed this way and that, rattling against one another beneath the light of Tulathan and Rhia.

Zaïde stood from Yndris's prone form, hands slipping behind her back and clasping as if this were a sparring circle, little more than their latest lesson. Her eyes, though, were intent on Yndris. They were angry, more angry than Çeda had ever seen them.

She turned to Çeda, who was being forced to her feet by Sümeya and

Kameyl. "Release her," she said, and the two Maidens did. "Why did you attack your sister Maiden?"

What could she say? "The asir are holy. Is it not so? Those blessed by the Kings and gods, both. And she killed one without thought. He didn't deserve it."

"*Unhhh . . .*" Yndris was trying to speak, but all that came from her were guttural sounds.

Melis helped Yndris to her feet, and Zaïde pressed her thumb to the places she'd struck, massaging slowly. "And you," Zaïde said to Yndris, "what justified the killing of the asir without my leave, and more importantly, without King Mesut's?"

"Thuh . . ." Yndris opened her mouth wide, lolling her tongue like a jackal. "Thuh . . . the asir was wild. It wuh . . . was coming for me."

"It had stopped."

"It was stuh . . . staring at *her*." She raised one trembling arm, pointed to Çeda, and swallowed several times before speaking again. "I know not what it saw, but I know it was dangerous." When Zaïde remained silent, Yndris's eyes widened and she spoke in one long slur, "By the gods who breathe, it *attacked* us."

Zaïde stared up at the moons, as if searching for wisdom, then released a pent-up breath and leveled her gaze at Yndris. "Your sister Maidens are the ones who need your protection most. It's true the asir attacked, but there was no need to slay it as you did." She turned to Çeda, her eyes afire. "And while it was against our laws to harm it, drawing a blade on a sister is a sin that cannot be forgiven." She motioned to the places where they'd been kneeling not so long ago, mere paces from where the dead asir lay. "Come. Yndris's vigil is a holy ritual I refuse to delay, but upon your return to Sharakhai, you will both present yourselves in the courtyard, where you'll receive ten lashes each."

"Yes, Matron," Yndris and Çeda said together.

Zaïde watched them as they knelt. Everyone clearly felt uncomfortable, including Çeda. But she, Çeda, had *felt* that man's life. She had *lived* his memories. The only thing remotely similar had been the emotions she'd felt from King Külaşan in the moments before she'd killed him in his hidden desert palace. She'd never dreamed of being connected to the asirim so strongly, or that they would remember so much.

And in truth the nature of her connection—the wound, the poison, the anger flowing like a river—didn't concern her as much as the magnitude of the asirim's suffering. For too long she'd thought of them as less than human, creatures without lives of their own. She'd known the truth of it, but until tonight, she hadn't felt it in her heart.

How foolish I've been. How thoughtless. They were victims four centuries ago on the night of Beht Ihman, and they were victims now. She'd been so fixated on the Kings, she'd forgotten about those who had lifted them to their thrones on Tauriyat. She would make that mistake no longer.

Late the following evening, Zaïde trudged up the dark, winding stairs of the Matron's tower toward her room. Her candle threw strange shadows as she wound her way upward. She was more tired than she'd been in years, and yet she wondered if she'd be able to sleep. Her mind kept drifting to that strange scene in the blooming fields. The asir. Yndris lopping off its head. Çeda attacking Yndris in retaliation. Later, she'd been unable to shake the memory of the scene in the courtyard, where Çeda and Yndris had received their lashes. Yndris had acquitted herself well enough, crying out near the end, but Çeda had been stone silent. With the sun rising in the east, she'd stared at the keep's outer gates, jaw set grimly, eyes watering from the pain. But she hadn't made a sound. Not once. Not even when Kameyl had whipped her harder near the end in order to make her do so.

Çeda could be so very stubborn. It was half the reason Zaïde had waited so long to speak to her. She wanted the girl to learn patience, but Zaïde now wondered if she ever would.

As she neared the fourth floor and her bed, her candle guttered. A draft, likely from Sayabim leaving her windows open again. "Tulathan's light," Zaïde said under her breath, "live on the mountainside if you love the cold so much." She was old as Tauriyat anyway. The two of them would likely get along fine, trading stories from dusk till dawn.

She laughed at her own lack of charity. *You're not so very much younger, Zaïde Tülin'ala.*

She'd have a word with Sayabim in the morning. Winter was on them. There was no sense risking the flu. And yet when she reached the landing of the uppermost floor, the chill washing over her feet came not from Sayabim's door, nor the other two Matrons', but from her own. She remembered then that she *had* closed her shutters that morning, just before she'd left for a bath and her midday meal.

Stopping short of her door, she reached out, felt a heartbeat from within the room. She recognized it immediately. Closing her eyes, she gathered what patience she could—*Nalamae lend me strength, why does the girl have to be so headstrong?*—then opened the door to find a dark form sitting in the chair beside the open window. She worried Çeda might have been seen stealing up the stairs of the tower, but when she looked at the open shutters, understanding dawned on her. Çeda had *climbed* here and had been lying in wait since. Clever. Tulathan had already set, and Rhia shone in the east, which had given her all the shadows she'd needed to remain hidden during her climb. More clever still, she'd left the shutters open, a subtle cue to warn Zaïde so she didn't cry out and alert any of the other Matrons on this floor.

Zaïde stepped inside and closed the door. The latch set home with a soft clink. "Explain yourself," she said in a bare whisper.

Çeda pushed herself to her feet. With the candlelight wavering, she looked as old and merciless as Sayabim. "I'm not the one who needs to explain."

Zaïde took a step forward, thrust a finger at Çeda's chest. "I will not have you—"

But her voice trailed away, for Çeda was holding out a folded piece of papyrus between two fingers. When Zaïde made no move to take it, Çeda shook it, and when Zaïde *still* refused, Çeda took her hand and placed it in her palm. That done, she stepped back and lowered herself gingerly into the chair, sitting stiff-backed to avoid putting pressure on her fresh wounds. She motioned to the note. "Read it."

After taking a moment to let her anger subside, Zaïde took the candle to her bedside, sat down, and by candlelight read.

I know not how much you know of the asirim, but know this: I felt them last night. I felt the mind of the one who was killed. I felt his life before he was given as sacrifice by the Kings to the desert gods. I felt him as a man, felt all his hopes and dreams, felt them as they burned to ashes and were lost to the wind so that the Kings could secure their place in the desert.

The asirim have waited four hundred years for justice. While you and I remain warm and sheltered in a tower of the Kings' making, they wait still. And they suffer.

No longer will I stand aside. Teach me or I will take matters into my own hands.

Zaïde read it again, then set it to flame and let it burn along the candle's brass base. There was anger in her over Çeda's presumption, over the risk she'd taken in coming here, but in truth she'd felt this confrontation coming for months. She knew Çeda's nature, and knew as well she would not rest forever.

"You felt so much?" she said after a time.

Çeda nodded.

There had been a day when Zaïde had felt similar things, but those days were long gone, and she'd never had visions as strong as Çeda seemed to. She'd lost the ability long ago, well before she'd taken the Matron's white. She'd never understood why. Perhaps her own deep-rooted fear of the asirim. Or perhaps the asirim themselves sensed her hesitance and distanced themselves from her because of it. Whatever the case, it was clear Çeda was more gifted than Zaïde had guessed those months ago when she'd saved her from the adichara poison.

Zaïde motioned to the dying flames. "You shouldn't have penned those words. If you'd been found and searched—"

"We cannot speak," Çeda cut in. "We cannot share words. What can we do, Zaïde? When do we act?"

"Only when the time is right. We must take care, and move with precision."

"And while we *take care*, the asirim die."

"They are already dead." She immediately regretted the words.

Çeda paused before speaking again. "Do you believe them less worthy than us?"

"No. But if you have their welfare in mind, then you must know that all can be unraveled if we act brashly, as you have done tonight."

Çeda stood, grimacing from the effort. "We unravel ourselves if we wait too long. I am not advising that we act in haste. But we must *act*, Zaïde. And soon. Our kin have waited long enough." She moved to the window and crept up onto the sill. "I'll give you one week."

Zaïde's spine stiffened at Çeda's tone. "Or what?"

Çeda spun on her toes, seemed to gather herself before speaking again. "Are you aware that a man breached the walls of Tauriyat three weeks ago?"

"Everyone in the House of Kings is aware."

"Are you also aware that the assassin gained the walls of Eventide? That he attempted to kill several of the Kings? That he scratched the Confessor King's cheek with a poisoned arrow?"

Any annoyance Zaïde had felt over Çeda's tone vanished with these words. Zaïde *was* aware of the assassin, but Çeda shouldn't have been. The information had been shared with only a handful outside of the Kings themselves.

When Zaïde chose not to reply, Çeda said, "The assassin was no man." And then she was gone, climbing down the tower, though along what handholds and footholds Zaïde had no idea.

A slow burning rage built inside Zaïde at the implications of what Çeda had said. Çeda was the assassin. She'd taken matters into her own hands without ever speaking to Zaïde about it. And what had come of all that risk? A Spear dead. A Maiden fallen.

And yet . . .

She'd come close. By the account King Ihsan had given her, Kiral might have been killed without Mesut's quick action. Husamettín had protected himself with his usual deadly skill, but *Cahil's* life had been a very near thing. The poison had acted quickly and might have finished him had a healing elixir not reversed the damage it had caused.

And she'd done it all on her own. Was Çeda right? Was she being too cautious? She could remember only dimly now the sorts of visions Çeda had mentioned. A woman running over the sand toward the gathered might of the desert tribes. She remembered the howling, the glee, the terrible thirst for blood.

That old life of hers felt so close at hand, as if she could take it up again if she wanted, make a difference by the might of her own sword arm. She knew at the same time that her day in the sun had passed, and it brought on the feelings of failure she felt so often. "What have you done in all your years, old woman?"

Little enough. Despite all her hopes to the contrary, the might of the Kings had always felt too large for her to stand against—a ceaseless windstorm, she but a grain of sand.

Zaïde closed the shutters, then returned to her bed and blew out the candle. She lay awake for hours, haunted by her decades of failure. She found sleep only after she decided what she must do next.

Chapter 6

Thirteen years earlier...

Çeda woke to the sounds of the city coming alive. She got out of the bed she shared with her mother, taking the blanket with her. Her mother always snapped at her for getting the blankets dirty, but she wasn't around to yell at Çeda just then, was she? She shuffled over to the window and pulled the heavy curtains aside, then breathed out and watched the fog of her breath dissipate in the cold winter air. Outside were the streets of the Red Crescent, the neighborhood that surrounded the city's small western harbor. Beyond the buildings she could see the tops of the ships' masts, dozens of them, bare and sharp like the legs of some strange, overturned insect.

Far to the east, bells began to ring. It came from Tauriyat, little more than a mound in the distance. The palaces would ring their bells first, followed by the House of Maidens, then the manses scattered across Goldenhill. It traveled through the rest of the city as people paid honor to the asirim, the city's sacred defenders, and the men and women they'd taken as tribute during the holy night of Beht Zha'ir. The asirim protected the Kings, the legend went, but also the city itself.

Protected the city from what, Çeda wasn't quite sure. Some said the threat of the desert tribes. Others said the kingdoms that neighbored the Great Shangazi. Whatever the case, the story said they were the blessed, beloved by the gods themselves, but how could creatures as terrifying as the asirim be beloved by the gods? Her mother, Ahya, said some stood vigil on the night of Beht Zha'ir, waiting, hoping to be chosen, but Ahya never did and Çeda certainly didn't either. She huddled in their home when the holy night came to Sharakhai, often with her mother, but sometimes Çeda was left to clutch her blanket alone, listening in fear as the asirim howled across the city—like last night, when Ahya had gone to the desert to collect her petals. She'd never admitted her purpose to Çeda, but Çeda knew. She'd seen her mother pressing the pale blue adichara petals in her small book of poems more than once.

Through the window, Çeda could see a goodly length of the Waxen Way, where she and her mother had moved only a few weeks before. She wished her mother would appear along the street below, bringing home fresh goat's milk, some fruit, or a loaf of bread, but Çeda knew better. If Ahya hadn't returned by now she'd probably be gone until early evening. She wouldn't want to be seen returning from the desert early enough for anyone to suspect she'd spent the night outside the boundaries of Sharakhai. To be found guilty of being out on Beht Zha'ir would earn you a public flogging. To be found near the blooming fields would mean death.

Part of her was glad her mother would be gone. There was a boy she'd recently met. Emre. He was fun. And funny. And his friends had all taken to her right away. All but the one called Hamid. He was always so quiet it made her wonder what he was hiding.

A short while later, as she was shoveling a handful of pistachios into her mouth, several clattering noisily onto the floor, she saw him. He was walking with Demal and Tariq. She quickly picked up the pistachios she'd dropped and stuffed them in her mouth while shedding her night clothes. After pulling on a pair of boy's trousers and a shirt that had seen better days, she sprinted out and down the stairs, winding around and around until she reached the ground floor and headed out into the street.

"Hello, Emre," she said as she came near.

"*Hello, Emre,*" Tariq echoed with a sneer. He had dusty blond hair and hardly more meat on his bones than Çeda had on hers.

Emre gave Tariq a shove. He looked like he was about to say something when Demal broke in, "We're already late. Bring your new girlfriend if you want." He gave Çeda a friendly wink as he spoke, then continued down the street.

"Where're we going?" Çeda whispered to Emre as Demal and Tariq led the way.

"Off for a bit of fun. You in?"

Glancing back at the empty window of her home, Çeda shrugged. "I'm in."

Demal turned as he walked, giving Çeda a flash of his bright smile. "Another added to my growing flock." He was well older than Tariq and Emre, who Çeda was pretty sure were both her age, seven or thereabouts. She'd only met Demal the other day, but she could already see the swagger he had about him. He knew what he was about, a confidence that ran much deeper than Tariq's defiant cockiness.

With the morning wind kicking up a bit of desert dust, they marched along the Waxen Way to the Spear, then made their way eastward toward the Wheel, stopping once so that Demal could buy them each a warm meat pie filled with ground lamb, onions, and a gravy so thick and savory it made Çeda's mouth water with each and every bite. "Never let it be said my wrens go without," Demal said as he licked his fingers clean.

They passed a squad of eight Silver Spears heading in the opposite direction. They'd done nothing wrong, and yet Çeda's heart began to thump in her chest. Emre and Tariq stepped aside and waited. Çeda moved behind them, eyeing the Spears, standing stock-still. But Demal removed his white woolen cap and bowed with a flourish. Çeda didn't understand why he was doing it, exactly, but she knew it was rude. The lead Spear stared at Demal, and looked like he was nearly ready to do something about it, but then he leaned into his comrades and mumbled something. They laughed, staring at the lot of them—dirty, threadbare gutter wrens, one and all—and continued on their way.

When they'd passed, Demal spit onto their path, though not, Çeda noticed, when any of them were looking. Soon they reached the Wheel, the grand open circle in the center of the city. Already traffic was busy, carts and horses and people flowing through the circle from one of the four streets that crossed here in the center of the city.

Demal turned around and sized the three of them up. "A bit more rough and tumble, methinks." Immediately Emre and Tariq took dirt and rubbed it over their hands and face. Demal snapped his fingers at Çeda. "You as well." Çeda complied, but stopped when Demal laughed. "Dear gods, you're meant to look like a west end urchin, not a bloody golem from Malasan." He wiped off some of the dirt, sized her up anew, and then nodded. "Well enough."

Demal ordered them to the edge of the Wheel, but not so far that those passing through couldn't still see them. He looked to Emre. "You can enlighten our young wren?" Emre nodded, and then Demal headed into the crowd looking for all the world like a little lost dove.

"Keep your eyes on him," Emre said to Çeda, "and look sad."

"I do look sad."

"No, you don't. You look like the jackal who swallowed the finch."

Çeda laughed. She tried hard to hide her excitement, but Emre's look made it all the harder, and soon she was laughing outright, the crowd staring at her and the others as they strode or rode past.

"Gods, just send her home," Tariq said.

"No, I can do it." But she didn't actually stop smiling until she got a sour look from Demal. The look made her feel small and childish, and she felt bad for disappointing him.

After a good long stare, Demal seemed satisfied and proceeded to stop random passersby and tell them stories. A tale of woe, she later learned. Their mother had gone to a caravanserai to pick up their ailing grandmother. She'd been robbed at the caravanserai and could no longer afford the return passage home and could they spare a sylval or two to help?

Sharakhai was famous for how many ships arrived the day after Beht Zha'ir. Who would want to arrive just *before* Beht Zha'ir, after all? As Demal began working his magic, Emre went on. "The richest among these fine, wide-eyed does," he said, "often have their purses cinched tighter than Tariq's arse." Tariq scowled and gave him an elbow. Emre shot him a quick smile before putting his sad face back on. "And the crews of the sandships have little enough to spare. It's the people like them." He pointed to the couple in green finery speaking with Demal, who held his woolen cap tightly in his hands. "They're the ones ripe for the plucking."

Demal got nothing from that first couple, but he moved on, undaunted.

He changed the story for each couple he stopped, and it was *always* couples. If a Malasani merchant was walking the Wheel, Demal might say their mother was lost in Ishmantep, a caravanserai they'd likely passed through on the way to Sharakhai. If it was a Qaimiri lordling, it would be Mazandir. And he would change the caravanserai based on how rich they appeared to be: the poorer the lord and lady, the nearer the serai was to Sharakhai, and so, the cheaper the passage; the richer, however, and their fictional mother was magically transported to one of the farthest serais along the path to their assumed country of origin. Two women wearing green silk dresses even gave Demal a *rahl*, a full piece of gold, and this after they'd given him two sylval and Demal had been bold enough to ask for more, explaining that the fare from Rienza was expensive indeed.

They did well that day. Very well. Çeda saw coins pass to Demal's hands several times an hour. They moved locations now and again, sometimes to try their luck in a new place, other times because a Silver Spear told them to shove off or catch the flat side of his blade for the trouble. Near midday Demal bought a sprig of yellow jasmine from a vendor at the center of the wheel, near the pool of water. "You hardly look like a girl," he said to Çeda as he put it in her dark brown hair.

She could feel her face flush as he went back to his business. She felt foolish wearing it. Her mother had never been one for putting on airs, so after a few more *prunings*, as Demal put it, Çeda threw the jasmine into the dirt behind her. Soon after, she caught Demal looking at her hair, but he made no mention of it, so neither did she.

They finished a few hours before sundown when the traffic had wound down and most of those freshly arrived in Sharakhai had made it to wherever they'd been headed. As they were starting back toward the Red Crescent, Demal put one arm around Emre's shoulder, the other around Çeda's. "Well, my little wrens, *one* of you must certainly have pleased Bakhi." He squeezed Çeda's neck and hefted his leather purse. All of them heard the satisfying clink. "Tulathan's bright smile, I've never seen the like."

Demal was not a gutter wren. Not really. His father was a stevedore at the southern harbor. His mother was dead. He was the de facto head of his household, and did things like this to make a little extra, to help his father and brothers and sisters. Perhaps that, and the fact that they'd managed to take so much that day, was the reason he did something no one in Sharakhai should do in plain sight.

He opened the purse and began to count the money out. Tariq received his share first. Then Emre. Before he could count out Çeda's, there were three men standing before them in the street, blocking their way.

"Hello, Demal," said the nearest, a shirtless man with a red vest and an expression that made him look calm, like an old friend happy to be reacquainted with someone he'd missed. Except he was no friend. If Demal's expression of poorly masked terror wasn't enough to tell her that, the looks on other two men—utterly blank, like a pair of wild dogs closing in for the kill—would have. The one who'd spoken was Çeda's mother's age. Thirty summers, perhaps. The other two, grizzled men, the both of them, looked years older.

Demal was silent. Grim-jawed. Wide-eyed. He stared at the men as if he knew exactly who they were and deeply regretted that he was now standing before them.

The red-vested man motioned to the alley on their right. "Let's go have a chat, shall we?" Without another word, he walked down the alley, while the other two men remained, watching Demal closely.

Demal glanced over to Tariq on his left, then Çeda on his right. "Alando, there's no need to involve them."

"Bring them all," the red-vested man, Alando, called over his shoulder.

With familiar ease, the larger of the two toughs pulled a straight, slim knife from the leather bracer he wore on his forearm. It was keen-edged, Çeda saw. Well kept. "You heard the man," he said, jutting his stubbled chin toward the alley.

Demal swallowed, then worked his tongue around in his mouth. His cheeks were aflame. He looked ready to bolt, but after only a moment's pause he nodded and followed.

Ahead, Alando had reached a courtyard of sorts. He whistled three high notes and stared upward, a common signal that no one above should watch lest they risk the street toughs' wrath. Çeda and the others soon reached the courtyard, and indeed, the windows above them were all empty save for one three stories above, where a tabby cat lay along a sill, watching them with casual interest.

Alando waited, hands behind his back. Only when Demal and Çeda and the rest came to a stop did he begin to speak. "You've been going to the Wheel for a while, now, haven't you, Demal?"

"A few weeks is all. No more."

"A few months," one of the men called from behind him. "Near a year now."

Alando tilted his head, regarded his man, then settled his cold stare back on Demal. "A few months, he says. Near a year." He paused as if trying to remember some crucial fact. "When did we speak last, Demal?"

"About a year ago," Demal said, "but I haven't—"

"About a year ago," Alando cut in, "and when we spoke, what did I tell you?"

When Demal replied, his tone sounded defeated, like he'd already given up. "I haven't made much." Even Çeda knew he shouldn't have said it. Give, and they'd ask for more. Give them that, and they'd take everything.

"Doesn't look like *not much* to me," Alando said. "That look like not much to you, Meshel?"

"Not to me," said the one with the thin knife, still held loosely by his side.

"Doesn't look like much to him." Alando considered Demal, looked him up and down like a cut of meat he hadn't quite figured out if he was going to buy or not. "The way I see it, Demal, you owe Farah tribute for a year, plus interest." He jutted his chin toward the purse at Demal's side. "We'll take that as the daily amount and extend it from there. You know what that's going to add up to by the time you're done?"

"What I made today was triple any other day this year! And I don't go every day! I've got a family to take care of. Tansu's come up sick. The medicine's expensive. And father needs the salve for his knees more than ever!"

Çeda heard the man coming up behind her. She should have moved, but she was so worried for Demal, what would happen to him and his family, what Alando would do if Demal didn't pay him the money, that her feet were like lead. Meshel, the one with the knife, grabbed her hair and slipped the knife easily under her chin, the tip pointed upward. All he need do is lift it and she'd be done. Her terror drove her up on her tiptoes, but Meshel kept the tip pressed lovingly against her skin. All she could think about was how long it would take to die when Alando decided enough was enough and Meshel did the deed. Gods help her, she *squeaked* in fear like a frightened little mouse, but what was she to do against such a big man?

Demal turned halfway toward her, but kept his eyes squarely on Alando. "Please, don't. Leave her be. She only came with us today, this one time!"

"If you didn't want her involved, Demal, then *you* shouldn't have involved her." He nodded to Meshel, at which point the big man tightened his grip on Çeda's hair and pressed the knife deeper.

This time Çeda shouted from the fright and the pain. She'd never been so afraid, not even when the asirim came howling. But just like those nights, she hated herself for giving in to the fear. Her mother was no victim, and neither was she. Before Demal could say another word, she gripped Meshel's wrist and put all her weight and strength into pulling the knife down. The moment it was free of her skin, she jerked aside and shoved the knife upward as hard as she could.

He wasn't ready for it. The knife drove into the underside of his jaw. How deep it went she wasn't sure, but the moment he loosened his grip on her hair, she dove forward, grabbing a blue, castoff bottle as she rolled back to her feet. As she turned to face Meshel, she felt a burning on the underside of her jaw. The knife *had* cut her, she realized, but she ignored it.

Meshel was holding his throat with his free hand, eyes wide in disbelief. He was half coughing, half choking as he staggered toward her. He swiped clumsily as Çeda ducked. When she came up, she swung the bottle broadly over her head. It crashed into the side of his head and shattered. Çeda felt stinging pain along her palm where the glass cut her. Meshel staggered backward, coughing, eyelids blinking like a butterfly's wings. Then he fell to the dry earth like the broken mast of a sandship, the sounds of his moist gagging filling the small space.

A sound like a hammer on stone preceded the world tilting away. The ground swung up and struck Çeda full on. The only sound in the air was a keen ringing. And then the pain came, something small that blossomed like a newborn sun at the back of her head. Her skull felt like it had been put into a vice and was squeezing, squeezing, ever harder.

As she rolled over, she saw Alando standing over her. "You're a fucking disgrace, Meshel!" He was shouting, but the words were soft and distant, dreamlike in the fabric of the pain that enveloped her. She could understand little. The windows above her seemed impossibly far away, doorways to other worlds. Alando's knife, however, seemed oh so close. He held a *proper* knife—a kenshar, curved and keen, flicker-edged.

He gripped Çeda's hair and lifted her head until the two of them were eye to eye. There was regret in his eyes, as if he knew this had gone too far. He pointed to Meshel with his blade. "He might *die* girl. I can't let this go. You know I can't." Which seemed a strange thing to say since he was the one holding the knife and could do just about anything he pleased.

He was breathing hard now, perhaps working himself up like she'd seen boys do from time to time. But then there came a long, piercing whistle. Alando's head snapped up and his look of indecision became one of confusion. Confusion and a touch of fear.

"This is no business of yours," Alando said, though who he might be speaking to Çeda had no idea.

"My daughter *is* my business," said a voice.

It took a long while to register who had spoken, and still she didn't understand. Why would her mother be here? How could she have found Çeda?

"Your daughter's just taken a knife to my man."

"If your man can't protect himself from a seven-year-old, then perhaps he *deserves* to die."

Footsteps approached, the sound gritty. Alando stood, and finally Çeda could roll over to see. Her mother wore a simple blue dress. A fighting dress, cut at the sides, strips of boiled leather worked into it. She held her shamshir at her side with ease, at the ready. She had always done so when the two of them had practiced at swords, but something had changed. Never had Çeda felt ill intent from her mother. But she felt it now, a *will* to do harm. The signs were all over her. From her half-fighter's stance to the way her body was poised to the way she was ignoring-but-not-ignoring Alando's other man.

Most of all, though, it was in her eyes. There was a dangerous quality in them Çeda had never seen before, not even when she was shouting at Dardzada the apothecary, arguing with him over this or that.

Ahya turned to where Emre was standing and stared straight at him. "You know where we live?" she asked.

Emre nodded.

"Go, then. Take my daughter home."

"You can't have her," Alando said, holding the kenshar so tight his knuckles turned white.

Ahya said nothing. She merely stared him straight in the eyes, the tip of her sword waggling as she dropped incrementally into a proper fighter's stance. She was a bowstring drawn, a black laugher ready to charge. And Alando knew it, good and well. He held perfectly still and said no more.

Emre came to Çeda's side and helped her to stand. With Tariq and Demal following, Emre supported her as they walked unsteadily from the courtyard and returned to the buzz and bustle of the Spear. As the thoroughfare made way for them, subsumed them, caught them up in its ever-flowing currents, Emre whispered into Çeda's ear. "What's she going to do?"

"Never mind."

She might have heard a shout. She might have heard a scream of pain, cut short a moment later, but she couldn't be sure. The traffic along the Spear was too loud.

In the days ahead, Çeda would hear rumors of a rival gang eliminating another in the Red Crescent. She would hear of three of their men being killed in vicious fashion. She would hear of their leader, a particularly ruthless woman named Farah, who'd been found face down in the Haddah's riverbed, both of her little fingers missing. She would hear that the remaining few members of Farah's crew, having no idea who'd murdered their leader, had moved on to a rival gang before they too were given back to the desert.

In the days ahead, she would learn those things and more, but that night Çeda knew none of them, and when her mother came home safe and whole and stitched Çeda's wounds, the two of them lay with one another long into the night, Ahya stroking her hair while Çeda cried herself to sleep.

Chapter 7

ALONG THE SHORE OF the Austral Sea in the castle of Viaroza, Ramahd sat within a coach, waiting for the train of horses and wagons to begin the trek toward Almadan. A cold wind blew. Dozens had come from the castle to bid them farewell. They waved, but their eyes . . . Mighty Alu, there was a haunted quality to them that made Ramahd wonder what could have caused it, and in so many of them!

Just as he turned to Meryam to ask her about it, Lord Hamzakiir's tall form strode past his window, blocking the sun momentarily. Ramahd's heart lifted to see him, but Hamzakiir didn't so much as glance his way as he made for the front of the train.

Like Ramahd, those gathered in the courtyard at the foot of the castle stairs—the steward, the guards, the page boys, the cooks, the maids, the smith and his massive wife, the stable master, and over a dozen children—all basked in Hamzakiir's presence. They looked mad with glee, and for a moment, Ramahd saw himself in them and wondered, *Is that how* I *look?* The thought unnerved him, but the next moment he was waving to the gathering and leaning back into the padded bench as the coach lurched into motion and rattled beyond the walls.

Across from him, Meryam was picking at her nails again. "Stop it," he said. "You'll ruin your hands." Indeed, her nails were already bloody, the cuticles a torn, red mess.

She stared down at her hands, placed them in her lap, where rust-colored stains now marred the robin's egg blue cloth. A moment later she was back at them, picking, scratching. "There's something strange about him."

"Hamzakiir? Don't be foolish, and lower your voice." He motioned up to where the driver and guard were sitting. "You know how the others talk, and you know how very loyal they are to him."

"I know," she said softly. "It's only . . . something has happened. I just haven't been able to work out what."

A handsome man, staring Ramahd in the eye, holding a knife. "Meryam, stop it."

"In the dungeon. Dana'il was with me. You'd gone for a swim. I was speaking with him, though why we were in the dungeon I can't recall."

That same man, lying on the filthy floor, his body bent at odd angles, as if he'd died in terrible pain.

"Meryam, I told you to *stop it.*"

"We were looking into one another's eyes. I was speaking to him, but he . . . he was whispering. At first, I could barely hear it, but then it was all I could hear."

What was his name? Meryam had said it only a moment ago. He'd been a dear, dear friend, hadn't he? Now he was a man with no grave because Ramahd hadn't seen fit to give him one. Though Ramahd couldn't explain why, a surge of rage rose up inside him. He lifted his hand and backslapped Meryam. She reeled, but then looked him in the eye with a dread anger. She seemed ready to speak, so he slapped her a second time. Blood trickled from her split lip, down along her chin. It pattered against her dress, mixing with the older, smaller stains.

She blinked, ran a finger up the trail of blood, brought it to her mouth and licked it. Her nostrils flared. Her eyes went wide, as if she'd come to some new understanding, and then her look grew worried, frantic. "What have we done, Ramahd."

The cold dread in her words sent a shiver up Ramahd's spine. "We've done nothing. It's only your nightmares. You've been having them again, haven't you?"

Meryam seemed to shrink into herself. She was edgy as a rosefinch, her face aghast. It made Ramahd nervous just to look at her. "They're with me all the time." Her words came in a thin rasp, so desperate Ramahd wanted to weep for her. She was staring through the coach window. The humid air blew in and threw her fine hair across her face. She ignored it and blinked, a tear streaming down one cheek. "All the time, and yet when I put my mind to it I remember so little. I see glimpses. Echoes of a life I once led."

"They're dreams, Meryam. Things have been difficult. We'll go to Almadan and attend our lord as he bids us, and when we return, I'll see if we might not take a carriage ride to see the gardens of Dalasera."

"He's done something terrible."

Ramahd lowered his voice. "I told you to hold your tongue."

"He did something to Dana'il. He made him do it."

The man on the dungeon floor, a red smile across his stomach, knife lying forgotten in a lifeless, bloody hand.

As he had so often this past week, Ramahd pushed the strange memory away. It made him irrationally angry to do so. Why, he wasn't sure. All he knew was that Meryam was the common thread; these things only seemed to happen around her. His anger at his own confusion and Meryam's small disobediences had been accreting like snow along a mountainside, each one making it more and more ponderous. Now the snowpack began to fracture, to fall in a rapidly growing avalanche. Before he knew what he was doing he'd wrapped his hands around Meryam's scrawny neck. Her eyes bulged as he squeezed, as he used his weight to press her back against the padded bench. Her blood-stained fingers clawed at him, but she was too frail to stop him. Her face went red. She tried kicking at him, but his body was too close to hers for it to do any good. She struggled. She squirmed. And still Ramahd squeezed tighter as the wind blew through the cabin, throwing her dark hair across her face.

That look. He'd seen it on another woman's face. He'd been standing on a wide veranda. His wife, Yasmine, long dead now, her bones buried in the desert. A girl had been standing beside her. Precious Alu, his daughter, Rehann. He'd forgotten how very small she'd looked as Yasmine led her through the dance steps of the seguidilla while Ramahd and Meryam watched. They'd clapped in time and hummed the tune while Yasmine and Rehann whirled and spun, their path curling over the veranda's red stones.

When they'd finished, Meryam had clapped, her eyes filled with pride, and said, "That was *perfect*, little one. You'll be the envy of them all." Rehann's smile had filled him with light for days.

It had been windy that day, and as Rehann had come to the table to finish her plate of dates and honey, Meryam had scooped her up and set her on her lap. The wind had played with Meryam's hair. How different the two of them were: the Meryam of old, strikingly pretty, her face elegantly full, and the Meryam of now, so gaunt she looked like the starving beggars of Sharakhai.

Meryam was still clawing at him, but her strength was flagging. As her eyelids began to flutter, Ramahd snatched his hands back, his chin quivering. *By the gods who breathe, what's happening to me?* Why was he always so angry? Why did he blame Meryam for it? None of this was her fault, was it?

But if not hers, whose fault is it?

Meryam took in a long, hitched breath, then began coughing heavily, eyes red and watery as she stared at him, shocked as she was pained.

Ramahd sat back on the bench as the coach bounced along. He looked out to a day so pleasant it begged to be watched. They were passing a farmstead. A man and his son stood from their work and waved to the train. Ramahd waved back, wondering who could be angry on a day such as this.

"Don't worry," he said to Meryam without looking at her. "We'll reach the capital soon. We'll have a grand time, and the two of us will forget any small tiffs we had along the way."

Meryam said nothing, but Ramahd knew they would.

Surely they would.

Four days later, they reached Almadan. The city rose above the green landscape and the nearby forests like some leviathan of the sea. They rode through the vast city, its citizens stepping aside for the train of coaches and horses. When they reached Santrión, Almadan's stout castle upon its hill, it was not Ramahd's footman who came to set the stairs in place, but Hamzakiir.

"My lord?" Ramahd said.

Hamzakiir touched the back of his neck and whispered something into his ear. The moment he did, the world blurred. He was led into the castle proper. Lords and ladies greeted him, men and women who looked so very familiar, and yet he could neither place them nor remember their names. Despite this, he found himself holding conversations with dozens, singly or in groups, as if he were nothing more than a puppet.

For a day or more this went on. He moved from place to place, eating, talking, even dancing at a formal ball, and all the while he felt as though he were lost in the sort of deep fog that rolled off the sea in spring and swallowed Viaroza for days at a time.

But it all changed when he was given an audience with Meryam's father, King Aldouan. Meryam came as well, as did Hamzakiir. They supped in a grand room covered in tapestries. The fire snapped in the broad hearth behind the king, as they were brought roast venison with blueberry sauce, black mushroom caps stuffed with rice, mango, and sweet lobster meat, a squash soup with a currant-pepper spice he'd missed terribly while traveling in the desert. More courses came and went, but at last the king, a thickset man with a dark beard and eyes very much like Meryam's, bid all the servants to leave the room. The king spoke to Meryam and Ramahd almost exclusively, all but ignoring Hamzakiir. He asked detailed questions about how long they had questioned Hamzakiir, what he had divulged of the Twelve Kings of Sharakhai, and how, in the end, they had broken him.

What a nonsensical question, Ramahd thought. They hadn't *broken* Hamzakiir. They had merely traveled with him to the capital from his estate along the coast. And he'd divulged nothing to Ramahd. Why would he? And yet Meryam answered the king as if Hamzakiir had, telling her father how long it had taken in the dungeon, how she'd worn him down, how she'd used Ramahd to lure Hamzakiir out and chain his mind to hers. "In the end, I broke down his walls, and there was nowhere left for him to hide."

"And your hands?" Aldouan asked, clearly concerned over Meryam's partially healed fingers.

Meryam hid them in her lap. "It was a stressful time, father."

The king's expression was one of ill-concealed disgust. "Well I daresay it's over now, Meryam. Get ahold of yourself."

"Of course, father," she replied easily.

"You're sure that he's ours?" Aldouan asked.

Meryam nodded with the sort of enthusiasm a maid reserves for suitors asking her to dance. "Would you like to see?"

"I would," Aldouan replied, his eyes betraying his deep-seated curiosity.

"Well then," Meryam said to Hamzakiir. "Come, the king wishes to see a demonstration."

Hamzakiir nodded and complied, pushing his chair back to stand beside Meryam.

"Bow to your king."

Hamzakiir bowed low, but he did not drop his gaze, as one should before the king. Instead, he stared at Aldouan with a look of hunger. If Aldouan was concerned, he didn't show it. But *Ramahd* was concerned. This wasn't right. None of it was right. Why was his mind so muddled?

"Now serve him wine."

Hamzakiir rose and strode proudly toward the head of the table, where King Aldouan sat. Feeling an indescribable fear, Ramahd made to rise from his chair. He'd managed to grip the chair's arms, to push himself off the padded seat, before he found himself sitting silently once more, his body trembling.

Hamzakiir was his lord. Hamzakiir was his enemy.

I can't let this happen. I can't.

Hamzakiir retrieved the wine from its silver platter at the serving table behind the king. He filled Aldouan's half-empty glass. "In truth," Aldouan said to Meryam while lifting his glass, "I thought we'd be forced to kill him."

Hamzakiir set the bottle of wine back on its platter, but instead of returning to his seat, he stepped behind Aldouan's chair.

"Don't!" Ramahd called.

It was the only word Ramahd managed to utter. Hamzakiir's eyes were on him, and he was silent once more, watching a scene unfold that was always going to play out in just this way.

Aldouan set down the wine and turned to see what had so shaken Ramahd, but Hamzakiir's left hand was already clamping over Aldouan's mouth while his right snatched the king's wrist and pressed a thumbnail sharp as a badger's claw deep into the king's flesh. Blood poured from the wound. Aldouan tried to use his free hand to scratch Hamzakiir's face, but Hamzakiir was fiercely strong and it was all too easy for him to maneuver away from the king's clumsy swipes. Legs flailing for purchase, Aldouan struggled as Hamzakiir held his bleeding wrist over the freshly poured glass of wine. Blood dripped. Aldouan seemed transfixed, so much so that he stopped thrashing for a moment. As understanding dawned on him, however, he struggled all the harder to escape.

It was Meryam who came and stopped him. She grabbed his free hand and held it tight against the table. "Shhhh. It will all be over soon."

A glow of flame formed in the palm of Aldouan's hand, the one Meryam was holding. He was accomplished in the ways of blood magic, but he was surrounded by two adepts. Meryam leaned down and banished the burgeoning spell with a puff of breath from her pursed lips.

All this time, Hamzakiir had been watching Ramahd. His mere gaze held Ramahd in place. *Fight him*, Ramahd called to his King. *Deny them, or we are all lost!* But nothing Ramahd did would allow him to speak again. He was well and truly trapped in the fetters Hamzakiir had placed on his mind in the dungeon of Viaroza.

"I must admit, I'm impressed," Hamzakiir said to Ramahd while holding Aldouan steady. "I doubt there's been one like you in generations." At first Ramahd had no idea what he meant by that, but then he thought he understood. His resistance to Hamzakiir's will. Had there been others like him? It would perhaps explain why Hamzakiir's commands, this grand ruse he'd sewn within Ramahd's and Meryam's minds, had been imperfect at the seams and had never quite taken hold of Ramahd.

"But now," Hamzakiir continued, "it's time we went on." He released Aldouan's bloody wrist and snatched up the wineglass while keeping his other hand firmly over Aldouan's mouth. Aldouan swiped at the glass, managing to bat it once. Wine splashed over the plate of half-finished food and the fine white tablecloth. But Hamzakiir kept his hold on the glass and brought it to his lips. He downed it in three long swallows.

Aldouan fought all the harder, his muffled screams sending a chill down Ramahd's spine. The king managed to snatch his arm from Meryam and shove her away. He tried desperately to wrest himself free, wriggling like a fish in the bottom of a boat, but soon his movements grew less frantic, then pathetically weak, until at last he was sitting in his chair, staring along the length of the table, blinking as if he'd just woken from a terrible dream.

Hamzakiir released him, at which point King Aldouan looked down at the table, at the spilled wine and spilled blood, then ran his hands down his rich clothes as though that would clean it all up. He took up the napkin in his lap and began furiously rubbing the blood from his fingers. "Call for the servants, won't you?" he said to Meryam. "Have them bring us our dessert."

Meryam did, and what followed was surreal. The servants entered with confusion plain on their faces, cleaning the mess as best they could while staring with sidelong glances at the four gathered for dinner, then bringing roasted pears with cinnamon-ginger cream drizzled over the top. The king ignored them all, constantly dipping his napkin into his water glass to clean more of the blood from his skin and clothes. Meryam and Ramahd stared at one another. Ramahd was living the script Hamzakiir had written for him while also watching it play out. He'd become both spectator and actor in the most horrifying play ever written.

Ramahd could see from Meryam's expression she felt the same; there was a composed look on her face, but also a sickened gleam in her eyes, a defiant quiver on her lips. All the while, Hamzakiir watched with a level of satisfaction that made Ramahd want to crash his skull in with a mace.

He had trouble remembering what happened after that. Hamzakiir was much more careful, knowing now that Ramahd had found some way—or had inherited it by dint of blood—to resist the domination of his mind. Even so, it was different than before. Ramahd now recognized who Hamzakiir was: the son of King Külaşan, a blood mage, a man who threatened the King of Qaimir; indeed, a man who threatened the very monarchy. And yet having that knowledge did him no good. The puppet show continued, Hamzakiir feasting in the halls of Almadan, King Aldouan praising him to any and all who came for an audience, Ramahd and Meryam playing along, trapped within their own minds.

And then came the most troubling realization of all. In one lucid moment, Ramahd heard King Aldouan bidding his chamberlain to make arrangements for travel to the Shangazi Desert. They would travel by land, then take a sandship from Ur'bek and over the amber sea.

It wasn't the fact that Hamzakiir would return to the desert—Ramahd had reasoned he would do that eventually—nor was it the fact that Ramahd and

Meryam would be joining him. What troubled Ramahd was the fact that for the first time in his life, King Aldouan would be taking to the sands as well.

Ramahd's days blurred. His nights became unending pits of terror. He seldom woke from the fugue Hamzakiir had placed on him, but it did him little good. Hamzakiir had become adept at noticing when Ramahd was beginning to wake, and when that happened, he would come, he would whisper in Ramahd's ear, and the world would return to its dreamlike state.

He saw them preparing to leave Almadan. Saw them travel cross country and into the mountains that bordered the Great Shangazi. Saw them pass through the Last Keep and down the divide toward the desert proper. Soon they had reached Ur'bek, a collection of sandstone buildings radiating outward from a deep well and a set of stone piers where sandships were berthed. In short order the *Blue Heron* was being outfitted for a long voyage over the sands.

"Please, my Lord King," his cousin, Duke Hektor, was saying. "Surely I, along with Meryam and Ramahd, who have done so well in Sharakhai, can carry out your will in the desert."

Aldouan gripped Hektor's shoulders and held him at arm's length, the two old men staring at one another with emotion in their eyes. They loved one another dearly, Ramahd knew, but it was a false display on Aldouan's part, more tragic than anything else.

"My Lord Duke," Ramahd said.

All eyes turned toward him, including Hamzakiir, who stared with eyes ablaze.

"Yes, Ramahd," Hektor said.

The dry desert wind played across the deck of the ship, sending a biting spray of sand along with it. Ramahd swallowed. This was his last chance. *Hamzakiir plays you falsely. He plays us all falsely.* He tried to say the words, but no matter how he tried to coax them out, they would not come. "I will lay down my life, if it comes to that. As will Meryam. We will see our king safely home. This I swear to you and to Qaimir."

Hektor seemed confused by his words, but Aldouan smiled and clapped Hektor's shoulders. "You see? All will be well."

"And if, Alu forbid, you don't come back?"

"Then my daughter Meryam shall be named queen," Aldouan said. And when Hektor asked the next logical question, seeing as Meryam was there with him, he waved him off, and said, "If I don't come to an accord with the Kings of Sharakhai, the succession will be the least of our worries."

Soon they were off, onto the endless sands. Ramahd woke again as the ship rocked back and forth, the swell of the dunes like the roll of the waves on the Austral Sea. He sat up, groaning. "Dana'il?"

Quezada was coiling a length of rope beneath the gunwale. He looked at Ramahd as if he were mad. Rafiro glanced over to him from where he stood at the pilot's wheel.

And then it all struck Ramahd like a hammer.

Dana'il wasn't here. He'd died in the dungeon of Viaroza, and Ramahd had been complicit in his death. If the gods were kind, he was no longer there, but for some reason Hamzakiir had killed him brutally, feeling it necessary to make an example, perhaps, or lashing out petulantly as he regained himself.

Ramahd stood, bracing himself on a belaying pin. After the anguish of the previous night, he was surprised to find himself in control of his faculties. Even so, finding his sand legs wasn't easy. The ship kept throwing him around as he strode forward, hand along the gunwale like a useless landsman. Looking over the landscape, he tried to get his bearings. He'd been here before, he was sure, but his mind was so muddied he couldn't place it. Somewhere near Mazandir, perhaps?

Ahead, Hamzakiir stood at the bow, watching the way ahead, ignoring Ramahd and the crew. As Ramahd approached, he looked for something, anything, that might give him some advantage. He might be able to draw the small kenshar hanging from Hamzakiir's belt. Or perhaps he might run and crash into his back, launching him over the gunwale . . .

"Come, come," Hamzakiir said, "you're not so foolish as that."

With those words, the realization that this journey would end exactly as Hamzakiir wished it fell over Ramahd like a heavy cloak. He nearly threw *himself* over the gunwale. Instead he asked, "What will you do with us?"

Hamzakiir half-turned, the wind angling his shoulder-length hair across the curious look on his face. "Meryam is gifted. Her father, if I'm being honest, is but a pale imitation. But you . . . How could your parents have let your potential go untapped?"

"My mother was from Iliatoré."

"Ah," Hamzakiir said with a knowing nod. He'd spent time in Qaimir generations ago, learning the ways of the blood magi from the people who had conceived and nurtured its practices. He would have learned of Iliatoré, the easternmost province of Qaimir where the ways of the magi were not only avoided, but in some places shunned. "Your father held no sway over her?"

"Some, but it was always a losing battle. She was a determined woman."

Hamzakiir smiled wanly. "I know the type."

"Qaimir was your ally once. Do you think you owe us nothing, to take the king and his daughter against their will?"

"I am the son of Külaşan, the Wandering King, now the rightful heir to his throne. If the king's daughter wanted special consideration, she shouldn't have tried to take *me* against my will. And don't pretend he isn't complicit in his daughter's crimes. He knew very well what she had planned to do, and condoned every step of it. You are the one I have some sympathy for, Ramahd Amansir. You knew little enough of their plans. You were but a piece on the board, as I was for a time. But now I am a player. You might be too."

While Hamzakiir gazed across the sands with a placid expression, Ramahd's ire grew. "I would *never* join you."

"Do you know the king and your Meryam had many conversations about you? They considered you headstrong. Too focused on Macide Ishaq'ava for their tastes. Always bucking when the king tried to rein you in."

"He killed my wife and daughter."

Hamzakiir nodded. "I understand your pain. But know this. They had conversations about leaving you behind. Giving you back to the desert, Meryam once said."

Giving someone back to the desert was not only a Sharakhani term, but an ancient custom of the desert tribes, giving their dead to the dunes, which would draw their bones down and embrace those to whom they'd given birth. It was sometimes used in Qaimir by those who thought someone had turned their back on their own country and had come to accept the Shangazi as their home.

"Meryam loves me."

"We can love and still betray for the greater good, can we not? And what of your king? Can you say there was ever any great love between the two of you?"

It was true. There never had been. His arranged marriage to Yasmine had been one of convenience for the king, who at the time had been facing threats from the seas, and needed to secure more of the ships Ramahd's father controlled. But Aldouan had never loved Ramahd for it. The marriage may have been convenient, but it had forced Aldouan to marry off his eldest daughter to a lord who, at that point, had not been greatly respected in the halls of Santrión.

"Did you allow me on deck merely to watch me suffer?" Ramahd asked.

"I am granting you truths that you might make important decisions. You've shown yourself worthy. And you still have a goal, do you not? You still wish to take your revenge, a thing even you will admit was slipping further and further from your grasp well before I was awoken in the catacombs of my father's palace."

"I will not stand by your side."

"Don't, then. Take your prize and return home to Qaimir."

"My prize . . . ?"

"Macide."

Unbidden, a host of chilling memories ran through Ramahd's mind. His wife running across the sand, an arrow taking her through the chest, their daughter dying of thirst as he and the other survivors of the Bloody Passage struggled to reach the nearest caravanserai. Ramahd pinched the bridge of his nose, driving away the memories that Hamzakiir himself had surely drawn up. "You would give me Macide, and let me go?"

"If that is what you wish. But I could do more. I could see to it that Qaimir *itself* falls into your lap."

The ship rose over a dune. As the *Blue Heron* crested it and sailed down the far side to more shallow sand, Rafiro called out orders to trim the sails.

Ramahd had dreamed of sitting the throne of Qaimir. What lord hadn't? But it wasn't something he yearned for. He would complete his business here and return home. Find a wife. Raise children as he'd always meant to do. "Why would you do this for a man who's your enemy?"

Hamzakiir turned and looked him up and down. "I don't consider you my enemy. As I said, you were caught in a web much larger than you'd ever imagined. Take what I offer and go home if you don't wish to remain in the desert. Or remain by my side and we'll explore how you're able to . . . blunt my attentions. You have only to agree, and it shall be so."

Alu grant him grace, he thought about it for a moment. The pain and confusion of these past weeks had worn on him, and he would give much to have it gone. But he would have to give up too much in order to attain his freedom. Meryam. King Aldouan. They may not have been forthright with him at all times. They may have even discussed sacrificing him like a kulthar piece in a game of aban. But he knew his place in life. He accepted it. He *was* a kulthar, and if his country would be safer for his sacrifice, then he would gladly make it. And his crew, who had been nothing but faithful to Ramahd. How could he abandon them? And then there was Dana'il . . .

"Why did you kill Dana'il?"

"Who?"

"In the dungeon of Viaroza. Why would you force him to use his own knife to kill himself?"

Hamzakiir shrugged. "There was anger in me."

"No. That was not anger. That was cruelty. Dana'il was a loyal friend. I loved him, and you treated him like a dungeon rat."

"Well," Hamzakiir said, looking genuinely disappointed, "I see you've come to your decision."

Until this point, Ramahd had been free, but Hamzakiir once again placed the shackles upon him, and he found himself suddenly speechless. He was forced belowdecks, to the small hold at the rear of the ship, where he and Meryam and King Aldouan slept or sat on the dirty floor. He felt his mind retreating to the small space that Hamzakiir left for him, or perhaps it was the place Hamzakiir couldn't reach. Whatever the case, he reflected on how very tired Hamzakiir had seemed. The man was not without his limits, then. He may have control over them from the blood he'd taken from each, but it still took effort to exert his influence. It wore on him, day by day, which was perhaps as good a reason as any other to offer Ramahd free will, as well as a bit of sanity to contemplate where Hamzakiir was taking them, and why.

With light coming in through the small, shuttered window at the back of the hold, Ramahd could see his king sitting beside Meryam, their backs against the sloping hull. They watched Ramahd with haunted eyes, as if they were pleading with him to do something. But what could he do? They were trapped. Whatever weakness Hamzakiir might have shown, he was too powerful to oppose.

As the rise and fall of the ship over the sands sent the three of them leaning this way then that, Ramahd fought to get words through gritted teeth. "How long?"

Aldouan and Meryam stared at him with hollow eyes.

"How long?" he said again, louder this time.

Both of them looked as though they dearly wished to speak. Their eyes glistened like distant stars. Their mouths quivered.

In the end, it was Meryam who said, "Seven weeks."

The words struck him like a hammer blow. Sweet Alu, seven weeks . . . Could it truly have been so long? All that pain. It had taken place over the course of weeks, not days as he'd assumed. What was worse, though, were the implications. It meant that they'd traveled well beyond Iri's Teeth. They certainly weren't headed for Mazandir; they could easily have reached Sharakhai in seven weeks.

This area of the desert . . . How familiar it had looked. And then, as he stared into Meryam's horrified face, he remembered.

Breath of the desert, they had to free themselves. They had to leave before they reached that blasted plain. He began fighting Hamzakiir's hold on him as he'd never fought before. His desperation gave him strength, but he struggled even to reach his feet. Pain built in him as he moved toward Meryam. He reached out his hand to her, but she merely stared, tears streaming down her face. She couldn't help in this fight.

It was up to him, then. He would have to take Hamzakiir. Somehow, he would have to do it. He walked toward the door. Each shivering footstep that brought him closer brought with it waves of pain. They shot up his legs like lightning, making him shiver from it. Sweat was gathering on his forehead by the time he reached the latch, and it was pouring from him by the time he gained the forward cabin.

Inside, he found a kenshar he'd had for years, a gift from the Kings of Sharakhai to the ambassador of Qaimir. He stalked back down the passageway and climbed the stairs up to the deck. When he reached it, Hamzakiir was still at the bow, looking out over an expanse of desert that looked dark, almost glasslike. His men saw him, but he ignored them. He would rush Hamzakiir. He would send steel deep into his flesh and watch him bleed.

But he'd not gone three steps before he fell to the floor, writhing in pain. As he screamed, the ship slowed.

"Bring them," he heard Hamzakiir call.

He realized he'd blacked out. The ship was no longer moving. He, Meryam, and King Aldouan were thrown down to the sand. Nearby was a vast plain of black stone. They were dragged onto it, the ground cutting their clothes, slicing their exposed skin.

"Far enough," Hamzakiir called after a time. "Stand them up."

"Aye," Rafiro called woodenly, and he, Quezada, and Hernand lifted the three of them, propping them up like drunks standing for the judgment of their lord.

Hamzakiir took the ornamental knife Ramahd had been holding a short while ago and used it to pierce the tip of his thumb. Blood welled there. He came to stand before Meryam, and while whispering words Ramahd couldn't quite make out, drew a bloody symbol on her forehead. Ramahd had stood on this plain with Meryam months ago, and she'd done the same with the blood of a sacrifice, a man, a tanner they'd brought from Sharakhai for the express purpose of summoning an ehrekh. She'd used the blood to protect Ramahd and his men, to give them strength to withstand the presence of Guhldrathen, but this was something wholly different. Hamzakiir was giving them no sign of strength; he was marking them with a sign of summoning, a sign meant to attract Guhldrathen, to make it clear he was giving the beast an offering.

He meant it, perhaps, as a way to release his own debt. Hamzakiir had made some bargain with Guhldrathen in the past to grant him the long life that had saved him in the catacombs of his father. Whatever he'd received, he'd betrayed Guhldrathen, a fact Meryam had exploited to find how she might be able to reach Hamzakiir. It had worked, for all the good it had done them. The tables were now completely turned, and it was Meryam, her father, and Ramahd who would pay the price.

Hamzakiir repeated the ritual before King Aldouan, and then came to stand before Ramahd. There was a saddened look in his eyes as he painted the mark on Ramahd, and when he was done, he met Ramahd's eyes for a moment. "You should have taken my offer."

Ramahd managed enough control to spit in Hamzakiir's face.

Hamzakiir wiped the spittle from his cheeks and chin with the back of his sleeve, then backhanded Ramahd so hard he collapsed to the ground.

"Come," he heard Hamzakiir say. The sound of footsteps resounded over the glasslike stone, then began to fade. "Let the winds bear us to Ishmantep."

He heard the ring and rattle of a ship being readied, of sails being hoisted. A bell was rung. Soon after came the shush of a sandship's runners skimming over the surface of the Shangazi.

Then all was silence save for the haunting wind.

Until dusk neared. That was when Ramahd first heard it. The rhythmic sound of thunder in the distance, pounding, booming, coming nearer and nearer.

Chapter 8

IHSAN THE HONEY-TONGUED KING strode into a room with a cavernous ceiling. Taking a bite of the quince he'd plucked from his garden, he made for the far end of the room, where bright patches of sapphire, emerald, and ruby sunlight splashed against the stone floor from the mid-afternoon sun, which slanted in through a row of tall, stained glass windows. Three sides of the room were occupied by shelves filled with thick tomes, large tables with glass contrivances, and cabinets with a myriad of drawers filled with ingredients so rare they would put any apothecary in Sharakhai to shame.

King Azad stood before one of the many tables, nursing the contents of a flask with a glass rod. He wore a simple flaxen robe with the cowl laid around his narrow shoulders. As he stirred, he dropped a measure of red powder into the brew. The tinkling of the glass and the soft bubbling of the rose-colored liquid mingled with a soft hissing coming from a lidded pot in the far corner. He glanced Ihsan's way as he neared. "You know I don't like to be disturbed."

"And I detest sandstorms, yet they strike the city on their own schedule, not mine." He took another bite of his quince. The fruit was overly crunchy, not quite ripe but deliciously cool after such a hot day. After one last bite, he shot the core into the basket filled with thorny branches and a scattering of blue-white petals, wilted and browning at the edges. The air was thick with the sweet smell of desert flora and other, more bitter scents. "For the love of the gods, Azad, the air has nearly as much bite as my quince." He moved toward a closed window nearby.

"Leave it," Azad snapped. "I'll not have the dust of the city invading this place."

"I swear, one day I'll find you unconscious on the floor." And yet Ihsan made no move to open the window; this might be *his* palace, but allowances were made for projects such as this. "I suppose a bit of thick air is a reasonable price to pay for immortality." He moved to Azad's side instead, where nearby, a mound of thorny branches, cuttings from the adichara, were stacked on the table. He picked up one of them, examining its length. "So what of it? You've reported little progress of late."

"I've only just begun experimenting with the roots you secured from Kundhun. But I *have* made strides."

"And time grows short."

"I'm doing all I can." Azad motioned to the boiling liquid. "My voles are already responding well."

Ihsan laughed as he tossed the branch back onto the pile and picked up a dried adichara bloom from a similar pile beyond it. "We are hardly voles, my good King."

"Laugh if you wish, but the ones I feed it to live twice as long as those I don't. And the ones I cut heal twice as fast."

"Well, well," Ihsan said, "progress indeed. But I will consider it nothing more than an incremental step until you tell me you're ready to test it on man."

Azad paused. With his hands gripping the edge of the table, he scanned its length, as if by doing so he might solve the problems that had plagued him for months. Then he seemed to deflate. From a nearby pitcher he poured a healthy amount of white wine into a glass still wet with the last pouring. After taking one long swallow, he turned to face Ihsan. "I need more time."

"Time . . ." Ihsan would have laughed, but Azad looked so very serious. "As well ask for my head on a platter. You may have all the adichara you could wish for. Any ingredient you like, no matter the cost. You may have all the voles in the desert, or for that matter, all the men and women. Our dungeons are brimming with any number you might wish to call upon. What I *cannot* give you is more time."

"And yet that's what I need. Delay our plans if you must."

"Wheels have been set in motion and, just like time, they cannot be turned back."

After emptying his glass of its wine and pouring another tall measure, Azad stared into Ihsan's eyes with a mixture of anger and worry, the two combining like alchemical components in one of his flasks. How like the old King this Azad looked. Külaşan and Sukru had done an impeccable job in the transformation. No one would notice the imperfections. But in the set of Azad's fiery eyes Ihsan could see not the old but the new. In his voice as well. The deception was nearly perfect, especially after the long months of coaching Ihsan himself had delivered to the actor who had learned, bit by bit, to wear the guise of Azad like a veil. Even so, certain words were shades different from those of the King who'd died twelve years ago. They might be dangerous—clues to those who had known the old Azad well—but Ihsan treasured them. They were subtle nods, the wink of an eye from the imposter who stood before him.

Ihsan reached out and took the glass from Azad's cupped hands. Surprisingly, Azad allowed it. And then Azad's look softened. "I will do all I can," he said evenly, "and if the gods permit it, I will find the key to the elixir we all so desperately want, but I cannot go faster than I already am."

"What if you had help from the collegia?"

"The scholars?" Azad's brow knitted. "You said the risk was too great to involve them."

"If they were allowed to remain in the collegia, yes. But a certain event approaches, one in which some might reasonably have been thought to have vanished."

"Vanished . . ."

"Just so, my good King," Ihsan said.

"How?"

"There's little need for you to worry about the details. Just tell me if it would help."

"These scholars. What would happen to them when their usefulness ended?"

"Now why would you ask such a question when you have no desire to know the answer?"

"Don't presume to tell me my mind. I *do* wish to know."

"No, you don't. Not truly. You wish to rule. To guide Sharakhai to a greater place. Isn't that what we've always planned?"

"It is—"

"Of course it is. Let *me* worry about what happens to the scholars." Ihsan waved to the wealth of apparatuses around them. "*You* worry about the elixir."

Azad looked ready to speak, but just then his gaze swung toward the entrance. Hearing footsteps, Ihsan turned as well, and Tolovan, Ihsan's towering vizir, stepped into the room.

"My Lord Kings," Tolovan said, bowing deeply, "the Matron Zaïde has arrived. Shall I tell her you'll meet with her in your study?"

"No," Ihsan said, "send her here."

"Very good." Tolovan bowed his head, but paused, glancing at Azad and then back to Ihsan. "There is more, my Lord King."

"Then out with it."

"You said to bring you this news whenever it came to me." He was now pointedly *not* looking at Azad, a choice that made his intent perfectly clear: that he wasn't sure whether he should speak in front of Azad or not.

There may come a day when I need to conceal more from Azad, but for the time being we are in this together, for better or worse. "Speak," Ihsan said.

"Word has come that the ship that smuggles the ingredients from Kundhun was attacked."

Ihsan was taken aback. "Attacked?"

"The captain was taken from behind. He was unable to identify his attacker definitively, but suspects it was a woman."

"A Maiden?"

"He couldn't say, my Lord."

"And what was taken?"

"As far as the captain is aware, only a leatherbound journal that contained the captain's personal thoughts on his travels."

"Nothing more? Nothing that might give some clue as to what we were smuggling?"

"The captain believes not."

The captain, a stubborn but loyal Kundhuni, would probably have told the truth, not only for the money Ihsan was paying him, but because honesty was in his blood. "Very well," Ihsan said.

And with that Tolovan bowed and left.

"Could you not meet Zaïde elsewhere?" Azad asked, clearly annoyed. "I have enough to do without constant interruptions."

Ihsan flourished to the now-empty doorway. "One of the aforementioned wheels set into motion."

Azad snorted. He returned to mixing the elixir, then crouched and blew out the burning lamp set beneath it.

"Besides which," Ihsan went on, "you should hear this. I'd like your counsel."

In little time the matron, Zaïde, entered the room in her white robes. Her cowl lay about her shoulders like a mantle, revealing gray hair and a regal, sun-wrinkled face with tattoos along her forehead and cheeks and chin. "My Lord Kings," Zaïde said with a low bow.

When she rose, Ihsan motioned to Azad. "I received your note," Ihsan told her. "You mentioned the disturbing events of young Yndris's vigil. Please, tell us both what happened."

"As you say, My Lord Kings, I joined Sümeya's hand to attend Yndris's vigil. Things were quiet until we reached the killing fields. I could tell well before we arrived the asirim were agitated. Several were nearby when we began the ritual, but one was nearly mad, straining at the chains upon him as we were whispering our devotions. In fact, the very moment Çedamihn was giving hers, the asir broke free."

"This is nothing new," Azad said. "We've seen this sort of behavior before."

Zaïde nodded. "True, what made me pause was that it was linked to the anger within Çeda. I could feel her feeding it to the asir, and the asir in turn feeding its anger back to her. For a time, the two of them were as one. I've never seen the like, in an aspirant or a Maiden. Last night, she stole into my room and confessed she'd *felt* the asir's thoughts. She claimed she saw Beht Ihman through its own eyes."

Well, well, thought Ihsan. When he'd agreed to allow Çeda to live and arranged for her entry into the Maidens, he'd hoped there might be a bond forged between her and the asirim, one that might allow her to break the bonds that had been slowly weakening over the generations since Beht Ihman, but it was still a pleasant surprise to discover he'd been right.

"The asir?" Ihsan asked.

"Beheaded by Yndris when she realized it had targeted her. Çeda fought her afterward, incensed, claiming that it was because of Yndris's disregard for the life wasted."

"There's little surprise in that," Azad said. "Çeda was avenging one of her own."

Ihsan nodded. "Still, I'm surprised she'd be so bold."

Zaïde frowned, her brow knitting. "It wasn't boldness, Your Grace. She was swept up by emotion. She had almost no choice, I suspect. She would have killed Yndris had we not stopped her."

"What else did she say?" Ihsan asked.

"She demanded that I train her that we might free the asirim sooner."

"And what did you tell her?"

"That I would think on it, at which point she threatened to leave the Maidens if I thought on it overly long."

"She *threatened* you?" Azad asked, bristling.

Zaïde nodded. "A threat I believe she'll uphold. She'd been so affected by the asir. She was haunted by the notion of them lying beneath the blooming fields, suffering, and the more they reach out to her, the worse it will become."

Ihsan mulled this for a moment, weighing it against the news Tolovan had brought a short while ago. "May I ask where Çeda was four nights ago?"

"Gone," Zaïde replied. "Sent on a mission by Yusam."

"Do you know where?"

"I wasn't told, my Lord King."

No doubt to the desert. No doubt to a Kundhuni ship that had smuggled in the ingredients for Azad's draughts. "So, the blade we put to the fire has survived." He turned to Azad. "She's been tempered, but we always knew she would one day need sharpening. The question is, has that day arrived?"

Azad may not be a true King, but he was shrewd, and would have as much sway in Ihsan's plans for Sharakhai as anyone. Ihsan needed not only Azad's involvement, but his true belief that this would all go as planned. Too much was at stake to do otherwise.

Azad considered, his eyes moving to a green-tinted splash of sunlight. "I don't like it. To *threaten* a Matron . . . Let her leave."

"We've put much effort and risk into her."

"She can still prove a valuable tool from within the Al'afwa Khadar," Azad replied.

Ihsan made a face. "I'm not so convinced as you that she'll throw her lot in with the Host."

"And *I'm* not so convinced your interpretations of Yusam's visions are accurate, at least where it comes to her." Azad shrugged. "Besides, where else would she go but the Host? Her Emre is there."

Ihsan turned to Zaïde. "And you?"

"I've been thinking on it since she left my chamber. I think if we allow her to go now, we'll lose her forever. Let me train her. She's ready for it. We can always make other . . . arrangements should my assessment prove faulty."

Ihsan took this in and nodded. "With apologies to Azad, I too believe she is ready. Let's see what you can make of the White Wolf, shall we?"

"I'll begin at once." Zaïde bowed and left.

When her footsteps had receded, Azad returned to the flask he'd been tending earlier. "I'll work on the elixir as quickly as I'm able."

"Don't be angry with me."

Azad nodded. "Arrange for the scholars to be brought to me. I'll speak with them."

Ihsan took a step closer. "We can use her."

"As you say."

Ihsan ran his hands down along Azad's dark brown hair, until he shrugged Ihsan's attentions away. When Ihsan trailed his fingers down to his neck, however, Azad made no move to stop him. "Come, share your thoughts."

Azad turned, looking up to Ihsan, his eyes unreadable. "I tire of wearing this skin. It drives me mad. I want to walk in the light of day with you, hand in hand."

"You always knew this would take time," Ihsan said. "We need only a little more. And despite your fears, Çeda will be a part of this. We know as much from Yusam's visions."

"We don't *need* her."

"Need is the wrong word. She is a tool, one of many, and I will use all that are available to me until we have what we want." He took Azad's hand, stroked the skin along the backs of his fingers. "I have lived for over four hundred years. I have seen what comes of bold action and what comes of waiting. I like to think I know the benefits and detriments of both. Believe me when I say Sharakhai is ready for this. It is a fruit that has reached perfect ripeness. If we wait, it will surely begin to rot. Better to pluck it from the tree and eat of it now, don't you think?"

Instead of answering, Azad lifted Ihsan's hands to the carnelian necklace around his neck, which was an answer in and of itself. Despite himself, Ihsan found his heart beating faster. With care, and after stealing a glance toward the doorway where Zaïde had exited, he pulled the necklace over Azad's head. Azad blinked, his breath coming faster, just like Ihsan's. His nostrils flared as Ihsan stepped in and kissed him.

Ihsan liked feeling the change. He liked holding Azad when it happened. He felt himself stiffening as the two of them embraced, as their hands roamed. He felt Azad's hips widen, felt his waist narrow. He reached up and cupped one breast as it formed. It swelled as their passion bloomed, and soon the two of them were pulling off clothes, standing before one another as man and woman.

When Ihsan pulled away and stared into those eyes, eyes with such fire in them, he found not the visage of a King who'd died a dozen years ago at the hands of an assassin, but Nayyan, Azad's daughter, the Blade Maiden who'd taken his place. Nayyan stared back, but only for a moment. Soon she had pulled him close and kissed him once more, pulling him down toward the floor.

For a time the two of them were little more than two lovers, lying amongst their discarded raiment, free of the fears and responsibilities of Kings. Their mouths met, then traveled along one another's frames, pleasuring the other with kisses, with licks of the tongue, with teasing between the lips. He ran the tips of his fingers over the places where the colored lights shone down on her. Emerald along one shoulder. Ruby down her long, rounded stomach. Amethyst over her supple thighs. He stopped at a long scar there, one of the many wounds she'd taken in killing the ehrekh in her youth. "What a day that must have been."

"A day long past," she said huskily. She'd never told him about what had happened, how she'd killed the creature. But when she took his wrist and led his hand up until his fingers were rubbing between her legs, he decided he didn't much care. She took the middle finger of one hand in her mouth and sucked on it as he slipped its counterpart deep inside her. He placed kisses along her lips, spreading them with his tongue, sucking them in, tugging playfully. He flicked his tongue slowly upward, then traced the tip of his tongue around her silken pearl, enjoying the hitch in her breath as he timed those movements with the gentle presses of that place inside her she liked so much.

He kissed his way up her body, taking one breast into his mouth as she reached down and stroked his shaft. He felt the swell of her, soft like sand dunes. He moved to her other breast, then her neck, and then, as she guided him inside her, she kissed him, clutching his hair and drawing him close as if in that moment she couldn't get enough of him. Her breath came sharply as she used her legs to draw him rhythmically inside her. Then she arched back and released a cry, writhing to the throes of pleasure like a leaf being tossed on a strong summer wind. Ihsan followed soon after, clutching her hair in return, biting the skin along her neck, thrusting as she bucked beneath him.

Slowly, they fell from the heights of their love, and Ihsan lay by her side, his head cradled on one arm. Nayyan stared at the arched roof, idly raking her fingers along his scalp, her cheeks flushed. Ihsan simply studied her, taking her in before she donned King Azad's skin once more.

It had not been easy, choosing someone to take Azad's place and hiding it from those outside the House of Kings, but it had been necessary. And it had been as easy as convincing Kiral, the King of Kings, that to show weakness was to reveal a chink in the vaunted armor of Tauriyat. Once Kiral had agreed, the rest had followed. They had only to choose someone to play the part and for Külaşan and Sukru to work their magic.

They might have taken anyone, but Ihsan had put Nayyan forth. Despite all his rules about mixing love with war, she was a woman he'd come to believe in. She could help him in his quest, he knew. He'd arranged for her to visit him that very night. Her build was right, and she was Azad's daughter, which would give those who might complain about her legitimacy little reason to gripe should her identity eventually be revealed.

"Nayyan," he said wistfully while running the tips of his fingers across her belly.

She stared deeply into his eyes. "Why do you speak it so?"

"Because I relish fine food. Because I savor the perfect glass of wine. Because I love few things more than contemplating a masterful work of art when I find myself standing before one. You're a work of art, Nayyan, a wine I would drink of forever."

"I am none of those things."

"No? Then, pray tell, what are you?"

"I am a mask, Ihsan. Another of your tools."

"But the winds shift, my love." Ihsan stood and pulled the carnelian necklace from underneath Nayyan's outstretched arm. "A great storm builds in the distance. Soon it will fall upon our shores. A tool you may be now, but I promise you, when the winds die down, when the sand no longer bites, it will be you and I who stand alone on Tauriyat." He swung the necklace back and forth, admiring it for a moment, then handed it out for Nayyan to take.

Nayyan stood, naked, and eyed Ihsan with a hesitance that spoke both of suspicion and hope. She held her lofty position at the mercy of the Kings, who all knew her nature, but Ihsan had fought the hardest to place her there, so he could understand her continued hesitance.

He shook the necklace, the blood-red gem swinging like a pendulum against the backdrop of her smooth belly and curved hips. "I will never betray you."

Still she watched him, her jaw jutting for a moment, but then she snatched the necklace away and pulled it over her head.

The transformation took little time. Kings once more, the two of them began to dress.

Chapter 9

"**H**OLD," BARKED SAYABIM, the sword mistress who'd been instructing Çeda in swordplay since she'd entered the House of Maidens. Sayabim wore her white Matron's dress. The cowl, pulled up to shield her eyes from the morning sun, accentuated her dove-gray hair. Sayabim's merciless ally, the simple white stick she used to correct Çeda's errors, was held behind her back so that the tip of it peeked over one shoulder like the head of a curious snake.

As Sayabim had instructed, Çeda held her pose, her shamshir lifted high, right arm across her body at the end of a cross block. Sayabim knew the position was painful for Çeda—the welts on her back were only a few days old—but the sword mistress showed little compassion. "A Maiden fights in pain as well as in good health," she'd said the morning after Çeda's visit with Zaïde in the Matron's tower. "There's no excuse for poor form in either case."

The barracks courtyard where they worked was largely empty. Sayabim and Çeda stood at one end. A group of four other Maidens practiced wrestling at the opposite end, beneath the shade of an acacia. One Maiden, a brute of a woman with massive arms, was shouting in one corner, breaking bricks with the palm of her hand. Around them, darkened windows and doorways stared down from the stark faces of the surrounding buildings.

With her stick, Sayabim tapped Çeda's sword arm. When Çeda lowered it, she tapped the insides of her ankles, so she adjusted her stance. Sayabim breathed a snort of disgust. "Now begin again."

"Yes, siyaf," Çeda said, giving her the ancient word for sword master. As she stepped through the opening moves—blocking, thrusting, advancing, retreating—she spotted Zaïde and Yndris walking side by side toward the ring where she practiced. She ignored them as best she could, treating them as if they were but one more ache, one more thing to ignore. She spun, twisted, her blade a blur.

When she finished, Sayabim stood stock-still, her stick beneath one arm. She didn't grunt. She merely nodded. "The lumbering oryx has found some small amount of grace, it seems. But you're inconsistent. One moment you do it well, and the next you're like wood." She came and touched Çeda's stomach with one hand, her back with the other. "You flow from here. Flow, always, like the Haddah just before she bursts her banks. Do you understand?"

"Yes, siyaf."

Sayabim snorted. "I doubt it, but one day you might. Now begin again." She motioned Yndris into the ring. "But this time with her."

Çeda returned to the ready position. Yndris, eyes afire, fairly jumped into the ring and drew her ebon blade, the skirt of her black dress flowing in her wake. The two of them hadn't spoken since her vigil five nights ago. The part of Çeda that thought it wise to draw as little attention as possible was tempted to apologize, but the rest of her refused to bend. What Yndris had done was inexcusable. There had been no need to end the asir's life so callously.

What concerned Çeda more than Yndris, however, was Zaïde. She hadn't spoken to Çeda since their conversation in Zaïde's room. Çeda had meant what she'd said. She would leave the Maidens if she felt she would get nowhere, or progress so slowly that it made no difference. She'd make an attempt on the life of another King if she could, whoever she could manage, and then go to the desert. She would try to reach Nalamae and beg for her guidance. The need for secrecy was great, the goddess had said, but surely she would listen to reason. Surely she would know what might be done about the asirim. In truth, though, Çeda didn't wish to take that step. If she left the House of Maidens, there would be no going back. But what was there to do about it now? She'd thrown down the gauntlet. It was left to Zaïde to pick it up or not.

When Çeda raised her sword, Yndris did the same. As the Maiden being trained, it was Çeda's prerogative to choose when to begin, but Yndris cared little about such things. She was already moving, swinging her ebon blade from on high. Çeda had no choice but to respond, blocking and sliding out of Yndris's center.

She slashed at Yndris's midsection. Yndris blocked, a grin on her face as she moved easily through the form. Çeda made several mistakes in the opening sequence, but Sayabim said nothing, and the two of them continued, Yndris pressing harder than was necessary, Çeda doing all she could to keep up. Yndris was hoping to embarrass Çeda, to force her into improper form or hastily raised countermoves, but it was having the opposite effect. Instead of worrying so much about every movement, every position, Çeda fell into the movements as if she were separate from her body, as if she were the river Sayabim had spoken of, her body and sword mere currents in that greater flow. On and on they went through the sixty-six moves of the form, Çeda little more than sweeping arcs, sharp thrusts, ringing blocks, until they'd reached the very end. The two of them held their final move, waiting for Sayabim to order them to relax.

Yndris seemed disappointed, which was hardly a surprise. Çeda had done well. Zaïde's expression, something like satisfaction, or even vindication, was more difficult to read. Sayabim, however, was plain as an open book. She had a pinched, almost angry face, as if she'd bitten her own lip and then sucked on a lime. She looked Çeda up and down like a caravan master at the slave blocks, willing to pay for goods but displeased with what she'd found. "If I'd known all it would take was a childish rivalry to make you concentrate, I would have pitted you against her months ago."

As Sayabim stepped into the ring, Zaïde bowed her head. "Sword mistress, I believe it's time that I took her."

Sayabim's eyes went wide with shock. "Who? Çedamihn?" When Zaïde nodded, her eyes widened even further. "Now?"

"Unless you'd rather I wait for the desert's final days."

Sayabim ignored the gibe as she appraised Çeda, shaking her head and clucking her tongue. "I'm nowhere near done with her."

Zaïde stood straight, hands clasped behind her back. She looked regal before the churlish Sayabim. "You say that of everyone."

"I say it because it's true."

"We cannot wait until she's ready to take the Matron's white for you to consider her ready. I asked if I may have her."

"Seems to me you *told* me."

Zaïde shrugged, her jaw set. .

Sayabim considered, her mood darkening. "If you wish to take on an unbroken foal, so be it, but don't come running to me when she throws you."

Zaïde stretched her mouth into a forced smile. "Very well. In the meantime, I'd be pleased if you'd take Yndris beneath your wing."

Yndris's eyes widened. Her cheeks flushed. She opened her mouth to speak, but Sayabim talked over her. "Another rough plank needing sanding, hmm?" She tapped Yndris's hips with her stick, then her shoulders. "Very well, very well."

And Çeda saw in Sayabim a pride she hadn't noticed before. She loved this, the honing of new blades, and even though Çeda had been hoping for it for months, it gave her pride that Sayabim approved of Çeda enough to let Zaïde take her.

"Coming?" Zaïde said, motioning Çeda out from the sparring circle.

Çeda glanced at Yndris, who stared back with her lips pressed into a thin line. Hiding a smile, Çeda sheathed her sword and bowed her head. "Of course, Matron."

Zaïde led her to the largest building in the compound. It was where the Matrons and the wardens had their offices and where Maidens were trained in the softer arts of history and the written word, even in art and tattooing. It was where the library was kept and, if rumor were true, a special set of rooms deep below the earth that was said to house the annals of the Maidens—journals and other recorded histories of the campaigns and wars the Maidens had fought, including the silent campaigns elite Maidens undertook on behalf of their Kings. What Çeda wouldn't give to dig through those records, but she'd had no opportunity to enter the building until now, and she suspected that anyone who *did* came under closer scrutiny by Kings and Matrons both.

As they entered the building, the heat of late morning was replaced by a chill breeze. Çeda worried that her assumption had been wrong, that Zaïde was merely handing her off to another Matron to be trained in calligraphy or some such. "Matron, I would speak with you of—"

She stopped when Zaïde, without so much as looking Çeda's way, grabbed her left hand and gripped it to the point of pain. The hall was empty, and Çeda heard no one near, but it seemed paramount to remain silent. Zaïde continued walking as if Çeda hadn't spoken at all. The message was clear: *speak of nothing, not now.*

They soon came to a room with high windows that shed golden light onto the rich, wooden walls. Spaced around the room were racks brimming with different types of weapons—swords, staves, spears, shields, fighting sticks, chained weapons, and more. They were made for practice, but for all that they looked well made and well maintained. *Well loved,* as her mother used to say of the simple wooden shinai she'd given Çeda when she was young.

"Remove your shoes," Zaïde said. After slipping her sandals off and setting them on a rope matt near the door, Zaïde took one step further into the room and then slapped her hands against her thighs and bowed. Çeda did the same, and only after did Zaïde step onto the padded canvas mat that dominated the space and kneel at its center. When she motioned to the space opposite her, Çeda mirrored her until the two of them faced one another, their knees almost touching.

"Do you know what this place is?" Zaïde asked.

"Zaïde, I—" But Çeda stopped, for Zaïde was shaking her head. "This is a savaşam," Çeda replied. "A training hall." She could only assume that Zaïde feared the King of Whispers, or perhaps King Yusam and his mere.

Zaïde nodded with a wry smile, as if nothing were the matter. "It is," she said, looking to the walls, motioning to the weapons, "but there's much more to it than what you see." She paused a moment, gathering her thoughts, then nodded toward Çeda's right hand. "Do you remember what I said to you when I revealed your tattoo?"

"That I must fight with my heart."

"You must fight not *with* your heart, but *from* your heart." Zaïde gestured to the room around them with a look of reverence. "Within these hallowed walls we are taught what it truly means to be a Maiden. I will continue to teach you how to use your sword properly, for Sayabim was right. There is work to do yet." She leaned forward and pressed her hand over Çeda's heart. "But I will also open doors that have been closed to you. Let's begin with a simple exercise." She stood, motioning for Çeda to do the same. "You must learn to look deeply into your own heart, and through that you will learn to see into the hearts of others."

When the two of them stood opposite one another, Zaïde put out her right hand, palm open, fingers lax. It was the first position in open-hand sparring. Çeda mirrored her, shifting until the backs of their hands were touching. They were close enough that they could strike one another. Their knees were bent, their bodies loose.

"Using only your right hand, prevent me from touching your neck."

When Çeda nodded, Zaïde remained stone still for long moments, the wrinkled skin around her eyes and mouth relaxed, and then her hand shot out and her fingers brushed the skin of Çeda's neck.

Çeda's head jerked back reflexively. The strike had been light, but she started coughing. It felt as if an olive were stuck in her throat. Gods, she'd hardly seen Zaïde move.

"Again," Zaïde said.

Çeda cleared her throat and returned to the ready position. Again Zaïde was almost too fast to follow, and this time her fingers pressed deep into Çeda's throat. Çeda coughed harder and backed away.

"You're watching my hand," Zaïde said. "Watch *me. All* of me. Again."

Çeda tried. She was used to watching her opponents for any sign of an attack, but there was something about being in this room, waiting for only one strike, that was making her focus too narrowly. She had to remember that even though Zaïde was not out to harm her, this was as much a fight as the ones she'd waged in Osman's pits.

As she stepped into the ready position again, she relaxed. She took a deep breath and felt the way the back of her hand touched Zaïde's. She took in the Matron's eyes, her face, her shoulders. She watched her stance. She tried, however imperfectly, to study the entirety of Zaïde's form.

And then she saw it—the tightening of muscles along Zaïde's neck and shoulder—and she reacted. She used the palm of her hand to swat away the first of Zaïde's thrusts, then the back of her hand for the next. The third was a feint. Zaïde's arm swung below Çeda's following block and snaked in toward her throat, catching her with the brush of a butterfly's wings.

Çeda had failed, but Zaïde was smiling. "A fair enough beginning, young dove, something we can build upon."

"Zaïde, I'm grateful you've brought me here, but—"

Before Çeda knew what was happening, Zaïde was rushing in, grabbing the front of Çeda's dress, and throwing her over her hip onto the canvas. Zaïde's face was inches from Çeda's, looking more intense than Çeda had ever seen her. "You will speak when spoken to, child. Do you understand?"

Çeda nodded.

"Good." She released Çeda and came to a stand with a well-oiled ease that defied her many decades in the Shangazi. She reached down and offered her hand, which Çeda accepted, then Zaïde pulled her upright. She immediately lowered herself into the starting position again. "Now wipe that smile off your face."

Was she smiling? She supposed she was, and it took her a moment to realize why. Things were moving at last. She would still need patience, but she was sure it would come. She put the back of her hand against Zaïde's, lowered herself into the starting position, and managed, at last, to stop grinning like a fool.

"Now see if you can do it again," Zaïde said, and struck for Çeda's neck in a blur.

When Çeda returned to the barracks it was well past nightfall. She'd never felt more exhausted. She'd never felt more exhilarated, either. She went to her hand's common room and poured herself some watered wine, grabbed a clutch of grapes from the bowl on the table, which was always filled with some fruit or another, and made ready to head to her room and pass out the very moment she'd wolfed down the grapes and finished the wine. The only other person in the room was Sümeya. She was sitting at a table, reading from a sheaf of papers. As Çeda waved and headed for her room, Sümeya said,

"This arrived for you," and shoved a small, oddly shaped bundle wrapped in fine linen and tied by a pale green ribbon.

"What is it?" Çeda asked.

"I've no idea, but it came from the Mirean embassy." Sümeya eyed her more closely now. "Making friends, are we?"

Çeda smiled back, trying her best to hide the sudden nervousness blossoming inside her. "An admirer, perhaps."

"Perhaps. Why don't you open it?"

Çeda allowed her exhaustion to show through. "In the morning. I'm just off to bed."

With little fanfare, Sümeya set down her reading and regarded Çeda. "Open it."

An order. Çeda might refuse her, but it would arouse suspicion, which she couldn't afford, not now that she was finally making headway. So instead of arguing, she stepped up to the desk and untied the ribbon, hoping Juvaan had not left anything to chance. She lay the linen back, revealing a short stack of reed paper, a bottle of ink, and a steel-nibbed pen. They were clearly Mirean in origin, and of the highest quality, the sort befit for a queen.

"An admirer, indeed!" Sümeya said. "But who?"

Çeda picked up the note:

For the Blade Maiden who's stolen my heart, to use when your thoughts turn my way. Or if they don't, perhaps to light a flame.

"A bit melodramatic, don't you think?" Sümeya asked when Çeda showed it to her. She handed it back and returned to the papers she'd been reading. "Best get to sleep if you're so *very* tired."

"Yes, First Warden." After stacking everything on the paper—her wine, the grapes, the ink and pen—Çeda cradled them all and headed back to her room. Once there, she lit a candle and sat at the small desk near the window. The wine and grapes all but forgotten, she stared at the paper, felt it between her fingers, *smelled* it.

To use when your thoughts turn my way, Juvaan had written. And then the mention of flame. They were instructions, of course. Though she wasn't quite clear on it all, and had no idea how he might communicate back, she took up the pen, grabbed one of the papers and wrote:

Your gift received. What now? When to converse?

Then held it to the flame. The corner of the paper took to it, slowly at first, but then a blue flame rushed across the sheet with such speed Çeda dropped it onto the desktop with a small yelp of surprise. The paper hadn't burned all the way through, however. A gossamer-thin layer remained, charcoal at the center, burning blue at the edges. The words she'd penned were gone, erased by the flames. A moment later, however, something new appeared on the burned surface: thin, blue-green flames lit along the upper portion. Like a pen with ink made of arcane flame, words appeared, flowing with a quick, confident script.

Name the place where I first saw you, and the man you faced.

The words remained for a moment, burning low, but then spread just as quickly as the first flame had. In a burst of blue flame, it was gone. All of it. No smoke. No soot. No ash from the paper itself on the desk.

"Gods," Çeda whispered, and knocked back a long mouthful of wine.

She took another paper and wrote:

The Pits. Ramahd Amansir. A test for you as well: Name the occasion of our second meeting.

Then burned the page as she had the first.

She waited, watching the slowly burning page. This time she held her hand over the flames and felt only light warmth. Soon, penned in blue flames, were new words:

The Sun Palace, moments before you received your blade.

Let us waste no more of these. Take great care to conserve them, as no more exist in Sharakhai but those I've delivered to you. But don't fear to use them if the information is important. Let us try to write when the moons are dark, but know that they will be monitored all hours of the day.

I hope to hear more when the time is right.

Çeda stared at the words, then watched as the sheet lit and burned itself to nothing. She stared for long moments at the empty space where the paper had been, her anger rising. She took another sheet.

And what of the scarab I asked for?

She lit it and waited. It took a long while for Juvaan's response.

These are more precious than you can imagine. Do not use them frivolously again. There is nothing I can share as yet. Such things are difficult to attain. Be patient! I'll give you what I have each time we speak.

Do take care to conserve these!

Then the page lit and was gone.

Çeda popped a grape into her mouth, chewing it noisily for a moment. *Take care . . .* She finished off the wine in one swallow. *Take care I don't show up at your house and beat it from you.*

But really, what was she to expect? He'd spoken true. It would likely take time before he had any word of Emre. So, after putting the paper, ink, and pen into her desk and stuffing a few more grapes into her mouth, she fell into bed.

Chapter 10

IF SHARAKHAI WERE A CROWN lying in the center of the desert, its famed collegia was certainly one of its brightest jewels. Its two oldest buildings—a mudbrick hall of learning and a small dormitory—predated the rule of the Twelve Kings by three centuries. Others had been built as time wore on, the collegia eventually splitting into different fields of study, with halls and scholars dedicated to each. It was one of the few places in Sharakhai that held a reverence quite separate from that of the Kings and the Maidens, of Beht Zha'ir and the asirim. The collegia was part of *old* Sharakhai, the one settled by a mismatched group of wanderers who had, for myriad reasons, tired of the ceaseless travels of the desert tribes. The collegia was rightly regarded a part of the bedrock of Sharakhai, one of the wonders that made it unique.

The collegia had from its earliest days steadily collected wisdom, first from the wise men and women of the twelve desert tribes. Its more formal name, the Collegia al Shangazi'ava, showed how the early settlers thought it a place that reflected the collected wisdom of the desert, not merely Sharakhai. Later, as the city had grown and more travelers had come to settle, it attracted more of the learned from all the Five Kingdoms until eventually scholars and laymen alike, whether native to the desert or not, recognized it as the undisputed leader in dozens of different fields: mathematics, astrology, the lesser forms of alchemy, engineering, irrigation, mining, and so much more. That in turn made it one of a very small handful of academies where one aspired to go in order to dedicate oneself to higher learning. Kings and queens, emperors and empresses, lords and ladies, all vied to place their sons and daughters there, for it was a mark of high prestige to attain the laurel wreath of a collegia scholar.

It was so well respected, in fact, that it was one of the very few places considered sacrosanct, safe from harm or violence, even by the scarabs of the Al'afwa Khadar, who had sworn oaths to harm the Kings in any way they could. No formal treaty had been signed, nor even uttered, but neither had anyone ever been attacked on collegia grounds, which made the latest request from King Yusam all the more unusual. More curious still was the fact that he'd called on all five in Çeda's hand to attend him in his throne room and bid them to go to the provost's office that very morning.

"What should we expect to find, my King?" Sümeya had asked.

Yusam, staring at her with his piercing green eyes, had pursed his lips and sat deeper into his throne. "Expect conflict. Swords at your sides, Maidens, loose in their scabbards."

Yusam's dictates were often thus: confusing, inscrutable before the fact. It sometimes took the event itself, even for Yusam, to understand the vision he'd been shown in his mere. Some of the things he'd been asking them to do since Külaşan's death had been strange indeed—queries asked of caravan masters, watching the passage of ships entering and exiting the vast southern harbor, digging up bones far into the desert—but Çeda had the impression that the grand vision Yusam seemed to be fixated on was starting to come clear. They'd been going on missions that seemed to be leading to *something*; Çeda just had no idea what.

With the black veils of their turbans hiding their identities, the five of them left Yusam's palace and rode down the slopes of Tauriyat, through the gates of the House of Maidens, and into Sharakhai proper. The day was unseasonably warm, the heat wavering from the tops of the amber stone buildings as the crowd parted for them like waves before the prow of a ship. They reached the collegia stables a short while later and left their horses with a stable girl. Sümeya bade them each to take an adichara petal. Sümeya,

Kameyl, Melis, and Yndris retrieved one from small clamshell holders that hung from their belts, but Çeda took hers from the flame-shaped locket hanging around her neck. As the floral taste filled her, and the verve of the petal rushed down her limbs like a spring flood, they made their way through the outermost buildings, swords swinging easily at their sides.

Sümeya led the way, with Kameyl and Melis following and Çeda and Yndris bringing up the rear. As their leather boots crunched into the gravel path, scholars and students all stepped aside, bowed their heads, and crossed their arms over their chests. In short order, they reached a wide open space, a grand oval with flowering bushes and pathways and stone benches, where people sat talking or studying in the shadows of the tall date palms. When the flaxen-robed students and collegia scholars in their hooded robes and saffron belts spotted them, they stopped what they were doing and paid obeisance to the will of the Kings in Sharakhai.

Sümeya led them through the well-tended courtyard and into one of the buildings directly off of it, the hall of records. They soon came to a large atrium open to the sky above. Six sets of stairs were spaced at the corners of the atrium and halfway along its length, allowing access to the floors above. As before in the courtyard, all stopped what they were doing, faced the Maidens, and bowed their heads, though some few did not cross their arms—likely foreigners who were unaware of or unused to the rituals of Sharakhai.

When Sümeya neared the center of the atrium, she stopped and took in the scene as if she were memorizing each and every face, as well as their positions in the atrium. Çeda tried to do the same. Clustered in one corner was a flock of students who hardly looked old enough to be entering the collegia. To their right, a group of tall Kundhunese men in togas and sandals stood by two young women and a boy who hardly came up to their knees. One of the men was bent down and shushing the boy, who was talking and pointing at a pair of finely dressed Sharakhani men who'd just stepped off the nearby stairs. The boy paid no attention until finally the man pinched his ear and he began to cry. Other scholars, administrators, and students stood about, but Çeda saw nothing of note.

Though Çeda had spent very little time in the collegia proper, she'd come once to speak with the old scholar, Amalos. Later Davud, a boy from the bazaar who'd grown into a proper young man within these halls, had shown her the tunnel that led all the way from the neighborhood known as the Well to the collegia's scriptorium. She'd visited dozens of times after that, but had been limited to a single room beneath the scriptorium, devouring the texts left there by Davud for her to read. She'd no more begun sifting through those memories than she saw him, Davud, a student with dirty blond hair and an infectious smile, standing beside two other students—pretty girls, the both of them. It was like a gift from golden Rhia, come when she'd least expected it. Gods, how he'd grown these past four months. He looked a proper young man now, the remains of his boyish features replaced by more masculine ones.

"You may take your ease," Sümeya called loudly.

In fits and starts, the crowd returned to their business and the sound throughout the atrium rose to a suffused and roiling din. The girls near Davud—both Qaimiran from the look of their lighter-toned skin—began speaking to him, but he hardly seemed to hear them. He was staring at Çeda as if he'd recognized her, even in her veil and turban. Çeda gave him the smallest of nods, a thing he returned before turning to the girls and smiling. He walked away with them, chatting all the while. He didn't look back.

Sümeya was eyeing the levels above, studying those who stood at the railing. "Yndris and Çeda, with me. Melis and Kameyl"—she pointed to where the two main hallways adjoined the atrium—"watch the exits. Be wary."

With that she headed for one of the stairwells. Çeda and Yndris followed, and together they made their way up to the second floor. They came to an open doorway, beyond which was a long marble desk with two men and a woman opening and sorting wax-sealed letters behind it.

"I've come to speak with the bursar," Sümeya said.

The nearest of them, a fellow with a crooked back and a strange, gourd-shaped head, stood and bowed.

"Of course," the man said with a noticeable slur to his words. He moved out from behind the desk with a heavy limp. "If you'll follow me."

"Remain here," Sümeya said to Çeda and Yndris, and then followed the man to an office at the rear of the large room.

The remaining pair of clerks returned to their business, but they were noticeably quieter than before, and they made sure never to look in the direction of the entrance where Çeda and Yndris stood. Çeda eyed them for a while, still wondering what Yusam might have seen, and why he wouldn't have told them. If he had, would the vision fail to come true? Would some other reality have presented itself? How difficult a burden it would be to know so much, yet be afraid to approach it for fear of its taking wing like a skittish lark. Little wonder he was so mercurial.

Outside the office, Çeda could see a wide swath of the atrium below, plus the balustrades and rows of doors opposite where the bursar's office was situated. Some few people were peeking out, sending glances toward the doorway where Çeda stood. A pair of men were climbing the stairs directly across from her. Neither glanced her way as they wound their way up, but she recognized them from the atrium below: the little boy had been pointing to them before the Kundhuni man had pinched his ear.

Çeda whistled softly, drawing Yndris's attention. She nodded toward the stairwell. When Yndris stepped over and looked, Çeda said, "I saw them downstairs."

"What of it?"

"When we arrived, they were headed out, yet here they are, climbing the stairs after two Maidens were posted at the exits."

Yndris watched as the men continued toward the fourth floor and were momentarily lost from sight. Yndris swung her gaze to the bursar's office then out to the atrium again. "Watch them," she said. "I'll tell Sümeya."

As she headed for the back office, Çeda stepped onto the balcony. The two men had reached the top floor and were walking along the hall that would take them to the far left corner of the building. *And where might you be headed?* The men might be here for perfectly innocent reasons. Or they might be *pretending* to be on proper collegia business until the Maidens left. Or it might be they had another way to escape. She looked for another set of stairs between the pillars and the scalloped arches along the upper floor, stairs that might lead up to the roof. Seeing none, she scanned the roofline, looking for a ladder or . . .

There, hanging from one corner of the roof's opening, she spotted a rope. It blended in well with the building's white stone but hung below the ceiling of the upper level, far enough for someone to stand on the marble balustrade and reach it. A moment later, one of the men did just that. He stood, grabbed the rope, and began climbing with surprising ease toward the roof. Neither was watching her, and she had the distinct impression they no longer cared if they were seen. They'd judged the regular exit too dangerous and were praying none of the Maidens saw or, perhaps, that they'd be far enough ahead to escape even if a Maiden discovered them.

Were these men scarabs, agents of the Moonless Host? It seemed likely. So many of Yusam's visions revolved around them. Çeda stared down to the atrium below. Neither Kameyl nor Melis was looking up; they were scanning the comings and goings of the people below. She thought of letting the men go. She could let the Moonless Host have whatever it was they'd come for. Except it would weaken her position with the Kings. It would weaken her own grasp on the situation as well. The Host had raised Hamzakiir for a reason. And she was sure that this was somehow a part of it: their plans for him, or perhaps *Hamzakiir's* plans for the *Host*. It was very possible, perhaps even likely, that the power structure had shifted and Hamzakiir now pulled the strings. Macide and his father, Ishaq, may have shattered a gemstone, releasing a demon that would better have remained trapped.

The first man had nearly reached the roof. The other was just about to grab the rope. He looked down at the lowest floor first and caught sight of Çeda watching him. His eyes went wide and he climbed faster, his body swinging wildly from the effort.

Çeda leaned over the balustrade and whistled sharply. When Melis and Kameyl looked up, Çeda pointed to the corner, where the first man was just levering himself over the lip of the roof. Kameyl and Melis sprinted for the nearest exit—they knew they couldn't make it up the stairs in time, and were trusting that Çeda, Sümeya, and Yndris could.

After directing another sharp whistle into the bursar's office, Çeda sprinted after them. When she neared the corner, she leapt onto the balustrade and propelled herself through the air toward the trellis that ran from the ground floor all the way to the topmost. A shout of surprise filtered up from the crowd as she crashed into the trellis. The slats shattered beneath the weight of her right foot. Splintered bits of wood spun lazily down, but the trellis held, and soon she was climbing for the roof as fast as she could.

One glance back saw Sümeya and Yndris stepping out from the bursar's office. They fairly flew along the hall toward her. As Çeda reached the third floor, she heard the rattle of leaves and the snap of vines as Yndris and Sümeya leapt onto the trellis below her.

Above, the younger man was nearing the edge of the roof. "Hurry, you fool!" the other rasped as he shook his hand and leaned down as far as he dared.

Just as Çeda gained the topmost floor, the two men clasped hands, and the one climbing kicked against one of the bronze torch holders along the wall and was dragged over the lip. Knowing time had almost run out, Çeda stepped off the trellis, onto the balustrade, and sprinted along it, arms windmilling to keep her balance. The men tried to pull their escape rope up, but before it could snake out of reach she jumped and grabbed the end of it. The rope, drawn down by her weight, slid through the younger man's hands, burning them. He released it, sucking air through his teeth noisily, and the rope snapped taut, straining against whatever it had been tied to above.

The elder man, meanwhile, drew a knife from within the sleeve of his khalat, and slipped it under the rope. He sawed at it feverishly. Desperate, Çeda drew her legs up, caught the wall's decorative coping, and powered herself away from the wall just as the knife finished its work. The world spun. With one hand still holding the rope, Çeda snatched its opposite end and snapped it like a skip rope toward the nearest torch holder. It wrapped around the curling base and, thank the gods, held.

She dangled in midair, planning to use the holder to climb up to the roof, but she stopped when the man with the knife approached. Knowing he could easily reach the rope, Çeda gripped both ends of it with her left hand and drew River's Daughter with her right.

The man froze, eyeing her sword.

"Come," the younger man rasped. "Quickly now."

After one last glance at Çeda, he complied, perhaps hoping that by the time she managed to reach the roof, they would be well away. Gripping her sword between her teeth, Çeda climbed, feeling like an ungainly sack of potatoes as she maneuvered herself atop the torch holder and then up to the roof at last. The men were sprinting with abandon toward the corner of the flat roof. As she watched, they leapt toward another of the collegia's buildings, arms spinning as they spanned the gap. She nearly charged after them, but knew that would be foolish. She didn't know if they'd have others lying in wait; they likely did, the Host long ago having been forced to become adept at conducting such operations.

She leaned over the edge and found Yndris and Sümeya standing on the fourth-floor balustrade, waiting. She dropped one end of the rope to them and held the opposite end tightly, bracing herself as Sümeya and then Yndris climbed to the roof to join her. Then all three of them were off, chasing after the two men. Sümeya whistled—two sharp, rising trills, an alert for Kameyl and Melis so they'd know their position—then did so again after they'd leapt the gap between the buildings.

Ahead, one of the men was walking a rope, balancing with his arms as he stepped quickly but expertly across the span to one of the collegia's dormitories. As the other followed, the first kneeled and lifted a contraption that looked like a crossbow, except instead of a single bolt in a groove, nine bolts protruded from a rectangular wooden box. The bolts themselves weren't tipped with broad-heads, but what looked to be wads of black cloth or paper. As the taller man dropped to the roof and drew his knife across the tightrope he'd just used, the other triggered the crossbow. Nine bolts flew through the air, one of them trailing red powder as it arced off target.

"Hold your breath!" Çeda called.

The bolts pounded against the roof where Çeda, Sümeya, and Yndris were crossing. As each one struck, a cloud of red dust coughed into the air in a funnel-shaped spray that rushed toward them. In a blink, the air was thick with it. Çeda managed to take a hurried lungful of untainted air, but as the cloud swept over her, her eyes began to water. The very air burned. It scratched at her nose and throat so badly she coughed from it while trying to escape. She *couldn't* escape, though. The powder was so fine it had spread over most of the roof.

The wind was not strong this day, but Çeda reckoned it was strong enough to move the cloud, so she made for the cloud's windward edge, and eventually the air began to clear. Eyes watering terribly, she scanned the opposite roof. She had only enough time to register one of them—the younger, kneeling, aiming something at her—before her instincts sent her twisting away. She dropped toward the roof as the lathe of the crossbow snapped and something flickered toward her. It ate up the distance almost too fast for the eye to follow. Something burned its way across her back, hardly more than a tug at first, but then bright pain blossomed in a line just below her shoulder blades.

Her first thought was that the bolt had been poisoned, as hers had been for the Kings in Eventide, but she couldn't worry about that now. Yndris and Sümeya reached her side while, on the far building, the two men were slipping down yet another rope they'd prepared.

Sümeya tried to whistle again, but she was coughing so horribly she couldn't manage it. Çeda whistled for her, then did so again as she stumbled to the edge of the roof, where a terra-cotta downspout ran from roof to ground. She began shimmy down it, but it was unsound. The clay fractured as she went, sections of the downspout crumbling as she tried to hold on. She leapt away from the building to avoid the debris, and rolled as she struck the brown lawn, but she still hit hard, and when she came to her feet, her right ankle was screaming from the pain. Sümeya was whistling again from the roof above. A reply came from somewhere beyond the building Çeda had just climbed down.

Çeda looked up, unsure what Sümeya wished her to do, but when Sümeya pointed toward the escaping men, Çeda ran, powering through the flaring pain in her ankle. The petals were wondrous things, though. They numbed aches. They granted strength. And soon she was flying over the collegia grounds.

After crossing the road that circled the collegia she headed down an alley, the most likely place for the men to have gone. Ahead, a woman and a little boy were walking toward Çeda. The woman looked at nothing in particular, her eyes distant as Çeda approached, but the boy kept glancing back, past a bend in the alley, until his mother tugged sharply on his arm and he stared stone-like, straight ahead.

They'd gone this way then. Çeda continued, faster, and it was clear that they were headed toward the Shallows, the poorest section of the city and the one that most sympathized with the Moonless Host. She leapt through a break in the city's old wall, little more than a crumbling arch, and continued down the narrow street until she saw them well ahead, running fast through a crowd.

"*Lai, lai, lai!*" Çeda called, more a demand for all to stand aside than for the men to stop running.

The men and women she passed obeyed, clearing a path, but few bowed their heads, and some seemed slow in their movements, perhaps hoping to delay Çeda in any way they could. Çeda wove between them and saw the men took different paths at the next intersection, a small square where five alleys split off like the spokes of a wagon wheel and ran along drunken, misaligned rows of houses.

Çeda followed the elder, the taller one, if for no other reason than she thought he might have more information than the younger.

"Hup, hup!" the man called as he ran. "Hup, hup!"

They were into the Shallows proper now. Refuse and barrels and disused crates filled the streets, some freshly knocked over by the shadowed forms of men and women ducking into their homes.

Çeda dodged what she could, leaping or somersaulting when she couldn't. The rage was building inside her for those who were trying to keep her from reaching the man, and she realized only then just how badly her right hand was throbbing, worse than her ankle. She ignored the pain, knowing it was fueling her anger; a year ago *she* might have been the one throwing crates into a Maiden's path to slow her down.

Ahead, a cart lay without a mule. The man, who was beginning to flag, ran up along the inclined bed and angled himself over the eaves of the nearest, half-repaired roof. Çeda launched herself after him and chased him over the roofs of the ramshackle homes. Knowing he was caught, he turned to face her, knife in hand, his breath well on him now.

Çeda was ready for him. She dropped, spinning, and caught him around the ankles. He fell to the roof in a crashing heap. It was child's play from there to take his knife from him. He was no fighter, this one, but a thief, a trickster sent to gather information for the Host. Why, she didn't yet know. But she would.

She stood him up, his arm locked behind him. He hardly struggled. In fact, the only reason he seemed to fight her at all was to look east, more or less toward the collegia.

That was when Çeda saw the silhouette. The sun was in her face, so she didn't at first realize a man was standing fifty paces away across a sea of brown and red roofs. But when he registered at last, she saw the bow he was holding, saw his right arm tugging back, as if he'd just loosed an arrow. In the split second that followed, his hand returned to the string, nocked another arrow, and released.

The arrows she never saw, not until both of them were sprouting from the chest of the man she held in her arms. He groaned. His body went slack. Her first thought was to let him drop to the roof's broken tiles, to chase after this newcomer, but she already knew she'd never catch him. He was too far away. So instead she held her prisoner up, using him as a shield should more arrows be launched her way.

Slowly, she lowered the dying man, peering over his shoulder. Then she stared, mouth agape. The assassin's bracers. The wide belt around his waist. By the gods who breathe . . .

A whistle called her attention elsewhere. Yndris was climbing up to the roof, Kameyl just behind her. They took in the dead man at her feet, then turned to look in the direction Çeda had been watching. But the bowman was gone.

"They shot him," Çeda said simply.

Kameyl kneeled and snapped the arrow shafts where they'd entered the man's chest, then threw them aside. "I would've too, were I them."

"The other?" Çeda asked.

Kameyl shrugged. "Melis and Sümeya went after him."

When Çeda stood there, unmoving, Yndris stepped over and looked the dead man over, then regarded Çeda. "What did you see?"

Çeda shook her head. "A man with a bow."

Yndris accepted the answer, but Çeda could tell she was watching her whenever she thought Çeda wasn't looking. And well she might have. Çeda would have done the same had Yndris been as visibly shaken as Çeda in the moment she'd recognized the man with the bow.

The bracers. The wide belt. His stance and his way of moving. She'd recognize them until her dying day.

It was Emre. And he'd just shot the man who had stolen secrets from the collegia.

Chapter 11

WHEN EMRE SAW THE TWO MEN climbing onto the four-story roof of the bursar's office, he knew it had all gone wrong. He'd watched as Melekh and Iliam had traipsed across the collegia rooftops, watched as the Blade Maidens had survived the fire-dust, watched as one had caught a crossbow bolt across the back and had continued the chase.

The gods are cruel to make the Maidens from iron while we are but flesh and blood.

It had seemed like such a simple operation when Macide had laid it out for them. Get in, get the list of names from their agent in the bursar's office, and get out.

"Why spend so much effort on contingencies?" Emre had asked. "It'll attract attention, tipping our hand to the Kings when we should be holding our cards tight to our chest."

Macide had stroked his long beard and given Emre a look of sufferance. "It may seem foolish, or costly, but we know the right way to do things."

As it turned out, Macide had been right to be cautious, and all too soon, Emre found himself watching Iliam flying up to the rooftops, a Maiden nipping at his heels. Emre drew his arrow back to his cheek, ready to fire the arrow into the chest of the Maiden, but then Iliam drew his knife and the Maiden took him easily with a quick sweep of her leg. He released the tension on the string the moment the realization struck him. He knew her. The Maiden. By Tulathan's bright smile, it was *Çeda*. He was certain of it.

A nervous laugh nearly burst from his throat. He'd been set to take any Maiden chasing him. Of course he couldn't now. But he also couldn't let Iliam be taken either. Macide had made that clear over and over again. He was to protect them if he could, but if it came to it he was to take Iliam or Melekh rather than allow the Maidens or the Silver Spears to capture them.

Çeda stood Iliam up. She had him in an armlock. Any moment she'd drop him below the roofline and Emre would have lost his chance.

The old feelings of fear returned, feelings born of his inaction when his brother, Rafa, had been murdered by that Malasani dog. But this wasn't fear for himself, but for Çeda. The thought of killing her, of even harming her, made him go cold. But he blinked hard and shook his head. He was a cowering fool no longer. He was a man reborn.

With reflexes he'd been honing day after day, he lifted the bow, aimed while drawing the string to his ear, and released. Faster than it took to draw breath, he lay a second arrow across the bow, drew, and released. He knew before the first arrow struck that there was no need for a third. Both arrows struck true, sinking deep into Iliam's chest.

Despite the shell he'd tried to build around himself, Emre felt the cold knife of regret driving through his chest. He'd known Iliam. Known him well. They'd traded stories over fires. They'd cooked for one another. Iliam had defended Emre several times to some of the other scarabs who hadn't yet come to trust him. And now he'd sunk arrows into his chest. He'd killed him. Under orders, true, but that made it no easier. For a moment he felt no better than Rafa's killer.

Çeda—he was certain now it was her—stared at him for a moment. He stared back. How he wished he could walk across these roofs and speak to her. Hold her. Take her from the House of Maidens.

But he couldn't. No more than she could take him away from the Moonless Host.

When a piercing whistle rose above the bustle of the city and Çeda looked down to the alley, Emre dropped from his perch and lost himself in the cramped byways of the Shallows.

Arcing along the curve of Sharakhai's great southern harbor were dozens of massive warehouses that stored goods delivered by incoming ships. Sometimes those goods remained for mere hours, moving after a quick sale to other merchants from the neighboring kingdoms or to middlemen in Sharakhai who would hold them and sell them to their own contacts over time. Other shipments would sit for days or weeks, the caravan's agent in Sharakhai waiting for the right moment to sell if the price for their goods were volatile and presently low. There were several small auction blocks as well for trading among the many merchants who came to Sharakhai or called the city home. There were pens and paddocks for animals in and near the warehouses, the sounds and smells equally raucous. Stevedores entered and exited with all manner of carts from the dockside quays, sometimes choking the roadways as they headed to and from their assigned ships, merchants and their gangs of workers milling through the warehouses and among the cityside streets. Weaving among them all were day merchants who roamed with food carts, their own children threading through the crowd with samples on sticks, crying, "The best to be found in the Amber City!"

It was a constant hive of activity, an ever-changing collection of sounds, smells, languages, and cultures, which in some ways made the harbor the perfect place for the Moonless Host to meet. It was difficult for the King of Whispers to hear their words when the sheer volume of conversation tended to drown them out. Even King Yusam and his mere, Emre suspected, might have trouble sifting through the threads that wove together here.

And yet, however well it might suit their needs in some respects, the truth was that the lion's share of money moving in and out of Sharakhai traveled through the southern harbor, so of course it attracted the Spears. Like bees to flowers in bloom, they swarmed about the harbor and its streets, its warehouses and ships, following the scents of currency and graft and crimes against the Kings. Like falcons through flocks of starlings they cut through the crowds in their white uniforms, many, though not all, looking for ways to line their *own* purses. Occasionally they even kept the peace.

Even now near end of day, while Emre was heading toward the safe house and the roar of the harbor's workday was starting to fade, he passed three pairs of Silver Spears. He recognized a few who had been bribed by the Host to avert their eyes from Emre and others like him, but Macide couldn't bribe them all. Even if he had all the money in the world, too many Spears had been harmed, directly or indirectly, by the Host. They were the ones fiercely loyal to the Kings and to the Lord Commander of the Silver Spears. It made the selection of who to bribe tricky to say the least.

Emre continued past the safe house. He wandered a bit, making sure he wasn't being followed, then circled back and made his way to a small warehouse with a livestock pen near the harbor's eastern edge. Seeing the way clear, he hopped over the fence, dodged a number of sows, as well as their piles of shit, and headed in through the pig's entrance. The smell struck him hard. He'd come to hate it, not because it was foul, but from his days working in a shambles. Those had been dark days, days he'd tried and failed to work through his self-loathing after Rafa's death, and the smell reminded him of his failures.

Inside the warehouse, a space opened up with pens for animals. Several were filled with short Qaimiri workhorses. A man waited just inside, a rangy fellow using a rasp to file one of the horse's hooves. He stood when Emre entered and stared.

Emre looked back at the entrance. "One day the dunes will shift, yes?" A common refrain among the Host, referring to the day when the Kings would fall.

The man grunted and pointed with the rasp toward the nearby cellar door, then returned to his work. Emre took the stairs down, and there found a room perhaps three paces by five, lit by a lone lantern in the center of the seven men and women. Half of those gathered had been assigned to key positions around the collegia in support of Melekh's and Iliam's joint mission. Melekh was already here. His worried look made Emre's gut churn. He'd always been good at burying his emotions, but staring at Melekh, his regret came rushing back, stronger than when he'd sent the arrows into Iliam. He'd taken a life today—a *friend's* life—and no amount of rationalizing was going to change that.

His childhood friend Hamid squatted on the far side of the lantern, watching Emre's approach with sleepy eyes. He motioned to a place across from him. Emre sat there, and the rest gathered round. "Tell us," Hamid prompted.

And Emre did, from the things he saw on the tower to the chase, to shooting the arrows into Iliam's chest. As he said these words, he stared directly into Melekh's eyes. He wouldn't hide the truth from him. Iliam had been Melekh's blood, and he deserved an honest telling. "My tears for your loss," he said when he'd finished.

Melekh swallowed hard, then nodded. He wiped tears away with the back of his hands. "The stubborn bastard would've demanded no less."

Perhaps, thought Emre, *which only serves to deepen the ache.*

The others told stories as well, but Melekh was the only one with news of substance. He'd been successful. He pulled out a roll of papyrus he had stuffed inside his kaftan. He handed it to Hamid, who looked it over by the yellow light of the lantern.

"Very good," he said, then looked to all those gathered. "This is what we risked our lives for. Indeed, this is what Iliam gave *his* life for. Our hearts may be heavy, but that's fitting, as I see it, for we've done the heavy work. Now go." He motioned to the cellar steps. "No contact with your commanders for seven days," Hamid told them. They nodded and left, but Emre stayed behind.

Hamid stared at him, emotionless. "If you wish to know what Melekh found, I can't tell you."

"It isn't that," Emre said, though he was more than curious about what Iliam's blood had bought them. "It was the Maiden who caught Iliam, the one who held him as I shot the arrows."

Hamid stuffed the roll of papyrus into his own kaftan, eyeing Emre with a look of mild curiosity. "It was Çeda, wasn't it?"

Emre's head jerked back. "How—"

Hamid blew out the lantern and headed for the cellar stairs, tugging Emre's sleeve for him to follow. Soon they were out and into the city streets. Dusk had fallen over the desert, the first stars piercing the gauze of a darkening slate-blue sky. "I could always tell when you were mooning over someone, Emre."

"I wasn't mooning," Emre said as they headed south, skirting the edge of the warehouse district. "I worry over her. That's all."

"I know you two were close, but she's chosen her path. What good will your worry do her now? It'll only distract you. Misstep in this game we're playing, Emre, and it isn't a finger you'll lose from the Spears, or even a hand. It'll be your life, or worse, an intimate chat with the Confessor King. Stop worrying about Çeda and start worrying about us."

Emre snorted. "What *are* we doing? We hide. We run from the Kings."

Hamid shrugged. "Retreat is not defeat."

"But what we did in the desert, in Külaşan's palace, it was all for nothing. Hamzakiir was taken from beneath our very noses. And the Kings have been hounding us ever since. More are taken every day."

"Taken only from the fringes. People who know little of our inner workings. We've remained as intact as we could have hoped."

"For what gain?"

"What fool told you to always expect gain? We fight our battles. We'll lose some, there is no doubt, but we will win this war."

As they passed the Trough and continued along the same street, Emre noted just how smug Hamid seemed. He was good at hiding his emotions—much better than he'd been as a child—but Emre could still see the signs. "Something's happened."

He shrugged. "We have a bit of information. More than we had yesterday."

"No, it's more than that."

A smile tugged at the corners of Hamid's mouth.

"Tell me."

"Our journey to Külaşan's palace . . . It may not have been so fruitless as we thought."

"Hamzakiir?" When Hamid didn't react in any way, Emre understood. "He's been found?" Hamid half nodded, half shrugged, as if he could neither confirm nor deny Emre's assertion. Emre pointed to Hamid's kaftan, where the list was secreted away. "He asked for that, didn't he?"

"Nothing like this happens in the Al'afwa Khadar without leave of our leader, Ishaq."

It told Emre much. That Hamzakiir had indeed returned. That he was now plotting with the Host's leader and Macide's father, Ishaq. "But the collegia?"

"Tell me, Emre, if you hoped to strike at the very heart of the Kings, what would you target?"

Emre wasn't sure what he was getting at. "Their sons and daughters."

Hamid smiled. "Go on."

The Blade Maidens were the most obvious answer. They were the pride of the Kings, firstborn daughters, each and every one. But the Maidens were a particularly thorny group to target. Emre had seen some truly talented soldiers in the Moonless Host, but there was no denying the Maidens were the most skilled swords in the desert, and they had a penchant for exacting revenge in a way that showed they weren't merely good at it—they reveled in it, took glee in it. Surely even Macide would grudgingly acknowledge that when the scales were weighed, the Maidens often came out ahead. Emre doubted the Host were ready for another confrontation after the campaign of murderous retribution waged by the Kings after Külaşan's death.

So if not the Maidens, then who? Of course the answer was right in front of him. "We'll take their brightest minds."

"As they take ours," Hamid replied.

The collegia. Hamzakiir was targeting its students. Emre had known few people who had risen to enter the collegia, much less become a scholar. But he, like many in Sharakhai, considered it a noble calling. "Are we sure about this? The collegia?"

Hamid didn't flinch. "Nearly everyone who enters those halls are rich, the sons and daughters of the lords of Sharakhai or those who hail from foreign noble families. Good riddance to them all."

What he said was true. Each year, some few of the collegia's robes were granted to promising students from the poorer quarters of the city, but more and more it was difficult for the common man to reach those hallowed halls. "Good riddance," Emre echoed, "and now we can do it at our leisure, take them one by one."

"That," Hamid said with a sidelong grin, "would be altogether too slow for our purposes."

Chapter 12

WHEN THE GROUND BEGAN SHAKING like the beat of a heavy drum, Ramahd knew what was coming, but try as he might his body refused to move. He stood at dusk by Meryam and King Aldouan's side, for all the world another stone in the desert. Along the western sky, the sun burned, a molten copper splash, where the rest of the sky was the color of a darkened bruise, a vast remembrance of pain and torment. A figure approached, lumbering forward, the sounds of its passage delayed ever so slightly from the fall of its long strides. Pebbles and sand on the glasslike surface of the ground skittered.

As it came, Ramahd fought. He fought to escape. Fought to choke down his fear. Fought to speak so that he could, perhaps, release Meryam or his king. But nothing worked.

Guhldrathen neared. Like a wolf stalking its prey, the ehrekh's form was hunched, its nostrils flared. Its eyes, set into blackened skin, were sallow. A crown of thorns adorned its head. Its forked tail swished in hypnotic patterns, the pace of which quickened as it neared. When it came within ten paces, it stopped and stared at the three captives, offerings to a false god. It gave them a wide berth as it circled, eyeing each in turn as if deciding just what to do with them, and in what order.

When it approached at last it hunched lower, the muscles along its arms rippling as it spread them wide. It came to a stand before Meryam. "Is it so? Thou comest unprotected with sigils upon thy skin?"

Meryam said nothing, but Ramahd could hear her breath rasping through her nostrils, quick as a desert hare.

Guhldrathen moved to stand before Ramahd. It lowered its head until the two of them were eye to eye. Ramahd could smell its fetid breath, but could not rear back, could not look away. "The pup who chaseth the White Wolf." It smiled, blackened lips receding, yellowed teeth now bared.

It stalked to Ramahd's right, coming to a stand before Aldouan. Ramahd could see only its tail, which twitched in rhythmic patterns. "And a third." Ramahd heard the king gasp, heard a sound like the puncturing of skin, then a smacking sound like a child licking honey. "Blood of thy blood," the ehrekh said.

It resumed its pacing, circling them, stopping before Ramahd several times to examine the mark upon his forehead, doing so before Meryam and the king as well. The sky continued to darken, and still the ehrekh paced. It was wary, Ramahd realized. It surely knew by now that Hamzakiir had been the one to deliver them. No doubt it could smell Hamzakiir's scent from the sigils on their foreheads, painted with his blood.

Ramahd wondered if he might use that to his advantage, but how? Hamzakiir's bonds were still in place, and nothing he did, no matter his desperation, no matter his anger, seemed able to dislodge them.

With Tulathan cresting the horizon in the east, Guhldrathen slowed, then came to a stop before Aldouan. Its breath was coming in great huffs now. At last Ramahd managed movement. He was able to turn his head to see the ehrekh staring at Aldouan. The beast stretched its neck out, then slipped a forked tongue between its black lips and lapped at the blood laid by Hamzakiir upon his skin. It closed its eyes and shivered, as if savoring the taste.

Ramahd knew what would happen next, knew there was nothing he could do to prevent it. Yet still he railed against his bonds. *Touch not my king! Take me! Take me, foul demon!*

But the ehrekh was intent on King Aldouan. With no preamble, it clutched the king's shoulders and pulled him in while clamping its wide jaws over the king's chest and collarbone. When the beast's head withdrew, the sounds of cracking and tearing went with it. A dark mass of red was revealed. Blood spurted from Aldouan's neck, spraying his chin as his head jerked back reflexively. Dark trails of blood arced over the twilit sky, pattering against the translucent stone a moment later.

Leave him! Take me and leave him!

But it was too late. The ehrekh's lips pulled back, revealing blood-stained teeth. And then it was on the king with an abandon it hadn't shown before. Thank the gods for small favors, he pushed Aldouan to the ground. Ramahd could no longer see his king, but he saw the beast's head jerking back, over and over. He heard the silken sound of fresh meat being rended. Guhldrathen was devouring the King of Qaimir before his very eyes, and there was nothing he could do about it. Nor would he be able to prevent it when his turn came. Alu forgive him his cowardice, but he hoped it would take him next, not Meryam.

From the corner of his eye he saw Guhldrathen plunge a clawed hand into King Aldouan's chest, saw it ripping Aldouan's heart free from his rib cage, which lay shattered, open for god and man alike to see. It ate until sated, and then paced along the stone in some unknowable pattern. It slowed, bent down, put a finger to Aldouan's ruined form, then drew a symbol on the stone with fresh blood. It drew another symbol next to it, an ancient form, a word of power perhaps only the desert gods still knew. It moved from place to place, marking the stone here, then there, stopping to inspect its handiwork or snuffing in displeasure before laying more blood to correct the growing, infernal device it was laying on the stone.

It took a long while, but as the ehrekh's work continued to expand there was a quieting, a dwindling of the keen ringing sound Ramahd hadn't entirely been aware of until then. It was Hamzakiir's presence, he realized. It was not gone, but it was certainly diminished. And he could see it in Meryam as well, for it was then that she fell to the ground, sobbing. Her frail form crawled to where her father lay. She threw one arm across the ruin of his chest as if to hide the carnage, or to protect her father in some small way after failing him so perfectly.

Ramahd found that he could move as well. His limbs begged him to collapse, to lie in a fetal ball to await his death. His knees shook, and he was so unsteady he staggered merely to remain upright. But stand he did. He had to. He could show no weakness to Guhldrathen, now of all times.

"Enough," Ramahd said, lurching forward until he stood directly before the ehrekh. The beast was half again his size, but hunched over as he was, still feasting on Aldouan's heart, Ramahd was able to look him in the eye. "Leave this place, Guhldrathen."

The ehrekh stopped chewing. A low chuckle escaped him, the sound of thunder in the darkest hours of the night. "I was given thee to do with as I please, and so I shall."

"You've taken what was offered, a life in forfeit if she failed to bring Hamzakiir to you."

"Her *own* life hath been offered."

"And you took her father's, which was worth much more to her." Ramahd stepped aside, motioning to Meryam, who hadn't yet moved.

She sobbed as she touched her forehead to her unmoving father's. "I'm sorry," she whispered. "I'm sorry, I'm sorry, I'm sorry."

When Guhldrathen took a step toward her, Ramahd blocked its path. "Our lives were offered by Hamzakiir, the one you seek. The one who owes you *his* blood. You would accept from him trinkets when a chest of gold is owed you?"

A mischievous twinkle appeared in Guhldrathen's eyes, a reflection of Tulathan, bright now in the east. "Thou and yon woman are but trinkets?"

"To you, yes. You want *Hamzakiir*, the one who betrayed you, the one who stole from you as if you were a fool and a beggar."

The ehrekh's nostrils flared. "Much is owed."

"And you will have it. You have taken a life. You have supped upon her father, a king in his own land brought to the Great Shangazi by trickery and betrayal. We seek revenge against Hamzakiir as well. In this we are aligned."

Guhldrathen looked him up and down. It stood to full height, and when it huffed like a bull, its head and shoulders shook.

"Give us time. Take our king's blood and be glad, knowing that we will return with more."

"And if thou fail?"

"If we fail, I will deliver myself to you."

Guhldrathen craned its neck, then shook its massive head. "My wish is no longer for thine own blood, nor the daughter of thy king."

"What then? Name it, and it shall be yours."

"I will have the blood of the White Wolf."

Ramahd's head jerked back. "What did you say?"

Guhldrathen didn't respond. It only moved its head back and forth, a black laugher sizing its prey.

"Her blood is not mine to give."

The ehrekh blinked. Its gaze flicked beyond Ramahd to Meryam.

Gods, the hunger in those eyes. Meryam had told him how the ehrekh could become fixated on certain men or women, living through them, sating their hunger for the touch of the first gods. He remembered how Guhldrathen had acted the last time they'd stood in this place. It had sniffed about Meryam, Ramahd, and his gathered men, spending the most time on Ramahd himself, and then it had told him if he wanted to find Hamzakiir, he need but follow the White Wolf. Had *he* been the one to set Guhldrathen on her scent? Had its infatuation started in that very moment?

Mighty Alu, he didn't know what to do. The thought of promising Çeda to Guhldrathen made him go cold. To wager one's own life was one thing. To wager hers was quite another. But what else could he do? He must right the scales. He must see Qaimir safe. And if all went as planned, he would have Hamzakiir and he would deliver him to Guhldrathen and none of this would ever matter.

"Don't, Ramahd." This came from behind him. He turned and found Meryam staring up at him, her pale face blood-streaked but otherwise strangely bright in the moonlight. Her look pleaded with him to simply let this all end. "My time has come."

She wasn't thinking straight. This was merely a moment of weakness. She would recover. He would make sure she did. And then they would find Hamzakiir.

He turned to Guhldrathen, pulled himself taller, and said, "Very—" He swallowed, licked his lips. Gods, how dry his mouth had become. "Very well. Should we fail, the White Wolf's life in forfeit."

The ehrekh turned its gaze on Meryam for one weighty moment, as if sizing her. Something inside Ramahd turned over and over, like an eel trying to free itself from a fisherman's hook. To gamble with another's life was a foul thing. It gave him no pride whatsoever, and yet it was little different than what he did as a lord. Little different than what a king did with those who served him.

"By thine own blood dost thou forge this bond?" Guhldrathen asked.

"By mine own blood," Ramahd said, holding out his arm. Using the sharp point of the silver ring on his thumb, he pierced the skin of his wrist. Blood welled and trickled down his hand. As Guhldrathen took his hand and lapped at his bloody fingers, Ramahd felt his fingers and toes go cold.

"So it shall be," it said.

Taking Ramahd's head in its hands, it licked the blood clean from his forehead with a tongue so warm it made Ramahd's stomach turn. Hamzakiir's taint was slowly lifted. The keen ringing that had diminished with Aldouan's death now vanished. His flesh and blood no longer corrupted, he stood straighter, saw the desert around him with new eyes. He took a deep breath. For all the painful memories of the past months, Ramahd felt like a man reborn. The night air had never smelled so sweet.

Meryam, as if realizing it couldn't be avoided now that the bargain had been struck, stood bravely on shaking limbs. Perhaps she was unwilling to face the ehrekh as a mewling child might, or perhaps she'd sensed what had just happened to Ramahd, and wanted the same for herself. Whatever the case, Guhldrathen repeated the ritual with her, then strode away.

Meryam went through a stunning transformation. She was frail as ever, but she stood to her full height for the first time in what seemed like years. She breathed deeply, then released a discordant laugh, a sound that evinced both sorrow and relief.

When the ehrekh's booming footsteps had receded, then faded altogether, Ramahd held his hand out to Meryam. "Come."

She looked to the body of her dead father. She bent down and took off his ring of office, his golden necklace as well. After secreting them away inside a pouch at her belt, she took Ramahd's hand, and the two of them began walking across the desert, northeast toward Sharakhai.

Chapter 13

CEDA RODE AT A FULL GALLOP, third in their line of five horses as they sped along the Spear toward the House of Maidens. Ahead, the House's outer gates stood open. Four Maidens stood on the ramparts, watching the line of people and carts and wagons awaiting entry. Below them, eight Silver Spears inspected those at the head of the line.

As their horses powered over the dry street, Sümeya stood in her stirrups and waved her ebon blade. "Clear the way!"

The line reacted quickly, bowing their heads as the first four horses passed by, but many lifted their eyes, some gaping openly, at the woman being dragged over the ground behind the final horse, Kameyl's. A Sharakhani man in a bright orange thawb shielded his daughter's eyes while, just ahead of him, a pair of Qaimiri ladies in a covered wagon lifted kerchiefs to mouths. During open displays of the Kings' power such as this, failure to pay obeisance to the passing of a Maiden was often overlooked. Allowing the lowborn to see such things only added to the mystique of the Blade Maidens. That it also added to the hatred of them was viewed as a fringe benefit. The Kings dealt in many currencies, after all; gold might be the most valuable, but respect and fear were not far behind.

The woman alternately moaned and screamed as she was scraped roughly over the stone and packed earth. Her light linen dress was tattered, her legs torn and bloody. They'd found her in the bursar's office. She was the officiant who'd tended to the two men, the agents of the Moonless Host. She'd denied any wrongdoing, but after a few short minutes of questioning, Kameyl had grabbed the woman's hair and dragged her all the way to the collegia stables, at which point she'd tied the pleading woman to her saddle and set out for the House of Maidens. Çeda had tried to think of a way to stop her, but she knew Kameyl wouldn't listen. Not after they'd lost her prize: the scarab who'd escaped them in the maze of the Shallows.

Somewhat unexpectedly, King Yusam strode to meet them as they rode for the paddock. They gave their horses over to the stable girls, at which point Kameyl bowed to the King and asked leave to bring the woman to the interrogation rooms, a request Yusam granted with a wave of his hand. The rest of them—Sümeya, Melis, Yndris, and Çeda—stood before him while Sümeya recounted the tale, Çeda and the others adding details where Sümeya could not. He paid particular attention to Çeda's story of the bowman. Çeda didn't use Emre's name, and tried to be as general in her description of him as she could, but Yusam pressed, his eyes studying hers carefully. He asked for details, *any* details, and so Çeda told him of the bracers in case Kameyl or Yndris had seen as much, figuring to give that up would mean little. But when she described them, Yusam's eyes relaxed, as if there had been a tension building up in him that was released with that information, perhaps confirmation of something he'd seen.

Please, Nalamae, deny him Emre's scent.

When they were done, he beckoned to Çeda. "Come. I would speak awhile." Yndris stared at Çeda with naked resentment, but strangely, Sümeya did as well. In all her months here in the House of Maidens, Çeda had never felt jealousy from Sümeya. Anger, certainly. Resentment of her presence, especially early on, but not jealousy, not until now, and suddenly she wished Yusam hadn't singled her out so openly from the others. *But what is there to do but swim with the current?*

She followed as he strode to a tower built into the nearby curtain wall. Inside the tower, they took the stairs up to the wall and walked east, side by side, toward King's Harbor, where the royal clippers and ships of war were kept. Every few hundred yards they would pass through another tower. The tower's interior would shade them for a moment, the sun's absence feeling cool but not cold, and then the heat and the brightness of the Amber City and the desert beyond would return.

"You've been among the Maidens for some time now," Yusam said.

"Yes, my Lord King."

"Have you found your place?"

"If you mean, do I feel like this is my home, in truth I would say no, but it is coming. My sister Maidens have welcomed me."

"But only after proving yourself."

After killing a King. After lying to them and telling them it was Jalize. "Yes, my Lord."

"Tell me of your childhood."

"What do you wish to know?"

"Tell me about your mother."

She'd told him of Ahya many times before, but she did so again, giving him the same story she'd given him and several of the other Kings: that her mother, Ahya, had come from the desert when she was young; that she'd done much in her time: seamstress, translator, poet, sword mistress; that after Çeda was born they'd moved about the city often, her mother never finding comfort in one place.

"Do you suppose she did so because she missed the desert?" Yusam asked.

The thought so struck her that she stopped for a moment. They were at the edge of King's Harbor, which sprawled to their left, a mass of ships crouched along dozens of piers, as if they yearned for the wind to fill their sails, for the sand to rush beneath their skis. On her right, the desert sprawled endlessly. How much *had* Ahya wished to return to the desert? She'd come to Sharakhai with purpose, to see to the downfall of the Kings, or at least to orchestrate it with Çeda as a necessary instrument, but how much had she given up to do so? It was clear she'd cut almost all ties to her family. Çeda had met only her grandfather and only when she was very young. Ahya hadn't even introduced him as such, but Çeda had seen him again in the visions from Saliah's tree, seen him in the reflections of those chiming crystals, her grandfather with tattoos on his face, golden rings in his nose, a vicious scar running down his neck.

Who else had Ahya left behind? And how much had she come to regret doing so?

For years Çeda had dreamed of sailing the desert, visiting the desert tribes, hoping to connect with those of her blood, and the call was never greater than it was now, standing on a wall that protected the Kings, staring out over the Great Shangazi.

"Have I struck a nerve, young one?"

"My apologies," Çeda said, resuming her pace until they were again stride-in-stride. "I suspect you're right. I think she dearly wished to return to the desert."

"Then what prevented her?"

What, indeed? She had to be careful here. Yusam was far too intelligent, and too gifted at sifting through disparate, seemingly unrelated clues. "A family divide, I suspect."

"Ah," Yusam said, "a thing that happens to all of us from time to time. But we are nothing without our family, our tribe. Is it not so?"

"Indeed, my King." It was the truest thing Yusam had ever said to her.

To their right, the Taloran Mountains were a jagged black line along the horizon. Cutting the desert in two between the mountains and the harbor was the aqueduct, which carried precious water from the mountains—from a lake, it was said, nestled between the peaks like a sapphire hidden in the nest of a carrion crow. They continued along the wall of King's Harbor, climbing the stairs to the massive gates, crossing them, and climbing down the far side. It soon became clear Yusam was going to lead her around the entirety of Tauriyat, the mountain upon which the House of Kings was built. As they walked, Çeda could feel Yusam's eyes on her, and on the harbor as well, as if he were considering the two of them together. It sparked a memory, of war ships sailing over the sand. She looked to her right, examining the amber dunes that made their way right up to the very gates of the harbor, trying to determine whether, and indeed *how*, the two of them were related.

It seemed as good a time as any to broach a subject. "My King," she said as they moved beyond the harbor and toward the northern slopes, "I've wondered about your mere, the visions it shows you."

He nodded his assent, striding with hands clasped behind his back.

"You've sent each of us in Sümeya's hand on various tasks, and I wonder:

Did the visions themselves show you the danger we face, or is it the outcomes that do so?"

"In truth, both. Think of our combined future—yours, mine, Sharakhai's—as a grand tapestry." He gripped his hands before him, as if by doing so he could shape the very things he spoke of. "A tapestry that is constantly being torn apart by the whims of the gods, indeed, by the whims of man, threads that are woven and rewoven. The mere grants me some small insight into the colors and shapes within that tapestry, but only a glimpse, and an imperfect one at that, for the tapestry may be torn and remade by some monumental event, or even a host of smaller ones. Or even—given time—one tiny event that like a landslide triggers others. It is up to the viewer, then, to determine how soon the event might occur, and to move as quickly as possible to gather views of other, nearby threads so that a larger picture might be formed. Wait too long, and I'm pulling together an image from different times, from different tapestriers, in a way of thinking. Wait too long and the view becomes flawed, and eventually useless."

"So you must move quickly."

Yusam nodded. "Yes, there is that. Simple, straightforward briskness. But there are times, young dove, when a particular future is all too likely. It comes on strong. So strong, in fact, that it almost feels a certitude. And when one of these visions comes to me, I know it, and I have learned that I can take more time. I can be patient, for the thing ahead is massive. Unlikely to easily change."

"That's what we're doing, helping you to see something important to the Kings."

"Not just the Kings, Çedamihn, but the entire desert. What is coming will shape the way of the world. I know it is so. I simply don't know what form it will take, this threat."

"But you will."

Yusam made a gesture like *who can tell?* "With diligence, and the favor of the gods, yes. But we can never rest."

"Have you learned anything from what we've done? Can you not see the *nature* of the threat?"

Yusam smiled, his bright eyes glancing Çeda's way. "Do you wish to look in the mere yourself?"

"No, my Lord King. I only wonder if the Maidens could help more. If *I* could help."

"Your enthusiasm commends you, child, but this a broth best left to a single chef."

"Is it to do with the harbor, a threat from the desert?"

Çeda had expected some response from Yusam. What she hadn't expected was for him to stop and spin her to face him. "Why did you say that?"

She'd wondered how much she could say without putting herself in danger, but she could see now she'd better tell him most of it, or a near enough facsimile that he wouldn't be able to tell the difference. "I've been given to dreams from time to time, my Lord King."

He peered more deeply into her eyes. "Yes."

"In one, I saw ships sailing over the dunes. Dozens of ships. Perhaps hundreds. I'd never known what it meant, but since entering the House of Maidens, since seeing King's Harbor with my own eyes and the dunes beyond, I wonder if that wasn't what I saw—a threat to our house."

"Tell me about them, these ships."

Çeda shrugged. "The dream was a long time ago. When I was nine, ten. I can't remember anymore. But it was vivid, and it's stayed with me ever since. I don't recall much about the ships themselves, only that they were of varied types. That they were sailing over the dunes on a moonlit night."

"Under the twin moons?"

"I think so, yes."

"And these dreams, do you have them often?"

"No. Only a handful of times in my life."

In truth, they hadn't been dreams at all. Not in the normal sense. They'd been visions from Saliah's tree, deep in the desert. Saliah, the goddess Nalamae in disguise. Or if not in disguise then at the least in a new skin that Nalamae herself did not completely understand. The visions had come the day her mother died, and they'd shown her a number of things, some of which had already come true. The granting of her ebon blade by King Husamettín, the tattoo placed on her right hand by Zaïde in order to save Çeda from the adichara poison, the truth of Çeda's heritage as the daughter of a King of Sharakhai. No matter that the final one had been a vision from the past. She now believed that all of them would one day come true. In fact, they now felt inviolate, as if she *must* play her part or risk the displeasure of the fates.

"What else have you seen, child?"

Çeda told him of Husamettín granting her her blade, of Zaïde tapping the tattoo into the palm of her hand. She told him of the Blade Maidens raising their swords in triumph. She wasn't sure whether to share with him this last vision—she had no idea whether it might be related to the ships on the moonlit sand—but he seemed so intense she thought it might lighten his mood.

And it did. They resumed walking, and soon the view to their right was dominated by the terraced rice paddies on the mountain slopes and the fields of grain and vegetables fed by the glinting reservoir beyond. Yusam's intense curiosity faded, replaced by a contemplative look. "You were headstrong when you came to us."

"Some would say I still am, my Lord King."

"Yes, but perhaps this gives me some insight as to why."

"I suspect it has more to do with my mother than any visions. I had no idea they would come true then."

"And now you have some confirmation."

"Yes, but as you say, who can know whether a vision will come exactly as it's shown?"

"You may have more of them. Will you come to me if you do?"

"I will, my King."

"Very well. It's good you've shared with me what you have."

As they continued, Yusam's mood continued to lighten. As they rounded Tauriyat and approached the House of Maidens once more, he pointed out the parts of the city that were young when he was a child in Sharakhai, before he'd become a King. The old wall, which still existed in many places but that had long been outgrown. Ancient bathhouses, the auction blocks, Bent Man Bridge and the Wheel, where the city's largest streets, the Spear and the Trough, met. "How it's grown," he said, his eyes bright, and for a moment Çeda wondered at all he'd seen. Here was a man who'd lived for well over four hundred years. It wasn't right. No man should live so long, certainly not while standing on the graves of those he'd sacrificed.

No sooner had the thought come than a well of hatred surged up inside her, a thing tied to the blooming fields that ringed the city. It became so great she nearly screamed. Without even realizing when it had happened, she saw her own kenshar gripped in her right hand, the very one given to her by her mother when she'd turned six.

"My dear child, what are you doing?"

She blinked. She'd just drawn a knife in the presence of a King. The poison in her hand had done it. Or rather, the link she felt to the asirim sleeping out in the desert. She'd first known of the bond it had created shortly after Zaïde had saved her from the poison. What she'd never expected was that it would control her, force her to do things against her will. It had happened at Yndris's vigil in the desert, and now here. Gods, was she becoming a tool of the asirim? Would they use her as the Kings used *them*? They would if she didn't learn to control it. And then where would she be? Dead. Lost beneath the sand. Forgotten like her mother.

Bearing down against the pain that was now running all along her arm, Çeda showed the blade to Yusam. "I'd forgotten one last vision," Çeda lied. "I remembered it only when you were speaking of the bladewright just now, the one who made your first sword for you."

None of the concern had left Yusam's face. "Go on."

"I saw a woman, perhaps me, perhaps another, driving this knife into the heart of a false King."

"Why do you say false?"

"Because when he fell to the ground, the crown upon his head rolled away and withered."

Yusam swallowed. His eyes searched hers. He took the knife from her and examined it, then handed it back to her as if it meant nothing. "Come, Çedamihn Ahyanesh'ala. We've talked enough of meres and dreams and knives this day."

They completed their circuit, and Yusam delivered her back to the courtyard of the Maidens. Sümeya, with a sour expression on her face, was there to greet them.

"What is it?" Çeda asked before she could think to allow the King to speak first.

After a look of chastisement for Çeda, Sümeya addressed Yusam. "My

Lord King, my apologies, but there's been an incident with the woman we brought from the collegia."

"An incident, First Warden?"

Sümeya nodded. "She poisoned herself, most likely before we took her from the bursar's office." Sümeya paused, glancing uncomfortably at Çeda. "She's dead, my King."

King Yusam didn't appear angry at this information. Rather, he seemed to weigh it, to turn it about to inspect it from all angles as if it were but one more piece in the grand puzzle he was solving in his mind.

"You have my thanks," he said absently, then strode from the courtyard.

Çeda slept only lightly. Her chest was filled with the flutter of moth wings, not only over the strange conversation with Yusam, but with what she was about to do, the hope within her that might be crushed.

After listening for some time for any movement from the other Maidens' rooms, she got up and moved to the desk in the corner of her room. She lit a candle and retrieved a piece of the reed paper she'd received from Juvaan, then took out the inkwell and pen. She wrote in clipped sentences in the smallest script she could manage. She recorded her initial meeting with Yusam, their chase after the two men, the death of one of them. She did not name Emre, but she made it clear she'd seen the scarab she'd been searching for but had no idea where he might be now. She wrote of the woman being dragged back bloody to the House of Maidens, and finished with her long walk with Yusam.

She lit the corner, feeling a hundred times more exposed than their last exchange. A plot was afoot, and she needed to know what, and she desperately wanted to know how Emre was involved. The page lit, blue flames rushing across it in the blink of an eye. It rested there, the flames licking the edges, the ghostly sheet seeming to ripple above the desk's wooden surface. She waited for long minutes, her nervousness growing.

Letters appeared, inking the page in elegant curves and blue flames:

Very well. I did find that the Kundhunese ship you told me of, the Adzambe, *which has been smuggling in rare herbs and roots for Ihsan, things the grass witches use before taking one of their week-long sleeps beneath the earth. Why would he want such?*

Her heart sank a bit as the page burned up moments later. Why wouldn't he mention *something* about Emre?

She took another paper. *I've no idea why Ihsan would want them. What of my other concern? Has there been word of the scarab? Do you know what they're doing?*

As she lit the fresh page, she heard the creak of a bed. It was likely one of her sister Maidens shifting in her sleep, or getting up for a drink of water or to relieve herself, but it felt as if they were going to burst into her room at any moment. She readied herself to smother the flames with the square pot she had on one corner of the desk, a thing she'd prepared for that very purpose.

But then writing appeared on the burning page—

I've nothing on that as yet. Report more when you can.

—and it burned up, just like her hopes.

She fumed, wondering whether she should use another sheet to press Juvaan. Surely he knew *something*, even if only rumors. Staring at her dwindling supply of the magical paper, she decided to give him more time. It may be that the Host had gone quiet before the mission at the collegia, which she'd learned was often the case.

Give him time, she told herself. *Give him time.*

A bitter leaf, but what was there to do but chew and swallow it?

Chapter 14

WITHIN THE SAVAŞAM, ZAÏDE UNLEASHED a series of moves that had Çeda on the defensive, barely able to keep up. Çeda blocked them all, but when she tried to spin away to regain her distance, Zaïde caught her heel with a well-timed snap of her foot. As Çeda fell, Zaïde launched herself forward and brushed the vein running along Çeda's throat, ending with a perfectly executed shoulder roll to return to her feet. It was a reprise of the drill they'd been performing this past week. Zaïde had managed once again to score a strike, but Çeda was somewhat pleased that it was taking her longer and longer to do so.

Çeda kicked off the mat to reach her feet. "Do you never tire?"

No sooner had she spoken the words than Zaïde's ghostly pallor registered. She was standing perfectly still, her breath coming heavy, a discomfited look on her sweaty face. As Çeda ran to the edge of the room and fetched water from a ewer, Zaïde's brows pinched, distorting the crescent moon tattoos between them. Her eyes were fixed on some point beyond the wall ahead of her, as if she were concentrating, willing her body to recover. Indeed, by the time Çeda returned with a glass of water, her breathing had slowed and the distressing ashen color of her skin had flushed a rosy hue.

As Zaïde sipped the water, Çeda wondered if she should fetch help. It was easy to forget that Zaïde was more than twice Çeda's age, perhaps even thrice as old—she'd never divulged her exact age. But here was a sign that perhaps Çeda should be more careful lest she lose her one and only ally in the House of Maidens.

"Wipe that look from your face," Zaïde said as she ambled toward the edge of the mat.

"What look?"

"And don't patronize me." She drank more from the glass, then set it on the table and returned to their starting position. "I'm not ready to see the farther fields just yet."

"It isn't that," Çeda said, taking her time moving across from her.

"Oh, what is it then?"

"I'm only annoyed that you won again."

"You're a terrible liar, Çeda."

"I'm speaking the truth."

"A half-truth to hide your thoughts. Now come," she said, taking another gulp of water, "it's time we try something new."

"Shouldn't we rest first?" Çeda asked.

"Well of course, my precious child. And would you like someone to rub your feet as you lie upon your divan?"

Part of Çeda wanted to laugh, but it felt too much like deflection on Zaïde's part, or worse, deathbed humor, which was preposterous, of course. Zaïde was healthier than most people half her age. And yet there it was, a worry about Zaïde that went deeper than the mercenary notion of losing an ally. She'd come to enjoy her time with the Matron. Çeda had promised herself she'd make no friends in the House of Maidens, but if there was anyone who might hold that title, it was Zaïde.

In the end, Çeda moved into place across from Zaïde, at which point the Matron lifted her hands into starting position. Çeda followed suit, the back of her right hand touching Zaïde's.

"Now close your eyes."

Çeda stared. "Why?"

"I said close your eyes."

Çeda did, confused, feeling very exposed with the two of them poised to fight.

"Now, feel your heartbeat."

Çeda had little choice—it was still pounding in her chest—but she expanded her awareness to feel more: the momentary surge of blood through her body, particularly in her temples and along her hands and fingers; her breathing as well, but only in relation to her heartbeat, one a staccato rhythm, the other a legato swell.

"Good," Zaïde said, as if she could sense how deeply Çeda was in tune with her body. "Now feel mine."

Confused, Çeda opened her eyes. She moved her hand away, an act that earned her a scowl. Zaïde grabbed Çeda's hand and snapped it back into place.

"Sorry," Çeda said. She shut her eyes and enveloped herself in her own rhythms once more. For the life of her, though, she had no idea how she might sense Zaïde's heart.

"Come, Çeda, you like to think yourself a clever girl. Prove it to me now."

Çeda pressed her lips tighter, but then forced herself to relax. Zaïde was always pressing her in different ways: physically but also with insults and the occasional nasty trick. *Your enemies will never let you rest. Why should I?* She'd put them in first strike position for a reason. The backs of their hands were touching, so Çeda focused her attention there. She felt Zaïde's warmth, felt her sweat-slicked skin. Felt the pulse of her blood.

"Yes," Zaïde breathed.

Their heartbeats were out of sync, Zaïde's moving slower than Çeda's, no matter how out of breath she might have seemed moments ago.

"Now slow yours to match mine."

Çeda tried, but each time she did, it only seemed to speed her heart, not slow it down. This was strange magic, what Zaïde was asking her to do. It might seem simple, but Çeda knew very well it was for some greater purpose. Mastery of this would lead to more, perhaps to the very secrets that made the Blade Maidens so mysterious to the populace of the desert: their ability to know the minds of their opponents, their ability to cow those who would stand against them.

And there was another aspect that made her heart race. In the last moments before King Külaşan's death, he had used this against her. He had synced their heartbeats, then *pressed* upon her, stifling the beating of her own heart, until the hatred of the asirim had revived her. Through her, the asirim had vented their long-suppressed rage for the Kings, allowing Çeda to turn the tables on him.

"I said slow your heartbeat." Zaïde was perturbed, yet perfectly in control. Her heartbeat had hardly changed, while Çeda's rhythm swung wildly.

Çeda concentrated once more. She reduced herself to sinew and bone and blood and muscle—not her memories, nor her emotions, but her physical self. Like this, she managed to slow the pace of her heart, and though for a time the two of them, Matron and Maiden, struck a cadence that was slightly out of sync, Çeda was able to weave them closer until the two were as one, a single soul in this place of sweat and learning.

When Zaïde's hand withdrew and reached out to strike Çeda's neck, Çeda felt it, almost in advance.

Eyes still closed, she blocked one strike, then two, then a third. Zaïde advanced, and Çeda retreated, blocking blow after blow. Then she stood her ground, blocking a flurry of movements that made the sleeves of their uniforms snap from the ferocity of it.

Then Çeda felt a *tug* on her soul. A thing that made her cough, made her cringe both inside and out for how feeble it made her feel. Like turning an opponent's hold against them, Çeda tried to turn their shared bond against Zaïde. Indeed, she heard a light cough from Zaïde just as Zaïde reached past her defenses and connected at last.

Çeda remained standing there, eyes closed, the touch of Zaïde's fingers still fresh on her skin. She realized the two of them were still in sync, that she was in fact finding it difficult to unchain herself. And finally, whether it was her own doing or Zaïde's, the feeling was gone, and she was herself, alone in her skin once more.

She opened her eyes to find Zaïde staring at her with something like awe. She recovered herself a moment later, the stern look she wore most often returning, but it was too late. Çeda knew that something strange had happened. Something unexpected.

"What?" Çeda asked.

"Have you done this before?"

"No," Çeda lied. She couldn't tell the truth about Külaşan's death, not here, so close to the House of Kings.

Zaïde didn't seem convinced, but after a moment, she nodded. "You did well, Çeda. We'll continue with this another time." She looked about the room, staring into the corners. "For now there are other things we must discuss." She spoke in a voice so low Çeda could barely hear her. "You've gathered, no doubt, that there are times when it is unwise to speak freely. One day I'll teach you how to know when you can and when you cannot, but not today." Çeda was about to respond, but Zaïde held up a finger. She kneeled and motioned for Çeda to do the same, and then she did something most strange. Her lips pinched, lending her a sour look, as if she'd bitten into something horrible. Çeda soon understood that she was biting the inside of her lower lip, enough to draw blood. She ran her finger against it until it was covered in blood, then she ran the tip of it over Çeda's lips. "Stick out your tongue."

Çeda did, and Zaïde touched it with her bloody finger. The Matron repeated the motions over her own lips, her own tongue. Çeda could taste Zaïde's coppery blood, but she could also feel a tingling throughout her mouth.

"Now," Zaïde said, "if the gods are kind, this conversation goes unnoticed."

By Thaash's bitter blade, this was blood magic, a thing forbidden to all but the Kings themselves and some few magi who answered only to them. "One day soon we will speak of your night in Eventide, but you have earned the right to ask me questions. So, Çeda. Ask what you will."

Çeda was unable to speak for a moment. She'd been so eager these past months that the sudden removal of Zaïde's restrictions made her nervous, which only served to remind Çeda how risky all of this was.

"Are you of the lost tribe?" she finally asked. Strangely, her words sounded flat to her ear, deadened, as if they were bound to them and them alone.

"I am, though my blood is not so thick with it as yours. And there are others here as well."

"Among the Maidens?"

Zaïde nodded.

"The House of Kings as well?"

Another nod.

"How many?"

"That I cannot reveal, but know this—you are not alone. We've been working our way into the Kings' lives for a long while. I have the ear of one, who offers us some protection."

"Which one?"

Zaïde shook her head. "That secret must remain with me."

"Are you in league with Ishaq, then? With Macide?"

"That's a complicated question with no simple answers. For now let me say yes, Ishaq and I work toward the same thing, the downfall of those who sit the thrones. We simply believe there are different ways to achieve it."

"He's violent," Çeda said.

"He is violent, yes. And prideful, as if he alone has inherited the legacy of the thirteenth tribe. Make no mistake, though. There is no way around it. Rivers of blood will be spilled before the Kings step down from Tauriyat. But there is more to it than that. I believe you are aware that there is a poem, one uttered by the gods themselves on the night of Beht Ihman."

"The bloody verses," Çeda replied.

Zaïde nodded soberly. "Do you know the one that applies to the thirteenth tribe?"

"Yes."

"Recite it."

It felt strange to utter it here, and terribly foolish, but she did as Zaïde asked, starting with the first stanzas she'd found in her mother's book. *"Rest will he 'neath twisted tree, 'til death by scion's hand. By Nalamae's tears and godly fears shall kindred reach dark land."*

Zaïde nodded. "That is one stanza of what we believe is the final verse of the poem. In full, it reads thus:

One King betrayed,
one King unmade,
King of Thirteenth Tribe.

With withered skin,
and fallen kin,
his fate the Gods ascribe.

Rest will he
'neath twisted tree,
'til death by scion's hand.

By Nalamae's tears
and godly fears
shall kindred reach dark land.

Zaïde paused. "You know who the King of the Thirteenth Tribe is."

Çeda's skin prickled. "Sehid-Alaz." To speak of this after being silent for so long, and with someone who might know more than she did—it made her worry that Zaïde was trying to trap her, to get her to speak against the Kings for some hidden purpose. But that made no sense. Dardzada had confirmed Zaïde's identity, and Zaïde had done much to help her so far.

Zaïde went on. "You're also well aware who the kindred are."

"The asirim."

"It is that first line you recited that you and I and many from the lost tribe are most concerned with. A line that Ishaq scoffs at. *'Til death by scion's hand . . .* I believe, as others do, that there will be one of our blood who releases the asirim that they may find peace and pass on to the farther fields at last."

"And Ishaq?"

"Ishaq . . ." Zaïde's expression soured. "Our efforts in the House of Maidens began well before Ishaq was born. He argues that they are seeds that have borne too little fruit, and there's some truth to that, I suppose, but it doesn't negate what we do here. We cannot know which of us might free the asirim from the bonds placed on them by the gods on the night of Beht Ihman. It may be none who are living now. It may, in fact, be your daughter, or Macide's or someone else's we're not yet aware of. There are, after all, those of the blood who do not realize it. I can only have faith that the goddess will see us through."

"Nalamae."

"Yes, Nalamae."

"She came to me that night, when I was out in the desert."

Zaïde was a composed woman, at ease with the world around her, so it was with no small amount of surprise that Çeda watched her rear back at this news like she'd been struck. "She *came* to you?"

Çeda nodded. "I've seen her before, as well. She called herself Saliah. My mother took me to her house in the desert many times when I was young. I went there myself early this year, in spring."

"You've spoken to the goddess . . ."

She seemed to have said the words more to herself than Çeda, but Çeda answered her anyway. "I have. She saved me in the blooming fields. Goezhen came with a pack of black laughers, though I know not why."

"Tell me, Çeda. All of it."

There was a moment's hesitation. Again the mistrust for Zaïde, a habit born from a life of worry, of being taught to take care from the earliest days of speech. She knew it had to end somewhere, though. She could not do this alone, and she refused to become like Dardzada or even Amalos—someone who stood rigidly in place for fear of taking the smallest misstep—so she told Zaïde of her childhood visits to Saliah's home, the way she was summoned by the chimes, how Saliah's cheek had been cut by the crystal that had fallen and shattered against a stone. She finished with the night she'd been left in the desert, when Nalamae had led her into the waiting arms of the adichara, how they'd waited together as Goezhen came and inspected the very ground upon which Çeda had stood.

For the first time, Zaïde seemed unsure of herself. "She wasn't merely some desert witch? A woman touched by godsblood?"

"Do you think a desert witch could hide from Goezhen himself?"

"It's just . . . we've long thought Nalamae lost."

"Well it isn't as though she could move openly, is it? She's been chased throughout the centuries by the other desert gods."

"Yes, it's only . . ." Zaïde was crying, but there was a haunted smile upon her lips that echoed the naked amazement in her eyes. "We thought . . ."

"You thought what?"

"That she might have been killed, once and for all."

"The gods cannot die," Çeda replied.

"How little you know, child. Nalamae has died many times since Beht Ihman. Among the gods, she alone wishes to help us, to undo what her brothers and sisters have done. And the others know. They've always known, else why would Tulathan have named her as she spoke that poem to the Kings on the night of their dark bargain?"

Suddenly all the stories Çeda had read about Nalamae made sense. How the other gods had seemed to be chasing Nalamae down, how she had returned as a little girl, and other manifestations. "The other gods hunt her," Çeda said. "There are stories over hundreds of years."

"Yes," Zaïde said, "and they've found her. They've killed her, or tried to. She returns, but we never know when, or even who she'll be. It might be years or decades, even generations before she's ready to help us once more. Don't you see? If Nalamae has begun to stand against the other gods, it means she's ready to help us."

The news struck Çeda in the chest. "She'll know, then. She'll know the poems and which Kings they refer to."

"Perhaps, but I suspect you may be disappointed. When the goddess is reborn, she remembers little from her prior lives. The memories come back to her a little at a time. So we may find her, and if we do we will ask her what she remembers. But the chance of her deciphering the poems is small." Zaïde paused, considering. "How many did your mother find?"

"I know of three. One was for Külaşan, who lies dead. The second is certainly for Mesut."

"Recite it for me," Zaïde said.

"The King of Smiles,
from verdant isles,
the gleam in moonlit eye;

with soft caress,
at death's redress,
his wish, lost soul will cry.

Yerinde grants,
a golden band,
with eye of glittering jet;

should King divide,
from Love's sweet pride,
dark souls collect their debt."

Zaïde's brows pinched in concentration. "You said it is *certainly* for Mesut. Why?"

"He wears a band of gold with a jet upon it."

"Would you bet your life that the poem refers to that stone and that stone alone?"

"There's more." Çeda went on to tell Zaïde about the strange ritual in Eventide, how Mesut had used that golden band to summon the ghostly spirit that had then been drawn into the woman's form, how the soul of the asir had reached out to the others in the blooming fields and how it had sensed Çeda after.

By the time Çeda was done, Zaïde's face had gone pale. "Breath of the desert . . . The asirim have been difficult to control in recent years. I thought it a sign that the days of their rule were nearing an end. But if Mesut is able to create more . . ."

"And they're using blood of the thirteenth tribe. I'm sure of it. Sacrificing our people yet again."

Zaïde nodded, her eyes distant. "I'll think on this." A tear slipped down along her cheek, and she wiped it away. "Now give me the last."

"Sharp of eye,
and quick of wit,
the King of Amberlark;

with wave of hand,
on cooling sand,
slips he into the dark.

King will shift,
'twixt light and dark,
the gift of onyx sky;

shadows play,
in dark of day,
yet not 'neath Rhia's eye."

"Beşir," Zaïde said, "the King of Shadows."

Çeda nodded. "And it implies that he cannot use his ability to shift between shadows when Rhia is full."

Zaïde's eyes were afire, moving this way and that. "And yet I wonder . . ."

"What?"

"Does Tulathan's light *weaken* him? Or does she negate her sister's effects? We must be very careful of the bloody verses. The Kings think them largely forgotten or obscured to the point that they'll have no meaning to those who discover them. The true, untainted verses are like water in the desert to those of us who strive against the Kings, but to tip our hand early—"

Zaïde stopped, tilting her head. She raised one finger to Çeda, a warning not to speak, then raised her hand into the starting position in a rush, motioning for Çeda to do the same.

No sooner had Çeda done so than Yndris slid the door to the room open without announcing herself. She stood at the edge of the padded canvas mat and spoke to Çeda as if *she* were First Warden. "We've received word that we're to leave in the morning for the desert. Sümeya bids you return to the barracks."

Çeda stifled her annoyance as Zaïde nodded to her. "Practice what we've done," she said to Çeda. "Live within the beat of your heart, and those of your sister Maidens if you can manage it. We'll continue another day."

"Of course, Matron."

Then she bowed and followed Yndris from the room.

Chapter 15

WITH NIGHT FALLEN AND RHIA swelling in the east, Emre watched as five drunk women wobbled down an otherwise empty street, gossiping and tittering as they went. When they'd passed around a bend and the street was silent once more, Emre headed for the open doorway of the warehouse across from him. He didn't go with the cockiness he'd learned from growing up in the city's west end, but with a tentative step, hands fiddling before him, a persona he hoped matched the modest robes and curl-toed shoes he wore.

Inside the warehouse he found a small office where a man leaned back easily in a chair, copying tallies of the day's receipts into the master ledger by the light of a bright yellow lamp. A large bottle of what looked to be pombe, a Kundhunese beer, was near to hand, as was a gourd cup filled with the frothy beer.

Against the far wall leaned the night captain of the warehouse's guardsmen, a brute of a Kundhunese with scarred black skin and closely shorn hair. He'd been whittling a lion woodcarving, making the small shells on his vest rattle and the muscles along his arms bunch and cord, but upon Emre's entrance he stopped and studied him with deceptively casual interest. When

Emre bowed his head and waited, hands clasped respectfully, the captain soon went back to his whittling.

The man at the desk raised one finger, not yet prepared to look Emre's way. He dipped his quill and continued writing, finishing one last line. When he was done, he marked the last of his figures with a spot of ink and pulled the spectacles from around his ears. His annoyance was clear as he turned to take Emre in. "What do you want?"

"Are you Serkan?"

Without looking, he picked up his gourd cup and took a long, healthy swallow. He glanced at the guard, then nodded once to Emre, suspicion growing in his eyes like ironweed.

"I've been told, by a, uh . . ." Emre licked his lips. "By a close associate of yours. That . . . Well . . ."

"Dear gods, man, get on with it!"

"I've been told that you deal in, uh, certain goods."

Serkan rolled his eyes at Emre's bumbling, put his spectacles back on, and turned back to his ledger. "I have no idea what you're talking about. Now get out."

"I'm afraid I can't do that."

At this, the Kundhunese stood from the wall, his woodcarving forgotten while his right hand held the knife in a particularly unsubtle grip.

Serkan turned back to Emre, taking his spectacles off with much more deliberation than he had the first time. "There are many paths to tread in the desert, young falcon. Are you sure you wish to tread this one?"

Emre knew very well he dealt in *certain goods*, but Serkan was a wary man, and for good reason. He worked for a woman named Hülya, a Sharakhani with Kundhunese blood who traded exclusively with the Thousand Territories. She'd spent her life doing so, as had her mother, who'd left her not only the caravan ships and the warehouse when she'd died, but its longstanding trade agreements as well, the most valuable of the lot by far. The allegiances of the Thousand Territories of Kundhun were like constantly shifting sands, what with the wars that spread like wildfire over the hills and plains of the grasslands. But Hülya had learned from her mother. She navigated their politics with poise. Like a creeping vine, she forged new relationships when old ones were severed. She brought much to Sharakhai that other caravan masters could either not obtain or else paid for exorbitantly, while she enjoyed the prices of a close ally, a privilege normally granted only to other Kundhunese.

Serkan was her master of books, who negotiated contracts with various merchants in Sharakhai and other caravans who took the goods Hülya imported, the rarest of which were tabbaqs, shipped in crates and divided into smaller bags before being auctioned off to various other merchants. It was a process easily skimmed if one were dishonest. Emre doubted Serkan was dishonest by nature, but the Host had learned he'd fallen on hard times, and there was nothing quite like personal hardship to spin the dial of one's moral compass.

For months he'd stolen a bit from the batches coming in, then replaced it with a slightly inferior—and much cheaper—tabbaq. And suddenly Serkan had his own supply of unadulterated, highest-grade smoke from the richest producers in the known world.

Emre bowed his head to Serkan three times. "My most sincere apologies, *hajib,* but anything your creative minds might dream up for me will be nothing compared to what my master will do should I return to him empty-handed."

"You underestimate Agabe's abilities." The man—Agabe, presumably—took a step toward Emre, but at a raise of Serkan's hand, he stopped, still eyeing Emre with that coldly casual look. "Pray tell why your master would treat you with anything but the utmost delicacy."

"My master is a tenement lord in the Shallows. His name is Alu'akman. You may have heard of him."

Alu'akman was one of the most feared men in the Shallows. He ruled his tenement houses fairly, but for those who didn't pay, or broke the rules, he was ruthless. He was the same with those he did business with, which made him simultaneously sought after by those who dealt above board and shunned by those out to cheat him in even the smallest ways. He might have met an untimely end before now had it not been for how diligent he was about paying his taxes, making him the golden child of the city's tax lords and, by extension, the Silver Spears.

"I fail to see what business that is of mine."

"Well," Emre continued. "His mother has taken ill. She has terrible pains in her knees and ankles. And my lord Alu'akman has learned that a particular tabbaq from Kundhun can alleviate her pain."

Serkan nodded, granting the point. "There are many fine purveyors of such tabbaqs along the Trough."

"There are, indeed," Emre replied quickly, "but my master finds their prices unfair. He is prepared to buy in some quantity and the merchants along the Trough are often . . . inflexible, even when buying in bulk."

Serkan inserted one end of the spectacles into his mouth and considered Emre's story. "The cost of such tabbaqs is dear, even when purchased in bulk."

Emre took the bag from his belt and opened it, revealing the topmost layer of the golden rahl within. "My master is prepared. He asks only that the price be fair, all things considered."

Serkan looked at Emre, but his eyes betrayed him when he glanced sidelong to his man, Agabe, who stood very much at the ready to do whatever Serkan wished. Given the amount of coin within Emre's purse, even Serkan might be thinking of betraying whatever code of ethics he held dear and simply take it from him, but that was why Emre had put forth the name of Alu'akman for this caper. Had Emre been sent by some unknown lord in the Shallows, Serkan might take the money and bury Emre in the sand, and should anyone come calling claim he'd never seen him. But Alu'akman was a different story entirely. The likelihood of receiving righteous retribution over it was simply too high.

"The name of this tabbaq?"

"Laulaang, from Yaramba province."

"And how much does he desire?"

"Three pounds."

Serkan glanced down at the bag of coins. "Such a sum might be found, but for no less than twenty-eight rahl."

Emre considered this. It was a slightly higher price than one might pay for bulk tabbaq of that rarity and quality but would not be considered unfair. "Very well."

Serkan nodded. "Wait here."

Emre shook his head. "Forgive me, my lord, but my master was adamant. I'm to collect it myself, ensuring he gets the best from the bulk." Serkan hesitated, but Emre went on. "He's aware that you keep it at the back of the warehouse. There's no harm in allowing me a closer inspection on behalf of my master." In truth his purpose here had nothing to do with the tabbaq.

He'd been sent to act as a diversion. The tabbaq was merely the excuse he needed to get inside the warehouse so that Hamid and Frail Lemi, the simpleminded brute who'd accompanied them, could get an alchemycal agent for Macide.

"I *never* allow such things," Serkan said.

Emre waited for a moment or two, to see if Serkan would change his mind without another word being spoken, but when he didn't, Emre nodded and closed the strings of the purse. "I understand."

"But," Serkan said as Emre was tying the purse to his belt, "for a man of Alu'akman's stature, if there are guarantees that more orders might be placed, I suppose an exception might be made."

Emre pasted on a smile like Serkan had just saved his life. "A most generous allowance, my lord. *Most* generous."

"And since you're choosing whatever you wish, it seems appropriate that thirty-five might be paid."

Emre pretended to weigh Serkan's offer, and eventually countered with, "Thirty-two, *hajib*, and I'd say we have a deal."

Serkan stood and smiled, nodding as he took Emre's hand in a congenial shake. Grabbing the lantern at his desk, he led Emre to the rear of the office, through a doorway, and into the darkness of the warehouse at large. Once inside, Agabe whistled. From the darkness emerged a short, reed-thin man with two long knives strapped to his thighs. As Agabe whispered to him, Serkan motioned Emre toward the back of the warehouse. The four of them—Serkan and Emre, followed closely by Agabe and the other night guard—walked among the tall shelves filled with crates and burlap bags and cloth-wrapped furniture, many burned by the brands of the Kundhunese craftsmen who'd made them and the caravan sigil of Hülya.

Serkan walked all the way to the opposite corner of the warehouse, as Emre knew he would, and there he had Agabe and the thin Sharakhani drag out several crates. The air was thick with the smell of tabbaq—earthy, pungent, even floral. When Agabe had dragged three large crates aside, Serkan pried up several boards of a false floor, revealing a clutch of smaller, hidden crates.

As Serkan worked to pull one up, Emre glanced over his shoulder to the front of the warehouse, where he saw the silhouette of a rope snaking down from the darkness above. A moment later, a form dropped, spider-like, soon lost in the shadows among the shelves. By then Serkan was cracking open the lid of a crate. Within was a cinched leather bag, which he tugged open. Stepping back, he waved at it, allowing Emre to inspect the tabbaq.

Emre crouched beside it and smelled, good and long, making a show of it, as if he were some connoisseur. Using the spoon within the bag, he lifted some of the tabbaq, and allowed it to pour back in, being careful not to touch any of it with his fingers and making sure none of it spilled from the bag.

"This is from Yaramba?"

Serkan answered with a clear note of pride in his voice, "Every last leaf of it."

"It doesn't smell like it."

Serkan laughed bitterly. "Believe me, my mistress fought long and hard for the rights to buy from tribe Hidindi."

Emre placed the spoon carefully back in the bag and faced Serkan. Seeing a crate being lifted at the far end of the warehouse, he cleared his throat, coughed several times. "You'll forgive me, I hope, but Alu'akman is a very particular man. I'm not nearly as accustomed to tabbaq as he is, but I *am* familiar with it. He had me smell the leaf he bought along the Trough, many times, over the course of days, before he allowed me to come here to you. And *this*"—Emre waved to the crate—"is not Yaramba tabbaq."

"I'm afraid you're mistaken," Serkan said, clearly flummoxed. "The shops you speak of along the Trough, where your master bought his Yaramba leaf, all of them purchased their leaf from this very warehouse."

"Might you check the crate again? There may have been a simple mistake. Or we could open the larger, and take it from there."

"You'll take from the crate I opened for you or none at all."

Emre resisted the urge to stare as a second crate was lifted on the far end of the warehouse. From the corner of his eye he saw it rise from the darkness of the aisles toward the open ventilation window above where Frail Lemi was pulling furiously at the rope. Only one crate left, then Hamid himself had to escape.

"I can see that I've caused offense. You'll forgive me, I hope. My master is not a merciful man, and if I came back with the wrong leaf, it would be worse than if I came back with no leaf at all."

"Which is exactly what will happen unless you take what I've offered. And now the price *has* increased to thirty-five."

Emre was raising his hands. "Yes, of course. Let me just take another look." He knelt down again, clearing his throat several times to cover the momentary buzz of the rope rubbing against the windowsill. He sniffed the leaf with long, exaggerated inhales, each time stopping in between and blinking while staring off into the distance as if he were considering. "Hmm," he said, dropping the tabbaq from the spoon again. "Could you bring that lantern closer?"

Serkan stared down at him. He picked up the lantern, but made no move to bring it closer to Emre. "You're wasting my time," he said, and turned away.

"Wait, please!" Emre ran forward and grabbed his sleeve as the third crate was being lifted away from the front of the warehouse. "I think perhaps I was mistaken. I'm sorry my master is so difficult, but surely you can see it isn't *my* fault."

Serkan had turned back toward Emre, but his face was now a study in disgust. "Take him out back," Serkan said, ripping his sleeve away from Emre, "and show him just how particular *caravan* men can be."

Emre managed to grab Serkan's sleeve one last time as Hamid's form was being hauled up by the rope. Frail Lemi was strong as three men put together, but there were still times when Emre was amazed by him.

Agabe and the smaller guard stormed in, wrenching Emre away from Serkan. Agabe pulled him up and drove a fist into his stomach. The smaller man knocked him across the jaw, a thing Emre rolled with, but not enough to make them suspect that they were playing their part in this heist. "This has been a complete misunderstanding!" He raised his hands to Agabe as Serkan walked away. "Please!"

Emre saw the rope being pulled up as Serkan's form walked away in the darkness. As Agabe approached once more, he fell for the mere show of it, taking some kicks to the legs, to the back. The pain didn't bother him. He'd seen his brothers safe, and that was enough.

Chapter 16

THE MORNING FOLLOWING THE revelations with Zaïde in the savaşam, Çeda and her entire hand stood amidships on the royal cutter *Javelin* as its sails began to fill with a stiff easterly wind. All around the ship, standing like troops on display, were fifty more ships of war: carracks and caravels and several massive galleons that looked so ponderous Çeda wondered how they could ever manage to sail the sandy seas. And this was but half the royal navy. This many ships or more patrolled the desert or were harbored at the caravanserais sprinkled across the Great Shangazi.

There were smaller vessels as well: the Kings' yachts or sleek scouting ships like the *Javelin*. Even more impressive than the ships, though, were the walls arcing around the eastern border of the harbor. The towers spaced along the wall's length looked like sentinels ready to lumber forth and trample the Kings' enemies. And the gates looked as though Thaash himself had built them—two tall monstrosities, one of which was open to allow them passage.

Nalamae's sweet tears, Çeda thought, *what the Kings have built.*

Melis was laughing at her.

"What?" Çeda asked.

"You may as well put on a pretty little dress and tie ribbons in your hair,"

Melis said, chuckling good-naturedly, referring to how Çeda looked like a wide-eyed girl.

Yndris, who'd surely seen the harbor a dozen times before, scoffed, but Çeda didn't care. Taking in the entirety of it, the harbor, its defenses, the palaces that watched from above, she wondered who could stand against the Kings were they to assemble for war. *No one, which is why so many approach Sharakhai like jackals, waiting for the Kings to weaken or fall lifeless to the desert floor.* Who, then, had she seen in the vision she'd shared with King Yusam? The desert tribes? The Moonless Host? She didn't know, but she couldn't see how they might prevail.

After sailing beyond the walls, the gate groaned behind them, booming home as their ship moved out into the desert proper. Sand stretched in endless amber waves beneath a sky of lapis blue. The scent changed almost immediately from one of mules and men and sunbaked wood to one more redolent of the early days of the world. Portside, like an arrow flying from Thaash's great yew bow, Sharakhai's aqueduct raced over the desert toward the mountains in the distance.

"Come now, my little doves," Kameyl called while striding up to the forecastle deck, "come stand at the bow."

Sümeya and Melis shared a look, as if both were worried how their two youngest Maidens would handle the coming ritual, but neither said a word as they took the ladder belowdecks. Yndris immediately headed for the raised foredeck, but Çeda could see the stiffness in her gait and, before she'd turned away, had glimpsed the worry on Yndris's face, echoing everything Çeda was feeling inside.

Below the gaff-rigged sails that heaved with the morning wind, Kameyl motioned to the bulwark. "Yndris, stand there. Watch and listen, but do not speak. Çeda, face the way ahead." As Yndris gave a quick bow and complied, Çeda took her place so that she was looking directly out and over the bowsprit. Pointing to a small scar at the center of her palm, Kameyl asked, "Do you know why it's our hands we poison?"

Çeda shook her head. Yndris snorted, but Kameyl went on as if she hadn't. "It's because the asirim are the holy defenders of our city. They are the swords of the Kings themselves in the desert. And it is we, the Maidens, who wield them." She took Çeda's hand and touched her scar at the center of the blue tattoos. "Through this you can feel the adichara, and through that you will feel the asirim."

"I already feel them," Çeda said.

They were there, below the adichara in their sandy graves, waiting to be called on. Some were torpid, oblivious to her. Others ignored her. Others still were hungry and animalistic in their rage, though whether it was directed at her or the Kings or their miserable lot she wasn't sure.

"Mesut has granted each of you one of the asirim. Find the one that feels brightest, Çeda, and draw it near. With the King's blessing, you'll find it easy enough."

Indeed, Çeda sensed two that were fully awake and not so far from the ship. One was nearer, brighter in her mind. Surely that was the one Mesut had chosen for her.

Come, she called to it, feeling sick to her stomach for doing this. *Come, for I have need of you.* Like a wolf that had caught a strange scent on the wind, the nearer one turned its attention on her. When the asir's presence strengthened, however, Çeda's breath caught in her throat.

She recognized it, the doomed woman she'd seen transformed in the courtyard of Eventide. *You . . .*

Why by Rhia's grace would Mesut have chosen this one? Did he know something? Was he testing her? But when she thought about it a moment, it made some sense. If the Kings planned to use that same ritual to create more asir, would they not want to test the asirim's obedience? And who better to test them than an untrained Maiden like Çeda? If *she* could do it, then what trouble would other, more experienced Maidens have?

The asir was confused for a moment. It didn't know how to react at first. Çeda immediately worried that it would warn Mesut, as it had when it lifted its finger and pointed to the tower where Çeda was hidden, the string of her bow drawn, a poisoned arrow ready to loose against the Kings. The asir made no move to warn Mesut, however, not that Çeda could sense. Instead, it reached out to her, a simple gesture of bonding. Was it bound to do so? Did it have any will whatsoever?

As if in response to her unspoken questions, her thumb began to ache. She felt the asir's anger grow. Felt its hunger. It approached, but there was another asir that followed. Not the one meant for Yndris, but one that pined for the soul bounding over the dunes toward Çeda. Çeda could feel the love between them. It was a distant thing, almost buried by the weight of the compulsions the gods had lain across their shoulders, but it was there. They might have been lovers once. Or brother and sister. Çeda couldn't tell.

Come if you wish, Çeda said to the second.

She felt relief from that tortured soul, but also hatred that it was forced to beg for permission. Together, the two crept closer to the ship, their wails falling across the dunes like a dark host hungry for war.

"Two," Kameyl said. "That's more than most could do their first time."

That's nothing, Çeda thought. *I could have summoned a score of them down on this ship had I wished.* They were straining against their bonds even now. They were ready to heed her call. But then Çeda felt another presence, this one at the center of all the others. She turned, looking back the way they'd come.

It was coming from Sharakhai.

Long moments later, Çeda realized someone was shaking her. She turned to find Kameyl staring, an expression of awe on her face. "You *sensed* him?" Kameyl said, her voice low, almost a whisper, perhaps so that Yndris wouldn't hear.

"Sensed who?"

"Mesut, the Jackal King, Lord of the Asirim."

Çeda shrugged, confused as to why Kameyl was shocked. "I sensed *something.*"

"It is the King who grants us the asirim."

"I know. I was only summoning them, as you told me to do."

"Yes, but it is by his leave that you're able to do so. Without his consent, you would be able to do nothing."

No. I could take them from him if I wished.

No sooner had the thought occurred to her than a whisper played within her mind, something so distant, so soft, she barely heard it.

Provoke him not.

Sehid-Alaz . . . King of the Thirteenth Tribe. She knew it was him. She also knew it would be beyond foolish to reach out to him, or to reply in any way.

Slowly, she relaxed her mind and withdrew lest Mesut learn too much.

Soon her world diminished, and she could sense only the two asirim once more. *Come,* she called to them. *Come, for I have need.*

She heard their answering wail far ahead across the desert, the sound of it little different from what she heard each night of Beht Zha'ir. This time, though, it felt as though *she* had caused it, as if *she* had fed them to the adichara to twist into those pitiful, shriveled forms.

She wanted to tell them she would free them if she could, but she couldn't risk Mesut hearing her, so she remained silent. Whether they felt it within her she couldn't say, but their cries became that much more desperate, and she found tears coming to her eyes.

"Why do you cry?" Kameyl asked, wiping away Çeda's tears. It was an unexpectedly intimate gesture from Kameyl, who was always gruff and grating, but it only served to show how deeply Kameyl cared for her sister Maidens beneath her hard exterior.

"Because they are brave," Çeda replied, hoping Kameyl pressed no further.

"They are. Now keep them close. Don't let them go until I tell you. Understand?"

Çeda nodded.

"Good. Now come"—Kameyl made an impatient, beckoning motion to Yndris—"and see if you can do as well as your sister."

As Çeda stepped over to the bulwarks, Yndris took Çeda's place. She was trying to hide it, but Çeda could see her look of jealousy. How very hard she drove herself. Was it for her father, King Cahil, or to impress Sümeya? Whatever the case, it was a dangerous combination: an immature girl with the power of an ebon blade and all that entailed.

On the fifth day of their journey, Çeda sat with the others in their shared cabin, feeling the rise and fall of the dunes as they headed east over the desert. Yndris was reading a worn, leatherbound copy of the Kannan, the Laws written by the Kings and based on the much older laws of the desert tribes. Kameyl was carving minute sigils into the shaft of an arrow, one of many she had laid out on a blanket. Sümeya and Melis were sitting on Sümeya's bunk, a game board between them. They were locked in a tight battle with one another, but after a quick flourish of moves, Sümeya had won.

Melis, her wild hair pulled back into a loose tail, set up the pieces of the aban board again, each coming down with an angry clack. As they started with their opening moves, Çeda rubbed her right hand. The pain was worse each day, and she knew very well why. She might not be able to see them, but she could sense them, the asirim. Like flaming brands felt but not seen, they bounded over the desert, pacing the ship, tireless, wailing their pain, their hunger, their sorrow. She could also feel, though to a much lesser degree, Yndris's asir. She'd tried to summon two, as Çeda had, and it had caused her to lose concentration, preventing her for a time from summoning even one. But eventually she'd mastered her emotions and managed to draw the asir Mesut had chosen for her near.

The hatred from that one emanated like stink from rotting flesh, which made Çeda wonder: Did all the Maidens sense the same from them? Surely the asirim fought the yokes placed on them as strongly as they did with Çeda and Yndris. Mesut understood very well why the asirim wished to throw their yokes free, but what about the Blade Maidens? Were they unable to feel the anger? Perhaps so. Perhaps the asirim simply didn't share with them as they shared with Çeda—one of their own, blood of their blood. Or perhaps the Maidens *could* feel it, but told themselves it was hatred from a different source. They'd been taught since birth that the asirim were holy defenders of the Kings' god-given right to rule Sharakhai and the desert. So if they felt their hatred at all, perhaps they thought it the burning anger of the asirim toward the enemies of the Kings. Çeda refused to believe the Maidens would continue to use the asirim if they knew the truth.

No, she amended while staring at Yndris, *some would. But certainly not all.*

Nearby, Melis stood from the bed, staring down at the aban board in disgust. She glared at Sümeya for a moment, then hopped up to her own bunk above Sümeya's and picked up the intricate leather bracelet she'd been weaving over the past several days.

"Come," Sümeya said to Çeda, motioning to the place on her bed where Melis had just been sitting.

"I wouldn't make a very good opponent," Çeda said. "I've never been properly taught."

Sümeya's wry smile was chiding. "And when has that ever stopped you?"

Çeda couldn't help but return the smile. She shrugged, gripping her right hand, and sat down.

"How bad is it?" Sümeya asked, nodding at her hand.

It had been sore all morning and was getting worse as the day wore on, but she didn't want Sümeya or the others to know the full extent of it. "It's sore, nothing more than that."

Sümeya arranged the carved pieces on the board, a mixture of ebony and ivory of several different shapes and sizes. She held up the largest of them. "These are aban, the first, the gods of old. There are three of each, and they're trying to reach the opposite side of the board where the farther fields lie. But they cannot do so alone." She held up the second type, the midsized ones. "These are urdi, the second, the young gods. There are seven. The aban must make them, forge them from the stuff of creation that falls from the heavens. The cost is dear, but the urdi are powerful indeed. They will help the elder gods, but they cannot follow to the fields beyond."

"Why not?"

Sümeya smiled a knowing smile. "Who knows the ways of the gods?" She held up one of the smallest pieces, of which there were many. "And these are kulthar, the third, men and women, villages and cities. The playthings of the gods. They help the old gods and the young, and they can go to the farther fields as well. The more that reach the heavens, the more glorious your victory might be, but it leaves those behind weaker."

Sümeya showed her how each of the pieces could move, how the old gods would visit special places on the board to create the young gods, how, after having enough of the young gods, they could create kulthar. It was confusing at first, but she soon started to sense the ebb and flow of the game, how it took time to build one's base of younger gods, how moving to the farther fields might give you an early edge, but leave you weakened.

Sümeya won the first game handily. She quickly set up another and motioned to the board. "Now, make the first move." She leaned against the angled hull, her legs folded underneath her. It was as intimate a posture as Çeda had ever seen from her. It felt strange, and stranger still that Çeda was some-how comfortable with it.

Çeda chose her opening move with care. "Do you know where Yusam's scryings are pointing us?" A question she'd been meaning to ask for weeks.

For a moment, movement in the cabin stopped. Melis glanced back to-ward Çeda, as did Kameyl. Sümeya looked at the others, then regarded Çeda levelly. "Not as yet."

"He must know something by now," Çeda replied, looking over the board, trying to appear nonchalant.

"When we're meant to know, we'll know."

"Of course. I only meant that I'm confused by what he's looking for, and what he hopes for us to find on this journey."

"None can know but the King himself." Sümeya made a bold opening move, daring Çeda to move her pieces to stop it. "And do not place so much upon his shoulders. King Yusam is gifted, but he cannot see everything. Far from it, which is why we act as his eyes and ears. We must be vigilant, for anything we gather for him might be the key he needs to unlock another of the mere's mysteries."

"Wouldn't we be better able to help if we knew more?"

When Çeda said this, Yndris looked up from her reading and stared at Sümeya. Although trying to appear uninterested, Yndris seemed as curious about the answer as Çeda did. Kameyl and Melis, on the other hand, only seemed annoyed.

"You know," Çeda realized. "You all know, except me and Yndris."

Sümeya sat up straighter. "You barely know how to summon the asirim. You have yet to replicate all of our hand signals or whistles on command. And you complain that we don't yet trust you with the world." She made another move, the piece clacking loudly on the board, another bold move. "Concen-trate on your studies. Learn and progress. Above all, however, remember that trust is forged of verity and tenacity—an alloy rendered brittle by demands and shattered by falsehoods."

Çeda was fully aware that she'd overstepped her bounds, but just then her poisoned thumb was burning so badly it was affecting her mood. It made her testy when she knew she shouldn't be. She replied to Sümeya's moves—clumsily, she saw, after Sümeya moved an aban, summoning two urdi in a move Çeda hadn't known one could make.

"Guard the points near the locus," Sümeya said, pointing to the empty spaces Çeda had left free.

Çeda made a sequence of moves that raised Sümeya's eyebrows. "Good," she said, "but you used up your urdi too quickly." In the next five moves, Sümeya took three of the five urdi she'd raised, leaving her all but defenseless.

Çeda had no idea why, but there came unbidden a fury deep within her, a rage hidden but close enough to call upon. The poisoned mark on the meat of her thumb flared so quickly she snatched her hand back from the move she was about to make and shook it in hope of alleviating the pain. That only seemed to make it worse. When she looked at it, she could see the wound itself was red and puffy.

Sümeya sat up. "You'll not be able to fight if that flares up at the wrong time."

"I'll manage."

Sümeya made the game's final move, taking the last of Çeda's aban. "Will you?"

Hardly realizing she was doing it, Çeda stood, one leg on deck, the opposite knee resting on the bunk, and stared down at Sümeya. The ache in her hand was no normal ache. Not any longer. How she longed to wrap her fingers around the hilt of a weapon. To stick it into Sümeya's throat. She could do it. She could kill Sümeya and Melis and perhaps even Kameyl before Yndris even knew what was happening.

Sümeya seemed to understand that something had changed. One leg dropped to the floor. "Sit down, Çeda." She was still seated, but Çeda could tell she was ready now.

When Çeda made no move to comply with the order, Sümeya glanced toward the opposite bunk and nodded. Before Çeda could even turn, Kameyl was powering her across Sümeya's bunk until her head crashed into the hull. As pain blossomed along the right side of her head, Kameyl held her in place with a hand to her neck. In her free hand she held the knife she'd been using to cut the symbols into the arrows. She pressed the tip to Çeda's cheek. "You're too arrogant, little wren." Grabbing a fistful of hair, she pulled Çeda's head away and slammed her into the hull again. Çeda felt blood tickling its way into her ear. "Keep your questions to yourself. When you've earned the right to question the warden of your hand, you'll know it."

Sümeya watched the exchange calmly, silently. Melis was the same, though she seemed to regret what was happening. Yndris, however, watched with eyes alight and barely contained glee. Çeda cared little for her, however. Her mind was drawn to the asirim. She felt them more strongly than she had at any point over the past days since leaving Sharakhai. The hunger was still strong within them, but so was disappointment, as if they'd come close to fulfilling their desires but had been denied in the end. It was bad enough—the realization that she could lose herself to them so easily—but it was their calm assurance that shook Çeda the most. They were angry, but they were patient as well. With Çeda, they felt assured they'd yet have their chance.

As Çeda nodded and Kameyl released her, Çeda nearly said as much to Sümeya. But she held her tongue. The chance of her giving away secrets unknowingly was simply too great.

"I'm going up to deck," Çeda said, grabbing her turban and opening the cabin door.

"You do that," Sümeya replied. "Cool off with the evening wind."

In the gangway, Çeda passed one of the crew, who was taking a tray of food to the Maidens' cabin.

He cast his eyes down immediately when he saw Çeda wasn't yet wearing her veil. "Would you care for food, Maiden?"

Çeda ignored him and went topside, pulling the turban cloth around her head with practiced ease. She left the tail hanging down, though, refusing to cover her face. She reveled in the feel of the hot wind over her cheeks. Most of the crew was belowdecks, having their own meal before preparing to anchor for the night. She headed to the starboard side and leaned against the gunwales. Far in the distance, she could see them, dark forms bounding along the dunes like tireless hounds.

She rubbed the wound on her thumb and tried to reach out to them, to communicate with them in some way. *Who are you? What do you want?* But the asirim were silent, their anger sated for the moment.

Zaïde had warned her that she'd be fighting the poison and the pain in her wound for the rest of her life. She'd never mentioned fighting the asirim as well, but perhaps she hadn't known. It made Çeda wonder if things would get worse. She was being taught how to control the asirim, but would the reverse be true? Would *they* learn how to control *her*?

Just then, one of them wailed, a long, lonely call. On and on it went, sending a chill through Çeda that somehow deadened the pain in her hand. Soon it was hardly more than a distant ache. The pain had been with her for so long, her body so tight from it, she felt exhausted by its sudden absence.

"It doesn't forgive what you did," she whispered to the dark forms.

The wail ended, and silence fell over the desert once more. And then all Çeda heard were the runners sighing over the amber sands.

Chapter 17

ARLY THE FOLLOWING MORNING, Çeda felt unease brewing within the asirim. She went to Sümeya and told her of it.

"Where?" Sümeya asked.

And Çeda realized she knew. She aimed her finger.

"Two points larboard!" Sümeya called over her shoulder.

"Two points larboard!" echoed the pilot as he guided the ship around a sharp jutting stone in the sand.

With that one command, the mood of the crew transformed. They set about making the small adjustments needed to catch the westerly wind. There was no doubt they'd run the ship smartly since leaving King's Harbor, but now they hardly seemed different than the fore and aft ballistae they were loading with grapnel hooks, or the bows they hung on hooks along with quivers bristling with black arrows. The ship and its crew had always been a weapon, but now it was poised, ready to draw blood.

"Be wary," Sümeya said to both Çeda and Yndris. "They'll try to break free, but you must hold their leashes tight."

They nodded, calling the asirim closer to the ship. The three dark forms bounded ahead over the smooth amber sands, eager for whatever lay along the horizon.

From atop the vulture's nest on the mainmast, the first mate called, "Ships ho! Dead ahead!"

As the *Javelin* sailed hungrily on, sails appeared along the horizon. The captain studied them through his spyglass, calling out minor adjustments to their course. Kameyl and Melis came from belowdecks, the two of them buckling their sword belts. As they moved to the foredeck, Sümeya pulled Çeda aside amidships. "Are you sure you're ready?"

Çeda put her hand on the pommel of River's Daughter. "I am."

Sümeya looked down at Çeda's tattooed hand. "You're in control of yourself?"

"I am."

"*And* the asirim?"

"Yes, First Warden."

Sümeya weighed her for a moment. "I'll take them from you if necessary, but I'm loath to do so. The effects are unpleasant, for both you and the asirim."

Çeda nodded. "You can trust in me."

Apparently convinced, Sümeya brought Çeda back to the foredeck, where Kameyl stood by Yndris's side. Melis had moved to the ballista near the bowsprit, where she was carefully coiling the rope attached to the grapnel.

Along the horizon, wavering from the heat coming off the sand, Çeda could just make out a line of three ships. Yusam had told them to look for a plain of rock southwest of Sharakhai. Nothing more. But surely these ships were related to the King's vision. Even if they weren't, now that they'd been spotted, there was no way Sümeya would simply sail on. There was the occasional story of ships lost or blown horribly off course by a storm, but Çeda knew—as did everyone else onboard—that the ships they'd spotted were pirates. The royal navy were allowed to sail this part of the desert, but all others were forbidden deviations from the prescribed shipping lanes to Sharakhai. If they wished to sail on to another port, they would first need to pay a tariff on their goods. Anyone attempting to skirt those laws risked having their cargo taken, perhaps the loss of a hand for the ships' captains as well. If it turned out they were smuggling goods forbidden by Kings' law, however, the entire crew would be killed and the ships taken or burned.

"You'll keep the asirim from attacking until we're ready," Sümeya said to Çeda and Yndris. "Allow them to range ahead, near enough that there will be no mistaking the Kings' will in the desert. The asirim will strain at their leashes, so you must be ready. When we near the ships and I give the word, allow them free rein. They'll do the rest."

"Yes, First Warden," Çeda and Yndris intoned.

Çeda already felt the hunger, the excitement, from the pair of asirim she was bonded to. She could even feel it from Yndris's, so murderous were its thoughts. She bid hers to run ahead of the ship, but to remain near. They obeyed, the nearest making a strange yipping sound as it bounded forward.

The *Javelin* took an intercept course, the gap between the ships growing ever smaller. The skin along Çeda's arms prickled. Excitement from the asirim now mingled with a strange sort of fear, a thing Çeda imagined a wolf might feel when baring its teeth at a newfound enemy.

"A final word of warning," Sümeya said while watching the three asirim dovetail ahead of the ship. "Never release them entirely. They're difficult enough to control once their blood is up, but infinitely worse if you free them."

Yndris watched the way ahead hungrily. "And if by accident I do?"

"Then be prepared to see everyone on those ships die. Let's see that it doesn't happen. Leave their captains alive if possible, their officers if not."

"Who are they?" Çeda asked.

Sümeya shrugged. "We'll find out soon enough." She gave a signal to the captain, after which a crewman began ringing a large brass bell with a wooden mallet, a warning for the ships ahead to slow and submit to inspection. The ships were still distant—a league or more away—but Çeda saw they were turning now.

"They've made their choice, captain!" the crewman above called. "They mean to flee."

"Aye," the captain called back.

All three ships curved north. The wind was with them, and they looked to be sleek ships, but they'd lost speed with their turn and were only now regaining it.

"How do we know they're not ships of the desert tribes?" Çeda asked.

Sümeya, standing on the gunwales, balancing herself with the nearby shroud, glanced down. "It doesn't matter. Run from the royal navy, and you'll be taken down."

The ships were quick, but the *Javelin* was an impressive craft. It was sleek, well-balanced, built for speed. A ship made for war, not hauling cargo. Its runners—the most important parts of a sandship by far—gleamed under the sun. They were smooth and well maintained, protected by wax of the highest quality. The ships ahead stood no chance of outrunning them, and perhaps they realized it, for Çeda could see them gearing for battle—bows being readied, a catapult on the aft deck of the rearmost ship had just been lit aflame.

"Enemy pots lit!" the crewman called from above.

"Well-noted!" the pilot shouted back.

As the *Javelin* approached, the pirates launched the catapult.

"Flame away!"

"Aye!" the captain called.

A clay pot flamed into the sky, trailing black smoke.

The *Javelin* heeled, groaning as the pot neared. It wasn't going to be enough, Çeda could see. They'd aimed well. If it didn't hit the deck, it would strike the side of the ship, which would force them to deal with it lest the ship be set ablaze.

Melis stood near the bowsprit with a drawn bow, sighting along the length of a black arrow. As the pot reached its zenith and stormed toward the *Javelin*, Melis let fly. The arrow streaked toward the pot, a line of black on a field of blue. Melis shot a second arrow, then a third. The first two struck with sounds like stone chipping, and bits of red earthenware fluttered away from the pot, but the third crashed through the pot in spectacular fashion, the flames blossoming like an imperfect sun, spraying the sand to the port side of the ship. Some of it caught the port runner, but several of the crew converged there with buckets in hand, throwing blue sand that doused the flames in less time than it had taken for Melis to launch her arrows.

The *Javelin* sailed now at the edge of bowshot. The asirim ran just ahead of the ship. They strained mightily at their leashes, but Çeda and Yndris held them in check. When Sümeya called, "Now!" Çeda did as she'd been told;

she allowed her two asirim to bound ahead while making sure not to release them entirely.

She immediately gripped her stomach, retching from the dark urges that roiled up inside her. In the days since she'd first bonded with them, their desires had been stifled every bit as much as their abilities to act on them. Now, though, their emotions were unsuppressed. They'd been given the freedom to act, and with it came deeper desires, ones that made Çeda tremble both inside and out. She could feel it churning in her gut like a feast of rotted meat. She wanted nothing more than to put the yokes back on the asirim if only to lessen it, but she wondered if she even could. This was nothing like days past. They were like forces of nature now, nigh uncontrollable.

She looked over to Yndris, who was watching it all unfold with an expression that made it clear she'd been unprepared. She had her hand over her stomach as well, and then she was running to the gunwales, vomiting her morning meal over the side of the ship.

The three asirim wailed. They flew over the desert like jackals, sand kicking up in tails behind them. The pirates loosed arrows. One struck the nearest asir, taking it in the midsection, but the asir merely broke the arrow with a swipe of its arm and leapt to catch the edge of the lead ship. A man charged forward, spear raised high, but before he could bring it to bear, the asirim howled in a way that rattled Çeda's bones, even this far away. Sand billowed up behind the asir. It flew at the ship in a stream, flowing around the asir, over the ship, over its crew, blasting the men, the rigging, and the sails in an unending torrent. The plume it sent into the sky was like a fount of gold against an azure sea.

The second asirim came just after, leaping up and over the aft gunwales to land behind the pilot. It grabbed the man's arm and tore it free in a single, savage movement. A stippled arc of red followed the man down to the deck. Çeda lost sight of him then, but the asir was visible as it rose above the bulwarks and was lost from sight once more, its movements both rhythmic and animalistic. Dear gods, it was *feeding* on the pilot. She tried to pull the creature back, refusing to allow it to continue, for its own humanity as much as the pilot's life, but the asir was too far gone. Its desire to slake its thirst on the blood of the living dwarfed Çeda's ability to control it.

The third asir, Yndris's, galloped beyond the rear ship in the enemy's line and approached the second. Instead of trying to reach the hull, it leapt upon the port-side ski. It stood upon the skimwood runner as the crewmen—men and women wearing flowing desert clothes—leaned over the gunwales and shot arrows or hurled pots of fire down at it. The asir took arrow after arrow, and a pot of oil burst just behind it on the wide runner. The oil splashed its legs, but it seemed oblivious to the pain. It focused all its attention on the ski's thick support, its blackened, withered hands pressed to either side of it, as if it were trying to hold itself steady.

Çeda had no idea what it was doing. More arrows sunk into its arms and its thighs. Surely it would fall to the flames if nothing else, but then she saw what was happening to the support. Bits of it were flaking away like ash from a windblown fire. It was only a small amount at first, but soon more and more of the wood fractured and was blown by the wind like autumn leaves in a storm.

Çeda could hear the crew of the pirate ship yelling, rallying others to fight the asir. But before they could react, the wooden support split. The ship heeled sharply, the entire deck dipping sternward on the port side. Seconds later other support rent under the strain. A sound like thunder fell over the desert as the ship's forward shoulder dove into the sand. Screams and shouts mingled with the rattle of rigging being shaken and torn, mere moments before a tremendous crash of wood and sand and stone drowned out all else. It was a surreal sight, the masts and white sails tipping sharply downward, the rigging whipping along with it. The entire ship seemed to explode in an amber cloud of sand and dust.

The rearmost ship managed to steer wide of her fallen sister, but Çeda's asir were wreaking havoc over the deck, men and women screaming as they tried to fight the holy defenders of Sharakhai.

The *Javelin* steered wide as well, heading now toward the lead ship, a cutter with patchwork sails that was nevertheless swift. Even from this distance Çeda could see the look of fear on the pirates' faces. She wondered what they'd been told. Surely they'd heard the stories, how deadly the asirim could be, how viciously they fought to protect the interests of the Kings. But perhaps they hadn't believed it, or perhaps they thought the chances were small they'd be caught, or that the rewards far outweighed the risks.

Whatever the case, they were surely praying to their gods for their lives—or at least a quick death. No one wanted to be taken in chains to Sharakhai, where they'd be subject to the attentions of the Maidens, or worse, the Confessor King.

Ahead of the fleeing ship, a black swath ran across the desert. Stones marked the earth, forcing the cutter, and then the *Javelin*, to avoid them. They might have thought the *Javelin* unable to easily follow, but in this they had misjudged the skill of the Kings' crew. The *Javelin's* pilot seemed to navigate with ease. The enemy shot arrows, but they'd only managed two volleys before Melis cried, "Grapnel away!" and released the ballista she stood behind.

The ballista's swing arms snapped, thudding against the stanchions. The grapnel flew, the rope Melis had coiled so carefully unwinding with a soft buzzing sound. Then it snapped taut. The grapnel, arcing high over the enemy ship, shot downward, aft of the foremast and across the rigging lines.

"Now!" Melis called.

"Brace!" bellowed the captain.

At the rear of the ship, a massive wooden beam was released. It fell backward on a hinge and crashed, the iron fork at its tail end biting into the sand, the foot-long teeth digging deep furrows and braking the ship. The *Javelin's* deceleration caused the grapnel to pull on the pirate ship's rigging. It caught the lower part of the mainsail, hauling two dozen of the ship's lines with it. The smaller ones snapped. Others were pulled free of their stays. Most importantly, many held, slowing the ship right along with the *Javelin*.

Soon both ships had come to a halt. Some few of the enemies' crew leapt down from the tilted deck, ready to defend the ship, but just as many simply turned and fled.

Sümeya whistled two sharp, rising notes, the signal to follow her, then jumped down to the sand. Çeda followed along with Yndris and Melis. Kameyl didn't jump, but instead balanced herself and ran along the grapnel's rope. So taut was the line, it carried her weight, hardly bending. In five long strides she was to the ship and flying through the air, ebon sword held in both hands as she thrust its tip through the mainsail's canvas. It ripped beneath the sharpness of the blade, lowering Kameyl into the battle. She dropped to the deck, into the very center of the enemy, her body and blade a deadly blur. She drew much of the pirates' attention as Çeda and the others approached.

The rest of the *Javelin's* crew had bows at the ready. They released two volleys before Sümeya and her Maidens neared the ship. Most of the pirate crew simply dropped their swords, fell to their knees, and raised their hands. Only two actually dared to raise weapons to the Maidens, and these men Sümeya and Kameyl felled with brutal efficiency. Melis watched the others warily. But Yndris ran toward the nearest, a boy her own age, perhaps seventeen. His eyes went wide and he held his hands up, shouting, "No, no, no!" in Malasani. Yndris didn't listen. She was going to take him down as she'd taken the asir on the night of her vigil.

Çeda sprinted between them, holding River's Daughter out to stall Yndris's charge. "He's no danger to us."

Yndris rounded on her. "That's the second time you've stood against me." She tried to go after the boy again, but Çeda placed herself in Yndris's path, sword at the ready. "He deserves no *mercy*," Yndris shouted.

"He may have information we need."

"Him?" Yndris laughed. "You're a fool if you think so."

At a sharp whistle that meant, *to me*, Çeda and Yndris turned and saw Sümeya pointing to them.

"Aiyah! Aiyah!" Melis called, swinging her ebon blade in a wide arc. The simple threat forced a dozen pirates to stop and drop to their knees for fear of being taken down by an ebon blade.

As the navy crew from the *Javelin* approached, bows at the ready, Yndris and Çeda both complied with Sümeya's order. Sümeya, with a glance toward the boy, guided Yndris away from the kneeling men and women, but before she went too far, she pointed Çeda toward those who'd fled toward the blasted black stone. "Go to them. Offer life to any who come willingly, or death in the desert to those who flee. And by the gods, call your asirim to heel."

Çeda nodded and ran toward the dwindling forms in the distance. As she did, she summoned the asirim. They defied her at first, which made her insides twist into knots. She could feel how hungry they still were, but they'd killed many aboard both ships, and the feeling wasn't so strong as it had been. Eventually they came, slinking toward her like scuttling crabs. When they'd put a hundred paces between them and the ship, their hunger faded, and they rose, running with speed until they'd caught up to her. She forced them to stay close at heel now. Their instinct to hunt was on them, though. They'd sensed those running ahead, a group of eight men and women.

Those fleeing had given themselves a good head start, but they were not conditioned and were slowing already. And then Çeda realized several had stopped. She had no idea why until she came closer. A body lay on the black stone. At first Çeda thought it one of the pirates, but as she came closer she saw the body's raiment was too rich for a simple pirate, and the cut was not Malasani, but Qaimiri, and in the royal colors of saffron and crimson with viridian piping. Few would wear such colors together, for in Qaimir, red and gold were set aside for the royal family alone.

The pirates watched her warily as she approached. They stared at her ebon sword, which was drawn and ready but held in no hostile manner. They backed away as Çeda came to stand before the body.

It was a man with a light beard, his sightless eyes, now clouded and desiccated, staring skyward toward the heavens, perhaps to his own soul, who walked in the farther fields. His chest was a perversion of blood and bone and torn clothing, as if his heart had exploded. Or been torn out. She stared at the withered fingers, the drawn skin, wondering how long it had been here. Surely a week at least. Dried blood lay all around the body, and now that she was standing before it, she could see that there were constellations of the gods drawn in a circle around his dead form. There were ancient symbols as well. She was well-versed in the languages of the desert. They'd been drilled into her by her mother. But she recognized few of these sigils. She saw one for betrayal above the man's head, another for lure at his left hand. When she saw the one by his feet, however, she gasped. She sheathed her sword and crouched down, reaching a hand out, but she found herself unable to touch it.

By the gods who breathe, it was the same symbol that was on her back, the tattoo Dardzada had given her when she was twelve, turning thirteen. She had thought it meant *bastard child*, but she'd found out later the older meaning—*one in many*, and *many in one*—revealed to her by the King of Swords, Husamettín himself.

How could this be? Who would have done such a thing? She'd like to think it had nothing to do with her, that it was some strange coincidence, but she knew it would be foolish of her to ignore it.

This was what Yusam had seen in his mere, she realized: this body, herself finding it. It was too improbable for it to be otherwise. What it meant for her, for the Kings, she had no idea. Why would a lord from Qaimir have come here to the desert? And what by Goezhen's dark crown had happened to him?

Çeda studied the symbols, memorized their placements, then stood and stared at the pirates, the eight of them fretful, nervous, watching her and then the asirim, sometimes glancing back toward the deeper, darker part of this blasted land. "What do you know of this?" she asked them.

The one closest to her, a woman ten years Çeda's senior, shook her head. "Nothing, my Lady," she said in halting Sharakhan.

Of course they knew nothing. Çeda turned toward the asirim, drawn by their shift in mood. Their hunger had been replaced with a wariness she'd never felt from them before. They crouched, backs arched, eyes staring wildly at the land beyond the pirates, like hounds that had suddenly become aware of some primeval danger mortal man could never hope to understand.

"What you will do with us?" the woman asked, the sound startling Çeda from her reverie.

Çeda pointed to the body. "Take him. We'll return to the ship. And by the gods, say no more until we're off this stone."

Together, the two young men dragged the body, Çeda motioning them and the others to walk ahead of her. The asirim came behind, and slowly they all moved off the dark stone and onto the blessed sand of the desert.

Sümeya met them there. She stared down at the body. "We found it," Çeda said, "just lying there on the stone."

Sümeya pulled her eyes away from the bloody corpse and took in Çeda anew. "Do you not know who this is?"

Çeda shook her head.

"Here, in the forgotten corners of the Shangazi, lies the King of Qaimir."

A tingling sensation ran through Çeda's fingers and toes. Her first thought was for Ramahd. He'd come to Sharakhai at his king's bidding. He was one of Qaimir's primary diplomats. Her second was over the upheaval the death of the king would cause.

The sands are shifting, Çeda thought. *One day they may overwhelm Sharakhai.*

Two days into their return toward Sharakhai, just as they were anchoring for the evening, Çeda was alerted by a cry from the pirate ship behind the *Javelin*. Many were moving about the ship, preparing it for the night, which looked to be windy, but all were now flocking toward the deck of the pirate cutter.

"Make way!" Çeda called, pushing her way through. When she reached the deck, she found a boy being lifted from the hold of the ship. The boy's head lolled back, his body twisted at odd angles; a doll of string and bones. The gathered Malasani prisoners wailed, and a woman fell to the boy's side, holding his cheeks between her hands as he lay lifeless on the deck. It was the same boy—a young man, really—who Yndris had nearly cut down when they'd approached the ship.

Sümeya stood nearby, watching the scene unfold. Her face was hidden by her veil, but there was concern in her eyes.

"What happened?" Çeda asked Sümeya, who, along with Yndris, had been aboard that day, interrogating their officers.

"I don't know. He may have fallen into the hold."

"Did anyone see it?"

Sümeya shook her head. "No one seems to have."

To her right, Çeda saw a form coming to a halt on the gunwales—Yndris in her black Maiden's dress, turban and veil hiding her expression. She stared at Çeda for the span of a heartbeat, and then, one hand gripping the shroud, the other the pommel of her ebon blade, she dropped to the sand and strode away as if the wailing on the deck were nothing more than the howl of the wind.

A cold hatred flared to life inside Çeda. "She's a disgrace."

"You don't know that she had anything to do with it."

"I do. And so do you. She had no right to do it. She's nothing more than a child, unfit to wear the Maiden's black."

"As though you're one to judge." The words sounded bitter, but they were hollow, and Sümeya likely knew it. Çeda could see it in her eyes.

"I know enough to know that women like Yndris are a cancer. Best to excise her now before she infects others."

Çeda expected Sümeya to grab her, to snap at Çeda for questioning her authority, or that of her father, King Husamettín. But she didn't. She merely watched the woman grieving over the boy, and then turned and stepped onto the gunwales, much as Yndris just had.

"Come. Let them grieve in peace." And then she dropped to the sand and headed for the *Javelin*.

Chapter 18

KING IHSAN TAPPED THE INK FROM his quill and wrote the final entry in his journal. He sprinkled salt over it, then lifted the edges of the journal to gather the salt into the gutter and funnel it into a salt cellar. As it was the end of the day, he gave the cellar a quick shake, then took a pinch and placed it on his tongue, reliving the day, in a manner of speaking. It had been a day that had seen him speak with a dozen of his courtiers, those most loyal to him. Soon all the work he'd done, all the positioning, would begin to fall into place.

Azad was close to perfecting the serum Ihsan and his closest allies would need in the coming years. He was hopeful that the collegia scholars he would soon secure would help Azad to finish the job. And then at last the royal pruning that was centuries overdue could begin in earnest.

He rang a bell from his desk. Footsteps followed, and soon Tolovan loomed in the doorway. "Prepare my bed," Ihsan said.

"Would you care for some tea, my Lord King? Some araq?"

Ihsan was just about to ask for both when a bell of a different sort rang. A low bell. One that could be heard over all of Tauriyat, and a good amount of the city as well. It was a bell that hadn't been rung in twelve years.

Tolovan looked to the open windows, to the darkness beyond. There was an accepting look on his face as the bell rang again, as if he'd long expected its return. "Shall I have your coach brought around, My Lord King?"

"That would be good of you, Tolovan. Thank you."

"Of course, my Lord." He bowed and left.

Soon, Ihsan was sitting in his royal coach, being bumped and jostled past the palace walls. As it moved beyond a curve in the stone-paved road, the southern face of Tauriyat was revealed, and the tolling of the bell sounded clearer. Ihsan chuckled as the coach approached the central road, the one that led to each of the palaces in turn. Four hundred thirty-two years on this earth, and here he was, summoned like a vizir to bow before the King of Kings. He had no one to blame but himself, he supposed. He might have tried to sway the other Kings to choose a different man to lead them on the night of Beht Ihman long ago—himself, perhaps, or Yusam, a figurehead he might have more easily swayed over the years—but there had been an impetus around Kiral's claim to the high throne that Ihsan hadn't at all been sure he could preempt. He'd been so new to his powers he hadn't wanted to overplay his hand.

More fool me.

But the river flowed, as they say. Things had changed since then. The time to act was nearly upon them, and then *Ihsan* would be the one ringing that mighty bell, summoning his chosen to attend him.

Many minutes later, after working through a series of switchbacks, the coach arrived at Eventide, Kiral's high palace. Upon entering, Ihsan was led by a servant in rich dress to an opulent room where Kiral and nine other Kings had gathered to one side. Husamettín studied Ihsan with something like annoyance. Cahil, their Confessor King, seemed eminently bored. The man was over four hundred years old, yet the expression of tedium on his boyish face reminded Ihsan of young royals throughout the ages forced to suffer through one ceremony too many. The rest, however, looked impatient, restless to get to business. He was relieved to see that the Feasting King, Onur, had not come. *Well and good. What need have we of a man who most days can't be bothered to wash himself?* On the other side of the room, standing with hands clasped behind their backs, stood two Maidens wearing their black fighting dresses but not their turbans. One was Sümeya, First Warden of the Blade Maidens, and the other, perhaps not surprisingly, was Çedamihn, a young woman whose fate seemed more entwined with Ihsan's by the day.

Lying on a table between the Kings and Maidens was a body, bloody and broken, wearing the raiment of a Qaimiri nobleman. The ribs were splayed wide, innards missing, the skin sprinkled with a fine white powder—natron, if Ihsan didn't miss his guess. At first he thought the body might be a high-ranking member of the Moonless Host in disguise, but as he reached the foot of the table he recognized the form of King Aldouan shan Kalamir, Lord of the Sovereign Lands of Qaimir these past thirty-five years.

"Good of you to come," Kiral said, a look of sufferance on his pock-marked face.

Ihsan bowed his head to the degree he felt appropriate for the minor shame of having arrived last. "I was unavoidably detained. What, pray tell, have the Maidens found?"

"Tell them what you told me," Kiral said to Sümeya.

Sümeya nodded. "We found him in the desert, far to the southwest of Sharakhai."

"Surely you didn't find him by chance," said stout Zeheb, the King of Whispers.

Sümeya shook her head. "We were guided by King Yusam to a small pirate caravan sailing the forbidden paths through the desert. Some were chased onto a plateau of blasted stone, where Çeda found the king's dead body."

As she spoke, Ihsan studied Çeda. How she'd changed in her time with the Maidens. She had looked so out of sorts when she'd entered the House of Maidens. A babe among jackals. Now, while she might not have the same sort of calm confidence as Sümeya, she was not far off. She studied each of the Kings without really seeming to, and when her eyes met his, she didn't stare wide-eyed as she might once have done. She merely gave him a perfunctory nod.

Ihsan nodded back, then returned his attention to the body and the ruined cavity that was once its chest. This wasn't the work of a black laugher, Ihsan knew. There was order in this chaos. There was intent.

Kiral unrolled a piece of parchment and laid it across Aldouan's thighs. "This was around the body."

The Kings—even Cahil, who had been leaning against the wall, staring with dispassionate eyes—gathered around the parchment. Near a crudely drawn outline of a body, dozens of symbols were laid out in a rough circle, some smaller, some larger. Constellations, Ihsan saw immediately. There was Goezhen's near the top, where Aldouan's head would have been. Bakhi's lay near Aldouan's right hand, and just inside of that symbol was Alu's, the Qaimiri god who hadn't set foot in the desert since well before Ihsan had been born. Strangely, Nalamae's constellation was present, east on the compass rose, but well outside the circle formed by so many of the other symbols. Interestingly, there were some symbols Ihsan could attach no meaning to, ancient sigils from when the first gods still walked the earth.

"Who made this?" Ihsan asked, flicking the corner of the parchment.

"Çeda," Sümeya supplied.

"While you were there, at the scene?"

"No, my King," Çeda said. "On the ship, once we were underway."

Almost of their own accord, Ihsan's eyebrows raised. "This is complex. Placement will be important."

"It's accurate," Çeda said, with all the confidence of a master scribe penning a scroll she'd copied thousands of times before. He was about to challenge her when she repeated it. "It's accurate, my King."

He found he believed her.

"This"—Husamettín pointed to a symbol Ihsan recognized, the ancient pictograph for unity: one in many and many in one—"appears on your back, does it not?"

Çeda nodded to him. "It does, my Lord King."

"How did you find the body?" Kiral asked.

"Sümeya bid me chase a handful of the Malasani pirates. They had stopped when they came across Aldouan's body, clearly afraid to continue."

"And did they know what might have done it?" asked King Mesut, the Jackal King, Lord of the Asirim. He had a reedy voice, a remnant from a bout of whooping cough he'd survived when he was young. Like Cahil and Sukru, he was normally a man who preferred to watch, to follow, but not because he wasn't as bellicose as the others. He was, at heart, a man who preferred the sword to the olive branch. But he was also a very deliberate thinker. He studied a thing from all angles before deciding, which made him in many ways more pliable than the rest of Kiral's lackeys. Now, he was strangely intent on Çeda and what answer she might have for him.

Çeda replied, "No, my King, they had no idea. There was fear in them and little else. They knew there was a good chance that the Kings' justice would take their lives, and yet their hope of fleeing had transformed into a plea for the Maidens to deliver them from that cursed place."

"Have you no guesses of your own?" Mesut went on.

"Surely the Kings would know better than I."

"That wasn't what I asked," Mesut replied easily, his breath a harsh whisper.

"I suspect, my Lord King, that it was an ehrekh."

Mesut paced like a master at the collegia might do with a prized student. "And why do you suspect it was so?"

"The symbols are the old script." She pointed to several of them in turn and spoke a word as she touched them. "Fallow. The unending well. The wonder of the gods. Stave, or sunder."

Mesut smiled, a strange thing to see on his pinched face, but he looked to the other Kings. "A learned woman, our young Maiden. But there are many, as you have just proven, who might know the old script."

"True," Çeda replied, "though few but an ehrekh would feast on the heart of man, as I suspect happened here, for they believe that to do so will give them a glimpse of the man or woman in the next life as they walk the farther fields. They hunger for such things, for in them Goezhen lit a desire for the touch of the first gods. And despite what *I* might know, the symbols are known to few. Fewer still would know where to place them on a circle such as this. And only a handful of souls would dare place the constellations of the gods along with them"—she pointed again—"Bakhi, Goezhen, Alu, thereby risking their wrath. And there is the strange stone we walked upon. The ehrekh are said to favor such places. There was a feel to it, my Lord King, a thing most unnerving. A feeling like the end of days was near. Any one of these things presented alone might indicate something else—a blood mage perhaps, a blood shaman of the desert tribes—but together, they point to an ehrekh or I'm a stonemason's son."

Ihsan laughed. Kiral was annoyed by it, but Ihsan couldn't help it. Çeda was always surprising him. And he hadn't failed to notice that she'd avoided calling attention to Nalamae's constellation, though certainly she'd seen it.

"No doubt you are correct," Ihsan told her. Then he turned to Kiral. "But what now?"

It was Çeda who spoke next, however. "Is it to do with the names from the collegia?"

Several of the Kings exchanged glances, but Husamettín pulled his attention from the parchment, pulled himself up to full height, and focused his dark eyes on Çeda. "Explain yourself."

"The Host were after names. Perhaps they were looking for names of Qaimiri students"—she waved to the body on the table—"perhaps some who'd been related to our newly departed king."

Kiral, standing by Husamettín's side, frowned. "There is much that might be done with blood." He looked to Zcheb, the King of Whispers. "Look into it. See if any of the students from Qaimir have gone missing."

Zeheb nodded. "At once."

The shuffle of footsteps sounded behind Ihsan. *"At once . . ."* a deep voice said in a sneer. Ihsan turned and found Onur's massive form standing in the open archway behind him. He stared at the body on the table with porcine eyes as he waddled forward on legs wide as tree trunks. He towered over all the other Kings, even Kiral and Husamettín. Black hair hung in lank strips down his forehead. He had the stink of black lotus on him. "At once," he repeated, "as though you command the Spears."

"Only," Zeheb replied, "when my Lord King finds himself indisposed."

The implication was clear to everyone in the room. The Silver Spears were Onur's to command, but his office was so often vacant that Zeheb, in addition to coordinating the movements of the Kings' spies, had taken command of the Spears as well.

Heaving his bulk forward with his characteristic limp, Onur treaded closer. He scratched the stubble along his jowls and stared down at Aldouan's body with dispassion, the sort one might give to an uncooked rack of lamb. "What do we care if a young scholar has gone missing?"

"Other than the obvious," replied Beşir, the King of Coin, with forced patience, "that all four kingdoms pay handsomely to have their children taught by our collegia masters. If they fear for the safety of their young they may call them home and send them to other institutions. The money that would normally accompany them would go elsewhere. Are you not worried that a plot might be unfolding beneath your very nose?"

Onur sniffed. "This may smell of a plot, but what of it?" He turned to King Zeheb. "What have the whispers told you?"

"Nothing as yet," Zeheb replied.

"Nothing," Onur scoffed. "They oppose you at every turn." He swung his gaze to Yusam. "And you? Has your mere not granted you some small insight into this grand plot?"

All eyes turned to Yusam, who was still staring at King Aldouan's body, transfixed. Onur snapped his fingers, and Yusam drew his eyes up, his distant look replaced by one of annoyance.

Onur laughed. "What use is a pool that grants foresight when the one who peers into it flits and flutters like a hummingbird?"

"The mere brought us this body," Yusam replied.

"And what of it?"

A pensive look overcame Yusam, a look of uncertainty. He looked to the body, then Çeda, then Ihsan, who he considered with a look of calculation, but also uncertainty. A chill ran down Ihsan's frame. Had he seen enough of Ihsan's carefully laid steps to guess what he was doing?

"All is not yet clear," Yusam said to Onur, "but the gods will provide. It will come."

"There is more we should discuss," Ihsan said before Onur could lead the conversation further astray, "including what we can expect from Qaimir now that their king is dead."

"If they even know," Zeheb added.

Ihsan tipped his head. "If they even know. We should prepare the body and bring it to their embassy house. I can speak to them, offer aid in the investigation."

Kiral considered, then nodded. "I won't have them thinking it was our fault. Offer to have them come and examine the king, question the Maidens."

"Offer them nothing," Onur countered. "*Our* Maidens found their king. Give them his body, then wait. We'll learn who takes Aldouan's place and by his response learn what he's made of in the bargain."

If Zeheb were watching Onur with an irritated expression, Azad could barely conceal his anger. No small wonder given how fastidious he was; he hated everything about Onur. Cahil, however, still standing with his back against the wall, seemed impressed. Sukru, the Reaping King, seemed pleased as well. He had a hungry sort of look on his pinched, vulpine face. The rest guarded their expressions, perhaps waiting for Kiral to make his thoughts known.

"His daughter, Meryam, is next in line," Ihsan said, "though since the Bloody Passage, she and Lord Ramahd Amansir have been here as often as in Qaimir. I wonder if Aldouan's brother, Hektor, will allow her to take up a crown he covets. And for that matter, given Meryam's fixation on the Moonless Host, I wonder if she'll even wish to lift the crown from her father's dead brow."

"It seems there's no reason to make the decision tonight," Husamettín said, motioning to Aldouan's body. "I daresay he'll keep until morning."

Onur flung one meaty arm toward Aldouan. "Will no one say it? We sit here and talk of appeasing a country that would take us the moment they saw weakness in the heart of the Shangazi. We grow weaker every day. The vultures have begun to peck at our dying corpse. It's a wonder they haven't already come, Qaimir or Malasan or both. And surely we're all aware the hungry gaze the bitch queen of Mirea has upon Sharakhai." He paused, sweeping his eyes over them all before resting on Kiral. "The gods have laid the King of Qaimir at our *feet*. Can you think of a clearer sign that they wish us to march south?"

"Whatever you may think, Qaimir is not a plum ripe for the picking," Husamettín said evenly.

"No, but soon *we* will be. Our asirim are dying. They become more erratic every day."

He said this to Mesut, who waggled his head. "Some few have rebelled . . ."

Onur laughed and leaned forward. "Some few . . ." He stared at Mesut as if he were a mummer in a play making a grand joke. "Some days I wonder if you hear the shit that spills from your mouths. Keep dickering, my good Kings, and it won't matter what power we still hold. It won't be enough. Soon, Mirea will ally itself with Malasan, or Qaimir. And then where will we be?"

"Onur's words have the ring of truth to them," King Sukru said, his pinched face watching Kiral and Husamettín carefully. "We would be wise to consider them."

"Consider, yes," Ihsan said. "But let us not be hasty. There is time yet."

Onur spun, swaying slightly before looking Ihsan up and down. Then he looked to the rest of the Kings with an expression that might better be saved for prattling children. Finally, he turned to the Maidens, looking at Çeda with bald hatred. "Consider all you will," he said without taking his eyes from her, "but when the spears of our enemies close in around Sharakhai once more, you'll remember my words." With that he strode from the room, leaving a dark mood in his wake.

Ihsan broke the silence. "Can we agree to meet midday at the Sun Palace to discuss our next moves?"

There was general agreement, after which the group began to disperse. Some remained behind, but Ihsan walked with most out to the carriage circle, where a host of horses, coaches, footmen, and drivers awaited. Onur's coach was just rumbling away as Ihsan motioned Zeheb nearer. "Ride with me?"

Zeheb agreed and sent his own coach away, and soon the two of them were riding along the switchbacks, down from the heights of Eventide, the lights of the city twinkling below. "An interesting occurrence," Ihsan said. "A king killed by an ehrekh."

"Do you know what those signs meant?"

"I suspect they were a plea to Goezhen, a way to make its voice heard by the God of Beasts, or if not that a way to summon a future it desires."

"Or both."

Ihsan sat deeper into the bench, feeling the cool night air wash through the cabin. "That I doubt. What I do know is that Yusam is coming nearer to *something*. I can see it in him, that look he gets when a grand weave begins to make itself known. The Maidens would not have stumbled across the body were it not so."

"You said you could control Yusam."

"I can. But if his mere leads him to the plans of the Al'afwa Khadar, there's no telling what he might do."

"Then what? Back away?"

"No, no, my good King, we speed things up." Ihsan stared up at Eventide, lit brilliantly by a host of lanterns and braziers. "It's time the scarabs came scuttling from their holes."

Chapter 19

THIRTEEN YEARS EARLIER…

IN THE CENTER OF SHARAKHAI, along the banks of the River Haddah, a crowd of three hundred joyous friends and family were gathered to celebrate the crossing of Demal, a handsome boy of thirteen with gangly limbs and an infectious smile. Winter storms had come, and the river was flowing in a clear, bright stream. The burbling sound reminded Çeda of the times she'd splashed in it with Emre and Tariq. The crowd laughed and joked. They ate and sang. A drum played while women danced around it and boys watched shyly. The girls would pull the boys in from time to time. No one did this more than Sarra, who always chose Demal, and together, they would dance over the river stones, laughing when they spun too fast.

Çeda's mother, Ahya, was speaking with a man who looked fresh from the desert, from the way his turban was tied, to the amber sand in his orange thawb, to the dust that marked the creases in his skin. He had a long beard, which made his handsome face look longer than it truly was, tattoos on the skin alongside his eyes, and more that were lost in his brown beard. Most interesting were the two shamshirs he wore on his belt. She'd never seen anyone with two. When Çeda asked him about them, Ahya had smiled and sent her away, which seemed rude, especially since she'd also refused to introduce them.

After a while, though, she didn't care. There were so many people to watch, and she liked listening to the music. And her mother . . . Tulathan's bright eyes, what a change had come over her. She was normally so strict. So grim. But here she was, chatting with this man from the desert, *smiling*. She even laughed now and again, her eyes far away as if she were reliving a story they'd both had a hand in crafting. There was a look to his face that was not so different from Ahya's. A man from her father's tribe visiting the Amber City? A cousin, perhaps? Ahya wouldn't say. Of course she wouldn't. She'd just shoo Çeda away again so she could talk in peace.

Higher along the bank, walking in from the western quarter of the city—the poorest by far—were Hefhi, Demal's father, and his six brothers and sisters. Demal's mother had died years ago from dysentery, leaving Hefhi to raise their children alone. Demal was the eldest, though, and everyone knew that he had shouldered his responsibilities well. He was the head of the household when Hefhi was working in the southern harbor, moving freight to and from the ceaseless influx of ships in from the southern kingdom of Qaimir, or the eastern kingdom of Malasan. He even worked on the occasional catamaran favored by the desert tribes.

Demal had changed since Çeda had first met him a season ago. He no longer ran the streets. He directed his brothers and sisters now, some of whom were gifted at stone carving. They made small but artful statues of oryx or falcons or rearing desert asps, things one would buy while in Sharakhai and return home to give to children, or put on a shelf and remember the distant, golden land they'd once visited. The other siblings, including Demal, scoured the aisles of the bazaar to sell them to the ceaseless droves of visiting patrons. Demal also cared for those who were sick, and not just the members of his own family; he made time for those in the tenement where they lived, and those from the neighborhood as well. He took them to the physic, the one who lived in the Shallows, who everyone knew was favored by the gods for her unguents and salves and balms. They worked wonders, and Demal sometimes shared what was left over from an application and gave it to others who might benefit. He had become a treasured child of the Shallows. And it showed in the sheer number who had come to the river this day.

"He's already been promised to another," Çeda's mother said with a chiding smile, nodding to Sarra, who was even then laughing at a quip from Demal.

Çeda realized she'd been staring for some time. She looked around for the man her mother had been speaking to, and found him at the edge of the crowd, crouched down as he spoke to three wizened men sitting cross-legged on the bank of the river. "I don't *care*," Çeda finally said. "I don't want to be promised to anyone anyway."

"You don't?" Ahya asked, her smile widening. "Not even to Emre?"

Çeda had been spending more time with Emre lately. Truth be told, she sometimes pretended that she and Emre had married, but she didn't want her mother knowing it. She feigned a sullen shrug and said, "*You* don't need a man. That's what you keep telling me."

Ahya pursed her lips as she leaned her body into Çeda's and pulled her close. "Need? No." She kissed Çeda's forehead. "But we all want love. We all want family."

"Where's *our* family?"

Ahya nodded to the crowd around them. "Right here."

"No, where's our *real* family?"

"You don't understand," Ahya said. "This *is* our real family."

She was always saying things like that, but Çeda knew it was just a way to deflect Çeda's questions. They'd come from the desert. Çeda knew that much. But she had no idea from which part, or why Ahya had come—or been *forced* to come—to Sharakhai. She had yet to meet another soul from her family. She'd not met her father. Nor her grandfathers or grandmothers. Nor her uncles or aunts or cousins. That is, if there were any alive to meet. Her mother would never say.

"Is *he* our family?" Çeda asked, pointing to the desert man.

"Shush," Ahya said, jutting her chin toward the crowd. "It's about to begin."

Demal's father, Hefhi was making his way down the bank. In his right hand he held a freshly cut branch from a fig tree with three ripe figs dangling among the green leaves. In the other he held an unsheathed sword—a fine shamshir with rich leather wrapping its hilt, the pommel in the shape of a desert fox, ears standing tall. As he came, the crowd made way, parting like water. Hefhi shared a toothy smile, his pride shining like a brand in the night. Demal's grin, on the other hand, faded, an anxious look replacing it. He'd been dancing earlier, acting the fool, but the time had come for him to show his mettle. All eyes were on him.

The crowd formed a rough circle as Hefhi and Demal met at their center. The men howled while the women cried *"Lai, lai, lai!"* Holding sword and fig branch in one arm, Hefhi wrapped the other around his son's shoulders and spun him about. "A thousand thanks for all who have come to see my Demal pass into manhood." Again the cries rose up, louder than before. Demal's cheeks were ruddy from the attention, but there was an eagerness in his eyes and bearing that made it clear he was ready for the dance. "That you, his friends and loved ones, are sharing this day with him means much to me, to all our family." Hefhi spun around, turning Demal with him, and took everyone in. "Blood of our blood," he said.

"Blood of our blood," the crowd replied, including Ahya, who had slipped her arm around Çeda's shoulders.

Hefhi now broke away from Demal. The crowd whistled and stomped their feet as Hefhi held the sword and olive branch high, presenting them both to the sun. He then flipped the sword in a graceful move, laying the blade along the sleeve of his arm, holding the hilt out for Demal to take. The moment Demal took the sword, two drums struck a lively beat.

As Demal began an intricate dance with the blade, turning and spinning, his blade glinting under the winter sun, the crowd cried out, and this time Çeda joined in with them. *Blood of our blood,* she thought, smiling, feeling, at least to some small degree, what her mother had been talking about. One might be powerless over one's family—in this, the fates gave what they gave—but you could spread your arms and embrace those you loved. That much you could do.

Demal began a series of spinning moves that drew a roar of approval. Then he approached his father and slashed out with the blade, slicing one of the figs cleanly from the branch. The crowd gasped as Demal completed the move, snatching the purple fig from the air before it struck the ground. Many laughed their approval, some calling for the fig to be theirs. But it was only in jest. The first was always given to the one holding the branch, often the boy or girl's father.

Demal gave it to his father with a smile and a half bow. Hefhi accepted it and took a huge bite from it, then held it up high, his pride clear to gods and man alike.

As the drumbeat came louder and Demal picked up the dance again, Çeda wondered what it would be like when it was time for *her* crossing. Would the gods be watching when she danced? Would they bless her? This was an ancient ritual that had been brought to Sharakhai from the desert. The people of the tribes claimed Sharakhai had not been anointed by the desert gods, but Sharakhai still stood, did it not, despite the anger of those who still sailed the sands and forged a living from the Great Shangazi? Surely the gods favored Sharakhai, and if that were so, perhaps they would smile on Demal. Perhaps they would smile on Çeda when her day came.

She hoped it was so.

Demal spun away, then came closer to his father once more. The blade swung out and cut another of the dark purple figs from the branch. Demal caught this one cleanly as well. This one would normally have gone to his mother, but as she had passed to the farther fields, Demal was free to give it to whomever he chose. He didn't hesitate. He made straight for Çeda and offered it to her with a bow.

As Demal's youngest sister began to cry that she hadn't been given the fig, Çeda could only stare at the plump fruit in his hand. Many laughed. Others smiled, waiting expectantly.

"Take it," Ahya said.

"But why?" Çeda asked.

Demal winked. "Because you seem so very sad."

Had she? Had she seemed sad?

She reached out and took the fig, feeling the heat rise in her own cheeks. Çeda took a bite from the luscious fruit, the sugary taste and the crunch of the seeds filling her mouth. The crowd clapped and whooped, her mother as loud as any of them. Demal then roughed her hair and strode back to start the final movement of the dance.

The crowd grew intense now, watching closely. With this final cut, and the offering given, Demal's crossing would be complete. Demal had acquitted himself well so far, but the highest blessings were bestowed upon those who cut all three figs cleanly, to those who caught all three, and to those who made wise choices with their offerings.

Demal spun and twisted, raised his hands high, then brought the sword low. He approached his father and lashed out with the sword with an uppercut to slice the fig free in a move that was so fierce, so swift, it made Çeda gasp. Demal caught the fig so calmly, so elegantly, she wouldn't have been surprised to learn that he was Thaash reborn, for surely this was how gods looked like when they walked the earth.

Demal held the fruit in one hand, considering carefully who he would give it to, but Çeda could tell it was all an act. He knew exactly who he would be giving it to, and so did everyone else, for when he turned to Sarra, many of the gathering whistled in the way one did for young lovers.

Before he could take two steps, however, there came a disturbance from the far side of the gathering. Hefhi turned to see what was the matter, and that drew everyone's attention to the riverbank, where a cadre of Silver Spears led by a Blade Maiden were navigating the rocky slope downward toward them. The Silver Spears wore conical steel helms with a curtain of mail hanging from sides and rear. Their bucklers and breastplates and vambraces were bright and polished, and bore the same royal designs as their leaf-shaped spearheads: a shield with twelve shamshirs fanned around it.

The lone Blade Maiden, though, seemed infinitely more dangerous than the city guardsmen. She wore a black thawb and a turban that covered all but her eyes. Her ebon blade hung sheathed at her side, her left hand resting loosely on its pommel. An intimate friend was that ebon blade, a thing she might have known for all her life. It was her bearing, however, that made her seem so deadly, like a cobra, raised and hooded, poised to strike.

The drumming ceased. A young boy gasped. Ahya's hand took Çeda's wrist in an iron grip, an echo of the constant care Ahya took to avoid the Kings and the Maidens in the light of day. Çeda and her mother's eyes met. Ahya shook her head. The time had not yet come. They would draw too much attention to themselves if they tried to leave now. Çeda looked to the old men by the riverbank, looking for the man from the desert, but he wasn't there. She couldn't find him anywhere.

All attention was now focused on the Maiden, whose kohl-rimmed eyes were fixed uncharitably on the gathering. Men and women grabbed their children, shielded them with their own bodies as if the city guard was about to launch a volley of arrows into their ranks. Faces happy only moments ago had turned to stone.

The fig branch still held in his left hand, Hefhi raised his arms high in a gesture of peace and strode toward the Maiden. The crowd parted, and the Maiden came to a stop two paces in front of Hefhi. The Silver Spears spread out behind her in two ranks of ten, shields at the ready, the hafts of their spears leaning toward those who had peaceably gathered.

"I have come for Demal Hefhi'ava," the Maiden said, staring past Hefhi toward his son, who stared back with a defiant look.

"For what reason?" Hefhi asked.

"The Kings' business is none of yours," was all she said as she stepped around him and made straight for Demal.

Hefhi ran past her and placed himself between the two of them, arms still raised. He backed up, placing himself ever in her path, as the Maiden veered this way then that. Then the Maiden stopped and regarded Hefhi. Gone was the look of sufferance she'd had when she'd reached the riverbed. Now there was malice in her dark eyes. "Remove yourself from my path ere I cut you like a river reed."

"It is his day of crossing. Please. Let us finish, and I will bring Demal to you myself, wherever you say. We'll stand before you and answer any questions you may have."

"It is not for you to decide whom the Kings will question and whom they will not. If, as you say, this is the very threshold of Demal's young life, then take care for his sake. Step aside before blood is drawn."

Hefhi could not argue further. He knew it, and so did everyone else. He raised his hands again and bowed placatingly to the Maiden, stepping aside but remaining close at hand. He realized, perhaps only then, that Demal was still holding the sword in his right hand. Demal was breathing hard, nostrils flaring, hand gripping and regripping the hilt of the sword.

"Demal," Hefhi said carefully, "lower your sword."

Demal merely stared into the Blade Maiden's eyes. They were nearly of a height. Demal was tall for his age. And he was competent enough with a blade. But this was foolish. Even Çeda knew it. The Maidens trained day and night. They could see into a man's soul. She would see Demal's next move before *he* did.

"Demal, lower your sword."

"Listen to your father, boy," the Maiden said. "Talk is all we wish."

Demal's chest broadened and contracted, slower than before. His grip on the sword loosened and his shoulders relaxed. When he spoke, it was strangely calm. "We'll have you in the end."

"You?" the Maiden replied, drawing her sword from its scabbard with violence and fluidity. Her ebon blade shone dully under the noontime sun, glinting like a bitter, bloody smile. "You and your friends?" Her right foot shifted. She lowered herself into a fighting stance. "No. You'll be crushed beneath the heel of the Kings, as were your brothers and sisters before you, as you all shall be while the Kings stand proud upon the mount."

Hefhi waved his arms in the air, the fig branch tilting this way and that. "No! Please don't do this!"

"*He* chose this," the Maiden replied, "not I."

And then several things happened at once.

Demal burst into motion, raising his sword high, the third of his figs forgotten on the riverbed behind him.

"No!" Hefhi cried as he charged the Maiden, wielding the fig branch like a sword. He spread his arms wide, perhaps hoping to tackle the Maiden and bring her to the ground, but before his arms could slip around her, she had stepped to one side, batting his left arm away and distancing herself from Demal at the same time.

The blade arced up, then across her body in a swift motion, slicing across poor Hefhi's undefended neck. Blood gushed everywhere.

"*Noooo!*" Demal screamed.

His charge had stalled. His motions as he tried to renew it were uncontrolled, clumsy. He swung for the Maiden, who blocked it easily, and the second. When he came in for the third—a high strike, both hands gripping the hilt—the Maiden sidestepped the wild blow and sent a spinning back kick into his jaw. Everyone heard the crack of breaking bones.

Like a sack of sand, Demal crumpled to the riverbed.

For a moment, everyone stood, mutely staring.

Then all was madness. Men shouted and screamed. Women wailed. Some shook their fists in the air. Some picked up stones from the riverbed. Many closed in around the Maiden, but none approached her. She held her sword at the ready amidst them, low in her fighting stance, waiting to see if anyone dared approach. None did. But when the Silver Spears began making their way forward, the crowd formed a wall, hoping to prevent them from taking Hefhi's remains or the unconscious Demal. The Spears shouted for them to back away, but compliance came only when an old woman was stabbed with a spear for coming too close.

Dozens had come to the riverbank to see what was happening. A few ran when they saw, but many rushed *toward* the conflict, their faces intent, the people of Sharakhai's western quarter ever-ready to vent their anger against the Kings and their servants. All knew that if the Maiden were to die, many more would be killed in retribution—they were the Kings' chosen, anointed by the gods themselves—but there was a limit to what the masses of Sharakhai's poorest quarter could stomach.

Some began moving in behind the Silver Spears, others along their flanks. The crowd closed in around the Maiden, some raising their rocks high over their heads as they screamed at her.

The Maiden waited, ready. Then a stone flew. It struck her on the back of her head. She turned and charged, slicing from neck to stomach the man who'd thrown it, and cutting another who'd thrown and missed, and a third when he came in bearing a stone like a club, hoping to bash her skull in from behind.

"Now, girl," Ahya said, still gripping Çeda's wrist. "Come now."

She pulled Çeda up and ran across the shallow river, splashing into it and across to the other side in three long strides.

Çeda kept up as best she could, climbing the far side until her chest was heavy with breath. Ahya led them through the city, not toward their home, but west. They passed beyond the city limits and came to a shallow crystal cave, which they reached by dropping to their stomachs and sidling in. Çeda could still hear the sound of the fighting. It had erupted and was spreading across the city. For a long while, Çeda couldn't speak, and at some point during the long, fearful afternoon she fell asleep.

When she awoke, it was morning, and her mother was coming back into the cave bearing a skin of water. She handed it to Çeda, who took it and drank thirstily.

There were no sounds of fighting, no cries of lament, only the laugh of a jackal somewhere deeper in the desert.

"Is it over?" Çeda asked.

"For now," Ahya replied, "though it will live well beyond today."

"Why did she do it?"

Ahya's face turned sour. "Kill Hefhi? You saw with your own eyes, Çeda."

"No. Why did she come for Demal in the first place?"

Ahya considered for a time, perhaps deciding how much to tell her. "If you haven't guessed, child, he was a scarab, a soldier of the Moonless Host, and he was foolish about it. He let it be known to one person too many." As Çeda took another long drink, she heard her mother speak under her breath. "A mistake I will never make."

Çeda wasn't sure just what Ahya was saying. Was she part of the Moonless Host as well? Çeda didn't dare ask. She was too afraid of the answer.

Later that day, they returned home to gather a few things, then moved in the night to another part of the city entirely.

Two days later, Demal was found at the gates, hung, along with eleven others.

Chapter 20

A SHARP WHISTLE WOKE ÇEDA FROM HER DREAM. Gods, she hadn't thought of Demal in years. It still felt so vivid, as if *this* were the dream, not that terrible day on the banks of the Haddah. She stared up at the stone ceiling of her bedroom. She lay there on her bed—blankets tangling her legs, most of it tossed aside in the heat of the night—still hearing her mother's words, *a mistake I will never make.*

She had, though. She had misstepped, and it had cost her her life. The Kings had found her the night after Beht Zha'ir and strung her up below the gates of Tauriyat with ancient words cut into her skin, a mystery that dogged Çeda still. Which King had her mother gone to see? Which King had found her? Which had carved those symbols into her mother's skin and hung her at the gates of the House of Kings?

The whistle came again.

"I'm up!" Çeda said.

"Then hurry your hide," Sümeya called. "A King is on his way to watch you perform."

Çeda shot up in her bed. *A King?* She dressed hurriedly and buckled her sword belt, wondering which of them would come, and why. Likely it would be Husamettín. Perhaps he wanted to judge her progress, a thing he did with Maidens from time to time, particularly the newer ones.

She made her way quickly down to the barracks courtyard, where three dozen sparring circles were located. A handful were occupied, some with two or three Maidens sparring with bamboo shinai that blurred through the air and cracked when they struck, others fighting in tight quarters with vicious swipes from wooden daggers or powerful hand-to-hand blows that ended in a sharp *kiai*.

Kameyl, Melis, and Yndris were already standing at the edge of the largest sparring circle, the one at the center. "No steel, young wren," Kameyl said, motioning to River's Daughter.

Çeda removed it, leaned it against a nearby tree.

"What say you, oh Çedamihn, daughter of Ahyanesh?" Kameyl asked. "Are you ready to growl? To roll in the dirt like a dog?"

"Wolves have sharp teeth," Çeda said, trying to hide her nerves. "They'll draw blood if you're not careful."

Kameyl chuckled. "Nip at our heels, more like. Whine when they're whipped." She took one of the four shinai from beneath her arm, flipping it so that Çeda could grip the handle. "Perhaps I'll take myself a pelt this day," she said to Melis, "a white one to grace the floor of my room."

"A pelt would look lovely, indeed," Melis replied.

Çeda forced a smile as she accepted the bamboo practice sword from Kameyl, but her thoughts were too focused on Sümeya's words—*a King is on his way*. She was just about to ask about it when three forms strode into the barracks courtyard. Zaïde and Sümeya were walking beside Mesut, the Jackal King. Zaïde wore her white Matron's dress, Sümeya her Maiden's black—both simple, utilitarian uniforms. Mesut, in contrast, looked like a shaikh of old in his fine, slate-blue khalat and his silver turban.

When Mesut spoke, it was with a reedy voice, as if its timbre had been stolen by a trickster god. "You may begin," he said simply to Kameyl, his hands over his chest, as if *he* were ready to judge her in Husamettín's place.

Kameyl handed one of the shinai to Melis, then another to Yndris, who each took up positions at the edge of the circle.

Çeda, so worried over Mesut she still didn't understand what was happening, made to step into the circle, until Mesut raised his hand to forestall her. "A moment, Çedamihn."

Mesut had an aquiline nose and piercing eyes beneath heavy eyebrows. His mustache and sculpted beard lent him a certain intensity, as if he meant to do her harm, but when Çeda stepped to his side, he gave her a disarming smile and held out one hand. She raised her left hand in response, as her right was holding her shinai, but he shook his head and pointed to her sword hand. "If you would be so kind."

"Of course, my Lord King," she said, switching her sword and allowing him to take her right hand. He lifted it to his mouth. She thought he was going to kiss it, but instead he twice ran his thumb over the puckered scar, the place where the adichara had poisoned her, then put his lips to it and sucked. The sting it produced was so immediate, so piercing, she gasped, to the annoyance of Sümeya. The King, however, kept his lips where they were, as if he were drawing blood from a poisoned wound. It was a wound no longer, though. It had long since healed to look at it, but it hurt terribly sometimes. Today she'd hardly noticed the pain, but as the King sucked at it, his warm, wet lips pressed tightly to her skin, the pain flared like a geyser, so much so that she tried to pull away. The King, however, held fast, his grip sure, his strength undeniable.

Çeda gritted her teeth against it, so acute had it become, and finally the King pulled her hand away from his mouth. He examined the wound, running his thumb over it as he had before. The pain now spread from that central point to the meat of her thumb to her wrist and hand. It felt as though she were being poisoned all over again.

"Now," he said, waving to Kameyl, Melis, and Yndris, "spar with your sisters."

Çeda had no idea why he'd done this. Apparently she wasn't supposed to know, for Mesut merely stepped back and waited, and Sümeya motioned to the ring with a subtle nod of her head. Çeda complied, stepping into the ring, moving to its center, as Melis, Yndris, and Kameyl had taken up positions around the edge of the circle.

"As we practiced," Zaïde said to Çeda, with the nonchalance of a master who cared very much about how her student was about to perform.

Çeda nodded and prepared, stepping into the ready position. She began to feel for the heartbeats of the three Maidens surrounding her. Kameyl she felt immediately, a strong and powerful heartbeat. Melis's came next. And finally Yndris's, who, Çeda suspected, was trying to mask it to embarrass Çeda in front of the King. But hiding one's heart was not an easy thing to do, and Çeda homed in on hers soon enough.

It was difficult to maintain the sense of three nearby heartbeats, but Çeda had been drilling with Zaïde and her sister Maidens to expand her awareness. She felt Yndris advance. Strangely, she felt it through her *hand*, not her mind, as if her wound was now attuned to the blood of her sisters.

Çeda spun, blocked high, then sidestepped a downward swing from Melis. Kameyl charged in. Çeda positioned herself so that, for a few precious moments, Kameyl blocked Melis and Yndris's path to Çeda. They traded a flurry of blows, their shinais clacking loudly. She fell into a rhythm, blocking, striking, taking occasional blows that stung. And all the while the wound in her hand began to burn. It grew like a fire in a furnace, red hot, then orange, then white. And as it did, her movements became more erratic, wilder, but stronger as well.

Twice she saw Yndris cringe when Çeda's swings came down hard against her raised defenses. She saw Melis grit her jaw when Çeda's left leg shot into her midsection while simultaneously blocking a low swing from Kameyl. Even Kameyl grunted as Çeda ducked beneath a high strike and brought her sword hard into her left shin, then up to catch her wrist as she was trying to reestablish her line of defense.

Çeda absorbed blows as well, but the rage within her was so strong she barely felt it. She hardly knew what she was angry about until a glimpse of her dream returned to her.

Demal, collapsing on the bank of the Haddah.

With that connection, the rage in her transformed. It had been so unfocused a moment ago, but now it homed in on one thing. One person. King Mesut.

She continued to fight Kameyl, Melis, and Yndris, but in truth she was looking for a way she might sprint from the circle and take Mesut. If only she had River's Daughter in her hands. It was just there, leaning against the tree. She might reach it in time. She might lop the King's head off before anyone could do anything about it. The very notion of witnessing the death of a King—the blood, the look on his dying face—sent a rush of glee coursing through her veins. *Oh, to dance on the grave of a King!*

Despite her intensity, she was becoming careless, her movements wilder, more erratic still. She tried to bring her focus back to the fight, as blows she had been blocking earlier rained in against her legs, her back, her arms and head, until finally, a sharp whistle came from behind her. She swung three more times at Kameyl, but Kameyl simply backed away, blocking Çeda's inexpert swings with practiced ease.

Her breath coming in ragged gasps, Çeda lowered her shinai. She felt no one's heartbeat now, none but her own, pounding so heavily all she heard was its low-pitched thrum. She wasn't even sure when she'd lost them.

"She was like this?" King Mesut asked.

"Yes," Yndris replied immediately.

"Not so bad as this," Kameyl cut in, "but yes, my King. Like this."

Çeda stared at them, confused. What were they talking about?

"And your training sessions?" Mesut said to Zaïde.

"Yes," Zaïde replied, "from time to time."

"Have they been more frequent of late?"

Zaïde waggled her head, considering. "Yes, they seem to have been."

This clinical examination did more to bring Çeda back to herself than her own desire to stifle her rage. She looked between the Maidens and the King, feeling betrayed, but also worried over where the King's line of inquiry might be headed.

"Leave us," King Mesut said.

The Maidens bowed and left. Zaïde did as well, but not before giving Çeda a worried look, as if she too were unsure of Mesut's purpose.

"All of you," Mesut shouted to the courtyard, clapping loudly, "leave us."

Immediately the other Maidens stopped what they were doing, bowed to their King, and left, leaving Çeda and Mesut to occupy this grand space on their own. Mesut held out his hand, flicking his fingers. "Your shinai." She handed it over numbly. Mesut took it and leaned it against the tree just next to River's Daughter. The anger was still there, but buried more deeply, like a creature retreating into its cave.

With lithe steps, Mesut made his way across the sparring circle to the traditional starting position for unarmed combat. The sun angled in over the barracks roof, bathing him in golden light. He stared at her with a keenness that reminded her of a desert falcon—a look both regal and ruthless—then motioned to the space across from him. Çeda stepped into the ring as her confusion, not to mention the pain all over her body, grew in frightening increments. "Will we spar, my Lord King?"

His only reply was to motion again. As she took her position, he said, "I felt you out in the desert, when you called to the asirim."

And suddenly Mesut's presence here, his interest in her wound, became clear as sunlit rain. She'd felt *him* in the desert as well. She'd thought him unaware of her presence. But of course he hadn't been. She'd been foolish to think it. What might he have learned while she was bonded to the asirim? And now that he was wary of her, would he dig deeper? Would he learn her secrets?

"Zaïde is pleased with your progress, as is Sümeya." He motioned to her wounded hand. "But you cannot continue as you have."

Çeda shook her head. "I don't understand."

"Come," he said, lowering himself into a fighting stance and raising his hands. His body was loose but poised to strike. She could see in his form, in his eyes. He was a supremely confident fighter. Hesitantly, Çeda complied, and then the King said exactly what she feared he would.

"Now try to strike me."

"My King?"

His face pinched in annoyance. "Attempt to strike me, as you would an enemy of Sharakhai."

"I cannot strike a King."

"Unless he wills it."

She made a half-hearted attempt, but the King blocked it with ease and drove his palm into her chest. It was a movement so compact, so perfect, she could see it traveling up from his legs to his hips to his shoulders to his palm. It sent her flying backward and onto her rump.

He returned to the starting position. "I said, *strike me.*"

She got up and dusted herself off, then returned and lowered into a ready stance, controlling her emotions as best she could. She wasn't afraid of what the King might do to her. She was afraid of what *she* might do to the *King* were she to lose control again. She no more wanted to be controlled by the asirim than she did by the Kings.

She tried again, a faster flurry of blows, but each time, the King somehow wrapped his wrists around hers, twisting like a snake. He gave no ground, always sending Çeda backward with a strike to her head or chest or shoulders. And he was constantly altering *her* strikes, blunting their momentum by twisting them outward or inward and curling around her defenses until he could counterstrike.

Çeda tried to find her center, tried to touch Mesut's heart, but in this she failed miserably.

Until Mesut shot one hand in like a striking asp and grabbed her right hand. He twisted her arm painfully while pressing the tip of his thumb into her poisoned wound. Her world became pain once more. She felt as though she were at the top of a mountain with the world burning white all around her.

Mesut loomed over her as she fell to her knees. "I told you to strike me, child!"

He released her and kicked her in the chest, a blurring movement that was fluid as an autumn gale, powerful as a raging river. She fell hard across the sparring circle's thick rope border, the back of her head thumping against the ground.

She lifted her head, ears ringing, then returned to her feet. As before, the wounds across her body faded. She felt only the wild white fire burning in her hand. Her hatred—the *asirim's* hatred—had returned, but it was focused now. On the Jackal King alone. She returned to her place in the circle, feeling his heartbeat. As she had in the desert, she felt . . . No, she *knew* she could smother him, that she could bury him beneath the desert if she so chose.

But are these my thoughts or the asirim's?

Refusing to lower into her fighting stance, to *submit*, she struck at Mesut, giving herself to the pain and anger emanating from her thumb. She felt the world around her draw inward. Soon it was only the two of them, nothing else, arms powering forward, twisting as he twisted, waiting for the inevitable counterstrike. They continued, legs trading positions like dancers in the center of a vast, empty hall. His eyes taunted her, which only fueled her rage.

The poison took her then. Her entire world went white. She felt but did not see her hand strike Mesut, but she had no idea where. Then she was falling, something struck the front of her body. She screamed in rage, struggling to free herself, but something had her pinned from behind.

"Return to me, Çedamihn Ahyanesh'ala," came a low, rasping voice. "Return to me now." The pain continued to burn. "Return to me."

Like fog burning away, the courtyard resolved from the whiteness. She felt and heard her own harsh breathing. She sounded like a wounded dog, growling and mewling at the same time. She realized the King was on her back, pinning her right arm behind her. He was pressing his thumb against her wound again, but this time it was gentle, as if he were holding a compress to a cut to staunch the bleeding. Instead of making the pain flare, his touch was having the opposite effect. Slowly the agony faded, as did the anger, leaving Çeda a wreck. When Mesut let her go at last, she collapsed against the ground, unable to understand the emotions roiling inside her. She felt like the trees standing sentinel about the courtyard, blowing this way then that with the wind.

Mesut kneeled next to her, put his hand on her shoulder, then stroked her hair. "I blame myself for this. I feel the anger raging in you. The kiss of the adichara did so much more than poison your flesh. It poisoned your mind as well. It gave the asirim a pathway to you, and through you they have found a way to voice their rage." For a long while, he simply ran his hand down her back. Gods curse her, it felt good, a solace in this very strange storm. "Can you sit?" he asked after a time.

She nodded, and he helped her up to a sitting position. He sat cross-legged across from her, oblivious to the dirt soiling his fine clothes. It reminded her of Emre, the two of them sitting in their shared home before any of this had begun, the memories jarring when set against the experience of sitting here intimately before a King, as if the whole of Sharakhai had just been tilted on some unseen axis.

"The asirim are our heroes," Mesut went on. "Our protectors. You know now the rage they feel."

"Why?"

"Why what, dear child?"

"Why rage?"

Mesut reached out and brushed her cheek. She wanted to slap it away, but she couldn't. "Can you blame them?" he asked. "They've shouldered a heavy burden for four hundred years. That's a long time for anyone to shoulder anything, but the asirim in particular bear the brunt of securing our fortune in this city. They live. They see pain. They come for Sukru's chosen ones to honor the gods and their own sacrifice, and they do so willingly, but they still *feel*. Their rage sometimes seeks a voice in the wrong places. Which is why you must exercise control, Çedamihn. You must exercise control with them, over yourself, over your wound, and over the poison that still lies within it, for only in this will you be allowed to live."

He let the words hang between them like a body on a gibbet.

"Yes," he said. "There have been others who have gone mad while fighting the same battle you fight now. Most were put to the sword when they proved they couldn't contain themselves. I don't wish that to happen to you, Çeda. You're an asset to the Maidens, and I would not wish to see you tossed aside like a distasteful cut of meat, but you will be unless you can master the asirim. Do you understand?"

She wanted to say yes. She knew she should, but something had struck her, a realization so painfully obvious she wondered how she had not seen it before. She knew as she knew the grip of her blade that it wasn't a random occurrence that drove Maidens mad; it was blood. As sure as the dunes were dry, the women Mesut was referring to had been members of the thirteenth tribe, the blood of Çeda's people sifting like sand from the corners of the Great Shangazi into the House of Kings. Like a map charting their terrible history, there they were, sprinkled throughout the centuries since Beht Ihman, evidence that the thirteenth tribe had survived, yet no one knew of them, their voices drowned before they'd truly lived.

Mesut's expression hardened, a King with his subject once more. "Do you *understand*, girl?"

"I understand," Çeda said, trying to put enough emotion in her voice to make him believe her.

"Good." The King patted her knee, then stood. "Now see that you put it into practice."

And with that he walked away, leaving her sitting there, alone. When he was gone, she stood and brushed the dirt from her black dress. She stepped over to the tree and took up River's Daughter. After strapping the belt around her waist, she drew her ebon blade and began to flow through the movements of *tahl selheshal*. It had always calmed her and did so now.

As she moved, as her body sang with her sword, she wondered over those other Maidens, the ones who'd gone mad. How many had there been? How many had died without knowing their heritage? Like a facet of a terrible, intricate jewel, this was yet another aspect of the curse the Kings had handed down to the thirteenth tribe on the night of Beht Ihman, a curse the gods themselves had granted.

She closed the final movements of the dance, and came at last to the question that haunted her most. *Will I die too?*

Control. Just as Mesut had said, she couldn't allow the asirim to control her. She had to remain herself, or she would lose everything. And so it would be. She would learn control. She had to, or she was little more than a dead woman yet to find her grave.

Control, she thought. Then began the dance anew.

Chapter 21

"WHY LET THEM BEAT YOU LIKE A DIRTY CARPET?" Hamid asked Emre.

They were snaking their way through dark west end streets beneath a starry sky. Emre, walking by Hamid's side, was still limping from the beating Serkan's guards had given him. Behind them, towering a head and a half above them both, was Frail Lemi. A rope was slung over one broad shoulder, the three crates, one tied to the next, swung behind his back like a horsetail.

"You needed time to get off the roof, didn't you?" Emre had a bit of a slur. He'd chipped a tooth, but thankfully none were broken. He'd picked up a few cuts. A few bruises. On balance not bad considering the contents of the crates were far more valuable to Macide than the gold Emre had flashed to Serkan.

"Might've just walked in the front door with knives to hand," Frail Lemi said.

He'd said much the same these past few days, but this entire operation—not just *their* heist, but the other five that had been arranged for the coming attack on the collegia—was something they couldn't leave to chance. If all went well, it might be a week or more before their thefts were discovered. And even if one or two *were* discovered, it would be days or weeks before the

Silver Spears put it together. The one man they feared learning of it was Zeheb, but that was why they'd set up different sorts of capers for each heist. Keep the King of Whispers guessing with multiple tales, each contradicting the next. It was when too many men and women began speaking about the same subject that trouble came. It didn't matter if it was the Moonless Host or the Silver Spears or the civilians in this war being fought in the shadows; pluck a particular harp string often enough and it would eventually reach the Whisper King's ears.

The soldiers in the Host, even captains like Hamid, were rarely told more than they needed to complete their missions. And what little they *did* know they were told to keep to themselves. Frail Lemi, however, was a bit off. Had been since he was ten. He'd fallen from a granary tower and broken the fall not with his arse but with his skull. He hadn't woken for a month, and when he *had* regained consciousness he was . . . different. He fixated on things. He'd be quiet for long stretches, hours at a time, sometimes days, and then he'd work himself into a frothing rage at the smallest of things. Never at those he knew. Never at loved ones. Only those he disliked or didn't know at all. Sometimes complete strangers would suffer his wrath, and it was left to Hamid or Emre or others to talk him down from it. Sometimes even that didn't work. More than once Frail Lemi had left a body or two in his wake.

Sometimes that same night, sometimes days later, he'd break down and cry over it. It hurt Emre to see him like that. Deep down he had a tender heart. If it were up to Emre he'd have Lemi tending to the grandmothers, fixing them tea and the like, but he couldn't deny the man was good in a pinch. Hardly felt pain at all as far as Emre could tell. And he did what he was told, even if he groused about it now and again.

"Don't you think, Hamid?" Frail Lemi pressed. "Walk in the front door." He paused, face screwing up in concentration. "Slip a knife between their ribs, nice and slow."

"Might've done," was all Hamid said in reply, knowing that to engage or argue would only cement Lemi's line of thinking, or worse, touch a brand to the fuel and set his anger aflame. There was no telling what Frail Lemi might do if that happened. Might even turn around and do just what he'd said: walk back into that warehouse and leave it a bloody mess. And then where would they be?

"That's *right* we might've done," Frail Lemi said. His neck muscles went taut, pulling his lower lip down to reveal his stained teeth. "Take them out in the time it took to take a sip from his fucking cup of flatland beer, eh, Emre?"

"One sip," Emre agreed.

"One sip," Frail Lemi echoed.

Emre and Hamid continued on to the northwest corner of the city where the quarry lay. Several men stood at the ready at the top of the labor elevator, bowing their heads to Hamid after he gave them the callsign, at which point they stepped aside and allowed Hamid, Emre, and Frail Lemi into the cage.

"*Yip, yip!*" one of them called, taking a switch to the back of a mule. As the mule walked, turning an old, grease-stained capstan, the cage was lowered steadily into the quarry. Once they'd reached the bottom, they headed out and into a tunnel, taking several turns in what Emre knew was a vast warren of them.

A yellow light shone ahead. They arrived at a large room, more of a man-made cavern, really. The quarry master might have found a vein of something years ago and excavated the area to get as much of it as he could, but now the cavern lay unused, at least for mining purposes. In one corner, near where they'd entered, were a dozen men and women, soldiers of the Al'afwa Khadar. Several turned when they entered, among them Darius, who raised his left hand in a wave, drawing them closer.

"Late once again," he said, smiling even as he grimaced.

"Late once again," Frail Lemi said, smiling in that same strange way, as if he felt Darius's pain.

Darius had still not fully recovered from the assault on King Külaşan's desert palace. The remains of the force sent in to retrieve Hamzakiir had exited the same tunnel they'd entered, only to be attacked by Ramahd Amansir and Princess Meryam, the daughter of King Aldouan himself. Darius had taken an arrow in the chest, very near his windpipe, very near his major arteries. He was lucky to be alive, but his shoulder had never quite healed and his arm was almost useless. It hung in a sling most days, but today he had chosen not to wear it, likely so he wouldn't be seen as weak before so many of his brothers and sisters.

"We may be late," Emre said, "but we've brought a bounty with us. More than anyone else, or I'm a boil on a Maiden's fat arse."

Frail Lemi laughed so hard he sounded young again. "Fat arse." When it had passed, he lifted the three crates with one arm until his fist bumped up against the low ceiling. "Three crates we found, sitting untended like babes in the streets. Was a service we rendered, rescuing them."

"Bring them here," came a voice on the opposite side of the gathered crowd, "and those of you who've already delivered, leave."

The crowd dispersed, some waving to Hamid or slapping his shoulder on their way out, others glancing back with annoyance at the hunchbacked man who sat at a table with a myriad of glass contrivances. The man, Samael, was the Host's chief alchemyst. He swung his head around and absently scratched a bit of flaking skin on his bald head. "Send the big one away. I won't have him breaking things again."

Frail Lemi glowered at this, but Hamid immediately inserted himself between Lemi and Samael, raising his hands in that placating way of his that mostly worked to calm Frail Lemi's nerves. "Take this," Hamid said, reaching into his thawb and pulling out a folded paper packet. "Go home. Take it with araq, just like last time. It'll quiet the voices."

Lemi's eyes flicked between Samael and the packet several times. "Nights like this, they're fierce, Hamid. Fierce like a sandstorm."

"I know," Hamid said. "This'll help. It always does, doesn't it?"

Frail Lemi nodded, took the packet, and without another word walked off like a man who hated being late and just realized he'd forgotten something at home.

Emre had no doubt Frail Lemi heard things inside his head, but the main effect of the soporific wasn't for that. It was to make him shut that big rat trap of his. By the time he woke, he'd have forgotten nearly everything about what they'd done the night before. He was particularly malleable that way. Another reason he was so useful. Part of Emre even envied him. *There are a fair few things I wish I could forget.*

"Come, let me see," Samael said, nodding to Hamid and scratching another flaking red spot on his scalp.

Hamid and Emre brought the crates over while Darius watched, trying to hide his frustration over not being able to help. Hamid cracked open one of the crates with a pry bar, exposing a bolt of rich black cloth. Folding it back revealed a mound of what looked like clods of dirt. Emre knew them to be golange, or blackcaps, as they were better known, a Kundhunese truffle with mild hallucinogenic properties and an aroma treasured in fine Shara-khani cuisine.

Samael lifted one of the blackcaps, brought it to his nose, and sniffed deeply. He did so again, his frown vanishing. "Well, well. Fresh indeed."

Interesting, Emre thought. *Hangmen give more compliments than Samael.* The crates must have been freshly delivered from Kundhun to rate even faint praise from the alchemyst.

"Do you have enough?" Hamid asked.

Samael looked down at the two other crates. "The others have just as many?"

"Feels that way," Emre replied.

Samael bunched his lips, waggling his head from side to side, and seemed about to answer when a woman's blood-curdling scream cut through the darkness of the cavern. Emre turned back the way they'd come, a bitter chill running down his frame. Before he could say anything, Hamid gripped Em-re's wrist and shook his head. *It's nothing to worry about,* he was saying, and yet Emre *was* worried. He hated being in these caverns. They felt poorly built, ready to collapse at any moment. Add to that the screaming—some experiment being conducted in preparation for their assault on the collegia, no doubt—and it made Emre's mouth go dry.

The scream stopped a moment later. Samael seemed strangely unper-turbed by it but he did glance toward the cavern entrance before regarding Hamid coolly. "Not everyone was successful, but with this"—he raised one of the blackcaps—"we'll have enough."

Another scream came but was cut suddenly short. Samael looked at Emre with something like appraisal. "You'd better take this one to Macide," he said to Hamid, disengaging as if he weren't pleased by what he'd seen in Emre but had neither the time nor the will to do anything about it.

Hamid nodded. "Well enough. Everything else goes well?"

"It will if you leave me to my business," Samael snapped.

Hamid gave Emre a stone-faced look. "Touchy, this one." Then he shrugged as if to say he'd gladly suffer men like Samael so long as they pro-duced results, and turned Emre around with an arm across his shoulders. As they exited the cavern and were swallowed by the tunnel's gloom, another shriek came, a mixture of fear and rage and driving will. "Dear gods," Emre said to Hamid. "Like Goezhen himself come for vengeance."

Hamid nodded, a bit of emotion showing in his sleepy eyes. And then it was too dark to see. Until, that is, they reached a point where another light, hidden from them behind a curve in the tunnel, was revealed. Soon they arrived in a room where three men were standing, with a fourth kneeling next to the form of a prone woman. The kneeling man was dipping his fingers into a censer filled with what looked to be blood. Indeed, it looked to be his *own* blood; as he pulled the sleeve of his khalat back so that it didn't dip into the blood in the censer, a cut along the man's forearm that was revealed. Emre recognized him. He hadn't seen him since the flight from Külaşan's palace, moments before he'd been taken away by Meryam and the men from Qaimir. But here he was now, Hamzakiir, Külaşan's own son—returned to them, it was said, after sweeping into the throne room in Almadan and killing King Aldouan and a dozen of his family by plunging a knife into their chests.

A lantern on the floor cast an eerie golden light against the three standing men. They looked like the first men must have looked, regal and puissant, like the gods who'd made them. The nearest man Emre didn't recognize, but he certainly recognized the second: Macide, his arms crossed over his chest, revealing the viper tattoos on his lean, muscled forearms. The man to Macide's left was easily three times Emre's age. He wore a dark khalat, its exact color swallowed by the darkness. The cut was not like the lords of Goldenhill might wear today, but instead something from centuries ago. Its silhouette was older, the fabric coarser, but it seemed all the finer for it. Emre had never seen him before, but given the identity of the other men, and a not-inconsiderable similarity to Macide, Emre had a very good guess as to who it might be.

"Sharakhai welcomes Lord Ishaq," he said, bowing deeply.

Macide glanced knowingly at his father, then to the other man next to him, a man dressed in finery one might find in the palaces of the Kings. "Father, Lord Aziz, this is the one I told you about," Macide said. "Emre Aykan'ava, the one we took to the King's palace."

Something lit in Ishaq's eyes. He became much more intense than he had been a moment ago. "You know Çeda, then."

"I know her quite well, in fact," Emre replied, regretting it a moment later. It felt a betrayal, those words, though why that should be, he wasn't quite sure.

"Well then," Ishaq said, "we'll have to speak on it one day."

He nodded his head and said, "Of course." But inside he was wondering, *Why? What do you wish to know?*

The woman lying on the floor still breathed, but only just; her eyes were fixed on the ceiling as if she were staring through it to the farther fields. Emre thought surely Hamzakiir would speak to Macide and Ishaq, report to them whatever it was he'd been doing with the woman, but instead he stood and faced Emre, every bit as interested in him as Ishaq seemed to be, though surely not for the same reasons.

"Our young falcon has returned," Hamzakiir said. "Victorious, I hope?"

Emre nodded. "Exceedingly."

"Good, good." He glanced down at the woman, then at Macide and Ishaq and Lord Aziz, completely ignoring Hamid. "My lords, might I speak with young Emre alone?"

Ishaq spoke first. "Well enough, but come to us tonight."

"I would dream of nothing else."

Ishaq bristled at this, but said nothing else as he turned and strode away. Macide ushered Hamid behind him. Lord Aziz remained a moment. He was a large man, quite unlike both Macide and Ishaq. In fact, he had the look of Sharakhani royalty about him. His clothes, the cut of his beard, even the way he took in the ritual being performed, as if he were above such things. "We'll speak again soon?" he said to Hamzakiir.

"Of course," Hamzakiir replied, and there was a look exchanged between them, a knowing look, the sort that made it clear there were things to speak about, but not openly.

Soon Emre was standing alone in this room with a dying woman and a man who should long ago have been dead. Hamzakiir kneeled next to the woman and motioned Emre to a spot across from him on the stone floor. "Come."

Emre complied, noting how much Hamzakiir had changed. His cheeks had filled in. His skin was no longer dry as parchment. There was proper meat on his bones. Even his hair and beard had changed. They were no longer wispy as fleece, but thick, black, and healthy. There remained, however, the same undeniable hunger in his eyes, a thing that made Emre wonder why he'd asked Emre to remain while sending the others away.

Hamzakiir laughed, a sharp, grating thing in this hard place. It made Emre's skin prickle. "I'm not in the habit of devouring young men, in case you're wondering."

"Of course not, my lord Hamzakiir."

"Good. Then perhaps it's merely her." He waved to the woman lying on the floor. "Come closer. There's nothing to fear."

Emre did so, ignoring the insult, and stared down at a woman who'd seen no more than twenty summers. *Çeda's age.* A thought that chilled Emre to the bone. The woman had blood around her eyes, along her cheeks and on her forehead—a pattern drawn with a blood-soaked finger.

"Its been some time since I've done the ritual," Hamzakiir went on. "I had to make sure I remembered. That we were ready for the day."

He meant the day when the Host would unleash their latest attack against the Kings and their rule. Except now they had the son of a King on their side. It wasn't lost on Emre that Hamzakiir might fancy *himself* a King, might want to take the high throne in Eventide should they manage to rid themselves of the eleven kings who remained. And if *he* was aware, surely Macide and Ishaq had thought the same. But he couldn't worry now. Hamzakiir was a bloody blade held to the throat of the Kings, a weapon Ishaq would use if it might topple the Kings from their hill.

"And did you?" Emre asked without looking up. He was staring into the woman's eyes, who ignored him, staring at the ceiling instead.

"Well, let's just see, shall we?" He held his hand out. "Might I have your knife?"

He had one of his own lying propped against the censer next to the woman, but Emre shrugged and took his out, then flipped it and handed it by the blade to Hamzakiir.

Hamzakiir's sly fingers took the handle, then he held it above the woman so she could see it. "Take it," he said softly, "and end thy life."

The woman's nostrils flared. Her head turned toward Emre. Their eyes locked. Emre thought she might have shown fear, regret, anger at what was happening. But he saw only cold determination and undeniable pain, the two heated red hot and mixed like bitter alloys, one now inextricable from the other. She gave him that unyielding, flinty stare as if he'd offended her, as if *he'd* been the one to challenge her to do this. She reversed the knife.

Dear gods, she's going to do it. Emre saw his brother, Rafa, lying on the floor of their shared home, a Malasani pig hovering over him, grinning, a knife pointed at Rafa's chest.

"No!" he shouted, reaching for her wrists. But before he could, Hamzakiir grabbed *his* wrists and prevented him. He didn't look to be a strong man, but his grip was like stone.

"You don't have to do this!" Emre yelled.

"We do. We must know the devil's trumpet is perfect." Hamzakiir watched the woman with a fascination that sickened Emre. The woman embraced the knife, the sound of it entering her body the very same as when Rafa had been murdered. Blood welled between her breasts. She pulled the knife free and stabbed herself again, then a third time. Her face went from resolve and anger to pain to confusion, and then her body went slack and the light faded from her eyes at last.

Just like Rafa's.

"You knew she would do it," Emre said.

"No," Hamzakiir replied as he released Emre's wrists and pulled the woman's hands free of the knife. Gripping the handle, he pulled it free from her lifeless body. "I didn't *truly* know. And for this we must." He stood, prompting Emre to do the same. "Many have volunteered to die for our cause and go through the ritual she's just completed." He motioned to the woman lying between them. "But only twelve by twelve will be chosen. One hundred and forty-four, the same number as the Blade Maidens who protect the Kings. Will you be one of them?"

"If that is what you wish." And he meant it. He didn't wish to throw away his life—he hated that this woman had been forced to give hers to satisfy Hamzakiir's curiosity—but he no longer had a fear of dying. He hadn't since the ritual where he'd drawn the blade across Lord Veşdi's throat to fill the breathstone, the very stone that, brimming with the power of Veşdi's blood, had brought Hamzakiir back from the dead. When his day came at last, he would walk to the farther fields and embrace his brother and tell him he was sorry he hadn't done more.

"You would have no regrets?" Hamzakiir asked.

"Some."

"Name one."

Çeda, Emre thought. *I would hold Çeda one last time before I die. I would sail her away from the misery in Sharakhai and tell her that I love her.* "The desert holds countless delights," he finally answered.

"And yet I asked for but one."

"You misunderstand. I love the desert. I love Sharakhai. I will miss it when I walk among the farther fields."

At this, Hamzakiir paused. Then he smiled, a genuine thing, it seemed to Emre, tempered perhaps by their dark business in this dark place. "As will I." He handed the knife back to Emre. "You drew me forth from the darkness below my father's palace. You gave me the breath of life."

"I wish I'd done more. We'd hardly turned a corner and we lost you."

Hamzakiir spread his arms wide, as though he were standing in the open, welcoming a rare burst of summer rain. "And yet here we are."

"Hearty and hale."

A low chuckle escaped Hamzakiir. "These old bones might disagree." He motioned toward the tunnel. "Now go, young falcon. Live this day. For tomorrow, we go to war."

Chapter 22

CEDA WALKED EASILY THROUGH THE GATHERING CROWD in the collegia's grand, open-air forum. She wore a patterned dress she'd been given by the Matrons, one that combined the Malasani flare for colors with the long, flowing cut of a traditional desert dress. It was full-sleeved, and ran almost down to her ankles to hide the light armor she wore beneath. It felt strange wearing River's Daughter beneath her clothes, but Melis had given her a special leather sheath and shown her how to walk in it so that it looked natural. She'd shown her as well how to move and bend her legs so that the thin leather cords holding the sheath in place would snap, and so that the delicate stitching on the dress would rip, giving her all the freedom of movement she'd need if the day turned violent.

Around the forum, dozens milled about, sitting on the simple stone benches or talking beneath the shade of the myrrh trees that lined the grounds. They were the family and loved ones of the students who would soon receive their laurel crowns, the mark of a collegia graduate. Sümeya, wearing a rich dress of cream accented in azure, stood in a group of highborn men and women. Melis was near her, chatting with another group, laughing easily at a story being relayed by an aristocrat with thread-of-gold woven into her elaborately braided hair. Yndris strolled the edge of the forum, admiring the flowering shrubs, stopping occasionally to pick one of the blue flowers, smell it, and add it to her growing bouquet. Kameyl was not here but in the garrison building, which loomed like a monolith over the near end of the forum. She stood ready with three dozen Maidens, prepared to deliver a response should the Moonless Host be foolish enough to show themselves.

Çeda, like all of the Maidens now hidden among the crowd, had been ordered to take an adichara petal before coming. She could feel its raw potency coursing through her veins. Her senses expanded to encompass the world around her, often giving her more than she wished. She heard the wheeze of a child as his mother shushed him a hundred paces away. The day was warm, but she still sensed the heat from the bodies all around her. Rosewater and lavender and jasmine might waft from the women, the men might smell of sandalwood and honeypine, but the wind also carried the scent of unwashed masses, the sour smell of the collegia's brewery, and a sharp, moldy smell she couldn't identify. Such were the gifts of the adichara.

A pair of colonnades ran along the length of the forum. Chipped and aging, they were some of the oldest structures in all of Sharakhai, built shortly after the basilica to the west and the ancient garrison to the north. The students were gathered in the basilica, awaiting the sound of the kettledrums that would announce their march, but the masters had already arrived. They were easy to spot in their flaxen robes and freshly made laurel crowns. Some wandered, chatting with the families, while others stood like stones at sea, waiting for others to come to them. She saw Master Amalos among them, a bent man wearing the orange robes of a high scholar. One hand swept absently down his white beard as he spoke with a woman half his age—another high scholar whose mirthful eyes twinkled at Amalos's words.

An honor guard of Silver Spears was in attendance, a pair at each of the four corners of the forum—no more than would normally attend. They'd been told to act nonchalant, to chat with one another and the passing crowd, to wish them a good day, so that none would suspect anything amiss. Two dozen archers were stationed along the rooftops, the best the Spears had to offer. She caught a glimpse of one watching from behind a pair of statues atop a nearby building, but only because she knew to look for them.

The ceremony approached. Young collegia students began moving the

gathered groups toward the stone benches, leaving the central aisle clear for
the waiting students to stride along from the basilica. Çeda decided to stand
near the back, but still ended up being cornered by a man from Malasan with
a sweaty brow, a terrible smile, and worse breath. He leaned in as the high
scholars took to the steps of the stone dais and arranged themselves. "And
what house keeps *you* in Sharakhai?"

"I'm a guest of the Confessor King," she said easily. As she waited for this
to sink in, a line of drummers and sitar players took up a song, signaling the
start of the ceremony. The man's face was already blanching, but she leaned
in close anyway and said in a hoarse whisper, "He rather thinks he owns me,
but he doesn't. I'd rather be out among the streets, not traipsing about some
cold palace." A gong struck, and the students began walking in ranks of three
from the basilica doors. "And what house keeps *you*, my lord?" He cleared his
throat, his mouth opening and closing several times. He looked perfectly
miserable. When everyone turned toward the procession, including Çeda, he
shuffled away in haste.

The graduates were arranged at the very front, and everyone was seated.
Speeches were made, including one from King Azad's grandson, a man who'd
graduated from the collegia with honors and now lavished expensive gifts
upon it. The graduates, young men and women filled with hope, smiled as
they were led to the stone dais and laurel crowns were placed on their heads.
They were kissed in turn by each of the high scholars in attendance. At one
point Çeda caught Melis's attention, who was standing along the opposite
row of benches. Çeda gave a small shrug, which Melis returned before swinging her attention back toward the front of the assemblage, where the last few
students were stepping up the stone stairs.

Scholars, Çeda reminded herself. *They're now scholars.*

Most had gone back to their seats, but Çeda realized one had broken away
and was coming to stand by her. Tulathan's bright eyes, it was Davud. She'd
been struck in the bursar's office by how much he'd grown, and here it hit her
again. His curly hair, once brown, was now sunkissed, perhaps from more
work outside than Çeda would have given a young collegia student credit for.
She smiled, overtaken with joy at seeing someone, *anyone*, from Roseridge,
then took him into an embrace. She held him at arm's length, admiring him
properly.

"Well, well," she said softly as the closing speech began, "if the gods haven't shined on me this day."

"The pleasure is all mine," he replied easily.

And then she realized: around his neck hung a torc of fine gold wire, the ends shaped into ram's heads. It was a sign of a graduate completing his course of study with high honors. She shook her head, feeling like a proud sister. "You're *seventeen*, Davud. You can't be *graduating*."

He bowed his head, as a collegia debater might when conceding a point. "One of those assertions is most assuredly true."

She ran her fingers along the golden torc, then adjusted it, making the ends even over his collarbones. "And with honors!" She pretended to cry. "My little boy's all grown up."

Some of the old redness in his cheeks returned. "Master Amalos thought it time, is all."

"Well, I know Amalos well enough to say he wouldn't do such a thing if he didn't think you'd earned it. What will you do now? Return home?"

Davud brightened. "Master Amalos has agreed to keep me on. I'm to be given my own studies, and some day, my own students. But first I'll be visiting each of the four kingdoms' capitals." Davud ran his hand down his chest as if he were stroking a white, hoary beard, and said, in a white, hoary accent, "To deepen my pitiful understanding of their customs and histories."

She could hear Amalos saying those words. "And to learn their tongues?" she asked in Kundhunese.

"Not merely to learn them," he replied in equally passable Kundhunese, "but to *know* them." He returned to speaking Sharakhan. "I've chosen to study language. How it's changed, how it's *still* changing."

"Breath of the desert, how I'd love to do that," Çeda said.

She could see the look of optimism in his eyes, as if to say, *you could, you know.* "And you?" he asked. "Have you done what you'd hoped to do?"

To this, Çeda merely smiled, while at the front of the assemblage, the kettledrums took up a slower, more playful beat. The scholars formed a column in the central aisle, ready for their return march to the basilica. Their pride shone like the coming dawn.

"That's your cue," Çeda said.

He bowed his head. "Of course." He hesitated, as if he wanted to say more, but then repeated, "Of course," and left, waving once before jogging after the others.

Çeda felt relieved. It seemed Zeheb had been wrong. Or perhaps the Host had never been targeting this ceremony after all. Or perhaps they'd smelled the trap. Whatever the case, the last of the students filed through the basilica doors to receive their final words from the collegia masters.

Hardly had the doors closed, however, when a war cry came from Çeda's left. She turned as shouts of surprise were followed by cries of pain.

"Here! Here!" cried one of the Silver Spears.

The audience looked fearful and skittish, like a wing of skylarks the moment before they lifted into the sky. Çeda stood tall as she reached into the slit worked into her dress and drew River's Daughter. She crouched, neatly splitting her dress on both sides up to her thighs. Everyone nearby stared at her, waiting.

"To the basilica!" she shouted, pointing them, shoving some away.

The shouts came louder, the crash of battle rising above the growing fear. The crowd parted, most running toward the basilica doors where a group of Silver Spears stood at the ready, ushering everyone inside.

On the far side, from between two buildings, a loose unit of men and women loped toward the forum. They wore thick leather armor and iron helms with chain mail that lapped against their shoulders. They held shields at the ready, shamshirs carried low. Blood marked their eyes, their noses, their mouths, as if they'd been anointed in some way, prepared by Thaash himself for this very battle.

A dozen had charged ahead of the others, screaming, eyes maniacal, but many more trailed behind. The Silver Spears engaged, but they stood no chance against so many. Like gods of war stepping from mist, Sümeya, Melis, and Yndris emerged from the crowd, their ebon blades in hand. They joined Çeda, and together the four of them ran to meet the onslaught. Two more hands of Maidens approached while ahead, arrows streaked in from the Kings' bowmen stationed on the rooftops. One of the attackers fell when a black arrow drove through his knee, but he got up straightaway and limped forward. The others took arrow after arrow, hardly slowing their plodding gait.

Their eyes were crazed. They bellowed nonsensical words as they met the charge of the Maidens. There were so many that some merely ran past. It was clear their target was the basilica.

And then Çeda was among the enemy, sword swinging, the cries of her enemy rising around her. At first she maintained discipline, keeping the proper distance with Melis on her left and Sümeya on her right, but all too soon everything around her was madness.

She deflected a swing from the man before her and felt for his heartbeat, for the beat of the woman next to him as well. They came to her with surprising ease. The drums of their hearts played as she parried a swing from the woman, as she retreated half a step and leaned away from a heavy, overreaching swing from the man. Then she sliced River's Daughter, the blade cutting halfway through his arm. It hung ineffectively yet still he fought on, his face maniacal as he swung with his right and the woman lunged for Çeda's midsection.

After two ringing blocks of the man's sword, blood spraying in a river from his nearly severed arm, Çeda kicked the woman away, then brought her dark shamshir around and sliced the warrior's legs to the bone. He hardly seemed to care. He swung wildly for her, but fell, his wounds gushing red, eyes rage-filled as he screamed, "Death! Death to the Kings! Long live the Thirteenth Tribe!"

All around, the battle raged. The ring of metal on metal pierced the battle like the cries of an eagle. The heartbeats around her became a symphony of drums. Two more blood-marked warriors approached, though with more care than the others. Çeda engaged them, retreating, being saved by Sümeya more than once, moving to guard Melis's and Yndris's flanks when she found herself free of opponents.

She and her sister Maidens were soon surrounded. She took a cut along her hip that bit through what light armor she wore. She took another along her forearm. But strangely, this calmed her. With so many enemies near, with so much noise and the wildness of the battle, she'd lost her center, but the pain coursing through her hip and arm carried her back to the place she needed to be more effectively than mere concentration ever could. She felt those around her, the one ahead, the two behind, Sümeya on her right, Melis on her left. She narrowed in on the enemy, blending together sight and hearing, the feel of the heat from their bodies and the rhythmic pounding of their blades against hers. She brought herself in sync with the beating heart of the man in front of her and *pressed*. Despite his crazed expression, his wild movements, he seemed to catch himself and, in that moment, Çeda blocked his sword high and slashed at an angle across his neck.

She ducked and rolled away, feeling more than seeing the arc of a shamshir behind her. The sword slashed overhead, sinking deep into the rib cage of a hulking swordsman. The blade was momentarily caught, enough for Çeda to lift and swing River's Daughter across the woman's undefended midsection.

Others charged in, maniacal in their thirst for Maidens' blood, but Çeda and the others were in control. She felt them—Sümeya, Melis, even Yndris— and knew they felt her as well. In this moment they were one, a congregation of blades, spinning, twisting, biting through bone and muscle and armor alike.

Nearby, the enemy had thinned, but from the forum's northeast corner, near the stout garrison, more were arriving. They were met by Kameyl's unit of Silver Spears, who were now pouring forth from the monolith of the garrison. "Go," Sümeya said, pointing toward the basilica. "Protect the graduates." And then she was sprinting toward Kameyl, the skirt of her blood-streaked dress flowing behind her.

Melis pointed toward the stout basilica doors, where two dozen blood-fueled warriors were in a pitched battle with half as many Silver Spears. Together, Çeda, Yndris, and Melis swept over the ground toward them, Melis leading them screaming, *"Lai, lai, lai!"*

Strangely, there were no archers on the nearby buildings. Some stood on more distant rooftops, launching arrows to stall the enemy's advance, but none stood here. Çeda smelled the same curious odor as before—something acrid and foul—but all too soon she was engaged with no time to think on it. The men of the Moonless Host raged, shouting curses against the Kings. Çeda had only just crossed blades with the nearest of them when she spotted one of the Silver Spears to her left. He lay prone, arms splayed, with what looked to be a small tuft of red feathers sticking from his neck.

She blocked a blow and retreated, then saw a dot of red blossom on the back of Melis's neck. Melis immediately ducked and stepped away, feeling for whatever it was that had struck her. She tried to pull something free from her skin—a small dart, Çeda realized.

Çeda gave a rising whistle—*enemy behind, beware!*—as Melis slumped to the ground. Together, Çeda and Yndris retreated. Three of enemy's soldiers followed. As Çeda and Yndris engaged them, another red dart streaked in, narrowly missing Yndris and striking the woman she was fighting in the cheek. The woman stumbled, eyes blinking, confused, and Yndris took her down.

As Yndris engaged the last of them, a man with a long beard matted in blood, Çeda spun around. The myrrh trees, she realized. The dart had seemed to come in from a high angle, and the trees were well-tended and fully fledged in thick green leaves. Their mushroom-shaped tops could easily hide one of the enemy. Making sure to keep moving, she scanned through the leaves of the nearest. Soon she spotted the silhouette of a willowy man hiding within, saw something long and straight lift to his lips.

In that moment she took a deep breath. She raised her sword, the flat of the blade angled toward the tree, and released her breath as her heart synced with that of the man in the tree. She *felt* his puff of breath as a streak of red flew out from within the leaves. She adjusted the blade, heard a ping as something tapped against River's Daughter. The puffy red end of a dart appeared in the well-trodden ground at her feet.

Knowing she had only moments, she took three long strides, dropped River's Daughter among the roots of the tree, and leapt. Her shoes gripped the bark as she powered herself up between the lowest branches. In the shadows, partially obscured by the boughs, she saw not a *man* hiding in the tree, but a boy, hardly more than ten. He was loading another dart into his blowpipe with quivering hands. She never gave him the chance to finish. She snaked through the branches and then swung her body, legs first, catching him full in the chest.

He flew backward, arms flailing, blowpipe twirling away. He thumped hard against the ground, breath whooshing from his lungs. As Çeda dropped and collected River's Daughter, he rolled over, clutching his stomach, trying to regain his breath. He managed one wheezing inhalation before Çeda snaked her arm around his neck and squeezed until he lost consciousness. She left him there, limp but still breathing, and rushed back toward the basilica doors.

Yndris was still engaged with the same man, who was bloody from head to toe. She was hammering her shamshir against the man's own, her face as mad as the mindless scarabs around them. With a cry she disarmed the scarab with a powerful blow, then opened him up with a deep cut to the ribs. Only three of the Moonless Host's warriors remained, but they fought like mad-men, continuing to battle even with terrible wounds.

What drove them so? This went well beyond mere fervor or hatred for the Kings. Was it an alchemycal mixture of some sort? Or the blood on their faces, perhaps drawn by the hand of a red mage? *Either way, dear Nalamae, please see to it that Emre isn't among them.* Çeda cut the last man down from behind, wishing none of this were happening to her city, wishing she hadn't been forced to play a part in it. But these were hard truths. *War is war. The will of the Kings must be opposed, and the price they'd set for peace was blood.*

With the enemy nearby all fallen, Çeda hurried to Melis. Her pulse was weak. There was nothing to do about it now, though. She had to hope Melis would live long enough for the Matrons to attend to her. Çeda had just smelled the acrid odor again when one of the Silver Spears who'd fought with them collapsed. She thought it might be loss of blood, a wound of some sort, but as she stepped closer, the man next to him collapsed as well. Both had been standing near the basilica doors.

"Step away," Çeda said to Yndris.

Yndris stared at her as if she were craven. "Gather your courage, girl." When she moved toward the fallen men, Çeda grabbed the back of her dress to stop her, and Yndris spun and slapped Çeda's hand away. "What do you think you're doing? Accompany me into that building or my father, your Lord King, will hear of it!"

"Can you not smell it? Take one breath near that door, and you'll fall to whatever is leaking from the basilica"—she motioned to the unconscious men—"as they have."

"Then take a breath, you bloody mule, and follow."

Three times Yndris pumped her lungs like a forge bellows, then she picked up one of the spears dropped by the city guardsmen and ran for the door. Using the butt of the spear, she knocked out the small stained-glass window set eye-level in the center of the rightmost door, then reached inside and pulled up the wooden bar. With the bar gone, she pulled the door open and rushed inside. Çeda followed and was assaulted by a noxious smell, the same one she'd smelled earlier during the ceremony but hadn't been able to place.

There was no smoke or fumes that she could see, but her eyes immediately began to water, and her nose was irritated by a prickling sensation that was so strong she lost air to a short cough before recovering.

The center of the basilica was dominated by an arcade of impressive polished granite arches that supported three upper floors and a grand ceiling of elegant, crisscrossed supports. The lower floor had dozens of wooden desks and chairs with aisles in between. The center of the space was where the scholars were to have waited with the collegia staff. But they weren't there. The guards were, though all were unconscious, as were the masters. But the scholars? There were none.

Çeda thought perhaps they'd fled from the other exit, the one leading to the street opposite the forum, but she saw now the door was still barred. There were no signs of conflict or bloodshed. If the soldiers of the Moonless Host had somehow found their way here, the guards would have fought them. She supposed it was possible they had waited until everyone inside had been knocked unconscious by the gas, but if so, how could they have taken the students from the building without being seen?

Yndris stared angrily at Çeda, as if she were withholding the answers to the mystery. Çeda pointed to the upper floors. The graduates might have fled there if they'd feared an attack. And yet when she took one of the winding sets of stairs up to the second floor, there was no sign of them.

Blood of the gods, could they all have fled the building and someone barred the door behind them? Perhaps, but it seemed unlikely that *all* of them would have left. Surely some would have fallen to the gas. They might have been ordered to hide somewhere in the building Çeda hadn't yet searched, but if so, why wouldn't the masters have hidden in the same place? They had no more ability to fight than the scholars did. Less so, in fact.

In the end she and Yndris were forced to leave. They cleared the doors and headed into the wind to avoid breathing in any of the gas that might be blown in their direction. When they entered the basilica again, they searched for the source of the gas. In the northwest corner of the building they found it: two clay pots with a brownish liquid bubbling inside them. Çeda and Yndris took one pot each, then ran outside. After setting them downwind, clear of any of the nearby buildings, they backed away. They gasped, hands on their knees, as a wracking cough seized them both. Yndris vomited. Their eyes were reddened and puffy. Snot ran freely from their noses, forcing them to wipe it away with their sleeves.

On the far side of the forum the battle still raged, but Çeda and Yndris both knew the battle had been nothing more than a massive feint. The Host had been after the graduates all along. They were trying to pull off some grand trick, and Çeda was sure they had only moments to unravel the mystery before it was too late.

"Where could they have gone?" Yndris asked, staring at the basilica doors. "To a cellar, perhaps? To the roof?"

Çeda shook her head. "No. They were taken."

"How?"

How, indeed? Where might they have gone? As Çeda stared at the nearby buildings, her mind went to the tunnels beneath the city. Davud had shown her some to get from the Well in the western quarter of Sharakhai to the scriptorium tower's cellar. Why couldn't there be more? "Are there tunnels that lead to the basilica?"

Yndris seemed caught off guard. "Of course not." But her tone made it clear she wasn't certain of the answer. She too began looking to the other buildings, but Çeda was already running toward the fight raging on the opposite side of the forum. Çeda whistled a winding series of notes, the ones that identified their hand uniquely, a call for Kameyl and Sümeya to attend them.

Kameyl was deep in the battle, but Sümeya, fighting near the back, disengaged and ran toward them. "The scholars have been taken from the basilica," Çeda said when she came near. "All of them. Are there any tunnels leading to nearby buildings?"

Sümeya stared at the basilica, then swung her gaze to the old garrison, a dull stone among the brighter jewels of the collegia's more modern buildings. Sümeya's eyes were calculating. She glanced back at the battle, but then motioned Yndris and Çeda toward the garrison. "Come with me."

Over the gravel they flew, through the green bushes bordering the mall, across the cobblestone street. They reached the stairs leading up to the garrison's stout, iron-bound doors. Çeda expected them to be barred, but the rightmost door creaked open at Sümeya's touch. All three of them—Sümeya, Yndris, and Çeda, had swords in hand as Sümeya pushed the door fully open. Just inside, three guardsmen lay dead.

Down a short hallway, in a large, open room, stood a man by a barrel. He stared at the three of them with a sickening gleam in his eyes. He was old. Blood streaked down over his eyes and cheeks in a haunting pattern. His long beard was matted with dried blood. In one hand he held a brass lantern. In the relative darkness, it cast strange shadows against his craggy face.

Sümeya came to a halt, clearly wary. "Who are you?"

"The one sent to kill you," the man said, his voice cracking with age.

Sümeya took one step forward, her movements measured, neither too quick nor too slow. "Where are the scholars?"

The man smiled like a thief who'd just stumbled upon a bag of golden rahl. "Gone, gone, gone! Taken from beneath your very noses!"

Çeda tried to reach out, to feel for more who were here, but for some reason she could barely feel the man's heartbeat, let alone others. Yndris had moved to the left of Sümeya. Çeda stood on Sümeya's right. There was a trap here, but what?

With a dire grin, the man reached down and lifted something from the top of the barrel. And then Çeda realized there were no barrel rings around the barrel, neither along the bottom nor near the top. No sooner had she noticed than Yndris started running toward the man.

"Yndris, stop!" Çeda called, sprinting after her.

The man pulled the rope, and the barrel staves fell outward like the petals of a blossom. Thick, golden liquid spread in all directions. As it rushed over the floor like charging cavalry, the man lifted the lantern high.

Çeda managed to catch Yndris's arm and pull hard. Yndris was so fixated on reaching the man she fell in a tangled heap. The lantern shattered. The oil lit with a whoosh. In the center of this spartan place, a sun was lit, its center fixed on the man as he laughed, raising his arms high. "So the Kings tumble!" he screamed. "So the Kings fall!"

Çeda tried to pull Yndris to her feet, but Yndris fought her. "Release me!" she screamed, and fell backward.

The oil caught up with her, soaking into her left sleeve as Sümeya rushed in and pulled her up by the bodice of her dress. The oil caught Sümeya's skirt and crept beneath Çeda's shoes, but the two of them managed to pull Yndris to her feet and run.

The flames followed. The sound of it roared, drowning out the madman as his laughs turned to screams. They burst from the building as the oil rushed out and flowed down the stairs, making the garrison look like an elder god spitting fire and hatred. Çeda slipped her burning shoes from her feet. Sümeya used her ebon blade to cut her own skirt free.

Yndris's right sleeve was still aflame. She tried to pat it out, until Çeda grabbed a fistful of cloth at the shoulder and yanked downward in one hard motion, ripping the sleeve away. Sümeya did the same to Yndris's skirt, leaving her looking like a poorly made rag doll, but she was free of the fire.

For a moment, the man's screams reached a fever pitch, but then they simply stopped. The fire continued to rage. It burned with bright white intensity, with licks of darker colors, green and turquoise and blue. Kameyl rejoined them. The battle was nearly ended, the last of the Moonless Host's maniacal scarabs being cut down at last. As they fell, more and more of the Kings' warriors turned to look up at the garrison. Here and there along the base, flame was burning *through* the gaps in the stones. Those gaps widened. The stones themselves began to slump like blown glass.

"Back away!" Sümeya called.

And everyone did, moments before the front half of the garrison collapsed. Stone walls buckled, then gave altogether. Four stories crumbled, coughed away from the rest of the building, spreading like a fistful of pebbles dropped by a child. Stone and fire mixed, smoke roiling upward. The earth itself rumbled like the day of reckoning.

For the first time, Çeda truly saw the Al'afwa Khadar's destructive ways through the eyes of a Blade Maiden. She felt like the old children's tale, the moth in the maelstrom. She had so little control over what was happening to Sharakhai, to the desert. And she wondered where she and the city and all those she loved would wind up when it was finally over.

You assume too much, Çeda mused. *It may never end. This struggle may flow beyond your precious years.*

Some continued to watch the burning building for a time, but there was work to be done. Wounded to tend to. After watching perhaps longer than she should have Çeda turned away, to help as she could.

Chapter 23

THE MORNING AFTER THEIR ORDEAL WITH GUHLDRATHEN, during the false dawn, Ramahd waited on the dunes with Meryam by his side. A bare mist was forming, slipping over the dunes as the cool of the night was slowly replaced by the warmth of the day.

The desert was a harsh mistress, but Ramahd had been studying her ways for years. After the Bloody Passage, in which his daughter, and almost all the other survivors of that tragedy, had died of thirst, he'd promised it would never happen to him again, and so he'd found those watering holes that existed. He'd studied the flora and fauna of the desert so that he could, if need be, survive. Ignoring the objections from both Meryam and Dana'il, he'd tested himself in the desert for no less than seventeen days and seventeen nights.

It had meant days of travel over open sand as he moved from oasis to oasis, but he'd forced himself never to rely on a single watering hole. He'd painstakingly collected the tiny, bitter leaves from firebushes and eaten them for their hunger-sapping effects. He'd used a rock to form and sharpen a crude spear, which he'd used in the mornings to stab lizards as they crawled out from under the rocks they used for their warmth in the night. He'd found it grueling, and there were days when he wondered if he'd survive, but he had, and he'd returned to Sharakhai hardened. He'd built a fire on his last night in the desert and feasted on an addax calf he'd taken down with his spear. He hadn't been proud of taking such a young animal, but he'd thought it a sign from Alu or perhaps even one of the desert gods that he'd done well, and he didn't wish to insult them.

Ahead of where Ramahd and Meryam waited, forms scuttled from the troughs between the dunes, hundreds, thousands of them. They crawled up along the windward side, stopping just before they reached the crest.

"Watch them now," Ramahd said to Meryam.

She did, though with a numb expression. The beetles spread their wings, tipping their backsides toward the wind. The mist collected on their wing covers, at which point they'd close them and gather the water to drink.

Ramahd walked along the dune to the nearest of them, then picked up a beetle and sucked what moisture he could from it. It wasn't much. A drop or two. But it was something. He continued this way, beetle after beetle, motioning for Meryam to do the same. She stared at the beetles, then Ramahd, then closed her eyes and shook her head as if she were wondering how all this had come to pass. But when she opened her eyes again, there was some small spark in them. She trudged over, weak and shaking. Every time Ramahd had offered her help she'd refused, so he remained silent, ready to rush to her should she collapse. She picked up a beetle, sucked moisture from it with a pinched expression on her face, then tossed it aside like a pistachio shell.

"Eat some," Ramahd said, then crunched down on one of the wriggling things. "We don't know when we'll be able to eat again."

She stared at him sidelong. He thought she would refuse, but a moment later, she crunched down on one. She chewed and swallowed, taking rather a long time to do so, but ate another a moment later, faster this time.

Soon the sun had risen, burning away the mist. The beetles fled back beneath the sand, and the two of them were off toward the nearest of the drinkable watering holes he knew of, or as near to it as he'd been able to judge from the late evening stars.

Ramahd spotted it near nightfall. He might have missed it entirely, but he'd been watching carefully for any signs of birds, and a few had flown in from the south, passing overhead and gliding down toward it. It was a small

234

thing, secreted between two rocky strips of land. There was green vegetation surrounding the crescent-shaped oasis. Such a strange sight. Leagues of sand, but here, a strip of water reflecting the bright orange sky, emerald ribbons along the bank framing it like the setting for a flaming jewel.

They reached the water and drank deeply. It tasted foul, but it would sustain them until they reached the next.

Meryam plopped herself down on the bank, her dress fanning around her. She took off her shoes, set them carefully by her side, put her feet in the water, and stared intently into the crystal-clear depths as if it might reveal her future like King Yusam's mere. After a time, she pulled her legs up and hugged them, looking for all the world like a lost little girl.

"I am the queen," Meryam said after a time.

"What?" Ramahd asked, pausing in his task of collecting dates from a nearby palm.

"I am now the Queen of Qaimir."

It was true. Ramahd had thought of it several times that day, but hadn't wanted to bring it up; it made no difference, not until they reached the safety of Sharakhai.

Ramahd sat next to her. After removing his boots, then his socks, he put his feet in the warm water next to hers. "You are."

"What ever will I do with a kingdom? I wasn't meant for such things. Indio was meant for the throne, or Yasmine after he died. I never thought . . ."

"Well," Ramahd said, motioning to the dunes beyond the palms and desert ferns that lined the water, "who's to say that skinny little arse of yours will ever reach the throne?"

Meryam glared at him, but then looked out over the desert, a florid purple landscape with the sun's passing. And then she laughed. She laughed so hard she nearly fell in the water, and when Ramahd grabbed her arm to keep her from falling in, she lay on the grass and laughed at the sky. "The throne of Qaimir is years and worlds away."

It was a common refrain in Qaimir among its lords and ladies, referring to how very few would ever get to sit the throne, no matter how much they might like to. And here she was, the kingdom given to her by the callous act of a fellow blood mage—albeit a foreign one—and a merciless ehrekh.

Meryam seemed to feel this connection as well, for just then she rubbed her hand on her forehead, where not so long ago Hamzakiir's blood had marked her and Guhldrathen's forked tongue had licked the sigil away. She rubbed harder, then took some water up with one hand and did so again. Then she was splashing into the water, clothes and all, rubbing viciously at the place where she'd been marked.

"Meryam, stop it."

She didn't. She rubbed even harder, thrashing in the water, screaming in rage or impotence or both.

"Meryam!" He dropped into the water and grabbed her hands. "Stop it!"

"I've done a terrible thing, Ramahd." Her tears mixed with the water, and she cried, falling into his arms, sobbing against his chest. He held her, brushing her hair from her face, running one hand along her back as they listened only to each other's breath. Their toes squished into the mud. Nearby, beetles began to buzz.

"It was a mistake," he spoke softly. "He was more powerful than we'd guessed."

Meryam's hand reached up to touch his cheek. His neck. For a long while they remained this way, standing in the water, two souls comforting one another in an embrace that belied her years of cold, bitter behavior. She pressed her lips to his neck, merely resting there against his skin, but then she was kissing him.

He tightened, but it only made her pull him closer. She stitched ardent kisses across his neck. She raked his hair until she had a fistful of it. She craned his neck back until he stared at the sky, a willing prisoner to her affection. A bare few stars lit the field of dusty gray above. One, the brightest, felt like a soul he'd known—Yasmine, perhaps, watching his betrayal from the farther fields.

"Meryam," Ramahd said.

She ignored him, pulling his shirt out, her fingers now working at the ties to his trousers.

"Meryam."

"Be quiet." She shoved him backward against the bank until he was lying on the reeds they'd matted down. "Your queen wills it." She pulled his trousers halfway down. Still in the water herself, she stroked him while placing warm, wet kisses along his thighs, over his hips, over his stomach. Then she took him in her mouth, and he gasped in pleasure and pain as she—sometimes roughly, sometimes tenderly—ran lips and tongue over his hardening cock.

As he watched her, his pleasure mounting, he saw small glimpses of the old Meryam: the beautiful younger sister of his dead wife. He saw the Meryam who had been carefree, if inclined to dark thoughts. How far they'd come since then, their days spent in Viaroza or in the capital or occasionally traveling the country together, going from city to city and sampling the food, a thing he, Yasmine, and Meryam had all enjoyed immensely. And now they were reduced to this: Yasmine dead, Meryam a shadow of the woman she once was, Ramahd vowed to take the head of his wife's murderer but too often being swept along by currents he was unable to see, much less control.

Meryam climbed out of the water. She stripped and stood over him, naked, staring deeply into his eyes, daring him to turn his gaze from her, to deny her what she sought.

He didn't. He waited for her to lower herself down, then guided himself inside her. She gasped as she fell over him, her cold skin now pressed against his as he wrapped his arms around her and thrust slowly into her. He saw the star again, twinkling, shining bright. But now other stars joined it. More of the dead, gathered to see some small glimpse of those they would never touch again, not until they too passed beyond the darkling veil.

"I'm sorry," he whispered to the star.

Meryam rose enough to stare into his eyes. She looked so very desperate still, but something else had kindled inside her: a glimmer, like the most distant of fires. It wasn't passion, or not entirely. It was an undeniable lust for life, a thing he hadn't seen in her since the desert when she'd taken Hamzakiir in a clash of brightfire. "What is it?" she asked, halting her movements.

Ramahd couldn't take his eyes from her. He didn't want to. "Nothing," he said, then drew her to him.

Meryam kissed Ramahd deeply, riding him faster now, breath halting noisily through her nose. She shuddered once, twice. Her body convulsed, and then she broke her kiss and arched her back to look up at the sky. Ramahd kissed her breasts, holding her waist as he thrust into her over and over. As he was drawn over the edge as well, Meryam looked down at him with an expression of simple passion, of joy in the physical form. He'd never seen her look so beautiful.

After, they lay there a long while, their bodies becoming one as night fell over the desert and the chittering, buzzing insects came to life.

Ramahd and Meryam traveled from oasis to oasis, taking care to drink their fill and carry extra water in the hollowed-out bulbs of the small cacti that often grew along the wadis that funneled water into the oases. Eating was difficult, but Ramahd created a spear as he'd done on his self-imposed exile and managed to take a few lizards and snakes so they might fill their bellies with something besides beetles and sweetgrass.

He even made a fire one night using tinder from the bark and dried leaves of a date palm and a hand drill he fashioned with his knife. There was no fruit on the palm, but the fire was a welcome solace, a thing that felt so foreign the two of them stared at it for long hours, lost in thought. When it had died to embers and flickering flames, they lay next to it and made love, their own warmth mixing with that of the fire, creating something like comfort for a short while, at least until the two of them were lying next to one another and the very real possibility returned that they would die before they reached Sharakhai.

The days wore on, stretching into weeks. The food was spare, as was the water when he misjudged the distance between oases. But when that happened, they would rest for an extra day at the next one and gather their strength. They would gain nothing by rushing this journey, and they stood to lose everything if they took one misstep too many.

Ramahd thought Meryam might withdraw from him, seeing their love-making for the mistake that it was, but each night when the sun set and the stars stormed across the sky, she would take him in her arms, kiss him, draw him down to the sand or into the warm water of the oases. It seemed right, somehow, a part of this strange landscape they found themselves traversing.

Meryam seemed to be gaining weight. This in itself wasn't surprising; she'd been so thin, so skeletal, that any amount of regular sustenance was sure to put meat on her. More surprising by far was the fact that she was eating regularly. She never once complained about the food Ramahd offered her—no matter how strange or offensive—and she always ate as much as he recommended.

"I wish I had a plate of fekkas," she said one evening after chewing and swallowing a tiny live lizard. "How I'd grown to hate them, Ramahd, but I would eat a dozen platefuls were they set before me now."

"I'll make them for us when we reach Sharakhai."

She smiled then, a healthy glimmer in her eye. "When we reach Sharakhai, I fear I shall eat the city whole, every stone, every bone, every happy king's throne." It was a line from a nursery rhyme about a giant who was tricked by a witch into eating an entire city, the home of a king who had once done her harm.

"Now the only way out is to pay the old crone," Ramahd said, completing the line. She laughed, a sound that nourished his soul, and he laughed with her.

As they entered their third week of travel, rare clouds came, providing welcome shade for their daytime trek. They made good time to the next oasis, but Ramahd was almost certain they'd reached the last of the easily accessible watering holes they would find between here and Sharakhai. The rest were few and far between, and would be much harder to find.

"Leave that to me," Meryam said the next morning.

For hours she searched the ground carefully, looking for he knew not what. Eventually she picked up a stone that looked rather like the hull of a ship—rounded with a keel-like ridge on one side, flat on the other. She used one end of it to press deeply into her thumb, drawing blood.

Ramahd knew her nature, and yet the sudden return of her abilities felt strange. The two of them had been traveling almost as husband and wife for long enough that this sudden reminder of who they were and all they'd promised to do felt like a sudden storm from the seas, a thing that carried with it the troubles they'd set aside since Guhldrathen had stalked away on that cursed plain.

"It's better if we both do it," Meryam said, handing the bloody stone out for him to take.

"What will it do?"

She shrugged, as if this were nothing. "It should be enough to summon a ship, if any are near."

He continued to stare at it, not wanting to don that life once more. "You might have done it two weeks ago if that's what you meant to do."

"I might have died if I'd tried it then. And besides, if you think the ships of the wandering tribes go anywhere near that blasted heath, you're daft." She shook the stone at him. "Take it. The time is ripe, I think."

Ramahd took the stone and pressed it into his thumb. He knew as well as she that without the use of her magic, the chances of dying were high. They'd been lucky so far. To continue unaided was to gamble with their lives. And yet, it felt like doing this wiped the ink from the story they'd been writing these past many days, a story he'd hoped to explore further.

"What are you waiting for, Ramahd?"

He looked down at his hands. He hadn't drawn any blood.

"It's only . . ."

She looked at him as if she knew exactly what he was feeling. "It's only what, Ramahd?" she asked in that tone of hers, the one that seemed to devalue anything that stood between her and what she wanted.

It's such a very long road at times, he wanted to say to her. He wanted to erase all that had happened since they'd arrived in Viaroza. But he couldn't, and they both knew it.

He pressed the stone into his thumb until the edge bit and drew blood. He let the blood pool, then ran it along the red line Meryam had already drawn. It looked for a moment like a ship riding a blood-red sea. When he held it out for Meryam to take, she took it gently, emotion showing in her eyes—for him, for her father, for Yasmine, he couldn't tell—then she threw the rock toward the deeper desert.

It landed with a splash of amber, the sand somehow swallowing it whole.

A pair of ships arrived at the small oasis the following morning. They'd gone off course in a terrible sandstorm, they told Ramahd when they arrived, watching the two of them warily. Meryam greeted them politely, more reserved than she would normally be, knowing the tribes' propensity to distrust aggressive women. They spoke to Ramahd, asking him what happened, and he told them enough lies to convince them that a lord and lady from Qaimir might end up here: a whim to voyage to the Shangazi and see its grandeur for themselves.

The tribesmen—men and women of tribe Oran, judging from their flowing blue thawbs and dresses—had merely nodded, sharing looks as if to say: *And what would a man and woman of the rain-filled south know of the Great Shangazi?*

"We can take you on our ships if you wish," they said to him.

"Where are you headed?" Ramahd asked.

"To Sharakhai," came the expected reply, "to trade for steel. From there you can arrange your return home."

"We would be most grateful," Ramahd said, allowing some of the relief he was feeling to shine through. "To Sharakhai it is."

Chapter 24

DAVUD'S EYES FLUTTERED OPEN.

Sweat rolled down his scalp. Made his skin itch. It was morning, wasn't it? If it was this hot already, it was going to be a sweltering day in Sharakhai.

He felt strange. Sick. As if the world were spinning, as if the floor itself were pitching this way then that. A weight rolled against him. His heart beat like a tambour. No. It was *another* heart, not his own. A dream? It felt like a dark presence looming, a thief unseen yet palpably present.

I'm good and drunk, Davud decided. The celebrations after the graduation. He'd been invited to three. He'd accepted them all, not wanting to disappoint. He'd promised to go to Anila's in Blackfire Gate, but had decided to go there last in hope of spending a bit more time with Anila herself. His stomach turned over just thinking about it. Had he gone? Had he stopped by the others? Had he drunk so much araq he couldn't remember?

The floor pitched again, and a shushing sound entered his awareness, a sound he suspected had been there all along. Breath of the desert, it was so bloody *hot*. Sweat trickled down his temple, along the center of his chest, pooling there. He wanted so very badly to scratch it, but just then he was lying too firmly between dreams and waking.

He fought to find his memories, a battle that escalated quickly, with him on the losing side. He remembered going to the collegia grounds. He'd stood with his fellow students in the basilica. He'd hugged everyone. Smiles and laughing, talks of what the days ahead would mean for each of them. The sounds of drums had summoned them from the building. He'd received his laurel crown, hadn't he? Yes, because after, King Azad's grandson had delivered a speech. And he'd talked with Çeda. Gods, why did he always act like a little lost lamb whenever she was near?

And then it all came back in a rush. He'd been standing in the forum when the first of the bloodcurdling screams had come. Shouts had followed. They'd been funneled like goats into the basilica. A childlike fear of the unknown had followed. They all felt it, and as they'd stared into one another's eyes, their helplessness spun their fear into terror. They'd watched the doors, the high windows in the ceiling, the corners of the basilica's grand arcade, wondering when the attackers would arrive. They'd been warned there might be danger, but they'd also been assured they had the protection of the Kings.

Sounds of battle had approached. The clash of steel. Men and women dying, distant, then closer, then closer still. He'd smelled something strange. An earthy scent like mushrooms and garlic laced with the purest of alcohols. His eyes burned. The world around him had gone hazy. Colors trailed in his vision like paint smeared across canvas.

"Run!" he'd called, staggering toward the doors, blinking to clear away the muddiness in his mind. "It's in the air!"

He'd not gone five steps before the basilica floor had risen up and struck him in the face. It seemed only moments later when he'd woken here. But where *was* here? The groan of wood came. The lurching of the world around him. The snap of rope on canvas. Rigging, he realized. Gods, the rocking. The incessant hiss. He was on a *sandship*.

A thousand questions boiled up inside him. Where was the ship bound? Who commanded it? How many of his schoolmates were still alive? How many were here with him? How many of the enemy were there?

His breath was coming quickly now. Too quickly.

Calm, Davud. Calm. Calm yourself down.

Trying to reason with himself was only making matters worse. His throat constricted as the ship tipped upward and lurched as it crested a dune. He pushed himself up off the deck, stars swimming in his vision. Gods, he was going to pass out again.

It was the girl next to him that brought him back from the brink. Anila. She'd been lying next to him the whole time. She looked fragile, lying there with a circle of red just above her delicate eyebrows. And then a terrible thought occurred to him. He pressed his fingers against her neck. He felt nothing. He moved her so that she was lying flat on the deck where he'd been moments ago, then tried again. Thank the gods, he finally felt something. A pulse, but weak as the flow of the Haddah after a soft winter rain.

"Anila," he whispered in her ear. "It's Davud. Please wake."

She didn't respond. Nor did Jasur or Raji or Meiwei when he tried to wake them. But at least they were still alive. Collum was not. Kind Collum. Fair-skinned Collum. The boy from Qaimir, the son of a merchant who specialized in antiques from sailing ships of the southern seas. They sold well in Sharakhai. So many, even those in the kingdoms beyond the Great Shangazi, were fascinated by stories of the Austral Sea.

All of those trapped here in the hold had a circle of blood drawn on their foreheads, just above the eyebrows. He checked his own forehead, scraping away at the skin with a fingernail, finding flaking blood when he looked at it. Why had they all been marked? And why with blood?

The sound of footsteps passing just overhead pulled him from his reverie. They stopped, then went the other direction, aft. *Calm, Davud. Use reason to your advantage.* Clearly he and the others had somehow been transported to the ship, but how long ago? A day? A week? From the way they were all stacked here, thrown on top of one another like fish in a basket, it seemed unlikely that the crewmen above came down here to give them all drink. Davud's lips were dry, a bit chapped, but not overly so. The others were the same. They couldn't have been gone for more than a day or two, then. It might even be the same day!

Wait. He peered at the brightness on the dunes through the gaps in the hull. The ceremony had taken place in the afternoon, and it looked to be high sun now, so it was probably the next day. They might still be near Sharakhai, then. Perhaps close enough to return should he manage to escape.

He stood, cracking his head against the low beams above. He moved about the hold on uneven legs. He stepped over Anila, his other friends, to reach the rear, where a gap between the planks let in a good amount of light. He knelt and peered through the gap. He was at the aft of the ship, the golden sands of the Shangazi flowing away from him. As they crested a dune he scanned the horizon for any signs of Tauriyat, but there were none. Of course there weren't. They'd likely been sailing for six or seven hours, or more if the men who'd taken them had decided to sail through the night, which likely they had.

From somewhere above, a woman called, "Ho, tighten forward sail!" An echo of her command came moments later, "Aye, tightening forward sail!"

Davud picked at the dry rot on the wood. It practically powdered at his touch, flaking away and falling into the sand. He heard the squeak of a windlass being pulled, felt the ship list as they tilted over another dune, and all the while he scraped away at the wood. Larger pieces came free, falling dull and gray against the bright amber sand.

They'll see me. They'll see the pieces and come down here and bash my head in for trying to escape. By the gods, Davud, slow down! And yet the thoughts only made him move faster. The thought of widening this hole far enough to slip through drove him beyond the point of prudence. It felt as though one of the crew would come down the ladder and into the hold at any moment. Surely they came to check on them, to give them water. When they did, there would be no hiding what he'd done. It was now or never.

He pulled as much of the dry rot out as was going to come easily. The ship was old and in poor repair; the planks were not as sound as they once were, but he was weak and dizzy. It made for slow going. He gripped against the plank, his sandaled feet to the wood on either side, and strained, pulling mightily until it snapped.

He fell onto his rump, holding a hunk of wood the size of his head in his hands. The snap had been loud. And the sounds from above, movement, the shuffling of feet, had suddenly stopped.

He set the board down carefully. Looked to Anila, then Jasur, then Meiwei. He might try to stuff one of them through the hole first so that he'd have an ally. They could trek across the desert together.

But no, that was foolish. Even if he somehow managed to get one of them through the tight hole, they'd likely break their neck on the fall down to the sand, and even if they survived *that,* he'd likely be condemning them to death in the desert. He couldn't do that to them. Better to go on his own and get help, tell the Kings' men where the Host had gone.

"Farewell," he whispered, then angled himself through the gaping hole. His robe caught on the rough edges, but he managed to pull the snag free and inch further out. His hips were the most difficult, but a wale, a hull board thicker than the rest, ran just above the hole and he was able to grab its upper lip and work himself back and forth. He felt like a massive pickle being removed from a particularly stubborn jar.

"Captain," came a voice from above.

Davud froze, looking up toward the aft gunwale. He saw only blue skies, a piercing yellow sun.

"Yes, my lord Hamzakiir?" a voice replied, the same woman who'd called out the orders earlier.

"One of the scholars is attempting to escape through a hole in the rear of the ship."

The thud of booted feet. A woman's head peered over the side. She gave a broad smile, accentuating the scar running down across one eye, then she turned, looked up, and whistled, pointing down, where Davud was caught like a desert hare. A moment later, a man swung wide of the ship on a rope tied to the end of a yardarm, arcing expertly around the ship's stern.

Rhia's grace, the sailor was going to land right on top of him. Davud struggled to wriggle his way out, but his infernal robe caught again. He freed himself, swinging one leg out, ready to drop to the sand, but just then the swinging sailor clucked his tongue and fell hard across Davud's back. "Now, now, my little lizard," he said, the scent of his breath heavy with cumin and araq, "it wouldn't do to slither to the sand just yet."

Above, the captain whistled, flicking her hand up, and in as little time as it took Davud to cry out from the surprise of it, he and the sailor were hoisted upward. He tried to keep his grip, to remain in place, but was ripped free of the ship anyway. The two of them swung out over the sand, Davud's legs kicking like some naughty child who'd been swept up in his father's arms.

He and the sailor landed on the afterdeck, where a pilot manned the wheel, where the captain stood grinning, where a tall, gaunt man with a dark beard waited with hands clasped behind his back as if this sort of thing happened to him every day.

"What is your name," the gaunt man asked.

Davud looked around to the sailors gathering round, to the captain who waited with an aggressive sort of patience, then back to the man who was surely Hamzakiir, the blood mage, son of Külaşan the Wandering King. He thought of disobeying, of making a stand to retain his own free will, but after a moment, he decided to take another sort of stand entirely. "My name is Davud Mahzun'ava."

"And when did you awaken?"

"Half a turn ago," Davud replied. Then he shrugged. "No more than a full. It's difficult to remember."

Hamzakiir looked up to the sun, then to the wake the ship had made in the sand. He laughed silently, as if he found Davud's answer particularly amusing.

Davud pulled himself taller and said to Hamzakiir, "The blood on our foreheads is yours, isn't it?" He didn't know why he'd said it. He was more scared than he'd ever been in his life. But the vision of his friends lying there, marked, one of them dead with others likely to follow, spurred him.

Hamzakiir seemed amused by the question. "It is."

"Why?"

"Too keep you docile. To keep you safe."

"Safe . . ." Davud wanted to laugh. "Safe for what purpose?"

"A more salient question, don't you think? But I'm afraid you'll have to wait for the answer until we speak again." He nodded to someone behind Davud.

Davud only had time to turn his head before a hand was around his neck and a cloth was placed over his mouth. It smelled the same as it had in the basilica, an earthy, alcohol burn. He knew he shouldn't breathe it in, but in his terror he took in a lungful.

The brightness of the desert slowly went dark, and in those final moments, he saw Hamzakiir staring at him, not with anger, but with amusement.

Amusement, and curiosity.

Chapter 25

A
T HIGH SUN TWO DAYS AFTER the abduction of the collegia graduates, a horn blew from the uppermost tower of Eventide. It resounded over Sharakhai, a lamentation for the fallen who had been taken so unjustly by the Al'afwa Khadar. From her vantage in the courtyard of the House of Maidens, Çeda could see hundreds lining the walls of Kiral's palace, watching silently as the procession began. Among them would be the families of the dead, by and large the highborn of Sharakhai, but a number who hailed from the desert's neighboring kingdoms as well.

Another, deeper horn followed the first, this from Husamettín's palace. A third followed, higher-pitched, and a fourth, higher still. Çeda could see the mourners standing along the walls of those palaces as well. The cynical side of her wanted to believe that the Kings had ordered the attendance of their servants and soldiers to make their sorrow appear deeper than it was, but as she looked on the tearful faces of those who waited with her in the courtyard— dozens of Maidens and hundreds of Silver Spears—she knew it wasn't so. Too many in Sharakhai treasured the collegia. Even those in the Shallows revered it, considering it hallowed ground, for what greater pursuits were there in life than love and learning?

They've overstepped at last, Çeda thought. *The Moonless Host have reached too far in their thirst for revenge. They have driven a stake through the very heart of the city.*

The battle in the forum had ended shortly after the fire in the garrison. Inquisitors from the House of Maidens were dispatched to investigate, questioning survivors found on collegia grounds and in the surrounding neighborhoods. What they found with the help of the King of Whispers was that shortly after the battle had begun, three wagons had pulled up behind the garrison. Men poured from within, attacking the garrison's only other entrance. They'd gained entry in short order, and later one witness reported seeing young men and women being carried out from the rear of the garrison. They were laid in the wagons, stacked like cordwood, and then driven away. The wagons had been traced to the Trough and then to the Wheel, the city's largest open space where traffic was thick, the noise thicker, and the sheer press of humanity difficult for anyone to deal with. Little wonder the Moonless Host had taken their spoils there. It would be difficult for anyone to remember the passing of a few nondescript wagons.

Where the Host had taken the graduates from there no one knew. The bigger question was *why* they'd been taken. What did the Host have to gain by abducting the young men and women who would be the least likely to do them harm? Was it not the scholars who were urging for peace in the desert? They would never come out and ask for the Kings to treat with the Moonless Host, but it was implied in many of their pacifist writings.

Çeda wondered if this had been Macide's doing or his father's. This was bolder than anything they'd done in a long while. Perhaps they'd grown desperate. Or it might be due to Hamzakiir's presence? They'd raised him for a purpose, after all, and the scarabs *had* had bloody symbols on their faces.

More than ever, she wished she could speak with Emre. He might have answers, but the deeper part of her, the part that had known him since they were children, simply wanted to know he was safe. *Well of course he isn't safe. None of us are; not any longer.*

From the palaces above, new horns joined the chorus, each adding their own unique voice until a dirge of eleven horns were sounding in unison. All but dead Külaşan's now rang, but a short while later—a respectful pause to distinguish Sharakhai's recently departed King—even the Wandering King's ghost stood forth with the deepest of the horns, with a first son, perhaps, standing at the railing of his palace, looking down over the city.

At this, the final horn, the great western gates of Tauriyat swung open. They swung silently at first, then groaned mightily, as if what were issuing forth was not a host of Silver Spears and Blade Maidens, but the collected sorrow of the Kings. The Silver Spears marched forward, rank upon rank, dressed in white uniforms, conical helms with chain mail lapping at their shoulders, shamshirs at their belts, shields at the ready and spears held high so that they looked like a bed of nails marching forth.

Next came an honor guard of Blade Maidens. Sümeya rode among them, as did several other wardens. Twenty-four in all rode on tall akhalas, the horses' sleek coats of silver, bronze, gold, and metallic black rippling beneath the glare of the hot sun. Following them came six wagons with prison cages on their beds, each filled to the top with dead bodies. Men. Women. Some hardly more than children. Laurel branches had been split into thin strands, then used to tie each of them against the bars of the cages. Laurel leaves had been stuffed down their throats. Their eyes had been put out, and more leaves stuffed there. And in their hands they gripped laurel crowns, so that each looked as though they were about to place it on the head of a graduate.

It was a vulgar display. A travesty. The Kings had done what they'd always done, rounded up those they thought might have some small connection to the Host. And if they hadn't found enough, they'd simply gone to the Shallows and found more, using whatever flimsy evidence they thought sufficient to put chains around their ankles and lead them to King Cahil to be put to the question. How much information those poor souls had given the Kings Çeda had no idea, but she doubted it was much. And now here they lay, eighty-nine slain, a twisted echo of the eighty-nine casualties from the forum: forty-nine found dead after the battle, thirty-seven graduates taken, and, curiously, three scholars unaccounted for.

"Nalamae protect us," Çeda said.

"What?" Melis asked beside her.

Çeda's horse, Brightlock, threw its head back and shook, tack jingling. Çeda turned to Melis. "It's only that my heart weeps."

Melis's look was grim, but her eyes softened. "How can it not?"

Indeed, Çeda thought. *How can it not?* Holding her reins, she rubbed her right thumb absently. It ached terribly, and had since the attack.

"Control yourself," Melis said, noticing her discomfort.

Çeda nodded. Melis was right. This was no time to be thinking about her own ills. But the old wound was now so much a part of her life she hardly realized when she was rubbing it, or favoring it while sparring in open hand combat.

Soon the procession reached them. Ahead, Kameyl and Yndris rode forward. Çeda and Melis followed. A hundred more Maidens came behind, black-clothed, veils in place. As each pair of Maidens rode through the tall gates, they drew their ebon blades and held them, tip upward like black flames to honor the dead. They rode like this, horns sounding, horses clopping, wagon wheels clattering over the city stone. When they reached the Wheel, they rounded it and headed north toward the harbor. The streets were lined with mourners, men, women, and children dressed in white and veiled, so that the dead would not recognize those they knew and linger too long in the land of the living. It was important for the dead, especially those who had died gruesomely, to move quickly to the farther fields that they might begin their life anew, as free from the old as they could be.

For the same reasons, most would remain silent during such a procession, but the display the Kings had created—a message for those who sympathized with the Moonless Host, or one day might—caused many to gasp, to cover their mouths or moan. Some few cried out in rage at what the Kings had done, though they were quickly brought into check by those around them.

The procession reached the northern harbor, where it turned around and headed back south. The wails were louder now. The initial shock had passed and more shouted to the gods, *Why?* They would not deny the Kings' their justice, not within hearing, but they would also not suffer in silence.

They reached the Wheel again, and then headed to the western harbor, and here, along the Spear, the crowd became angry. Çeda could see it in their eyes, though nearly everyone was veiled. Some still wore white, but far fewer, as if those in the west end slums refused to let the dead pass gently. They wanted them to return, to attack the Kings, to haunt them until justice had been served. Near the northern harbor, no one had followed the procession, but here, so near the Shallows, home to nearly all the dead, a smattering of men and women began to trail behind. They kept their distance, enough that the Silver Spears at the rear, instead of turning and chasing them away, chose to remain with the procession.

As Çeda looked back, her worry grew, and she wondered at the wisdom in that decision. The crowd of mourners following them soon became a throng. The sound of their anguish, their anger, their lament, all grew until it drowned out the horns from the palaces. It became so loud it was difficult for the Spears or the Maidens to pass orders to one another. At Çeda's side, Melis made the hand sign for *be ready*.

They returned to the Wheel and headed south toward the city's largest harbor. The mourners lining the street were much the same as those who had watched along their northern trek. They were, generally speaking, affluent men and women come to pay their proper respects and to denounce the actions of the Al'afwa Khadar. But the crowd that had formed in the Shallows continued to grow; more and more were rushing in from the western streets and pushing their way through the lines of people to join the trailing column.

Çeda made the sign for *retreat*, following it with the modifier, her little finger crooked, to make it into a question. She meant the Kings' assembly— the Maidens, the Spears, the wagons—that they ought to abandon their plans and return to the safety of Tauriyat. Melis understood and signed back, *time is short*, which meant, rightly, that it was probably too late for that.

Along the curving quayside of the massive harbor stood four towers. Three were quite tall, but they were also thinner, unable to hold many men. The fourth, the one nearest the Trough, was a stout, burly affair that had decades ago been granted to the Kings' tax men for use as an accounting office. It was, however, still a holding of the Silver Spears, and it was to this building that the procession moved. The Silver Spears at the lead encircled the building, five ranks deep. The Blade Maidens' honor guard moved among them, still on horseback, ebon blades drawn.

A host of Silver Spears took the dead from the wagons and carried them to the base of the tower, where ropes awaited. One by one the dead were strung from the ropes by their feet and hauled up. Their bodies scraped against the stone, twisting and turning as they went. It looked, Çeda thought grimly, as though they were still alive and in the throes of terrible dreams. A dozen Maidens, including Çeda, Melis, Kameyl, and Yndris, slipped down from their horses and followed a squad of Silver Spears into the tower and up to its roof. Çeda had seen from horseback that the crowd was large, but they'd been behind her, hidden to a degree by the marching ranks of the Silver Spears. From the top of the tower, however, she could finally see its vastness.

The almighty weight of the crowd pressed in around the base of the tower. They gave the Spears a wide berth, but not so wide as Çeda might have guessed. More and more came behind them, a sea of Sharakhani, fists raised, their voices no longer calling to the gods, but to the gathered soldiers, the Maidens, the Kings in their palaces. Çeda realized how wrong she'd been earlier. Taking the graduates had been no mistake on the part of the Moonless Host; it had been a gamble that was paying off in spades. The Kings, tricked by their overzealous natures, had gone too far in hope of cowing their enemies. Their responses to the Host were always disproportionate. That was nothing new. But there was something about the graduates. Perhaps the people of Sharakhai thought the response dishonored the graduates in some way. Or perhaps this had been a well-orchestrated plan on the part of the Host, a campaign waged in the streets that had stoked the flames of those on the lowest rung of Sharakhai's social ladder. Or perhaps everyone in the west end was simply tired of being treated like chattel.

Whatever the reason, Çeda could already see this was ready to spiral out of control. The crowd's anger crashed against the stones of the tower like waves on a storm-swept sea. Even now, hours after their deaths, the wind tugged the laurel leaves from the gaping mouths of the dead. More fell from the crowns in their hands to flutter down among the crowd. Most would gasp and jump out of their path, fearful of being touched in any way by the falling leaves. But there were some who caught them midair, or picked the leaves up once they'd landed on the ground. Çeda got the impression these were the families of those who'd been killed, for without fail they held the leaves reverently, as if they now held a piece of their departed's soul.

Foreign witnesses to this might think collecting something so intimately related to their deaths a strange way of honoring them, but to a true Sharakhani it wasn't strange at all. The desert tribes saved the arrows, spears, or swords that had slain their fallen; such artifacts were kept as treasures, remembrances of their loved ones' lives even though the weapons had caused or aided in their deaths. Çeda's heart ached. It made her feel as though the old ways of the desert were not so distant after all.

When the first of the rocks were thrown, Çeda was standing on the eastern edge of the tower. She didn't see who had thrown it, but she saw the Silver Spear flinch, heard the captain's shout to set shields and ready spears. Like a sinuous creature of spines and thorns and chitinous armor, the white-garbed soldiers locked their shields and lowered their weapons, forming ranks to prevent any in the crowd from coming closer.

From farther back another rock flew. It struck one of the archers behind the front line full in the face. He reeled away as more rocks arced in. Soon there was a rain of them striking the men of the city guard. Some were launched at the Maidens who stood behind them, but they had room to maneuver and ducked or sidestepped.

An older woman wearing a faded brown dress and a niqab strode forward until she was a mere hand's breadth from a soldier's readied spear. She shouted at him with a fist full of laurel leaves.

Then she grabbed his spear.

The soldier tried to pull it away from her grasp, but she had no care for her own safety and allowed herself to be pulled among the Kings' soldiers. She lifted her hand high, shouting something, and threw the leaves into the soldier's face. As they fluttered to the ground at his feet, he thrust the spear sharply forward and pierced her belly. The woman gripped the spear's haft. Even from high above Çeda could see how white her knuckles were. Blood welled from the wound, spreading slowly down her simple dress like spilled wine. Her cries were filled with pain, but also a rage that made a chill run down Çeda's spine. The cry of a mother for a lost child.

The crowd erupted around her. They bulled forward, a thing alive. Hands grasped spear tips, pushed them up and away so that others might surge forward. Many were impaled, but for each that fell, three more rushed in. The second and third and fourth ranks of Silver Spears held their weapons steady while the front rank drew shamshirs, cutting those that came near. But there were simply too many. They were an endless horde.

"Dear gods," Çeda said. "Hundreds will die."

Melis, standing by her side, answered in a hard voice, eyes locked on the unfolding riot below. "*We* will die if they aren't brought to heel."

Some in the crowd were pointing to the closed tower doors, which were the only likely way to cut the ropes that held the dead. Strangely, it was at this point that Çeda felt the pain in her right hand vanish. It felt like those rare summer rains that passed through Sharakhai, lifting, at least for a time, the miserable heat waves. She hadn't realized just how much pain caused until just then, when it stopped. But it also made her wary. Why had the pain lifted? Why now?

She scanned the crowd below, seeing nothing she hadn't seen earlier. But then she noticed a tall woman with hair the color of the amber sands. The eyes of everyone below were fixed on the tower, but not her. She swam against the current, moving steadily across the quay toward the nearby docks, where ship after ship was moored in a grand and graceful arc. The woman was tall, taller even than most of the men, and while those around her moved with the unharmonious rage of a riled hornet's nest, she glided like a heron on wing. And not a soul seemed to notice her.

As sure as the desert is dry, here is Nalamae, the woman I once knew as Saliah Riverborn. And yet the goddess did not turn, did not look up toward Çeda, and Çeda found herself second-guessing what she'd been so sure of only a moment ago. But then, as she stepped onto one of the nearby docks, just before she was lost between two massive barquentines, the goddess turned and looked directly at Çeda. Çeda felt her skin go cold. It was as clear a sign as if Nalamae had whispered into Çeda's ear.

"I must get to that ship," Çeda said aloud, though no one heard her. *I must. But breath of the desert, how to reach it?*

Below, a great yell went up as one corner of the Silver Spears' line gave way to the surging crowd. A group of shouting men and women surged forward to reach the wall. Those at the head of the crowd pressed themselves against it. Others were helped onto their shoulders, and then a third row of their growing pyramid was added, all in the hope of reaching the lowest of the dead hanging from their ropes.

Çeda turned to Melis. "Come with me. We must reach that ship!"

Melis signed back, *Why?*

What could she say? What could she say to make Melis lend her strength and skill to the effort? "There's something aboard it."

Another sign. *What?*

And Çeda could only shake her head. "I don't know. But I know if we don't reach it, we will die."

Melis hesitated.

Çeda pulled her veil away so that Melis could see her, could read her earnestness. "I don't know how I know," Çeda said, "but I tell you it is true."

Melis's face was veiled, but Çeda saw her eyebrows pinch. She glanced to Kameyl, who had taken note of the exchange. "Come," Melis said to her. "Our sister has need."

To Çeda's utter surprise, Kameyl nodded and turned toward Yndris, as if to let her know as well.

"Leave her," Çeda said.

Yndris had taken up a bow and was shooting down indiscriminately, a hungry look in her eyes. *Her father's blood.* Çeda had half a mind to rip the bow from her hands, or better yet, kick her off the tower, but there was nothing to do about her now. The faster they acted, the fewer would die on both sides.

Çeda slipped over the side and down one of the ropes. Melis and Kameyl followed, Melis sliding down the rope to her left, Kameyl on her right. When they came to a stop twenty feet above the crowd, the crowd took note, their calls shifting as they pointed toward the three descending Maidens. Rocks rained in, a few striking painfully.

"They think we're coming to aide the Spears," Çeda said, "so leap as far away as you can manage and then make for the sands. Use no blades. Only scabbards. Once we push beyond them, we'll circle back to the ship."

Melis nodded.

Kameyl said, "I hope you know what you're doing, young dove," and then kicked away from the wall in a twisting, backward leap. Çeda and Melis followed, the three of them landing close to one another near the edge of the crowd, well beyond the safety of the Silver Spears. They pushed for the sand, but many in the crowd followed them, trying to hem them in. A chaos of yelling and hands grabbing and legs kicking followed. Çeda felt their closeness as much as she heard them. She returned punches and kicks, swiping with a sheathed River's Daughter—anything to gain some small space from those pressing in around her. She fell once, but screamed in rage and fear and was up again in a moment. She caught sight of Kameyl spinning, punching, kicking in all directions. A blur. But she couldn't find Melis.

She saw her a moment later, lying on the ground, a dozen around her kicking fiercely.

"Lai, lai, lai!" Çeda cried, bulling her way toward Melis. She managed to reach her, to try to lift her up, but then she was grabbed from behind. She fought to free herself as another seized her sword arm. The man behind her slipped his arm around her neck. She lowered herself, driving back to gain leverage, then flipped him over her shoulder, but more were already pressing in.

Beyond the row surrounding her, an ebon blade flashed. The crowd, which had been shouting triumphantly, screamed and backed away. It was Sümeya, Çeda realized. She'd come from the base of the tower and was forging a path with ebon steel. "What by the gods are you doing?" she asked when she reached them.

"I'll explain later," Çeda said. "Just help us reach open sand."

Çeda didn't wait for acknowledgment. She drew River's Daughter, for the threat it posed more than anything else, and held the wooden scabbard in her off hand. When anyone came too close, she used her scabbard to ward them away. She worked her way to Kameyl, Sümeya and Melis guarding her flanks, and then together the four of them fought their way free to the edge of the quay and down to the harbor's sandy floor.

"There!" Çeda said, pointing at the two barquentines and the pier between them.

Sheathing their swords, they sprinted across the sand. Çeda was the first to reach the pier. She felt sure Nalamae would be long gone, and yet there she was, stepping down into the hold of the ship on her left.

"Wait!" Çeda sprinted toward the gangplanks that led to the ships. As she reached the deck of the ship, she was struck by a sound she'd thought she'd never hear again. It was nearly drowned out by the roar around the tower, but she could hear it, the sounds of birds chirping. She dropped down through the hatch. "Goddess?" she whispered, praying the Maidens behind her wouldn't hear.

But she saw no sign of Nalamae. She found instead a hold brimming with stack upon stack of bamboo cages. Birds flitted within, easily tens of thousands of them, and they were all bright blue. Tufts of blue down and feathers littered the hold. Black and white shit layered the bottom of the cages. The combined sound of their chirping and the fluttering of their wings as they flitted about their cages was deafening.

Melis, Kameyl, and Sümeya dropped in just behind her. All three stared in wonder.

"Blazing blues," Melis said.

"A sign of peace," Sümeya offered.

Çeda nodded, dumbfounded, and drew River's Daughter once more. "Open the cages. All of them." Then she began slicing at the leather strips that held the cages shut.

The cages opened easily, the blazing blues fluttering into the hold and finally out through the hatch. She desperately wanted them all out, but there were so many. So very many.

The four of them freed more and more, throwing aside cages once the blues had flown out. They worked feverishly. The birds had gone strangely silent, as if they didn't wish to interrupt, but then chirped as they headed out the hatch and lifted toward freedom. The rice and water that had been set into each cage was scattered over the floor as the Maidens' ebon blades rose and fell, until finally it was done. The last of the blues flew up and out from the hold.

"Quickly now"—Çeda pointed to the far side of the hold—"grab a sack of rice and follow me."

Çeda hoisted one over her shoulder and took the ladder up to the deck. Above, the cloud of blazing blues were circling, but in no time at all they might leave. She dragged her sack of rice to the front of the ship, sliced it open, and began flinging it over the crowd. Kameyl, Melis, and Sümeya followed suit, cutting open their own sacks and throwing handfuls of rice as far as they could.

The first of the blues dropped, and then the air around them was a tempest of wings. The air became thick with them, occluding the sight of the tower. The Silver Spears in their white uniforms, the Maidens in their black, the patchwork of the crowd, all of it cast varying shades of blue as the birds dove for the rice.

It was so very different from the time she'd gone with her mother to the salt flat and seen these birds for the first time, but still, Çeda held a hand up as she had then, over a dozen years ago. The birds came, pecking at the rice lying on her outstretched palm. Dozens swept around her, but she felt only the barest touch of their beaks, the wind from their beating wings. Near the tower, the roar of the crowd grew quiet, then quieter still, until all she could hear were the blazing blues, their cobalt wings winking across their iridescent black breasts, making them look like a field of rapidly blinking eyes.

How long the feeding went on Çeda couldn't say. She merely held herself still and prayed the bloodshed would end. She prayed too that her mother might be doing the very same thing in the farther fields, feeding her own flock of birds as Çeda was doing now. After all, it seemed the sort of thing that might draw her mother's eye, a memory as strong as this one.

Eventually the storm of wings began to diminish, and then all at once they were gone, the flock flying up into the evening sky like a billowing cloud of smoke. It drifted northeast, over the city, and soon was gone, leaving a stunned silence in its wake.

At the tower, the Spears and the Maidens held their weapons loosely, staring at the crowd, ready to fight but clearly reluctant to do so. The crowd, on the other hand, looked shocked, as if they'd only then realized what they'd done, the sort of danger all of them were now in.

They began to break at the edges. Just as the actions of a handful had spurred the entire crowd into action, so did the choice of some few to flee. Soon everyone was running away, melting back into the city, leaving the wounded and the dead behind.

Then at last, the Maidens and the Spears were alone, with the dead on the ground and the dead they'd strung up.

Chapter 26

IHSAN SAT BEHIND HIS DESK AS TOLOVAN led the lithe form of King Azad, followed by the husky frame of King Zeheb, into his chambers. Tolovan had set two additional chairs by Ihsan's side for the other Kings, and they sat as Tolovan bowed and left the room then returned shortly with the young Maiden, Çedamihn. Instead of her Maiden's dress, she wore a bright blue jalabiya, her hair braided and wrapped into a bun behind her head, two hairpins holding it in place. She looked very Mirean.

"Please," Ihsan said, motioning to the chair opposite his desk.

"Of course, my Lord King," Çeda said. "How may I help?"

Again Ihsan noted how far she'd come. Months ago she would have stared at them all wide-eyed, a frightened little doe, but here she was, sitting before three Kings, knowing a questioning was to come, and she hardly batted an eye. There were still nerves—Ihsan could see it in the tightness of her frame—but she'd become more and more adept at disguising it.

"We wish, as you may have guessed, to speak to you of the riot."

"I am an open book."

Ihsan had to hide a smile at this. Ihsan knew many of her secrets, as did Azad and Zeheb, but Çeda didn't know that. He took a piece of paper with fine writing on it, an account of Çeda's recollection of the events on the day of the riot.

"As you reported it, you and three of your fellow Maidens left the relative safety of the tower and made your way to the open sand of the harbor. That done, you returned to a pier where a ship carrying hundreds of birds bound for Malasan was moored. Upon finding them, you and the others freed the birds in an attempt to quell the crowd."

Çeda bowed her head. "All true, Excellence."

"What you did not report was why you chose to leave the safety of the tower in the first place."

"My Lord Kings, we were headed for a massacre. I wished to avert it."

"To avert it."

"To shake it. To make the ground rumble, as my mother used to say. I wished to lift the crowd above their blood thirst however I could."

"This is ridiculous." Zeheb shifted in his chair, which groaned beneath his weight. "How did you know the blazing blues were in that ship?"

"I saw one escaping from the hold, Excellence."

Azad stared. "You left the tower because you saw a lone bird flying from the hold of a ship."

Çeda nodded. "The blues are prized in Malasan, and the ship was flying Malasan's colors. It didn't take much to realize the hold must be full of them."

"It seems a desperate act," Azad said.

"It was a desperate moment."

"But to risk your life, and the life of your fellow Maidens so."

Çeda opened her mouth to speak, but then closed it. Her eyes roamed, searching for the right words. "I hope you'll forgive me the question, my Lord Kings, but do you deal very much with children?"

A vision came to Ihsan, of a girl placing her small, soft hands in his. His own daughter, her eyes bright, her smile brighter. "Presume, for the moment, that we don't."

"You see, there are times when children become lost in thought. Sometimes in happiness, sometimes in fear, sometimes in anger. They can become so fixated on those things that it feeds on itself. Fear becomes terror. Anger becomes mania. I should know. I was once a very angry child. Sometimes I still am." At this, Azad chuckled. "Sometimes it is all you can do to convince them otherwise," Çeda went on. "Fighting fear by telling them there's nothing to be afraid of only draws their attention to the thing they were afraid of in the first place. And anger, if you're not careful, can turn to violence."

"Get to your point," Zeheb groused.

"Crowds like the one at the tower have often devolved. They're no longer thinking as adults do but as their baser selves. I've found that if you can approach that anger from another direction, you can often douse the fire before it grows worse."

"Reasonable enough words when spoken from the comfort of a King's palace," Ihsan said, "and yet you must admit it seems quite convenient that those birds lay in wait for you."

"Not convenient, my Lord Kings. Those birds were a gift from the gods themselves. They *meant* for the riot to disperse."

"What gods?" Ihsan asked.

Çeda merely shrugged. "Who am I to say?"

"A report was given by one of the Silver Spears near the barquentine where you found the birds. He said he'd seen a tall woman with blond plaited hair. She walked not *with* the crowd, but *across* them, much as you describe cutting across a child's anger to blunt their emotions."

Ihsan let the words hang, leaving the question unasked. Allowing a witness to fill in the question often told him as much about them as their answers. To her credit, Çeda said nothing. She raised her eyebrows as if she were confused. An act, he was sure, but a good one. He was half tempted to compel her to speak of that day, but he didn't wish to share his power with Çeda just yet. It was blunted when used on those with blood of the thirteenth tribe, and faded the more it was used. Which was part of the reason he preferred playing this game without such things; one never knew who was a descendant of the tribe and who wasn't.

"Did you see such a woman?" Ihsan finally asked.

"Forgive me, Excellence, but I did not."

Azad leaned into his chair, fingering the carnelian necklace hanging around his neck. "Why did you leave your fellow Maiden, Yndris Cahil'ava, alone on the roof of the tower?"

For the first time, Çeda's mask slipped, but only for a moment. "She was hardly alone, my Lord King. There were a dozen others there with her."

"Don't quibble. She alone from your hand remained while the rest of you dropped to the sand."

"There was simply no time. It all happened so quickly."

"And yet you had time to inform two other Maidens on the roof of that tower to join you in your quest."

"True, your Grace, but they were close to hand. Yndris was otherwise engaged."

"With a bow," Azad supplied.

"With a bow." Her face went stonelike. "Shooting into the crowd."

"You disapprove of her methods?" Azad pressed.

"I never said so, your Grace."

"And I never said you did. I'm asking you now. Do you disapprove of Yndris's methods?"

"They seemed, at the time, overzealous."

"And you disapprove of zealotry?"

"Forgive me, my Kings, but you are asking me to speak plainly, so I will. There are times to use the steel edge of a sword, to keep the peace, to drive away our enemies with the righteousness of the gods leading us, but there are other times when blood only begets more blood. I felt the riot was one of the latter. Yndris did not."

For a time, all three Kings were silent. Azad seemed displeased; no surprise given his alter ego's connection to the Blade Maidens. Zeheb gave away little, but seemed ready for this audience to be over. For Ihsan's part, his estimation of Çedamihn Ahyanesh'ala had just risen several notches.

"Very well," Ihsan said. "That will be all."

To which Çeda bowed and left the room.

"Do you believe her," Zeheb asked after she'd left and the door had been closed, "that she did not see Nalamae?"

"Of course I don't," Ihsan said. "I'm convinced the goddess has returned, and have few doubts she guided Çeda to that ship. What I'm more interested in is that fact that Nalamae seems content to let things play as they will."

Zeheb frowned. "You call her actions at the tower *playing as it will*?"

Ihsan shrugged. "A notable exception, to be sure, but you can't deny that, thus far, she's kept her nose out of our business."

"That could change at any time," Zeheb replied.

"Granted."

For a time they were silent, considering. "Should we tell Kiral what we've found?" Azad asked.

Now *there* was a question. If Nalamae was becoming active again in the city, what might it mean for the House of Kings and their entwined futures? More importantly, what might it mean to *Ihsan's* plans? "I think, for now, it would be best if we kept it to ourselves."

"Very well." Azad stood, smoothing down his fine green-and-ivory khalat. "Can we move on to other business? I have much to do."

"Ah," Ihsan said, standing and motioning the two other Kings toward the arched entrance to the halls, "that is exactly why I asked to hold this meeting here. If you would be so good as to accompany me?"

They left, heading down the grand, vaulting hallway. They followed it to the towering atrium at the center of the palace, and from there wound their way down six levels until they came to a cold hall lit by oil lanterns spaced along its considerable length. Two of Ihsan's personal guard stood there, bowing as the Kings walked past. When they came to a door, Ihsan unlocked it and entered. Inside was a man wearing a simple thawb. The top of his head was bald. The wild gray hair that grew along the sides and back was unkempt. He had a purple scab on his forehead, scrapes on his nose and left cheek, but otherwise looked unharmed.

"My good Kings, here we find Taram, a man particularly gifted, I am told, with the flora of the desert, their distillations, how they might be combined for different effects, and so on."

When Ihsan made no move to say more, Azad became irritated. "Do you expect me to conduct my questioning down here?"

"I do," Ihsan said simply.

Azad's face fell. His entire frame slumped. "This cannot continue. All of this would be infinitely easier in my palace."

"As would acting in the open," Ihsan replied. "But this is dark business, Azad, and I will not let them out of my proverbial sight. And before the question arises, no, the room where you conduct your experiments will not be moved from my palace."

"It slows everything I do," Azad breathed.

"Then it is slowed. I'll not leave this to chance, so you may as well move beyond it and ask whatever it is you wish to ask."

Azad stared. "I work better alone."

"Perhaps, but you're working too slowly for my tastes. We will conduct our questioning here, and I will oversee your work until we are done."

"But—"

"You said you were close," Ihsan broke in.

"I am."

"Then this will all be over shortly." Ihsan waved to Taram. "You may begin."

"Well." Zeheb smiled impishly at the two of them, an amused expression on his jowly face. "I leave my two good Kings to the task at hand."

Zeheb left, leaving Azad staring balefully at Ihsan. But Ihsan knew it would pass. It always did.

"Are there more?" Azad asked.

"Yes, there are two more scholars for you to speak with."

Finally Azad breathed out, scraped one of the empty chairs toward him, and sat. "Let's begin with what you know of the adichara."

What Taram must have thought of all this Ihsan couldn't guess. But he was an intelligent man. Likely he knew where this would all end. Yet he uttered no complaints. He didn't plead with them. He merely bowed his head, said, "Of course, my King," and began a recitation of the properties of the adichara—roots, branches, thorns, and blooms.

Very good, Ihsan thought. *Very good, indeed.*

Chapter 27

E MRE STRODE ALONG THE STREETS of the Shallows with a bagful of coin, Frail Lemi towering at his side. Five years ago he would've walked through this part of town and thought someone like him the perfect mark. He could picture the setup. A boy distracting him ahead, another behind, nicking the bag with a knife, more ready to nab coins if they fell. A few might get roughed up. One or two might even be killed for it, but a bag this size was the sort of thing the gutter wrens in the Shallows would take risks for.

Having Frail Lemi at his side was a deterrent, certainly, and a considerable one at that, but it wasn't the most significant. That honor fell to his status as a scarab, a soldier of the Moonless Host. Everyone in this part of the city knew that if they laid but a finger on him, they would answer to the Host.

There might be some newcomers stupid enough to make a grab at the bag, or challenge him for it—foreign toughs who didn't know any better, or the truly desperate—but if they did, everyone nearby would close in, knives in hand, and take care of things as quickly as they'd started. Emre could see it in the way they watched him with looks of respect, with the sort of careful nods he'd seen them giving to Hamid for months now.

Emre was just about to turn down an alley when he noticed a street tough leaning against a building, arms crossed over his chest. He wasn't doing anything threatening, just watching Emre and Frail Lemi, but he was watching *closely*. The hood pulled over his head hid his face, but there was something familiar about him.

Frail Lemi cracked his knuckles loudly. "Want him and me to have a little chat?"

A little chat . . . More than likely the man would end up bloody and writhing on the ground if Frail Lemi came within two paces of him. "No, leave him be."

It was only as the man began walking away that Emre remembered where he'd seen him. The sleeves of his shirt had hidden his arms, but when he'd pushed himself off the wall, Emre saw the scars crisscrossing his hands. The sun on his chin and neck revealed more scars, more than Emre had ever seen on a man.

It was Brama, a boy he and Çeda and Tariq had occasionally run the streets with. He'd been through something terrible with Çeda years ago, and everyone thought he'd died. But he'd returned to Sharakhai months later, sporting those scars. What had happened to him Emre hadn't learned. He only knew that Çeda had helped to extricate him from the trouble he'd been in. Now he lived in the Knot. Called himself the Tattered Prince. It was said he had a gang of some sort. Drugs, maybe. Emre didn't know.

By his side, Frail Lemi was growing restless. "How many more, Emre?"

"Two more," Emre said, giving the dwindling form of Brama one last look before heading down the alley.

"Two more," Frail Lemi said. "Two more. Then we're off to the baths, like you said. The one with the hot stones."

"Just like that, Lemi. Hot stones on our back, the two of us relaxing like Kings."

"Like fucking Kings." He stretched his neck, as he'd done the past dozen times he'd mentioned it. "Need it something fierce, Emre. Neck hurts bad."

"I know. We'll be there soon enough," Emre said as they walked into the open doorway of a tenement. They took the stairs up to the fourth floor, the smell of curry and lemon and roast lamb making Emre's mouth water. They wove through the halls, passing doorways in various states of disrepair, some with carpets or blankets strung across them, others open to let the breeze wander through the building. Many nodded at their passage. Emre didn't bother nodding back any longer, but Lemi nodded to every single one, a serious look on his face.

"How many more?" Lemi called.

"Just two. Wait here, Lemi." Emre ducked under the carpet that served as the door and entered a room with a grid of eight simple pallets laid out over the floor. Six of the pallets were occupied by young men, the other two by girls. Most were snoring. An old man was sitting by the window on a wicker chair, a pile of pistachios on the windowsill next to him. He took one, cracked the shell between his teeth. He spit the shells into his hand and dropped them between his feet, where a pile of them lay. The man's eyes were opaque and hauntingly white in the dimness of the room. As Emre navigated the floor, trying not to wake anyone, the man turned toward him, the wicker chair creaking under the movement. "Who's come?"

"A friend," Emre said.

"Ah." He chewed on another pistachio, white eyes staring sightlessly. "Come to pay for the souls you bought."

Emre had just opened the top of the bag slung from his shoulder, but he paused. Of the twenty stops he'd made already, this was the first to say anything against him, or for that matter even mention the reason behind the payment. "If that's the way you want to put it." Emre began counting out coins.

"Seems to me that's how it is. No sense dancing around it."

On the other stops, the money went to the families of those who'd given their lives during the attack on the collegia grounds. But not here. This man, Galliu, was different. He found orphans for the cause. He promised them they would find themselves princes and princesses in the farther fields. He promised them their friends or sweethearts would be treated with kindness by the Host afterward. He promised them their friends and family would be marked so that they could find their way to them when *they* passed beyond these shores.

"They've helped a greater cause," Emre replied. "They deserve to be paid for it."

"You believe that? That they serve a greater cause?"

"Don't you?" Emre still wasn't sure if Galliu was an earnest man or a swindler.

Galliu snorted while spitting the shells into his palm. "Here's what I know, though you likely don't want to hear it." He chewed and swallowed. "Our bones will be buried in the sand, as will the rest of the soldiers' in the Al'afwa Khadar, long before anything changes in this city."

"A King lies dead."

Galliu tilted his head, a perplexed, almost angry look on his face. Sunlight slanted neatly across his face, making him look like the god of chance, of light and dark. "And what does that prove?"

"If one can die, they all can. We're winning."

"Winning . . ." Galliu laughed, an old saw biting into fresh wood. "Let me ask you something. Were you able to kill all the Kings with but a wave of your hand, what do you suppose would happen?" He grabbed a nut and poked it at Emre. "I'll tell you what. Their sons and daughters would sit their thrones ere they grew cold, as the freshly crowned King Alaşan has already done with his father, the Wandering King's. They will extend the rule of their fathers over this city. The sands of the desert do not change."

"Even the mighty can fall to the shifting sands of the Great Mother."

"But will you and I be alive to see it?"

Emre finished counting out the coins and cinched the top of the bag. "I don't care if I'm alive. What I do now will help others."

"Or maybe what you do, what we all do, will raise their ire and give them four hundred years more."

Emre took Galliu's hand and placed the golden rahl into his palm. "Why do you find boys for the Host if you don't believe it will help?"

With incredible speed and precision, Galliu stacked the coins along the windowsill into eight neat piles, one for each of the young men he'd sent to battle, then took a single coin from each and dropped them into his own purse at his belt. "A man has to eat."

"You traffic in the lives of others. You're telling me it's not for coin and coin alone?"

Galliu leaned back in the chair once more, scratching the white stubble along his chin and staring across the city as if Emre no longer existed. "Make no mistake, my wayward son. We are the same, you and I. At least I'm man enough to admit it."

Emre wanted to say something, give him some sharp reply, but what did it matter? He didn't need Galliu's approval. The old man delivered the recruits Macide needed. It was as simple as that. And yet, as he left the small room with Frail Lemi following, he wondered. *Did* he traffic in lives? He wished it wasn't the case, but just then no words had ever felt truer.

"How many more, Emre?"

"Just one, Lemi."

They went to another house, where a woman no older than Emre accepted the last of the coins. She acted no differently than the others. There was gratitude in her voice and sorrow in her eyes, and yet Emre felt as though *he'd* been the one to kill her husband, as though he'd been the one to order the attack on the collegia that had sacrificed every last soldier the Host had sent to fight the Spears and the Maidens. Consumed by the devil's trumpet as they were, they'd fought until they were dead or wounded so badly it made no difference. And those who had by some miracle survived had been taken by the poison hours later.

"My tears for your loss," Emre said, a thing he'd said to no one else that day.

"Keep your tears." She held the coins tightly. "Keep them for the day we are all free, then weep with joy, for Adram walked with his eyes wide open."

A heartening thought, and yet it was Galliu's words that haunted him like a restless spirit. *Make no mistake. We are the same, you and I.*

As he left the building, Emre turned to Frail Lemi, who leaned against the wall, arms folded like a shisha den guard across his chest. "Now we go, right Emre?"

The grin on his face was wide as the Haddah in spring. In all honesty, after this day of paying for the dead, he was looking forward to the bathhouse as much as Frail Lemi. Emre was just about to tell him so when a ricksha rattled to a stop a few paces away. Emre was about to bark at the skinny driver to move along when he realized who was sitting in the seat, half-hidden by the canopy's fringe, wearing a fine desert khalat.

"Hold on, Lemi," Emre said as he took a step toward the ricksha. He nodded to Ishaq, Macide's father and the supreme leader of the Moonless Host.

Ishaq nodded back, his eyes expressive, curious, almost humorous. "Come, sit by my side, Emre. A talk between us is long overdue."

"Of course," Emre said, but he made no move toward the ricksha. He turned back to where Frail Lemi was standing and said, "Wait for me here, Lemi."

Lemi's gaze darted between Emre and Ishaq. "We're going, right Emre? We're going to the bathhouse?"

"We'll go a bit later. After I get back."

"You said one more. You finished them all, and now it's time to go." Lemi was flexing his arms, balling his hands into fists. "You said one more." Gods, his eyes. They looked confused, like a boy preparing to do something very foolish. The last time he'd seen Frail Lemi like this was at an oud parlor. He'd asked for a song from the musician, who'd played it with gusto. When Lemi had asked for it again, he'd nervously agreed and played it a second time, but when Lemi had asked for a third, the man had refused, and Lemi hadn't taken kindly to it.

Emre had been sitting there beside Hamid and Darius, all three of them watching the exchange, knowing what was going to happen. Hamid had just stood and was raising his hands, speaking calmly to Lemi, when Lemi charged and crashed his fist into the musician's face. He fell on the poor man, blow after blow thundering down, turning the musician's once-handsome face into a bloody cut of pork. By the time they'd left, the musician's clothes, his oud, the carpets in that corner of the room, had been layered in red.

"Lemi, I promise you, we'll go. Just a little while, and then we'll go."

"You're going to *leave*?" Frail Lemi pointed at Ishaq. "With *him*?"

Before Emre could answer, Ishaq whistled sharply, twice. "Come," he said, motioning Frail Lemi closer. Ishaq held out one hand, but Lemi ignored it, continuing to bunch his fists, the muscles along his arm rippling. His chest worked like a dirt dog's his first time in the killing pits, but Ishaq appeared not to notice. He flicked his hand again, and this time, Frail Lemi raised one meaty hand and placed it in Ishaq's.

"Orange peels," Ishaq said. "Do you like them?"

Frail Lemi blinked.

"Orange peels and clove. We take them into the caves far to the west of the Great Shangazi. We steep them in hot water for hours before pouring the mixture over hot stones. Some say it summons Thaash. It is a bold and sturdy scent, after all. But I've always thought it more likely to attract the notice of Yerinde, for whenever I breathe that air, I think my most ambitious thoughts. It's what I used the day before I came to the city." Emre realized Frail Lemi's free hand was no longer in a fist. It hung loose, and Lemi's eyes were reflective, almost calm as Ishaq continued speaking to him. "You and I will go when I return. Yes? We'll breathe those scents and wonder where the winds of the desert will take us."

Frail Lemi's eyes were awash with emotion. He stared at Ishaq. He blinked. And then nodded.

"Good," Ishaq said. "Wait here. We won't be long."

Frail Lemi nodded again, and Ishaq motioned Emre to take the seat beside him. Ishaq knocked a ruby ring on the wooden frame of the ricksha, and the driver, a middle-aged Mirean man —so thin Emre felt terrible for adding to his burden—leaned into the wooden rails, setting them into motion. Frail Lemi watched their departure, but Emre suspected he hardly saw them. He had that look about him, as if he were off, somewhere *else*.

The ricksha rattled and bounced. Ishaq glanced at Emre, running his hand down his trim gray beard. "In the catacombs, you told me you knew Çeda well. Quite well, I think you said."

"That's true."

"Tell me about her."

Months ago, Macide had implied that he'd known Çeda's mother, Ahya. Emre had that same impression now of Ishaq, a man who wasn't so much *discovering* things about Çeda as he was filling in gaps.

Emre wasn't sure where to begin. "She's strong-willed. She takes care of her own. She loves poetry and books. She's funny when she's not so wrapped up in . . . everything."

"And her mother, Ahya? Did you know her as well?"

Emre shrugged. "I knew her. She didn't know me, though. Not well, at least. She was always chasing me away from their home, wherever they'd taken up. Once she took a switch to my backside for coming to Çeda's window late at night." He could laugh now, but how it had stung then. "She said it'd be a carpet beater the next time. And a sword after that."

Ishaq smiled a melancholy smile. "And how long did it keep you away?"

"One night."

Now came a chuckle. "You enjoy taking beatings, then?"

"I was scared Çeda had received the same. I wanted to apologize."

"And did you? Apologize?"

"Yes, but I got her in trouble that same night. We snuck away to watch the fire eaters performing at the Wheel, and Ahya switched her again."

"Willful," Ishaq said as the ricksha turned onto the road known as the Corona, just short of the western harbor.

"My fault, probably."

"Perhaps, though her mother had enough willfulness running through her veins to share."

"You knew her, then, Ahya?"

Ishaq smile wryly. "Yes, I knew her."

"How?"

Ishaq remained silent, watching the way ahead as it curved gently around the western edges of Sharakhai. They came to a rise, where the ricksha driver took a short break to drink from a skin hanging from his belt. To their right, across the chockablock landscape of Sharakhai, loomed Tauriyat. Ishaq motioned to it. "Have you spoken to her since she took up her ebon blade?" When Emre glanced at the driver, he nodded. "You may speak freely."

"We spoke in Külaşan's desert palace, but only briefly."

"When Dardzada first told me about it, I wondered at the wisdom in letting her go there." He glanced to Emre. "I wonder even now whether we should let her remain."

As the ricksha lurched into motion, Emre leaned back further in his seat. "It seems to me she'd be in *more* danger if she left. Would the Kings not do everything in their power to punish such a betrayal?"

"They would, young falcon." He took a deep breath and released it, as if he'd been struggling with this himself for some time. "Well, I suppose that, for now, is a sleeping dog. Let's let it lie for the moment. I have another reason to speak with you. Macide seems to think you a trustworthy man."

Emre bowed his head. "I'm honored."

"That you would never betray him, or the true leaders of the Al'afwa Khadar."

"I would not."

"There is a new player afoot, as you're well aware. The son of a King, now resurrected by your own hand, by your own blood, if what I hear is true."

Emre wondered, not for the first time, what sort of power he'd given Hamzakiir when he'd offered the mage his own blood. "It is."

"There's no doubt he's a charismatic man. And powerful. But he's fresh from the grave. He knows little about the powers that shift in the desert sand. There are those who might be fooled by his charms, but make no mistake. There is no blood of the lost tribe in him. We cannot allow others to be lured away from our cause."

Emre considered. "You fear it's already happening."

Ishaq rubbed his ruby ring as if it were a talisman. "When you came to the catacombs, there was a man we were speaking with."

Emre remembered. The man with air of nobility about him. "Lord Aziz of Ishmantep."

"Just so. There is reason to wonder whether Aziz has been truthful with us. It may be that he's been lured by Hamzakiir's power. It wouldn't be the first time it's happened in the desert. Or it may be that Hamzakiir has done the unforgivable and applied the power of his magic to those in the upper-most ranks of the lost tribe. There are many unanswered questions surrounding Hamzakiir's recent actions, and we need to know the truth of it."

"You have only to command me."

"Good." They turned again, and headed back toward the tenement building where they'd left Frail Lemi. "How do you feel about turning the tables on a captain of the Silver Spears?" Ishaq asked.

"A Spear. A Maiden. A King. It makes no difference to me."

He watched Emre carefully, then nodded and patted Emre on the knee as they rounded a corner. "Very well, Emre Aykan'ava."

Ahead, they found Frail Lemi leaning against the wall where they'd left him, using a knife to clean beneath his fingernails. He stood when he spotted the ricksha and slipped the knife in a blink into its sheath on his forearm.

When the driver pulled the ricksha to a stop, Emre hopped out and Lemi sat in the place where Emre had just been. The ricksha creaked mightily as Lemi found a comfortable position. He dominated the bench, grinning like a Goldenhill prince on his birthday.

Ishaq knocked the wood twice with his ring. "Hamid will give you your orders," he said to Emre, and the ricksha pulled away, the driver struggling with Lemi's added weight.

Chapter 28

WELL BEFORE MORNING LIGHT, Çeda roused herself from bed. For each of the past many nights, she'd returned to the House of Maidens bone-tired but then hardly slept a wink. Last night, she and the other Maidens had again worked long into the night, searching for those who were felt to have instigated the riot, but had eventually left the rest to the Silver Spears. She had nightmares of blood and spears and a ceaseless wail of pain and frustration from the faceless thousands who surrounded her. She woke, breathless, her mind swimming with scenes of the terror at the harbor and the door-to-door searches they'd conducted at Husamettín's orders. She thought of the goddess as well. How dearly she wished she could have spoken to her, asked her some few questions before the other Maidens had arrived. But she thanked the goddess for her kindness. She'd saved the lives of hundreds, and many more from injury.

Her heart bled for Davud. Did he yet live? If so, where had the Host taken him? Or more importantly, *why* had they taken him and the others? She worried over Emre as well. Surely he'd been involved. Likely all of the trusted agents of the Al'afwa Khadar had been involved *somehow* these past few months.

Hearing nothing from the other rooms, she moved to her desk and lit a candle. After pulling out a sheet of the reed paper, she penned a new note, telling Juvaan what she'd seen over the past few days. The bloodshed. The maniacal fervor with which the Host's scarabs had fought. The fire at the garrison and the missing graduates. The riot at the harbor.

Satisfied, she took a deep breath, then put the corner of the paper to the flame. She held her breath, waiting. The reply came quickly.

Very well. Take great care. Leave the papers untouched for one month. With as much as had happened, I fear that the Kings will pick up the scent of our correspondence. One month. And then we can speak again.

She waited for more, but the words simply stopped, and then the page burst into cerulean flames, vanishing as though it had never existed.

Her hands bunched into fists. She shook with rage, and took up a new sheet of paper. Her lips pressed into a thin line, she wrote—

What of the scarab? What of the plans that surround him?

—then lit the page and waited. Again the reply came quickly.

I have nothing as yet. But I hope to when we speak again.

For a long while after the charred sheet had burned itself up, Çeda remained at the desk. By the gods, one month. *Six weeks.* Could he give her nothing before then? Like the page itself, the city would be afire with Silver Spears' enforcers, with the Maidens themselves, with Zeheb's spies. More bloodshed would come. It would be a sensitive time. But perhaps that was the *best* time for her and Juvaan to speak. With the chaos that was sure to rule the days to come, how likely was it for the Kings to learn of their communications?

Unable to sleep, she headed for the roof of the barracks, where she came at times to watch over the city. She didn't look out over Sharakhai, however. She looked east, beyond the walls that ran around the House of Maidens to the tall buildings beyond. The embassy houses. Malasan's, Qaimir's, Kundhun's. And there she saw it, a deep shadow north of the road leading to King's Harbor: the Mirean embassy house, built of stone, but in the style of its homeland, a tower of seven progressively smaller levels with red clay shingles on its roofs.

She wanted to believe that Juvaan was merely being sensible, but it didn't feel that way. It felt as if he'd been making her dance like a marionette from the start. She watched as the coming sunrise lit the horizon, the embassy houses little more than dark silhouettes against the golden dawn. Only after the sun had risen had intent finally replaced the frustration and anger roiling inside her.

"Soon, Juvaan," she said to the building in the distance, "you'll see what it means to toy with a Sharakhani."

As the bells tolled, calling the Maidens to rise, she left the roof and prepared for her day.

With the city in the throes of a terrible heat wave, Çeda and Zaïde were stripped down to the light cotton shifts the Maidens wore beneath their battle dresses. The two of them wove over the canvas, arms snaking under or over the other's defenses. They did not kick, but their legs were placed just so, to the inside of their opponent's stance, or outside of it, whichever gave them the best advantage. No longer was Çeda trying to score with a single swipe against Zaïde's neck, nor was Zaïde attempting the same with her. They had advanced to something that was deceptively difficult: to strike with enough force to knock their opponent off balance. It made the contest a dizzying mix of dance, tightrope act, and aban match. Çeda had the edge in strength, but Zaïde's form was perfection. There were no wasted movements. *Well-oiled*, Kameyl had said of her once, and Çeda agreed.

At last, when Çeda spotted an opening, she unleashed a palm strike. Like the snap of a rope, it traveled from heel to hip to shoulder to palm, but Zaïde anticipated the blow so well it merely glanced off her shoulder. Çeda leaned away from Zaïde's riposte, using her right hand to guide the blow up and well off target, following with a sharp strike that was sure to score her a hit.

But Zaïde was expecting it. She spun like a dervish, swiping Çeda's wrist to send her blow off the mark, then struck hard into Çeda's ribs with her trailing left hand—not as hard as she might have, but more than hard enough to send Çeda stumbling away. It was another loss, but at least Çeda hadn't fallen to the mat as she might have done weeks ago.

Çeda stood and bowed, preparing to listen to the litany of things she'd done wrong, but Zaïde actually seemed pleased. "Very good," she said after returning Çeda's bow.

"Good? I *lost*. Again."

"The difference between winning and losing is a very narrow thing." From a rack of bamboo shinai, Zaïde picked up two sweat-dampened towels. She threw one to Çeda, who caught it and mopped her brow and face.

It was then that Çeda sensed a change. Like a familiar weight felt only by its absence, something *lifted* from the room. It wasn't the air, which was hot and oppressive, but something else. A presence that had been here but was no longer. Çeda knew that the attention of King Zeheb had just turned elsewhere.

Immediately, Zaïde stood and motioned Çeda to one corner of the savaşam. When Zaïde pressed on a wooden panel between two weapons racks, a dull thud came as the panel moved inward. Zaïde swept the section aside to reveal a corridor of bare stone. Just inside was a shelf with small hand lamps and bottles of oil and a striker.

"Where are we going?" Çeda asked.

"You'll see soon enough. Quickly now." After striking one of the lanterns, Zaïde headed down the tunnel, setting a grueling pace from the start.

The walk through the tunnels was chill, especially after their sparring and the heat of the savaşam, but it wasn't a difficult trek. As their path twisted and turned, Çeda did her best to memorize the way in case she needed to come here again, perhaps without Zaïde. She judged they were headed roughly southwest, and although their path was winding, occasionally even circling back on itself as they climbed or descended, she figured they hadn't gone very far beyond the walls of the House of Kings, so she was hardly surprised when they reached a length of natural tunnel that looked familiar. Soon they arrived at the very door Davud had shown her those months ago, the one that led from the tunnel at the base of the dry well to the scriptorium, where she'd spent many long nights trying to unlock the riddles of Külaşan's poem.

Without pause, Zaïde opened the door and swept through it. Çeda should have guessed who they were going to see. She thought Zaïde had brought her to speak with another Matron in private, or a scholar, some ally within the collegia, but instead, when Zaïde led her to the room Çeda had sat in for so many nights before becoming a Blade Maiden, she found Amalos poring over a clay tablet at the room's lone desk.

"What's *he* doing here?" Çeda asked Zaïde.

Amalos shivered and lifted his head, eyes wide with fright. When he saw who it was, he visibly calmed and leaned back into the chair. It creaked as he regarded Çeda and Zaïde in turn. "I am here," he said in a raspy voice, "to help."

"You said you didn't *want* to help," Çeda replied. "That you were afraid."

He nodded, a simple gesture that somehow made him seem even more frail. "I was. I am."

He was here because of Davud, of course. His prized student had been snatched up by the Moonless Host, and Amalos felt responsible for it, or at the very least he felt angry enough at the Host that he was willing to set aside his fear. "Perhaps if you'd helped sooner, Davud might not have been taken."

She expected Amalos to be angry, but he only nodded. "A thing I've been struggling with, dear girl, since the day of the attack."

Çeda turned to Zaïde. "And if he changes his mind again?"

"Amalos is willing to help, and I trust him. Are those two things not enough for you?"

Davud, she told herself. *Davud and the others are what's most important.* Releasing a pent-up breath, she said, "Of course, Matron. My apologies."

They settled themselves, at which point Amalos licked his lips and frowned, as if wrestling with his thoughts. "You came here with Davud, Çeda, and you learned some things before entering the House of Maidens. You learned much more on the night King Külaşan died. Before we begin, I think it important that Zaïde and I understand what you know."

It felt so very strange to speak openly of something she'd so rarely spoken of with anyone, but it was also liberating to finally share, so she poured out her history before them, telling them how it had all begun. She started with her mother, how she'd rushed Çeda from their home and into the desert to see Saliah; about the draught of hangman's vine Dardzada had prepared for her; about the haunted look on Ahya's face as she'd left to meet with one of the Kings. "Which King, I never learned, but I know the Blade Maiden Nayyan was lost that same night. Surely the two are related." Çeda told them of how she'd fought the Blade Maiden the night she'd poisoned herself, how the woman had worn a necklace of thorns, which Nayyan was said to have owned.

"I suppose there's a chance the Maiden was Nayyan," Zaïde replied, "but we never learned what happened to her, nor her necklace. She simply disappeared."

Çeda was disappointed. She'd hoped to have her guesses either confirmed or proven false, but Amalos knew nothing about it and Zaïde refused to speculate, so Çeda moved on, telling them what she'd learned of the thirteenth tribe, the men and women and children who had been sacrificed by the Twelve Kings. Their lives had been stolen that night; their very culture, their collective soul, had been struck from the annals of history, amounting to no less than the loss of an entire people. She spoke of Sehid-Alaz and the kiss he'd given her, how it had led her on a strange journey to see Saliah, who was Nalamae in disguise.

Amalos's brow was furrowed. He looked worried. "How can you be sure it was the goddess?"

"She admitted as much. And she turned Goezhen's gaze aside when he came looking for me." Çeda told them how, on the night she'd taken Külaşan's life, Nalamae had come to her while she was speaking with Sehid-Alaz.

"And she came again on the day of the riot," she continued, telling them how Nalamae had paced through the crowd like a sacred spirit, none seeing her as she passed unobstructed to the pier that held the two large barquentines. She could still hear the sounds of the birds as she and the others freed them, could still see their beautiful blue wings flapping over their breasts. Even now she found it both difficult to believe and utterly natural that that wondrous event had broken the riot.

She stopped when she saw how awestruck Zaïde was. Her eyes were filled with wonder. Amalos was little different. "What is it?"

"She's decided to step into the sun," Zaïde said.

"What do you mean?" Çeda asked.

"The goddess," Amalos said, "has been hounded by the other desert gods since the night of Beht Ihman. She was not in their good graces before that, but after, they hunted her, slaying her current incarnation when they could."

"But why?" Çeda asked. "What do they have to fear from her?"

Amalos ran his hand down his white beard, settling it over his chest before speaking again. "That is the very heart of the question, is it not? We know that Nalamae did not go to Tauriyat when the thirteen Kings called upon the desert gods." It was so strange to hear *thirteen*, but of course Sehid-Alaz would have been among them. He would have been as desperate as the others to save Sharakhai from the might of the gathered tribes. The gods had not yet made their demand for sacrifice, nor had he and his people been chosen to fulfill the demand with their blood. "Nalamae has always been known as the god closest to mortal woman and man. Some say that alone is enough for other gods to be jealous of her. And I don't doubt it plays a part—they covet that which we have, the blood of the first gods—but I suspect the greater reason is that Nalamae knew the nature of the bargain her brothers and sisters would demand of the Kings and refused to participate. She knew they would not be swayed, and, further, that they would likely come for her once it was done. It may even be that they killed her *before* they went to Tauriyat."

Çeda frowned. "But as you say, the Kings had not yet made their demands."

Amalos spread his hands wide, as if to indicate the entirety of the desert. "Are the gods not gifted at manipulating man for their own purposes?"

Çeda chewed on this a moment. "If that's so, then might the gods not have fueled the anger of the desert shaikhs, a thing that could lead to the war itself?"

Amalos smiled his scholar's smile. "Very good, Çedamihn. I've long wondered that as well, though who can say now? So much has been lost."

The lantern flickered, making the shadows in the small office dance. "What's important," Zaïde said, "is that Nalamae has risen again. We've traced Nalamae's lives over the four centuries since Beht Ihman. She has been hunted and killed by the other gods a dozen times."

"More, as it turns out," Amalos said. "But she's more difficult to kill than the other gods suspected. She reappears some years later; sometimes only a few years pass, but sometimes as much as a generation goes by before she resurfaces. She often appears as a woman, but she has been known to be reborn as a man. Sometimes she is young, other times old. She has come as a seer and a prophetess, once as a mad sage in the deep of the desert. She either pretends not to know her true nature and her part in the history of Sharakhai or is blinded by her death and rebirth. We cannot say which."

Interesting that he used the word *blinded* to describe her. It made her think of Saliah in the desert, blind yet far-seeing. "I felt no deception in her when she wore the guise of Saliah Riverborn."

"You would know if Saliah were lying?" Amalos chuckled, in a way that made the young blush, for it called their wisdom into question. "You don't think it beyond the goddess to deceive you?"

"When my mother and I went to her, I sparked an augury. Saliah seemed not only surprised by it, but shocked. She had much the same look when I came to her again after you refused to help me." Suddenly Amalos seemed to find something in his lap terribly interesting, but he made no mention of their talk when he'd refused in no uncertain terms to help her in her quest against the Kings. "I'll grant you she might have deceived me," Çeda went on, "but I've been thinking on it a long while now. I believe she saw something in that vision the day before my mother died, and again when I went to her, things that perhaps led her to finding herself once more. It may even be that she willingly sacrificed my mother to learn more."

"What do you mean?" Zaïde asked.

"My mother begged her to shelter me. After I'd climbed her acacia and the chimes rang, she refused to even consider it. I think she knew my mother was going to die, and that I would one day return to her in the desert."

Amalos stirred at this. "Auguries are difficult to interpret, as you know from your time with King Yusam. She may only have been doing what she thought best—whatever would give you, and her, the best chance at succeeding."

"At the cost of my mother's life," Çeda said.

"Not all can be saved," Amalos countered, "especially as the other gods seem to be working against her."

Çeda knew it was so, and she'd given up on wishing things had gone differently that day. They hadn't. And, right or wrong, she was closer to the Kings than she'd ever been, more able to put a stop to their cruel ways. She hadn't asked to walk this path, but she stood upon it now, and she would make the most of it.

"Time grows short," Zaïde said. "We should speak of the Kings' poems. Recite them for Amalos."

And Çeda did.

"Sharp of eye,
and quick of wit,
the King of Amberlark;

with wave of hand,
on cooling sand,
slips he into the dark.

King will shift,
'twixt light and dark,
the gift of onyx sky;

shadows play,
in dark of day,
yet not 'neath Rhia's eye."

"Beşir, of course," Amalos said. "The bane of the desert tribes. He's long been known to slip into shadows in one place and appear from another."

Çeda nodded. "The poems seem to hide each King's gift in the opening verse and their weakness in the second. Külaşan was laid low by the adichara pollen. Could it be the same with Beşir and the light from Rhia?"

Amalos stroked his beard as if it were a sleeping cat. "It seems likely, but let me think on it awhile. The second?"

"The King of Smiles,
from verdant isles,
the gleam in moonlit eye;

with soft caress,
at death's redress,
his wish, lost soul will cry.

Yerinde grants,
a golden band,
with eye of glittering jet;

should King divide,
from Love's sweet pride,
dark souls collect their debt."

Çeda paused. "I'm sure it refers to Mesut. I've seen the band of jet he wears on his wrist."

"Take great care with your assumptions," Amalos said. "Never forget that the Kings know of these poems, and that they've had centuries to prepare themselves for their enemies."

"No, I *know* this bloody verse is his. I saw him in Eventide. He and Cahil took a woman there, perhaps a woman of the thirteenth tribe, and *made* an asir." She went on to tell Amalos about how the woman had been fed Cahil's serum, how Mesut had summoned a soul from his golden band. She shivered, recalling how the woman's skin had desiccated, how the wight had entered her, how she had joined hands with the other asirim. "She'd been beholden to Mesut, bound to him with chains stronger than those on the other asirim in the blooming fields."

Amalos scratched his chin, clearly shaken by this news. "But why?" His eyes searched Zaïde's for answers, all but ignoring Çeda. "Why sacrifice someone new?"

"Because the bonds on the asirim are weakening," Çeda interjected. "It's been happening for years, and the Kings know they'll lose more with each passing year."

"She's right," Zaïde said. "There have been reports of the asirim straining at their leashes. And rumors have been floating through the House of Kings for years now that Mesut goes to the blooming fields to cull those that no longer obey. It may be that he draws them into his golden band."

"And if he can now use them," Çeda said, "binding them to another form, it would shore up the Kings' waning power."

Amalos shook his head, his eyes staring through the stone walls as if he couldn't quite believe it all. "At the cost of yet more lives."

Zaïde stood and raised her hand when Çeda wanted to continue. "Come, we'll not solve all the world's problems today, and it's getting late. We must return to the House of Maidens."

As Zaïde and Çeda wended their way back through the tunnels, Çeda tried to concentrate on the path, but her mind was running wild with all they'd talked about. "Zaïde, what if I tried to learn more from the asir, about Mesut and his bracelet?"

"How?"

"In the desert, the asir I bonded with was the very one Mesut raised in Eventide. He chose her for me, I think, perhaps to ensure that it would be safe for other Maidens to bond with those raised in a similar manner."

Zaïde thought on this as they walked. "It's too dangerous. Besides which, it's not likely that you'll be bonded to another asir for some time, and even if you were, chances are Mesut will choose another."

They were nearing the savaşam. The time she had to speak to Zaïde openly was rapidly shrinking. "I might be able to reach out to the asir, the one I was bonded to, if I took a petal."

"It's too *dangerous,* Çeda. Mesut might sense it. For now, leave it be."

Light flooded the tunnel as Zaïde opened the panel leading to the savaşam. "Zaïde, please, if only I could ask her. Surely she would know—"

Çeda went silent. They weren't alone. Yndris was standing on the far side of the savaşam, just next to the peg where Zaïde's winter robe was hung. The rope that had been tied to the handles of the sliding doors earlier now hung loosely.

"Ask who?" Yndris asked casually.

"Why were you looking through my clothes, Maiden?" Zaïde asked her.

"I came in and found the two of you missing. I was looking for clues. We can't be too careful these days, can we?" Yndris stepped toward them. "Ask who, Çeda? And ask them what?"

But it was Zaïde who answered. "Why would you interrupt our training in the first place?"

Yndris shrugged. "I knocked, and when no one answered, I opened the doors."

"Did you slip that rope, Maiden?"

Yndris was a very pretty girl, but her expression of innocence, a thing that bordered on mockery, was revolting. "It was undone when I arrived," she said. "Does my father know that you take students into the tunnels?"

"Why would His Excellence care one whit where I take my students?"

"Forgive me, Matron. It only seems odd. Times being what they are, enemies all around, it does seem . . . imprudent, does it not, to leave a lesson to run about the hidden tunnels of Tauriyat?"

"What I do with any of my students is no concern of yours."

"Mine? No, you're right, of course. But my father has been consumed in an inconsolable rage over what happened at the collegia. He's convinced we haven't gone nearly far enough with the masses that teem over the west end like termites."

Çeda had met people like Yndris before. Traded words with them. Traded blows as well. But somehow, she'd never been angrier than she was with Yndris now. Yndris had grown up in the halls of her father's palace, and Cahil was one of the few Kings who kept his firstborn children in his palace if they wished it. *Family above all* was the refrain for those sired by the Confessor King. It was said Cahil had always doted on Yndris, a child born with jewels around her throat and gold around her ankles, and here she was speaking of the people in the west end as if they were insects to be crushed beneath her bootheel.

"What's more," Yndris went on, "he isn't pleased at all with your favored Maiden, allowing so many to flee when dozens should have been hung for their crimes."

"What I did saved lives," Çeda said, "which was a fair sight better than you, launching arrows into them as if they were targets on a range."

"They were guilty of *murder*, every single one of them."

"They were only reacting to—" Çeda began, but Zaïde stepped between them.

"You can rest assured I'm taking all the proper precautions, child. Now leave us. We've work to do. And if you ever go through my things again, it'll be lashes for you."

Yndris stared defiantly into Zaïde's eyes. "The whip is no stranger to the halls of King Cahil."

"Would you care for some now, then?"

At this Yndris was silent. She gave Çeda a look that had all the smugness of a sibling who knew she'd found something she could hold over her elder sister. But then she bowed her head and strode from the room, closing the door behind her as though she hadn't a care in the world.

After Zaïde slipped the rope back over the door, and they heard Yndris's footsteps fade, Çeda released a pent-up breath. "We'll never be able to use the tunnel again."

"Don't be ridiculous. It was a mistake not to make the doors more secure, but I'll have a Maiden I trust watch the hall to this room."

"She'll tell her father."

"I'll tell him first. One of the many things we'll be talking about is the flora and fauna of the desert. It so happens there are several type of fungi that we use in our ointments and salves. And there is a special place deep beneath Sharakhai that has a slow flow of water that is especially effective at treating ringworm. There are a dozen reasons more for us to be wandering the tunnels, so think nothing of it. If you're asked, play innocent. You have no idea when or how often we might visit the tunnels. Give Yndris no reason to suspect anything. But be vigilant as well. We cannot afford more mistakes."

"Very well," Çeda said, though her nerves were frayed.

"You will come for training six hours each day. I will continue to teach you the way to your heart, and others', but I will also teach you history, mathematics, and language—your King's script is passable, but you need much more work on the spoken and written forms of our neighboring kingdoms. We will deepen your knowledge of plants and herbs, how to make healing salves and a range of poisons. And courtly manners, child. Gods know you're a bull amongst babes. You must learn all these things, quickly and well if you're to have time to go to Amalos and search for clues."

"Why must I learn so much? If I could spend more time with Amalos—"

"Don't be foolish. If you do not, the Maidens—or worse, the Kings themselves—will suspect. And besides, you *must* be trained, Çedamihn. There is much that lies ahead, for all of us." She took Çeda by the shoulders and took her in from head to toe. "Now you are little more than unsharpened steel, but put a keen edge on you and a fine weapon you shall make."

"And if Yndris or someone else comes for me while I'm gone?"

"I will steer them wide. But few will come, and I'll make sure that Sayabim keeps Yndris busier than she has ever been in her life. The need to learn is a rite of passage taken seriously among the Maidens. Now, repeat after me." Zaïde proceeded to show Çeda a series of hand signs—basic directions for left and right and up and down—that would take her through the maze of corridors to the collegium historia. Çeda memorized the sequence and repeated it for Zaïde.

"Again," Zaïde said after she'd done it once. Then twice more until she was satisfied. "Good. You'll show me again when next we meet."

Chapter 29

DAVUD OPENED HIS EYES TO DARKNESS. His head was pounding. He coughed, his throat dry as sand. It was cold in this place. So very cold. He was lying on a bed of warmth-stealing stone that was moist, slick in some places. He pushed himself up off the floor and felt for the walls, stumbling across a bucket. He found water within, a wooden ladle as well. He drank from it desperately, downing as much as his stomach could bear. Only then did he continue his search for the boundaries of this place. He was in a tight cell, a few paces from wall to wall. The air didn't feel stale, but neither was it fresh. It smelled of the earth—rather like the tunnels below the scriptorium.

The collegia . . . Sharakhai . . . How far away they seemed. Worlds away. He reasoned he was still *somewhere* in the desert, but that could be anywhere. The Shangazi wasn't called the Great Mother for no reason. It was massive. It took weeks to sail from one end to the other.

Come, Davud. You can reason this out if you try.

He thought back to the few moments he'd had on the deck of that ship. It had been past midday. And by the angle of the shadows on deck, he judged that they'd been heading on a southeasterly course. Surely they'd been trying to get as far away from Sharakhai as they could. If they kept to the direction they'd been traveling—a suspect assumption at best, but he had to start somewhere—it would land them in the traditional lands of Tribe Kadri or Tribe Kenan. Kadri were nominal allies of the Kings, the Kenan were not, so Davud's best guess was that they were taking shelter in some Kenan stronghold. He remembered reading of old abandoned mountain keeps that they'd built in the years leading up to the war with Sharakhai. That would place them in the foothills of Iri's Teeth.

"All conjecture," he said into the darkness, the words echoing. "Guesses at best."

"And yet guesses can lead to the truth."

Davud shivered at the sound of the voice coming from somewhere above.

"Who's there?" But he already knew. It was the man who'd looked upon him so curiously on the deck of the ship. Hamzakiir.

He started as something flapped against the wall near him. He felt it graze his arm. A coarse rope, he discovered after waving his arms back and forth. He held it like an idiot, thinking Hamzakiir might lower himself down, or that one of the Host might.

"If you wish to remain," said Hamzakiir, "I can draw the rope back up. There is, as you can well imagine, more than one collegia graduate to occupy my mind."

Davud grabbed the coarse rope, tugged on it to ensure it was sound, then began to climb. He was no soldier, no pit fighter to climb such things with ease, and yet it came easier to him than he'd guessed, and soon he had reached the top and levered himself over the stone lip. Strangely, the aches and pains he'd felt upon waking had vanished, leaving him with a heady, exhilarating feeling he could only assume was due to being let out of that terrible hole. Dim light came from a tunnel to his left. High walls surrounded him, but the ceiling above was lost in a sea of darkness.

"Where are we?"

Hamzakiir began walking toward the tunnel. "As unimportant as a tally of the grains of sand in the Shangazi."

Davud followed when it became clear Hamzakiir would be content to leave him behind. "Where are my friends?"

"A much more interesting question. For now, let us leave it aside. We'll return to it, I promise you."

"Why have you brought me up from that hole?"

"Ah, now we're nearing the mark." They reached a room with a small wooden table, with a lantern upon it and another short tunnel that led to a winding set of stairs. Hamzakiir took up the lantern and walked to the stairs, then began climbing up. "You're a scholar now, is it not so?"

"Yes."

"Then tell me, how did your friends find themselves asleep within our ship?"

Davud remembered the screams, the rising panic when they realized they were being gassed in the basilica. That was the obvious answer, but from the way Hamzakiir had approached the question, he seemed to be looking for something more. From what he'd learned of the basic alchemy classes he'd taken, he suspected that such an application of gas would last only hours at best. They might have used the gas on them again. It would have been relatively easy to do so in the enclosed space. But he recalled no container or bag in the hold, and there had been no residual scent. More importantly, it would explain the marks of blood they'd all had on their foreheads.

"You forced us to sleep with blood magic."

"Very good," Hamzakiir said.

A rush of fresh air hit them as they reached a hallway—ground level, Davud assumed—but Hamzakiir continued up the winding stairwell. There was a strong urge to run down the hall, to find his way out and back into the real world, but what good would that do? Surely there were guards. Or if not, Hamzakiir would be able to stop him with a wave of his hand. He'd have betrayed himself for no gain. He needed to find his friends, to gain his bearings and recover from the ordeal of traveling here.

"Now, a rather important question . . . Why do you suppose it was *you* who woke while your fellow scholars did not?"

There seemed to be only one logical answer. "A mistake. The blood wasn't applied properly, or the sigil was malformed in some way."

Davud knew little enough about blood magic, but he'd read some texts of magi who'd attempted to share what they'd learned, to pass it along to others.

A blood mage conceptualized the effects they hoped to achieve when they applied or imbibed blood. In written form these effects were called sigils—complex symbols of power with layer upon layer of meaning—but the term "sigil" also applied to the layering the magi did within their minds to effect the spells. There were dozens of stories of magi applying sigils improperly, from haste or poor memory. Most often the spell would simply fail. Other times the intended effect would be altered or weakened. Rarely, the effect would be something unintended and potentially disastrous for the mage.

"Reasonable enough inferences, yet both are incorrect." Hamzakiir was becoming winded, as was Davud. "Have you no other guesses?"

Davud thought back to how he'd awoken, the strange dizziness, the heartbeat he'd felt that had seemed like someone else's. He'd thought it a remnant of some dream. But now, looking back, it felt wrong and unnatural. "I might have said *you* woke me," Davud finally replied, "but you were surprised when I was pulled up on deck, intrigued that I'd done so, so that can't be it."

After several more turns, they came to an upper room of a minaret, a lookout of sorts. The ceiling was made of the same reddish stone as the stairs they'd climbed, but the floor was covered in a beautiful, if somewhat worn, patterned mosaic. They were three stories up, and overlooked the desert in the distance and a jumble of buildings nearby. A desert keep, perhaps. But as Davud stepped closer to the stone balustrade, he realized how wrong he was. There were several dozen buildings, even a plot of land off to his left with green fields. They were in a caravanserai, though which it might be he wasn't sure. From the direction they'd been sailing, he guessed Ishmantep, or perhaps farther along the eastern caravan route to Tiazet or Ashdankaat.

Strangely, Davud felt more vibrant than before. *The sun,* he told himself. *It must be the sun and the heat of the desert breeze.*

"Let me tell you a tale," Hamzakiir said as he stepped beside Davud. "Many years ago, there was a young man born to the Kings of Sharakhai. A first son. He was trained in many things, and among them as a linguist so that he might follow in King Ihsan's footsteps, perhaps one day to work in his stead, negotiating trade agreements with the kingdoms that surround the Great Mother. One day he was taken to Qaimir, merely to listen, to learn from the Honey-tongued King as he spoke on topics that had long been discussed between Sharakhai and the southern kingdom. The Qaimiri king was of a mind to forge an accord that would, if enacted, grievously harm a family that had long been one of the proudest in their grand history but that had fallen on hard times as their monopoly on the southern shipping routes steadily eroded.

"The Qaimiri king met with Ihsan for long days, and eventually they reached an agreement. They had but to sign the documents that our young son drafted under Ihsan's strict guidance. That very night, a feast was held. Rich food was served. Red wine was poured. The conversation was gay, for many in Qaimir were set to benefit from the agreement. But as the dinner wore on, King Ihsan grew quieter, as did his retinue, all but our young man. He noted the odd behavior of his countrymen, but thought it a symptom of how very late they'd been working the past many days.

"But then he saw the Honey-tongued King take up a knife. The moment the King did, the others in Ihsan's retinue moved against those from Qaimir, and did so violently, pushing them away from the King's chair at the head of the table. The first son was confused, to put it mildly, but there was so much more to it than met the eye. He felt a tug on his soul like a deep craving for food, or for sex, only stronger, nearly undeniable. It was this, he knew, that the King and the others from his homeland had succumbed to. He knew that his King had no ill will toward the King of Qaimir, so he held him, shouted for Ihsan to return to himself."

Hamzakiir's gaze shifted, his eyes caught by a line of dark-hulled ships with sails like scythes. They were curving around a hill in the distance, heading for the caravanserai. Hamzakiir was talking about himself, Davud knew, this first son of Sharakhai, but for the life of him he still had no idea *why* he was telling this tale. *A tug on his soul,* he'd said. A compulsion, the sort blood magi can lay upon others. It was to do with the family, Davud understood, the one who'd been slighted, else why mention them at all? And with that simple connection, Davud began to understand.

"It was you, but your abilities had not yet manifested."

Hamzakiir pulled his gaze away from the approaching ships, a hint of a smile on his lips and at the corners of his wrinkled eyes. "Indeed, they had not." He turned away, brushing sand and dust from the balustrade as if it offended him. The sand fluttered away, taken by the wind to curl down toward the red roof below. "As it turned out, the Qaimiri family had several careful, if not particularly strong, blood magi in their employ. They had conspired to have their King Rejando killed, but failed when a man traveling with King Ihsan had the potential to become a magi himself. He would one day become quite strong, I'm not afraid to say, but on that day I knew nothing of my talents in the dark ways of blood."

There was only one conclusion Davud could come to that made any sense. Davud waking when none of the others lying in the hold of that ship had. Hamzakiir's strange reaction when Davud had been brought to the deck. This strange separation from all the others. The conversation they were having now. "You think I have the same potential."

"It has likely come as a surprise, for I can see now that no one has ever told you of your potential. But yes, Davud Mahzun'ava. You might become a blood mage. If you so chose."

"If I *chose*? Why by the gods' sweet breath would I choose that?"

"There is much given to the mage. More than you can imagine."

"I know enough. To deal in blood is to deal in misery, to drink of death."

Hamzakiir shook his head violently. "To deal in blood is to deal in *life*!"

"The edge of a blade brings only pain."

"And yet by killing an enemy you may save the innocent," Hamzakiir countered.

Davud laughed. "You speak of the innocent. What of the scholars you stole from the forum? Is this the life you spoke of, to wield them in some way against the Kings?"

"What do my purposes have to do with it? If I cut a man down with the swing of a shamshir, could you not use the same weapon to save a child?"

Some of the bravado had drained from Davud, and he began to feel alone and very afraid. "Where are my friends?"

"That must remain with me."

Davud stared out over the distant dunes, watched the people of the caravanserai walk about the streets, saw the docks where crews worked the ships, readying them to set sail. "Why would you want to teach me anything?"

"Do you know how the red ways were first brought to the Shangazi?"

"By the Qaimiri."

"True, but from whom did they learn them?"

Davud had no idea. He'd never had cause to study any of this.

"A child of Goezhen," Hamzakiir went on. "An ehrekh. One of the elder beasts made by the god of chaos in the early days of his dark experiments. Like many ehrekh, this elder hungered for the blood of man, for we are blessed with the blood of the first gods. The young gods are not, and the children of Goezhen are doubly damned, for Goezhen instilled in them much of his own hunger. The ehrekh went to Qaimir in the guise of a wizard. He lived among them for many long years, and although he tasted of their blood, there were also those he came to love. He allowed them to watch while he worked. It amused him to teach them his ways. Indeed, to see them prosper, to use their own blood in ways even he hadn't thought of. It proved his undoing. More than a century after crossing the border into Qaimir, he was killed by two of his disciples, twin sisters, both of them adepts."

"I care for my friends, not stories of Qaimir."

Hamzakiir pursed his lips, glancing at Davud in the way a man of the streets might size up an approaching threat. "Your impudence grates."

"I wish only to take leave of this place with my brothers and sisters by my side."

"A path no longer open to you."

"Then what? You expect me to be taught by you? Why would I ever allow such a thing?"

"The twin sisters," Hamzakiir said. "They had a brother who, as was later learned, might become gifted in the ways of blood. They didn't know it, but the ehrekh did, and because of some perceived slight, the ehrekh let the boy go through his change unaided."

"His change?"

Hamzakiir turned now to Davud, a most curious look on his face. "There are those who might become a blood mage and never know it. They go through life none the wiser. But there are those who, once awoken, are taken by it, by the very *need* for blood."

At last it was dawning on Davud why Hamzakiir had looked at him so strangely on the deck of the ship, with a look akin to pity, why he'd separated Davud from the other graduates, and why, most importantly, he was making this strange offer.

"You think I will die from this change . . ."

"If left alone, your death is a certainty. It's indisputable that the strength of the one who first touches you with blood will affect just how quickly the change will come—that and the potential of the one touched. I've seen many over the years who might walk the red ways. I've seen few with gifts such as yours. You might become powerful indeed, but only if you survive the change that is coming."

Davud shook his head. "Again I ask you why?"

Like a chef wandering the stalls of the spice market, Hamzakiir seemed to choose his next words with care. "Some have died from the change because they never knew and had no hope of being saved. Others died because it was their time, and the lord of all things had summoned them. But there are some few who perish even though their nature is very much known, to themselves and those with the ability to aid them. They die because in many parts of the world the red paths are shunned, and magi are killed for practicing it. And in some rare cases"—Hamzakiir paused to glance at Davud—"it is nothing more than a cold choice made for personal gain."

Davud knew Hamzakiir was testing him, but he didn't understand what he was getting at. He was sick of this game. He didn't trust Hamzakiir to tell him the truth. And yet the mystery Hamzakiir presented nagged at him. Had someone died who Hamzakiir cared about? Had he felt betrayed by it?

And then Davud understood. It was simple with all the pieces laid out. Hamzakiir was the son of Külaşan the Wandering King. He was also a very powerful blood mage, and he'd just told Davud how he'd stumbled onto his own abilities in Qaimir. But he hadn't been a mage at the time. He'd not yet gone through his *change*. He was a first son and, as such, would have needed permission from the Kings to get the training he needed, especially considering that at that time, generations ago, blood magi were persecuted in Sharakhai.

"Your father denied you your training," Davud finally said.

"*Tried* to deny me," Hamzakiir corrected. "In gratitude to my actions, the Qaimiri king offered it himself. But my father was a coward. He considered sons and daughters cheaply made, and reasoned that a dead son was less nuisance than having a blood magi walk the halls of his palace. So I fled Sharakhai and traveled to Qaimir on my own. I found my way into their halls of learning despite my father's demands that I return, despite the Twelve Kings applying steadily mounting pressure." He paused for a moment, considering, his piercing eyes weighing Davud more carefully than he had before. "So now you see. As surely as the sun does rise, you will die without my help." He raised one hand toward the bright oasis and the caravanserai surrounding it. "Do you choose to live and to learn?" His other hand he raised toward the dark set of stairs leading down. "Or do you wish to hide in a hole until your nature catches up with you?"

"Days ago you were ready to kill me."

He nodded, granting Davud the point. "A man can change his mind."

Davud felt his breath coming on him, felt his pulse pounding in his neck. "I would kill you had I the chance, in order to free them."

"I would expect no less."

Dear gods, what could he do? He didn't want to die. He wanted to travel. To learn. To see more of this grand world. But all that had changed. *The gods care little for your hopes and fears.* And then a thought occurred to him. "Free some of them, and I will do as you ask."

Hamzakiir shook his head like the stoic monks who lived in mountain monasteries and came from time to time to Sharakhai. "As I've said, their fate is sealed."

He thought of Anila and Meiwei and Jasur. Bakhi forgive him, he didn't wish to blaspheme by choosing the living from among the dead, but he couldn't stop without at least trying. "Give me three of them. What is a mere handful to you?"

But to this Hamzakiir merely shook his head again. "That I cannot do."

"Then return me to the darkness."

Hamzakiir seemed to be weighing Davud's words against this strange compulsion not merely to save Davud but to set him on a path neither of them would have predicted. "You will come to regret this."

"I don't care." The words sounded petulant, even to Davud's ear.

"The first days of the change may be kind to the body," Hamzakiir went on. "You may feel euphoric, your body as sound as it has ever been. As the days wear on, however, you will be plunged into an unending pool of misery."

He was right on the first count. Davud *did* feel potent. But he could not simply abandon his friends.

"So be it," Hamzakiir finally said, motioning to the stairs.

Davud thought of pleading one last time, but he could see that Hamzakiir wasn't going to change his mind, so after one last glance to the bright of the desert, the green of the nearby fields, the blue of the pool at the center of the caravanserai, he turned and headed into the darkness. Down he wound, ever lower, the chill of the earth clinging to him, until he found himself at the edge of the deep pit once more. He climbed down, sat holding himself as the rope was pulled up. Then Hamzakiir's footsteps faded, and Davud was alone once more.

Chapter 30

IN A COVERED ARABA PULLED BY A PAIR of short but stout ponies, Meryam sat on a padded bench next to Ramahd. The driver was whistling shrilly at a mule dray moving too slow for his liking, but a moment later, the araba lurched as the driver led them over a large pothole and moved past the dray.

The sun was bright, the air stifling compared to the wide open wind he'd grown accustomed to on the voyage aboard the tribesmen's ship. It felt strange to be riding along the Trough after being gone from Sharakhai for so long. He glanced over at Meryam, who sat on his left staring at the city with emotionless eyes. Stranger still after all that he and Meryam had been through since leaving the Shangazi with Hamzakiir, their prize.

Ramahd snorted softly, returning his gaze to the busy street as their araba forged its way through traffic. *Some prize*, he thought. *No sooner had we reached our home than our* prize *turned the tables*. And now it had cost them their king. It had cost Ramahd his best man in Dana'il.

Ramahd blinked away the vision of Dana'il lying dead on the dungeon floor and instead leaned out and stared up at the immensity of Tauriyat, the amber megalith standing to the east of the city center. He'd been sent to Sharakhai to keep an eye on the Kings, but he'd been driven by his thirst to avenge the deaths of his wife and child. And now his king was dead, his bones bleaching somewhere out on the sands of the Shangazi. Hamzakiir had played them all for fools.

"Did he allow himself to be taken?" he wondered.

"What?" Meryam croaked, still watching the crowd.

"Hamzakiir," he said softly. "Did he allow himself to be taken?"

"To what purpose?"

"To toy with us. Or to gain some distance from the Host so that he could approach them again on his own terms."

She turned to him, her sunken eyes aflame. "What matter is that now?"

Ramahd was ready to object, but Meryam's look was so fierce he didn't press. She got that look most often whenever her father was mentioned. Surely she felt guilt over what had happened, but she never said so. As Yasmine had always done, she was surely using it as fuel for the fire that drove her, a thirst that could never be quenched. It made him wonder just what she had planned now that they'd returned to Sharakhai.

"No matter," Ramahd said at last.

She looked him up and down, as if annoyed at his very presence, then returned her gaze to the throngs moving along the Trough.

They soon reached the Wheel, then went east toward the gates of Tauriyat. The Silver Spears manning it inspected them carefully. The two of them shared a dubious look, and seemed ready to send them away, when Meryam said, "Ask him," and pointed to a captain of the guard. Ramahd recognized him, and thankfully he recognized both Ramahd and Meryam. "Please accept my apologies, my lady," the captain said, bowing deeply to them. "If there's anything the consulate needs, I trust you'll have your servants inform me."

Meryam, lying back in the bench with a sour, pained expression, said nothing, but Ramahd waved to the captain, and soon they were off to the manor where they'd spent so much time in Sharakhai.

They were met with open-mouthed stares by their countrymen. Basilio, a distant cousin of Meryam's and the man who had taken Ramahd's place as the Qaimiri ambassador here in Sharakhai, led them in himself. "Please, is there anything I might do to help after your harrowing journey?"

Being treated as a lord after so long in the desert was so strange a thing that Ramahd didn't know how to feel about it. In some ways that moment months ago when Hamzakiir had first dominated his mind felt like it had happened only yesterday, the events since ephemeral, dreamlike mirages in the desert. But it also felt as though every day that followed had lasted an age, and that his life had stretched across every excruciating moment of it.

They sat down for a meal that evening with Basilio and his wife, Eloise. They were a fine couple. Handsome. Polite. But for some reason Ramahd couldn't stomach the idle chitchat after all that had happened. He ate of the blood-red elk medallions before him, he pecked at the baby parsnips, and tried his best to speak of things that weren't related to death in the desert or fallen kings. "Might we speak alone?" he said to Basilio when he could stand it no longer.

They'd not finished their meals, but Eloise immediately dabbed the corners of her mouth with her napkin and stood. "The three of you will have much to speak about, of course." She bowed her head to Meryam, then Ramahd. "My queen. My lord."

Alu's light, how strange to hear it. But it was high time Ramahd started using it himself. *Queen. Queen Meryam.* He was embarrassed he hadn't been using it all along, as befit her station. A memory flashed, Meryam naked in the water, speaking softly, huskily. *Your queen wills it,* before taking him in her mouth.

"Whether we wish it or not," he remembered telling Meryam that night, wondering at all they'd been through, "time is a river, ever moving, bearing us to new places."

"Until the water pulls you down," she'd replied easily, "secreting your bones beside the souls of those who came before."

As Eloise left, the servants swept in and cleared their plates. Meryam, as was her wont these past weeks, had eaten only a bird's helping, and the servants took away a plate nearly full. The wine, however, she drank deeply, and took her goblet up once more as the door closed, downing a fresh swallow with gusto.

Basilio ran his hand over his beard, then steepled both hands over his ample belly. He looked between Meryam and Ramahd. "I thought to wait until tomorrow to tell you, but as we are here now, there is news from Almadan."

"Go on, then," Meryam said, clunking her goblet against the table and falling heavily into her chair. She was not drunk yet, but was well on her way. Or so she wanted it to seem.

Ramahd knew just how much Meryam could drink. It was part and parcel of her condition, an indicator of how close to the edge she pushed her abilities as a mage. The closer she was to death, she'd told him once, the more able she was to harness the power in blood. She'd even said she could taste the very touch of the first gods, could smell the scent of the farther fields. He didn't believe that, but he *had* seen her drink two full carafes of wine on her own and still be able to walk a straight line.

Which meant she wanted Basilio to think she was beyond her senses. Which in turn meant she didn't trust him. Why, Ramahd wasn't yet sure, but he'd play along until he understood.

"There was some question over whether you were alive," Basilio said. "We all hoped and prayed for your safe return, you and your father both." He looked to Ramahd. "And you as well, my lord."

Ramahd nodded for him to continue.

"But the kingdom has needs, and so plans were made—"

"To pass the crown," Meryam said, leaning forward and staring Basilio straight in the eye, "over my father's dead body. Over mine as well. That was the way of things, wasn't it?"

"I mightn't put it so bluntly."

Meryam eyed Basilio, barking a laugh. "Then how might you put it?"

"You left under such strange circumstances, my queen. And this after *arriving* under such strange circumstances. There were those who were nervous from the beginning that we'd taken Külaşan's son and paraded him like a prize before the lords of our kingdom. They worried that we had displeased Mighty Alu, that ill would befall us."

Meryam laughed, a low chuckle that built the longer it went. "Well they were right on *that* count, weren't they?"

Basilio could no longer seem to hold Meryam's gaze. His balding pate furrowed like a field in spring as he slowly spun the base of his wineglass. "I wouldn't like to say, my queen, but the lords were wroth that they had been taken so, played with like puppets in a play for Hamzakiir's amusement. And they now know of Guhldrathen as well."

"How could they know?" Ramahd asked.

"Because Hamzakiir spoke of it in the capital before he left."

The gall, Ramahd thought. He'd told the lords of Qaimir exactly what he'd planned to do with their king, but they hadn't been able to do anything against him, ensorcelled as they were.

"Some few," Basilio said, "worried over your return."

"Worried . . ." Meryam pounded the table, making the silverware rattle. "Who? Abrantes? Gueron? Remigio?"

Basilio hesitated. "Among others."

"How low we've come." Meryam drained her glass in three loud swallows, then slapped it down. "Quaking in our boots at the mere mention of the Sharakhani Kings."

"I'm apt to agree with you, my queen. But those in Almadan view it differently. There has been talk of placing another on the throne even if you did return."

Meryam paused, but didn't seem shocked. In fact, she seemed to accept it, as if she'd known it was coming and had already made up her mind about it. All the fire she'd shown only moments ago seemed to drain from her, and she seemed small and frail once more. "Well, there's little surprise in that, I suppose."

Though Basilio tried to hide it, Ramahd caught a momentary look of disgust on his face at Meryam's sudden weakness. "My queen. One of our ships leaves in two days. If you wish to return to Almadan, I'll arrange for it. You have but to command me."

Meryam seemed to consider it. "There is unfinished business here in the desert. I would speak with the Kings first. Cement a new understanding between our two countries. Need I leave with haste to set things aright?"

"Far be it for me to deny you, your excellence, but you were the one who took Hamzakiir from this city. The Kings of Sharakhai may view you as an enemy."

"Is that what they're saying in Almadan?"

Basilio looked suddenly uncomfortable. "It has been said."

"By whom?"

"Who knows where whispers begin, or how they echo through castle halls? The point is that it is being spoken openly now."

"Are things so dire in Almadan, then?"

Basilio made quite a show of pondering the question. He waggled his head. His face soured as if he'd bitten into a Malasani lime and he toyed with the silverware before him. "Your people need you, my queen, and I don't advise leaving the throne for long. But yes, I believe there is time."

Meryam nodded, her eyes heavy with drink. "Very well. Send news with the ship that I am in Sharakhai and will travel home as soon as I'm able."

"Of course," Basilio said. "It will be as you say." He blinked his eyes, and ran his napkin over his lips and mustache. "It has been a long day for you, after many long, harrowing weeks. I'm sure you'll wish to rest."

When Meryam nodded, Basilio stood, bowed, and gave his farewells. The moment the door closed behind him, the glazed look in Meryam's eyes faded.

The transformation was so sudden Ramahd nearly laughed. "What was that all about?"

"Men like Basilio never give themselves away when someone with strength stands before them. But make yourself seem unsure and their true nature reveals itself. When given the choice of my returning to Almadan or remaining, he allowed that I could stay. No man as shrewd as Basilio would ever advise such a thing when there is so much uncertainty in Qaimir."

Ramahd paused. "You admit that what you're doing is foolish, then?"

Her expression turned dark. "I admit no such thing. It is a calculated risk. My point is that Basilio is little more than a tool for others in Qaimir. He and his entire family have long been the Abrantes' lapdogs."

"The Abrantes have long been overeager."

Meryam nodded. "My father kept them close, and for good reason. Their vineyards and their men at arms are too valuable to do otherwise. But now I've little doubt that they fought for Basilio's position here to control our presence in Sharakhai from afar."

Ramahd looked to the door at the far end of the room. "What will we do with our good Basilio, then?"

Meryam shrugged. "For now, nothing. The news of my return will put cracks in the foundations of their plans. It will be a while yet before they're ready to make their next move. They'll want Basilio to watch me, see what my inclinations might be. In the meantime, there's a larger game afoot."

There was a gleam in Meryam's eyes that Ramahd remembered from their time hunting Macide. It had been gone for a long while now. The journey back to Qaimir, their time in Almadan and later, Viaroza, the shock after their forced meeting with Guhldrathen and Aldouan's death, had all seen a different Meryam. But to see her old self return so strongly, so quickly, so completely, made Ramahd wonder at all that had happened, and why . . .

Like a root, the thought crept deeper and deeper into his mind. It was so foul and devious he felt embarrassed having thought it, but he couldn't shake it. While Ramahd had been acting as the Qaimiri ambassador to Sharakhai, Aldouan had often hampered their efforts. At every turn, he'd taken such careful steps it had given the Host time to adjust, time to escape. Even Meryam had found her father's strictures more and more difficult to live with. So what if Aldouan's control over her simply . . . vanished? With the power of the throne in her hands, what might she do then?

He shivered. Could she have done it? Taken Hamzakiir to Qaimir with that very thing in mind? Could she have *planted* in Hamzakiir's mind an unyielding directive before he returned to the Moonless Host? Might he have been *allowed* to go so that Meryam could follow his movements as he thought himself perfectly free? It would give Meryam so much information about the Host, more than they'd ever been able to glean before. But it was all predicated on the assumption that Meryam could take such a step, to kill her own father in order to gain more power, or at the very least more freedom. It seemed a stretch. She had seemed so distraught in the desert after Aldouan's grisly murder. Could that have been guilt in her eyes and not grief as Ramahd had assumed?

I've done a terrible thing, Ramahd.

"Ramahd Amansir, you look like you've stepped on your own grave."

Perhaps I have. "A game, you said. It made me think of Guhldrathen. The promise I made."

"The girl . . ."

"Yes, the *girl*, the White Wolf. She doesn't deserve that."

"Well, if you're so worried for her, all we need do is serve Hamzakiir up on a platter. The only question is how."

"I've been thinking on that." Ramahd rang the small silver bell on the lace-covered table.

Meryam's eyebrows rose. "We've been in Sharakhai less than a day and you've made plans. I am impressed, Ramahd."

A servant woman stepped into the room. "My queen."

"Send Tiron in."

The woman bowed and ducked out of the room.

Meryam refilled her goblet. With a steady hand, she examined the carmine contents. She took a slow swallow, then licked her lips. "Tell me."

After knocking back a swallow from his own goblet, Ramahd nodded. "You recall how I found the White Wolf?"

"Juvaan Xin-Lei."

"I believe it's time we learned what Queen Alansal is truly up to in the desert."

"Mirea . . ."

"Just so, my queen."

King Aldouan had refused to allow Ramahd or Meryam to look too deeply into Mirea's activities. But with his death, their shackles had been removed. There was sense in being prudent—Mirea was not a tiger one should poke without reason—but it was long past time they discovered more about her plans. And that meant learning more about Juvaan Xin-Lei, her primary agent in Sharakhai.

Again the thought prodded him. Had Meryam planned this all along?

He quickly shoved it aside. It was too cynical. Meryam loved her father dearly.

After a knock at the door, Tiron, a man of thirty years who wore a perpetual scowl to match his scruffy beard, stepped into the room and bowed deeply to them both. "My queen. My lord."

"Come," Ramahd said, motioning to the chair across from him, the one Basilio had so recently occupied. "Tell our queen what you've found."

Tiron frowned, which for Tiron was merely a sign of reflection. "As you bade me before you left the desert, I've been keeping an eye on Juvaan's movements, but he's a very careful man. Careful enough that I never see him go to the wrong places, or speaking to the wrong people. He spends most of his time in Tauriyat. We saw his man, Ruan, go to his contact in the Host only once after the Wandering King's death. And Osman, the owner of the pits, has gone nowhere near Tauriyat or Juvaan. They've not been seen anywhere with one another as far as we can tell." Tiron tipped his head to Ramahd. "Finding so little, we began following Osman's most trusted men. There are

Deha, Bahral, and Fa'id, but through none of them did we find the slightest ties to Juvaan."

Meryam looked from Tiron to Ramahd. "Dear Alu, the two of you treat secrets like diamonds the size of your own two stones. Spill your tale, Tiron, before I die of old age."

At last the glimmer of a smile showed on Tiron's face. "A young tough has been moving up the past few years. It seems Osman thinks his shoulders ready for a heavier burden."

Meryam considered this. "This man's name?"

"Tariq Esad'ava. And he's been seen in the company of those who ferry messages to Ruan, so I think we have the right man, but there's danger."

There was always danger in this sort of work. Tiron meant something unexpected. "How so?"

"I did some rooting around. It may not have anything to do with Juvaan, but Tariq has been known to visit the Tattered Prince in the Knot."

Meryam seemed unfazed by this, but Ramahd hated complications. "Who is the Tattered Prince?"

"A man who's built a reputation as something of a hero," Tiron answered. "For several years he's been helping the addicts there, and they love him for it."

"What do you mean? Helps them how?"

"Provides a safe place for them. Helps to free them from the smoke." Tiron shrugged. "Rumor says he was once an addict himself."

"He's no one we can't handle," Meryam said to Ramahd. She considered for a moment, absently pinching her bottom lip before taking Ramahd in with a look that made it clear she was ready to act. "Bring me Tariq."

"You're sure?" Ramahd asked. "There's time to consider your next move more carefully."

"I'm sure."

Ramahd nodded. "Then consider it done."

Deep in the back alleys of the Well, Ramahd and Tiron crouched beneath a garden arbor. Tiron was dressed as a west end beggar, his face dirty, his hair a filthy mess. The garden around them was green and vibrant, filled with a dozen types of flowers. Ivy choked the arbor's slats, hiding them effectively from the nearby alley and, more importantly, the street crossing only a short distance away.

Ramahd was glad to have Tiron by his side. He was one of the few still in Sharakhai—still *alive*, Ramahd reminded himself—from those who had joined the attack on Külaşan's palace. The rest were dead, or presumed dead. Quezada, Rafiro, and Hernand had all been left on the ship that Hamzakiir had sailed from the southern border of the Great Shangazi. They might yet draw breath, but if so they were in Hamzakiir's control and there was only a hare's chance in a wolf's den they'd make it through the experience alive. It comforted him to know Tiron and his brother, Luken, had a stake in this, that they along with Ramahd might have a chance at revenge.

Tiron shifted by his side, lifting his head. With a deeper scowl than normal on his face, he pointed down the alley, where several men had just reached the crossing. "There he is."

Three men were walking side by side. Two were simple guardsmen. Hired thugs. The third was dressed in clothes that were fine but steeped in the styles of the desert, the sort of clothes the prince of a desert tribe might wear. This, surely, was Tariq.

"Best get moving," Ramahd said.

Tiron nodded and left, leaving the garden quickly, then walking along the alley with a bit of a limp, a bit of a stagger, a very good approximation of a drunk turning sober and looking for money to fill his next cup. Holding a beggar's bowl before him, he approached Tariq and his bodyguards. One of the brutes, studded cudgel in hand, blocked Tiron's path. He said something Ramahd couldn't quite hear, but when Tiron made to bypass him, waving his bowl toward Tariq, he raised his cudgel and shouted, "One more step and it's a knock to the skull!"

It was then that Ramahd saw a form break from the shadows behind Tariq—Luken, his dark clothes blending in well with the mudbrick buildings, the dusty street. He padded quietly, a slim knife in hand. As Tiron attempted a drunken rush past the guards, the guard who'd shouted took a swipe at Tiron. In that moment, Luken reached Tariq's side, cut his purse from his belt, and ran quick as a jackal down a dark alley on the far side of the crossroads. Tiron immediately disengaged and ran down a different street as a group of gutter wrens, who'd been sitting on the stone stoop of a building, all pointed and laughed.

The guards seemed momentarily unsure what to do, go after Tiron or Luken or remain with Tariq.

"The purse," Tariq said in an exasperated tone. "Get the fucking purse."

Ramahd was already on his way. As the guardsmen lumbered after Luken and the stolen coin, Ramahd padded over the dusty earth toward Tariq.

Give Tariq credit. Ramahd was quiet as could be, and still Tariq sensed him. He turned just in time, twisting away as Ramahd bulled into him. He caught one of Ramahd's wrists and managed to throw Ramahd over one hip.

But Ramahd was no newcomer to street tussles. With his free hand he grabbed a fistful of hair along the top of Tariq's head. He used it, and the momentum of the throw, to pull Tariq down with him. Tariq landed hard. He tried to call for help, but Ramahd had slipped one arm around Tariq's neck on the way down and was now tightening it like a noose. Tariq tried to slip free, to pull Ramahd's arm away, but he had no leverage. All too soon he'd gone limp.

Ramahd rolled him over and sat across his hips. The gutter wrens were no longer laughing.

"If I were you," Ramahd said, "I'd take my chance to leave."

They took the hint. Every one of them left, leaving Ramahd alone in the street with Tariq. Ramahd spun a bulky ring on his thumb and pressed its sharp point deep into his own wrist. It pierced between the other, older marks, drawing a thin stream of blood. He held the dripping wound over Tariq's mouth, parting his lips with his free hand so that it pattered against his teeth and tongue.

Tariq swallowed involuntarily, drinking Ramahd's blood. Ramahd continued for a time, enough that it would give Meryam a few weeks with Tariq. If they didn't find what they were looking for in that time, he would have to think of a new plan, but he and Meryam both felt that things were coming to a head in Sharakhai. The rumors flying after the abduction at the collegia spoke of something larger in motion. And make no mistake, Juvaan was involved in it or Ramahd was a goat herder's daughter.

When Tariq began coughing, Ramahd turned his head aside so that he wouldn't be sprayed. Then he sent a sharp punch across Tariq's mouth, enough to cut the inside of his lip against his teeth. Tariq wouldn't remember getting hit, but with luck he'd think the blood his own. Who else's would it be?

Tariq began to moan, and Ramahd heard the men returning.

"Hey!" one of them called, seeing Ramahd sitting atop their charge. "Hey! Off him now!" Ramahd stood and ran, back the way he'd come. "I'll find you, thief! I'll find you and gut you like a desert snake!

Ramahd stopped at the mouth of an alley, and saw one of the guards helping Tariq to sit up, the other looked around as if he expected enemies to come charging through the twilight from all angles.

Well, Ramahd thought, *what a lively tune we've struck this night.* After the past months, it felt good to be *doing* something again. But this was only the beginning. There was much more to come.

Chapter 31

ZAÏDE HAD NOT LIED.

Çeda's training shifted to languages more than anything else in the weeks following the first meeting with Amalos. She would drill Çeda for hours in the ways of unarmed combat, but would never do so in modern Sharakhan. One day, all she would speak was Kundhunese, the next Mirean, the following Malasani, and so on. Çeda knew a smattering of each language from all four kingdoms surrounding the Shangazi, but little more than that. She knew King's script passing well. Her mother had owned a number of books written in it, and Çeda had read them all, but when she tried to speak it her tongue felt like lead, and when Zaïde used it she spoke so quickly Çeda had trouble keeping up.

But the interesting thing was that Zaïde was drilling Çeda in the very same things from weeks past, things Çeda knew by heart, so that while she might not know every single word, she understood the context, and slowly, as they went over things again and again, she began to pick them up. From there, her knowledge bloomed. She learned the bridge phrases that allowed her to learn the core of each language, and from those central linguistic locales, her knowledge broadened, then spread further as terms and concepts overlapped one another and the gaps in her understanding filled. She saw stark contrasts between the languages. Mirean was smooth and quiet, where Malasani was harsh and Kundhunese more guttural. Qaimiran was the language most similar to Sharakhan, and she found herself advancing the fastest on the days Zaïde spoke it. For all their differences, she saw similarities as well. The four languages had each affected one another to some degree. Roots were shared even if their meanings and pronunciations had changed. Structure varied from language to language, but many words stood only one or two steps removed from one another.

By the end of each day she was swimming in words and phrases and concepts. Not drowning, she realized. Swimming. It was a good feeling; she hadn't felt this sublime love of language since she and her mother had read books together in the homes they'd moved to all across Sharakhai. She had often been harsh, Ahya, but she loved words, and it seemed to Çeda that they were the closest in those moments when they shared stories with one another. Looking back now, it was, perhaps, because Ahya could set aside the troubles of the real world and simply enjoy life with her daughter for a time.

"What's wrong?" Zaïde asked in Malasani as they finished a grueling set of unarmed forms.

Çeda replied in the same tongue, though more slowly than Zaïde. "I was thinking of my mother."

"Have you thought on the fourth poem? Where it might be?"

Çeda had shared Ahya's book of poems with Zaïde, who had looked through it for several days, returning it to Çeda after she'd examined the poems and looked for other clues. She'd found nothing, and had seemed vexed by it, as if the fourth poem had some special meaning for her. To come so close to it only to be rebuffed seemed particularly frustrating for her.

"It must be to do with the key," Çeda said.

She'd shown Zaïde the key Dardzada had given her. It had felt particularly strange to do so. As if it were meant only for her, not to be shared. A foolish notion, which was why she had shown it to Zaïde, but it still felt like she'd committed a betrayal.

"You've had no more thoughts on it? On where the lock might be?"

Çeda shook her head, resting her hand on the purse at her belt that held the key, a thing that rarely left her side.

"And Dardzada?"

Çeda sneered. "He said he didn't know."

"He can be a cuddly sort of beast, can he not?"

Çeda laughed. "Cuddly, yes . . . Like a starving hyena. But in this I suspect he's telling the truth, and if so, I'm not sure I'll ever know the nature of the key."

Çeda continued to go to Amalos as well. Not every day, or even every week, but they met often enough. Enough for Çeda to read texts about the Kings that Amalos himself had chosen.

At one point, she looked up from the vellum scroll she was reading and saw Amalos crying.

"Whatever is the matter?" Çeda asked.

He blinked tears away. "It's only . . . Davud." He waved the large bone he held in one hand—the thigh bone of a black laugher, Çeda guessed. It had words etched along its length. One read the text lengthwise, turning the bone as if it were on a spit, until it ended where the story had begun. "He was a *wonderful* storyteller," Amalos said. "Did you ever hear him?"

Çeda nodded. "May I see it?"

He handed the bone to Çeda. As ancient as the bone was—with dirt and what looked like blood marked indelibly on its surface—the text was rather difficult to read, but she puzzled it out. It was a story of Bahri Al'sir, a traveling bard who wandered the twelve tribes for all his days, collecting stories and sharing them with the other tribes. Many of the tribes thought Bahri Al'sir to be one of the gods in disguise. Goezhen, some said, for he had a wicked sense of humor, and ran into trouble more than once when he played tricks on the wrong tribesmen. Thaash, others said, because his stories often spoke of vengeance and the settling of scores. Others said Bakhi, and Çeda agreed, for he often came at times of harvest and left when it was complete.

There was one small note at the end that gave Çeda pause. The shaikh of Tribe Halarijan said the bard might be one of the old gods who'd remained behind when the others had left for the farther fields.

"Do you think any of the first gods remain?"

Amalos sniffed, wiping his eyes with a corner of his sleeve. "What?"

"The first gods. Do any still remain in the world?"

"Who can tell anymore?"

"You've no guesses of your own?"

"What do *my* guesses matter?"

"Humor me, master scholar."

Amalos took a deep breath, looking toward the ceiling as if it or the sky beyond might provide some inspiration. "There were forty-nine first gods. We know this. *Seven by seven they came from the heavens.* We know that after aeons spent walking the earth, they tired of our world and were driven to create another. It is said all the old gods worked together, and furthermore, that they forbade the young gods from attending them. It sowed worry among the young gods, but what were they to do? The old gods continued with their plan, and eventually, as we know, created the farther fields. And then, one by one, they left, but not without feeling some yearning, some wistfulness, for this one. Those were the days in which some few of the younger gods were given life, Nalamae among them. And those few had a hand in creating man. Or at least were there to witness it. Before they left, the elder gods gave man blood of their own blood, a thing they hadn't seen fit to grant to the young gods. Who knows why? It was a treasure granted only to us, so that when we were done with our lives here, we would follow them and be reunited and tell them stories of the world they'd left behind.

"It is unknown whether the old gods left in one large exodus, as is sometimes told, or whether they left one by one. Most tales say that all of them left, not one remaining, but I ask you, Çeda, what are the chances that forty and nine creatures of free will would agree upon something like this in all ways?"

"It seems unlikely," Çeda said.

"It does, indeed. Surely there are one or two that still yearned for life here. I even like to think they come to Sharakhai from time to time. In the end, though, what does it matter? They haven't made themselves known, and if they haven't by now, I doubt they ever will. So put it from your mind. It's little more than a fancy and has nothing to do with us."

"I suppose you're right," Çeda said.

Unlike Amalos, though, she found it disturbing to think that the old gods might still be hidden in the world. If they were, and they held so much power, why wouldn't they step in to put down an evil such as the Kings of Sharakhai?

A short while later, Çeda came across another curious story, also etched into a bone. She read one particular section over again, then a third time, her fingers tingling as she rotated the bone. Her heart sank as she finished the tale.

"What is it?" Amalos asked. She handed him the bone. He began reading, twisting it like a haunch of meat over a fire. He too slowed, in what Çeda judged was the very place where the story had caught her attention. "The Lord of Laughs . . ."

"Yes," Çeda said. That was the line that had made Çeda pause as well. "Keep reading."

He did so, then looked up at Çeda with that pinched look of his, the one that told her that sharp mind of his was fitting pieces of the puzzle together, discarding them, trying new ones. "Tribe Narazid is a clue, yes?"

"It is."

He finished reading, and then he too frowned.

The story, written by the shaikh himself, told of a *Lord of Laughs*, how he'd come to a meeting of several caravan families in the center of a set of oases, hidden and known only to their tribe. They were a people Çeda had come to learn much about while reading the stories on these bones. Tribe Narazid called the southern desert their home. It was a desolate place, but there were several sets of oases, dubbed the Verdant Isles, which they guarded jealously.

In the poem that seemed to refer to Mesut, he'd been referred to as *the King of Smiles, from verdant isles*. Surely the Lord of Laughs referred to him, for the story told of how something precious had been stolen from him by a woman, called *a scuttling thief* in the story. It didn't take much imagination to connect a thief who scuttles to the scarabs of the Moonless Host. It went on to say how the thief had tried to use the stolen device against the Lord by *summoning the wailing horde*. They had indeed come, the shaikh had written, but when they'd arrived, they'd set upon the one who'd stolen their Lord's effects, killing her and all who stood by her side.

The Lord punished the entire tribe, ordering the death of the shaikh's eldest daughters—a just punishment, the shaikh had declared in the story, as he had five other daughters still.

"It smacks of propaganda," Amalos finally declared, handing the bone back to Çeda.

Çeda took it and shook it at him. "That's all you have to say?"

Amalos frowned. "What did you *expect* me to say?"

"I don't know. I'd hoped we would only need to take the golden band from Mesut, that his curse would be fulfilled when we did."

At this, Amalos's frown only deepened. "It seems you were wrong."

"Don't make light of this."

"I'm quite serious. All this means is that you haven't yet found the truth. But it's here." He motioned to the room, to the collegia hidden above them. "Somewhere."

Çeda nodded, if only to let Amalos get back to reading. She wondered what that girl had felt after she'd stolen Mesut's golden bracelet. She must have thought herself close to killing him. How fearful she must have been when the asirim—the *wailing horde*—had come for her instead of him.

The very same thing may happen to me.

They read on, until Çeda had to leave.

"Çeda," Amalos said as she placed the last of the bones she'd read back into their cloth-lined trays. When she turned to him, he stared at her with a look of concern, perhaps worry. "There's something I should have told you long ago."

"What?"

"Your mother. Ahya. I knew her before you came to me those months ago."

"You told me."

"Yes, well, what I *didn't* tell you was that I knew of her efforts. I knew she was searching for something."

"The bloody verses."

Amalos nodded. "I didn't know what they were at the time, but yes, the bloody verses."

"She came here? As I've been doing?"

"No. She had someone searching for her. A dowager named Eleanora who supported the collegia generously with her late husband's fortune, and came here often. To read of the city's great history, she would tell anyone who asked."

"And she was doing it for my mother?"

"For Ahya. For herself. Making good on a vendetta. Who can tell anymore? Eleanora killed herself shortly before the Silver Spears, and then King Zeheb himself, came here to ask about her activities. They learned little. We didn't need that sort of attention from the House of Kings. But some of us knew she was searching for the wrong sorts of secrets."

Killed herself. Of course she had. "Why are you telling me this now?"

"Because it's been eating at me. And you deserve to know." He blinked at her a moment, but then went back to his reading. She'd never seen him look more uncomfortable.

As Çeda left, part of her was glad to hear news of her mother. Any news. But another part recognized this as yet another dead end in her long search to know more about what her mother had been doing; that part wished he'd remained silent.

<hr />

On a fog-filled night that would start moonless and remain that way for several hours, Çeda finished her climb to the roof of a squat building within the Mirean embassy house's compound. This was a domicile for many of the servants, who by custom were not allowed to sleep in the same house as their masters. The embassy proper, a seven-story tower of stone and clay-tile roofs, loomed above her. Paper-shrouded lanterns, dreamlike in the fog, hung from iron hooks along the paved walkway surrounding the tower's base. Otherwise the tower was dark.

After scanning the wall for any signs of the lone guard she'd spotted earlier, Çeda reached inside her black dress and pulled out a roll of paper. She tugged at the twine on each end, then flattened the papers to liberate the inkwell and pen Juvaan had given her. After setting them before her on the slate tiles of the gently sloped roof, she pulled out a small ceramic pot from another pocket in her dress. She set it next to the paper and twisted the top off. Inside was sand that cradled softly glowing embers. She blew on them, making them glow a dull red. Finally, she unwound the blanket she'd wrapped around her waist and set it across her shoulders. Putting all but one of the sheets of paper into her lap, she dipped the pen into the inkwell and wrote.

I need to know the scarab's whereabouts. Tell me what you've found.

She could barely see the words as she wrote them. She knew it to be terribly sloppy. But that didn't matter. She pulled the blanket over her head and let it drape down so that it covered the earthenware pot. And then, spreading her arms like a sheltering tree, she touched the edge of the paper to the embers. As soon as it took, she dropped the paper to the tiles, pulled her head out from under the blanket, and scanned the tower above. She'd been quick about it, but her eyes were still blinded for a moment by the blue light.

The paper burned blue at the edges. The center was dark as coal. After a short pause, words began to appear.

Nothing as yet. And by the grace of the desert gods, wait for the time we agreed upon before speaking again.

Before the sheet could burst into flame, she brought the blanket lower to block its light and scanned the windows above her, but she saw nothing from the room she suspected was Juvaan's. It was possible he had a room facing a different direction, but she doubted it. The lords of Mirea revered east, the direction of the rising son; those most powerful in a household always had their rooms facing that direction.

She tried again.

This is no longer a request. I'll not wait any longer.

This time, she made sure to look away before it burst into flame. She tilted her head back as well, scanning the rooms above. A breath passed. Then two. And then she saw it. A flickering high up on the topmost floor. She'd been nearly certain that was Juvaan's room, but she hadn't known whether his papers—the twins to hers—were there, or if he'd be there tonight.

Words appeared on the charred sheet.

You're being reckless. Wait as I have asked. You'll receive no more replies until then.

Çeda rapidly tucked everything into her dress, wrapped the blanket around her waist, and moved to the edge of the building, where three silk ropes were secured. Dozens of lanterns were hung along the ropes for various festivals and holy days, the most recent the celebration of Mirea's new year. The lanterns were gone, but the ropes gave Çeda access to the tower. Checking one last time for the guard, she placed her foot on the rope and used her arms for balance. She was not as graceful as Kameyl, but she windmilled her way across the gap to reach the tower's fourth floor. From there she followed the path she'd mapped out earlier, scaling up along the decorative lions and dragons that graced the corners of the building.

Landing softly on the parapet outside Juvaan's room, she found a candle flickering behind the paper doorway. With deliberate care, she stepped down to the balcony and slid the door open. Within, she found Juvaan sitting at a desk, stripped down to a simple pair of cotton leggings. On the desk, leaning against the wall, was a large metal rack with several dozen sheets of the reed paper strung to it. Juvaan's head jerked toward her, his pale eyes wide, then he stood and spun to face her, his bone-white skin rippling with lithe muscle. Fear was painted all over him, in the way he looked to her, then the sword hanging from the wall nearby, to the way his body was positioned, ready to spring into action.

"I'll have my answer now," Çeda said in a low voice.

As she pulled her veil away, his fear faded, and fury rushed in to replace it. He glanced back at the desk where he'd been sitting, then over Çeda's shoulder to the darkness of the desert night. And then understanding dawned on his face. "You stupid girl!" He gave a short, piercing whistle. Only a bare heartbeat passed before the door at the far end of the room flew open and a Mirean man in light armor rushed in. "Take her," Juvaan said, motioning to Çeda.

The guard hesitated only a second, perhaps given pause because a Blade Maiden had suddenly appeared in his master's room. He drew a straight, double-edged blade and advanced. Çeda, meanwhile, backed away. She didn't think Juvaan would attack her himself—likely he wanted no bloodshed—but she wasn't willing to risk it. As the guard stepped forward, Çeda felt for his heartbeat, as she'd done so many times with Zaïde. As he neared her, she felt it, but instead of trying to attune hers to his, she *pressed* against his.

By the time he coughed, momentarily confused, Çeda was on the move. She swept in as he prepared to deliver a compact swing of his sword, then she leaned away, in perfect tune with the sword's arc. The tip slid past, a finger's breadth from her chest. She felt a tug, heard a ripping sound as it caught the fabric of her dress. And then she was on him, slipping beneath his elbow as he tried to recover, sliding past him to reach his side. A sharp knee blow to his stomach made him hunch forward, enough that Çeda could send a vicious cross with her free hand to his jaw. When he reeled, she followed, sending her right hand, still gripping River's Daughter, crashing against his exposed temple. He crumpled to the floor like a misshapen sack of limes.

She'd only taken her eyes off Juvaan for a moment, but when she turned back, she found the tip of his sword beneath her chin. He held it with both anger and confidence. Çeda, however, held her ground. He wasn't ready to draw the blood of a Maiden. Not yet. "You think what *I* did was foolish?" She let her eyes drop to the sword for a moment. "What you're considering now is *infinitely* worse."

"You don't come to my home and dictate how our arrangement will work."

"I've come, my good lord, to make my position more clear to you. The fault is mine, really. I've failed to convey just how important this is to me." The sword didn't waver, but a bit of the anger left his eyes. "I've gone through great pains to become the woman you see before you now. But I have not left my old life behind. Far from it. If anything, its absence has made it *more* dear to me, not less. So you'll forgive me if I've become frustrated at your reluctance to share with me what you know."

"As I've said, I know little."

"Ah, now there's a word. Little. While your replies would have me believe you knew nothing."

"Your impatience could lead to years of work unraveling."

"No, your unwillingness to confide in me could. And if you please, let's discuss this with your sword lowered. Unless you wish to find yourself lying next to your man there." When his eyes glanced down toward his guardsman, she slowly but deliberately reached one hand up and pressed the tip of his sword downward. Juvaan huffed his pent-up breath and lowered it all at once. In one smooth motion, he sheathed it and sent it clattering onto the nearby desk. Turning to her, he leaned back against the desk, crossed his legs casually, and folded his arms across his chest. His long white hair hung freely, the ends brushing the surface of the desk behind him.

"I am no confidant of the Moonless Host, to know this man's whereabouts or that man's intentions. They deal only through Osman, as they always have. And they're well aware of the arrangement. They're supremely careful. I supply them with what they need, and in the end it helps my queen's position here in the desert. I'll not jeopardize our arrangements over one man, no matter how important he is to you."

"And while all that you've said makes perfect sense, my impression of *you*, Lord Xin-Lei, is that you are also supremely careful, an impression that has only been strengthened by our dealings with one another. You wouldn't allow supplies or money or information go to the Host without a way to verify that it's paying off."

"It's not so difficult as you're making it out to be. You can see, as I have, that my dealings have furthered our goals." He waved at the papers on the wall behind him. "The very information you've sent to me confirms it. That doesn't mean I have an inventory of every scarab in the Host."

"What I've sent may provide you with some insight, but we both know that I'm hardly your only source of information. You have others in Sharakhai, and you've learned much from them, enough to ensure that your investments are sound. I've given you much, risking my life each time I've communicated with you. Give me a way to reach the Host, and I'll consider the ledger squared."

Juvaan paused. Çeda thought he was going to deny her. And if he did, she truly wasn't sure what her reply would be. But then Juvaan seemed to come to some conclusion. "There is, perhaps, a way to find another who would know more."

"Go on."

"A drop is being made soon. The elixir that was used on the scarabs in the collegia, the ones who fought so maniacally. There's more being made by an apothecary in the merchant's quarter, a man named Dardzada."

Çeda felt a chill. Dardzada. She hadn't seen him since the days following the battle at Külaşan's palace. "When?"

"Five days from now, near nightfall. That's all I can give you." He paused, then gave her a more contrite look. "But I meant what I said. I'll give you more when I have it."

Çeda nodded, walking toward the balcony. "I'll contact you again in a few weeks."

As she climbed down the tower, a strange mixture of emotions simmered within her. Part of it stemmed from the feelings she always had when she thought about Dardzada: the discomfort of all they'd been through coupled with the desire to speak to someone, anyone, so closely linked to her mother. But there was more, something deeper. *Stop being foolish,* she chided herself, yet the feelings remained. She realized why a moment later.

A terrible storm was brewing in the desert. It was gathering, preparing to sweep over Sharakhai. She wondered where they would all land by the time it was done.

Chapter 32

THREE DAYS AFTER SHE CONFRONTED JUVAAN in the Mirean embassy house, Çeda was granted a free day, the first one she'd had in weeks. She knew she needed to reach Dardzada's on the day Juvaan had indicated, but the leave she'd been granted was a full week later. "What would it take," she asked Kameyl that night, "to let me take your day instead?" Kameyl, she'd learned, had the day two days hence, the one Çeda needed.

Kameyl was sitting in a chair, legs pulled up, reading a book of bawdy Malasani limericks. Without looking up, she said, "I don't know that there's *anything* you could offer."

"There must be something."

"Why do you need it?"

"I've heard word of a troupe of jongleurs and acrobats from Mirea. They're leaving the city the day after." It was the truth. Çeda had learned of them that morning. When Kameyl lifted her head, her face slowly transforming into a look of disgust, Çeda shrugged. "My mother and I used to go to see them."

Kameyl rolled her eyes and went back to her book. "Gods forbid you'd miss the *jongleurs* prancing about in their pretty tights."

"Does that mean you'll trade?"

She waved her hand. "If it's so precious to you, then go."

Çeda ran to her and kissed her head. "My thanks, sister."

"I'm not your sister." Çeda waved and left to tell Sümeya. "And if you kiss me again I'll gut you in your sleep!"

Two days later, Çeda left the House of Maidens, but she knew she couldn't go straight to the merchant's quarter. She wasn't aware of having ever been followed, but she couldn't risk being discovered now, so she went to the spice market, as she always did. Once there, she wandered the stalls, not only to calm herself, but to look for any who might be following. She stayed for well over an hour, sampling araq-soaked honey-prunes infused with cinnamon and ginger and coriander, trying the ground spices at a stall she'd never seen before, tended by a pale woman in white clothes who acted as though each sniff she allowed should be regarded as a holy experience. She bought a bag of cashews coated in caramelized sugar and dusted with something smoky and spicy, then walked along the stalls to the south, the ones that specialized in flavored drinks. And all the while she watched from the corners of her eyes, studied the patterns of those around her.

Her instincts for noticing a tail had always been good. Even when she was young, she rarely failed to spot Emre or Tariq or Hamid in the games they played along these very aisles, seeing who could find whom first. And when there were *real* threats, she was the first to notice those as well—older children looking to dole out a bruising for having a purse nicked, or fruitmongers angry at having food stolen from their stalls. She'd warn the others with the signals they'd developed, or would outright shout if the threat was near, and then they'd be off.

And yet it took her nearly the full hour to notice that someone was, in fact, trailing her. A woman. Young from the look of her, though it was hard to know for certain, clothed as she was from head to toe in an indigo dress and matching keffiyeh. But Çeda had learned to identify people by telltale signs like silhouette, and the shape of one's hands or feet, even by the cadence of a gait, so she knew as surely as the sun did shine that the woman following her was Yndris.

She picked up her pace, but only slightly, as if she still had time to linger but would soon have to leave. She made her way toward the center of the grand, complicated space. Yndris was good. She stayed two aisles back, lost among the crowd. She never looked directly at Çeda, but instead browsed the stalls, pinching samples of spices and sniffing or tasting them. Çeda was careful not to look directly at Yndris, either, lest she realize Çeda had grown wise to her.

Çeda wondered who'd sent her. It might have been her father, King Cahil. More likely, though, she'd come on her own. Yndris was desperate to find Çeda doing something, anything, wrong. She wanted to discredit Çeda, though Çeda still didn't understand why. *Don't be such a fool. When have the highborn needed a reason to frown and spit upon those of lower birth?*

The spice market was filled with dozens of places one might hide, from slipping beneath a table covered in cloth to hiding in a carpetmonger's rolls of carpets to shimmying up the stone supports to the wooden beams above, a space that was hidden in relative darkness but that housed thousands of grape-sized spiders.

She was near a hiding place she'd used many times when she was young and never been caught. Near the old fort that was home to the spice merchants there was an alley of sorts that ran behind a row of stalls. The aisle leading to the alley was conveniently curved, so that by the time Yndris reached its entrance, Çeda would be out of sight. Çeda took it, moving swift and low past seven stalls until she came to Young Khava's, a place that sold exotic vinegars made from pomegranate and coconut, and rice from a particular mountainous region in Mirea that somehow made the vinegar taste like peaches. At the rear of the stall were three massive wine tuns. No one knew why they were there. Not even Old Khava had been able to tell Çeda why. "They were here when I first took this stall, and I like them," he shouted at her, hard of hearing as he was. "I'm not getting rid of them!" She hadn't bothered to say she wasn't asking him to.

The tuns were tight together, and a hole had been cut in the rear of each. Çeda ducked through the first, and immediately, the same old scent struck her, a fruity, oaky smell, strong from the heat within the enclosed space. Somehow it seemed much less pleasant than it had back then. Years ago she'd been able to stand tall, but now she was forced to hunch as she stepped forward, ready to peer through the narrow gaps in the tun's staves. Before she could, she stumbled into something.

She should have been prepared for it, should have looked, but in the darkness she hadn't realized she wasn't alone. A young girl, perhaps seven, was hunched down, small as a mouse, trying not to be seen.

"Quietly now," Çeda said to her while shifting to the far side of the tun. "Quietly, and all will be well."

The din of the market came to her muted. She watched as people strode past, as Young Khava spoke with his patrons, oblivious to her. And then Yndris in her indigo dress rushed by the front of the stall, past the patrons dipping some crusty bread into Khava's samples. She was in a hurry, craning her neck to look ahead over the shoulders and heads of the endless sea of patrons. Soon she had moved beyond Khava's and was lost around the bend in the aisle. Çeda ducked down to leave, but paused and looked at the girl.

"A good find, is it not?"

The girl only stared.

"Do you have money for food?"

The girl nodded, eyes wide.

Çeda laughed. "You're a shit liar, girl. Work on that." She reached into her purse and tossed two sylval onto the floor of the tun, enough for a gutter wren like her to eat for a month if she was careful. The coins landed with dull thuds. "Be well," and then Çeda left, heading in the opposite direction from Yndris, making quickly for the spice market's exit.

She wanted to head toward Roseridge, if only to see her old home once more, but she didn't want Yndris to find her there, so she headed south instead, planning on heading east once she'd passed beyond the Well. She was just nearing the Spear when she felt a familiar presence. She came to a stop in the middle of the street, absently rubbing the wound on her right thumb. It was throbbing again, but the pain felt good, like her legs after a punishing run, or her arms after an hour of sparring with Kameyl.

It was the asir, she realized, the one Mesut had chosen for her, the one he'd forged through ritual sacrifice in the courtyard of Eventide those many weeks ago. Why had it found her here? And why now? Çeda wasn't sure, but she couldn't let the opportunity pass. She had to know what Mesut was doing with the golden band, and more importantly how.

She beckoned the asir nearer, coaxed it, remembering what Mesut had told her. Control. She needed to exert control. Like wildfire rushing over the city, it drew nearer and nearer.

Do you remember who you are? Çeda asked.

Like a dog well acquainted with being kicked, the asir shied away.

Do you remember what he did? How you gained your new form?

The asir said nothing, nor were there thoughts or memories like she'd felt from the asir Yndris had killed in the blooming fields. There was only a cold rage burning.

Please, I only wish to help.

It was then that Çeda caught sight of a woman in an indigo dress. Yndris. Luckily she'd turned and was heading away or she'd surely have spotted Çeda.

Çeda should have hidden—Yndris might turn at any moment—but just then hiding was the farthest thing from her mind. She let the traffic flow around her, pressing the meat of her thumb, watching Yndris's form dwindle as she walked farther and farther away. Gritting her teeth against the growing pain in her hand, an image played through her mind: Yndris rushing through the spice market as if Çeda were a prize she hoped to string up like a desert hare and lay at the feet of her father, the Confessor King. How very proud she would be when she did it, desperate to win affection from a father who had lived to see dozens upon dozens of children like her in his four centuries spent walking the halls of Tauriyat.

Without knowing when she'd decided to do it, Çeda found that she was trailing Yndris. Her thoughts shifted from the spice market to the desert; the memory of Yndris killing the asir in the blooming fields was suddenly vivid in her mind. The simple glee she'd shown. The way she'd reveled in the blood. She'd shown her nature again with the pirates, killing that boy in cold blood when she'd been denied it earlier. And again on the tower during the riot, shooting arrows into the crowd with the sort of enthusiasm a child reserved for treacle sweets.

Yndris's actions no longer made Çeda's blood run cold. Now it ran hot. She moved faster, balling her hands into fists, building the pain in her right hand. As she wove her way through the crowd, her old wound ached, flared, spread beyond to her forearm, so that by the time she was nearing Yndris, her entire arm was on fire. It was deeply painful, but nothing she hadn't experienced before. The pain was sweet, because it offered a release for something that had been bottled up inside her for so long.

Ahead, at a crossing, Yndris seemed to come to a decision. She turned left and started jogging back toward Roseridge. Knowing she was doubling back, Çeda sprinted down a short alley, at the end of which, piled like children's blocks, lay stacks of old crates. She sprinted up the mound of crates, bounded from one wall, then from the opposite, and finally leapt up from an exposed piece of brick to latch on to the edge of a balcony on the third floor. Her right hand felt red-hot. Felt *glorious*. She realized only then that the brickwork was crumbling beneath her grip. She swung herself up to the balcony, releasing the stone before it gave way.

She leapt again, caught the edge of the roof, and pulled herself up with ease. The wind blew through her unfettered hair as she raced toward the building's edge. She fairly flew across the mudbrick rooftops, climbing like a lizard when needed, sometimes dropping a floor or two and rolling. Soon she came to the edge of the building she'd been aiming for, where she peered carefully to the alley below.

Yndris was there, staring down the alley from the nearby street. The alley twisted its way toward another, larger street, a path she could take to return to the spice market if she felt she'd lost Çeda. After glancing back the way she'd come, she took to the alley with purpose. Çeda waited for Yndris to pass beneath her, glad of the song a woman and her children were singing somewhere nearby. It masked her descent down the old tenement house's wall.

As soon as Çeda reached the ground, she padded toward Yndris, who turned just in time to see Çeda's fist crashing into her jaw. Yndris rolled with it, but Çeda was already on top of her, punching her face over and over, the feeling of release so great she started laughing with it. Blood spattered over Yndris's indigo keffiyeh.

And then Çeda connected with a blow so strong Yndris went limp. But Çeda kept pounding, with a glee she'd never felt before. An almighty release she hadn't realized had been trapped inside her.

Mesut's words drifted to her through the haze of hatred and anger. *Control. You must learn control.*

It made her laugh all the harder.

What was control when she could tap into the rage that sat like a vast underground lake along the borders of Sharakhai? What was control when she had *this* much power at her beck and call?

The veil of Yndris's keffiyeh had slipped free. Çeda, her chest working like a bellows in a wartime smithy, held her fists at bay. Suddenly she saw not an impudent child of a King, but a young woman of noble birth. A woman with deep, bloody wounds marring the contours of her face.

Çeda stared around her. Several who'd been watching ducked their heads back inside their homes.

Still straddling Yndris, Çeda pulled her knife from her belt.

Things had just changed. Çeda felt it like a brewing storm. Until now, Çeda had only *dreamed* about stopping Yndris. She'd had it coming for a long while. But she didn't deserve the knife. The urge to do it had been born of the hatred seething beneath the adichara, the asir with whom Çeda had bonded in the desert. As she stared at the fine edge of her kenshar, she realized how much she was being *controlled*, how often it had been happening.

"This isn't right," she said to no one in particular. She resisted the will of the asir, but she felt so very small before its righteous anger.

What care you for her, some whinging whelp, the get of the Confessor King?

Çeda didn't know how to answer. She cared little for Yndris, it was true. But to kill her in cold blood like this? Wasn't it what she had been railing against for so long? Wasn't it why she despised the methods of the Moonless Host?

And where has that got you?

She'd found her way into the Maidens. She'd killed a King. But there were still eleven more. There were still all the Maidens.

At the edges of her mind, the asir's anger worked, grinding her down like gristle between teeth. The anger felt so much like her own, but when she looked to Yndris's ravaged face, she felt a coward. Yndris deserved to be put in her place, but she didn't deserve this. And yet the anger within her refused to ebb. The bond with the asir was growing stronger.

You cannot leave her to be found, the asir said. *Do so and the trail will lead to you.*

The knife slipped closer to Yndris's throat. The pain in her hand had grown so intense, her entire body shook from it. Tears streamed down her face. And still the blade crept closer.

The moment she touched it to Yndris's neck, Yndris flinched. Perhaps involuntarily. No, from a dream. She could see the young Maiden's eyes rolling beneath her closed lids. She moaned softly, and sounded in that moment like a little girl scared in the night.

"She is a child of Sharakhai," Çeda said.

She is the foul afterbirth of Beht Ihman, an insect crawling forth from the putrid hive of Tauriyat.

"What fault is it of hers, to be born of a King?"

No sooner had she said the words than a searing white pain coursed through her. *You would* defend *her?*

Çeda watched Yndris's blood pulse. How easy it would be to end her life. A movement so sweet she would remember it to the end of her days. But she knew this to be the asir's feelings, not hers.

Not mine, she told herself, if only to ground herself in who she was. *Not mine.*

"She was raised in the Kings' house." Çeda spoke through clenched teeth, sweat pouring down her forehead and neck, her blade trembling against Yndris's neck. "Raised beneath their dark shadow. She did not sacrifice you and your loved ones. That was the work of her father. The other Kings. The gods themselves. She should not be punished for it."

The knife wavered. A line of red appeared beneath its edge.

Slowly, however, the tide turned. She was able to draw her arm away. She could feel the asir raging against her, but the feeling was not so strong as it once was. Finally, Çeda won her silent battle. She slipped the knife into its sheath, heedless of the blood on the blade, and stood at last. As the asir's presence faded altogether, Çeda looked up at the windows. Not a single soul was watching, which was good. The fewer that saw her, the better.

"Help!" she cried. "A woman here needs help!"

She waited at the corner of a building for two women to step from a darkened doorway and approach Yndris. When they called up to an open window, Çeda left, whispering a quick prayer to Nalamae that Yndris would not die.

Chapter 33

"STOP BEING SO MEEK," Çeda's mother said. "I've given you a dozen openings."

Çeda stood at the top of a dune far into the desert. She breathed heavily, the tip of her bamboo shinai lowering until it touched the sand. Ahya batted it, sending a spray of sand into the air. "You cannot always defend, Çeda. You have to learn when the time is right to attack."

"But you always hit me when I do."

"Because you're too slow about it. Because you don't disguise it well enough."

Most of the morning had been spent on forms, a thing that always made Çeda feel club-footed, a condition that always grew worse as the sessions wore on. They'd taken a short break for food and water, and then had started sparring. They hadn't stopped since. And for what? They were waiting here in the desert for *something*, but Çeda had no idea what, or when it might happen.

The uncertainty, her mother's refusal to speak of it, this infernal practicing, all of it made her frustration boil over. "I'm seven, memma." She threw her sword down, a thing that infuriated her mother. "I'm not meant to be fast."

"Well, how do you think you get that way, little one? By giving up? Now pick up that sword."

"No."

"Pick it up, Çeda."

"I won't."

"You pick up that sword or mine will meet your backside."

Jaw set, Çeda stared into her mother's piercing eyes. She wanted to scream at her, demand to know what they were doing here, but she knew her mother wouldn't answer, so instead she went to her sword, picked it up, and flung it away for all she was worth. It went spinning into the air, across the nearby trough, and splashed into the rise of the opposite dune.

In a flash, Ahya had her by the wrist and was squeezing it painfully. "You will get that sword and you will *learn*, little one."

Çeda was just about to spit back a reply when she saw something moving smoothly over the shallow dunes in the distance. Sails. A ship, though not a very large one. It had two masts and lateen sails but the hull was shallow, the runners long and sleek. A yacht, she thought they were called.

Ahya stood and released Çeda's arm. She went and picked up Çeda's shinai and returned to their skiff, tossing both shinais inside the hull. In short order the yacht had come to a stop nearby and Ahya led her there. "Mind your manners, Çedamihn. Speak when spoken to. Remain silent otherwise. And stop fidgeting."

Three women in loose thawbs were tying off the sails while another woman stood amidships. As Çeda and Ahya neared the ship, a gangplank was lowered into place and an old woman walked down with the help of one of the crew.

"Her name is Leorah," Ahya said, "and you will address her as such." She took the old woman's hand and kissed the golden ring on her finger, which had clutched within its setting a brilliant amethyst that sparkled beneath the sun. Çeda came forward and did the same. Leorah watched her not with amusement, but critically, as if she'd been watching the sparring from afar and had come away unimpressed. "You are Çedamihn."

"Yes, my Lady Leorah."

Leorah chuckled. She was a bent woman with skin like broken stone. Tattoos of crescent moons and birds in flight marked the skin around her eyes and chin and cheeks. Not so different than those her mother had around *her* eyes, as if they'd been inked by the same hand. Leorah was more aged than anyone Çeda had ever seen, but her eyes were sharp. They pierced, making Çeda feel naked before them.

"Salsanna, take Çeda for a walk?"

"Of course," said the woman who'd helped Leorah down the gangplank. She had dark eyes, a sharp nose and chin. She was Ahya's age, perhaps a bit younger. She put an arm around Çeda's shoulders and guided her toward their skiff. "I saw you sparring."

Çeda didn't know what to say to that. She looked over her shoulder. Ahya and Leorah were both watching her. It made the skin at the nape of her neck itch.

"I saw you throw your blade as well," Salsanna went on as they came to the skiff's side. She picked up the shinais and held one out for Çeda to take. "Why don't you show me what you've learned?"

"I've learned nothing."

"Take that tone with your mother if you wish." She leaned down, spoke softer. "I just want to spar. To pass the time a bit while their mouths flap. Believe me, it can be interminable."

"What's interminable?"

Salsanna laughed. "The two of them could outtalk Bakhi, child. He'd kill them and send them to the farther fields if only to free himself of their incessant chatter."

Her mother outtalk *Bakhi*? That wasn't the woman *she* knew. Ahya was always short and direct. Except, perhaps, when she got a bit of wine in her. Or when she got to talking to Dardzada about philosophy. Then, Çeda admitted, she could certainly talk awhile, enough that Çeda got bored and would leave to do something else.

"What say you, Çedamihn?" Salsanna shook one of the shinai at her again. "Shall we while the day away?"

Çeda took the sword. She was still angry with her mother, but there was something about Salsanna. She was quick to smile in the way that made Çeda feel like a baby. But she had a hunger about her too. For what, Çeda wasn't even sure. But she liked it. It made Çeda want to impress her. The two of them stood across from one another. They prepared, and then Salsanna nodded.

Çeda attacked immediately. Not a single one of her hurried swipes struck home. And there were plenty of openings for Salsanna, none of which she took, but Çeda didn't care. She pushed, much harder than she'd pushed with her mother. In fact, not since their sparring in the days after Demal's death, when Çeda had been so angry she could have broken stone with her teeth, did she release so much fury. All her anger at her mother, at her quiet ways when Çeda wanted to know so much more, at the way she always demanded more of Çeda, never smiling, never offering encouragement. It all came out in one violent rush.

Their swords clacked loudly. Salsanna gave ground, her golden desert dress flaring as she moved. What began as a surprised expression became one of amusement, and then she outright laughed at Çeda's efforts.

"Stop *laughing*!" Çeda cried, swinging her sword like a useless wetlander.

Salsanna continued to block more of Çeda's swings until Çeda was simply too tired to continue. Çeda stopped, her sword tip pointing at the ground, her breath coming in great, miserable gasps. She felt the fool, especially with Salsanna's wry grin still on her face, but she hadn't the energy to do anything about it.

"Well now. That was quite a display." Çeda didn't know what to say, so she remained silent. The wind picked up for a moment, the sand spinning off the dunes behind Salsanna. "Are you quite done?"

After a moment, Çeda nodded.

"Good. Now let's *really* spar."

Çeda nodded again, and the two of them went through a less heated session. Çeda could see how good Salsanna was. She moved like Çeda's mother. Smooth. Graceful. With power to spare when she wished it.

When they finished, Salsanna took Çeda for a walk. They talked. They ate dates and pistachios and drank water laced with some desert herb that made Çeda feel fancy. They took the skiff for a short sail. Salsanna even let her steer. Çeda knew Salsanna was merely occupying her so that Ahya and Leorah could talk in peace, but she didn't mind. She'd come to like Salsanna. Her stories of racing tall akhala horses in the desert, of how all the children of the tribe practiced at spear dancing, were brilliant. Çeda had always wanted to visit one of the tribes, and this made her want it even more.

"Do you know why I've been brought here?" Çeda asked when they seemed to have run out of things to talk about.

Salsanna eyed her for a time before speaking. "If your mother didn't tell you I'm not sure that I should."

"There must be *something* you can tell me."

"Macide said you were direct."

"Macide doesn't know me from Nalamae."

"He does. He saw you the day Demal Hefhi'ava died."

Çeda thought back to that terrible day, to the man Ahya was speaking to with a smile on her face, the one who wore two swords. How had she not pieced it together? Macide, the famed leader of the Moonless Host, was said to wield two such swords. But the idea of her mother talking to *him* had never crossed her mind. Why would it?

"Is Leorah part of the Moonless Host? Are you?"

"I'm going to share a truth with you now, child. Everyone in the desert, in one way or another, is part of the Al'afwa Khadar."

"They aren't either."

"They are, though some don't realize it, or refuse to. And others do work for them in only the smallest of ways. But I tell you this. All, *all*, in the desert hate the Kings and will rejoice when the desert tastes their bones."

"Then why don't they fight them?"

"You think it so easy? You're from Sharakhai. Have you not looked upon her walls and wondered how difficult it would be to scale them? Have you not looked upon the palaces of Tauriyat and wondered how many would die before one set foot within those halls?"

Çeda shrugged. "But there are endless spears in the desert. Everyone says so." She'd only heard it from Tariq and Emre, but surely others thought so as well.

Salsanna smiled sadly. "If only it were so, Çedamihn."

When they returned, the sun had set and a fire had been built near the yacht. As they approached, Leorah, sitting by the fireside, stood with great effort and then held her hand to Çeda. When Ahya nodded, Çeda took it and Leorah led her away into the darkness.

"Will *you* tell me why we've come?"

Leorah took her toward a large rock, the only feature in the area that wasn't endless sand. She stopped well short of it, sat down in the sand, and motioned Çeda to do the same.

"Will you tell me?" Çeda asked, refusing to sit.

"Enough, child. Stop being so impertinent. And by the gods, do so for your mother once in a while. You'll be the death of her if you keep this up. She's like to send you off to live in the desert with me. Would you like that?"

Çeda shook her head. She hated this, hated feeling like a prisoner to her mother's whims. She wanted to know why they'd come and what they planned for her because surely they had something in mind. But what was there to do but go along with Leorah until they told her of their own accord? When she sat, Leorah pulled a locket from within her dress. It was shaped not so differently from the amethyst on her ring. She pried the halves open and took out a white petal that glowed softly in the dim moonlight.

"Do you know what this is?"

She shook her head.

"It's a petal from an adichara. Do you know them?"

Çeda nodded. Everyone in Sharakhai knew of the adichara. "They're the twisted trees."

Leorah's chuckle was like an ancient door groaning open. "Yes, child. Twisted trees, indeed. I agreed to come here because your mother thought you were ready. After speaking with her, I agree."

Suddenly the small petal looked infinitely more dangerous than it had a moment ago. "Ready for what?"

"To imbibe the petal. Or part of it in any case." She broke off the petal's sharp tip. In Rhia's golden light it looked purple or dark blue. She shook it, apparently waiting for Çeda to take it.

But Çeda could only stare. She was suddenly and inexplicably afraid. "What will it do?"

"Perhaps nothing, child. Perhaps nothing at all."

"Perhaps something as well."

"Yes, perhaps something, but we needn't worry about that yet." She shook the petal again.

Çeda wanted to be brave, but this journey had been all too strange. She didn't want to be here anymore. She wanted to go home. She wanted to run the streets with Emre and Tariq and their friend Hamid. But what was there to do but obey? She held out her hand to take the petal, but Leorah moved her hand away. "Open your mouth, girl. Lift your tongue."

Çeda did, and Leorah placed the petal fragment beneath it. Immediately her mouth began to water. As did her eyes. The horizon, lit golden by Rhia's light, wavered before her. She blinked away tears as the fragrant taste filled her mouth.

"Tell me what you feel."

"I feel . . . bright. And warm. Like there's a fire trapped inside me."

"What else?"

Çeda's hands shook. She gripped them tight, but it wouldn't go away. It wasn't from nervousness—not any longer—but because what filled her was impossible to contain. It leaked from her every pore. "It's how Rhia herself must feel."

"Go on, child." Leorah stared intently, her eyes betraying nothing. The grim way in which she set her mouth, however, made Çeda feel as though Leorah were disappointed. Why, she couldn't begin to guess.

"The taste of it is like—"

"Not the taste. Tell me what you feel *inside*."

"I already said. I feel like a fire's been lit within me."

"There must be more."

"Why?"

"Just concentrate." Her voice was hard, almost desperate. Çeda didn't know this woman, but there was something that made Çeda want to please her. As she and her mother did before and after they sparred, she took deep breaths. She released it slowly through pursed lips. She searched for her *center*, as her mother described it.

As the cool wind playing over the desert fell away, as she tied herself more deeply to the earth beneath her feet, she felt it tugging at her insides: a feeling rather like the fear she had when her mother left Çeda alone on Beht Zha'ir, or when she returned cut or bruised and wouldn't explain why. Çeda would help her clean and dress the wounds, but she would worry until she fell asleep, sometimes for days, that someone was coming to get them. Or some-*thing*. It gnawed at her from within. That's how it felt now, and it had a clear direction. She turned and faced it, ignoring Leorah's inquisitive stare.

"What is it?" Leorah asked.

How could she describe it? "Something large. And deep." She lifted her finger and pointed. "Like a part of me is there. Like it's always been there, and the petal merely uncovered it."

"Yes," Leorah whispered. "Yes, child."

"Is it Sharakhai?" Çeda asked, unable to guess what *else* it could be.

"In a manner of speaking, yes."

Another wall between her and the truth. "Lady Leorah, why won't anyone speak plainly?"

Leorah stared a moment, but then laughed. "You will learn one day, Çedamihn, that there are times to share knowledge and times to hide it." She stood and took Çeda's hand, and together they walked back toward the yacht. "Our secrecy is for your own protection, and for others as well. Many, many people may be harmed if it were to slip into the wrong hands."

"But one day you'll tell me?"

Leorah squeezed her hand. "One day, child." When they reached the edge of the fire, the four women around it dropped their conversation and watched in silence. Leorah nodded to Ahya. "Take her to Saliah."

Ahya nodded back. She seemed pleased, but she couldn't hold Çeda's eyes. She looked away, anywhere but at Çeda. Ahya was somehow ashamed, but Çeda didn't know whether it was for something she'd done, or what she was *about* to do.

After they'd fallen asleep—Leorah in the yacht, everyone else in bedrolls on the sand—Çeda woke and made water on the far side of the ship. After waiting to make sure no one had stirred, she went to the ship, climbed onto the curving struts and levered herself over the gunwale. Heart pounding, she stole down and into the ship. She could hear Leorah's snores. The door to her cabin, thank the gods, was open.

She slipped into the cabin, quiet as a ghost, just like she and Emre and Tariq had practiced. Hands shaking, she reached into Leorah's clothes and pulled the locket out. Leorah's snoring remained steady, a rumble followed

by a reedy inhalation. Çeda pried the two halves of the locket open, seeing
the remains of the petal Leorah had fed her by the light of Tulathan coming
through the nearby porthole. She didn't know what Ahya and Leorah had
planned for her, but she deserved this much. A prize for all they were putting
her through. Let Leorah wonder where it had gone. Let her have a mystery
of her own.

After secreting the petal in her handkerchief and tucking it carefully inside the bag at her belt, Çeda left and returned to her bedroll near the pile of
softly glowing embers.

She and Ahya left in the morning on their skiff, but not, Çeda soon realized, for Sharakhai.

Chapter 34

ON AN OVERCAST DAY, with a chill wind blowing in from the northwest, a two-masted dhow sailed from the desert toward the entrance to Sharakhai's southern harbor. The ship's approach was noted by the two towering lighthouses, which stood on either side of the natural channel that led from the desert to the harbor proper. From the upper deck of the easternmost lighthouse, signals were passed to the ship via crimson and yellow flags. A brief exchange followed from ship to lighthouse and lighthouse to ship in which the *Emerald Ibis*, owned by Lord Aziz of Ishmantep, requesting berth overnight to offload goods, identified itself and the lighthouse replied that the harbor was open and that the *Ibis* could sail on for its berth assignment. The lighthouse then passed another message to a squat keep halfway along the channel's considerable length, a message that was immediately relayed to the harbormaster's tower, an octagonal monstrosity that stood at the rough center of the harbor's haphazard cluster of outer docks.

In little time, the harbormaster, sitting at her desk, her massive harbor log sprawled before her, received the news of the incoming ship, already the twenty-fifth to arrive that day. Normally she wouldn't think twice about routing such a small ship to the outer docks, a position that necessitated the offloading and ferrying of the ship's goods quayside by sleigh, an operation that cost time and, occasionally, money. The captains rarely liked it, but she had precious few berths quayside, and the day was only going to get worse. The lighthouses had reported over a dozen more sails on the horizon, surely a caravan, perhaps more than one.

She knew giving the *Emerald Ibis* a berth quayside would cause her grief later, yet she paused. The *Ibis* came to Sharakhai nine times a year, as predictable as the passing of the seasons. It was not a ship that would be carrying much cargo, small as it was, but its owner was not a man to be trifled with. She'd never met Lord Aziz, but she'd held her position long enough to know what was good for her. Aziz was high enough in the city's pecking order to make her life miserable if he was annoyed about how his ship was being treated. And rumor had it he'd come only recently to the city himself. He might still be in Sharakhai. So after a moment's pause, she made a note in her log that it would be given a berth that would be opening up in a quarter of an hour.

She passed her decision on to her master flagman, who relayed the news to the squat keep with a series of sharp signals. Normally the flagman would stand vigilant, waiting for more signals to make their way to the tower, but in this case he set his flags down, wrote a number on a flat stone and tossed it down from the deck. The flagman watched as the stone spun in the wind and splashed against the amber sand in a sailing lane in the outer docks. He watched as a girl ran out from beneath a nearby pier and clawed at the sand where the stone was buried. Assured the stone wouldn't fall into the wrong hands, he took up his flags and returned to the business at hand.

The girl, no more than ten summers, found the stone and returned to her place beneath the pier. Once there, she noted the number written on its surface and buried it deeply, smoothing the sand over so that no one could easily find it. That done, she launched herself onto her zilij, a board she'd made from a length of cracked, discarded skimwood she'd found behind a shipwright's workshop. She would kick once or twice, then glide along on the zilij. The skimwood, and the special wax applied to it, made the board's underside slick as a silverscale in the lazy flow of the Haddah, which allowed her to fairly fly over the sand. In a short while she came to the inner docks, where ship after ship was moored, the landsmen helping the crews to unload their cargo. At the end of one of the piers, however, were two young men, who sat watching, waiting.

"Seventeen," the girl said when she'd come near.

Both of the men stood, but it was the one with the sleepy eyes who took out a sylval and flicked it into the air at her. She caught it easily and slipped it into the leather purse inside her trousers. Then she was off, gliding back toward the outer docks while the two men headed up the pier toward the quay, dodging several crewmen as they went.

In a short while, the *Emerald Ibis* docked at berth seventeen. The two men stood at ease nearby, close enough to note those who came or went but a good enough distance away that their presence would attract no undue attention.

"Just like he said," Emre said, referring to Ishaq.

"Just like he said," Hamid replied.

The crewmen aboard the ship were moving smartly, seeing to the sails and the rigging, but Emre was watching the quay, wondering how it would all progress from here. "You don't think Aziz will come himself?"

Hamid shrugged. "Why should a lord be bothered to come when he has men he trusts?"

"I would if *I* were him."

"And by doing so you might draw more attention than it's worth. The goods he's ferrying in are skimmed from the caravans that bypass Sharakhai. He collects the Kings' tithe, but he collects his own as well, then sends the goods here to be sold."

"That's what I don't understand. Surely the Kings suspect?"

"Of course they do. Likely Beşir has arrangements with Aziz *allowing* him to cull what he wants in Ishmantep. Within reason, of course. What good is a lordship in the middle of the desert otherwise?"

"Then why would it matter if he came to the ship or not?"

Hamid slipped his arm around Emre's shoulder and pulled him close while motioning to the *Ibis*. "My dear Emre. It's like the jackals and the bone crushers. Whether the bone crushers brought the oryx down themselves or not, *they* feast first. The jackals, if they're wise, bide their time, waiting for the crushers to gorge themselves. Only when they're sleepy and slow do the jackals approach, taking what they can. Come too early, though, and they're as like to get their own throats torn out as they are to get a meal. Aziz can't very well flaunt it so that everyone sees, particularly when men like Kiral or Husamettín would take it badly if they knew, or worse, Onur or Sukru, men with the sort of greed in them that would push them to make an example of Aziz."

Emre shrugged. "Fair enough."

Along the quay just then were a squad of four Silver Spears in their white uniforms and conical helms, chain-mail hauberks lapping at the top of their gray boots. One of them, a beast who towered over the other three, stepped down the pier and, without asking permission to board, dropped onto the deck of the sleek dhow with a thud Emre heard even over the din of the harbor. "And so it goes, the Spears come to collect *their* tithe."

Hamid nodded. "You know him?"

"I know enough not to poke at him with a stick." Everyone in the west end knew of Haluk. He was a terror of a man, worse for having been beaten in the pits by Çeda in her guise as the White Wolf. Since then, he'd fallen in with Layth, the new Lord Commander of the Silver Spears, a man cut from the same cloth.

Haluk's white uniform stood out against the dark wood of the ship, against the dingy clothes of the crewmen. He spoke for a short while with the ship's captain, a squat, potbellied stove of a man, and then they lost themselves within the hold. Emre was worried they'd be in for a long wait, which made him nervous with the other three Spears still standing along the quay, but Haluk and the captain returned a short while later, Haluk carrying two small crates across his shoulders by use of a rope tied between them. Haluk and the captain shook forearms, and then Haluk was off, taking to the busy quayside and flanked by his comrades-in-arms like cocks in a henyard.

Now came the real questions. Where were the rest of the goods going? How was the money collected? And where in turn was the money being routed? Ishaq was certain there was a connection between Aziz and Hamzakiir. Emre and Hamid just had to find it.

On the deck of the ship, the captain was waving his hand, yelling at his crew, who were now busying themselves, handing up crates that were passed from crewman to crewman, over to the pier, and onto the waiting bed of a mule-drawn cart. The process took the better part of an hour, after which the ship was readied to pull out and take a berth at the outer docks.

"Best get moving," Emre said.

Hamid nodded. "Good hunting," he said, then walked along the pier and dropped down to the sand, where he whistled for a sleigh.

Emre, meanwhile, waited, following the wagon as it pulled away and took to the Trough. Were it not a busy day he would have worried he couldn't keep up, but traffic along the Spear was so choked he had no difficulty jogging behind it. He knew the wagon would eventually be headed to Aziz's fence, a man Ishaq apparently trusted. Ishaq was convinced, as Emre was, that the wagon would stop somewhere first and drop off a few of the crates to be sold, and that the money eventually make its way into Hamzakiir's hands with Ishaq none the wiser. But the wagon never stopped anywhere. It went straight to Ishaq's fence.

He wondered if Hamid would have better luck. Some of the crates might have been left on the ship; they might be taken later that night by someone else. But then a new thought occurred to him. And the more he thought about it, the more likely it seemed.

As the last of the crates was levered off the wagon and into the warehouse, Emre was off, running through the city, back toward the harbor.

That night, well after sundown, Emre sat at the back of The Jackal's Tail, a shisha den he wouldn't have had the stones to walk into a year ago. Now he was treated like royalty. His glass was always filled with araq whether he asked for it or not. His shisha was well tended and filled with a smoke that smelled like a jungle ablaze. He got more than a few looks from other tables, nods of respect, a sly smile from the woman tending the tabbaq. He was just about to ask her to sit with him when the door at the far side of the room opened. Two men strode in, both with turbans and veils hiding all but their eyes.

They strode immediately toward Emre's table, took seats, and unwound their turbans—Hamid first, then Macide, although he left his veil loosely around his face, only partially concealing his identity.

After more araq was poured and the three of them had each raised their glasses and taken a swallow, Hamid said, "I found nothing."

"I know," Emre replied.

Hamid gave a look like Emre had just spit in his araq. "Well, out with it, you bloody goat fucker."

Emre picked up his shisha tube and drew a long pull from it. Until, that is, Hamid knocked it out of his hand and grabbed the neck of his kaftan. "You don't treat me like I'm some fucking carpetmonger, Emre!"

Hamid raised his hand to slap Emre, but Emre snatched his wrist and half rose, grabbing a fistful of Hamid's thawb, ready to defend himself if Hamid wouldn't stop.

"Enough," Macide said. A single utterance, but it filled space between them, cutting through Emre's anger. It cut through Hamid's as well. He looked to Macide, a flash of embarrassment showing, but then he looked at Emre once more, that same look on his face, and slowly the two of them sat back down.

Macide held Emre's eye. "It appears, young falcon, that Hamid has had rather a more difficult night than you have."

Hamid downed the rest of his drink, staring at Emre, daring him to say something smart. It was then that Emre noticed the bruising around Hamid's right eye, the slight swell to his lower lip, the way he kept swallowing, as if his throat was bothering him.

"What happened?" Emre asked, a thread of concern creeping past his shroud of indignation.

"Never mind," Macide cut in. "Tell us what you've found."

Around them, the hum of low conversation returned. "I've found the link to Hamzakiir," Emre began. "I followed the wagon to the warehouse, but they delivered all of it. Every single crate. I worried that Hamid wouldn't find anything in the ship, that we'd reached a dead end. And then it struck me. Haluk."

When Emre paused, Macide waved for him to continue. "I know him."

"He'd taken two crates directly from the ship, and I wondered if *he* might be involved. I backtracked and asked around for him."

"Carefully, I hope," Hamid said.

"As a toad betwixt the legs of a crane. I found his escort, those three Spears, standing outside Grivalden's." Grivalden's was one of the more famous auction houses in Sharakhai. It catered not only to the to the richest families in the city, but also to caravan masters, dignitaries, visiting lords and ladies come to steal fruit from the tree of Sharakhai before returning home.

"So what?" Hamid snapped. "Layth needs to offload his goods somewhere. The man might have the temperament of Goezhen's children, but that doesn't mean Grivalden's wouldn't be happy to sell Layth's goods, as long as they're the highest quality."

"All true, but that's why I followed them. Haluk ordered one of the Spears to return to tell Layth that the crates had been delivered, then Layth and the other two went to a brothel along the Waxen Way. I spoke to the madam and, after a bit of convincing, she let me speak to Layth's girl."

Hamid stared at him. He snapped his fingers. "Just like that?"

Emre had no idea what had happened at the ship, but he was getting sick and tired of the prodding. "What can I say? She's a friend."

"You expect us to believe that she betrayed a client because the two of you are *friends*?"

Emre shrugged. "I may have applied *other* sorts of pressure."

A sly smile came over Macide. "Emre, did you *whore* yourself to that woman?" When Emre was silent, Macide reared his head back and laughed. "Well, I'd heard the women go weak in the knees when you're around, but I had no idea they'd abandon their beliefs at the mere thought of sharing a bed with you." He laughed again, and this time, Emre joined in. Hamid watched them with a look of sufferance, as if he were embarrassed for the both of them.

"In truth," Emre said, "she *wanted* to tell me. Haluk treats the girls roughly, but with Layth's shadow protecting him, there's nothing she can do. After a few suggestions that Haluk's days in the Spears might be numbered were we to get the right sort of information, she agreed."

Hamid sneered. "Just tell us what the girl said."

At this, Macide gave Hamid a sidelong glance, but then he nodded to Emre to come to the end of his tale.

"The girl told me that Haluk was bragging about the drop-off. He said he'd return tomorrow after picking up Layth's share of the sale, a piece of which would go to Haluk."

Macide was intent on Emre now. "He may have been referring to Layth's cut after Grivalden's takes their share."

"That's what I thought, but according to the girl, Layth kept going on about how much bigger it would be if it wasn't being split four ways."

"Four ways," Macide echoed.

Emre counted them off on his fingers. "Layth, Haluk, Grivalden's"—he held on the last, pinching his finger—"and a fourth."

Hamid's face had finally lost its look of annoyance. It had been replaced by a contemplative look, a calculating look. "Haluk picks up the goods so no one thinks to track them, and Layth sells them at auction and splits the proceeds for Aziz. I have to admit, it's cunning."

Emre nodded. "Now the question is, where are those proceeds going?"

"We have to get into Grivalden's," Hamid said.

Macide knocked his ring on the table, much as his father, Ishaq, had done in the ricksha. "Leave that to me." He stood, but before he left he bent over, grabbed the back of Emre's neck, and kissed him on the forehead. "You've done well." He leaned over to Hamid and did the same to him. "You both have." And then he was heading for the door. "We'll speak soon."

Left in Macide's wake was not only bright optimism over what Emre had found but also the sour stench of Hamid's mood. The two of them stared at one another for a time, the drone of conversation drifting between them.

"You going to tell me what happened on the ship?"

"Not a chance in the great, wide desert, Emre."

Emre took up the bottle of araq and filled Hamid's glass. "Then at least share a drink with me. We're alive. And we're one step closer."

A common refrain in the Host.

Hamid looked as if he were going to throw the araq in Emre's face, but then something inside him broke. He laughed quietly and picked up his glass in a toast. Their glasses met with an unimpressive clunk, so Hamid slammed the two together a second time, splashing a bit of the liquor, then downed the whole glass and poured another.

"Did you really bed her?" he asked, a smile breaking over his face.

Emre shrugged. "It was all for the cause, Hamid. All for the cause."

"Such a committed young man."

"Such a terrible sacrifice, but someone had to do it."

Hamid laughed, loud and long, like he used to, and like when they were young, it surprised the hell out of Emre. "Let's hear it, then. What was she like?"

"What's there to say?" Emre asked. He began with the shape of her hips.

Emre walked blindfolded, his hand on Hamid's shoulder, as Macide led the two of them through the warrens beneath Sharakhai. They'd been walking for nearly an hour along cold, damp tunnels. Macide had insisted on the blind-folds, a thing Emre had immediately agreed to while Hamid balked.

"It's for your own protection," Macide said, implying that the very knowl-edge might make Hamid a target of the Kings or perhaps of the Maidens.

And Hamid had agreed.

For most of the way the only sound was that of their own scuffing foot-steps, but occasionally they heard water dripping in the distance. A musty, mineral scent filled the air, but there was something else, a floral scent of some sort. He didn't mind the blindfold so much. It was the feeling of being so deep beneath the city. It felt like any moment now, they'd fall into some crevice, trapping them until they died of thirst or hunger.

"It's safe now," Macide finally said. "You can take them off."

Emre did, and his terror eased. Macide was holding a dim lantern, guid-ing their way, but to Emre's surprise he found that he could see the tunnel by the light thrown from the purple moss that grew here and there. He stopped and ran his fingers over one of the patches. It flaked away like ash, the purple glowing brightly for a moment, then dimming like cooling embers. Beneath the moss was what looked to be thin roots. Did moss have roots? He had no idea. But the moss was definitely the source of the floral scent.

"Come," Hamid barked.

Emre hurried to catch up. They soon came to a natural cave. Another lantern was lit inside, lighting the cave's rounded interior like a star caught in a bottle made of greenish-gray glass. On a mound of rock, sitting just next to the lantern, was Ishaq, Macide's father.

"Well met," Ishaq said, smiling a wan smile. His voice had come in a croak, and he seemed to be favoring his right side, as if he were curling around a wound, protecting it. As they came closer, Macide went to him and kissed him on the crown of his head, much as he'd done with Emre and Hamid in The Jackal's Tail three nights ago. When Macide went to another mound nearby and set his lantern upon it, Emre saw the abrasions on Ishaq's face, and the cut beneath his eye. His right hand was wrapped with a blood-stained bandage. The blood looked fresh.

"My lord, what happened?" Emre asked.

"A rather blunt reminder that the Kings are not to be trifled with. But this desert lynx seems to have retained his hide one more time." His eyes were defiant, but his voice was melancholy, as if he knew how narrowly he'd escaped the Confessor King's rack. "Perhaps for the *final* time, but that's nothing to worry about now. There is news to discuss. Plans to make." He motioned to Macide with his good left hand. "Tell them."

"The day after we spoke, I had an agent of ours, a gifted actress, go to Grivalden's and pose as a buyer. She went the day after as well, and the day after that. And that's when she saw the crates you described brought out on display for the elite crowd. Inside were shark teeth, perfect specimens, prized in Mirea especially, but also in Malasan and Kundhun. The two crates fetched a very healthy sum. As the bidding was winding down, our agent lost herself in the upper floor of the auction house and emerged late that night to examine the register. There were three entries beneath the sale. One notated the amount owed the auction house itself. One notated the amount owed to the Lord Commander of the Silver Spears. And the third listed the amount owed to a vizir, Xaldis, the most loyal servant to King Alaşan." Alaşan was King Külaşan's son, the one who'd been elevated to his father's throne after Külaşan's death.

Emre looked from Macide to Ishaq to Hamid. Hamid looked as confused as Emre felt, but Ishaq watched the two of them, waiting for them to piece together the clues. His first thought was that Layth simply owed Alaşan some debt or allegiance, but if that were so, Macide and Ishaq wouldn't have mentioned it at all.

And then the threads, so loose a moment ago, all wrapped together into a nice, tight weave. "Lord Aziz is funneling money to Alaşan, the son of Külaşan. And Hamzakiir is *also* Külaşan's son. He and Alaşan are brothers. But why would Alaşan be in league with Hamzakiir? Blood isn't a strong enough reason to betray the other Kings."

"All true, except for the fact that Alaşan *isn't* a King," Hamid said, his eyes distant, flitting in thought. "He's King in name only."

When Emre shrugged, confused, Ishaq broke in. "Alaşan has been shunned by the other Kings. He is looked upon as a poor imitation of his father, hardly better than an actor wearing clothes too big for him. They give him no say in matters of state. They give him a fraction of what had, for four hundred years, been Külaşan's share from the city's treasury."

"What, then, is a bold young King to do?" Macide continued. "He cannot stand against eleven others. May as well take a knife to his wrists and give himself back to the desert. But what if he were approached by another son of his father? What if he were promised a piece of the city when the other son stood alone atop Tauriyat?"

"Especially if he were a man like Hamzakiir," Emre said.

"*Especially* so," Macide replied.

There was an odd sort of glee building inside Emre. "It's beginning to happen. They're eating themselves from within."

"That may be true, but Hamzakiir's deceit cannot stand," Hamid said. "If he is not a servant of the Al'afwa Khadar, then he is an enemy."

"You'll find no arguments here," Ishaq replied. "But there are enemies and there are enemies. For the time being, our interests and Hamzakiir's align. There is much to do in Ishmantep. We cannot abandon our plans after all we've set into motion, not unless it's absolutely necessary."

"There will be no repercussions, then?" Emre asked.

"You take me for a fool. If we do nothing, others will be tempted to do as Lord Aziz is doing, putting money toward a cause they consider likely to survive me. They may already be doing so. An example must be made of Aziz so that others will reconsider their allegiances."

"And to give Hamzakiir pause," Macide added.

Emre's mind was afire. "But you don't want to jeopardize what's happening in Ishmantep?"

Ishaq nodded, his face cragged in shadow. "You have thoughts?"

"I do," Emre said. "I do."

Chapter 35

IT WAS JUST PAST HIGH SUN WHEN ÇEDA knocked on Dardzada's door. Soon the floorboards creaked. The heavy clomp of footsteps neared. The door flew wide, and Dardzada, his ample frame filling a voluminous thawb of orange and red, stared at her, his mouth agape. His eyes lingered on the bloody knuckles of her hands, and he frowned, but then he said, "Come," and laid a meaty hand on her shoulder to usher her inside.

She shrugged his hand off and stepped within the shaded confines of his shop. As Dardzada closed the door behind her, she passed from the front of the apothecary—a selling space with shelf upon shelf of medicinal wares—to the workroom, where she immediately took up the ladle from the tall clay water urn and drank. She had a headache she hadn't been able to shake since leaving Yndris in the streets of Roseridge, a thing she was feeling low about. Lower than she'd felt in a long while.

She deserved it, the asir whispered in her mind. *She deserves worse.*

Çeda said nothing in return, closing her mind to the asir as well as she was able, feeling the fool for reaching out to it in the first place. Thankfully, the asir's mind fell silent. She could feel it, though, waiting like an assassin in a darkened doorway.

After drinking her fill, she poured more water into an empty bowl. Taking a clean rag from a pile Dardzada always kept underneath his worktable, she dipped it in the water and set to cleaning the dried mixture of her own and Yndris's blood from the backs of her hands. *Gods, how am I going to explain this to Sümeya?*

Occupying the broad wooden table were seven packages, each wrapped in muslin and tied with twine. The packages were innocent enough—Dardzada had such things delivered all over the city—but taken with the clues throughout the room, they told a very interesting story.

In a wooden pail in the corner were several dozen spent stalks of green charo, the same infernal stalks she'd milked day after day for Dardzada years ago. She could also see brownish-orange peelings from a root, fox's clote. The root itself would have been minced and boiled and mixed with goat fat to form an ointment that would fight even the worst infections. The air smelled of beef broth and pistachios, both evidence of the restorative Dardzada was famed for. Most interesting, though, was a white ceramic bowl, for within it were the bodies of dozens of bright blue spiders the size of Dardzada's fat nose. Grimbrides, they were called, for their kiss was deadly, but mixed in the right amounts they made a hallucinogenic tonic that made one feel invincible before eventually causing death. Her suspicions were confirmed when she picked up the scent of truffles from inside a nearby box. As she'd suspected, inside were dozens of blackcaps, an ingredient that prolonged the effects of the spider's poison so that it would work for hours instead of minutes. All the ingredients for devil's trumpet.

It was a recipe few in Sharakhai knew, for it had long been banned by the Twelve Kings, though the tribesmen had been using it for centuries. If imbibed before a battle, the tonic would leave the one who took it nearly insane with rage. It could lead a warrior to fantastic, nearly impossible feats of human endurance, but it meant death for the one who took it. Even if they survived the battle, the toxins would do their work in the hours that followed, slowly but surely leading them to their grave.

How very sad it's come to this, Çeda thought.

It was a desperate concoction made for desperate times. Few in Sharakhai would take it, but many in the Moonless Host were fanatical enough to with but a word from Macide. Çeda had guessed that the tonic had been used in the abduction of the collegia graduates. And now here was more. Why? What would Macide think important enough to again sacrifice his soldiers in such a way?

As Dardzada stepped into the workroom, Çeda leaned to one side to peer over his shoulder toward the front door. "When are they coming?"

Dardzada took two lumbering steps into the room, crossed his arms, and rested his belly against the worktable across from her, a sight that brought on a wave of nostalgia so strong Çeda felt the same pangs of regret and sorrow over the loss of her mother as she'd had back then.

He motioned to her hands. "What's happened?"

"A bit of sparring," Çeda replied. He seemed ill-pleased by the answer, but let it pass without a biting reply. "The collegia," she continued. "I was there. Dozens dead. Men and women sacrificed by Macide." She waved to the table. "And here, another massacre to come."

At this, the strangest thing happened. Dardzada had never had trouble meeting Çeda's gaze, most often with a frown like an angry bull. But now he stared at the table as though it were a rock, a thing to save him from the tempest. "I don't know why the gods have seen fit to deliver you here today of all days, but there are things I would share with you. Things that may keep you safe."

"Go on," she prompted.

He paused, gathering words. "I was sent to Sharakhai with my father when I was twelve. I'm still here, living in this city by leave of Ishaq, because I'm valuable where I am, because I keep my mouth shut, because I honor the way things have to be. The Al'afwa Khadar is a living thing. Like a grand tree, there are boughs and branches that strike at the Kings. When they're cut, new ones grow. Over time, they flourish and split, creating new branches. But there is another part that lies beneath the ground. A vast part. A part that plots. A part that waits. It is the part that nourishes the branches and the leaves. I am one of these. A root. And I've long been resolved to that. What I want you to see, the thing you've never understood, is that you are too. Or you could be. You have found your way by the grace of the old ones into the House of the Kings. Be content with that. Work with Zaïde. Work with Amalos. Feed your information to us that we may feed the parts of the Host that need it. Do that, and we may strike at the very heart of the Kings."

"No matter what you think, I am not one of the Host."

Dardzada shrugged. "What does that matter in the end? You could help us. We've already helped you, and will continue to do so."

The very thought of her help leading toward another slaughter like what she'd seen at the collegia made her stomach turn. She felt a strange sort of hunger from the asir, an urge to tear at those like the Silver Spears and the Blade Maidens who protected the Kings. It made her feel all the worse.

Dardzada was right, though. As much as she might hate the actions of the Host, there was no denying they supported her, and had been for a long while. Together, Dardzada and Zaïde had saved her life—as much as Dardzada had been unwilling to let it happen at first, he arranged for her entry into the House of Maidens. "I make no promises until I've heard what you have to say."

Dardzada weighed this, then reluctantly nodded. "After you returned from the House of Maidens the first time, we spoke of your mother and the night she left for the palaces. We didn't speak of the night before."

She'd had just about enough of Dardzada's hiding of information from her. She wanted to rail at him, but she stifled the urge and waited in silence until he went on.

"That night, before she'd taken the hangman's vine, we spoke. I asked her what had happened, but she would say little, only that she was convinced that the only way to keep you safe was to return to the House of Kings, as an assassin. Near the end, after she'd taken the vine, she confessed she'd gone to the top of the mount to *find her treasure*." He had a faraway look to his eyes now. "She was drunk with the elixir at first, and I thought the confession a symptom of the vine. 'What did you say?' I asked her, and she said, 'The silver trove, Zada. I went to find it in the whispers, but I found only a mirage.'"

"I don't understand," Çeda said.

His eyes snapped back to hers. "Neither did I. I thought it nonsense at first, but the day you came here and told me a King lay dead, it reminded me of her words. She and I spoke of those poems very little over the years, but she always said they were the greatest treasure in all the desert. The silver trove. I think that's what she meant when she said those words, that she'd gone to find them. All of them."

"But she was drunk on the effects of the vine?"

"Yes, but I don't think it would have made her speak untruths. I think it merely gave her a candor that had earlier been missing."

Each word that spilled from Dardzada's mouth felt like the tightening of some infernal device meant to crack her skull. "There is undoubtedly some point to this, Dardzada, but for the life of me I can't figure out what it might be."

Dardzada frowned, the sort he'd given her when she was young and had forgotten some piece of a rote formula he'd been drilling into her. "I was never sure where she'd gone the night before she brought you to me. I'm still not completely sure, but I suspect now she made her way to Tauriyat, else why mention the mount? And I suspect she was convinced she'd found the poems."

Çeda thought about it. "*All* of them?"

He nodded. "The silver trove, named for Tulathan, who spoke for the gathered gods atop Tauriyat."

"You think it's true then? That it exists?"

"I know very little about what your mother had been doing in the months leading up to that night. I saw her rarely those days. But clearly she'd been in and out of Tauriyat. It seems strange to me that the Kings would leave any evidence whatsoever of what truly happened the night of Beht Ihman, much less a trove like the one your mother hoped to find. But I wouldn't put it past the Kings to leave false threads dangling for those who might come searching for them. It wouldn't be the first time the Kings had unmasked their enemies by planting lies. There's also the possibility that one of the Kings had sniffed her out and laid a trap for her, luring her to Tauriyat for his own purposes."

Çeda rubbed her temples. It was difficult to think with her head pounding as it was, but it seemed plausible enough. "But why lure her there only to let her go again?"

"You'll note that she returned the very next night."

"You're saying they left her no choice."

"Or they tricked her. Or they used their god-given abilities on her. Ihsan isn't known as the Honey-tongued King for no reason."

The very thought of it, her mother returning to Tauriyat on marionette strings, made Çeda's stomach go sour. "A Maiden went missing the night Ahya returned."

"Nayyan?"

"You *know?*"

"Very little. Only what you've already said, that she was apparently taken that same night. The Maidens were out in force the following day asking for her."

Çeda nodded. "She was First Warden at the time." Çeda told him what she knew, how Nayyan had apparently disappeared, that a search was waged under King Ihsan's guidance but little, apparently, was discovered. "It's a mystery that still plagues Sümeya. But it's too much of a coincidence. Ihsan must know more than he's telling."

"Perhaps Ahya killed her. The Kings might have wanted to cover it up."

"Then why lie about it to the Maidens?"

"You're sure Sümeya's telling you the truth? Not some lie concocted by the Kings?"

Çeda thought on it. "She seemed heartbroken by it. She loved Nayyan, who brought her up in the House of Maidens."

"Well, perhaps they lied to her as well, and they might for any number of reasons. They wouldn't, of course, wish it known that an assassin had infiltrated their palaces. And the vaunted Nayyan being felled by a lone woman . . . Perhaps they wished to spare her family. Or perhaps Nayyan made enemies in the House of Kings. This might have been a way to quietly dim her flame."

Çeda shrugged. "Perhaps. Why are you telling me all this now?"

"My thoughts have been half formed for a long while. In a way they still are." He waved to the packages on the worktable. "But the city grows more dangerous every day. It may be more difficult to speak before long, and you *are* in the House of Maidens. Perhaps you could learn more."

There was something he wasn't telling her, something he'd been building up to since they'd started talking. "But why *now?*"

Even now that it had come to it, it took him long moments to utter the words. "Because I'm leaving Sharakhai, Çeda."

Like a crack forming in the earth, the revelation formed a divide between the two of them. It yawned wider and wider the more she thought about it. Suddenly there was a ringing in her ears, a trebling of the pain inside her skull. Even after everything, all Dardzada had done to her, she wanted him to stay. "Where are you going?"

"I can't tell you that."

Of course, Çeda thought. *Of course he wouldn't share a single thing with her.*

"Just remember what I told you."

"That I should sit among my enemies and wait for men like you to tell me what to do?"

"Better that than to die for nothing."

"My mother didn't die for nothing."

"No, you're right, but she could have done so much more."

Çeda massaged her temples with thumb and forefinger, but it did little to quell the rapidly rising pain. It felt like a host of insects were trying to chew their way out of her. "Perhaps she might still be alive had she demanded more help. Or received it without having to beg."

"Ahya knew the kind of support she was likely to get when she came to Sharakhai."

Çeda's hand lurched away from her temples. "What did you say?"

"She knew the risks, Çeda."

"Not that. What kind of support? Who sent her?"

"No one *sent* her." Dardzada's face was growing angry. "Do you not remember your mother at all? She *insisted* on coming. And by the time her decision had been made, no one would sway her from it."

"But someone gave her leave to go. She wanted to come to Sharakhai but was *allowed* to do so. Who allowed it, Dardzada?"

"I can't tell you that."

"I deserve to know!" She sounded a fool, but just then she couldn't think straight.

"Your mother died because she came too close to the Kings. She grew reckless, as you are growing now. Don't think it hasn't occurred to the Host how dangerous it is for you to be there."

Çeda stood there, stunned. He meant that if the Moonless Host thought she might compromise them in some way, they wouldn't hesitate to kill her. "Have *you* thought that?"

Dardzada seemed genuinely shocked. "Of course I haven't, but don't think you can constantly bull your way through life and not pay a price for it."

Çeda had known the dangers when she'd entered the House of Maidens; certainly danger from the Kings, but she'd known she would be walking a rope, and that any misstep one way or the other could spell her doom. And not only that, the doom of others—her friends, those she loved, the only family she'd had since her mother died.

But for some reason to have Dardzada state it so plainly made the anger inside her flare even worse than when she'd been stalking Yndris. The pain in her skull grew terrible, a storm of dizzying proportions. Pinpoints of light played across her vision. Darkness swept in. She felt herself pressed down into that darkness. And in that moment, the presence of the asir loomed large. This was nothing like what had happened with Yndris. Then, she had been fueled by the asir's endless reserves of anger, but at least she had felt in control. Now it was as though she were being pressed beneath the surface of a dark, midnight lake, and the harder she tried to fight, the lower she sank.

She saw herself draw her kenshar. Her poisoned hand throbbed so badly the knife quivered below Dardzada's chin. "Who sent my mother here?" It was the asir, feeding off Çeda's desires. Çeda was horrified to see the knife at Dardzada's throat, and yet part of her hoped it would pry the truth from him.

Dardzada's gaze wavered between the blade and Çeda's rage-filled eyes. His lungs were working like a frightened rabbit's. He swallowed, and then began to talk. "If you wish to kill me, go ahead. Gods know I've done enough to hurt you in the past. But I've always done so with an eye toward your safety, and the safety of all those with blood of the lost tribe running through their veins."

"I asked you who sent my mother here."

"And I'm telling you you'll not get it from me."

The knife lifted.

No! she cried.

And a reedy voice replied. *Bound by the law of the gods I may be, but that doesn't protect this man from our anger.*

Harm him not!

Why? The anger burns within you like a long-forgotten brand. What has he ever given you but grief and heartache?

He is a harsh man, but we live in a harsh world.

It felt strange to be defending Dardzada, a man who'd never needed anyone else's protection, but she knew that to abandon him now would be to sacrifice him to her own blade.

Dardzada's nostrils flared as he stared into Çeda's eyes, but then his attention was caught by something over Çeda's shoulder, something beyond the nearby arch and into the front room.

Çeda turned just as a man was entering the room. He wore a long green burnoose, cut in the style of Malasan, and a turban, also wrapped loosely as the men from the eastern kingdom wore them. His eyes were piercing and he wore his long, pepper-gray beard forked. She could see little more than his eyes, but she knew this was Macide. His eyes widened as he saw the knife she held.

He said something to her, but Çeda couldn't hear him. The ringing in her ears, the pounding in her chest, the unadulterated rage coursing through her was nearly too much to bear. In a flash he'd drawn one of the two shamshirs he wore at his belt. He spoke again, and when she didn't comply, he strode across the front part of the shop toward her, brandishing the blade.

And then Çeda was lifted up from the depths of the cold lake. She felt herself entwined with the asir, as if the gods themselves were braiding the two of them together until she could hardly tell herself apart from the creature. In that moment, she had a glimpse of twelve men standing on a mountaintop. Before the men were six numinous forms. They stood in an arc, though one was closer to the Kings than the others, a woman in a diaphanous white dress with flowing silver hair. Her skin glowed beneath the moons, both of which were full and bright, almost difficult to look upon. The goddess—for surely this was Tulathan—spoke to the silent, standing men, who could be no other than the Kings of Sharakhai. She gave words to them in turn, each bowing as she stood before him and as she stepped away.

Her sister, golden Rhia, stood behind her. As did Thaash and Yerinde and Bakhi. And there was Goezhen, crouched on taurine legs, his crown of thorns bristling beneath the light of the moons. As surely as the gods lived and breathed this was Beht Ihman. What struck Çeda was how very many were present. They stood behind the Kings, well outside the inner circle. Men and women, some few children as well, had gathered to watch this event unfold, this dark pact between Kings and gods.

The vision was there one moment, gone the next, and suddenly Çeda was returned to the pungent smells and enclosed space of Dardzada's apothecary. She felt the asir turn her away from Dardzada to face Macide, who had just entered the open archway to the workroom. She caught his shamshir against the crossguard of her kenshar and drove forward, forcing the sword wide as its edge slid along her knife's guard and then, using a move she'd honed over the past months, slid beneath his arm, grabbed his wrist, and twisted. She was surprised he let his sword go so easily, but realized a split-second later he'd done it to so that he could regain his distance and draw his other sword.

His intense eyes studied her, much more wary than he'd been moments ago. He spoke again, and so did Dardzada, but their words were lost to the madness that had overtaken her. Macide had stepped into the tight workspace, and as she advanced, he retreated behind the table, forcing her to fight above it.

Stop this! Çeda pleaded. *He is not our enemy.*

And yet a vision came of a host of young girls strung along the battlements of a tower, a warning to the enemies of the Kings. One of them, a girl with eyes like jade, so innocent, had been caught between the schemes of the Kings and this man. Macide Ishaq'ava.

She hardly knew what was happening. She felt like a whipsaw, being drawn this way, then that, as her memories mixed with those of the asir to create an unstoppable rage.

Enough! she cried, but the demand was weak. Pitiful. *Enough . . .*

She felt herself swipe her stolen sword in a wide arc, once, twice. When she parried and tried to riposte, he locked his crossguard against her blade and ran her sword high, its tip digging deeply into the plastered ceiling. Her sword thus caught, he rammed his shoulder into her chest, sending her flying backward. She struck the cabinets. A drawer above rattled open, sending bits of dried rose petals sprinkling down around her as she beat away two thrusts of Macide's blade.

Dardzada rushed up behind Macide and grabbed his sword arm. "It's Çedamihn!" His chest pumped like a bellows while his eyes pleaded with Macide. "Please, this is Çedamihn!" Macide's kohl-rimmed eyes widened. "It's the adichara poison," Dardzada went on. "You know she nearly died from it."

It was Dardzada's obvious care for her that finally began to turn the tide. Like rain against a raging forest fire, the asir's anger, and Çeda's, began to ebb. With a feeling akin to regret the asir retreated, away from Çeda, away from Sharakhai, back toward the desert. And then it was gone, as simple as that, leaving Çeda feeling like a dried up husk.

Macide's grip relaxed. The tightness in him began to unwind. He looked down at her right hand, which still held his sword, and his look softened. With a deft movement he drove his shamshir back into its leather sheath, then held his hand out, nodding to the blade in her right hand. "Unless you still mean to slice my neck open."

Çeda looked down at it, then flipped it, caught it by the blade, and held it out for Macide to take. As he did, Dardzada said, "Çeda, go out back. Please. Let me speak with Macide alone."

She nearly laughed. When she'd come here to Dardzada's apothecary in the years before her mother's death, and in the years she'd spent here after she'd died, Dardzada had sent her into the garden or out front to sit along the street more times than she could remember. It felt as though she were twelve all over again, wishing she were older, angry and petulant when Dardzada gave her no leeway, even when she'd been good.

But she was a child no longer. She'd crossed a boundary here today. She'd attacked the leader of the Moonless Host. Whether or not they had some distant connection through blood, he would not overlook such a thing easily. There was still a lot of anger bottled up inside her, but she had regained herself enough that she could tell it was misplaced—that *some* of it was misplaced, in any case.

"Very well," she said, and headed out through the rear door to wander through Dardzada's garden.

She picked some mint leaves and pinched them, breathing deeply of their scent before chewing leaf after leaf and swallowing them. She chose a stalk of lemongrass next, chewing on the fibrous end as she paced. Eventually she calmed down enough to sit on the bench on the far side of the garden and think. Setting her right arm on her thigh, she flexed her hand over and over, feeling the ache but little of the anger that had burned its way through her only minutes ago.

Zaïde had told her she would be fighting the poison her whole life, but Çeda thought she'd meant the *pain*. Pain she could handle. To have such uncontrollable anger making decisions for her . . . It was the very thing Mesut had warned her about. *You must exercise control, Çedamihn.* For all her impatience, she knew Zaïde, Dardzada, and even Mesut were right. Boldness may have its place, but she needed to take care or all will have been for naught.

And the asir . . . Tulathan's bright eyes, how could it have dominated her so? That it had built and stored its anger over the centuries, leaving it with a nigh-unending supply, made sense, but if that were so, why wasn't it trying to exert its influence over Çeda now? Why wasn't it trying to do so in every waking hour? Perhaps it was her proximity to the Kings themselves, those the asirim both hated and were bound to defend.

She pressed on the puckered wound where the adichara thorn had kissed her. Ever since she was young, after her mother had begun feeding her petals from the adichara blooms, she'd had the indefinable sense that the asirim were out there, lying in wait beneath the blooming fields. Surely her mother knew that. She had given Çeda petals in anticipation of using Çeda as a weapon against the Kings. But what the poison thorn had granted her was a hundredfold stronger than the petals. And when it flared, it created a conduit the asirim could use to voice their rage.

Their rage was justified, but she needed to learn to control it *and* the poison. If she didn't, she would surely die, perhaps taking those she loved with her—sacrificed to the emotions she could no longer control.

It happens through anger. Always through anger.

Perhaps it was something she could use to her advantage. After all, if the asirim could use *her*, might she not use them as well? She had bonded with them—as the Maidens had taught her and Mesut prescribed—but the link through the poison seemed to be something outside of that traditional method. Was it the combination of the poison and the blood she shared with the asirim? She wasn't sure, but she would learn more in the days ahead. This she promised herself.

Macide and Dardzada spoke for a long while. At one point she heard their voices raised, but she couldn't tell what they were saying. Finally, as the sun was setting, Macide came out and regarded Çeda from the doorway. "We should walk awhile. There are things we need to discuss."

She nearly demanded to know what but she stifled the urge and simply nodded. They returned to the workroom where Dardzada was stuffing the clothbound packages into two burlap bags.

For a moment Çeda and Dardzada stared at one another. There were words of apology on her lips, words of farewell, but like a wraith hopelessly searching for the life it once led, the words could find no form. It looked as though Dardzada wanted to speak as well, but then he glanced to Macide and finished his work. Macide slung one of the bags over his shoulder, motioning for Çeda to take the other. Çeda tried to say something. Anything. But in the end, neither she nor Dardzada seemed ready for this conversation, so she merely nodded to him and coiled the second bag around her wrist. Macide pulled the tail of his turban loosely around his face. Çeda did the same with her veil, and then she and Macide left the apothecary, the two of them striding side by side through a city cast copper in the ruddy light of sunset.

Chapter 36

MACIDE LED THEM SOUTHEAST THROUGH THE CITY. He wove his way through little-used alleys and shortcuts, moving with clear intention but little haste. They neared the outskirts of Sharakhai, but before they reached the rocky plateau that dominated the land east of the great southern harbor, he cut under an old bridge with an acacia leaning drunkenly over the road above, then they slipped down a little-known trail on the far side, through a small grove of well-tended olive trees, and finally to the Corona, a street that had tried valiantly to complete a full circuit around the outer edge of Sharakhai. Its only failure was the city's imposing eastern features, where the arms of Tauriyat and King's Harbor created a gap in the Corona's grand ring.

For an outlaw from the desert, Macide knew the city quite well. Then again, perhaps being an outlaw was the very reason he'd been forced to learn. After all, a stroll along the Trough for any amount of time would surely lead him past several patrols of Silver Spears. The real danger, though, were the Blade Maidens. Çeda and all the Maidens were regularly shown artists' renderings of Macide and Ishaq and Shal'alara and other leaders of the rebel tribe. They stood a much better chance of recognizing him than the Spears, but Çeda had to admit Macide was good at what he did. The disguise he wore was subtly effective. The Malasani had a way of swaggering when they walked. If many in Sharakhai thought it a brash confidence, the desert tribes thought it a sign of arrogance. Of all the people from the neighboring kingdoms, the desert tribes hated the Malasani the most. And yet here was the leader of the Moonless Host, a man who'd sworn to cleanse the desert of their presence, walking like one of them. His clothes and slightly hunched shoulder completed a look that Çeda was sure she wouldn't have seen through had she passed him on the street.

It felt odd to be strolling with this man, the leader of a band of shadow soldiers who had the blood of hundreds on his hands, a man who would be slain on sight and yet who held so much power in Sharakhai and beyond.

"The gods work in strange ways," Macide said in his sonorous voice.

"A point no one would dispute, least of all me, but in what particular way do you mean?"

"I wouldn't normally have gone to see Dardzada myself, but I'd wondered if he'd heard from you through our friend Yanca. I've been hoping to speak with you."

"With *me*? Goezhen's sweet kiss, why?"

They sidestepped as a cart piled high with hay bustled its way up the street. "To talk about your future."

Why would he want to talk about her future? But then she understood. "You hope to control me."

"Yes, though don't be so indignant about it. You do, after all, control *my* actions to a degree." He caught her skeptical look. "Come. The two of us are in positions of power now, Çeda. And those in power exert influence on one another. Is it not so?"

"I suppose. What is it about my *future* you wished to speak about?"

"We'll come to that soon enough. For now, there's a confession I think is long past due."

They'd come to the top of a rise. Ahead, the whole of the southern quarter of the city was laid out before them. Like children sitting before a story-teller, rank upon rank of warehouses and other buildings huddled near the immensity of the southern harbor. A grand arc of ships curved along the quay. Farther out, hundreds of ships complicated the sand of the central harbor around a complex array of inner docks, at the center of which was a squat, octagonal tower that was so utilitarian in design it looked like a child had built it. Two fat ribbons of rock hemmed the harbor in, and led to the twin lighthouses atop jagged outcroppings of stone; from this vantage it looked as if a fallen giant had reached out to gather his toy ships, two unlit candles gripped in his fists.

Macide stared at the scene, perhaps drawn in by some memory. He glanced toward Çeda, though if he was embarrassed by his peculiar silence, it didn't show. "I've heard you enjoy stories."

Çeda's heart began beating madly. She wasn't even sure why. "When the time is right."

"Believe me, the time has never been better." He paused, gathering himself. "Nearly two hundred years ago," he said as they began taking the long slope down, "a rumor surfaced in the desert tribes that on the night of Beht Ihman, Tulathan recited poems to each of the Kings. Then, the thirteenth tribe had been nearly decimated. They were the diaspora of our tribe, the survivors from the massacre of Beht Ihman and the years that followed in which any of our blood were hunted and killed. The rumor of the poems was believed by some, discounted by others, but most cared little one way or the other, for it was thought that the poems the silver goddess recited merely described the power granted to each King. Those few poems that had been unearthed corroborated this. They spoke of blessings, not curses.

"Time passed, nearly a century, before a lost stanza was discovered by a woman who had inveigled her way into the services of King Kiral. The *King of Kings*," Macide said in a mocking voice. "A secret council of our elders was called to hear these words, to listen to what the woman had found. They went to the desert to meet, but none returned. Their bodies were found the next morning. With blood upon the sand they lay slain, their throats slit. Any who'd heard those fateful words died that night, cutting off one possible path to our retribution like a branch from a sapling tree.

"For generations following that night, it was thought that the story had been leaked by the Kings themselves, that no such verses existed. It was said they'd lain a false trail so that the King of Whispers could listen for those words and turn his ear toward us more easily, and perhaps he did. Perhaps that's how Azad came to find them before slaying them all. Most believed this version of the story, and that the only folly was in believing that the gods would reveal some weakness of the Kings on the night of Beht Ihman. Why would the gods do so? they argued. Why come at the request of the desperate Kings and grant such wondrous abilities they might use to defeat their enemies while at the same time reveal weaknesses?

"Like ironweed in the desert, however, the story persisted. There were those who believed it, and nothing anyone said could shake their belief. In fact, arguments against it seemed only to make them embrace the idea more ardently. They were few, but they worked diligently over the course of the following decades."

A high-pitched bell rang on the road behind them. "Make way!" called a young woman. "Make way!"

They stepped to the side of the narrow road as three mules pulling carts of grain trundled past. The driver, a fair-skinned woman with freckles jogging alongside the first mule, tipped her wide-brimmed hat to them as she passed. "Good fortune upon you."

When the wagons had gone a fair distance, Macide continued. "At first, they had little fruit to show for their efforts. Some of their number wandered the desert, collecting stories. Others were sent to spy. Some made their way into the collegia to gain access to that grand store of knowledge." The thought reminded her of both Davud and Amalos and she nearly laughed, but the churning in her gut stifled the urge. "They made their way deeper into the city, coming closer and closer to the Kings."

"My mother was a believer," Çeda offered.

"She was, though her father was not."

Her steps slowed. Her feet stopped. The light of the setting sun was inexplicably bright. The city seemed so much wider than it had only moments ago, as if it were ready to open up and swallow her whole.

Macide turned to her, but said nothing. He merely waited for her to utter the logical question they both knew would follow. But Çeda's mouth had filled with spit. She swallowed, unable to speak. *How cruel are the gods?* Since she'd been old enough to know what family meant, she'd wanted to know where she'd come from, and now she could hardly work her mouth to form the question.

"And who was her father?" she finally asked.

Macide, a burlap bag of medicine and poison slung over one shoulder, replied, "Ishaq Kirhan'ava."

"Ishaq . . ." She remembered the dreams she'd had in Saliah's garden in the desert, the ones that showed her mother, Ahya, speaking with a man Çeda remembered from her childhood. Dear gods, she'd been shown pictures of Ishaq by Sümeya in the House of Maidens, but they'd shown a much older man than her memories. Now that she knew, though, the similarities were undeniable. The intense eyes, the sharp nose, the very shape of his cheeks and chin.

Macide stared at her with a look that bordered on sympathy. She could see some of Ishaq in Macide, especially in his eyes.

"Ishaq is my grandfather," Çeda finally said.

Macide nodded.

"And you are my mother's brother. My uncle."

He nodded again.

Çeda felt powerful, as if she could wrest from Thaash his command of the heavens and release strike after strike of lightning. Her head swam with questions. But the first that won out against all the others was, "Why did you never come to us?"

"I did once."

The day Demal was taken by the Maidens. The day Hefhi was killed. "But you said nothing to me. I had no idea who you were."

Macide nodded. "Ahya insisted I come only rarely, for my sake to a degree, but more so for yours. In all her time in Sharakhai, we spoke only thrice, and each time she was desperate to make sure her identity, *your* identity, wasn't discovered. As well, my father forbid anyone from the thirteenth tribe from contacting her."

"He forbid it?"

Macide nodded and motioned to the road ahead. The two of them fell into step once more, passing an old man with a crook and five children in tow, each shorter than the last. "There was concern, not only from my father but many others, that doing what Ahya did was not only foolhardy, but reckless. They felt it put the lost tribe at risk over a fool's mission."

"But it wasn't."

"So you say." Before Çeda could argue, he went on. "You have little sense of what it's like in the desert, Çeda. Life is hard. We live on a knife's edge. You will know well by now the number of Blade Maidens who hound us at the command of the Kings. They are merciless hunters, and good at what they do. The Kings come at times as well, baying beside their daughters. It's why we travel like packs of maned wolves, never larger than ten or twenty, joining together only rarely. Those in the lost tribe feel, rightly, that anything that puts them at risk must be weighed carefully. Some might listen to your story and consider it dumb luck that Külaşan was killed. Others will hear it and perhaps believe, yet still think it a fool's errand, not worth pursuing."

"I don't understand. If Ishaq was against her coming here, why did he relent? Surely he could have denied her. He is the leader of the Al'afwa Khadar, after all."

Macide tipped his head to her, granting her the point. "True, but there are other powers in the tribe, Çeda."

"Such as?"

"My grandmother, your great-grandmother."

Çeda considered this. "She was one of those who believed?"

"Not merely believed. Leorah is our chief historian, our greatest link to our past."

It was all so much to take in that the implication of what he'd just said took a moment to register. "Breath of the desert, she's still *alive*?"

"She's seen ninety-two summers, but yes, she's still alive. She and Ahya were quite the pair. When we were young, before Ahya left for Sharakhai, the two of them could always be found together, reading stories to one another or repeating tales they'd learned from others. We were sure Ahya would eventually take her place."

"What happened?"

"You mean, why did she come to Sharakhai?" This was what he'd been leading up to all along, Çeda knew. "It is difficult for me to say. She was my elder sister, and when I was young I was often regarded as a nuisance. I would try to sneak up to Leorah's tent when they were sharing their stories, but I was always found out and sent away, sometimes with a switching for my trouble. As I grew older, I had many things to do at my father's bidding. I only know that Ahya and Leorah conspired with one another for many years, and one day they revealed their plan to my father, for Ahya to go to Sharakhai to find more of the poems."

"And what of me?" Çeda asked.

"What *of* you?"

"She went to Sharakhai to have a child from one of the Kings."

"You know this to be true?"

"I was tested by the adichara. I'm a Blade Maiden now. It must have been part of her plan."

They'd been heading steadily downhill, and now were entering the outskirts of the warehouse district that pressed against the harbor like beggars on a bread line. As the sight of the harbor and the desert was lost, their world was plunged into the shadows of dusk.

"I know only that she went to Sharakhai after she and Leorah had devised a plan. I know they withheld it from my father until just before she left. I know that my father felt aggrieved, and rightly so, after being set upon by his daughter and his mother with demands he'd never been consulted about."

"Surely he could have refused her."

Macide tipped his head to her. "He might have, but Leorah is a convincing woman. She has an indomitable spirit. And perhaps, in the end, they had the right of it and so my father relented. Whatever the case, Ahya came, but who are you to say that your birth was her plan all along? She might have lain with one of the Kings simply to receive his favor, and so gain access to things she could not otherwise. She might have been raped." Macide raised his palm to the sky. "Gods forbid, she might have fallen in love."

As they turned left down a side street and headed toward the docks, the sounds of the city rose around them like a flock of starlings taking wing. In the stream of the late-day traffic, a pair of Silver Spears approached. Çeda's heart beat madly for Macide's sake, but Macide wore his disguise like a mantle, changing neither his speed nor his swaggering walk, and the Spears soon passed them by.

"And you?" Çeda asked when they were out of earshot. "Why have you not told me this before now?"

"My father forbade me," Macide said. "He made me swear a vow. Once he'd agreed to their request, he refused to allow anyone to go to your mother in Sharakhai, a command echoed by both Leorah and Ahya. They wanted no interference, no attention brought to Ahya. There were days I desperately wished to break my vow and go to her. I loved my sister, and my heart was laid bare when I learned of her death. But I knew even when I was young that to meddle in such things would put us all in danger."

Çeda shook her head. "There's so much I don't understand."

"I know. We have time yet. Ask me your questions."

"The lost tribe," Çeda began. "How could our very existence be so effectively buried?"

"Ah," Macide said. "A question that would take a year and a day to sufficiently answer, but let me do my best to summarize. It's not difficult to see how the Kings could guide the minds of those who lived here in Sharakhai. They had complete and undisputed power here. The tribes presented a different sort of problem. They could not destroy all who stood against them, nor did they wish to. The Kings were, after all, the blood of the twelve surviving tribes. So they sent Ihsan, the Honey-tongued King, to treat with the shaikhs. He gave them an ultimatum. Speak of the thirteenth tribe and be hunted to the ends of the Shangazi and ground into dust. But speak as though they'd never been, and they would be allowed to live, to prosper, in fact, under the rule of the Twelve Kings. The Kings had no desire to rule every corner of the desert. What joy is there in lording over such vast desolation? But obeisance, they required. And as long as their secret shame was buried by the tribes, as long as they could control trade in the desert, they were content to let the tribes live as they would."

"And the shaikhs bowed to the Kings' will?"

"At first, no. They bristled at the very notion. Some few refused even to speak with King Ihsan, but when the asirim were brought to bear, and the Kings themselves murdered the shaikhs who ignored Ihsan's calls to treat with him, the sons who replaced them *did* listen. They were too hard-pressed after the losses in the war and the devastation of Beht Ihman to do otherwise. So eventually, one by one, all the shaikhs agreed. They were complicit in the loss of our people, our culture, our very soul. But I don't blame them. Not truly. The desert is harsh, but it harbors life, it secrets it away until the storms come once more."

He seemed to be waiting for her to answer, but when she didn't, he went on. "Once the Kings felt like they'd forced the tribes into line, they returned their gaze to Sharakhai, which was in the middle of rebuilding after the war. It was a slow process. It took generations to scour the memory of the thirteenth tribe from the populace, but scour they did. The Kings are patient men. They burned the books with any mention of the lost tribe. They created their Kannan and had scribes create one for every house in Sharakhai. They had learned women in fine raiment—the precursor to your Matrons—go door to door and teach their ways. And always they spoke of twelve tribes. Those who breathed of a thirteenth were killed, and there were many at first, but the Kings gave blades to their daughters and told them to silence those who spoke the wrong words, or went themselves to lay the law upon those who'd broken it. Dissenters were culled. And soon enough, no more than a few lifetimes, only a bare handful knew the truth.

"And in the desert?"

"In the desert, it was the same and it was not. The shaikhs followed the will of the Kings. And when they didn't, the King of Whispers heard them, for in those days Zeheb was most concerned with keeping the tribes attentive to the agreements they'd made. When they stepped out of line, those who spoke of lost tribes were found dead, grim smiles spreading wide across their throats. And when it happened too often in one tribe, it happened to the shaikh, or his wife, or his children. Soon enough they too fell silent, and that was all it took. In those days, few enough knew how to write, and in any case our histories were told around fires or beneath the twin moons, not written on scrolls or in the pages of books."

"You and I are speaking of the lost tribe now," Çeda said.

"True, but we have learned that there are particular ways, particular times, when we might speak openly. What looms largest, however, our greatest strength, is that the King of Whispers has trouble hearing us when blood speaks only to blood."

By *blood*, he meant those of the thirteenth tribe, of course. "It cannot be."

"Only with one another, mind, and it depends on how much blood you have, but it's been proven over and over again."

"Why would the gods have given them such a weakness?"

"Why would they have sacrificed our tribe at all? The Kings begged the gods to save them. In answer, the gods might have cleared the field of the amassed army, but they didn't. Instead they demanded blood. They demanded sacrifice. They allowed the Kings themselves to choose which ones would be taken, and when the Kings did they granted them power, but also weakness. Why do any of that?"

Why indeed? "I don't know."

"No one does. Perhaps we never will. It may be that it simply pleases them to see us squabble. Four centuries ago they set a grand aban board in place, the Kings on one side, the desert tribes on another, and they have been watching it play out since then."

"I'm no piece on a board."

"You are, Çeda. And so am I. And now all we can do is play our part."

I'm no piece on a board, and neither was my mother. "You said you would ask something of me."

"Indeed." He motioned ahead, where they approached a dead end, an alley of sorts between two wings of a massive warehouse. He stopped and motioned for her to hand the burlap bag to him. "Wait here," he said. "It would be better, I think, if the one who thought of it explained it to you."

"Who?" she asked.

He ignored her, walking toward the lone warehouse door ahead with a certain weariness that reminded Çeda of her mother on the days when Çeda had tested her the most.

A woman opened the door, swinging it wide to allow Macide entrance. The woman, of an age with Çeda, stared at her with hard eyes. Çeda stared back, refusing to be cowed. "Go on," Çeda said. "Make sure your master doesn't trip with those heavy bags."

The woman remained, looking Çeda up and down as if she just might step out and make a problem where there didn't need to be one, but then she glanced back inside, into the darkness, and closed the door behind her, leaving Çeda alone to wonder who Macide had gone to fetch. *Ishaq,* Çeda thought. *It must be Ishaq. Who else would Macide defer to in this way? Who else would put forth an idea that he would accept?*

The very thought of seeing her grandfather, the man who could tell her so much more about what had happened to her mother and why she'd come here to Sharakhai . . . It made her gut twist in so many knots she felt sick. But it made her feel glad as well. To know more of her mother felt like finding lost treasure in a mountain cave.

It took only a few moments more for a man's silhouette to darken the doorway. When he remained, silent, Çeda took a step forward. "Hello," she said, feeling the fool for speaking first.

"Has it been so long you no longer recognize me?"

Çeda's breath caught in her throat.

By the stars above, it was Emre.

Chapter 37

TIME PASSED FOR DAVUD IN ENDLESS MOMENTS. They bled into minutes, became hours, grew into days, one stacked on top of another like stones on an ever growing pile, becoming so tall, all around him, he could no longer discern its form. Had he been here for weeks? Months? Had months slipped into years? Surely not that long. Surely he would have died. He wished he had.

Cold stone beneath him drew warmth. It gnawed at him like a wight crouched at the edge of a boneyard, fingers curling, beckoning him closer.

"Were you truly there," Davud whispered, "I would."

He pushed himself up off the floor, the aches and pains he wore like an ever more burdensome robe accompanying his movements. He stood and shuffled to the bucket he'd been given to piss in, to shit in. It was cleared once a day. The food and water that had been lowered to him in another bucket hours ago sat on the opposite side of this deep hole, untouched. Both buckets were tied with only twine, and not nearly strong enough to support his weight to climb out of this place.

He thought of eating yet had no appetite. Every time he tried, the pangs of need, of simple desire, returned. The desire for what, Davud wasn't quite sure. Blood, he presumed. But why? Why would he desire blood? What was it Hamzakiir had awakened in him by the mere application of those arcane symbols?

He'd had little reason to study the red ways at the collegia. He knew what most people knew, that they used their own blood, sometimes others', and bent it for their dark purposes.

"No," Davud said, his voice echoing in the closeness. "That's unfair." Their purposes were not always fiendish. He was associating that with the magi because of Hamzakiir, but there were many stories of heroes of Qaimir who had turned the tide of battles, sometimes to aid Sharakhai. Like anything, blood was merely a tool. But he still wondered: what was it his body hungered for? The blood of the first gods, Hamzakiir had said. That was what the *ehrekh* hungered for, the thing that had never been given to Goezhen and Tulathan and Bakhi and the rest of the younger gods. Had their very desire somehow been passed on to the first of the magi? Had it in turn been passed down from one to the next to the next? It might make some sense. Was blood not passed down from a mother and father to their child? But what of the magi who changed spontaneously, those who hadn't been touched by another mage? Endless questions with almost no answers.

As Davud finished his business with the bucket and went back to lie down, he felt the beginning of another endless wave of agony. A long, pitiful moan escaped him at the very thought. It started deep in his chest, but spread quickly, reaching, clawing, until his entire form was alive with it. An itching, an ache, a deep desire that could not be sated. Not by mere food. Nor by drink.

He moved to the corner of the pit. Drove his head against the stones, if only to feel something different than the walls that were slowly tightening around him, squeezing, unrelenting. Again and again he thumped his head, in time with the beat of his heart. The skin along his forehead was already raw, bruised, bleeding. He didn't care. It was something *else*, and that was a thing he would maim for. A thing he might kill for.

The thought grew within him like a dark, choking weed. He'd thought it many times before. He could kill himself and be done with this, all of it, the pain of the change, the pain of being separated from his friends, the pain of knowing something terrible was about to happen to them. Or was happening. Or already had.

He felt warm blood trickling down his forehead. He let it fall, let it run through his eyebrows, along the edges of his eyes, down his cheeks. The warmth of it crept ever nearer his own mouth. He tilted his head that it might touch his lips, and when it did, this small rivulet of crimson, he ran his tongue across it, accepting whatever happened.

It tasted of salt. Of copper. Of younger days filled with skinned knees and bloody noses and sucking blood from his wrist when he'd cut it on the edge of his father's belt buckle. But there was no deep, hidden meaning. No well of power as he'd thought there might be. As he'd hoped.

He laughed, a maniacal sound that bounded over the walls in the deep of this cold, hard place. "What did you expect, you beetle-brained fool? Some miracle from tapping your own, childish veins?"

The pain was beginning to ebb at last. He was able to pull away from the corner of the pit and make his way to the center, the place he most often inhabited. He breathed more deeply, the ache receding, like a serpent into a night-darkened well, readying itself to surge forth when the time was ripe.

As he sat, he realized he was hungry at last. He tried to ignore it, knowing food would just come up again when the pain returned. But if he didn't eat now, he might not later, and he was feeling so very lightheaded. He crawled forward, and as he did, he heard a long moan of pain. He was so confused he wondered if it was his own pained utterance he was hearing or not. But it came again moments later, a shriek that twisted into a full-throated note of anguish. It was distant, but it consumed him. It bore him like a babe on a raging river. On and on it went, unending, until suddenly and simply it was gone, leaving him feeling strangely empty, as if a beautiful flame had been snuffed between his thumb and forefinger.

He struggled to recall their names. "Anila," he whispered. "Jasur, Meiwei, Raji, Aphir." On and on he went, naming all forty-eight other graduates, finishing with Collum, who'd passed to the farther fields in the hold of the ship.

The screaming came again moments later, descending the pit as another spasm overtook him. He worried he would go mad, that he would be consumed by his fear for his friends and the pain within him, but strangely, those distant screams often quieted his own. Like cool water against forge-lit steel, it tempered him, hardened him to his own pains. He screamed, for there was no way around the agony that gripped him, but he was able to grit his teeth against it, to shunt it away in hope of . . . he knew not what.

Untrue, you coward. He *did* know, of course. He was silently praying to the gods that he wouldn't hear one voice in particular. Anila's. It was unfair of him to single out any one of his fellow scholars, when each would be feeling the same pain. But there it was.

Davud shivered as the food bucket shifted, scraping loudly over the stones. It was pulled upward, clunking against the wall. There was a plea within him that he was desperate to voice, a new position in his bargaining with Hamzakiir. Perhaps he should have offered it before. Perhaps he should keep his mouth shut now. He had no idea what the right choice was, whether he was playing the coward or the savior.

Both, you beetle-brained fool, now out with it.

There were sounds from above: scraping, a grunt, perhaps the one who'd come was annoyed that Davud hadn't eaten what he'd brought last time, or annoyed he was here at all, dealing with some fool scholar whose most fervent wish, apparently, was to die in a hole. And still Davud remained silent.

It wasn't until the bucket thumped against the stone floor that Davud blurted out. "One!" He looked up through the impenetrable gloom, hoping to see some hint of a body, to appeal to him directly. "Tell Hamzakiir I will do as he wishes if he gives me but one!"

He thought he might have seen movement above, the subtle shift of clouds on a moonless night, but he couldn't be sure.

"Please, tell him!"

There was no reply. Only the scrape as a leather sole shifted on stone, the patter of grit as it fell against the stone at Davud's feet, and nothing more.

"Please!"

But he was alone. More alone than he'd ever been. At least before the bucket man had come he'd been resigned to his fate. Now he had hope. A foolish hope, no doubt, a hope that threatened to crush him, but a hope nonetheless.

Every so often, the pain inside him abated. It did so now, leaving him utterly spent. He thought of eating. He knew he *should* eat. That he needed water as well. But just then all he cared about was closing his eyes and putting the horrors aside for a short while.

As he lay there, the realm of sleep closing in around him, the screams began again. He couldn't tell if it was Anila's voice or not, but in his dreams, she died a thousand deaths.

Davud woke curled up in a tight ball like an insect waking from its slumber, ready to unfurl and scuttle across the sand. He was hungry. So very hungry. But not for food. The gnawing had grown worse. It clawed at him from the inside, as if it were willing to tear away whatever flesh and bone might stand between it and freedom. In some unknowable way, the gnawing felt deeper, as though it had bored its way into his soul, a thing infinitely more terrifying than mere hunger of the body.

His lips were dry and cracked. Bleeding, he realized. His breath was shallow and quick, like a heat-struck dog. He knew he should move to the bucket and drink some water. But he didn't wish to.

So he lay there, wondering how long it would be.

And then a new wave struck him so hard he realized that all this time since he'd awoken had been spent in the valleys of his pain, not the heights. The pain so consumed him the world all around turned bright red. He cried out in agony, he was sure, but the only thing he could hear now was a keen ringing.

On and on it went.

Until he woke once more. He hadn't even realized he'd fallen unconscious, but dear gods the pain was worse than it had been the last time he woke. He was going to die in this place. In this deep dark pit hidden away from the world. He'd never see Sharakhai again. Never see Tehla, or mother and father, or Anila. Or Çeda. He would die as Collum had: quietly and unobserved.

He might try to hang himself, but the twine on the buckets would simply break. He swallowed, and coughed from the tight emptiness in his stomach.

"Ah," a voice came from above. "You're awake."

Hamzakiir.

He'd been so desperate to speak to Hamzakiir, but now the doubts returned. The path that lay before him. The cost in the end.

"You haven't been eating."

Davud crawled away until his back was pressed against the wall, then he sat up and pulled his knees to his chest. He tried to speak, but all that came out was a strangled rasp. He swallowed again, licked his lips. "I'm not very hungry."

"I told you. You don't have to die down there."

He wanted to give a biting reply, but his mind was too muddled, and he didn't have the will in any case. "I can't simply abandon them," he said at last. "I couldn't live with myself."

A silence followed that seemed to stretch wider and faster the longer it went. It went on so long Davud thought Hamzakiir had made up his mind and decided to let Davud rot, but just when he was about to call up to him, Hamzakiir broke the silence. "One, you said."

He didn't know what he was talking about at first, but then he remembered his plea, and suddenly his indifference, his doubts, all vanished. "One," he replied.

"Which?"

Gods forgive me. "Her name is Anila."

A moment passed, but then Davud heard the rope snaking down once more. It slapped against the stones near his head. "Best to climb out now, before another fit overcomes you."

Davud tried, but he could go no more than a few feet before he halted, his arms quivering from the effort. Suddenly he found himself being pulled up, quickly moving up to the top, where Hamzakiir grabbed his clothes and pulled him over the edge.

He was led, Hamzakiir supporting him, to a high room in the caravanserai. What followed was a day of bright light and pain. He was fed broth, given sweet lemonade laced with peppercorns and mint. What he remembered most, however, was Hamzakiir sitting by his bedside, a short, sharp kenshar in one hand. He used the tip of the kenshar to draw blood from the palm of his hand, which he then used like a painter's well, dabbing a finger, then applying blood to Davud's forehead, dabbing, then applying more to his cheeks. On and on it went, Hamzakiir studying Davud like a caring uncle might, one who was tied by blood but not so closely that his emotions overcame him.

It took hours to complete, some grand work over Davud's face and chest and arms and legs. It felt as if his entire body was covered with it. And perhaps it was. He'd blacked out several times as relief and pain alternated in strange, unexpected waves.

At last, Hamzakiir was done. He wiped the palm of his hand. The blood sizzled, his palm now clean. "Rest now, Davud Mahzun'ava. It was a very near thing, but I think you'll live. Rest, and when you wake up, you can see your Anila."

He wanted desperately to see her now, but knew he couldn't in this state. He'd no more nodded and made the sort of grunt he hoped would be interpreted as assent than sleep had taken him once more.

Again he dreamed of Anila, but this time, it was *she* who killed *him* in a thousand different ways.

"Davud."

He felt something cold and wet against his forehead, wiping his skin. Then again along his cheek. Did he have a fever?

The cloth moved more quickly now, more forcefully. "Davud. *Please* wake."

He opened his eyes, squinting against the sun breaking through the closed shutters. He was lying in a bed, a young woman with black hair and expressive brown eyes at his bedside. Her nose and cheeks were covered with light freckles, pale now against her dark skin, a reminder of her youth, she'd said, when she couldn't get enough of riding horses with her father along the winding bridle paths in the Hanging Gardens to the east of Sharakhai.

"Anila," he said, his voice a hoarse whisper.

"You were dreaming." She looked down at the bloody cloth she held in her hands. "You were calling my name."

Davud shook his head. "I don't recall." A bald lie, but he couldn't very well tell her the truth.

She dipped the cloth into a bowl of water on the table at the bedside, wrung it out, and continued to clean his face. "You seemed scared."

"Wouldn't you be?"

"I wouldn't know," she said sharply. "I don't know what you've been through." A moment later she softened. "What happened to you, Davud?"

He wanted to tell her that he'd been through what *she'd* been through, and to a degree he had, but it would be enough of a lie that he couldn't let it pass his lips. She knew, or at least suspected, that things had gone differently for him than it had for everyone else who'd been taken here. And surely she was justifiably concerned over being taken away from the others—rescued, in effect—and brought here to find Davud covered in blood.

"The blood," Davud said as she wiped his neck. "What patterns were they?"

She shivered. "Sigils, written in the old script."

She was hiding something. He could see it in her eyes, and the way they refused to meet his. "What did they say?"

"I don't know all of them."

He grabbed her wrist. "Anila, what did they say?"

She looked about the room, as if by doing so she could find her courage. "They spoke of blood and binding, of unbreakable pacts."

Dear gods. And now she'd wiped them away. "Can you re-create them?"

"What? No!"

He sat up in his bed to look for a mirror, his body screaming from the effort. There was nothing he might use to see his reflection, however. "Please, you must try."

Despite his demand, she began wiping more of the blood away.

He grabbed her wrists. "Anila, stop it!"

"Why?"

"Because I must know what he wrote upon my skin!"

"It's too late. It's gone. I've already wiped the rest of it away. It was foul, Davud. I don't know why you would want to know of it. Just be glad it's gone."

He pulled the blanket back. It was true. Other than a red cast to the skin along his chest and arms and stomach, it was all gone. "How could you have done that?"

"Davud, you're hurting me."

He looked at her hands, saw how white they were. He released his hold immediately. "I'm sorry," he said, but he hardly felt the words. Hamzakiir had helped him through his change. That's what he'd said, wasn't it? He was going to help him to live beyond this stage, and then what? Fool that he was, he didn't even know. Perhaps he'd had the conversation with Hamzakiir. He might have. But if so, he couldn't remember a word of it.

"What have I done?" he whispered.

"Davud, tell me what happened."

"Where is Hamzakiir?"

"Who?"

Davud stared at her, uncomprehending. "Who brought you here?"

"I don't know. He was veiled." She motioned to the door. "They're down the stairs if you wish to speak with them."

Davud stared at the door, inexplicably afraid of stepping into the world again. "What were they doing to you?"

Anila's eyes, openly concerned for Davud a moment ago, became every bit as afraid and haunted as Davud felt. "I don't know. We were kept in a cell. They came for us, one by one. We heard horrible screams. It must have been torture, but what they were hoping to learn from us I cannot say." She paused. "Do *you* know?"

"No," Davud said, and it was the truth, but Anila stared at him doubtfully. "Were you with us?"

"Yes." He breathed a sigh of acceptance. "No."

"Davud, what are you talking about?"

"I was with you at first, but when we arrived here, I was kept in a pit."

"Why?"

"I don't know." He couldn't tell her the truth. He didn't wish her to know what Hamzakiir had done to him, what he *was* now. But Anila had seen him lying here with sigils painted in blood covering his entire body. He may have lived, but he suspected he'd done something he would one day come to regret. It all came down to power. He'd given Hamzakiir power over him, and that was something he should have died before doing.

"Davud, what were those sigils for?"

Just then the door opened. They both turned to find Hamzakiir standing in the doorway. "Well, well, the dead have risen. If you're well, I would have a word with you." His gaze rested firmly on Davud, excluding Anila from the conversation. Even his body language divided Anila from Davud as he moved to the foot of the bed, his back to her, waving Davud toward the open doorway, a clear indication that Anila would remain. He held a leatherbound book in one hand, a thin tome. The leather and pages looked freshly made.

Davud felt his insides churn as Anila watched him with a wary expression.

Hamzakiir gave him an impatient smile. "I suspect you'll find your legs to be in good working order."

Davud took the wet rag from Anila's hands and wiped away as much of the remaining blood as he could, then stood and pulled on his collegia robes, which had been washed and laid on a chair by the bedside. Any embarrassment he felt over being naked in front of Anila, who refused to avert her gaze, was dwarfed by the knowledge that he'd be leaving her to confer with a man who was, for all the evidence before him, torturing his friends and would likely continue to do so. But he needed to know what had happened to him. And then he would see about leaving this place, taking Anila with him, saving others if he could.

He left the room, and Hamzakiir closed it behind him. Anila opened the door immediately, shouting, "You'll not leave me behind!" but a man wearing a turban and desert clothes barred her way. There was another guard on the opposite side of the door. Together, they pushed her back inside the room.

As the door clattered shut, Hamzakiir, unfazed, strode along the bright ceramic tiles and reached a set of stairs heading down. "Time grows short," he said.

Davud rushed to catch up. They wound their way down to ground level and soon were standing in a courtyard at the center of the building. It was well past midday, the sun cutting angular shadows over the walls and onto the winding path through the garden. From beyond the walls, he could hear the sounds of commerce, men calling, women bartering, goats bleating, but here, the courtyard was empty, the windows that looked upon it shuttered, the many doors that led to it all closed.

Hamzakiir moved to a bench near the center, beneath the shade of a palm, not far from the old bronze pump at the center of the courtyard. When Davud sat beside him, Hamzakiir motioned back toward the building they'd just left. "It was a very near thing. You're strong of will, but you waited so long before reaching out to me."

"What did you draw on me?" Davud asked.

Hamzakiir seemed confused, even slightly affronted. He scratched his chin, then combed his beard back into place, before replying. "I would have thought that was clear. They were sigils, drawn to save your life. Sigils that will continue to work for weeks, sheltering you from the worst of the effects. Sigils that will hide you from those who might try to take advantage of a mage young to the ways of blood."

Just how someone might take further advantage of him, Davud wasn't sure, and he didn't care to ask just then. He made to ask another question, but Hamzakiir spoke over him.

"Your mistrust is understandable, and I don't blame you for it, but there are realities you must now face. Rituals you must perform lest you slip back into the pain and madness you felt in the pit. If you ignore it, you will die." He raised the leatherbound book. "Use this, and it will serve as your guide in the days and weeks ahead."

He held the book out for Davud to take. Davud did, holding it so that a pair of pages near the center of the book were revealed. Sigils were written there in the old language of the desert with ink of rusty red. Davud couldn't deny their beauty, but he was also quite sure that they'd been drawn in Hamzakiir's blood. "You wrote this," he said, more to fill the space between them than a question that needed answering.

Hamzakiir nodded. "Last night, after your ritual was complete."

He read over the instructions that accompanied the sigils. Detailed notes followed each, stating their purpose, the rites he must follow leading up to the drawing of the sigil, and the ones he would follow after.

"Those in the opening pages will keep you alive. The ones in the following pages will . . . help you rise above your station, should you so choose. Use them or not as you see fit, but do not ignore the first seven pages."

"Why?" Davud asked, flipping through the pages. "Why have you done this?"

"I was the spark that caused the change within you. I was honor-bound to complete it."

"That's all?"

Hamzakiir considered this for a time, as if deciding how much to share. "There was someone I recently made a similar offer to. I was fairly certain he would deny me. But still, I had hoped he would accept."

"And you think this somehow evens the scales?"

"Had we two been born in Mirea, both of us would believe so."

"But we weren't."

Hamzakiir smiled. "Had we met under different circumstances, I would continue your training myself. It is of course impossible now, for many reasons, but I advise you to find another mage when you return to Sharakhai. It won't be easy, and I suspect before long one will come to you, one you mightn't like to have as your master, so work quickly."

"I know of no mages in Sharakhai."

"You're resourceful and you're smart. You'll find one if you look carefully enough."

Amalos, Davud thought. *He'll be able to help.*

But would he? Amalos might have loved Davud once, but he wouldn't after this. How could he?

"You haven't saved me," Davud said. "You've cursed me."

"It is part curse, to be sure. I freely acknowledge it. But if you embrace the red ways, they are more freeing than you can ever imagine. We touch the blood of the first gods, the very stuff of creation. Isn't that worth what you've gone through?"

"What are you going to do to my friends?"

Hamzakiir stood. "I'll be putting both you and Anila on a ship tonight. You will sail for Sharakhai, but will arrive well after this business with your friends is done." He took one step toward the door through which they'd entered the courtyard. "Farewell, Davud Mahzun'ava."

"Wait! Tell me!"

Hamzakiir ignored him, striding for the stairwell. Davud stood and ran toward him, but as he did, a veiled man in dark desert garb broke away from the shadows of the doorway and intercepted him.

He shouted after Hamzakiir, "What are you going to do to my friends?" mere moments before the guard sent a fist crashing into his stomach. Davud crumpled, his breath whooshing from his lungs. He clutched his gut, his breath refusing to come for long moments, but then finally it did in one long, wet rasp, and pain came with it.

"One more shout like that," the guardsman said, "and I'll undo all the good work my lord has done. Do you understand?"

As Hamzakiir's form vanished into the darkness of the stairwell, Davud nodded.

All too soon the sun was setting and Davud was aboard a ship, a small, two-masted ketch, and had set sail. Anila had at first refused to go, demanding to know where the others were. She had screamed until the guard, the same brute that had punched Davud in the stomach, wrapped one arm around her throat and squeezed until her face had gone red and she'd fallen unconscious. By the time she woke the sun was setting over the desert. They could see it through the small starboard window of the cabin they shared, casting golden light, then a bloody, muddy red against the distant clouds.

"You bargained for my life, didn't you?" Anila asked as she sat on her bunk.

Davud was seated, leaning forward, hands in his lap, staring at the planks of the ship's hull. "Yes."

"What did you give up in return?"

I'm not even sure, Davud thought. Hamzakiir claimed he'd saved Davud because of an unwritten code among the magi. Perhaps it was, but he couldn't help shaking the feeling there was more to it. "I just wanted to save you."

"But not the others?"

"Of course the others. I tried to, Anila. I did."

"How hard?"

Not nearly hard enough. "We have to return to Sharakhai and let them know what's happened."

"They won't return us to Sharakhai until his plans have been completed."

"Then what we know may help bring him to justice."

Anila lay down and faced the curving hull. "I know you were trying to help me, Davud, but their faces haunt me already. Their cries. I cannot be free while they remain there, being tortured every day."

"Yet here we are."

Anila rolled over and glared at him in disgust, then faced the hull once more. "Not for long."

Chapter 38

RAMAHD FELT SOMETHING HARD nudge him in the side. "Come," came Meryam's voice, dragging him out of a dream he'd been having of a desert oasis. He'd been swimming with a woman—Meryam, he realized now. They'd been circling one another in the cool water, moving slowly closer. Ramahd had been trying to reach out to her, but she'd been playful, swimming away when he came too close. Gods, how he wanted her.

Again something blunt bored into his ribs. "Up, Ramahd!"

He opened his eyes to find Meryam poking him with her shoe as he lay on the couch in her room. They'd been working late again last night, and had been doing so for nearly a full day. Meryam had tried over and over to keep him up, reasoning that they might miss something important, but finally she'd relented when Tariq had gone to sleep.

He looked over to the nearby windows, where the light of dawn leaked in through gauzelike drapes. For a moment the drapes lifted in the warm, oddly humid wind. "Did it rain?" he asked.

"For a time," Meryam replied, moving about the room, setting a tray of marbled cheese, dates, grapes, and a golden, crusty bread with white and black sesame seeds embedded in its crust. She poured jasmine tea for him as he tore off a hunk of bread and slathered the soft, smoky cheese over the still-warm interior.

As he chewed and sipped tea, coming slowly awake, Meryam said, "I've been summoned to Tauriyat."

"By whom?" he replied around the sweet meat of a date. When Meryam didn't respond with a sharp retort, merely going about the business of making a plate of her own, Ramahd began to understand. "By King Ihsan?"

She pulled a nearby chair closer to the couch, sat, and pulled a grape from the bunch on her plate. "I suspect he'll want to know why the Queen of Qaimir has not yet called upon him."

"And will you go to see him, the Honey-tongued King?"

"Eventually I must, but I put him off for now, claiming a mourning period for my father."

"That's probably for the best, at least until this business with Tariq is done." Ramahd had met Ihsan many times, and knew him to be a dangerous man. He had a way of making one speak about things one didn't really wish to speak of. Meryam would do fine, however. There wasn't a woman or man alive he trusted more to keep secrets.

Meryam pulled up the hem of her skirt and put her feet up on the couch cushions in a gesture so relaxed, so intimate, that Ramahd nearly laughed. *The places we've been. The things we've done.* He wondered, not for the first time, where the two of them might be if he'd met Meryam before Yasmine. Never mind that her father, King Aldouan, wouldn't have allowed it. And never mind that the very thought made Ramahd feel as though he were betraying Yasmine's memory a thousand times over. He couldn't help but wonder if he and Meryam might have been happy. And if Yasmine might not still be alive.

But then he would never have had Rehann. Her life had been cut short, true, but he would trade those bittersweet years for nothing. "The gods cast the dice when we're born," he'd once told Rehann, "and we live the life they've decided for us."

"But who casts the dice for the gods?" she'd asked him.

Who indeed, my darling child?

"Are you ready?" Meryam asked, popping the last of the grapes into her mouth.

Instead of the tea, Ramahd grabbed a nearby bottle of brandy and tipped it to his lips. He took a healthy swallow, then set it down and wiped his mouth with the back of his hand. "Why not?"

As Meryam stood, her mouth became a grim line. "Don't look so wretched"—she waved her hands over her form with a look like she couldn't believe what had become of her—"if I had the chance to shed this skin for that of a younger woman like your White Wolf, don't think for a moment I wouldn't do it."

"You'd do no such thing." As the alcohol burned its way to his stomach, Ramahd lay himself down on the couch, made himself as comfortable as he could. "You're too driven, Meryam."

"Driven, yes, but what I wouldn't give for a body that's whole."

"And whose fault is that?"

She replied without hesitation. "Macide's." And with that name all sense of playfulness vanished. She was once more the woman he'd known since Yasmine's and Rehann's deaths.

"I'm ready," he said.

"Well enough." And with that she bit her lip, enough that a bit of blood might flow. She leaned down and placed her lips slowly upon his. He felt her tongue parting his lips. And then she was pulling back, leaving a lingering warmth inside him, the taste of blood on his tongue, and the redolence of a woman he'd do well to stop thinking so much about.

Every other time they'd done this, each day for the past ten days, she'd pricked a finger with a needle and fed him her blood by placing it on his tongue. Why the change, this sudden intimacy, he didn't know, but the effects swept over him like a sandstorm over Sharakhai. Meryam's presence roared through him. Through the bond he'd created with his own blood, she reached out and touched Tariq as well. Unlike with Ramahd, however, she was oh so subtle. Like a marionette being passed from one puppeteer to another, Tariq was blind to their presence. For days more that would remain the case, but with so many days having passed already, the effect of Ramahd's blood was waning. It was becoming more and more difficult to maintain the bond, and soon it would be impossible without exerting more influence, a thing they couldn't afford to do unless they wanted to reveal themselves to him.

Ramahd felt his form change. It distorted, became more lithe. He felt an energy he hadn't felt in years, even though Tariq had not yet fully awoken.

———————————— ⟵●⟶ ————————————

Tariq rolled over and kissed the woman sharing his bed, the stunningly pretty daughter of a goldsmith. Curly hair. Bright eyes. She studied him for a moment, bleary eyed, her waking smile turning to a concerned pout. "Still have your headache?"

Tariq nodded. "I'll be fine."

"You should see my father's apothecary. She's brilliant."

Tariq gave her a playful shove. "I said I'll be fine."

She frowned and rolled away, tucking the pillow beneath her head, leaving Tariq to gaze at her naked form. Tariq rubbed his temples, opened his mouth wide, trying in vain to drive away the pain. As he stood and began to dress, the woman said, "You could stay a while," as she slipped one hand beneath the blanket, between her legs.

"Can't," he said. A roll beneath the blanket was the last thing his pounding head needed. He took to the streets and immediately regretted his sharp tone, his dismissive ways. She deserved better. He'd make it up to her later. For now, he had to keep his wits about him. The Knot, where Brama kept himself these days, was no place to go with a dull mind.

The streets were busy with traffic, but everyone was bundled up with a cold wind coming in from the north. Tariq felt the cold as well, but it felt good against his forehead, which so often lately felt hot too the touch. He reached the edge of the Shallows, and took it to a street where few dared go. The streets seemed to curve in on themselves here. The buildings leaned in, supported one another. Chary eyes watched from doorways, from windows. Hungry faces leered. He paid them no more mind than he would an urchin begging for coin, but he marked each and every one of them as he passed.

He came to a dead-end street that was so narrow two people could hardly walk abreast without becoming intimately familiar with one another. After the dozens who'd seen him approach, the emptiness of this short street felt eerie, menacing in a way he couldn't define.

A piercing whistle broke the wintry air, sending a sharp stab of pain through Tariq's skull. It was picked up farther down the street, and then again, somewhere inside one of the ramshackle buildings. A gaunt man stepped out from a doorway and barred his path. He wore rags, things you might find on a man who'd lost himself to black lotus, and yet this man's eyes were sharp. And while his hands may have shook, it looked to be symptoms of long-term damage from the drug, not fresh withdrawal.

He looked keenly at Tariq, then motioned to Tariq's belt, momentarily revealing the crisscross of scars on the palms of his hands, the sign of the Tattered Prince.

"Do we really have to do this every time?" Tariq asked.

The man merely stared, jaw jutted like a black laugher, his gaze as humorous as one, too. Rolling his eyes, Tariq pulled the sword from his belt and handed it to the man. He gave over his knife as well. "No fucking nicks in it this time."

The man took them and handed them to a woman half his age who had scars on the palms of her hands as well. The man stared, then flicked his fingers again.

"Bloody gods, I've not come to *murder* him."

Another flick, and Tariq lifted his arms up, at which point the man patted his sleeves, his chest, his back, feeling for weapons. He finished with Tariq's sirwal pants, then grunted and strode toward the far end of the street, bow-legged as a stork wading through the Haddah. In the doorway ahead, a young girl presented herself. She raised both hands, at which point the man did too.

"Take him up," the man said with a voice like a Kundhunese rattle, as if the gods had judged him unworthy and stolen his voice.

"He's asleep."

"He left orders, girl. Now bring him up."

The girl, a waif with no more meat on her than a mongrel dog, glared at Tariq. Tariq had never seen her before, so was surprised when she reached out and grabbed one of his hands. She looked at his palm, tossed his hand away in disgust and turned to walk deeper into the darkness of the building.

Tariq followed. People watched from within darkened rooms, staring with nervous, angry eyes. Some even had the look of the lotus on them—eyes half lidded and fluttering as if they couldn't stand the sight of the world.

The girl led Tariq up a set of stairs at the back, some of it repaired with fresh wood. They went up four floors to the topmost, where it gave way to open sky. Much of the wood here was blackened, charred, lost to a fire that had nearly swept over the entire neighborhood. The sun shone down on them through the gaping hole in the roof, but was lost as they stepped up into a hallway that had gray swaths of smoke damage along its plaster. The smell of burned wood was still strong, as was the smell of mold.

It was at this point that Ramahd felt a disjoint between Meryam and Tariq. Up until now he'd hardly noticed himself or Meryam, but now, as the girl knocked on the door, Tariq felt a familiar unease, and Meryam experienced a distinct fear. Their emotions were so powerful Ramahd felt like a piece of papyrus being torn between the two of them.

The door opened soundlessly a moment later, and a young woman perhaps two years younger than Tariq stood there. "Balen told me to bring him up," the girl said to her. The woman, Jax, nodded, then turned the girl around with a hand on her shoulder and gave her a shove.

"Come," Jax said in her Malasani accent, stepping back to allow Tariq entrance.

Tariq did, and found the room more or less the same as the last time he'd been here, though as always, there were some knicknacks—tokens of appreciation from the lotus addicts he'd healed— stacked here and there. A rag doll. A brass ring. A leatherbound book, half-eaten by decay. There were several tables, a desk, a chest, and an opulent bed. A man lay on the bed, eyes half-lidded as they stared up at the elegant wooden beams running like the threads of a spider's web over the ceiling. The air was laced heavily with the scent of black lotus.

It was rare for memories to be transferred through this arrangement, but just then Tariq had one so strong it momentarily replaced the scene in the room. Tariq in a drug den near the center of Sharakhai, drawing lotus smoke from a shisha tube. The rush of euphoria in that single breath flared to life, igniting Ramahd's memories of his own flirtation with the drug. The next moment the memory was gone, replaced by the man lying in an opulent bed in a slum.

Jax glared at Tariq. "Brama said to leave you with him, but he's not been well, so don't be long."

Tariq nodded, and Jax left.

Near the bed was a table that could only be considered a piece of art, its grain rich and pure, the stain the color of fresh honey. Its top and legs and drawers were decorated with the intricate eastern designs of a master

Malasani wood artisan. Warring with the beauty of that piece, however, were several things scattered across its top: an inkwell and pen, the ink splattered over the wood's lustrous surface, an ivory smoking pipe, a clay bowl filled with ash, a box containing a black, tarry substance that was easily five years workman's pay worth of the powerful drug.

Tariq moved closer. Gods he hated coming here. He used to run the streets with Brama, but that Brama was long gone, somehow replaced by the travesty of a man Tariq saw before him. "Brama, can you hear me?"

Brama's head lolled toward the sound, his curly brown hair obscuring the scars on his face for a moment. The scars looked like a mis-made quilt, a landscape as terrible as the blasted lands found far out in the desert. Only once had Tariq asked him what had happened. *Why, I've made my face anew. Don't you like it?* He'd said it nonchalantly, but there had been a look in his eyes. A devil's grin. Even now it made Tariq shiver inside to think about it. Tariq had heard rumors, though. Of a creature Brama had run into in the dark corners of Sharakhai.

Like a newborn child Brama's eyes refused to focus, but soon his attention had been drawn to something over Tariq's shoulder.

Leave, Ramahd heard Meryam say, jolting him from Tariq's mind. And yet she made no move to withdraw. *Ramahd, we must leave.* The terror in her was building, but they couldn't leave yet. Tariq was close to something. He could feel it.

Tariq came to the bedside. "Gods, Brama, you can't save them all."

Brama blinked, turned his head vaguely in the direction of Tariq, but his eyes still swam.

We must leave, Ramahd.

"Osman's worried about you," Tariq said. "I am as well."

Brama eyes fluttered, took Tariq in, then fluttered once more. He reached one arm out, presumably to take Tariq's hand, or his shirt, but he was well off the mark and grabbed only empty air. "Who's come?"

"It's Tariq. Osman's sent me. I've come for the caches." When Brama didn't respond, Tariq went on. "Have you found them yet?" Tariq felt a right shit for asking it so plainly.

Brama rolled back and stared at the ceiling. "There's another."

"Another what?" When Brama didn't reply, Tariq began looking over the table, opening the small wooden boxes there, then the drawers. "Another what, Brama?"

Brama's eyes closed, his mouth agape. He went so still Tariq checked the pulse at his neck. Word was Brama used a gemstone to do what he did: to heal those lost to the lure of black lotus. Tariq pulled his shirt away from his chest and caught a glimpse of it, a bloody great sapphire wrapped in a leather cord. He immediately let the shirt drop back. He'd heard tell of people who had tried to steal that gem. Within a day or two the thieves returned glass-eyed and handed the gem right back to him, gutting themselves with their own knives afterward. "They're hopeless addicts, Brama, and they're going to be the death of you."

At this Brama laughed, a slow thing, as if he were made of clay. "You've profited enough from it."

"There are as many ways to turn profits as there are souls in the desert," Tariq said. "You of all people know that. You've saved enough drug-addled children by now, haven't you? At least enough to even the scales with the gods for whatever sins you committed when you were young. Leave them behind. Find your salvation by giving to those in need if you must. But mark my words. The dark path you tread leads only to the boneyard, and unless I'm mistaken, the lord of all things already walks by your side. The only question is whether you're ready to take his hand or not."

Brama laughed again as his head rolled away. Frustration over the lack of answers thrummed inside Tariq like a rattlewing beetle. "At least tell me Lord Rasul's came to you. The last thing either of us needs—that *I* need—is to go to Osman empty-handed again." He rifled through the clothes piled on the floor beside the bed. "He's like as not to send me back to running packages if I don't come up with something soon, and I can't say I'd blame him." He stood and rubbed his temples for a moment before moving to the table inlaid with mother-of-pearl on the far side of the room and rummaged through that as well. "So please, tell me Rasul knew, and that you have the palaces." No longer pretending at courtesy, Tariq opened the chest at the foot of the bed and tore through its contents as if they'd insulted him.

As he did, Ramahd felt *something* in the room. He couldn't quite define it. It was akin to the feelings of despair after waking to find yourself inexplicably alone when your dreams had been filled with loved ones and joy; or the beckoning feeling of death that came from staring into the depths of the sea long after land has been left behind. It was a dangerous thing, a pitiless thing, a hunger that could swallow Tariq whole. This was what Meryam had sensed, though he could put no name to it. It had no form save this room.

As Tariq stood, Brama moaned, his head tossing from side to side, hands grasping for gods knew what. "There is another," he moaned.

"Fuck your mother, Brama, another *what?*"

And then Tariq saw it.

Ink marking the palm of Brama's right hand. He moved quickly to Brama's side, then pried his fingers back. It was so sloppy Ramahd could barely recognize it as writing, but after a moment he recognized them. The names of three Kings.

Ihsan. Zeheb. Kiral.

In that moment, as relief washed over Tariq like the Haddah's clear spring waters, Brama's hand shot out and clamped over Tariq's wrist. He twisted Tariq's arm, lifted his head until the two of them were eye to eye, the scars over Brama's face and neck so close Tariq couldn't help but wince. "There is another *here*"—he pressed his forehead to Tariq's—"with you."

"No," Tariq replied easily, as if he'd done this with Brama before. With deliberate force, he wrenched his wrist from Brama's grasp. "I've come alone."

For a moment, the haze in Brama's eyes vanished. He became as intense as Meryam when she was taken by the power of blood. He propped himself up on one shoulder, and as he did, something slipped along his hairy chest, the necklace with the sapphire wrapped in braided leather. Most of the gemstone's facets were occluded with soot or dirt—all but the largest, the one staring outward. *That* facet was nearly but not completely clear, and it gave view to the space within, a blue hollow that for a moment felt larger than it had any right to, a sense that grew by the moment. It felt large as the room, then as this leaning building, then larger than the Shallows beyond. It felt as though that strange gem were a gateway to the farther fields themselves. And there was something within: the presence Ramahd had felt but could not yet define.

Brama's low voice filled the room. Tariq's chest thrummed with the sound of it. "Someone watches you."

Tariq grunted, putting his hand to his head as a new wave of pain struck him. The headaches. It was to do with the headaches, he understood now.

By the grace of mighty Alu, Ramahd, we must leave now!

Ramahd now shared her desperation. He had no idea what lay hidden within that sapphire, and he had no desire to find out. He scrabbled away, but something held him in place.

Who are you?

It came from nowhere, everywhere. A terrible voice. Brama. The beast within the gem. Ramahd wasn't sure. But it had a note of familiarity to it. A feeling he couldn't quite place, until he thought of the desert, of Meryam's father, of the creature that had killed him. Guhldrathen. That's what the presence in the gem felt like.

He tried to scrabble away, to leave, to shed Tariq's body like a cloak and return to his own. But he couldn't. Dear gods, he couldn't. And Meryam was transfixed. The beast was staring into her soul.

Leave her alone! Ramahd tried to fight it, but what could he do? He was not gifted in the ways of blood. In this, he was little more than Meryam's beast of burden.

He felt Meryam's defenses falling. Any moment the beast would have her, and then it would be his turn.

"Brama?"

A woman's voice, filled with a strange concoction of confusion and concern. Brama turned, as did Tariq, to find Jax standing in the doorway.

And then the vision was gone and Ramahd was in another room in another building in another part of Sharakhai entirely.

Gasping for breath, drenched in sweat, heart pounding like the hooves of a prized akhala, he whispered to himself, "I'm in the embassy house. I've returned to the embassy house." At first the mantra was merely a hope, the voice still echoing inside him, *Who are you?* But slowly his words became a reality, a confirmation that he had somehow, perhaps improbably, escaped.

Meryam lay next to him, her entire body quivering as if she'd been taken by a terrible fit. Her eyes were rolled up into her head. Her head was arched back, her throat convulsing like a lizard trying to swallow a desert asp.

"Meryam!" Ramahd called, shaking her, holding her head in his hands to try to calm her. "Meryam!"

But she either would not or could not respond. Her breathing became labored. She began to gasp.

Ramahd gripped her by the arms and shook her fiercely. "Meryam, tell me what to do!"

Her movements slowed. Whatever battle was being fought, Meryam was losing it.

He looked at her lips, at the trace of blood still there from earlier. In a fit of desperation, he bit his own lip as she had done. He kissed her, spreading his blood around in her mouth with his tongue. He held her close, keeping their mouths pressed, an act as coldly dispassionate as the strike of a headman's axe.

At last, Meryam's muscles unclenched. And then all at once, her body went slack. He laid her down and looked her over carefully. Her heart still beat, her lungs still drew breath, though both felt weak and shallow. It was similar, in fact, to the deep sleeps she took after overusing her talents with blood. Which, considering all that had happened, was about as well as Ramahd could have hoped for.

He fell onto his own couch, knowing they had narrowly escaped with their lives. "Mighty Alu, what wicked soul lives within that gem?"

He half expected Meryam to wake and tell him, but this was a mystery that would have to wait for her to regain consciousness. His body begged him to lay his head down and sleep, but instead he levered himself up on unsteady limbs, left the room, and shouted for the house physic.

Chapter 39

ÇEDA STEPPED TOWARD EMRE OVER THE DRY, packed earth. Months ago, a random meeting like this had happened in the Qaimiri statehouse. Ramahd had arranged to bring them together, and they'd immediately fallen into one another's arms. This time Emre stared at her as if he hardly knew her. And perhaps he didn't. Really, how well did the two of them know one another anymore? They'd both changed so much over the past months, and it had formed a gulf between them.

Çeda felt suddenly chilled. Something had been lost between them, and it made her wonder whether they could ever get it back. She was reminded of the times they'd sat together atop their home, sipping cheap wine and talking late into the night.

"One day the Kings will be long forgotten," Emre had told her once.

"Perhaps," she'd replied, "but what if it's only after everyone else has gone to the farther fields?"

He hadn't answered. She'd wondered then and she wondered now what part the two of them played in this vast, unfolding drama.

"I saw you that day, on the rooftops," she finally said to him.

"I know."

"That was quite a shot." She left unsaid that the shot had killed a man. She could see even in the darkness that he was not proud of what he'd done. Somehow, that comforted her.

"Darius has been drilling me." He shrugged. "I've taken to it."

They'd tried bows once when they were young. Çeda had been passable. Tariq as well. Hamid had been deadly with it. He'd been so shy back then, and yet as he stared at the gourd they'd all been trying to hit, something lit in his eyes. A hunger that rarely came out of him, but when it did, it made Çeda's skin crawl. Arrow after arrow had sunk deep into the center of the gourd, and after, Çeda and Tariq had pestered him, trying to find out who'd taught him to shoot like that, but he'd said nothing, and then grown sullen and angry until finally they'd stopped asking. Emre had remained silent through Hamid's display. He'd been miserable at it, and Çeda thought he wouldn't want any more attention drawn to his efforts.

But Emre had changed. He'd shied away from violence back then, where now he seemed to embrace it. *Time is the hammer that shapes us all.*

Çeda took two steps forward so that she could see him better. She saw bruises along his left eye, a cut half-healed on his chin, but made no mention of them. "I worried you'd been killed at Külaşan's palace."

He smiled, a faint echo of the bright smile he'd always shared with her. "I nearly was."

"I'm sorry I couldn't help you."

"Gods, Çeda, will you listen to yourself? You saved us all. You came when Külaşan was ready to bury that bloody great morning star of his in our skulls."

It was Çeda's turn to shrug. "Still, I thought I'd done it all for naught. I thought you'd been buried alive, or taken by the Spears."

He spread his arms wide. "I am more alive than I've ever been." There was a confidence in his eyes and in his stance she'd never seen before. A year ago it would have looked like false bravado, a front to cover the pain of his brother Rafa's passing. But not now. Scar tissue had formed over that wound at last, leaving him changed. A man Çeda did not wholly recognize.

"Macide said you had a plan."

As he lowered his arms, a sheepish look overcame him. He waved back to the warehouse door. "I'm sorry. I know you don't like me being with them."

She couldn't help but think of Yndris, shooting arrows down at the crowd during the riot, or Kameyl dragging a woman behind her horse, or a thousand other things the Maidens had done that Çeda both hated and had done nothing to stop. "We've both chosen our paths, Emre."

"Well then." He strode to her side and held out his hand. "We have a bit of time. Let's walk."

She paused, then smiled and took his hand. Her fingers slipped between his, the calluses on their fingers and palms rubbing against one another, and suddenly all the worries of the past few moments drained like sand through the eye of an hourglass. It felt right, like a fire in the chill of the desert night, warming her soul. She wondered if he felt the same. She hoped he did.

He led her back the way she'd come, toward South Harbor Road. "It isn't *my* plan," he said softly. "Not really."

"Just tell me about it."

He bowed his head in exaggerated fashion. "Of course, my lady. But first, I have a question. Your mother's book had that poem. You said you might find more if only you could make your way into the Maidens. Have you?"

She had, within that very same book, but her old urges to protect Emre were so ingrained she had already begun forming a denial. She had to accept the fact that he was in the Host. *He's chosen his path,* she reminded herself. "I have," she finally told him.

He glanced back they way they'd come. "Well, I've convinced them to help you."

"Macide? What do you mean?"

"There's something big coming. The poems might help you to kill one of them, but you'd have to reach him first, right? And you'd want a way to do it without everyone knowing. Well, soon there will be so much chaos in the House of Kings you may just have such an opening, as you did with Külaşan. But there's a lot to do before that. A seed must be planted, and trust gained."

"What are you talking about?"

He squeezed her hand. "All in good time. I'm to deliver a message to the Maidens. I will tell them that there will soon be an attack against the city's aqueduct. The Host have targeted it, I will say, because of the drought. The reservoir is lower than it's been in living memory, and if the Host can destroy it, it will put incredible pressure on the city's water supply."

"But the attack is a feint."

"No, it will be real. We need to make the Kings stretch their resources, which is why the aqueduct is the perfect choice."

"You think they'll put themselves at risk for it?"

"They will if they're wise. And I'll guide them in the logic if they don't see it. Without the aqueduct, the reservoir's reserves will continue to drop over the winter, and when that happens, who do you think the Kings will favor with what remains? They'll ration it, but give the lion's share to themselves and those on Goldenhill. The rest of the city will whither like grapes on an untended vine, and if that happens, the ranks of the Host will swell, which is the last thing they need."

She couldn't deny it. The Kings would likely react just as he described. "You said *suspect* an attack. What's the real target?"

"I wasn't told."

She stared at him, waiting for him to say more. "Gods, you're a terrible liar. You want my help? Tell me the real target."

"Do you think for a moment they'd tell me when *I'm* the one about to speak to the Maidens about the aqueduct?"

"Wait, you mean to deliver the message *in person?*"

He nodded, grinning as if it had been obvious all along.

"Absolutely not!" Çeda said flatly. "I'm not letting you anywhere *near* the House of Kings."

"You have to, Çeda. It must come from me. A written message would never work, and you couldn't tell a story like this yourself without suspicion falling on you. There are too many details that come from deep within the Host."

"And why by Nalamae's sweet tears do you think they'd believe *you?*"

"I've lived in the west end my entire life. If the aqueduct attack succeeds, hundreds, thousands may die. I'll tell them I've had a change of heart, that I'm willing to do what I must to protect those I love."

Dear gods. *Thousands may die.* The words lay between them like an open grave. It was what she hated most about the Host, and Emre knew it, and yet he held her hand as if he hadn't just admitted that what Macide was planning would kill people they knew. She pulled her hand from his, silent now as they continued to walk.

"I know what you're thinking, Çeda, but it's going to happen."

"It doesn't have to."

"Macide's mind is set, as is his father's."

My uncle, Çeda thought. *My grandfather.* "Innocents will die."

"Don't you see? That's why I thought of you. If we can work together, the Kings' reign will end that much sooner."

"They'll kill you, Emre, but only after the Confessor King has taken his tithe."

Emre shrugged. "They'd be foolish to do so. I'll be too valuable to them."

"As what?"

The noise level rose as they reached the Wheel and began moving along with the evening traffic. The clatter of wheels, the rolling murmur of conversation, the water splash of children playing in the pool at the Wheel's center.

"Please don't tell me you're as beetle-brained as all that," Emre said. "I'll make them believe that I'll be their agent in the Al'afwa Khadar. I'll tell them about the attack, how they're willing to sacrifice so many and how I can't allow it to happen, that my friends will die, my family, that they're taking things too far."

Çeda's stomach had turned sour. It felt like he'd taken her thoughts and made them his own, but was using them now as a tool, as a way to manipulate her. "Just like that? You think they'll simply accept what you say and welcome you with open arms?"

"Of course not. I'm going to give them clues that they can verify. I'll tell them to search in Ishmantep for signs of Hamzakiir. And when they go—"

"*If* they go . . ."

"*When* they go, they'll see that I was telling the truth. It's all been worked out, Çeda."

"Where along the aqueducts, then? They're twenty leagues long."

"I don't think Macide has decided yet, but they're hoping to make the Kings commit as many resources as possible there, which will only help if we're able to isolate one of the Kings on the night of the attack. The only question is, which one?"

"Let me think on that awhile, Emre. I haven't fully decrypted the poems."

Emre shrugged. "Fair enough. We'll have time in the days ahead to talk further. And when we return from Ishmantep—"

"They'll never allow you aboard their ships."

"In truth I think they'll insist. I'll tell them that I don't know exactly where in Ishmantep Hamzakiir is hidden, but if I go, I'll be able to find it. We can make plans on the way, and when we return, I'll feed that information to Hamid."

Hamid, whom Emre looked up to now. "He used to be so shy."

"You don't know the half of it. He acts as if he's Macide's chosen."

"Isn't he?"

Emre shrugged. "I suppose he is. Hamid the Cruel, they've started calling him."

"Strange where we've come, isn't it? Tariq, too."

Emre laughed ruefully. "A bunch of gutter wrens preparing to run this city."

She nearly told him then, that she and Macide were related, that Ishaq was her grandfather, but she didn't know how to say it. For so long she'd considered Emre the only family she had. And now there was a whole new world of people she'd promised herself to learn more about. She felt connected to the Al'afwa Khadar in ways she'd never expected. She felt *responsible* for their cruelty even as she strived to accomplish the same goals.

"We might have been gutter wrens once, Emre, but not any longer."

Emre laughed more loudly, drawing the attention of two women balancing massive bales of cotton on their heads. "What are we, if not hopeless little wrens?"

"It sounds foolish when I say it aloud, but there are days when I feel like Sharakhai is alive. I feel like we've been chosen to protect it. To liberate it."

Emre's eyebrows rose so high he looked like one of the drunks leering along the river on Beht Revahl. "Well, if that's so, then it follows that you've come to see those I work with as necessary."

Çeda bit her tongue. The last thing she needed was an argument over the virtues of the Moonless Host, in public no less. "What else, Emre?"

"That's as far as your role goes. I'll do the rest."

The tightness inside her was so strong she could stand it no longer. She grabbed his wrist, and spun him around to face her, heedless of the crowd steering wide to get past them. "You don't know them like I do," she rasped. "I'm telling you, they will find you out."

He shrugged, a fateful expression on his face. "Then they do. It's worth the risk. And if you refuse to help me, then I'll be forced to go alone. It'll be harder, though. I'm not sure they'll believe me. Wouldn't you rather be there to explain to them, to *make* them believe?"

"You can't do this to me!"

All the humor drained from Emre's face, and he lowered his voice. "We are at *war*, Çeda. When are you going to accept that? You can't protect everyone. All you can do is to pitch yourself into the battle and save as many as you can once it's done."

"How very pat, Emre. Did Hamid tell you that?"

"No, that's all mine. And I rather like it."

"*Don't* do this." Her stomach turned, hoping Emre would agree, but he merely stared, cocksure, eyes half-lidded like Hamid, and she knew she wasn't going to change his mind. "Bakhi damn you, Emre Aykan'ava."

And then, before she knew it, he had swept in. It was so sudden she heard herself gasp. But then his warm lips were on hers. She wanted to kiss him back. She'd dreamt of this very thing in her room in the barracks. But this was wrong. She pushed him away. "Not like this, Emre."

"Like what?"

"Like it's the last thing we'll ever do."

The Emre of old might have shown his hurt. This Emre merely shrugged, an unreadable expression passing quickly over his face, before taking her hand once more. As they headed east toward the House of Maidens and its towering gates, Emre said, "Bakhi may damn me, Çedamihn Ahyanesh'ala, but if he does, at least I can ask him why he's been so cruel."

The whole incident, and his ability to move on from it so quickly, left her feeling cold, but what was there to do about it? *She* had denied *him*. "Tell me why they chose Ishmantep," she said, not wishing to linger on Bakhi. "It's two weeks by sail."

"It's as good a place as any. Better, really, as far as that goes. It's far from the gaze of Tauriyat."

As they took a slight curve in the Spear, a massive cart trundled past, its bed overflowing with wooden crates and bolts of leather. The city lay cloaked in the shadows of dusk, but high above the sun still shone on Tauriyat, lighting the upper palaces in a light so golden even Çeda had to wonder if the gods truly *did* watch over them.

"What are we doing?" Çeda asked.

"Stepping into the maw of a demon." He stared up at Eventide, the highest of the palaces, with a strange sort of hunger. "Just look at them, perched on their hill. It will be a wonder when they fall."

"There's much to do before that happens, Emre."

"So there is," Emre said. "Now, here's what we'll say . . ."

Chapter 40

As Çeda reached the gates of Tauriyat, worry ate at her. It turned in her gut like a snake as she raised a hand to the Maidens atop the wall. She'd convinced Emre to let her speak to Sümeya first. He would return in the morning, and by then she'd have arranged a meeting with the First Warden to discuss his news. A difficult thing in and of itself, made all the more difficult because of what she'd done to Yndris. Çeda had left her in the streets of Roseridge, beaten bloody, unconscious. She thought she would know how to explain it when the time came, but none of the stories she'd come up with sounded the least bit convincing.

She might tell the truth: that her hatred of Yndris's actions had boiled up inside her and she hadn't been able to contain it. She would be whipped for it. She might lose a finger from her off-hand to let the lesson sink in. But she would likely remain a Maiden. Wasn't that the most important thing?

But then Mesut's words came back to her: After his demonstration in the barracks courtyard, he'd implied she would be put to death if she couldn't learn to control the asirim. If she admitted to giving herself over to anger, how long would it be before Mesut pieced together the truth? It made her wonder, not for the first time, at how difficult everything had been since entering the House of Kings. She knew who her family was now. Could she not do more outside the city? Could she not search for Nalamae and plead for her help?

A coward's thoughts, Çeda mused, *the fears of a woman unwilling to die for her cause.*

As the gate creaked open, Çeda marched inside and was met immediately by Kameyl, who wore her Maiden's dress but no turban, no veil. "Why are you late?" Kameyl asked. Her face was tight, serious.

"I lost track of the day," Çeda said, trying to keep her story as simple as possible. "It won't happen again."

She looked Çeda up and down. Çeda thought she was going to press, but instead she shot a look back toward the infirmary. "Yndris was attacked today."

For a moment Çeda was speechless. They knew about Yndris, but if that was so, how was it they didn't know about Çeda's role in it? "Is she dead?"

"No," Kameyl snapped, "but she was beaten badly."

"Is she *awake?*"

"She woke a short while ago." Kameyl stared more deeply into her eyes. "Do you know something?"

"Gods, no!" The lie tasted bitter on her tongue, but by some strange miracle Kameyl didn't seem angry with Çeda, which meant they hadn't yet discovered the truth. "What happened?"

"Come," Kameyl said. "Sümeya is with her now."

They went to the infirmary, Çeda's home for her first several weeks in the House of Maidens. It was strange to see it again from a wholly different vantage: as a Maiden. Even stranger to walk toward Yndris, who lay in a bed with Melis, Sümeya, and Zaïde standing over her. Yndris was awake and speaking to Sümeya, who had an expression of deep anger.

"Our lost little wren has flown home," Kameyl said as she stepped to the foot of Yndris's bed.

Çeda crossed her arms to hide the wounds on her knuckles—wounds received while punching Yndris's face over and over—and stood by Kameyl's side. She looked down upon Yndris, guilt roiling inside her. Bruises marked her lips and nose and cheeks. Small cuts were mingled within them like daubs of paint from a particularly cruel artist. Çeda nearly confessed. The words were on the tip of her tongue, ready to spill from her mouth like bitter wine, but it was Sümeya who spoke first. "Yndris was attacked in the western quarter today. Did you go there?"

Çeda nodded. There was no sense denying it. They all knew she'd been raised there, and enough might have noticed her presence that they could trace her to the spice market and the bazaar if they wished to.

"Did you hear news of an attack on a Maiden?" Sümeya asked, waving to Yndris.

And it struck Çeda then how altogether emotionless Yndris was. Çeda had been so wrapped up in her own thoughts she hadn't noticed, but Yndris wasn't staring at Çeda with enmity or hate, but rather with curiosity, as if she too wished to know the answer to Sümeya's question.

Çeda shook her head. "I heard nothing of an attack."

Sümeya held her gaze, then looked down upon Yndris. "Surely it was the Moonless Host, or an opportunist with a grudge against the House of Kings, though how they might have identified her, we're not sure."

"We should beware . . ." This had come from Yndris herself. Her words were horribly slurred. It pained her merely to speak, and little wonder with the surfeit of wounds marking her face like mountains on a map. "We should beware," she began again, slower this time, "allowing Maidens out alone."

"That's nothing for you to worry about," Sümeya said. "Rest and take to Zaïde's ministrations. Listen to her, for I fear you'll try to be up and about too soon, as you always do. Don't this time. We'll have need of you in the weeks ahead."

Yndris nodded, a small frown on her face as though she were disappointed in not being allowed to return to the barracks that night.

Goezhen's sweet kiss, *why*. Why would Yndris hide what had happened? "Do you remember nothing?" Çeda asked her.

Yndris gave a small shrug. "Little enough. I remember . . ." She swallowed several times. "I remember going to the bazaar. And when I arrived I thought of Hasenn talking about a small tea house near there, Alam's Glade. I was headed there when someone struck me from behind."

Well, at least Çeda knew she was hiding some portion of her story. She'd been heading for a tea house like Çeda was a highbrow Mirean whore. She had been following Çeda and, for whatever reason, wasn't willing to admit it.

"You heard nothing?" Çeda pressed. "No clues about who might have attacked you?"

Yndris swallowed several times, wincing as she did so. "I remember being struck. The sound of it was like the sundering of the desert. The next thing I knew, a pair of Silver Spears were standing over me. A cart arrived and delivered me back to the House of Maidens."

That look on her face. So innocent. So utterly fake. Could no one else see it? Of course they couldn't. Neither Çeda nor Yndris were giving them the true story, so why would they think anything was amiss? "As you say, we'll have to take care from now on."

"We will," Yndris agreed, revealing a momentary glimmer of hatred, emotion masked a moment later by pain.

"Come," Zaïde said, making shooing motions with her hands. "Leave her in peace."

They turned to find the doors being opened by two manservants and King Yusam sweeping into the room in a brilliant khalat of vermillion and gold, and a matching turban bejeweled with a massive white diamond. He eyed Zaïde and the approaching Maidens, coming to a stop so that *they* could approach *him*.

As one, the Maidens came to a stop two paces before him. Zaïde joined them and together they bowed their heads. "My Lord King," Zaïde said, "what brings you to the Maiden's infirmary?"

Yusam sent a nonplussed glance toward Yndris. He took in each of the five women standing before him with a look that bordered on curiosity, though Çeda had the impression he was trying to hide it. "I've come to speak to my hand of Maidens. There is work for us to do in Ishmantep."

"Very good, my Lord King," Sümeya said. "What is it you wish us to do?"

Çeda's heart was already racing. She knew Yusam could see much. She'd seen it with her own eyes. So the mere fact that he knew something was happening in Ishmantep was no real surprise. What worried her was that he might have looked into his mere and seen *Emre*. She worried he'd bid them to take him, and if that happened, she knew there'd be no chance of saving him. *Nalamae's sweet tears, Emre, I wish you'd never said anything to Macide.*

"We'll speak in a moment," Yusam replied. "Await me in my carriage outside. We'll retire to my palace." His green eyes glanced meaningfully at Yndris. "For now, I would speak with our wounded dove."

"As you wish," Sümeya replied.

They all made to leave, but as Çeda walked past, Yusam held his hand out to her. The rest continued as Çeda stopped and held her hand out for Yusam to take. Zaïde paused in the doorway until the King's servants closed the twin doors, bowing their way out and sweeping Zaïde away with them.

Yusam held Çeda's hand in a dancer's grip. Then he turned her hand this way then that, a jeweler inspecting a stone. "You play rough." He held out his other hand, and she was forced to give him that one as well. He inspected the cuts along her knuckles the same way he had her other hand. "And so fresh!"

"Only a bit of sparring, my Lord King. With a dirt dog today, near the pits."

"Maidens do not spar with Bakhi's chosen, Çedamihn."

He said it not as an admonition, but as if he knew very well that she had not, in fact, *sparred* with anyone.

"Old habits die hard," she replied.

"That may be true"—he released her hands—"but there comes a time to turn the page, and how can we do that if we keep rereading the last, hmm?"

"Lose sight of the past, my Lord King, and we lose our direction completely."

A smile broke over Yusam's fine features. "As you say, young Maiden. Now leave us."

And Çeda did, but not before seeing the look of naked loathing on Yndris's face. As Çeda strode from the room, she wondered if she hadn't made a terrible mistake by not killing Yndris there in the streets of Sharakhai.

The following morning, Çeda sat on a stone bench in the largest building in the House of Maidens. It housed most of the Maidens' training rooms, where they learned the finer details of sword and spear and open-hand combat, but was also where Sümeya, as First Warden, kept her offices. Çeda sat in a hallway outside her door, wishing she could hear the conversation within, but since the moment Emre had stepped inside, she could hear little but the calls of the women as they fought one another in a nearby room. Had she taken an adichara petal she might have been able to hear Sümeya's and Emre's conversation, but she'd decided against it. The chances of Sümeya's noticing the effects were simply too great.

So she was forced to sit and fret, wondering what Sümeya was asking Emre, how he in turn would reply. Strangely, what she'd perceived last night as a clear disaster—King Yusam pointing them to the very place Emre wished them to go—was now a potential boon. If *Yusam* thought there were things to find in Ishmantep, why then wouldn't Sümeya believe Emre's story?

A chill went down her spine as Sümeya raised her voice. Emre was trying to paint himself as a sympathizer of the Kings, a potential agent for them in the Moonless Host. There were stories all over Sharakhai of traitors in the ranks of the Moonless Host, but Çeda wondered how many had come willingly and how many had been found out by Zeheb, the King of Whispers, and forced to give up their secrets, or work for the Kings under threat of violence to their family. She had to admit, though, that Emre could spin a good tale. She could only pray that things went well with Sümeya.

King Yusam was another matter entirely. Her strange mission out to the ship, the chase at the collegia, the battle in the forum . . . Like a man feeling his way in the dark, he was weaving his way toward a sound. That sound was something neither she nor Macide nor even Hamzakiir could easily shake. Where was his mere leading him? Macide's plot? Çeda's betrayal? Something else entirely? She didn't know, but what she wouldn't give to kneel by his mere and peer into its depths.

She stewed for an hour more before the door opened at last. Emre stepped into the hall, followed by Sümeya. She pointed to the bench where Çeda was sitting, and barked, "Sit there," and motioned for Çeda to follow her. Çeda got up, noting the very serious look on Emre's face. When Sümeya's back was turned to him, however, Emre winked at her. She'd taken the bait, then. Or was inclined to. Now it was up to Çeda.

Çeda soon found herself alone with Sümeya inside a large room with a desk at its center and a map of the Shangazi hanging on the wall to her right. She'd seen smaller maps of the desert before, but it was interesting to see it writ large like this, with all the caravanserais marked along the great trail that ran north to south, along the eastern passes and the northwestern valley that led to the Territories of Kundhun.

Sümeya moved around to the far side of the desk. She noted Çeda's interest in the map, but made no mention of it. "Sit."

Çeda did, taking one of the two padded chairs. Sümeya remained standing. "Trouble follows you, little wren."

"I'm not a wren."

Sümeya sniffed. "You're in the Maidens for less than six months and you lay an intricate plot at our feet."

"Would you rather I hadn't?"

"You must admit it's a strange bit of luck."

"As was the gods saving Sharakhai on the night of Beht Ihman."

"Don't blaspheme."

Çeda couldn't lie down for her—do that, and Sümeya would know. "I only meant that fortune shone down that night on the Kings and Sharakhai. And perhaps that's what's happened here."

"Perhaps." She began to pace slowly back and forth. "But before we get to Emre, let's speak of Yndris."

"What of her?"

"Watch that lip of yours." She motioned to Çeda's hands. "You leave here and return with cuts and bruises along your knuckles. I have little doubt that were I to press them against Yndris's face, they'd match like the pieces of a broken urn." Çeda started to speak, but Sümeya spoke over her. "I don't care what happened. Yndris appears willing to let it pass, and so do you. But I tell you this: it ends here. From both of you." Sümeya paused, perhaps waiting for a comment from Çeda, but Çeda could tell it wasn't over. "Zaïde asked us not to take Yndris on our journey to Ishmantep, but I've denied her request. Yndris will come, and each day, the two of you will spar, and then you will tell one another stories."

"Stories?"

"You will come to know your sister Maiden, and she will come to know you. You will *understand* one another if nothing else. And after that, there will be no more conflicts. You may not love her, and the gods know she has little love for you, but you will accept her. Is that understood?"

"Yes, First Warden."

"Dear gods, Maiden, I asked if you *understood*."

"Yes, First Warden!" Çeda repeated, more sharply this time.

"Good. Now"—Sümeya glanced over Çeda's shoulder toward the door—"tell me about Emre. How did he find you?"

"*I* found *him*," she said, as she and Emre had agreed on the way back last night. "He often goes to the spice market to find odd jobs. I didn't think I'd have much chance of finding him, but there he was."

"But not to haul spices."

"No."

"Do you believe him? That he's joined the Moonless Host so that he can report back to us?"

Çeda knew she had to play this part perfectly. "He has never held great love for Macide and his ways, even less so when one of his friends was murdered last week for refusing to let a wounded rebel into his home." It was true. Emre had told her about it. It was the perfect spice for this dish because it could be verified. And she could see how angry Emre was with the killer, but she could also see how loyal he was to Macide. "Truth be told, though, I'm not sure I believe him."

Sümeya paused. "You think he's lying?"

"Not lying, no. I merely think there's another, greater truth behind all of this."

"Which is?"

"That he cares for me. Perhaps too much."

Sümeya stared more deeply into her eyes. "Are you trying to say he loves you?"

It wasn't hard for Çeda to feign discomfort. "Yes."

This was the part of the tale they *hadn't* agreed on. She hadn't even brought it up with him, because she knew he'd be uncomfortable with it, perhaps even wounded, and she couldn't have him trying to talk her out of it. In fact, the less he knew about it, the better. He might have acted carefree yesterday after they'd kissed, but if he were confronted with this by Sümeya, his hurt would show, and that would be enough to convince her of the truth of it.

Sümeya stared into Çeda's eyes, weighing her words. "Yes, I believe he does. Do you love him?"

"Of course I do."

"No," Sümeya replied easily. "Do you *love* him?"

"Yes. Once."

"No longer?"

Çeda shrugged. "We've gone our separate ways. There is no place for love in the service of the Kings."

Surprisingly, Sümeya softened at this. Sümeya, outside of Kameyl the most severe woman Çeda had met in the House of Maidens, looked sad in the way one does when remembering a cherished heart taken too soon. The look was there one moment, gone the next, yet still Sümeya said, "Love can be found in the strangest places, Çedamihn Ahyanesh'ala."

"As you say," Çeda replied, if only to fill the silence and get her to move off the subject.

"Emre tells me that there is a man, a master of one of the Kings' own caravanserais, who has proof the Moonless Host plan to attack the aqueducts."

"That's what he told me."

"And that further details might be found in Ishmantep."

Çeda nodded. "He overheard Macide speaking to another." It was the same story Emre had given her, and no matter how much she'd pressed, that was all he would say.

"It smells strange to me, I'll admit."

"To me as well," Çeda said, staunchly refusing to mention Yusam's directives. That was a thought Sümeya would need to arrive at on her own. "The Host are devious. But we have only to go there to determine if he's right. I only ask that you leave Emre here."

Another agreed-upon piece of their tale, but one Çeda desperately hoped Sümeya would heed. Çeda knew immediately from Sümeya's stern look that she wouldn't.

"We will go. We have no choice in the matter now. But so will your friend."

"We don't need him."

"He's too valuable to leave behind."

She shook her head, picturing Emre strung up like her mother at the gates of Tauriyat.

Sümeya laughed silently. "I thought you would fight me harder, girl."

"Emre is stubborn, and so are you. I know when a battle is lost, First Warden."

And now Sümeya laughed out loud. "*You?* Know when a battle is lost? Sooner will Goezhen find forgiveness from Tulathan."

A knock came at the door, forestalling Çeda's words.

"Come," Sümeya called.

The door opened and Zaïde stepped inside wearing a thawb of pure white. She looked worried. "I need her, now."

Sümeya leaned back in her chair and nodded. "We're done." Çeda had just reached the door when Sümeya added, "And Çeda?" Sümeya's eyes were flint and steel. "If I find that Emre's been lying to us, I'm going to run my blade across his pretty little throat." Without waiting for a response, she took up a quill and began writing. "That will be all."

Chapter 41

"YOU SHOULD HAVE TOLD ME about your plan with Emre," Zaïde said to Çeda as they strode down the hall toward the savaşam.

"There wasn't time."

"There's always time. You're a resourceful girl. I think you could have managed it if you'd a mind to."

"It came up suddenly. An opportunity that couldn't be passed up."

"That's all the more reason to step lightly. You don't dive into a pit of vipers head first." She looked up to the corners of the hallway. "Not *here*."

Zaïde wasn't being unreasonable. What she and Emre were planning was dangerous. But Çeda wasn't going to change her mind, then or now, so there had been no point in bringing it up with Zaïde. "It won't happen again."

Zaïde stopped, pulling Çeda around by the sleeve until they were face to face. The anger in her, along with her wrinkled, tattooed skin, made her look like one of the desert gods come for vengeance. "Don't make promises you don't mean to keep. It makes you look childish and paints me the fool. Do you think me a fool, Çeda?"

"No, Matron."

"And whatever happened with Yndris cannot happen again. If it does, best to kill her and be done with it." She resumed her pace, her fury showing in the very set of her body, the tight swinging of her arms. "What you did attracts *notice*. It's the last thing we need. I've worked too carefully for too many years to see it all unravel because you decided to pull on a loose thread, or worse, tear the weave by poking at it in the dark like an infant."

Zaïde was acting strangely. She was angry, but there was more to it. "Something's happened."

"Yes, something's *happened*. Mesut wishes to speak with you. About what, I cannot say."

Gods, Mesut . . . Çeda felt everything she'd done to get here falling apart. *I would not wish to see you tossed aside like some distasteful cut of meat,* Mesut had told her, *but you will be unless you can master the asirim.*

"You said you had the ear of one of the Kings," Çeda said, her desperation beginning to grow. "Could you not ask for his protection?"

As they came closer to the savaşam, Zaïde composed herself and whispered, "It is not yet time to play that card. Be careful. Watch your tongue. Gather all the manners you can manage and by the gods *use* them." By the time they'd reached the savaşam, Zaïde's look had transformed into one of calm deference. She slid the door wide, stepped inside, and bowed her head low.

Çeda entered, expecting King Mesut to be standing there, but instead she found a tall woman with black hair bound in an intricate golden headdress. The woman stood in the center of the padded mat that dominated the room, her hands held easily behind her back as she took Çeda in. She wore a khalat, though it had been fitted to her feminine frame—a Mirean import, this particular cut of clothes, a recent addition to fashion in the palaces of Sharakhai. Her eyes weighing Çeda coldly, the woman waited for Çeda to bow to her, which Çeda did. After the customary breath of deference, Çeda raised her head, as did Zaïde.

"Çedamihn," Zaïde said, "this is Verdaen, vizira to King Mesut."

"Vizira," Çeda said, tipping her head again, only long enough for it not to be considered rude.

Verdaen chose not to return the pleasantry. Instead, she took in the room as if it were the first time she'd set foot in a savaşam. And perhaps it was. She looked as if she'd lop off her own hand before mastering a dozen swings from the *tahl selheshal*. And she was still wearing her fine sandals on the mat, a grave insult. It grated on Çeda's nerves, but given the woman's station, she wasn't sure whether it had been done with purpose or through simple ignorance.

Finally Verdaen returned her icy gaze to Çeda. "King Mesut would speak with you," she said, as simple as that, and then she was striding toward the still-open doorway.

"Might I ask the reason?" Zaïde's voice betrayed no sense of worry, but the way her eyes flicked to Çeda did.

"You may not."

"We were set to train, and with Çeda leaving on the morrow, I'd hoped to—"

"Are you denying your King his request?"

"Never," Zaïde stated simply. "Only wondering when she will return."

"She returns when she returns." And with that Verdaen swept from the room, expecting Çeda to follow.

Çeda said nothing as she followed the vizira from the building to the grand courtyard of the House of Maidens. There, footmen opened a gilded araba for them. Verdaen sat across from Çeda as the araba pulled away. Melis and Kameyl were just stepping out from the shadowed halls of the infirmary. Kameyl hadn't noticed Çeda, but Melis did. She watched both Çeda and Verdaen with a confused expression. She shrugged her shoulders at Çeda, a silent query, but Çeda could only shrug back.

They rode beyond the inner walls of the House of Maidens and along King's Road. Ahead, the road forked, the left fork leading up to the palaces, the right winding around the southern shoulders of Tauriyat to reach the Royal Harbor. To her surprise, the araba took the right fork.

"The harbor," Çeda said.

"The harbor," Verdaen replied.

For whatever reason, Çeda could feel the asirim beneath the blooming fields. They were restless, though why, and why now, when Çeda had been summoned to attend a King, she didn't know. "Is King Yusam aware that I've been summoned?"

Verdaen pulled her gaze away from the cityscape. "Why would he need to be?"

"I am his Maiden," Çeda said.

"You are new yet to the ways of Tauriyat, so let me speak plainly. Mesut needs no excuse to summon you for any reason unless, perhaps, Yusam had expressly forbidden it." The road curved around a great mound of amber rock, revealing the first of the ship masts and beyond them the towering wall that surrounded King's Harbor. "Has King Yusam forbade King Mesut from summoning you?"

"Forgive me, vizira, it's only that I leave tomorrow to do King Yusam's bidding in Ishmantep. There is much to do before we depart in the morning."

Verdaen gave her a patronizing smile. "I don't expect this should take long."

The harbor opened up before them, the ships of war, great galleys, clippers, and yachts, standing like soldiers at attention beside the piers that raked outward from the curving quay. Above were several palaces, including Eventide, King Kiral's. They looked like a pack of jackals to Çeda, hungry and smiling, lounging on the rocks.

As the araba pulled to a halt at the wide circle, the nearby sandsmen stopped and bowed. At a wave from Verdaen, they returned to their work, and soon the footman had opened the door and Verdaen was leading Çeda down along one of the piers. Çeda thought Mesut was waiting aboard one of the ships, but she kept walking past the gangplanks.

And then Çeda saw him. Out in the harbor, close to the towering doors that led to the desert, a man was moving gracefully through the forms of unarmed combat. Çeda couldn't see his face, but she recognized Mesut's lithe figure. Verdaen waved toward the ladder at their feet that led down to the sand. She wore a smug look that, years ago, Çeda would have wanted to slap from her. Now, though, she cared little for Verdaen. There was something afoot, and she wanted desperately to know what it was before Mesut sprung it on her.

Rather than take the ladder, she somersaulted down from the pier, then strode across the soft, shifting sand. Mesut wore sirwal trousers, but strangely, they were made from simple linen, the sort one might find a boy from the desert wearing. From the waist up he was naked save for his dark purple turban. He was shoeless as well, and was moving with ease and power through one of the oldest combat forms in Sharakhai. Its origins lay not in the tribes of the desert, but in the hills of Mirea, where hidden monasteries housed men and women who dedicated themselves to physical and spiritual oneness. It was an elegant form, and Mesut's mastery over it was complete. As she neared, she marveled at his prowess, at his well-defined form. Sweat, sometimes difficult to come by in the dry desert air, made his bare chest and arms glisten. By all accounts he looked to be Verdaen's age—forty summers, perhaps—but he was in top physical condition. He was like the flower in the bottle from children's tales, caught in time, ever blooming.

On his wrist he wore his golden band with the stone of jet, the same one she'd seen him wear when she was fourteen. Her impression of Mesut had changed much in the years since, but not her impression of that bracelet. It had seemed other-worldly then and it seemed so now.

When she came close enough she stopped and bowed, electing not to say anything that might interrupt him. He continued through the last moves of the form, legs bent and spread, fists held before him, every muscle taut, and then he relaxed and spread his arms wide, tilted his head back, eyes closed, to take in the sun. Then finally he composed himself and turned to Çeda.

"My Lord King," Çeda said.

From a small pile of folded clothes Mesut retrieved a towel. He ran it along his chest, arms, and the back of his neck, while studying Çeda. He looked completely at peace, which made Çeda wonder just what emotions he was feeling behind those placid brown eyes. The question was no longer *if* he knew about what Çeda had done, but *how much*, and what he would now do about it.

"Word has come that you're set to leave the city."

Çeda breathed deeply, calmed herself as she would before a bout in the pits. "I am, my King."

"Something to do with the poor souls taken at the collegia."

"We hope that's true, yes."

Mesut nodded. "Well, Yusam does see far." Finished with the towel, he folded it carefully and placed it back atop his black thawb and white tunic. "I'm glad that we have this chance to speak before you go."

"Is it something to do with the voyage to Ishmantep?"

He waved Çeda to a spot before him, then dropped into a fighting stance. "To a degree, yes, I would say that it does."

Çeda removed her sandals, tossing them near Mesut's carefully laid clothes, then moved to stand before him. They inched toward one another, dropping into a stance that brought Çeda to a place of familiarity, of calm. She felt the nervousness of the ride here melting away as she shifted her feet back and forth, settling herself into her stance, into the proper frame of mind.

Mesut nodded meaningfully toward their hands. "When we last sparred, I made a request. Do you remember?"

And just like that, the worry was back, ten times stronger. "You said to exercise control." This was why Mesut had brought her here. Control. Over the asirim.

"And have you been?"

"I have tried, My King, as well as I've been able."

"Have you truly? Tried, I mean."

"I have."

"Show me, Maiden."

Mesut launched himself forward. Çeda retreated, blocking his opening strikes, sidestepping another and sending two quick punches toward his chest and throat.

As they traded blows, Çeda felt the grand ring of the blooming fields around Sharakhai. Except this time, there was something wrong. A flower missing a petal. A beetle with one lost limb. She tried to understand it, to sense what it might be, but Mesut was pressing his attack with such ferocity she had no time.

"Despite the common assumption," Mesut said as he retreated out of reach, "I cannot hear all the asirim at all times." He reengaged, connecting with her ribs, while Çeda struck a glancing blow with her palm against his head. He spun away from an overextended punch, sent a hard jab into Çeda's side, then slipped out of reach once more. "And though rumor says otherwise, I cannot speak to all of them at once. The heroes of Beht Ihman, just like you and me, are at times difficult to control."

Heroes, Çeda thought. *They were victims, one and all.*

"Any King can call the asirim to heel. As can a properly trained Maiden." Mesut blocked a flurry of blows from Çeda before snatching her wrist like a striking asp. "What is rare, however"—he twisted her arm up and around, slipping beneath it as he went, forcing Çeda to roll with it or dislocate her shoulder—"is for an asir to reach out to a King. To *any* King, myself included. Even more rare to reach out to a Maiden."

At these words, she felt a growing presence, the same she'd felt when she'd beaten Yndris bloody in the streets, the one that had urged her to kill Yndris. It was urging the same now.

Kill him, the King of Smiles, the King of Lies. Kill him!

The anger came on so strong, so quickly, she had little chance of preventing it. She didn't know how to, and by the time the rage was pumping though her veins, she no longer cared to.

She knew Mesut had somehow masked the asir's presence, and perhaps that might have given her a clue to his purpose, but she was too taken by emotion to give it a second thought. She stormed in, sending blow after blow against the King. She blocked his attempts at fending her off, then punched him in the chest, sending him flying. He rolled backward, sand spraying in an arc above him, and reached his feet. "As I suspected," he said, "it would appear your control is not so complete as you claimed."

She could barely hear his words. The rush of blood through her head nearly drowned them out. She could think only of what the Kings had done. To slaughter so many in the desert on the night of Beht Zha'ir, to assign so many others to a fate worse than death. The asirim, the forgotten members of the thirteenth tribe, now scattered like seeds in a ring around the Amber City. For their sake, she pushed beyond her boundaries. In this moment, she wanted nothing more than to twist this King's neck as she had Jalizc's in the palace of Külaşan. She would drink his blood. She would grind his bones.

And then suddenly the presence that had been so overbearing simply vanished. Like waking from the worst of dreams, it was there one moment, gone the next. But the memories remained. It left her breathless, coughing, as something inside her shrank and disappeared.

That was when Mesut snaked in. He slipped an arm around her neck and flipped her over his hip. She struck the sand hard. Part of her—the instincts she'd honed in the pits—told her to fight, but it was a rote response, as distant as the Austral Sea. Whatever Mesut had done had taken all the wind from her sails. She simply lay there as Mesut stared into her eyes.

When he saw she was not fighting, he released his hold on her neck and came to a stand. "Rise."

The presence. The asir. It hadn't wholly vanished, as she'd first thought. It was still there, just . . . muted. Muffled. And now she could tell exactly where it was coming from. She turned to stare at the tall harbor gates—just beyond them, that's where the asir was.

"Yes," Mesut said. "That one has been calling to you for some time."

Çeda ignored him, for she sensed someone else now. Someone standing near the asir, a source of great hatred to the creature who was once a living, breathing woman.

A heavy thud resounded over the entire harbor. A rhythmic clinking followed, and a groan that sounded like the awakening of some hidden desert titan. Çeda turned and saw the leftmost harbor gate swinging inward. It stopped a moment later. All sound in the harbor had ceased. The snapping of pennants on the war galley mainmasts filled the dry desert air.

And then a man strode through the gap in the gates. Even from this distance, she recognized King Cahil's cocksure stride. He was dragging someone behind him. An asir, thin with dark, shriveled skin and lanky hair, which Cahil used to drag her forward. She struggled, but not as much as Çeda might have thought. It reminded Çeda of the night she'd been inducted into the Blade Maidens. An asir had been dragging a woman from Sharakhai toward the adichara trees. Now a King was dragging an asir, but the two events rang in sympathetic tones. As then, Çeda wished desperately she had the power to prevent what was to come, but as was true those many months ago, she was little more than a puppet in a gruesome play.

As Cahil and the asir came closer, old urges whispered in Çeda's ear. *You might fight them. Even if you die, it would be better than allowing this to unfold.* But those were the callow words of youth, the hopes of someone who knew nothing of the way of the world.

Cahil tossed the asir at Mesut's feet, then stared at Çeda with a face no older than her own. The face, but not the eyes. Those were ancient, atavistic. He watched Çeda with a primal hunger, as if he wished he could take her in return for the asir.

"Do you recognize her?" Mesut asked in a conversational tone, waving a hand easily toward the asir, who lay curled in a tight ball before him.

Çeda nodded. "I bonded with her before sailing for the pirate ships."

"Good. When did you first recognize that the anger within her was affecting you?"

Did he know the answer already? Had he been watching her all along?

She doubted it, or he would have done something before now. She painted on a confused expression for the Kings' benefit. "I think she's been doing it since the day we first bonded."

Mesut glanced at Cahil, then crossed his arms over his chest, the golden band and jet stone glinting beneath the sun. "You haven't answered my question. It's most important, Çeda. *When* did you realize?"

It was a test. She saw how eager Cahil was for her answer. That combined with Mesut's patient questioning could mean only one thing: Mesut was offering her an excuse for what she had done to Yndris. "In truth," she said, "I didn't realize it fully until now."

"You're sure?" Mesut asked.

"I've been"—she blinked, stared harder at the asir—"confused since we were first bonded."

"What do you mean *confused*?"

"Random fits of anger." Çeda stared at her knuckles, still bruised from Yndris's punishment. "Times when I've found myself wandering with no idea where I'm going. Other times when spells of sadness overcome me."

Mesut turned to Cahil. "Did I not tell you? The asirim's influence can be difficult to discern, even more difficult to resist."

Cahil took it in with a frown and a stare. He seemed unconvinced, but apparently wasn't ready to outright deny Mesut's conclusion, either.

"It has been a long while since the night of Beht Ihman," Mesut went on, turning his attention back to Çeda. He waved to the asir, whose jaundiced eyes were staring at Mesut's shadow on the ground. "Even the asirim, our holy avengers, can grow weary of their task. It is a heavy burden, and the weakest among them sometimes bend, while others break."

Cahil pulled the asir's head back, baring her neck. And now the asir was staring directly into Çeda's eyes. Gods, the emotion. She displayed none of the hatred Çeda had felt from her so often. Instead her look was one of deep sorrow, a thing that struck like a spear into Çeda's very soul.

Though she knew it might give the wrong impression, she knelt before the asir, giving her what courage she could. *Blood of my blood. This is all my fault. I called to you.*

You could not have denied me if you tried. A milky tear streaked down the asir's blackened skin. *Fear not for me. I go to see my children.*

From his belt, Cahil drew an ornamental knife, a kenshar of unsurpassed beauty. Gleaming steel, ruby pommel, inlaid hilt. He lay it across the asir's throat. The *woman's* throat, Çeda corrected. She was no monster. Or at least, a monster was not *all* she was. Her soul, though chained, still lived. There were still hopes, if not for herself, then at least for those who would survive her, the people of her tribe and their offspring.

"You don't have to do this," Çeda said to neither King in particular.

"Ah, but we do," replied Mesut. "For you see, if we allow her to continue, she *will* take your mind. It's happened before, and may happen again. We cannot allow it."

Çeda's instinct was to look away, but instead she took the asir's hand. *Your name?*

Havva, the asir said, grateful to be asked.

Havva, you are the brand that kindles my hatred.

Keep that. But find love as well, child. Havva's hand tightened on Çeda's. *Use the dying fire of our lives to give birth to a new tribe.*

From the ashes shall we rise, Çeda said.

From the ashes.

In one fluid motion, Cahil stood and drew the gleaming blade across her throat, leaving her to fall against the sand like an oryx slaughtered in sacrifice. Blood the color of Mesut's jet stone poured from the wound. It stained the harbor sand a deep ochre, like the desert caught in the throes of dusk. Despite her wish to show her self-control before the Kings, tears slipped easily along Çeda's cheeks. They fell to the sand to mingle beneath the surface with the blood of one of her tribe. Slowly, the asir's grip lost all tension. Her eyes went soft. Çeda felt her presence fade like the time-washed memory of a loved one.

As Havva's life dimmed and was lost altogether, Çeda forced herself not to stare at Mesut's bracelet. She could feel the unrest there, could feel those other souls screaming from within their prison. *Yerinde grants a golden band with eye of glittering jet. Should King divide from Love's sweet pride, dark souls collect their debt.* This was how Mesut had done what he'd done in Kiral's palace. These were the dark souls, the souls of the dead, trapped within Mesut's golden band. He'd chosen one of them, Havva, and given her new life so that she might be chained to the Kings anew.

Çeda had the sense Mesut could have harvested Havva's soul once more;

she could feel the yearning of the other asirim for him to do so. But he did not, knowing perhaps that Havva's was a will too strong, a soul no longer useful to him. Indeed, she was powerful enough that Çeda suspected she might infect the others trapped within that gem, inspire them to rise against the Kings as she had.

"Stand," Mesut said.

Çeda complied numbly, still staring into Havva's lifeless eyes.

"Look at me."

She turned to stare at Mesut's stony face, tears still streaming down her cheeks. She wiped them away.

"Now listen to me well," Mesut said. "Other asir may try the same, but you cannot allow it. You must exert your power over them, for only in this will our most treasured remain steadfast in their duty to protect us. Do you understand?"

Çeda nodded. *Keep your gaze level. Do not stare at his wrist, not even once.*

"Good. Understand that if this happens again, *your* blood will mingle with that of the unfortunate soul you've shown your weakness to."

With one last glance at the dead body, Mesut picked up his clothes and walked away, leaving her before Cahil. The Confessor King strode up to her and his hand shot out, taking her by the throat, his grip so tight she couldn't breathe.

She did nothing to prevent it.

Cahil stared into her eyes. Such a beautiful face, she reflected. Such haunting eyes. *Did you torture my mother? Did you carve the symbols into her skin with that very knife?*

The blade, still dark with blood, he raked roughly across the front of her dress—once, twice, a third time, the last nicking her neck. Blood welled from the wound, trickled down her neck to the ridge above her collarbone. Cahil thrust the knifepoint toward the body of the asir behind him. "Mesut would have me believe that creature urged you to attack my daughter. Yusam would have me come to him with any grievance over the Maidens he's chosen as his own. But know this, Çedamihn Ahyanesh'ala, if you ever take your hand to my daughter again, none of that will save you. I'll take you to the brightness atop my palace and see that you know the meaning of agony before I toss your body to the killing fields."

He shoved her away so hard she tripped and fell, then he walked away, not in Mesut's wake, but toward the towering harbor gates. Soon he had stepped back through the gap, into the desert, and Çeda was left alone with the body of the asir. The clanking of the gate's inner mechanisms resumed, and a moment later it boomed shut.

Creature, he'd said of the asir, not hero, as the other Kings were careful to say. A subtle betrayal of the truth. No surprise from the King who took so much pleasure from others' pain. *One day*, Çeda said to the great harbor doors, *all that you've sown will return, hungry to even the scales.*

She turned to face the dock. Mesut was climbing the ladder up to the pier. Verdaen was standing on the quay, waiting for him. The two of them spoke for only a short while, and then they climbed into the araba, which took them back toward the palaces.

Tomorrow, Çeda was bound for Ishmantep. She would go, she decided. With her sister Maidens she would go and see what she could find in the caravanserai. She would speak further with Emre.

Which one? Emre had asked her, meaning which of the Kings would she choose to kill. Her life was a shambles, stones sliding down a hill; the gods only knew where they would end up when the dust had finally settled. She knew one thing, though. She would take that band from the Jackal King. And then she would see what debt those souls might come to collect.

As the sounds of the harbor resumed—men working, the rattle of wagons—Çeda went to the asir. *She will have a proper burial, by the gods.* Cradling the too-light body in her arms, Çeda bore her toward the docks. *That much she will have.*

Chapter 42

DAVUD STOOD AT THE STERN OF THE *BURNING SAND*, the ketch he and Anila had been sailing since leaving Ishmantep. The dunes were alive with the wind as they headed westward. From the skin strapped across one shoulder, Davud dribbled a bit of the day's ration of water onto the turban he wore, then more along the back of his neck. He glanced up, giving the sun a baleful stare, a thing he'd been doing so often the ship's crew had taken to calling him Kingfisher, for the way the birds would crane their necks to down the fish they'd caught.

The ship's name was particularly apt. They'd been sailing for nearly two weeks now, though not along a straight path as near as he could judge. They were nearing winter, but the days were some of the hottest he could remember. It grew so hot that the men of the Al'afwa Khadar, who'd been ordered to keep both Davud and Anila locked in their cabin, hadn't had the heart to keep them in a space that might roast them like a brace of desert hare.

A laugh came from the fore of the ship. Anila stood there talking with Tayyar, the red-haired brute who'd punched Davud in the stomach, the one who'd threatened to cut off a finger if he asked to escape the furnace-like heat of the ship's belly again, the one who'd scoffed at Anila's demands for some propriety. "You'll eat like we do in the desert, sleep like we do in the desert, and damned if you won't shit like we do in the desert."

Anila had been overtaken by emotion the first few days out from Ishmantep, crying constantly. She'd pressed Davud again and again over what had happened between him and Hamzakiir, and when he hadn't answered, she'd tried to bully him. "How *dare* you barter for my life like I'm a prized akhala. You probably think you own me now! Do you, Davud? Do you think you own me?"

"Of course not."

"Well you don't," she'd said, as if he hadn't spoken at all. "Now tell me your part of the bargain. What could you possibly have that Hamzakiir would find so valuable?"

He hadn't told her, and he never would. He was too ashamed of it. She'd tried to browbeat him, telling him she'd have his father hauled before the Silver Spears the moment they returned. She'd even tried to beg. But what could he do but answer her requests with steadfast silence?

On the morning of the third day, things changed. After heading up to deck to eat their breakfast of olives and bread and limes, Anila had taken to occupying those parts of the ship where Davud was not. If he went astern, she would walk aft. If he came down to the heat of their cabin, she would head up to deck. And she began talking more to the crew, mostly the men, but the women as well. Small things at first, asking how the ship was run. Asking how she might help. And she did, working to hoist the sails and lower them at the end of the day. Helping to prepare food, handing it out when it was ready, and cleaning up when they were done.

Most of the crew ignored her. Some would send sidelong glances her way with clear, if brief, mistrust. But Tayyar had taken a shining to her. They began to sit by one another while eating. The captain of the crew, a woman named Rasime, the very same captain who'd commanded the ship that had borne the imprisoned collegia graduates to the caravanserai, would frown from time to time, but beyond that no one seemed to care. Davud had the impression they found it amusing: a desert wolf romancing a groomed lynx from the palaces of Sharakhai.

One evening at dusk, the crew built a fire among a host of dark standing stones. There they sat and passed around araq and sang songs to the deepening veil of stars. It was a holy day for the crew, a day their tribe celebrated, they said. They hadn't mentioned the *name* of their tribe, but the holy day itself was a clue. Davud was almost certain they hailed from Tribe Salmük, the Black Veils. Of all the twelve tribes only they had a holiday of significance on this particular day, a day celebrating the end of a three-year drought that had nearly destroyed their tribe. Adding to the evidence of their origin, their songs hailed from the eastern edges of the Shangazi, the center of which, due east of Sharakhai, was traditional Salmük territory.

"Ho, Kingfisher!" Tayyar called to Davud as he entered the circle. "Come have a drink!"

Davud tried to ignore the invitation, but it became all the more difficult with Anila laughing while leaning into the big dolt as though she thought him a sweetheart. Davud accepted the small cup and tried to drink more than he should have. He ended up coughing from the burn of it, which brought on peals of laughter, the loudest of which came from none other than Anila.

His face reddened as Tayyar said, "Minnows beware the snap of the fisher king!" But it was infinitely worse when Anila slapped Tayyar's knee and told him to stop, the way an older sister might do to protect her bothersome little brother.

"Might we speak?" Davud asked her when they were done eating. This was going completely and perfectly wrong. It couldn't go on, not if he wished to see her safely returned to Sharakhai, and that was exactly what he'd promised to do. But he worried now that she was turning her back on her city, being drawn into this life after the harrowing experience at the caravanserai. He needed to make her see that what she was doing was dangerous.

In answer, Anila stared dispassionately as Tayyar swung one meaty arm around her shoulders and the two of them leaned back against the smooth stone behind them. "What about?"

Davud didn't know what to say to that. How could she treat him like this? How could she favor *Tayyar* over him? As she held out her cup, and Tayyar poured more araq, Davud merely bowed his head and left the circle. "It's nothing."

He heard her whispering as he headed into the darkness, and when he'd been swallowed by the night, they laughed like two drunkards along the Haddah on Beht Revahl. His face burning like a brand, Davud returned to his small forward cabin in the ship, a place Anila rarely spent any time in now. After striking a lantern, he pulled out the book Hamzakiir had given him and opened it to the first page. He no longer needed to reference the first several symbols, but he did anyway. It helped not only to cement them, but to expand on their meaning.

He used the short knife to cut into his palm, then dipped his finger into the welling blood and read Hamzakiir's words. *To enact the spell, the first and most important for all magi, you need but summon those memories that bring you meaning. It brings you nearer to your core, the center of your soul, and for this spell of sounding, that is sufficient.*

With the blood he drew the sigil around the wound. It was meant to bring the mage in touch with their own blood, and so, their body, their soul. It was an anchor, Hamzakiir had said, a bridge to the first gods. It was the simplest of the sigils by far, a mother symbol, so to speak, one that needed very little concentration on the part of the mage. It was the only one Davud had been able to master. The rest had proven too difficult. He knew he had to visualize the sigils, but he wasn't sure how. Everything he tried produced no feeling whatsoever. Which was perhaps why Hamzakiir had felt secure in sending Davud off with such a book. Giving him the sigil to light a blaze would have been unwise had he any inkling that Davud might actually master them on the journey back to Sharakhai.

Davud used a bit of water to wash the blood away, then tried the one for warmth again. The instructions told him to summon thoughts of burning and binding. Burning was simple enough. He'd burned his fingers on enough candles to summon any number of memories. Binding, however, was another matter entirely. It was a common thread through many of the spells: the marrying of a concept to a memory. Binding. Also turning. Rebuffing. Subsuming. Hamzakiir had explained each along with the sigils. A student who'd been properly introduced to the red ways might understand, but Davud did not.

His head was starting to pound with a terrible headache when he heard someone gain the deck of the ship. He placed the book beneath his pillow as footsteps came down the hatch stairs. He was just washing away the blood when the cabin door flew open.

Anila rushed in, heading for her bed, but stopped as she saw Davud trying to hide his right hand beneath his rough woolen blanket. "You don't have to, Davud. I don't give a copper khet anymore." From the drawer beneath her bunk she grabbed a small leather bag—the type a collegia student would use to keep small mementos before graduation—then slammed the drawer shut and headed for the door as quickly as she'd come.

Davud sat up, heedless of the red still on his palm. "Anila, please, wait."

She stopped in the doorway, her half-hidden expression making it clear just how little patience she had for him.

"I'm doing what I can. I'll get us home as soon as possible and then we'll see about sending help for the rest."

The expression of sufferance on Anila's face faded, leaving only the rage. "You know Rasime won't bring us home until it's too late."

"Perhaps not. But they'll find out who did it. The Kings will make them pay."

"They know very well who did it. Hamzakiir himself seems happy to flaunt it beneath the noses of the Kings every chance he gets."

Suddenly all the looks from the crew, the laughs, the titters from Anila herself, all bubbled up inside him. "Well, why don't you bed the rest of the crew? Maybe that will get us home even faster."

"Do you know why I'm with him, Davud?"

"I'm sure I couldn't say."

"Because when I am, I can forget about those screams for a while. Can *you* help me forget them? No, because you left them all there to rot. You're the reason I have those nightmares."

Davud's cheeks flushed like a summer rose. "I . . ."

"Or perhaps there's some spell you might cast." Before Davud knew what she was doing she'd shot her hand beneath his pillow and grabbed the book. She threw it onto his lap. "Perhaps something from this little book from your new master."

Davud stared at it, held it tight though it sickened him. How long had she known? Probably since the beginning. She'd probably saved the knowledge for the moment she felt it would do the most damage, a skill at which she was particularly gifted.

"Nothing to say now?" Anila asked.

Davud could only stare. What was there to say?

"As I thought." And with that she spun and left the cabin, leaving the door open.

Davud got up, closed the door, and returned to his bunk, where he stayed long into the night, wondering when the crew would return. His shame, and Anila's words, haunted him, but instead of retreating from them, he absorbed it. He took it in, for he deserved it.

Pulling his solitude around him like a cloak, he opened Hamzakiir's book, and began reading it again.

Judging from the positions of the stars and the crude sextant he'd fashioned, Davud was sure the caravanserai where they'd been holed up was in Ishmantep. It was confirmed when he heard Captain Rasime, who was handing the wheel over to her second. She'd been pointing ahead off the starboard bow, and Davud distinctly heard the words *the handle of Breyu's sickle*. Rasime had noticed him watching and had immediately stopped.

"And what are *you* looking at?" she'd said, glowering.

"Nothing." Davud had turned and headed for the foredeck, hiding a smile as he went.

Breyu's Sickle was a land formation to the southeast of Sharakhai, and its handle lay along the path that led to Ishmantep. From here it would take only ten or twelve days of sailing to reach Sharakhai, but Rasime had been taking her time so far, sailing across the desert in a zigzag fashion, and he saw no reason the pattern would change. Likely they were biding their time before reaching a certain location on a certain date.

He was proved right on the twenty-fifth day from Ishmantep. They crested a dune and spotted a line of blue water that cut the desert like a knife. The crew raised their hands to the sky and yipped like jackals. One stood on the mainmast yardarm and took off his turban, whipping the cloth over his head in celebration as his long hair flapped behind him. High grasses, bushes, and palm trees edged the oasis. And there were three other ships resting near it: a large schooner and two smaller dhows.

"Who are they?" Davud asked Rasime.

Anila was on deck as well, and closer than Rasime, but Davud had given up on talking to her. These days, his questions to her were answered in one of two ways: monosyllabic grunts or cold stares.

Rasime grinned at Davud, her auburn hair flowing in the wind. "Our brothers and sisters, if you hadn't guessed."

"Why are we meeting them?"

"By the gods, Davud, there's no need to look so *scared*." This had come from Anila.

Rasime gave Anila an uncharitable look, then regarded Davud with a strange mixture of sympathy and something like disgust. She thought Davud should stand up to her. And maybe he should, but he didn't have it in him. He'd gotten Anila into this. She had every right to be angry.

"Our purpose is our own," Rasime said, and then set to ordering the crew to prepare for meeting the other ships.

Davud had some guesses about why they'd gathered here, the most likely being that they were transferring information, and perhaps orders, from Hamzakiir. Another, much more worrying possibility was that they'd come to transfer Davud and Anila to some other ship. Davud didn't know whether he should be nervous about the possibility, but he *did* know that Rasime's crew hadn't treated them unkindly, and he'd much rather they remain where they were.

The *Burning Sand* had soon joined the other three ships, the four of them creating a border of sorts. Between them, a celebration began. A fire was lit. Two small skiffs that had been sent out scouting returned with a bone crusher nearly falling off the back of one skiff's transom. It was quickly butchered and placed on a spit to turn, other cuts of the meat skewered with onions, carrots, and dried prunes. Pots were set to boiling and turnips and rice and onions were thrown in. Dried fruit and pickled vegetables were laid out and flatbread served.

As the sun was setting, the food was ready at last. Rasime called out, an ululation picked up by the other women, who easily outnumbered the men. More and more gathered, perhaps four or five dozen in all. They ate and shared stories. They danced around the fire while a rebab, an oud, a flute, a rattle, and a host of skin drums played lively songs from the desert. Davud had heard many of the songs, but not like this. In Sharakhai, they were often composed, rehearsed affairs. These were more loose in nature, allowing those who joined in some freedom to grant the song their own energy and emotion. Away from the fire, five women danced on their own, shoving away any man who dared come near, laughing each time they did so.

Liquor flowed. Mostly araq, but also rice wine from Mirea, whiskey from somewhere south along the Austral Sea, and a sour eastern wine that Davud had to admit was quite good. Many gathered around a boy who ground dark kahve beans and mace together to make a hot drink that tasted rich and smelled richer. More than the kahve itself, which was wonderful, the boy ground the beans in a rhythmic, almost musical pattern. It was common in the desert tribes to do so. In fact, each tribe had its own unique rhythm, marking it for those who knew how to pick them out. The boy's rhythm was Tribe Kadri's, which didn't necessarily invalidate Davud's theory that Rasime and her crew were from Tribe Salmük. The Moonless Host, after all, counted men and women from all twelve tribes among their soldiers.

Shishas were set upon the sand, and around each, a ring of rich carpets. Many flocked to these, sitting and smoking and telling stories or listening for a time. The smell of the tabbaq was so heady in some places there were those who simply stopped to admire it, allowing the smoke to pass around them. Davud didn't smoke, but he sat by a shisha that gave off a particularly rich smell. Rasime was near him. Thick, gray smoke trailed from her nostrils. She smiled like a great mountain dragon while holding the stained ivory mouthpiece for Davud to take. He was about to decline when she poked him with it. The others lying along the carpets laughed, including Anila and Tayyar. After a moment, Davud laughed as well, and accepted the shisha pipe.

How very strange, Davud thought as he drew a deep breath. He had no doubt everyone here knew who he and Anila were, knew as well the orders surrounding them, but no one acted aggressively toward them. In fact, it was as if they were both *part* of the Al'afwa Khadar. He felt the tingling burn of the smoke as it filled his lungs. He coughed, which prompted more laughs, but then he took a deeper pull and blew it up and into the dusk-filled sky.

"And now you must tell a tale," Rasime said, her eyes full of mischief.

Davud was more than a little tipsy, and wasn't sure he'd heard her right. "Pardon me?"

An old man across from Davud, lying on a carpet in a voluminous khalat, chuckled, his whole body shaking from it. The rest smiled, but Rasime grabbed the back of his head, pulled him in, and gave him a big wet kiss. He felt her tongue slip softly between his lips, tasted her and the smoke of the tabbaq they'd shared. When she drew away, a thing Davud suddenly and strongly regretted, she regarded him anew. "And now it must be a love story," she said, and shoved him away.

He fell backward onto the carpet, his feet kicking up sand as he struggled for purchase. The laughter rolled louder as Davud pulled himself back up, joining in on the laughter himself. "A love story . . ."

Many nods as the shisha was passed round.

"Very well," he said. "A love story it shall be." He waited for a moment, knowing already the story he would tell but pretending to fumble a bit to build the anticipation. "An age ago," he finally began, "there was a man named Bashshar, favored by Tulathan, blessed by Rhia." Immediately, several around the circle, who hadn't been paying much attention, turned and took note. Some whistled, while others slapped their knees in appreciation. Bashshar was a famous figure in the eastern desert, and was credited with many great feats, not the least of which was gathering and leading those who would one day be known as the Salmük tribe. "Bashshar had decided when he became a man, he would travel the desert, circling the Great Mother before returning to his homeland in the east."

Rasime's eyes shone through her drunken haze as she took in Davud anew. Davud felt his heart skip—Rasime was a beautiful woman—but he was deep in the story now, and continued without pause.

"Bashshar first went south, traveling always by moonlight so that the twin goddesses might shine down upon him, and there he found the deepest and bluest lake in Iri's Teeth. He swam to the very bottom, and there found a ruby. It gleamed like a drop of blood drawn from the first gods themselves. He continued west and found in a vale a staff of yew standing from the ground with berries on its head that did not poison, but heal. In the ruins of an ancient temple he found a turning gust of sand that never failed to stop, an efrit that had been left and forgotten since the great exodus. On he went, finding more wondrous treasures, a length of string that could cut wood, a stone that made the earth tremble, a flute that drew any animal he might name to kneel before him. Twelve treasures did he find, until at last he came near his homeland in the east once more."

His gaze roamed the gathering, meeting every eye. They were caught now, entranced. Even Anila. Even Tayyar.

"There," Davud went on, "walking across the desert beneath the glare of the sun—for he no longer had need to hide—he spied a woman in the distance. Her form wavered in the heat, and though he carried the greatest treasures in all the desert, he feared her. When the woman stepped beyond the mirage, however, he saw that she was beautiful, that she had only kindness in her eyes, and his fear vanished, but only for a moment, for in the next, she asked him, 'What have you there?'

"Luckily Bashshar had put away many of the smaller treasures. The staff, however, he had to hand, so he showed it to her and offered her some of its berries. She ate them, and thanked him kindly. 'There is a tribe of my people who might use such berries.' She pointed along the path he'd taken. 'In the black foothills. May we walk a while and bring them some?'

"Bashshar was entranced by this woman. She was tall, with green eyes and a thick plait of honey-blond hair that hung over one shoulder." Davud saw many among the circle nod. They knew who the woman was, for they'd heard the story before, or one like it. "Bashshar said, 'Of course I'll accompany you.' And together they walked, talking of a great many things, chief among them the sights Bashshar had seen on his trek around the desert. When they arrived at the tribe's camp, the woman asked if he might leave the staff with them, only for a short while, and while they held it, would he walk farther, to another tribe that had asked for her help?

"Bashshar again agreed, and they trekked to another tribe hunting in the foothills of the mountains, then another at a salt flat with water as smooth as glass, and more beyond. They made love beneath the stars. They made poems the likes of which have never been heard again. They walked the full length of the desert once more, taking the reverse path, and all the while Bashshar became more and more enchanted with the goddess Nalamae, for he knew by now that it was her. Each time they arrived at a new tribe, he secretly hoped she would ask him to leave one of the grand wonders he'd found with yet another tribe, for he wanted nothing more than to remain with her for as long as she allowed.

"But when at last they'd returned to Bashshar's own tribe, he was left with but one thing, a harp of gold that struck the purest of notes. She bade him take it back to his people. 'There is disquiet in your tribe,' she said, 'and the harp will calm them.' 'But I would stay with you,' Bashshar told her, for he knew she would not accompany him, and that if he left her side, he would never see her again. Nalamae kissed him and looked into his eyes and told him, 'One day we will again stand face to face as we are now. This I promise.'

"And so it was that Bashshar returned to his tribe, heartbroken. It is said he lives in the Kholomundi Mountains still, playing his harp at the break of day and when the sun sets, and if you go there, you can hear it and feel his sorrow."

Rasime looked at him, her face sublime in the firelight, thoughtful. "I asked for a tale of love, of romance."

"It was not, perhaps, a tale of romance, but it *was* a tale of love. When I was first told this story, I wept. For Bashshar, certainly, but more so for Nalamae, for her love of the people of the desert, a love that saw her weaving her thread among them, drawing them closer that they might be one."

Rasime studied his face, perhaps trying to absorb all that he'd said, and then she grabbed a hunk of hair at the back of his head and pulled him in for another kiss, a much longer one this time, more ardent. One that Davud returned. The entire gathering laughed, some whistling. Some time later, another story began, but Davud was so lost in Rasime's kisses he couldn't say when, or what the story was even about. Rasime raked her fingers through his hair, kissed his neck, placed more along his jaw and then licked his ear, her breath came hot and heavy. He was so lost in her he nearly missed Anila standing, taking Tayyar's hand, heading off to one of the skiffs, where Tayyar set sail beneath crescent moons and took her on a romantic cruise through the darkening night.

Bakhi take her. She could lie with Tayyar if she wished.

Davud stood and held his hand out to Rasime. To his surprise, she took it, to more whistles from the circle, interrupting a new story that the fat man in the khalat had just begun. Davud took an unoccupied carpet and led Rasime away, far beyond the borders of the circled ships, and laid it down on the far side of a shallow dune. The two of them lay there, pulling the clothes from one another with increasing speed, pressing more kisses, both wet and warm. Rasime might be the captain of a ship, but she worked harder than any of the crew. Her body showed it. Her arms and legs were well defined, her stomach smooth. Davud had slept with few enough women, but there was something about being here in the desert, away from Sharakhai, away from the ceaseless gaze of the collegia scholars, that freed him.

That and he was good and drunk. A drunk the likes of which he'd never experienced before. He released himself to it, kissing her everywhere, moving slowly from her tight breasts to her stomach to her thighs. Then he moved between them, savoring the sounds of her rapid breaths, giving himself to the pain as she gripped his hair and held him in place while grinding her hips in a rhythm they shared.

Her breath caught once. Twice. Then she cried out into the night, pulling him tighter to her than she had before. They both heard whistles from the other side of the dune, men and women laughing. She and Davud laughed as well.

"A story of love, you said."

She let out a biting laugh. "You call this love?" She rolled him over and sat across his hips, running her now-moist lips along his cock, slicking his skin. "This is nothing like love." She leaned down to kiss him fully, deeply, slipping her hand between her legs to guide him inside her. She rode him like the swell of the sands, slowly at first but building like a storm. And then it was his turn to twist his hips, to grip the edges of the carpet, to cry out, more loudly than he'd meant to.

More laughing came, mostly from the women, and Davud felt his cheeks burn even as he held her hips and pulled her tighter against him. They lay there for a long while, silent, Davud not wanting to ruin this moment.

And soon they'd fallen asleep.

Davud felt a hand clamp over his mouth. He opened his eyes to see a dark form looming over him. He thought it was Tayyar at first, but the silhouette was too slight. He struggled, which only made the one above him clamp his mouth tighter.

"Be quiet, you fool!"

Breath of the desert, it was Anila. He relaxed, and she slowly pulled her hand from his mouth. He could see her finger over her lips, then she motioned him to follow.

Rasime still lay next to him, naked, but she snored softly, and did not move as he lifted her head and pulled his arm free. He stood, trying to pull his clothes on, but promptly fell over. The stars above swam. The horizon kept wanting to tip upward along the edges.

Anila waited, impatience written all over her posture, but when he finally finished dressing, she took his hand and held him close, as if the two of them were lovers walking over the dunes. He tried to pull away, but she wouldn't allow it. "If you want to get away from here alive, Davud, hold me like the moon-eyed calf you are. Pretend I'm Rasime."

He obeyed, if only to give himself time to regain his bearings. The four ships' masts and rigging towered in the night, though their hulls and the celebration that had been held between them were largely hidden. Anila was taking them steadily toward the oasis. He had the impression she wanted to run there, but would not, for anyone might be watching from the darkness of the ships, or perhaps from the bushes along the water's edge. Davud played his part, putting one arm around her shoulder, drawing her tight to him. He even tried to take her hand, to hold it like lovers might while they walked, but Anila slapped his hand away.

A bridge too far, then.

When they reached the edge of the oasis, Anila guided them to the left. They curved around several turns in the small body of water, the ships coming in and out of view as the foliage blocked them. When they passed beyond a clutch of trees, however, all but the tops of the masts were lost from sight entirely.

Immediately, Anila grabbed Davud's hand and sprinted across the sand.

"Where are we going?" he rasped.

She didn't answer, but he soon found out. In a trough of rocky ground, nearly hidden from view, was a skiff, the one she and Tayyar had taken for their midnight sail.

"But where . . ."

His words trailed off, for just then he saw the body lying near the water. Davud walked toward it as Anila headed for the skiff. It was Tayyar, naked, lying on a section of matted grass. The striped blanket beneath him was stained dark, a great, bloody rose blooming around his head. Davud bent closer, sickened but too curious to just leave. Tayyar's skull was a matted mess of blood and hair. Bone stuck out in several places. A stone the size of a melon lay nearby, dark along one side, making it look like a third crescent moon fallen from the sky.

"Hurry, Davud!"

"How many times did you strike him?"

"Enough to make him stop moving. Now help me move this skiff or they're going to do the same to us!"

Davud turned away to find Anila muscling the skiff slowly toward the stony ridge. He ran to the opposite side and helped to push it, and soon they were nearing open sand. Davud studied the darkness, wondering who might be watching, certain someone nearby would sound the alarm, and dozens would wake. And then the chase would be on. They'd be brought back and hung from the yardarms. Or they'd be dragged behind the ships—sand whipped, they called it—until clothes, then skin, then muscle was slowly stripped from their bodies.

Then Davud looked to the wave upon wave of silver sands ahead. "We'll not make it three days," he said, "not without water and food."

"It's a hunting skiff, Davud. It's provisioned with water and hardtack and dried fruit, enough to last weeks if we're careful."

They hopped in and pulled up the sails. Anila sat aft, her hand already on the tiller. Neither of them were good sailors, but a year or so ago they'd been given tutelage on one of the Kings' royal clippers, and they'd both seen the handling of the *Burning Sand* over the past several weeks. They'd do well enough as long as they didn't do anything stupid.

Davud turned suddenly, watching the way behind, seeing the ships dwindle in the distance. And then a knife of fear stabbed through him. "My book!"

"It's in the bag, there." She pointed to a sack lying beneath the thwart he sat on. "I brought it, your kenshar, and your sextant."

A sigh of relief escaped him, which was more than passing strange. A week ago he would have scoffed at blood magi, considered them foul, or at least distasteful, and now he was dependent on their ways, sucking off a red teat. He shook his head from that bitter thought, from the celebration, from Rasime and Tayyar and Hamzakiir, from everything that had happened since the battle in the forum. "Why didn't you *tell* me?"

Anila scoffed. "Because you wouldn't have played your part well enough."

"I might have helped."

"You would have doomed us both." She adjusted course, the hull creaking, the sand shushing beneath the skis. "You are many things, Davud, but you're no actor."

He grew bitter at those words, but didn't have the heart for it. He knew she was right. He might not have played it well enough, and Tayyar might have caught on, and then where would they have been?

The skis and the rudder left a trio of wakes behind them, but there was wind enough that by the time the sun rose, all signs of their passage should be erased. He took a deep breath of the cool night air. It smelled of danger, to be sure, but also of hope. "You did well. Together we should be able to navigate our way to Sharakhai well before our supplies run low."

As the skiff crested a dune and tipped to the other side, Anila spat words in disgust, "We're not going to *Sharakhai*." He was about to ask here where they *were* going, but just then he understood, his horror confirmed a moment later when Anila laughed bitterly. "Oh no, Davud. We're returning to Ishmantep!"

Chapter 43

Thirteen years earlier...

In a rare fit of generosity, Ahya allowed Çeda to guide their skiff over the amber sand. Çeda took the job most seriously, riding the shallow dunes as her mother had taught her, being careful at the crests and troughs especially, trying to catch the stiffer sand in order to keep her speed up while watching for any rocks that might scrape the runners, or worse, run them aground.

In the distance, the only feature to be seen was a crooked tower of stone. After they'd passed it and it had dwindled to a mere finger on the horizon, Çeda asked, "How much longer?"

"How many more times are you going to ask me that?"

"How much?"

"A while yet. We'll get there when we get there, Çeda. Now be quiet a moment. We're going to see a woman who does not often see outsiders. She may refuse to see us. Or she may hide her home from us entirely."

"She's a witch?"

"She isn't a witch. And she won't take kindly to ill-mannered children invading her home." She raised a finger between them. "This is important, now. You will be on your best manners."

"Like with Leorah."

"Different than Leorah. Saliah knows the world as Leorah does not. And she will know your nature at but a word from you."

Çeda stared around the desert, suddenly feeling as though the sand had eyes, but the only thing she spotted was a family of oryx in the distance walking in a line. Shortly after, the skiff's runners scraped over a rough patch of amber stone she hadn't seen. She cringed, adjusting the tiller, while her mother pursed her lips.

"Why did you need Leorah's permission for me to see Saliah?" Çeda quickly asked, hoping to draw her mother's thoughts to safer ground.

After a moment, Ahya replied, "It wasn't *permission* I was seeking. I will do with my child as I will. But she is wise and I sought her counsel, nothing more."

"She frightens me."

Ahya turned. "Leorah? She's no one to be frightened of. Not by you and me, in any case. Her enemies, however, have every right to fear her."

"The man you were speaking to at Demal's crossing. The one with the snake tattoos. Do you love him?"

Ahya blinked. "What?"

"The way you smiled at him. The way you nudged his shoulder with yours. You don't do that with anyone else."

She looked uncomfortable, as though she'd been caught in a trap, but then she shrugged. "Yes, I love him."

"Then why doesn't he come to Sharakhai and live with us?"

At this, Ahya gave a silent laugh, the sort that made it clear she thought this was something Çeda could never understand.

"Or another," Çeda went on. "I want a father."

Ahya's face immediately hardened. "What need have we of men, you and I?"

Çeda shrugged. "*Tariq* has a father."

"Tariq has a *drunkard* for a father. A man who gives his children bloody lips when they talk back. Is that the sort of father you want?"

What could she say? "I only—"

"Stop it, Çeda. Your father will never have you. A thousand times I've told you, and if you ask me a thousand more, the answer will always be the same."

"But why? I want to know him."

"Enough, Çeda. I'll not argue with you again."

"Were you disloyal? Is that why he hates me?"

"Yes," Ahya said simply, her expression dark.

"Well, it isn't fair."

"You're right." Ahya turned her attention to the fore of the ship and the way ahead. "But we do what we must, Çeda."

They sailed in silence for a long while. Ahead, an expanse of flat rock appeared, and on it, a homestead. After anchoring the skiff, Ahya picked up a handful of sand. "As I showed you, now. Pray to Nalamae for good fortune."

Çeda gripped a fistful of sand as well and allowed it to sift down in a stream as she slowly opened her fingers. "Please, Nalamae," she whispered, "shine on us this day, whatever we're doing. I'm sorry I don't know more, but when it comes to secrets, my mother's lips are tighter than a frog's arse."

She'd whispered the words too loudly, she realized. Her mother was smiling but trying to hide it. It was something Tariq had said and she'd laughed at, but now she felt foolish. If Nalamae *had* heard her, she might be smiling too, but just how likely was the goddess to grant favors to a stupid, prattling child?

"Hail!" Ahya called when they neared the mudbrick home. "Saliah Riverborn?"

From the far side of the walled garden came the sound of goat bells clanking. Ahya was headed for the entrance to the garden when they spotted a woman kneeling on the ground behind the dwelling. As they moved toward her, Ahya took Çeda's hand. "Perfect manners now, Çeda."

"Yes, memma."

The woman, Saliah, had her back to them. She was kneeling on stone, but she was just next to a patch of sand. She cupped the sand in both hands and lifted it sharply into the air. The sand sprayed in the air above her. For a moment she looked like a phoenix rising from the ashes. Most of the sand fell, but left behind was a cloud, a glittering remnant that flowed through the air like seeds on the wind. The air was blowing west-east, however, and the glimmer in the air was spreading in all directions. As it fell over Çeda and Ahya,

Çeda felt a prickling over her skin—not the sort one feels when the air was cold, but those kindled when hearing the stories of gods who meddle in the lives of men, dooming them or those they love.

Thrice more did Saliah throw sand into the air. Only when the glimmer had faded did she take up the staff by her side and use it to reach her feet. "Who comes?" she asked as she turned to face them.

"It is Ahyanesh, and my daughter, Çedamihn. I believe Leorah came here and told you our tale."

"She did." Saliah turned her head toward Çeda but did not look her in the eyes. She looked *beyond* Çeda, as if she were blind as the beggars along the Trough praising those who'd tossed a few khet into their brass pot while staring right past them. Saliah stabbed the butt of the staff into the ground halfway between herself and Çeda. "This is she, then?"

"Yes," Ahya said, but with a look like she was confused, unsure of herself. Saliah held out her hand. "Come, child."

Çeda did, and when Saliah leaned the staff against her body and held out her large, callused hands, Çeda placed her own hands in hers. Saliah ran her thumbs over Çeda's palms, touching in turn the creases that marked her like a map. She did this over and over, moving along one crease, then the next, slowing down each time until it felt as though Saliah were robbing her of something she should be perfectly unwilling to give up. The feeling became so acute Çeda snatched her hands back, balling them into fists and holding them beneath her chin lest Saliah try to take them back.

Ahya opened her mouth to speak, perhaps to order Çeda to be still and let Saliah do what must be done, but Saliah talked over her. "Let us speak alone, Ahyanesh."

At this Ahya's face changed. She looked to Çeda as if she feared for her. Why, Çeda had no idea, and she had no chance to ask. Ahya nodded and told Çeda to remain here so that she and Saliah could speak in peace. She vowed to ask her mother about it, but she was glad to be alone for a time. She didn't wish to be near Saliah any longer.

When Ahya and Saliah were lost to the shadows of the mudbrick house, Çeda wandered the rocky landscape. She picked up a handful of rocks and threw them at the occasional yellow lizard that crept from its hole. She didn't go far, however; there was something she wanted a closer look at. When she returned, she squatted down by the sand Saliah had been tossing into the air. After glancing back and finding the doorway empty, she ran her hands through it. It was fine, almost like dust, but it didn't otherwise strike her as anything strange. She lifted some of it and let it fall between her fingers. Then she cupped some between her hands and threw it into the air as Saliah had done. When nothing happened, she threw it higher—too high, for the wind blew it right back in her face. She turned away, feeling like a beetle-brained fool as she blinked the stinging sand from her eyes and spat it from her mouth. When she was finally able to see again, she glanced back, worried her mother had witnessed it, but thankfully the door was still empty. Again and again she tried to summon that same feeling inside her as when Saliah had done it, but for her the sand was merely sand.

"She is *so* a witch," Çeda said under her breath.

"Çeda?"

Her face flushing, Çeda stood and faced her mother, who stepped out from the shadows of Saliah's home. She came to Çeda and took her hands, rubbing them much as Saliah had just done, but with an infinitely more tender touch. "There's something I'm going to ask you to do," she finally said. "It won't be fair, but life isn't fair. None of this is fair."

The hairs along Çeda's arms stood up. "What is it?"

"There is someone who needs our help. Who needs *your* help. Macide came to Sharakhai to tell me of it. I spoke with Leorah on the matter because I would be too blinded, but she agreed with me."

"But why must *I* do it?"

"Because you are unique, Çeda."

"How?"

"That doesn't matter."

"Then who am I to help?"

"A man who has lost his way. A man who stands on the brink of madness."

"What *man*?"

"In many ways, he is the father of our tribe."

"Memma, what *tribe*?" She didn't understand any of this.

"That isn't what matters. We need him, and we cannot allow him to go as others have gone. *This* is what I went to speak to Leorah about. It's what

Saliah and I have been discussing. And they both think you can help. So do I, Çeda. I know this makes little sense, but I must ask you to be brave. Can you do that for me?"

A directionless fear was growing inside Çeda, but she nodded anyway.

"Good," Ahya said.

Çeda wanted her to say that all would be well. But she didn't. She merely stood and led Çeda into the cool interior of Saliah's home, where they ate dense black bread and drank watered wine. For hours they spoke of inconsequential things. Çeda had never felt so awkward. The thought of whatever she would have to do kept gnawing at her. Why wouldn't they speak of it?

They left well before sundown in their skiff, sailing northeast toward Sharakhai. Çeda had tried to remain brave, but that all changed when they neared the Amber City. Ahead, lit by the bright moons above, were dark patches. Trees, Çeda realized. Groves of trees.

Breath of the desert, they weren't going to Sharakhai at all. They were going to the blooming fields.

Chapter 44

ON THE FOREDECK OF THE ROYAL CUTTER *Javelin*, Çeda and Yndris circled one another, shinai at the ready. Kameyl was watching the two of them silently, almost brooding in her intensity. When Çeda blocked a flurry of downward blows from Yndris, who often resorted to pure brawn, Kameyl threw one hand in the air and bellowed, "Enough! You'll be the death of me, the both of you."

She moved to stand before them as the ship crested a shallow dune and rolled down the opposite side. She glared at Yndris. "You might as well pen her a letter as ill-disguised as your swings are. And you!" She turned on Çeda. "She's given you a dozen openings, and you took none of them!"

Çeda had seen them. "I'm feeling a bit off today."

Kameyl stabbed a finger at Çeda. "Don't bloody lie to me. *She* has an excuse. She's hurt. But you! You might never hold a candle to Melis or Sümeya, but you're in fine enough condition, and when you and *I* spar, you might be an ox with a sword, but at least you're an ox with decent reflexes." In a burst of movement, Kameyl grabbed Yndris's shinai and attacked Çeda. Çeda hurriedly blocked her three opening swings, but then counterattacked, going for Kameyl's leading wrist, then her thigh, both of which Kameyl turned aside with ease.

"You see? Defense balanced with attack." She threw the sword back at Yndris, then stared at them both like a mother whose children had driven her to wit's end. "I can't stand to watch you for another minute. Go. Both of you. Tell each other your precious little stories as your mother bade you."

She stormed from the foredeck, leaving Yndris and Çeda to stare at one another. Çeda shrugged and sat against the bulwarks, resigned to her fate. Yndris, however, remained standing, perhaps thinking she might disobey, but she knew as well as Çeda how inflexible Sümeya had been on this particular condition since their voyage began five days ago, so after a moment's pause, she sat cross-legged by Çeda's side.

For a time they simply fidgeted. Their stories were ridiculous at first, Yndris telling Çeda of a wooden doll she'd once owned, a thing she'd broken and her father had replaced immediately. She'd broken it many times after that, on purpose, and her father's vizir had replaced it each time until Yndris had finally grown bored of the game. Çeda told Yndris tales of the spice market. Of sampling spices or breads or oils, often without leave, but sometimes saving up and having a feast of bread and cheese and marinated olives, a pauper's banquet Yndris probably found pathetic. Without fail, no matter which of them was telling it, their stories were without substance, meaningless to them both.

Today, however, Yndris jutted her chin toward Emre, who was holding a bolt of stained cloth and a jar of what looked to be deck oil. He was having a lively conversation with the quartermaster, who'd taken a liking to him, not leastwise because Emre was so helpful about the ship. "Tell me about him," Yndris said.

Çeda shrugged. "What is there to say?"

"Well I'm sure I wouldn't know."

Çeda shrugged again, wholly uncomfortable with telling Yndris anything about Emre. "He's nice."

Yndris laughed. A more grating sound Çeda had never heard. She wanted to punch Yndris in her throat if only to stop her laughs from invading the crisp desert air. "Your commander ordered you to tell a *story*. I hardly think *he's nice* qualifies, do you?"

Gods how Çeda wished she could just leap off this ship. Better to snap her own neck on the fall than suffer through another day with Yndris. "One day," Çeda began, just to get it over with, "Emre and I were running the streets near the western end of Hazghad, by Nalamae's old temple. You know the area?"

"No, but go on."

"We had our sights set on a fruit cart that came by the same time every week. We were hungry, and it didn't take much to nab a melon or two off the back." Yndris rolled her eyes, but Çeda continued as if she hadn't. "The fruit-monger was a lady with a limp and a cane. Years later we all secretly decided the limp was fake, that she was just doing it to catch would-be thieves off guard. We didn't think so at the time, but we'd heard the stories. She was fearsome if she ever caught any of the gutter wrens who plagued her. That day, I was clumsy. I tripped off the back of the cart when I was grabbing for one of the largest melons I'd ever seen. I ran, but the monger came storming after me, faster than I'd ever guessed she could move, but before she could reach me, Emre came running out of the nearby alley and launched himself at her. Just threw himself on her, body and soul, so that I could get away."

"And you escaped?"

Çeda nodded, watching Emre dip the rag into the jar and then smooth the oil over the deck. *She* hadn't been the one Emre had saved. It had been Hamid, but she couldn't very well tell Yndris that. The rest was true, though. Hamid had escaped and Emre had taken a beating fit for a demon.

"Well," Yndris said, standing and staring at Emre. "He deserved every thump from that woman's cane and probably more." She might have had a sparkle in her eyes for him earlier, but now her look was one of revulsion, the sort one gave to hair in soup.

Çeda let her leave without comment and watched Emre as he oiled the deck. Others might see a man who was bored, helping because he didn't have much else to do, but Çeda knew this was simply Emre. Always willing to help. Always willing to share a story.

Çeda's eyes were drawn to a pair of black forms loping like wolfhounds over the dunes: asirim, both bound to Kameyl. Çeda could feel them both, but especially the one that had just bayed. He was the second she'd bonded with on her last voyage, and she could feel his grieving, the hatred he nourished over the death of Havva, his sister asir, who Cahil had murdered in King's Harbor. She could feel the creature's resentment toward *her* as well.

I'm sorry, she said, more to herself than the asir. *I couldn't stop him.* She didn't know if he heard her words or not, but he stopped on the dune and howled once more.

Unlike their last voyage, neither Çeda nor Yndris had been allowed to bond with the asir. In Çeda's case, it was for obvious reasons: King Mesut didn't trust her. Which was all for the best, Çeda supposed. As strong as her fury had been after the events in the harbor, she might have done something rash, or the *asirim* might have done something rash *through* her. She wasn't too proud to admit that the combination of her own seething anger and the poison in her hand might have allowed them to do whatever they wished.

Yndris was another matter. Çeda was surprised Cahil hadn't demanded that Yndris be bonded, if only to set his daughter above Çeda. But if Çeda had learned anything in her time in the House of Maidens, it was that the Maidens were not the simple appendages of the Kings she once thought them to be. They served the Kings, true, but there was protocol—unwritten protocol in most cases, but protocol all the same. Without more evidence, Cahil had likely taken his vendetta against Çeda as far as he could without suffering retribution from Yusam or Husamettín. Which meant that for the time being Sümeya and her hand were the Jade-eyed King's to command.

As the days wore on, one blended into the next, their ship heading steadily southeast over the desert toward Ishmantep. Sümeya had ordered the captain to take them over the southeastern route from Sharakhai, over the lesser-used trails. It was shorter as the hawk flew, but much more treacherous than the well-traveled path straight south from Sharakhai and then east, and thus took more time. It was necessary, though. Sümeya didn't want to risk having a ship spy them and race ahead to warn the caravanserai they were coming.

In the mornings, after a light breakfast of dried fruit or spiced flatbread, they would practice swordplay against the rising of the sun. Sümeya, for her part, would only occasionally oversee Çeda's sparring. She spent most of her time practicing her forms—which Çeda had to admit were utter perfection—or reading on deck, or writing in her small journal. She spoke to the other Maidens, but to Çeda she would only speak in clipped phrases, passing along orders for the day, a command to correct Çeda's fighting poses, barking at her to listen to the asirim as Kameyl reined them closer or farther away from the ship.

The threat she'd uttered in the House of Maidens echoed in Çeda's mind—*If I find that Emre's been lying to us, I'm going to run my blade across his pretty little throat*—especially when she seemed in poor spirits. Surely it was only from the challenges they faced, the mystery of what was waiting for them in Ishmantep, but it never felt that way. It felt as if Sümeya were on the edge of making good on her promise, and Çeda would find Emre hanging from the end of a rope before they reached the serai.

For several hours each night in the Maidens' cabin at the front of the ship, Melis continued to teach Çeda and Yndris the hand signs they used to communicate with one another silently. The first few were simple—a closed fist for *move in tighter*, the little finger pointed down for *danger is near*, the thumb between her first and second fingers meant *prepare to retreat*—but they quickly became more precise and difficult to differentiate. More complex signs were founded on the basics. A closed fist bent backward told them to move into a formation that would allow them free movement of their swords, a sign not only that danger was near, but that conflict was imminent. The little finger pointed down but crooked slightly said *call upon the asirim, draw them near*, not merely a warning, but a command. Slight variations on *retreat* would tell her *where* to retreat, and commands would change based on the terrain around them. If high ground was near, or a barricade, or a trench, it was understood that an ordered retreat would be made there; if none such was near, they would move to where there were no enemies, or where they were fewest.

As Çeda and Yndris learned, Melis also began teaching them whistles that corresponded to each hand sign. The Maidens often found themselves out at night, or in situations where it wasn't practical for one's sisters to see a hand signal, such as when they were locked in battle. They used whistles in these situations. Çeda had a horrible time with some of them. She could whistle, but not in the trilling way she needed to indicate north, south, east, and west. Nor could she add the strange warble that was required for *wounded, need help*.

Yndris did well with them, but seemed strangely understanding about Çeda's inability to reproduce them. She even *helped* from time to time, which drove Çeda mad. *What are you doing?* she wanted to scream at her. *Fight me and be done with it.* She knew the two of them needed to speak, *really* speak, and soon, but it never seemed to be the right time.

Emre was rarely allowed on deck during their sparring sessions, but once they'd had their midday meal he was allowed to come up from the stifling interior of the ship. It was nearing winter in the Shangazi, but they'd hit a miserable hot spell, which made her feel for him, especially when the wind picked up and cooled her skin.

"You look like a drowned rat," Çeda said to him one day.

They were leaning against the gunwale at the rear of the ship, feeling the subtle rise and dip of the *Javelin* as it traversed the shallow dunes. Emre's long black hair was drenched in sweat. The wind played with it as he closed his eyes, arms out to catch the wind. "Rats wouldn't be dumb enough to get caught belowdecks in a ship as hot as this."

"That bad?"

He shrugged. "No, not so bad." He took in the way ahead, a rough section of desert they were crossing with care. "How much longer?"

"A week, Sümeya said."

"Then Ishmantep." He said it with a note of worry, but before she could say anything he took a deep breath and said, "Remember when we used to dream about sailing the desert?"

"Yes, though I distinctly remember it being only the two of us in that dream."

"What's a few Maidens here or there?"

"There's a bloody *plague* of them from where I'm standing."

Emre laughed. One of his *old* laughs, the sort that showed his teeth and dimples, both. She remembered that kiss he'd given her after talking along the Trough. She wanted to return it now, but she couldn't. Not in front of everyone.

Sümeya was speaking amidships with the ship's captain and the commander of the Silver Spears who had joined them on the journey. Melis and Kameyl were sitting cross-legged on the foredeck, braiding ropes, while Yndris stood on the bowsprit, her black Maiden's dress flapping as the foresail above her bowed in the wind.

"Tell me true, Çeda." Emre leaned in closer, looking toward them. "Do you think she'd marry one such as me?"

"Which?"

"The tall one."

Çeda couldn't help but laugh. "Surely, my lord, they, like all the women of Sharakhai, can discern the sort of treasure you are with but a glance."

"She can have more than a glance if she wishes."

"*Kameyl?*"

"She's ruggedly handsome."

"She's a gods-damned viper, Emre."

"Maybe you simply don't know her well enough."

"Oh, I think I know her more than well enough." Çeda nodded to the foredeck. "Why not Melis?"

Emre waggled his head. "Why not indeed? I am but a rat on a ship. Who am I to quibble?"

She slapped his shoulder. "You're foul."

"Make up your mind, Çedamihn, rat or fowl."

"The face of a rat and the legs of a hen."

He pushed himself away from the gunwale and headed across the deck. "Well, let's just see if dear Melis agrees, shall we?"

"Emre don't," she hissed. "She'll gut you."

He strode onward, skipping down the steps to the main deck and then gliding up to the foredeck, where he sat easily and began chatting with Melis and Kameyl, occasionally glancing toward Çeda with a grin, the sort a baby might give upon discovering how pleasantly squishy its own shit was.

"Mind the stink," Çeda said under her breath, though whether she meant it for Emre or Melis, she wasn't quite sure.

Chapter 45

ON THE EIGHTH DAY OUT FROM SHARAKHAI, the ship anchored early, and the crew, the Silver Spears, the Maidens, and Emre all built a fire and shared food and drink, each raising a wooden glass of araq to the rising of Rhia in the east. They did so again when Tulathan followed. It was Beht Firahl, the day Rhia had saved Tulathan from Yerinde's tower and both had risen to the sky. Rhia was a golden coin, filled with righteous anger, while Tulathan was a silver sickle, still weak from her imprisonment.

They ate beneath the stars, shared tales of times they'd gotten themselves or others into trouble, and how they in turn were saved by a father or brother or sister. Most seemed to be enjoying the night's celebration, especially Emre, who she often saw smiling from ear-to-ear. But not Sümeya. She'd given her assent for the night's festivities, but spoke little and ate less. Her eyes often drifted to the horizon, even when the crew started to dance around the fire. In fact, she began to avoid meeting anyone's gaze when they started to talk and laugh. While everyone else drank araq, she drank lustily from a bulging skin of wine.

A drum and flute and rebab were brought out. Some began to sing. Emre joined them with gusto. He'd always had a lust for song, especially those that embarrassed Çeda. But this time he sang a song of a bumbling jongleur who'd come to rob the desert tribes of their famed wealth but ended up loving the Shangazi so much he'd remained with the very first tribe he'd come across till the end of his days. As the araq warmed her fingers and toes, Çeda's mood brightened. It let her forget, at least for a short while, how drastically their lives had changed since they'd last sung songs together. When he finished, everyone shouted and whooped, raising their glasses and downing a healthy swallow.

"Now you," Emre said to Çeda from across the fire, his eyes alight with mischief.

Çeda stared at him and as whoops and whistles and ululations rose up around her, she said, "And so I shall." The whistles and shouts grew louder—Emre the worst of them—until she held her hand up. When silence fell she took up the song of Bakhi when he'd become drunk on his own wine and began to dance around the desert, until he came to Thaash, who stood on a mount like a statue, arms crossed. Bakhi decided to play a trick on the dour god. He sang a foolish song and made the fickle god smile, then laugh. Bakhi stole his laughter and fled to the western edges of the Shangazi. There he planted Bakhi's laughter. What grew soon after were the fire palms that region of the desert was famed for. What Bakhi hadn't realized was that a bit of Thaash's ever-burning anger had been caught as well. The fire dates the tree gave off were a wondrous fruit, and rare, at least in Sharakhai. They warmed the limbs and made the very heart sing, but were hot as Kundhuni peppers.

Everyone clapped. Someone spilled ale into the fire, making it sizzle as a young crewman took up a new song. Then, without warning, Kameyl stood and took one of the Silver Spears by the hand, a beast of a man, and led him off into the desert. Whistles chased their passage into the darkness. To Çeda's horror, Melis stood next, and held her hand out to Emre. Emre looked to Çeda, as if asking her permission.

"Well, what are you waiting for?" she asked, though they were the last words she wanted to say.

From across the fire he blinked at her, the alchemy of Melis's action and Çeda's words mixing to create a look of half shock, half hurt. But then his face hardened, and he took Melis's hand. More whistles followed them as

Çeda sat, staring sullenly into the fire, wondering if everyone could see the flush in her cheeks.

Sümeya stood as well, but instead of going to choose a man, she came to a stop before Çeda. Wineskin in one hand, her scabbarded sword in the other, she said, "Come. And bring your blade." Without another word, she trudged over the sand in the opposite direction the others had taken. Swallowing, Çeda buckled her sword belt and followed. No whistles followed their departure. Instead, a tense silence was left in their wake, at least until the two of them passed beyond the borders of the firelight and a new song began.

Sümeya hoisted the wineskin and drank as she walked, then turned and tossed the skin back to Çeda. "Drink!" she called, stumbling for a moment, sand sliding down one face of the dune like a growing landslide, the sound of it strange, like a creaking door. Çeda took up the skin but only slung it over one shoulder. Sümeya glanced back. "I said *drink*, Maiden." Words spoken in her warden's voice.

Not wanting a fight for no reason, Çeda complied, taking a healthy swallow of the crisp pear wine, but she worried about Sümeya. She'd never seen her drunk, or anything close to it. Sümeya was always cool and composed.

When the sound of the revelry had become but a murmur in the distance, Sümeya spun unsteadily—a top ready to topple—and held her hand out for the wineskin. When Çeda didn't immediately hand it over she snapped her fingers as if Çeda were her servant.

Çeda gave it to her, and Sümeya drank deeply. Then she stood there, staring at the trough between the dunes to her left. A drop of wine fell from her lips, a glint of gold falling to the desert, swallowed whole by the sand. She looked more haunted than Çeda had ever seen her. She turned to Çeda and seemed startled that Çeda was there. "You're doing well in your swordcraft." She spoke slowly, the pace of a woman who'd just realized how drunk she was.

"Thank you," Çeda said simply, unsure where any of this was going.

"Kameyl and Melis have both told me so. Zaïde has said the same of your open-hand training. And your mastery over your heart's rhythm as well. It makes me wonder if you've done it before."

"I never—"

Sümeya held up one hand. "I know. I've come to believe you are who you say you are." She took one more pull from the wineskin, then tossed it away.

"Sümeya, why are we here?"

In a move so fluid it surprised Çeda, Sümeya drew her ebon blade. The curved length of steel was so dark it seemed ready to devour the night sky. "Let's see if my Maidens are correct in their assessment, shall we?"

"First Warden, I don't think we should—"

Sümeya charged, sword raised above her head, but it was child's play for Çeda to avoid her downward swing. It took her down the dune, though. Sümeya followed, brandishing her shamshir.

"Draw your sword, Maiden!"

She came on fast. When she swung her blade across her body, Çeda retreated, but dove in immediately after, hoping to grab Sümeya's wrist and disarm her, but Sümeya surprised her. She ducked beneath Çeda's reach and punched her in the side so hard Çeda lost her breath for a moment.

Sümeya's sword moved so fast it flickered darkly in the moonlight. Çeda fell back. The sleeve of her dress was neatly cut near her shoulder, but she felt nothing along her skin.

"It's the last time I'll ask you, young dove."

"I'll not draw my sword against you."

Sümeya whipped her sword across her body, forcing Çeda back. "Will you not?"

Çeda took a deep breath and fell into the training she and Zaïde had gone over again and again. "I will not." She felt Sümeya's heart beat. She could also tell Sümeya was trying to mask it. Had she not been drunk, she might have been able to but not like this. It was all too easy for Çeda to sense her.

"The gods are watching, Çedamihn. Bakhi will not think twice of coming for one who offers herself so easily."

Sümeya came again and again. Each time, Çeda felt more in tune with her movements. Then a swing came that overreached. As the blade swept wide, a dark arc against the gold-dusted landscape, Çeda darted in, grabbed Sümeya's wrist, and used the momentum of Sümeya's own swing to fling her down the slope of the dune. Sümeya's blade flew away, twisting awkwardly before splashing against the sand. Sümeya herself rolled down the dune, coming to a sliding stop near the trough.

Çeda waited for her to rise, but she didn't. She lay there, facing away, looking like a lost child dying in the desert. Çeda knelt by her side. She wasn't sure what to say to a woman who opened up so rarely, and who had never, ever showed this sort of weakness.

And then Çeda realized she was crying, so softly it could barely be heard above the sounds of revelry in the distance.

Çeda placed her hand on Sümeya's shoulder, an awkward thing, a gesture between strangers. "What's happened?"

Sümeya lay there, silently sobbing.

Çeda squeezed her shoulder, trying to lend her strength. "Sümeya, tell me what's happened."

Sümeya pushed herself off the sand and sat up. She wiped away her tears, sniffing, avoiding Çeda's eyes. She stared up to the moons, a silent plea to the twin goddesses, though for what, Çeda wasn't sure. "There was another who had the mantle of First Warden before me, did you know?"

"Nayyan."

Sümeya turned to Çeda, her eyes looking over Çeda's face like a vintner might examine the first glass poured from last year's harvest. "Nayyan."

The reverence in her voice . . . *No, not reverence. Love. She loves Nayyan as I love Emre.* "Tell me about her."

"She was a wonder." Sümeya's voice was lusty. "Gifted in so many ways."

"All say she was the best in a generation with sword in hand," Çeda offered.

Sümeya shifted on the sand until she was sitting across from Çeda, their knees nearly touching. "There was that, but that was the least of it. She played the harp, taught to her by her mother. It was enough to make you weep. And how she could dance, without a blade somehow more beautiful than with. Would that I could hold her hand openly once more."

Through the haze of araq, something began to tingle inside Çeda. The night she'd gone to the blooming fields to poison herself. Çeda had nearly been caught by a woman in a Maiden's dress. She'd worn a necklace of what looked to be long black thorns, and it was said Nayyan, before she'd become First Warden, had killed an ehrekh in the desert, and made a necklace from the thorns that bristled like a crown on its head. Nayyan was thought to be dead, but she'd disappeared on the night Çeda's mother, Ahya, had been caught by the Kings.

Ever since learning more of Nayyan, Çeda suspected the Maiden with the thorn necklace had been her. And now Sümeya had said something most strange. *Would that I could hold her hand openly once more.* Not simply *hold her hand once more,* as one might say of a dead loved one, but hold it *openly.*

The tingling in Çeda's chest spread to her limbs at the very thought of what she was about to do. It could very well get her killed, but Çeda stood anyway and held out her hand to Sümeya. "How would you dance with her if you could?"

Sümeya looked up from her seated position, blinking for a moment before focusing on Çeda. Then she reached out and allowed Çeda to pull her up. As the music from the ship played in the distance—a tune that began slowly but picked up speed as it went—the two of them began to circle one another, Sümeya keeping her eyes on Çeda the whole time, a sultry look Çeda wondered if she was even aware of.

They spun and turned, dipping and turning their hips in time to the music, each of them throwing one hand in the air when the song called for it. The melodic calls of the crew came to them, but softly, as if they two were mere wraiths in the desert, remembering the lives they once led, envying those that still breathed. More than once Çeda had to steady Sümeya, but Sümeya didn't seem to mind. She laughed harder each time it happened, and then she *did* fall near the end of the song, tipping headlong onto the sand, Çeda coming with her.

They lay there side by side, out of breath as they stared at the stars. Sümeya reached out and took Çeda's hand. She rolled onto her side, stared at Çeda instead of the stars. "I see some of her in you, you know."

"What could you see of her in me?"

"You are gifted in blade and blood, as she was. You are willful, as she was." She reached out one hand and touched Çeda's cheek, ran her fingers along Çeda's jaw. "You are beautiful, as she was."

Sümeya paused, waiting for Çeda to turn to her. When Çeda did, she raked her fingers through Çeda's hair. Çeda shivered from the simple, gentle touch of another. She'd been so long without it in the Maidens' House that its sudden return made her think of Emre, of Osman, of Ramahd. More than anything, though, it made her wonder whether she might lie here with

Sümeya, a woman none would deny was beautiful, and forget for a time all that lay ahead, all that lay behind.

Before Çeda knew what was happening, Sümeya had crawled on top of her, slipped her hand behind Çeda's neck, and drew her in. For a moment she stared into Çeda's eyes, but then she leaned in and pressed her lips to Çeda's. Çeda stiffened at first, but the kiss was long and warm and immediately began melting her resistance. Sümeya was a chiseled woman, both in mind and in body, but by the gods her lips were soft as velvet. Çeda relaxed. She knew it was the wine speaking, but it felt so good to lose herself in another person's flesh, even if for completely wrong reasons.

When Sümeya broke the kiss at last, it was with an audible smack that left Çeda wanting more. She threaded her fingers through Sümeya's hands, not allowing her to leave, struggling for words that would raise no suspicion. "Why don't you go to her if you miss her so?"

Sümeya kissed Çeda's neck, then whispered into her ear. "You think it so easy?"

"It can be if you wish it so," Çeda whispered back.

"An assassin's blade took her from my side. You might think it uncomplicated to love a woman who's become a King, but I tell you it isn't."

As Sümeya stitched more warm kisses along Çeda's neck. Her hand slipped beneath Çeda's dress and crept slowly up her thigh. Çeda, however, remained perfectly still. She swallowed uncontrollably. *By Bakhi's bright hammer, Nayyan a King?* But which one?

Çeda moaned as Sümeya put her lips to Çeda's dress and exhaled, her hot breath spreading through the cloth and over the skin of her breast. She gasped as Sümeya's hand slipped beneath her small clothes. Sümeya ran her fingers like one might apply oil, with long strokes at first, then in ever tightening circles. Like a falcon riding hot desert currents, the pleasure rose with each turn. Sümeya was an artist, her skillful fingers bringing Çeda higher, then letting her fall, then bringing her higher still.

Dear gods, I can't do this. Sümeya is First Warden.

And yet despite her own thoughts, Çeda arched her back. She pulled her dress down over one shoulder, grabbed a fistful of Sümeya's hair, and pulled her head against her bared breast. As Sümeya used her tongue to circle Çeda's nipple, used her teeth to make playful bites, Çeda spread her legs wider. She leaned into the movements of Sümeya's fingers until the two of them were in perfect sync. When Sümeya slipped two fingers inside her, Çeda grabbed her hand, drew her deeper while pulling Sümeya in for another kiss. Their breath mingled. Their lips and tongues met with greater need. The wind cooled Çeda's skin where Sümeya's mouth had been.

Sümeya had just pulled Çeda's dress down to her waist when a blood-curdling yowl rent the cool night air. The sound was eerily similar to the call of the jackals that roamed this part of the desert and yet it was inescapably human. Çeda stiffened from it. Sümeya lifted her head, looking to the top of the nearby dune. Çeda craned her neck and saw the asir, the one that had been so vocal these past many days. It crouched there, watching the two of them.

It made her skin crawl just to look at it. As she quickly pulled her dress back on, she felt Sümeya trying to warn the asir away. She felt the asir's cold indifference. It continued to creep closer, low to the ground, arms akimbo, spider-like. Çeda had no idea why it had become so hungry, but she knew that murderous thoughts now drove it.

As the asir approached, scuttling like a beetle over the sand, Sümeya stood and took a step toward it. "Leave," she said, reinforcing the silent command she'd been giving it. The asir slowed, but now looked more akin to a starving panther that was weighing just how wise it would be to leap.

Keeping her eyes on the asir, Sümeya sidestepped to where her sword had fallen, then crouched and picked it up. She advanced on the asir. "I said be-gone!"

Shall I press the life from her? the asir asked. *Will you watch as you watched Havva die in the harbor at the hands of the Confessor King?*

Leave, Çeda said to it, dearly hoping this wouldn't end in bloodshed. *You'll solve nothing by killing her.*

That woman deserves to lie breathless beneath the sand.

Now is not the time.

It crawled forward, then raised itself up onto thin, blackened legs. *And when will that day come, favored of Sehid-Alaz? When will you finally work to free us?*

As Sümeya stepped forward, brandishing her ebon blade, Çeda felt herself being drawn into the emotions of this creature. As it had been with Havva, she felt the asir's burning desire to choke the life from a Blade Maiden. Any Maiden would do, but this one would be particularly sweet.

What is your name? Çeda asked.

My name, it spoke with clear pride, *is Kerim Deniz'ava al Khiyanat, cousin to our King, Sehid-Alaz, and Havva was my love, my wife, the mother of my children.* Khiyanat meant betrayal, or the betrayed, in the old tongue.

Kerim, I promise you, the day will soon come.

The asir paused, then glanced at Çeda, which made Sümeya do the same. Whether she could sense that some conversation was being played out between them Çeda couldn't say, but soon Sümeya had turned back to the asir. Çeda could feel her exerting her will, though it was doing little. Çeda worried that Mesut might be drawn to this meeting of wills, or that Sümeya might reach out to him, but she felt no other presence than herself, Kerim, Sümeya, and the second asir, curled in a tight ball somewhere out in the dunes, alone, confused, angry.

Go, Çeda said. *You've done enough damage this night.*

Still the asir waited, obstinate, but they both knew it would not harm Sümeya. Not this time.

Go, before she suspects I'm to blame.

Finally, with an inhuman wail, a sick twisting of its neck and shoulders, Kerim son of Deniz turned and fled into the night. Sümeya watched it gallop away, sword still at the ready. Something in her seemed to break then. Her sword tip lowered. Her shoulders slumped. She looked about her, to the wineskin, to the imprint she and Çeda had left in the sand.

She turned toward Çeda but didn't lift her eyes. Then, after sliding her ebon sword home in its scabbard with a clack, she walked to the wineskin and snatched it up from where it had fallen. She held the neck to her mouth, took a long pull from it, and without another word walked away, back toward the ship.

As Sümeya crested the dune, Çeda wondered if she'd just made a horrible mistake not letting the asir drink Sümeya's blood. It was only a fleeting thought—there and gone in the flick of a butterfly's wings. She knew she wouldn't kill any of her hand, not even Yndris. Not without provocation, in any case.

"Would you join me if you knew the truth?" Çeda said to Sümeya's retreating form. Most Maidens would not, but there must be some who would. She had to believe that. If there was no humanity in those who held power in Sharakhai—the Blade Maidens, the Silver Spears, the sons and daughters of the Kings—then all was lost no matter what she did.

Çeda waited—for what, she wasn't sure. Answers from the desert, she supposed. Didn't the old tales speak of the Great Mother answering one's most fervent prayers? The wind blew harder for a time, pulling spindrift from the dunes like spray upon the sea. Sümeya was but a dark form now, cresting a distant dune. Hearing no answers, Çeda pulled her veil into place and set after her.

Chapter 46

"**I** NEED A FIRE, ANILA," Davud said at the end of a long day of travel. The day had been cold and windy, and the night promised to be worse.

Anila was nearby, pulling their bedrolls from the skiff they'd stolen before fleeing the gathering of the Moonless Host. Every night since fleeing the *Burning Sand*, the cold had settled in Davud's bones as he slept, making any movement feel like spikes were being driven into his joints. It was only the lingering effects of his change, he knew, but it made him crave warmth. He might have asked Anila to sleep next to him, but he couldn't find it in himself to ask. She was still so very angry with him.

Instead he'd requested a fire, only a small one, enough to warm him for a time before falling asleep. Every day for the past week she'd denied him, judging it too dangerous, but this time she stopped what she was doing, turned, and stared at a brilliant horizon that somehow made Davud feel colder, as if the retreating sun had stolen the very warmth from the desert, leaving all things within it to suffer.

"Very well," she said.

Davud hid his relief. Anytime he'd showed softer emotions, be it relief, happiness, or the occasional attempt to share a joyful reminiscence of their fellow scholars, she'd become despondent. She felt guilty, of course. Their friends had not been as lucky as they. They'd suffered terribly while Davud and Anila had escaped. "We'll find them," Davud said to her. "We'll free them." Though how they might do that he had no idea.

Anila said nothing. The comment only made her seem more miserable. They both knew they had little hope of achieving the goal she'd set for them. In all likelihood they'd both die and Hamzakiir would use the survivors from the collegia attack to unveil his plans like a storm over Sharakhai. They'd have thrown away their lives for no gain at all, but there was nothing for it now. They were committed.

While Anila prepared their bedrolls and their rations of hardtack and water, Davud built a fire in the trough between two dunes. Soon they were sitting across from one other, the fire between them, their bellies contented if not full. As the fire snapped softly in the desert night, Davud held his hands over it, glad for the warmth, glad for the golden light as well. Anila watched in silence, contemplative, her knees pulled up to her chest. She was thinking again, worrying over what would happen in Ishmantep, but treating it like a problem to be solved, not some unassailable wall.

It enhanced her beauty, knowing her mind was working. She had a brilliant mind. A quick mind. It made him proud to know her, a thing that had been true practically from the moment they'd met. If only he could have said so before all this.

"Show me the ritual," she said suddenly, breaking the stiff silence between them.

"What?"

"You said you have an exercise to bring you in tune with fire."

"I do, but—"

"Then show me."

"I thought you hated the red ways."

"I do." She stared into his eyes, the firelight playing across the contours of her face. She swallowed hard. "But we're going to need it, Davud."

She meant in Ishmantep. She might be right, but they both knew his abilities would make no difference at all if they were pitted against Hamzakiir. Davud couldn't hold a candle to the blood mage. How could he? Hamzakiir had been trained by magi in Qaimir. He'd mastered it over the course of many decades, longer than Davud had been alive. What was Davud but some bumbling fool with the misfortune of having tainted blood?

He took the small kenshar Anila had had the foresight to bring—a simple, bone-handled knife that Davud now considered part of his everyday existence—and drove its point into the palm of his left hand. He felt the now-familiar prick of pain.

Setting the knife in his lap, he watched the blood well up. When there was enough of it, he touched a finger to it and with practiced strokes drew one of the sigils from Hamzakiir's book onto his palm. The sigil was really a combination of two master sigils: *fire* and another that meant *assimilate* or *subsume*. Like two shades of color combining to form a third, one sigil was laid over the other, the two acting in harmony.

Satisfied, Davud held his hand over the fire once more. He lowered it slowly as Anila watched hungrily. It was a familiar look to anyone who knew her. It stole over her in philosophic debates with Master Amalos, or during algebraic instruction with Master Nezahum. "It's like sunlight passing through colored glass, then? It's the symbol that performs the magic?"

"*Sigil,*" Davud corrected. "And no, it does not."

As he lowered his hand, and the heat began to rise, Davud concentrated, holding the concept of fire to him like a talisman. "The sigil is merely a starting point, a familiar frame of mind. It is the place where mind, body, and world meet and become as one." He willed the fire toward his heart by way of his open palm, and the fire began to swirl.

Anila watched. Her face might be like stone, but her eyes were bright and full of wonder. She found this abhorrent but the student within her found it too fascinating to ignore.

Davud lowered his hand. The fire swirled faster. Licks of it were thrown from the building maelstrom like moths bursting into flame. The heat on his palm built, but not nearly so much as it would have without the sigil.

"What's different now?" Anila asked.

Davud wiped sweat from his brow. "It enters through the palm, but it goes well beyond. It suffuses me, like the feeling you get after a run."

Anila smiled a wicked smile. "As though you *run.*"

"I *run,*" Davud said with an indignance that was only half felt.

"To your mother you run, after I've spanked you in yet another debate."

"Do you wish to learn about it or not?"

"Well then"—she bowed her head and flourished a hand—"please continue, Master Davud."

And so he did, telling her how it continued to spread through him until he was burning from it, how if he didn't release the power it would make his muscles ache, or eventually blister his skin. He showed her how he could make the fire dance beneath his palm. How he could bring it to life between his fingers at a mere thought, but not if he waited too long and the heat slipped away.

"Can you throw it?"

"The fire?" he asked. "I haven't tried."

A bit of a lie. In truth he'd been afraid to. Hamzakiir had warned him explicitly not to attempt it. Many had died from doing so before they'd understood the nature of fire and the sigils and the way they and the body interacted. *They are threads held in delicate balance,* he'd written. *Toy with them before you're ready, and you're as like to boil your own mind as bring about the effect you're looking for.*

"Try," Anila said. She was staring at him as if she knew exactly what she was asking—*risk it,* her look said, *or this will all have been for naught.*

He knew he shouldn't. He promised himself he would wait until he returned to Sharakhai, where he might be taught by those who knew better. She didn't have the right to ask this of him, but he couldn't shake that look of hers. *You owe me.* And she was right.

"Very well," he said.

After taking a deep breath, he summoned a mote of flame. It was tiny, almost insubstantial, floating over his palm like two warring moths. He made it grow to the size of a grape, then a walnut. "I'm not really sure how to throw it," he said after a time. When he moved his hand, the flame moved with him.

"If you can draw the flame into you, then you can force it away." She motioned to the slope of the nearby dune. "Try there."

Davud closed his fist. He stood and faced the dune, then summoned the fire again. It wavered more than it had the first time, but at least it wasn't the size of a gnat. He licked his lips, tried to stabilize it, but that only seemed to make it worse. Anila watched him with hungry eyes, as if she desperately wished *she* were the one wielding the flame. It made him entirely uncomfortable, though he couldn't have said exactly why.

"Is it so different from alchemy," she asked, "finding the balance between components?"

"It is nothing like alchemy," he replied. Like a dust devil, the swirling flame dissipated, then reconstituted a moment later, brighter than before. "The balance you have to maintain is so delicate."

"It's only that the components are different."

"That's like saying a painting is merely shades of color."

"It is."

"Stop being such a deconstructionist. Art is more than its base components. True art touches the artist's soul, and that in turn touches others'. Why else does it affect those who view it years or even centuries later?"

Her brow knitted, but her eyes lost none of their intensity. She said no more, waiting for him to try. But it was so difficult merely to maintain the effect. It was not as though the flame were some physical object he were holding. He could *feel* it, but it wasn't like his hand or his arm. It was as if the flame were an opening to another world—a world inside him, perhaps, or another plane of existence, he couldn't tell which—and what he was doing was merely allowing some small part of it to manifest.

As he drew his arm back, preparing to fling the fire toward the dune, the flame wavered. He reformed it with conscious thought. The doorway to that *other* place was so difficult to shape and maintain; if he wasn't careful, the floodgates would open and too much would pour forth.

That one small doubt became a worry, that worry, fear, and all too soon the fear became a certainty, a self-fulfilling prophecy. The delicate balance within him shifted. His mind went wild with terror that he'd harm himself, that he'd harm Anila, and suddenly it was all he could do to contain it.

The sleeve of his kaftan burst into flame. Anila shouted, backed away from him, but he could spare no concern for her. He was too busy trying to contain the fire threatening to run wild within him. Anila returned, a gray blanket trailing behind her like a dead man's cloak. She lifted it into the air, shouting something to him, when it all became too much. His world became fire and fear and a black pit that yawned open beneath him.

Davud screamed. His mind scrabbled for purchase. And yet down, down he fell, the darkness calling, its arms wide, welcome and waiting and so very, very hungry.

———— ● ————

Davud woke with a start.

It was still night. He stared at the sky for a long while, realizing Tulathan had risen, had moved halfway across the sky, in fact. He lay next to the fire, which was burning more brightly than was wise. Anila lay behind him, her arms draped over his body. The bedrolls cocooned the two of them. The smell of burnt hair was strong.

And he was cold. So cold.

He remembered the chill feeling sweeping over him even as his sleeve caught fire. How fast it had happened! How dissonant the cold was against the blaze of heat. He remembered falling as well. The sheer terror within him, blotting out all other emotions and conscious thought. Now that he was distanced from it, though, he could set aside the fear and see the sort of thing he'd held in his hand. Never in his life had he wielded real power. Amalos always told him that *knowledge* was power, and that was true as far as it went, but this . . . The fire coursing through him. The sheer rush of it. The things he might do if he could master it. The wrongs he might right. The very thought sent a chill down his spine.

Anila stirred. "Are you awake?" she whispered.

"Go back to sleep," he whispered back.

She pulled him closer. The smell of her skin, her hair, her cheek against his neck. It made for a heady mixture, indeed. "I thought you were going to die."

"I tried to do too much."

"I shouldn't have pushed you."

"I knew better, Anila. I shouldn't have relented."

"I'm sorry, Davud."

"We'll be more careful next time."

"No. I mean about Hamzakiir. You were trapped, just like I was. Just like all the rest. How were you to know what he would do?"

"I wanted to save everyone."

She ran her hand along his chest, then leaned in and kissed his neck. It felt like lightning running through him. "I know."

The sun was brightening the eastern sky.

"We'd better get moving," Davud said.

"We will." She hugged him to her. "Soon enough."

For a time they lay like that, sharing one another's warmth. The fire died down, became embers—golds within reds, nestled in a bed of black. The sun had just touched the horizon when Davud rose and kicked sand over the fire lest it smoke.

"Davud?"

He spun at the sound of panic in her voice. She was staring at the horizon. Davud saw only wave after wave of rolling dunes. But then he spotted it. From this distance they looked like sharp blades—the lateen sails of a sand-ship. The *Burning Sand*. He knew her lines well.

"They might not know we're here," Davud said. "Sail now and we might give our position away."

They were hopeful words but also naive, and they both knew it. Without either of them saying another word, they burst into motion. In less than a minute, they were in the skiff and sailing across the sand. Davud checked their position using the sextant and the stars still visible, adjusting course once he was satisfied with the path they were taking toward Ishmantep.

Anila watched the trailing ship as Davud steered. "By my estimate," she said, "we have four days of sailing before Ishmantep rises over the desert."

Davud nodded numbly. "They'll not rest at night now that they've found our scent. But at least the skiff is faster."

"Not by much. And the moons will be bright. The way ahead is clear. They'll be able to sail all hours while we—"

"We'll trade off," Davud said, not at all confident they'd be able to sail for three more nights straight and not risk getting caught in one of the deep furrows between dunes, or worse, catch on a rock and lose one of the skis. "We'll be fine."

Anila was crying. She wiped away her tears, her eyes locked on the trailing ship, a ship filled with men and women who would likely kill them the moment they caught up with them. "I should have let them take us to Shara-khai," she said. "I should have been content with telling the Silver Spears what happened and let them go in force to Ishmantep. Now we're going to die on the sands, Davud."

"Anila." She remained as she was, eyes filled with regret. "Anila!" he shouted at her. She turned to him. "You were right to do it. I should have done it myself. I should have done more in Ishmantep. You and I?" He stabbed one finger toward the *Burning Sand*. "We're going to stay ahead of that ship. We're going to reach the caravanserai before them. The gods will see to the rest."

The fear in her was palpable, but at his words, she sat taller and nodded. They sailed throughout the day, and for a while it seemed as though they were distancing themselves from the *Burning Sand*, but after midday, the wind grew stronger, and the trailing ship started to gain on them. Neither he nor Anila said a word about it, but they both knew their fates now rested with the fickle wind. The skiff had the advantage when the wind was low, but when it blew stronger, the sails of the two-masted ketch could catch more and power their ship faster over the grasping sands.

They jettisoned what they could. A length of rope. Canvas they might have used to patch the sails. The two small axes they'd found in the supplies. They upended the crates that held their remaining water, hardtack, smoked meat, and other provisions into the hull of the skiff, then threw the crates over the side as well.

From what Davud could tell, it made little difference. Captain Rasime was gaining on them. Davud thought surely the ship would catch them by nightfall, but they were still a half league out when the sun set. And then, thank Goezhen for his kindness, the wind lost some of its fury.

They sailed through the night, Anila first, then Davud, one sleeping as the other steered. Day came again and they led much the same chase as they had the day before: the *Burning Sand* catching up over the course of the day, the wind dying and the skiff putting distance between them at night, except this time, they'd come within a quarter league of their skiff. The crew climbed the masts and the rigging. They called and whooped. *"Lai, lai, lai, lai!"* A simple enough statement to understand: *Flee as you will, we'll dig your sandy graves all the same.*

Davud and Anila ate sparingly. They spoke seldom, but as the sun broke the horizon the following day, Anila said, "They'll catch us today if the wind is the same."

"It will be different."

"And if it isn't?"

Davud kept his eyes focused ahead, hoping. "It will be."

"Davud, don't delude yourself."

He tore his gaze away from the horizon. "Well, what do you *suggest*? I can't very well make the ship go faster!"

"But you *could*, Davud." She motioned to Hamzakiir's book in the bottom of the skiff. "If you tried."

"It's too dangerous," he said. "I nearly killed myself last time."

"We're going to die if they catch up with us, and it won't be a quick death, not after what I did to Tayyar."

For a moment, the vision of Tayyar lying on the matted grass, bloody, skull caved in by a rock wielded by Anila's hand, came to him. He pushed the image away. "The wind will favor us."

But it didn't. The wind blew across their bow with the sort of zeal that made it seem as though the desert itself were eager to find out what would happen when the *Burning Sand* caught up to them at last. Indeed, slowly but surely the trailing ship was closing the distance, a half league, then a quarter. At midday, Anila took the book and held it out to Davud. "Use it, Davud."

He stared at it for a long while, then glanced back at the looming ketch. Gods, it was getting close. He took the book and allowed Anila to take the tiller, then shifted forward. He began poring over the sigils for *wind* and *command*. He practiced drawing it in the sand collected at the bottom of the skiff.

"Enough," Anila said an hour later.

"It needs to be perfect."

"It *is* perfect. You were always the best of us with ink and quill, Davud. I know you're stalling."

"I can't do it, Anila."

"What, the spell? Of course you can."

"No, I can't do it."

"Why not?"

"Because I need blood!"

One's own blood gives power, Hamzakiir's book mentioned more than once, *but not nearly so much as another's.* He could tell by Anila's sudden nervousness that she knew exactly what he meant. Her jaw stiffened as she held out her hand. "Take all that you wish."

"It isn't that simple."

She shook her hand, eyes defiant, black hair blowing in the wind. "It *is* that simple. You need it. I have it. Take it, Davud, and save us both."

A horn blew behind them. Davud could see Rasime standing far forward along the bowsprit, one hand on the rigging, the other holding a curving horn. Like a revenant, she was, looming at the head of a ghost ship. "We'll bury your bones!" came her faint voice. "We'll bury your bones and the Great Mother will grind them for a thousand years then a thousand more!"

Davud swallowed, trying to ignore their incessant clashing of swords. "Very well," he said, and took up his knife. He took Anila's wrist and pressed the sharp tip into her forearm. Blood flowed. He placed his lips over the wound and tasted her blood while summoning the sigil to the fore of his mind. He drew more and more still, the metallic clang of the swords becoming rhythmic, a perfect match to the cadence of Anila's heart.

He felt Anila's body. Her very soul. He felt her fear, but also the exhilaration coursing through her as she fed him magic. The skin along her arm was chill to the touch, but her heart was an inferno. "Now, Davud. Do it now!"

He stood as a black arrow streaked in and speared into the hull of the skiff. Another tore through the sail's canvas as Davud slipped one arm free of his kaftan, then the other. After shrugging the kaftan so that it fell around his hips, he took more blood from Anila's arm and used it to draw the sigil on his pale, bared chest.

"Take him down!" Rasime shouted, pointing at him with the tip of her swinging shamshir. "Take him down!"

The few arrows loosed so far had been in warning. But no longer. Now a dozen men and women stood along the starboard bow, launching arrows in a high arc.

"Get down," Davud said. His voice shook, but he didn't care. As Anila obeyed, crouching low and guiding the skiff over the lip of a dune, Davud drew the symbol deeper in his mind, calling the wind, forcing it against the ketch.

It came slowly at first. A subtle shift in the wind that made their sail thrum. A lifting of spindrift that spun in the air like a nautilus shell before dissipating. A gust that rolled over the *Burning Sand*'s rigging like a hand plucking notes from a harp.

More arrows flew. Some splashed harmlessly into the sand. Others knifed into the hull. Anila was low, crablike, her eyes wide with fear. "Davud, Hurry!"

Davud tried to ignore her. The last thing he needed was—

Bright white fire tore into his left leg. He looked down and found an arrow sprouting from his thigh. He screamed, one hand reaching down reflexively to clutch at the wound. His fear was as great as Anila's, but now there was anger, too. Anger over all that had happened since Sharakhai. The sleeping gas in the basilica. Waking on a ship and finding Collum dead. Being given the ultimatum from Hamzakiir. Being toyed with. Being driven to choose between his own death and saving Anila. Being chased by this infernal ship! It built like a storm, then swept forward so quickly it was on him in moments.

A fresh volley of arrows stippled the sky. Days ago, with the fire, Davud had had trouble finding the balance between drawing too little and too much. Not so today. Either his anger or Anila's blood or the simple repetition of the experience allowed him to raise one hand and brush the arrows aside. Like leaves caught in a summer gale, they were thrown well wide of the skiff. Then Davud concentrated on the *Burning Sand*.

Power raged through him, consuming Anila's blood. Sand and wind drove against their enemy's ship, rippling the sails, pulling at the rigging. Rasime's orders were nearly swallowed by the howl of the wind, but Davud could hear the fear in her voice. He was glad for it, glad she could feel fear as *he* had felt it. Ropes snapped. Sails ripped. As the ship tipped up the side of a dune, a crewman on the mainmast fell and was lost to the billowing sand.

The *Burning Sand* began to fall behind. Davud released his hold on the gale, allowing it to expend the last of its energy unaided. He spared some small amount for their skiff, though, pushing them onward at a speed he hadn't realized a skiff could reach.

Anila had been watching with wide eyes, but as the *Burning Sand* was lost from view entirely, swallowed by the massive cloud of dust Davud's spell had drawn from the desert, she stood, heedless of the unattended tiller. Throwing her hands into the air and tipping her head back, she shouted, then laughed with complete abandon, her face toward the sun in an exultant display of emotion.

"You were *brilliant*, Davud!" She took him into a tight embrace. "Do you hear me? Tulathan's bright eyes, you were bloody brilliant!"

This time, when she began to laugh, Davud joined her.

Chapter 47

AFTER RAMAHD'S NARROW ESCAPE from the Tattered Prince, the days became interminably long. Meryam would not wake. Ramahd thought she might be have been caught by the strange presence they'd felt within that deep blue gem around drug-addled Brama's neck, but he started to think otherwise when her sleeping rhythms settled, becoming more akin to those she had after drawing overly on the power of blood. It was certainly cause for hope, but when it went on, day after day, he worried she would stay this way until she died of malnutrition.

She was well cared for. The servants of their house knew how to deal with her condition. But if her sleep continued too long, even their skills would prove insufficient and Meryam would eventually pass. Ramahd could even see it in Basilio's eyes, a certain well-masked hunger as he asked after her. Ramahd wanted to drive a fist into his face for it, but for now it was best if Basilio didn't suspect they knew of his allegiance to the cabal in Qaimir that plotted against Meryam.

He had other things to worry about in any case, not the least of which the possibility that Tariq—and by extension, the crime lord, Osman—had learned of their identities. Osman wasn't known for assassinations, but

Ramahd wasn't so green that he thought him above it. And even if the repercussions proved less drastic, neither he nor Meryam needed the attention.
Their greatest weapon in Sharakhai had been the care they'd taken to hide
their true purpose. If Osman found out, he might try to make life difficult
for them, either by blackmailing Meryam, or worse, selling their secrets to
the Kings. Ramahd resigned himself to that possibility. If it came to pass, they
could likely weather such a storm. The Kings knew of Meryam's abilities, but
thought they were being directed, as Ramahd had hinted on several occa-
sions, toward the capture of Macide and others in the Moonless Host.

More troubling by far was Brama himself, as well as the presence Ramahd
had felt within that gem. It was deeply powerful. And Brama was somehow
using that power for his own purposes. That feeling returned, the one he'd
felt deep inside while staring into that depthless gem, the feeling so like
Guhldrathen's presence in the desert. Was it an ehrekh hidden there? He
wasn't sure, but it was fortunate Brama had been stupefied by the black lotus.
Had he not been, he would have sensed their deception even sooner and
found Ramahd and possibly even Meryam.

As the days passed with nothing untoward happening on any front, Ramahd suspected, mighty Alu be praised, that he hadn't. The gods shone on
him again when, twelve days after their strange encounter, Meryam woke.
Ramahd sat by her side as the servants cleared the room. It was nearly midday, but the room was dark, the heavy curtains drawn over the windows. The
door to the veranda was opened a crack to allow for a little light, and it
showed Meryam was terribly weak, quivering and confused. Hardly a surprise
after what she'd been through.

"Get me up," she rasped.

"You should eat first," Ramahd replied, "regain a bit of strength."

"I'll take food"—she struggled to sit up, grunting from the simple
effort—"but if I don't feel the sun on my face soon, I'm likely to order someone's head off. Get me up Ramahd, or it might be yours."

He would never admit to it, but it felt good to hear her biting humor. He
lifted her into a sitting position, then carried her to the far side of the room,
using the toe of his boot to lever the door open. Sunlight crashed down onto
the rich red carpet as he maneuvered her out and onto the veranda. He set
her carefully in a padded chair beneath a trellis choked with white jasmine,

then ordered food for them both. They sat for a while, drinking hard cider and nibbling on wine-cured olives and long mustard-seed breadsticks they dipped into saffron-laced honey. Meryam ate in silence, lost in thought. A thousand questions fought to find voice, but Ramahd was so glad to see her awake and with an appetite that he let her alone.

Soon Meryam was looking better, and she finally spoke. "Bring me the vials, Ramahd."

He knew immediately what she meant. "You're sure you should do this so soon?"

She nodded, chewing noisily around an olive before spitting the stone out onto a waiting plate. "We must know more about this Brama."

He returned to Meryam's apartments and retrieved an ornate wooden box from a bureau by her bed. When he delivered it to her, she set it on the table and tilted the hinged lid back. Within were three glass vials cradled in red velvet. She lifted the one on the right and pulled its stopper free. The red liquid within, wine mixed with blood, sloshed as she tipped it back and drank it.

She barely had time to stopper the vial and set it back in the box before her eyelids began to flutter. The three vials were from three other blood magi in Sharakhai. The four of them—the three whose blood resided within those vials and Meryam—had decided long ago to trade their blood in order to protect one another from the Kings, from other magi, from anyone who might hinder them.

Meryam was doing so now, speaking to one of the three. Their identity remained hidden to Ramahd. He'd asked their names many times, but Meryam had always denied him. "None of them are open about their nature, Ramahd. This is a secret I cannot share, even with you."

As the desert breeze tugged at Meryam's dark hair, her lips moved. He heard the barest whisper from her, but he could discern no words, nor even the language she was speaking. She was conversing with the other mage about Brama, the threat he posed, he assumed. After nearly an hour, Meryam's eyes sharpened again and she sat higher in her seat. She immediately took a glass of water and downed the lot, then stared at the horizon with a calculating look, all but ignoring Ramahd.

"Come, Meryam. Out with it."

She glanced at him, nodding with a surprisingly contrite look. "I'd heard rumor of the Tattered Prince several years ago. A few magi had run afoul of him, apparently. At the time, I had no chances to look further—we had other things to occupy our minds—but I see now I should have looked deeper." She motioned to the vials in the box. "When he first became known to the others, he simply appeared. At first they thought him a magi like any other. It happens often enough. Magi are drawn to this city from distant lands. They thought him likely to leave as quickly as he'd come, but when he remained, they grew concerned and attempted to track him down. They learned that he was young—very young, in fact, to be so powerful. They found nothing more than this, however, for those who tried to follow his scent through blood were found dead within days of reaching out to him. Those who attempted to track his physical whereabouts disappeared."

The horrible scars over Brama's face came back to Ramahd, the raw power within the sapphire he wore. "Is he dangerous to our cause?"

She looked intense, as though she'd been struggling with that question since she woke. "Like the others, I thought it best to let a sleeping dog lie. He's never harmed anyone who hasn't come for him directly. Now that we *have*, though . . ."

"He sensed us the moment Tariq arrived."

"Aye, Ramahd, he did."

Far out in the desert, beyond the cityscape of Sharakhai, a cloud of amber dust lifted as if shaped by the hands of the elder gods. Such clouds were often an indicator that a larger storm was brewing, but even as Ramahd watched, the dust began to settle. Ramahd poured himself more hard cider from the glazed pitcher, then offered it to Meryam. She declined with a raise of her hand. "Well," he said after downing a healthy swallow, "I'd be insulted if he thought us too inconsequential to bother with. As addled as he was, he likely couldn't tell who we were, or where."

She dipped one finger into the remains of her cider and ran it over the rim of her glass, drawing a note that sounded strangely pure in this uncertain world. "Did you feel it, Ramahd? The deeper presence in that gem?"

"I did." The memories came unbidden, made him dizzy all over again. The gem had seemed bottomless. Boundless. A well that led to another world.

"And what did it remind you of?"

"An ehrekh," Ramahd immediately replied.

"An ehrekh." Meryam turned away from the desert to look at Ramahd, her sunken eyes as intense as he'd ever seen them. "Hiding, or trapped, perhaps ripe for harvest."

Her tone, and the implications of her words, rippled outward like the scent of war on the wind. "We're lucky to be alive, Meryam, and you would have us go after Brama and his gem?"

"Had he been more out of sorts, we might have taken it from him then."

"*Taken* it? Meryam, we barely escaped Guhldrathen. You would tempt fate in hope of controlling another?"

"It is the very threat of Guhldrathen's power that drives me. What better way to control it than with another of its kind?" For the first time in ages, he saw fear in her eyes, in the way her lips pinched, downturned at the edges.

"You are a queen now, Meryam. You have more to think about than your thirst for revenge. We need to find out what's happening here in Sharakhai and deal with it before it threatens Qaimir."

When Meryam didn't respond, Ramahd thought he'd made a mistake by mentioning their homeland. She rarely responded well to pressure. All too often she fought him simply to fight, logic be damned, but this time there was no biting reply. "There is wisdom in what you say. We have much to worry about."

Relief flooded through him. "Three Kings," he said, hoping to move away from the topic of ehrekh as quickly as possible. "Three Kings' names were written on his palm."

Meryam's eyes searched his. She hadn't remembered, but as he watched recognition lit within her. "Ihsan. Zeheb . . ."

"And Kiral," Ramahd finished. "And Tariq mentioned caches, asking Brama where they could be found."

"Their palaces?" she asked.

"Most likely, yes. The question is, caches of what?"

"Very good, Ramahd." Her eyes were suddenly alive. "The answer to that question will tell us why the Host have been maneuvering so boldly in Sharakhai. It will tell us what Hamzakiir meant to do after he left us, for as sure as the sun shines brightly over the desert, he's guiding Ishaq and his son, Macide, toward those caches."

Ramahd stood and began pacing beneath the shade of the trellis. "To risk so much, it would have to be something vitally important to the Kings. It won't be money. And if they speak of caches, it isn't something that will threaten the lives of the Kings. Not directly."

He realized how quiet Meryam was. When he turned to her, he saw that she'd changed. No longer did she slouch in her seat, nursing her ravaged body. She sat up straight, hands clasped in her lap, no daughter of a King, but the Queen of Qaimir. And she was staring at him with a look of such intensity Ramahd stopped his pacing and faced her.

"We need to know," she said. "The very fate of Qaimir rests on it."

"I may be able to help. When Tariq was rummaging through Brama's things, he mentioned Rasul. Do you remember?" Meryam nodded, keenly interested. "Kiral, King of Kings, has a grandson named Rasul. He is young, yet. He's seen only eighteen summers, and yet Kiral favors him. He's been seen in the courts since he was twelve, and Kiral has clearly been grooming him to stand by his side as his vizir."

"Ramahd, I'm impressed!"

"Don't be. I thought it wise to look into him while you were recovering. Rasul is smart. He's ambitious. He's extremely loyal to Kiral and Sharakhai."

"And yet," Meryam said.

"And yet, there have been whispers. Years ago, rumors surfaced that he visited some of the most exclusive drug dens in Sharakhai. No sooner had the rumors reached Sharakhai's upper crust than his glaring absence from those drugs dens was noted. All seemed well for a year or more, until Rasul was taken ill. The official word was that he had been taken by the white plague that had, if you'll recall, a small but contained outbreak that winter."

"I'm guessing our Rasul had a miraculous recovery."

Ramahd smiled. "Top marks to the queen. This last bit of information was difficult to get. One of the maids apparently reported bloody sheets being collected from Rasul's rooms in Tauriyat. They were burned, a common enough thing when the taint of the white plague is about, but the blood was from vomit."

Meryam frowned—intrigued, he was sure, and perhaps vexed she hadn't already solved the riddle. "And?" she said calmly.

"Bloody vomit is not a symptom of the white plague. It *is*, however, a symptom of black lotus addiction. I'd consider the information suspect under normal circumstances, and it only partially supports our supposition that

Rasul is a lotus addict, but when coupled with the earlier rumor and our visit to Brama's keep, I'm willing to bet more than a few rahl that Rasul had fallen to the lure of the lotus then, and fell to it again only recently, when Brama, conveniently for Osman, came across his path."

"And what of it?" Meryam said, vexed now. "You've clearly formulated a plan, so out with it."

"You have yet to meet with the Kings in your new role. I reckon it would be proper for you to do so now."

Meryam caught on. "Kiral would likely not come. Not to a first meeting. Ihsan will represent the Kings. A few other Kings may come. But we might arrange for Rasul to attend."

Ramahd nodded. "I've begun formulating the list of stand-ins for all twelve Kings. I'll stress how important it is to her highness that their seconds be present if the Kings are unavailable."

For the first time since they'd reached the veranda, Meryam seemed to relax a bit. "And if we find ourselves alone in a room with young Rasul? What then?"

Ramahd smiled. "Why, we tell him the truth."

The scene in the Qaimiri embassy house's ballroom was a grand one. As expected, King Ihsan, as Sharakhai's chief of state, had come. It was little surprise that King Beşir, Sharakhai's master of the city's finances, had joined him. But strangely, King Sukru, the Reaping King, a man who rarely bothered with social functions of any sort, had accepted their invitation as well.

The list of seconds Meryam and Ramahd had suggested to the Kings in their invitations had worked perfectly. The Kings had all sent replies and sent the men and women requested, except for Onur, who hadn't bothered to reply to the invitation at all. *Which is just as well,* Ramahd thought, *for there is a man who infects anything he touches.*

In the week since Meryam woke from her ordeal, she had transformed herself, at least as much as a woman could who was malnourished as she was. She had eaten properly. She had put on a few pounds, which, as emaciated as she'd been, had made her look merely gaunt instead of skeletal. Another woman might have appeared weak before the Kings, but Meryam stood tall, and she had an indomitable gleam in her eye, the one Ramahd knew all too well by now, the one that dared anyone to look upon her and call her easy prey.

Interestingly, Juvaan Xin-Lei was in attendance. The ambassadors from Malasan and the Thousand Territories of Kundhun had been invited, but the invitation to Mirea's ambassador, Juvaan himself, had purposefully been lost. Most times, Juvaan would have used it as an insult to wield against Qaimir at some future date, but in this instance, when he'd learned of the reception for Meryam, a servant had been sent immediately to "request clarification." Apologies had been made in abundance, owing to a servant who had taken ill and thereby lost the invitation that had been meant for Juvaan himself. Whether Juvaan believed it or not, it was telling that he thought it important that his presence, and that of his queen, be felt here.

Meryam handled her meeting with the Kings deftly, speaking with them in turn, making it seem as though each were her sole concern. She spoke with the Kings' seconds as well, talking of Qaimir and the long history of cooperation with Sharakhai, along with her most genuine hope that their prosperous past could continue well into the future. And why shouldn't it? There was trouble in the desert, and there was trouble in Qaimir, but what could two kingdoms not do together if their rulers clasped hands?

Largely, Ramahd let her be. She was handling herself well, and he didn't wish to put his clumsy feet into a dance where they weren't welcome. He relegated himself to wandering the crowd, offering a dance here and there, speaking with those in the Kings' retinue and rarely venturing to exchange more than pleasantries with the Kings or their seconds.

But he watched. Especially Rasul, who had come dressed in a brilliant silk khalat of forest green and aged ivory. He was jaunty, smiling broadly with everyone he met, talking loudly, with more than a passing resemblance to his grandfather, the King of Kings. His wife, a stunning young woman wearing a matching dress—ivory with tasteful accents of jade—was on his arm, every bit as adept at juggling a conversation as he was. They were, Ramahd had to admit, representing King Kiral admirably, but it was that very fact, his utter control over this situation, that convinced Ramahd he had a chance to pull this off; men who stood to lose the most were often the most malleable.

Dinner was superb. Roast amberlark stuffed with celery, water chestnuts, and truffled rice. A salad of smoked palm hearts, candied dates, and a lemon sherry vinaigrette. Rosewater iced cream over a warmed tart of pickled ginger and pears. Twelve courses of the best Qaimiri cuisine to be had in the desert, with more than a few traditional Sharakhani dishes to honor those from the House of Kings.

When the dinner was complete, Meryam made a short speech and a toast to Sharakhai of the sort any ruler new to the throne of Qaimir would make to the Kings of a powerful desert city state. Ramahd hardly listened. He was watching the reactions. Ihsan smiled politely, nodding at just the right moments. Beşir, a quiet man with a long face, seemed bored but sat through the speech well enough. Sukru, however, watched Meryam with barely contained disgust. Why he'd accepted the invitation Ramahd had no earthly idea. He looked like he'd rather eat grubs than suffer through a social affair like this.

When the dinner was finished and the food cleared away, Ramahd made his way through the crowd. "I'm afraid your wife may be a while," Ramahd said to Rasul, whose wife was speaking to Meryam, the signal Ramahd and Meryam had agreed upon to approach the young lord.

Rasul raised his glass and nodded. "Lord Amansir, I'm glad we could find some time to talk."

"As am I." Ramahd raised his glass in return and motioned Rasul to a dark corner of the room. "Changes are afoot for Qaimir, it seems."

Rasul followed Ramahd to the corner, then raised his glass again. "Indeed. My condolences to you and yours." They clinked their glasses and drank in honor of King Aldouan's passing. "The life you and your queen have led these past months! I could scarcely believe it when I heard the tale."

The official story was that Aldouan had died of a poor heart on a voyage to the desert. He'd wanted to see it, had ordered it, in fact, but the heat had proved too much for him.

"Well," Ramahd said. "Time marches on, does it not? And while we in Qaimir have changes ahead, I trust it won't be the same for Sharakhai."

"Gods willing," Rasul said, again raising his glass and taking another swallow.

Ramahd, however, did not return the gesture. "In truth, my good Lord, there is something I hoped to discuss with you this evening. It's rather"—he glanced toward King Ihsan—"delicate."

Rasul paused, his curiosity plain in the narrowing of his eyes, the set of his suddenly knitted brow. "Go on."

"There's trouble brewing in Sharakhai. The entire city knows it."

"The Al'afwa Khadar?" Rasul laughed. "Rest assured, they'll be dealt with in good time, as will all in the desert who stand against the will of the Kings."

"A common refrain, and an apt one at most times, to be sure, but I wonder if the undeniable strength of Sharakhai will hold if they are betrayed from within."

Rasul's smile crumbled. "Do you have evidence of such?"

"I do."

"Then tell me."

"A state secret was leaked"—Ramahd spoke lightly, as if he were recounting the story of a day sail on the Austral Sea—"a secret so dear to the Kings they would kill for it. They would go to *war* for it. And the man who leaked it—"

Rasul swallowed.

"—was you, my good Lord."

Rasul's face went stone-like. Just then, two from Rasul's retinue—coxcombs, the both of them—approached. Both stopped when they saw Rasul wave them away, and moved stiffly toward the smiling form of Basilio instead. Rasul returned his attention to Ramahd. "Now tell me what you mean before I draw the knife from my belt and drive it through your heart."

"You know the Tattered Prince?"

Now Rasul's face went white as bleached bone. "I . . . Who . . ."

"Or perhaps you know him as the Torn Man. He helps those who've developed an . . . unhealthy fondness for black lotus. I believe he has recently helped you. The only question is: Why would he have aided you, of all people?"

Rasul stared like a man standing on an ice floe drifting out to sea.

"The son of Kiral himself," Ramahd went on. "One who might have access to information as dear to Sharakhai as anyone but the Kings themselves would possess."

"I don't know what you've heard, Lord Amansir." His voice quavered as he spoke. "I may have dabbled in smoke, that's common knowledge, but that hardly means—"

"The man who helped you is a collector of information. He helps those in Sharakhai who've fallen under the influence. But he does so with the help of a gem. A sapphire. Have you seen it?" Rasul only stared, pulse pounding in his neck. "No doubt you've felt it as well. He took the urge from you, did he not? Took it into himself? Likely you paid a handsome amount for it. What he didn't tell you is that he lingers long after the ritual is done. A part of him remains, watching through your eyes, listening through your ears."

"He could not."

"He did. I'm telling you this as a *friend*, Lord Rasul. I'm telling you because neither my queen nor I have any love for the Al'afwa Khadar. *That* is common knowledge. And through you, the Torn Man has found a way into the House of Kings. He has found a terrible secret."

"*What* secret?"

And now it came to it. The gambit he and Meryam had agreed upon all hinged on just how scared Rasul would be at the news that his indiscretions had been discovered. He seemed not merely scared, but terrified, but that didn't mean he would share his secret. Ramahd gave a meaningful glance toward the Kings, who were listening to Meryam recount their carefully constructed story of the death of her father. "The caches," Ramahd said under his breath. "It is known that they're secreted in your grandfather's palace, as well as King Ihsan's and King Zeheb's."

Rasul closed his eyes. He nearly stumbled, but Ramahd smiled and clapped him on the shoulder affectionately, as if they were sharing a humorous tale. "Don't lose hope," Ramahd said. "There is reason to believe the information will not reach the Al'afwa Khadar."

"How? How can you be assured of such a thing?"

"Because we've intercepted the man who was to deliver it to them."

The haunted expression on Rasul's face betrayed the fear roiling inside him, but there was some small amount of hope in his voice. "You have him?"

"We do. But we don't know if he's told anyone else. We might take him to King Cahil, but in the questioning I'm afraid your indiscretions would become clear."

"I—" Whatever Rasul was about to say died on his lips.

Ramahd gave him a soft smile. "I've smelled the lotus's scent. I know its taste. Believe me when I say I'm familiar with its lure. It traps a man, does it not? And it grates that a man such as you, respected by all, would be brought low by such a thing."

Rasul swallowed. He seemed to choose his words with the sort of care a chef might give his ingredients before a Beht Revahl feast. "And why would you care, Lord Amansir?"

"We are allies, are we not?"

"Come. There's more to this than being allies, fast or not."

Ramahd paused, just enough to make one think he was considering how much to reveal. "My Queen would be wroth with me for admitting it, but we need all the allies we can get in Sharakhai."

"Go on."

"You see"—he nodded almost imperceptibly toward Meryam and caught her glancing his way, but it was so fast no one but him would have seen it—"our position in Qaimir is perhaps not as solid as we might like it to be. But were we to return to Almadan with a nod from the King of Kings himself, it would go a long way to securing her the throne."

"And you think *my* favor will secure it for you?"

Ramahd laughed. "My good lord, it couldn't hurt!"

At last, the indecision and distrust in Rasul seemed to melt away. He took in a deep breath and nodded. "What do you propose?"

"Do you see the beautiful young woman over my shoulder standing in the corner?"

Rasul looked. Then nodded.

"Her name is Amaryllis. When the night is done, do not return to the House of Kings. Take a coach to the Wheel. Amaryllis will be waiting for you along its western edge." Rasul looked uncertainly toward the corner. He was a man adrift, the currents dragging him further and further from the shore. When he'd nodded, Ramahd continued, "We'll take you to Tariq to discuss the matter with him."

"And then?"

"When we know all that he knows, I'll take care of the rest."

Rasul considered, but not for long. "Very well."

It was then that Ramahd noticed King Ihsan watching his conversation with Rasul. They'd spoken long enough. Perhaps too long. But, Alu's golden light, Rasul appeared to have taken the bait. That more than made up for any small amount of suspicion he might have raised from the Kings.

"Fear not," Ramahd said as he walked past Rasul. "All will end well."

Chapter 48

IHSAN LAY NEXT TO NAYYAN AS MORNING light broke through the white fog that lay over the desert. He could see it from his bed through the nearby doorway, an echo of the chill of winter in the desert. It reminded him of the winters he'd spent in Tsitsian, the interminable snow, the howling wind. He shivered at the thought.

He lay on his side, running his fingers over Nayyan's form. She'd come in late last night. He'd stirred, more exhausted than he'd been in many months, but when she'd lain next to him and ran her hands over his naked form, he'd woken fully. They'd made love, simply, beautifully, without a word spoken, and then both of them had fallen asleep.

"I'm cold," Nayyan said, pulling the blankets back up.

He pulled them back down. "It isn't so cold as that. And I would look upon you." His fingers roamed, touching the skin of her thigh, her hip, the curve of her stomach. He cupped her breast. Leaned in and sucked her nipple, which was taut from the cold. He warmed it as he could, and her breath came faster, but instead of turning to him as she'd done last night, instead of kissing him as she'd done in the throes of their passion, she took his hand away from her breast, pulled it to her stomach, and pressed it against her belly. Then she spread his fingers and pressed again.

She held it there. Waiting. Her heart beating. Her chest rising and falling with her breath. She stared not at him but at the painted ceiling of his bedroom. *Their* room these past many weeks. She was waiting for him to say something. Fool that he was, he didn't understand why until she pressed his hand more fully against her belly.

His first instinct was to recoil, to pull his hand away. He'd had a child once. A daughter. Ferrah. It meant *child of beneficence* in the old tongue. How his heart had sung when her hand was in his. How his ears rejoiced merely to hear her speak. She had grown into a beautiful woman and had given her heart to one of the thirteenth tribe. Their marriage had come shortly before the conflict with the desert tribes. When the two of them, Ferrah and Abdul-Azim, had been married in the desert, it had been a grand affair, with thirteen Kings and their thirteen queens and all their houses joining for a vast celebration, days of games and feasts on ships that sailed the dunes of the shifting amber sea. What joyous days those had been, even if Abdul-Azim had not been his first choice as a son. He brought joy to Ferrah's heart, and that had been enough.

And then the shadow of war had built on the horizon. The desert tribes had banded together, unforgiving of the way Sharakhai had grown, how it prospered, how its people had abandoned the ways of its ancestors. They called for higher tribute, and when it wasn't given, they called for blood.

Ihsan had worked so hard. He'd built the city, along with the other Kings, from a glorified caravanserai to a bustling metropolis, and he wasn't about to give it up. But Ferrah. Gods how he'd wronged her. When the desert tribes gathered for war, the way ahead looked bleak. The caravanserais were taken, one by one, and then the tribes closed in on Sharakhai. An endless sea of swords and spears assailed the walls, and though the city's defenses held, all knew the walls would soon fail.

And then Kiral said he'd found a way. He called them all to his audience chamber in Eventide. All but Sehid-Alaz, who had never loved Kiral, and whom Kiral in turn despised. "Tulathan came to me in the night," he said. "She offered me—she offered *us*—a way to avoid the bloodshed that lies ahead. If we come to her, she will deliver us not only Sharakhai, but the whole of the desert, until such time as we tire of its amber waves."

"At what price?" Ihsan had asked.

"But one of our number," Kiral had replied.

"One tribe," Ihsan had corrected.

To this Kiral merely nodded, as if he couldn't even bring himself to say it. The words fell over the gathering like a cold winter gale. *But one of our number,* the words had implied, *and the rest could live.* And it was all too clear which of their number Kiral meant to give. Tribe Malakhed. Iri's Chosen. Of whom Abdul-Azim was one.

Some of the Kings had quickly agreed. Sukru first. Then Külaşan and Mesut. Yusam followed, as did Zeheb and Beşir and Azad. Only Ihsan himself, Onur, Cahil, and Husamettín remained. If only Ihsan had said something sooner. All had watched Husamettín, knowing he would be the deciding vote. But Husamettín was a man of numbers, a man of calculation, always weighing the odds before making decisions. Ihsan should have known his answer well before he opened his mouth. He should have spoken against the King of Kings.

By the time Husamettín had nodded his head, throwing in his lot with Kiral and the rest, it had been too late. Soon Ihsan, Cahil, and Onur had all agreed. Ihsan prayed Kiral was merely making up a story to give them heart.

He hadn't been, though. That night, when the moons were full, he'd called upon the gods at the top of Tauriyat. And they had come. Tulathan first, her silver eyes alight. Then golden Rhia, her sister. Dark Goezhen had come next, twin tails swishing through the moonlit air. Then Thaash and Yerinde and Bakhi. A tribunal. They'd stood before the Kings, hearing their plea from the mouth of the King of Kings.

"Give us the means to drive the disloyal from the shores of Sharakhai," he'd said. "Give us the means to storm over the desert to the very mountains that contain it."

And when the gods had demanded blood, where could they turn but the thirteenth tribe? Those who had come to Sharakhai last. Those who had the closest ties to the desert still. Those who challenged Kiral's right to rule at every step, every turn.

Ihsan had been a coward, watching as the gods had granted their dark appeal. He'd tried to shelter Ferrah from it, but she had fallen into a dark depression following Beht Ihman, then taken her own life in the night, a knife to her wrists while sitting on Ihsan's own throne. He'd gone to the room alone, unable to face her with anyone watching, even his wife, Ferrah's mother.

All of this washed over him as Nayyan held his hand to her belly. "A child," he said, caressing her skin as the sun began to break the fog over the city.

"A child," she echoed.

Ihsan already knew it would be a girl—it could be no other way—and he knew he would not fail her as he'd failed Ferrah. "How the sun and stars will shine on the day of her birth."

Nayyan turned to him at last, stared into his eyes. "I wondered if you might not love another child." She knew some of what'd had befallen Ferrah. Not all, but enough. She wiped tears from his eyes, tears he hadn't even realized had gathered.

"I was not looking for it," he said after a time, "but those who look for miracles never find them. They come unbidden, at only the right moments."

"It is a sign," she said.

"What is?"

And she laughed, a deep, resonant affair, a window into her soul. "I came in so late. I meant to tell you, but I wanted to wait until you were awake so we could rejoice together."

"Tell me what?"

"The elixir, my love. I've found it. With the help of the scholars—Taram, especially, but Süleiman and Farid as well."

Ihsan hardly knew what to say. "You're certain?"

Her smile was the most beautiful thing he could ever remember seeing. "*Well* certain." She took his hand and pressed his forefinger to a light scar that ran along her right forearm. It was long as a knife, but pale, a shade lighter than the rest of her skin. It looked years old, but Ihsan knew the mark of scars mended by use of Azad's elixirs.

He continued to run his hand over the scar. "You did this to yourself?"

"I had to."

A vision of Ferrah, wrists slit, blood pooling at the base of his throne, swam before him. "With our child inside of you?"

"I had to know, Ihsan. I had to know."

He sat up. "You could have died, Nayyan!"

"Taram was tested first. He asked to be allowed to do it. But I couldn't leave it to him."

He grabbed a fistful of her hair and shook her. "You foolish woman!"

"Ihsan, you're hurting me!"

"You will *never* endanger our child again, do you hear me?"

She slapped his face, then punched him in the throat. When his grip loosened, she rolled back off the bed, naked, and when he came for her, she grabbed his wrist, lifted it, and punched him hard in the kidney. Pain blossomed. His body curled unbidden around the punch. He tried to grab for her with his free hand, but this time she punched him like the Blade Maiden she was.

He fell back on the bed, ears ringing. Nayyan straddled him. She gripped his head and shook him until he opened his eyes and looked at her.

"I know about your daughter, my Lord King. I know more than you think. It will not happen with ours. Do you hear me? We will take this city like a raging fire. The fire will spread, farther and farther, until we have all the Great Shangazi in our grip. Perhaps we will look beyond, you and I. Perhaps we'll travel the sand with our daughter. But by then it will be up to us and us only. Not other Kings. Not some bitch queen of Qaimir or Mirea. Not the mad King of Malasan nor the thousand crowns of Kundhun. Us and us alone."

Tears were streaming from the corners of his eyes, trailing into his hair. Nayyan was beautiful, but the only thing he could see in that moment was Ferrah, eyes lifeless yet somehow staring deeply into his soul.

She shook him again until his eyes met hers. "The elixir needed to be perfect, and now it is, Ihsan." She kissed him. "We are ready."

He nodded slowly. "We are ready."

She took his hands, both of them, and placed them on her belly. "We are ready."

Chapter 49

T HE DAY AFTER THE BEHT FIHRAL celebration was the most difficult day of sailing the *Javelin* had endured yet. A cool wind blew in the morning, ominous after so many days of heat. Barely an hour later, a storm struck. The captain advised Sümeya to find high ground or risk having their runners buried in the blowing sand, but Sümeya steadfastly insisted they sail on. All had the veils of their turbans wrapped tightly across their faces. Many who might have chosen lighter clothes instead wore tunics with long sleeves to ward their skin against the biting wind.

Çeda worried over just how much Sümeya remembered of the night before. But other than her orders being given more crisply than usual, there was no difference in the Sümeya she'd known these past few months. She was First Warden once more. Whether she remembered and was suppressing the revelations of the previous night or had truly forgotten, Çeda had no idea.

Near noon the ship began to slow, a strange feeling indeed after such smooth sailing during the past ten days. The deck seemed to sink beneath Çeda's feet. She tipped forward as the ship slowed.

"Slip-sand!" someone called.

"Grab hold!" replied the captain.

And everyone did. They'd been warned. The ship's crew had drilled the proper reaction again just this morning. But Çeda still had no idea how quickly a ship of this size could come to a halt. As Çeda shot one arm through the rope of a nearby shroud, the *Javelin* slowed further and then, like a child might do with dolls on a toy ship, the deck seemed to be pulled out from underneath her. All about the deck, coils of rigging rope slithered away like a host of snakes. The masts creaked as the sails leaned forward and snapped back, making the canvas thrum. Something above gave with a loud crack.

Some of the crew immediately moved about the ship, reefing the sails while the captain shouted, "To the sand! Quickly!"

The ship shuddered as it came to a full stop. The crew and the Maidens wasted no time. Two dozen souls dropped from the sides of the ship and headed for the prow, lining up to pull at two great ropes anchored beneath the bowsprit. The sand carried on the air was so thick the ship looked as though it were being swallowed by an efrit. The sand beneath Çeda's feet grew soft at times, forcing her to churn her legs or get pulled down. The dunes were shifting as she watched. If they allowed the *Javelin* to be caught in a trough for more than a few minutes, the runners would be overwhelmed, effectively grounding the ship until the sand passed. Some ships were half buried and took days to dig out. Other ships had been overwhelmed entirely, dragged down and lost to the swells of shifting sand, only to be revealed years or decades later when the wind hollowed the dunes in that part of the desert once more.

"Heave! Ho!" a crewman shouted. "Heave! Ho!"

And heave Çeda did. There was something about a storm so bad as this, and the thought of being lost in it, dragged beneath the grasping surface, that made her desperate to see them free. She could see the same look in the crew, and Emre. Even Sümeya looked like she regretted her decision to press on, but there was nothing for it now.

Inch by inch they towed the ship, dozens pulling, three crewmen at the end of each of the two ropes stabbing a great towing spear into the sand and levering backward to help free the skimwood runners.

When they finally pulled the ship out of the slip-sand, only the mainsail was still unfurled, and only halfway, so that they wouldn't lose control when the towing had done its work. Even so, the ship gained speed quickly. Two by two, everyone who'd jumped down ran alongside the ship and climbed up rope ladders to the deck.

Three more times that day the *Javelin* became stuck, but none so bad as that first. By the time night was nearing, the storm had finally begun to die down. They found no good rocky ground to moor near, but the captain, surveying the way ahead, declared it safe enough to stop for the night so long as the guards were careful to watch for the shifting dunes.

Çeda breathed a silent prayer for how quickly the day had passed. It meant she hadn't had to face Sümeya. Or Emre. Not directly, in any case. Not alone.

As she and the other Blade Maidens settled down for the night in their cabin at the fore of the ship, though, she finally had a chance to think about what Sümeya had said the night before. It nagged at her, so much so that, even though she'd rarely felt so exhausted, she woke in the hours before dawn.

All of the Maidens except Yndris were light sleepers, but none woke as Çeda pulled her blankets back and stood. The wind scoured the ship, the shrill sound masking the creak of the floorboards as she crept toward the door. She left as quietly as she could and treaded her way along the passageway to the stern, where Emre's cabin was situated just next to the captain's. The door was unlocked. She slipped inside with little more than a soft click and a groan of the deck boards to find him sitting up in his bunk, eyes wide in the golden light of the small candle by his bedside. She'd surprised him, but he relaxed as she entered and closed the door behind her.

His cabin was small, but there was enough space for her to kneel next to his bed. He turned over in his bunk so that he faced her. Though the air coming through the porthole was cool, he wore no shirt, and from the waist down was covered only by a thin sheet.

"You always were warm as a bloody ox," she whispered.

"And you were always cold as well water," he shot back.

They both smiled.

His scent filled the cabin. By the gods, how she'd missed it, and so many of the small things about how they used to live with one another. Their thrown-together meals. Walking to the bazaar to share a loaf of Tehla's bread. The songs they'd sing as the musicians in the neighborhood played. All of it gone now, perhaps never to return. Part of her wished to relive those days with him, but instead she put her hands in her lap and said, "We need to talk."

"Çeda, I'm sorry."

She waved his concern away, knowing he was talking about his night with Melis. "That isn't why I've come."

"It was a joke and it was cruel and—"

Her next words caught in her throat. "A joke?"

"When I was talking with Melis and Kameyl the other day, they saw how you were watching us. Kameyl joked that one of them should take me off to the desert, if only to . . ."

"If only to what?"

"She said she could see it in you. In us. That we wanted to be together. I laughed and said you'd left those days behind, but Melis insisted we should find out one way or the other. She'd ask me to go with her and thought you'd object and take me yourself. Kameyl laughed and said no, that you'd stew in your stubbornness for an age before saying a word against it."

For a moment, Çeda could only stare. *They'd been laughing at me. Even Emre.* "And what did *you* think?"

He shrugged, suddenly very interested in a stray thread on his woolen blanket. "I thought—"

"Never mind. It doesn't matter. That isn't why I've come."

"I hoped you would object," he blurted, "but I knew Kameyl was right. I still shouldn't have done it, though. It was cruel. We stayed only a short while, and then came back, but you'd already left with Sümeya."

Gods, am I so transparent? "Think nothing of it."

Emre took her hand as he had along the Trough. "Nothing happened."

"I don't care."

"I mean it. Nothing happened." He stroked her knuckles with his thumb. It felt good, but also wrong.

"Emre, stop apologizing."

"I'm not." Even in the dim light, she could see the color in his cheeks. "Well, I am, but—"

"Emre, this *isn't why I've come*." She snatched her hand back. "This is important."

He blinked. Licked his lips, clearly embarrassed. But then the look was gone, as if their conversation had never happened. She knew he was good at masking his feelings, but she was surprised to see him do it so quickly, and so very effectively, with *her*.

"You're right," he said. "What is it?"

"Last night," she began, "Sümeya revealed something to me." She continued, telling him everything, from their swordplay to Sümeya's confessions about Nayyan to Sümeya's advances. Surprisingly, the fact that she and Sümeya had kissed was not the hardest thing to speak of. It was the struggle between herself and the asir, how close Sümeya had been to dying, how tragic it was to send the asir away despite Çeda's promises to help them. But she moved beyond it and returned to the night's biggest revelation. Nayyan. "Sümeya said an assassin's blade took Nayyan from her side. She implied Nayyan is now posing as one of the Kings."

Eyes distant, Emre took a moment to digest it all. "Could it be? Ahya?"

Çeda nodded. "She killed one of them. I'm sure of it."

Emre glanced up as the deck creaked under a fierce gust of wind. He spoke very softly now. "A King dead I could believe. But to then *disguise* a Maiden as one of them? It makes no sense. Everyone would know."

"The gifts of the gods protect them, Emre. You think it impossible that they could conceal her nature?"

Emre shrugged. "I suppose it's *possible*. Which King, though?"

"I met all of them in the Sun Palace just before accepting my blade from King Husamettín. None of them had been wearing a veil or mask. So it could be any of them. But in truth that isn't what's bothering me. It's the other mysteries of that night and the night that came before it. My mother was so fateful. She told Dardzada she'd gone to find the silver trove." Before Emre could ask, she continued. "The poems, Emre. Tulathan read one for each of the Kings on the night of Beht Ihman. She hoped to find them that night."

"Do you think it's real?"

"I don't know. I need to think on it more, ask Zaïde about it when we return. What interests me more is that she returned at all. Why? And why was she so concerned with finding a place for me to stay?"

"You said it yourself. She escaped, but thought they might find Ahya and you together. She went to remove suspicion, to save you."

"But Emre, she was *allowed* to do it." She'd been worrying at this mystery since leaving Dardzada's, but now that she was able to voice it aloud, to finally *speak* with someone about it, more and more ideas were rushing toward her. "Who would have done so, Emre? Who would have let a woman leave when she clearly meant the Kings harm?"

"Perhaps they *didn't* know. It might have been your father, whichever King he was. Maybe he loved Ahya. Perhaps she was caught and he couldn't bring himself to kill her, so he let her go."

"That's rather convenient. The very next night a King is killed and a Maiden put in his place?"

"Then what?"

"Ihsan," Çeda said, staring at the hull planks. "The Honey-tongued King. He might have found her. Gods, he might have laid a trap for her, spreading lies about the silver trove to see who would come to find it. He might have whispered his honeyed words in her ear and told her to return."

"But he wouldn't have done that unless—"

Çeda looked at him and saw in his eyes that they'd come to the same conclusion. "Unless he *wanted* her to kill a King. He might have chosen Azad himself."

"Goezhen's sweet kiss, Çeda, could it be?"

Çeda shrugged. "Why not? They are men, and men scrabble and scratch and claw, even those who wear crowns. *Especially* men who wear crowns. Men who've lived for centuries, building grudges and burying hatred along the way. What I'm really wondering is whether he knew about *me*."

Emre considered this. "It seems likely, doesn't it? If he had a chance to speak to Ahya for any length of time, what are the chances he wouldn't have asked about it?"

"And if he knew about me, he likely allowed my entry into the Maidens as well. There's a chance he knew about *Külaşan*. Or hoped for it, at least."

"Do you think he foresaw you becoming a Maiden?"

Çeda's mind raced. "Who can tell? Perhaps King Yusam is in league with him. And why not? If one could plot to overthrow the other Kings, why can't two? It seems unlikely that Ihsan, even with his gifts, could stand on his own. He'd need allies, and what better ally than Yusam?"

"And your hand is assigned to Yusam. Have you seen them talking?"

"No, but they wouldn't be so foolish as to speak in front of us."

"Gods, Çeda, he might aid us, for a time at least."

"Ihsan aid *us*? As well make a bargain with a black laugher, Emre."

"The enemy of my enemy."

"Is in the end no friend at all. Not truly." But then she remembered Zaïde's confession in the savaşam, that she had the ear of one of the Kings, that he might offer his protection. Could it be Ihsan? Could Zaïde be in league with him? It made sense . . .

"What is it?" Emre asked, noticing her hesitation.

The thoughts were too half formed. She needed time to reflect, so she said, "You're right. Let me think on this awhile. Ihsan could be a valuable piece on the board."

The entire ship creaked from stem to stern, a strong gust of wind, pressing, howling. A river of fine amber dust drifted down by the candle's flame, creating a diffused glow that dissipated a moment later. She prepared to stand, but stopped when Emre said, "You could stay awhile."

She thought of his kiss along the Spear with the House of Kings watching them from atop Tauriyat. And then she thought of him walking away with Melis. She believed what he'd said, that he regretted it, yet still she couldn't get the image of him leaving the fireside, hand in hand with Melis, out of her head. "The sun will be coming up soon."

"Can you come again tomorrow?"

She shook her head. The shrill whine of the wind turned to a hollow moan. "Tomorrow we'll be in Ishmantep. I'll find my way here on our return."

When she left, she was surprised to find the most difficult thing wasn't leaving; it was the realization that parting had been easier than she'd expected. Part of it was the sting of Kameyl being right—why *hadn't* she fought for Emre?—but another was the knowledge that she and Emre were on entirely different paths.

She stood there awhile after she'd closed the door, wondering if she should go back, stay with him awhile. But after a moment's hesitation, she turned and headed for the Maidens' cabin.

Chapter 50

THE DAY FOLLOWING THE TERRIBLE SANDSTORM, the *Javelin* continued sailing toward Ishmantep. It was sunny but unseasonably cold, as if Thaash's anger had finally been spent and all that was left was cold brooding. Ahead of the ship, far off the starboard side, Çeda could see one of the asirim. *Kerim*, she reminded herself. *He has a name.* From this distance he looked like a black beetle scuttling over sand. A moment later he was gone, lost behind the far side of a dune.

The other came a moment later, moving like a hound on the hunt. The two of them were in deep pain, as the asirim always were. The pain fed their murderous thoughts. They ached to rend flesh, to sink long nails into the heart of another, if only to feel a heart beat as theirs once did. They could do none of these things, however. Not without leave, for the power of the gods compelled them, bound as they were to Kameyl until she released them or the Jackal King took them from her control. At the very thought, Kerim wailed. The sound rose above the incessant shush of the ship's skis, making the hair at the nape of Çeda's neck stand on end. *How can I sit and watch them suffer?* she thought. *Why not free them here and now?* She would die if she did so—the Kings would certainly sense it—which was a sound reason not to, but just then the knowledge was a cloak that did little to warm her.

On the foredeck Sümeya stood by Yndris's side, pointing to the left of a hill that looked like the hunchback curve of a black laugher's silhouette. "There lies Ridgeback, with Ishmantep just beyond." Only a few more minutes' sailing and they saw a caravanserai resolve above the wavering horizon. Like Sharakhai, Ishmantep had outgrown its defenses. A smattering of homes and a patchwork of green fields and farmsteads carpeted the terrain below high stone walls. There were trees—lemon or fig, most likely—and fields of onions, garlic, and turnips. There were even rows of grapes unless Çeda missed her guess. Within the walls, mudbrick buildings were built beside larger ones made of stone the color of a dusty rose. Years ago, before joining Sümeya's hand, Melis had been assigned to Ishmantep under a Maiden named Dilara. Thanks to her drilling, Çeda could already pick out the small keep for the lord of Ishmantep, the trade houses, the auction block, the stables, the barracks. At the center of it all stood a large, square building with masts from at least two dozen ships surrounding it—the caravanserai proper, the first building built and the heart of trade and commerce in this corner of the desert. Emre stepped up to the foredeck, a thing Sümeya noted but said nothing against.

"It's funny," he said to no one in particular, "in Sharakhai, ships dock at the edges of the city, but here they sit inside the walls, the center of everyone's attention."

Which only seems proper, Çeda thought. *In the caravanserais, life is sustained as much by the endless stream of sandships as the water from its wells.*

"It's larger than I would have guessed," Emre went on.

"Ishmantep was a city once," Melis replied.

Indeed, it was the largest of the caravanserais along the northern trail leading to Malasan—the Spice Road, as it was often called—a region that grew some of the most fragrant spices found anywhere in the world. In the distance, on either side of Ishmantep, two of the Great Desert's mountain ranges closed in, their foothills rounding the terrain before giving way to a tumble of black, jagged monoliths. To the left, north of Ishmantep, were the Taloran Mountains, with Mount Arasal visible in the foreground, the very mountain that fed Sharakhai's great aqueduct. And to the right, southward,

was a spur of the Kholomundi Range, the Black Teeth of Iri, the unending
string of mountains that walled the Shangazi to the south and east.

"Hundreds of years ago," Melis went on, "in the weeks leading up to Beht
Ihman, the desert tribes were marching toward Sharakhai but paused when they
came to Ishmantep. The city was four times the size you see before you now,
and well armed. But the tribes' host was numerous indeed. They gained the
walls and took the young city, slaughtering every man, woman, and child they
found before burning the buildings to the ground. That is what we fight for."

Sümeya turned to look at the Maidens, and Emre as well. "Lord Aziz has
lasted two decades as the governor of Ishmantep, rising from a lowly stable-
boy who worked those very stalls to the man he is now. The Kings have even
allowed him to buy land, a thing nearly unheard of for those without royal
blood. He is wily. He has the ear of the Kings, especially Beşir, who granted
him the land. He is well protected, so you'll wait for a signal from me or
Kameyl before you act. And by the gods' sweet breath, you'll treat everyone
with respect until we have reason to act otherwise. Do you understand?"

Ishmantep was special among the caravanserais. Most were little more
than a cluster of stone or mudbrick buildings where ships could stop to gain
access to water and rest for the night. Ishmantep, however, was one where
ships coming from the north or east could bypass Sharakhai as long as a tariff was paid for doing so. Most caravans preferred to sell their goods in Sharakhai to the highest bidder, and to buy from the wealth of goods offered at the
auction blocks and the spice markets and the bazaar, but there were trade
routes that had been set up generations or even centuries ago—shipments
between kings and queens and khans of distant lands. Such established trade
meant much to the Kings, which in turn gave the master of certain caravanserais power. They were trusted men and women. *Rich* men and women.
Which in turn meant they had to watch their step with Lord Aziz or risk the
wrath of the Kings who supported him.

They all nodded, even Emre, at which point Sümeya turned and headed
for the ladder leading belowdecks. "Come, it won't be long before we moor."

The sun was lowering as they passed through the gates and approached
the caravanserai proper, a squat monstrosity with piers jutting out from it like
a sunburst. The crew stopped them well short of the berth assigned to them
by the harbormaster. As a team of mules towed them toward the dock,

Sümeya ordered them all to take a petal. It felt strange for Çeda to do so. She'd never been this far from Sharakhai when she'd taken one. She felt some of the same verve she'd always felt, but it wasn't so frantic as it was closer to the blooming fields. It was a subdued sort of energy, the sort she felt after a fiery sparring session. She felt Sharakhai, but only distantly, like the sun in the hours before dawn.

No sooner had they docked than a man in a rich brown kaftan with thread of gold came bustling down the pier. Behind him came a train of seven veiled men wearing blue kaftans that seemed to glow against the stone-and-sand canvas of the caravanserai. Sümeya leapt to the dock. Kameyl and Yndris followed, with Melis and Çeda coming last. Emre remained on deck wearing a black turban with a veil across his face to hide his identity. Sümeya had thought this best—he would, after all, be a valuable source of information from within the Moonless Host should his claims hold true.

"Welcome to Ishmantep," the man said. "I am Şaban, aide to Lord Aziz Salim'ava." He spread his arms wide and bowed so deeply his graying beard nearly brushed the sunbeaten boards of the dock. "What we have is yours."

The other men, much younger, bowed as well, but none nearly so deeply. When they rose, Çeda could see how calm they were, almost *too* calm. A sudden visit like this should strike fear into men such as these, but they hardly batted an eye. And then she realized how similar they looked. Each of their bright blue veils was loose, revealing the set of their eyes, their sharp noses, the color of their skin. Brothers, perhaps. But seven of them?

"We were not expecting you," Şaban said with a broad grin, "but it is a bright day indeed when the presence of the Kings graces us."

"Take us to Lord Aziz," Sümeya said.

"Of course, of course." Şaban bowed his head and took a half step back, but made no move otherwise to lead them into the shaded stone halls of the caravanserai. "May we know your purpose? I'll have my men run and tell my humble master."

Sümeya strode past him. "Kings' business."

Şaban stumbled and then ran to keep ahead of her. "Beşir sent his coin counters only two weeks past. They found everything in order."

Yndris and Melis followed, and Çeda made to as well, until Kameyl took her by the elbow and held her back a moment. Yndris glanced their way, clearly confused, or perhaps annoyed, but did as she'd been instructed and followed Sümeya. When they were out of earshot, Kameyl squeezed Çeda's arm to the point of pain and whispered, "I've no idea what you're doing, or how, but I want you to stop it. Now."

She meant the asirim. She could see them through the gates they'd sailed through. They were closer than Çeda had realized. Their hunger had grown like the sun rising over the desert. They would not be stopped if they came much closer, so she pushed them back. *Not these, blood of my blood. Not today.*

The asirim sang their jackal songs, but then began to retreat, their forms dark in the distance over the golden dunes. Şaban glanced toward the sound, but seemed to think little of it. Surely the Maidens visited this place often.

In an effort to maintain some sort of decorum, Şaban rushed ahead of Sümeya and waved her beneath the arched tunnel that led into the heart of the caravanserai. They followed the passageway for a short distance and found themselves in a central courtyard, a place filled with green palms and lime trees and a well with a large bronze pump at its center. A portico bordered the entire courtyard, which lent dark, slanting shadows to a space that would be bright indeed under the noontime sun.

Şaban took them to the far side of the courtyard and back into the expanse of the building, which was much larger than Çeda had realized. They took several turns and found themselves in a hall with a stone dais at one end. On the dais was a wooden chair, a throne of sorts, a thing not so ostentatious that the lord of this place would be thought to consider himself a King, but certainly a thing that impressed with its beautiful pearl inlay and carvings of falcons at its shoulders. The chair sat empty, as did the rest of the room.

Şaban looked to the Maidens, but particularly at Emre. "My, but you *are* a strange Maiden, aren't you?"

Sümeya walked to the center of the room. "Where is your master?"

"Ah, forgive me, but as I've said you've caught us unprepared. We'll send for him presently." He snapped his fingers at the seven veiled men. "It will be but a moment. Until then, let us offer you drink, or food if you're hungry."

Sümeya shook her head. "Your master. And be quick about it."

"Of course, of course." He bowed low as he headed for the door, one arm against his chest, the other flung wide. He reminded Çeda of none so much as Ibrahim the storyteller, who was theatrical to a fault. Şaban was this way, stepping near but not quite crossing the line that divided amusing from offensive. "But a moment, I beg." He paused after stepping across the threshold, leaning back into the room at an awkward angle. "A moment only."

And then he was gone, and Çeda, the other Maidens, and Emre were left alone in the room.

"I like this not at all," Çeda said, looking about the room to the four sets of doors, to the shutters, half closed.

"Don't fret, little wren," Yndris said. "All will be well."

"That man—" Çeda tried to reply.

But Sümeya cut her off. "Lord Aziz has always been a strange man with strange tastes, but he's filled the Kings' coffers well enough despite it."

"You know this Şaban, then?"

"I do not." She turned to Emre. "Do you?" It was a cold and insistent stare, as if she thought it high time he show his worth, but Emre appeared not to notice as he shook his head. Sümeya continued, "I'm not surprised Aziz has chosen someone eccentric to wait upon him, but in the end it changes nothing. As we agreed then." She motioned Emre toward the door to the courtyard. "See what you can find."

Emre nodded and left, looking about as if he were admiring the designs on the walls when in reality he was looking for signs of the Host while Lord Aziz was occupied.

A short while later, the scraping sound of footsteps came from the stone-lined hallway outside. The doors opened abruptly, and in strode a score of men and women, most in rich finery. At their rear was a large man with golden clothes and curling jeweled slippers and a turban with a bright red ruby in its center. "Welcome, my friends. Welcome, and please, please, forgive my late arrival. The Kings' duties do take time."

The men and women all watched raptly, but none said a word. One of them, a woman wearing an embroidered khimar over her head, hiding her face in deep shadows, seemed to be watching them more intently than the rest.

Aziz spread his hands wide, bowing his head. "Pray tell, what can the Master of Ishmantep provide for the Kings?"

"Our business with you is private," Sümeya said.

"Private? Of course. We'll rest but a moment, and then—"

"Now," Sümeya replied.

Aziz's round face grew worried. He looked to the others, the men and women who'd accompanied him here. They, however, appeared calm, amused even, by what was taking place.

Şaban, who seemed to appear out of nowhere in the corner, began clapping his hands. "As the Kings command, so must we obey. Come," he said, clapping more loudly. "Out, and we will return for a feast when the sun has set."

Hushed conversation followed as they filtered from the room. Şaban held the door open for them, and when they'd all left, closed it behind them and moved to stand by the throne. Aziz sat down in it, perhaps trying to regain the air of nobility he'd had only a moment ago with his court surrounding him. Sitting there with no one but a single servant to attend to him, however, he looked ridiculous, a man naked, lost in the desert, hiding his cock lest he look foolish to the buzzards.

Lord Aziz smiled, a thing that bloomed and faded quickly. "Now, what might I provide for the Maidens of Sharakhai? You have only to name it."

"I would speak with Maidens Dilara and Rana for a start," Sümeya said.

"Ah," Aziz said, clearly put off by this request, "forgive me, but they are gone."

"They are assigned to this post," Sümeya countered.

"Be that as it may . . ."

"Gone where?"

"East. They left for Ashdankaat two days ago."

For the first time since arriving, Sümeya seemed off balance. Dilara and Rana were meant to remain here in the caravanserai. They watched the trade. They kept order. They were a reminder that the Kings were the power that ruled the desert and no other, and as such they were a stabilizing influence across the trails and caravanserais. For them to have gone east to another serai without Sümeya or the Kings knowing it was strange indeed.

"Was word sent to Sharakhai?" Sümeya asked.

Aziz bowed his head. "I do not presume to know the affairs of the Maidens. They may have sent word on the patrol ship that left a week ago, but if so, I do not know of it."

Sümeya turned to the other Maidens. "Melis, take Çeda and examine their rooms." As she said this, she made the sign for *danger* with her right hand where Aziz couldn't see it.

Melis bowed her head and led Çeda away.

As the two of them headed for the door, Sümeya snapped, "I'll see your ledgers."

"My ledgers?" As they left the room and closed the door behind them, Çeda heard Aziz's muffled reply, "I assure you, they are in order. Beşir's man came not two weeks back."

Melis led Çeda along the portico that bordered the lush courtyard. The sun was even lower now. The moons would not rise for some time, which lent this place—with its play-at-King master and his odd servant—a strange air indeed. They came to a heavy, nail-studded door carved with the official seal of Sharakhai, a shield with twelve shamshirs fanned around it. Melis took an iron key from the small bag at her belt, which she used to open the door.

Çeda stepped inside and found an office with two simple desks and a table with stools. Beyond, through an archway, was another room with eight beds, four along each side.

Melis glanced outside, then closed the door. "I like this not at all, Çeda. Dilara and Rana would not have left, not without sending word to Sharakhai." She moved to the nearest desk, sat down in the chair, and opened the shallow central drawer. From it she pulled a journal, which she set before her and began paging through. "It's possible some note they sent may have crossed paths as we came here, but the timing seems odd, doesn't it?"

Çeda looked to the shutters, to the gap at the base of the door, both of which would allow some air to flow through the room even if both were closed. She pulled back a nearby chair. "Would the Maidens have cleaned diligently?"

Melis frowned. "Of course. Why?"

Çeda motioned to the brown glazed tiles on the floor, and the space where the leg of the chair had been. "A bit more than two days, don't you think?" There was a fine layer of dust coating the floor, as there would be anywhere in the desert unless the room had somehow been sealed. It would depend on how many sandstorms had passed through the area, but it looked to Çeda like almost a month's worth of buildup.

"Yes," Melis said. "Dilara was fastidious about such things."

"Where might they have gone?" Çeda asked.

Melis paged through the journal, reading the early entries within it. "The gods may know, but I certainly don't."

While Melis scanned the pages Çeda moved into the next room. There were no signs that Maidens were using the room, or had in recent days. All the beds had woolen mattresses with neck rolls and two sets of sheets and blankets folded carefully atop them. None of the shelves above the beds held anything. No books. No mementos. Nothing.

There was, however, a strange smell in the room. Something like spoiled cabbage, with the sharp smell of vinegar cutting through it. She'd smelled similar things in Dardzada's shop, but those had always seemed natural, even if they had made her stomach turn. *This* odor made her feel as though the room had the taint of the dead upon it.

She heard Melis mumble something in the next room.

"What?" Çeda asked as she moved to the corner of the room where the smell was strongest. When Melis didn't respond, she got down on her knees and ran her hands over the floor. There was a discoloration. A darkened area—blood, perhaps, but with an oily sheen to it. When she put her nose right up next to it and sniffed, she reeled back. Something foul had soaked into the floorboards here, and no amount of cleaning would undo it.

Melis mumbled again, something about Dilara.

"What did you say?" Çeda asked when she returned to the front room.

Melis looked up from the journal, which was open to a page that contained only a handful of entries. "This isn't Dilara's writing."

"Rana's, then?"

Melis shook her head. "You misunderstand. It's been doctored, made to *look* like Dilara's writing." Melis stood and closed the book. "A forgery, and not a bad one, but it isn't hers." And then she tucked the book under one arm and headed for the door, grim determination in her eyes. "Come with me, and keep your sword loose in its sheath."

Chapter 51

WHILE LEAVING THE CARAVANSERAI PROPER, Çeda took note of the docked ships. There were eight besides the *Javelin*. Most had no crew on deck, but two were being readied for sail, and both flew the pennant of Ishmantep: a green, spread-wing falcon on a field of gold. One of the ships was a mid-sized cutter, the other a sleek yacht with well-oiled runners that looked is if it would fairly fly across the desert.

Çeda give a short whistle—*dangerous?*—and nodded to the ships.

Melis looked, then walked toward the *Javelin*, which was close, and got the attention of the captain of the Silver Spears. She pointed to the ships. "Do not let those ships leave. Put the crew in chains if you need to."

"It shall be so," the captain said, and called orders to his waiting men.

Melis and Çeda crossed the sandy ship path circling the caravanserai and strode down a wide street. There were people about, but Çeda was so used to the weight and press of Sharakhai that Ishmantep felt like a boneyard, ghuls wandering about looking for fresh graves to unearth. Melis took them farther down the street to a small shop. She didn't knock. She merely stepped inside, causing a small bell to tinkle above the door, to find a room filled with a variety of antiques—clay lamps, ornate hairpins, vases made from what looked to be jade. And there were books. Many books. Different sizes with bindings that ranged from wood to leather to metal.

At the back of the room, behind a workbench, sat a wizened man, bent over a book, wrapping what appeared to be snakeskin over the front backing board. "But a moment," he said without looking up. "I'll be with you in but a moment."

Melis, a forbidding look on her face, stepped up to the desk, raised the Maidens' ledger high, and crashed it onto the desk.

The man's head shot up, eyes wild and impossibly large behind his round spectacles. He swallowed, then unwrapped the spectacles from around his ears and stared at Melis, who towered over him.

"Tell me what you know of this ledger," Melis ordered.

He looked down, then at the book he'd been working on, then at his hands, now streaked with backing glue. He swung his gaze back up to Melis and smiled awkwardly. "Melis, isn't it?" When Melis nodded, he went on. "It's been a few years, assuming my addled mind has it right."

She stabbed her finger at the book. "The ledger, Belivan."

"This?" His voice was tremulous, the voice of an old man, but there was also fear, confusion. "What about it?"

"You worked on this book, didn't you?" Melis took it up and pointed to the binding. "The cover is old, the original, unless I'm mistaken, but the paper is new. New, but made to *look* old. Did you distress the pages before finishing this for Lord Aziz?"

The ancient man now picked up the ledger, held it in his shaking hands. He looked it over, but there seemed to be something melancholy about the way he did it. He made a show of walking his fingers over the pages, turning them slowly, running his hands along their length.

He stared up into Melis's eyes. Licked his lips. Sniffed wetly as his eyes turned rheumy. "I knew you would come. One day, I knew . . ."

"Why, Belivan? Why did Aziz have you create another?"

"It wasn't Aziz. It was Şaban, his servant."

Melis glanced at Çeda, confused, concerned. "Şaban then. Why did he want a replica?"

Belivan shrugged, a pained expression on his face. He looked beyond

Melis, toward the door. "I know not what happens in that place. Şaban . . . I . . . The serai hasn't been the same since his arrival."

"When did he come?"

"Seven weeks ago. Eight."

"And since then?"

"One night . . ." He blinked and shook his head, as if trying to clear a vision. "One night I heard *noises* coming from the caravanserai."

"What sort of noises? Tell me what happened, Belivan."

"I was walking home from my sister's house. We aren't supposed to go through the caravanserai, but I've done it from time to time and no one has ever said anything against it. I was walking through the courtyard, and by Bakhi's good grace, I heard it. Wailing. Calls that would wake the dead from their sandy graves."

Outside, the wind picked up. It whined beneath the closed shop door as a chill crawled down Çeda's skin. Melis glanced at it. Çeda could tell she was ready to leave, that she wanted to return to the others. Çeda did as well—Emre was in danger—but they needed to know more. Melis caught Çeda's eye, and she made the sign, *be ready*, so only Çeda could see, then turned back to Belivan. "How often?"

Belivan's brow pinched as if he were trying to solve a particularly difficult riddle, but Çeda recognized it for what it was—pain over his inaction, pain from hearing the wailing and doing nothing about it because there was nothing he *could* do. It was a look that everyone in Sharakhai was intimately familiar with, for it happened every night of Beht Zha'ir, when men and women huddled in their homes, unable to do anything to stop the culling of human lives, the sacrifice the asirim took from their city. "I should have stayed away," Belivan said. "But the sound was so desperate. I hoped I'd been dreaming . . ."

"But you hadn't been," Melis said.

He shook his head. "I went back the next few nights and heard nothing, but on the third night, I heard them again. And again two days later." He squeezed his eyes, tears falling against the Maidens' leatherbound journal. "I don't know who they've taken, but I fear for their souls."

"How long have the Maidens been gone? When was the last time you saw them?"

"Five weeks ago. Perhaps more."

He was about to speak further when Melis whirled and whispered, "Sümeya," mere moments before the sound of shouting and swordplay filtered in through the shop's front door.

Melis rushed into the street. Çeda followed and together they ran back toward the caravanserai. There were people in the street now, some of them stumbling from their mudbrick homes. Some grabbed their children and headed back indoors. Others watched as Çeda and Melis ran with swords drawn. More shouts came—shouts of anger, not pain—followed by the ring of steel.

In little time Çeda and Melis reached the dock surrounding the caravanserai. "Go to the ship," she said to Çeda, "bring the Spears and whatever crewmen can come. And by Goezhen's dark kiss, keep your eyes peeled for danger."

As she sprinted away, Çeda ran for the *Javelin*. The soldiers had heard the sounds of conflict, but it still took time to get them organized and off the ship. With Çeda leading the way, they charged along the dock, a dozen of them in all, swords at the ready. She led them down the short tunnel to the courtyard when all sounds of swordplay abruptly ended, as if one of the old gods had returned and swept them away with a wave of his hand.

"Be wary," Çeda said to the soldiers behind her, then led them into the courtyard, leery of an ambush. But they found the courtyard empty.

Except . . . The bronze pump at the center of the courtyard was *rotating*. Beneath its base, Çeda saw a hole with stairs leading down into the darkness, but the hole was slowly being covered by the pump's stone base. She sprinted forward. "Quickly now," she said as she sat on the dusty stone and set her feet against the base. As the men closed in around her, she held the lip and heaved, pressing with her legs. The men followed suit, bellowing as they shouldered the pump's handle or the patina-covered mouth or strained at the base.

In the end, the mechanism was too strong, and Çeda was forced to release the stone before her fingers were severed. The pump set home with a boom that shook the very ground.

"What shall we do, Maiden?" one of the Spears asked.

They all stared at her, awaiting orders. Gods, what could *she* do? A year ago she would gladly have left a Blade Maiden to whatever fate awaited her, but she knew she couldn't do that. Not any longer. She turned to the doorway where Sümeya had been questioning Lord Aziz. "Come," she said. "Be wary."

Even before she gained the room, she noted the sickly sweet smell in the air, the same odor she'd smelled on the floorboards of the Maidens' barracks. When she rushed through the open doorway she found Aziz lying unconscious near the center of the room. Emre lay just next to him, blinking groggily and pulling himself up off the floor. Lying next to them like fallen dolls were three bodies, swords near to hand. Blood stained their blue kaftans. Swaths of red painted the inlaid floor beneath their still forms. These were the men Şaban had brought with him to the docks when the *Javelin* had arrived. His servants. Or his assassins. Çeda knew not which. As Emre sat up and coughed, she moved to each of them and pulled their veils away. By the gods. They *were* the same as one another. The *very* same. From their lips to their chin to the mole on their right cheek.

"What happened?" she asked Emre as she knelt by his side. He stared at her with a look of confusion. He took in Aziz's prone body, then the dead men. His eyes were heavy until she gripped his jaw and forced him to look at her. "What *happened*?"

When he spoke, his words were slurred. "Şaban . . . He stormed in with his men. They were devils with swords, Çeda. They fought the Maidens, and for a time held their own. But when it looked like the tide was turning, Şaban threw something down in the center of the room. There." He pointed to the floor where bits of glass lay like the pieces of a shattered star. "The room filled with smoke, and . . . that's the last thing I remember until I heard you screaming in the courtyard. I thought you were dying, Çeda."

Çeda smiled grimly. "Not yet, gods willing."

Just then Emre's eyes went impossibly wide. He crawled backward as the sound of labored breathing came from somewhere behind Çeda. She turned and found the two asirim standing hunched in the doorway, faces gaunt, eyes sallow, their long, blackened fingers flexing. The Silver Spears stood at the ready, but looked on them with naked fear. They practically tripped over themselves to make way as the two sad creatures slouched into the room, arms twitching, eyes assessing everyone with a hunger Çeda could now feel.

"Take Emre and Aziz back to the ship," Çeda said to four of the Spears. "Stay there until we return. The rest of you, light lamps and come with me."

She returned to the pump. The asirim obeyed her silent command to follow, but slowly, grudgingly. She pointed to the pump. "Open it." When they didn't respond, she shouted, "Open it!"

She could feel Kerim, the closer of the two, his amusement over her command even as the yoke the gods had placed across his shoulders pained him. *I am not bound to you, daughter of Ahyanesh.*

It was true. Kameyl still commanded them. Apparently there hadn't been enough time to draw them near. Kerim wouldn't obey her, not without being forced to. He'd decided she wasn't worthy. She had no time to worry about his feelings now, though. She knew it to be a grave insult to do so, but she pressed her will upon Kerim. He resisted, and Çeda could feel Kameyl's bond to him as well, but soon both the existing bond and Kerim's will gave before Çeda's need.

Kerim's rage burned bright as a bonfire, not just for the Kings and the Maidens, but for Çeda—*especially* for Çeda. *I didn't wish it to be thus,* she told him. When he gave no reply, she turned to the other. *Tell me your name.*

The asir ignored her, stretching its neck as if the very question pained it. Its yellowed eyes flicked toward Kerim, perhaps asking for permission. "Your *name*," Çeda said aloud, to the confused looks of the Silver Spears.

The asir swallowed, then emitted a gurgling sound that made Çeda's heart weep. The asir tried again, and this time, Çeda heard it. A name uttered with the insect buzz of a voice that hadn't been used in decades. "*Mynolia.*" Çeda was surprised to hear it voiced aloud, but she could hear the strong note of pride in the asir's voice, could see it echoed in her fierce, bloodshot eyes.

Will you join me, Mynolia?

Join her willingly, she meant. She didn't wish to force Mynolia as she had Kerim. She thought she might have to, for her question was met with silence, but then at last she nodded.

Like a knife pressing between two halves of a walnut, Çeda slipped her will between Mynolia and Kameyl. It was easier than before, but still difficult, and she was sure she'd have to explain herself later—to Kameyl and Sümeya and surely Mesut as well—but there was nothing for it now. She needed the asirim's help.

She headed back to the courtyard and pointed to the pump. *Turn it,* she bid them. Mynolia immediately obeyed, grabbing the pump's handle with one hand, the throat with the other. Kerim crawled low to the ground, yip-ping like a hyena. His fingers gouged the earth, but then he set to it, wrap-ping his arms around the base and straining against the pump's hidden weight.

"Shall we help them, Maiden?" the captain asked, though it was clear from his look that he hoped it wouldn't be necessary.

Likely Kerim would not attack them, but she didn't want to chance it unless it was necessary. She pointed to a decorative stone near the base of a date palm instead. "No. Just roll that closer, and be ready to wedge it in."

The asirim's muscles pulled taut as shroud lines. Their lips pulled back in rictus grins, revealing chipped, yellowed teeth. Slowly, the pump turned. When the stairs were revealed, the Spears rolled the stone into place, wedging the way open. One of the Spears, a bull of a man, offered Çeda a lantern. She took it and headed down along tight, winding stairs. The asirim followed on all fours, moving like dogs eager for the hunt. The eight Silver Spears came last. They reached a landing some thirty feet below. On level ground at last, Çeda drew her ebon sword and rushed along a limestone passageway that wavered beneath the lantern's uneven light.

Soon they reached a point where the passageway split, but the fresh blood dotting the floor made for an easy trail to follow. They twisted through this place, and it quickly became clear that this was no mere underground lair; it was a carefully constructed place with markings that spoke of ancient days. Perhaps a temple to the elder gods, or one of the earliest made in honor of the young gods.

A darkened doorway yawned to their left. The rotted smell from that room was so strong it was difficult to approach. The asirim went before her, sniffing, yapping their way deeper into the darkness. Putting her sleeve across her face in a vain attempt at stifling the smell, Çeda followed. Along the right side of the room, wavering in the lamplight, stood dozens of copper vats and iron implements on stands. Their utility Çeda could only guess at. In the center of the room were six stone beds, and upon them she could see glisten-ing remnants. Raising her lantern high, she could make out the outline of legs, torso, arms, and head.

She felt light-headed. It was the smell, she knew. It might overwhelm her if she wasn't careful, so she looked through the rest of the room quickly before heading back into the hallway where a blessed breeze was clearing the smell from the air. Somewhere far ahead, a battle cry echoed through the catacombs, and again came the sounds of steel on steel.

"Go," she called to the asirim. "Find them. Protect my sister Maidens."

Conflict raged within the asirim. Some part of them wished desperately to rend the flesh from her and the Silver Spears, but they also relished the mere thought of inflicting pain on *anyone* to appease their ever-gnawing hunger. They ran ahead with a loping gate, faster than Çeda could run.

They came at last to a vast room with mammoth pillars running along its length. Each pillar had a lantern hanging from it, but the thing giving off the most light was a body burning with strange blue-green flames that filled the air with thick smoke and an acrid smell that made Çeda's stomach turn. On the far side of the room stood a statue that towered fifty feet high. It had the form of some forgotten god, kneeling, hands resting on its knees, palms facing upward. The god had the head of a jackal, its opaline eyes bright and mischievous.

Beyond the flaming body, a dozen dead men wearing the garb of the desert tribes—thawbs and ghoutras and keffiyehs—littered the floor. And beyond them a battle raged near the base of the god. Sümeya, Kameyl, Melis, and Yndris were all there, their ebon blades arcing, fending off blows from a dozen enemies.

As she ran toward them, Çeda caught movement from a darkened tunnel to the right of the towering statue. Her breath caught as she saw the naked, fleshy form issuing from it.

"Bakhi save us," one of the Spears intoned.

The creature might have been a man once—she could see its shriveled cock wag as it shambled forth—but now it was an ungainly, corpulent thing, staggering with half-healed scars complicating a strange topography of gangrenous skin. A second lumbered out from the tunnel, another man, and then a third, a woman, each like foul simulacrums of wool-stuffed dolls, the soldiers of a mad child.

By the gods, Emre, what have you got us into?

She knew they were the collegia students, turned by blood and the wicked hand of a mage into the poor, shambling creatures she saw before her. She knew that Hamzakiir had presided over their ghastly transformation. But

Goezhen's sweet kiss, *why*? Why take young men and women, peaceful souls, and do *this* to them?

The shambling forms advanced with an awkward gait, as if they could barely remain standing for the pain it caused them. Their faces, too, echoed a horror Çeda could only guess at.

Her terror rose with every step they took. "Them," she said to the asirim, pointing. "Take them down."

The asirim immediately heeded her call, wailing as another form darkened the tunnel. It was Şaban, studying the scene with something akin to satisfaction before receding into the darkness of the tunnel. Rhia's bright eyes, it was never Lord Aziz who had the answers. It was Şaban, who was surely Hamzakiir in disguise.

Çeda made for the tunnel, hoping to catch him. Ahead of her, as the asir approached the nearest of the shamblers. The man's porcine eyes widened, a host of emotions playing across his face: mostly fear, but anger and confusion as well. His flesh turned a dark shade of yellow. He shook violently, skin shaking miserably, fists quivering before him. A moan escaped him, low at first but rising quickly to new heights. It was a call that sent a cold spike of fear through Çeda's heart. The thing bent over, and bore down, his midsection widening to degrees Çeda would never have thought possible.

Çeda gave a piercing whistle. *Danger! Right flank!* Melis, Sümeya, and Yndris immediately disengaged and retreated. Kameyl, however, did not.

Mynolia leapt upon the shambler moments before it burst with such violence that it shook the entire chamber. The very air pressed against Çeda, sending her back a step. Far, far worse was the effect it had on those closer. A sickly ichor bloomed from the point where the shambling man had once stood. It spattered over Mynolia, who'd been flung free in the burst. It sprayed over the statue of the god and the other lumbering creatures. It coated many of Hamzakiir's men. Kameyl, though partly protected by the men in front of her, caught some of the dark liquid across her right side.

The low thrum of the eruption died down, but following it, depthless howls of pain filled every corner of this forgotten place. It came from Hamzakiir's men, from Kameyl, and especially from Mynolia, who lay writhing on the floor, her black skin hissing as the viscous substance ate its way through her. Even the stone of the god's knees smoked from the foul liquid, whatever it was.

The two other shamblers appeared unharmed. They were shaking now as well, their color deepening. Çeda whistled—*back!*—a split second before Sümeya gave the very same order with a whistle of her own.

This time Kameyl listened. She was covering her face and favoring her left side, but she still held her sword in hand. Hamzakiir's swordsmen scrambled backward, too, eyes wide with fear. They hadn't been forewarned, then. Hamzakiir had forsaken them.

Çeda was just able to draw Kerim back through a force of will driven by her quickly building fear. The two remaining shamblers burst—*thoom, thoom*—spraying their deadly ichor over the temple steps and the two fallen men. The screams of the fallen soldiers rose to new heights, but they fell silent soon after. Their bodies stilled as a grayish-green gas rose from their lifeless forms.

The five surviving tribesmen stared wide-eyed at the devastation, at their fallen brothers. Their weapons hung limply in their hands. When they realized how outmanned they were—five Maidens, an asir, and eight Silver Spears standing ready to oppose them—they dropped their swords. All of them had been splattered to one degree or another by the ichor. They grimaced, sucked air through gritted teeth. They stared first at the Maidens, then at the gelatinous remains of the howlers, things controlled by a man they had no doubt considered an ally.

Kameyl stood before them, sword still in hand, the embodiment of cold steel, Kings' law, and righteous anger. The body that had been burning when they entered was no longer aflame, leaving the lamps to light the massive space, but, despite the relative dark, Çeda could still see the burn marks on Kameyl's face and right hand. Kameyl's lips were pressed in a thin line. Her nostrils flared as her breath came short and quick. But she did not flinch. She merely stared with diamond-glint eyes at the nearest of the Moonless Host.

Then her eyes went wild with rage.

"No!" Çeda cried, but before she could move to stop her, Kameyl raised her ebon sword and brought it down like the blow of an axe against the nearest of the men. The sword's dark edge seemed to sneer at his hastily raised defenses. It sliced through his arms, cleaved his skull in two, and wedged between the broken remains of his collarbone. Chest heaving with her labored breath, Kameyl lifted one leg and kicked him free of her sword. As he fell, limbs twitching, the remaining men backed away. They did not, how-ever, run. Like the Haddah giving up its water at spring's end, their will to fight had been drained.

Her entire body shaking at Kameyl's cold violence, Çeda studied the cleaved man. Had he been one of the lost tribe? Had he been some distant cousin? Did it matter either way? Regret replaced anger, and the thought of Emre falling to the stroke of a sword. Was that what awaited him? Surely it was what awaited many in the Host. This seemingly endless conflict between the Kings and the Al'afwa Khadar left her feeling small and insignificant, a child watching helplessly as a brawl played out in the streets. *Yerinde's grace, we're better than this.*

After giving Çeda a disgusted look, Kameyl walked away. Melis began ordering the Silver Spears to take the prisoners. Yndris went with her, leaving Çeda alone with Sümeya.

"He might have told us something," Çeda said.

Sümeya was wiping the blood from her blade on the turban cloth re-trieved from a fallen enemy. She shrugged and said, "You'll find, as I have, that Kameyl is gifted at drawing the truth from men such as these, and to-night she'll have more incentive than ever." With a fluid motion, she drove her sword home into its scabbard. "I've no doubt we'll learn everything he might have been able to tell us."

"It's wasteful," Çeda said, "and heartless."

Sümeya laughed. "Heartless? You think these men have *hearts*? Two of your sisters are most likely *dead* because of these men." She stepped forward and stabbed her finger toward the remains of the strange shambling creatures. "They had a hand in turning our scholars into those abominations. You? You still have your Emre, the only family you have—isn't that what you told me?—so don't speak to me of being heartless until you lose something you hold dear."

A vision of her mother swinging from the gallows swam before her. *I have lost something I hold dear.*

"Now come," Sümeya said to her Maidens, making for the tunnel down which Hamzakiir had fled. "Take the lanterns. We may yet catch him."

Melis and Yndris took up two lanterns and followed as Sümeya and Kameyl led the way. Çeda stopped near the asir, Kerim, who was staring at

Mynolia's remains. His hands reached out, not unlike a father for his child, a brother for his sister. It was an expression of deep pain for someone they dearly loved, or perhaps it was confusion over the cruelty of fate.

"Come," Kameyl barked, but Kerim did not move. "Come," Kameyl said again.

Could she truly not know that Çeda had taken Kerim's reins? *Go,* Çeda said to him. *There's nothing to do for her now.* Slowly, the asir turned toward Çeda, as if he hadn't realized he was the one being spoken to. The look in his eyes broke Çeda's heart. It was then, as she stared into the asir's eyes, seeing this strange mix of sadness and a thirst for revenge, that Çeda remembered. The ships flying the flag of Ishmantep . . . they'd been preparing to leave. Çeda had set the Silver Spears to watch the ships, as Melis had bid her, but the Spears would stand no chance against Hamzakiir, not if he meant to escape Ishmantep.

Kerim understood as well, or guessed it from Çeda's thoughts. His body shook. The very notion of Hamzakiir escaping summoned a wail that began deep inside him. His rage found escape as he tilted his head back and howled to the darkened ceiling far above. And then he began loping toward the passageway Hamzakiir had used to escape.

"Stop!" Kameyl called. And then a look of confusion passed over her. She focused her eyes on Çeda, and understanding dawned. She thrust a finger toward the asir's retreating form. "Control it!"

Çeda tried. She had no idea what the asir was going to do, but she didn't want him running wild. Try as she might, though, she could do nothing to stop him.

"Release him!" Kameyl shouted. She grabbed Çeda's dress by the shoulder and shook her. "Do it *now!*"

"I can't!"

The bond to Kerim—tenuous as they'd taken the stairs down to the tunnels—now felt as though it were braided through her being, a part of her. Perhaps it was the asir's anger, or her own emotions, but just then asking her to release Kerim felt like to trying to forget her own name, to stop loving her mother. She couldn't simply sever her bond.

Çeda could feel him now, running through the darkened tunnel. But then she heard a rumbling, both through Kerim's senses and—a split-second later—her own. Pain ran through her. Fear. A sound like the world was rending. And then her bond with Kerim vanished.

The rumbling continued for some time. Dust coughed from the opening. They'd never make it back to the surface that way. "Quickly," Çeda said to Sümeya, and ran in the opposite direction, back the way they'd come. "Şaban is Hamzakiir in disguise. Unless we hurry, he's going to escape on Aziz's ships."

After a moment, Sümeya followed, then the rest. Through the passageways they went, Çeda remembering the twisting turns they'd taken on the way here. Soon they came to the winding stairs. Ignoring the burn in her thighs, Çeda powered herself up to the caravanserai's courtyard. She heard the sounds well before she reached open air. A roaring. A crackling. She gained the courtyard and saw smoke rising into the air on all four sides of the caravanserai. It billowed into the courtyard, scratched at her lungs, made her eyes water. The docks, she realized. The docks and the ships were on fire.

She sprinted down the short tunnel leading to the docks and was greeted by a wall of fire. The pair of berths that had held Aziz's ships, the cutter and the yacht, sat empty, but gods, the rest—the *Javelin*, the caravan ships, the piers, one corner of the caravanserai—were all aflame. Near the *Javelin*'s pier, beyond a wide swath of fire, a Silver Spear waved to her. "What is it?" Çeda shouted.

He gestured wildly to the *Javelin*. "They're in there!"

A cold knife of fear slipped into Çeda's heart. "*Who's* in there?"

"Some of the crew. Lord Aziz and the Spears who brought him belowdecks. And your friend, Emre."

No, no, no. "Why haven't they left the ship?"

"They can't! The hold doors were locked moments after the fires began, and they held like iron. It was Şaban, Lord Aziz's servant. I saw him, gods as my witness, fire flying from his open palms and striking the ships."

"And the ships you were told to guard?"

He pointed over Çeda's shoulder. "Three dozen men stormed the pier and slew the men we had assigned to watch Aziz's cutter and yacht. They sailed away in moments."

Çeda heard his words, but could only stare at the fire raging across the deck of the *Javelin*. She could hear the screams of the men within. She might have heard Emre's among them, but couldn't be sure.

Her attention was drawn to the men and women who'd formed a line from the well to one of the burning caravan ships. "Tell them to try to break out any way they can," she said to the Spear, then somersaulted down to the sand. She was ready to run to the water brigade and order them to shift their attention to the *Javelin*, but stopped when she saw a skiff approaching. There was a woman with straight black hair and a purposeful look on her pretty face sitting at the front of the skiff. And in the back, a worried-looking young man.

"By the gods," Çeda said. *"Davud?"*

Chapter 52

"**D**AVUD!"

Anila's voice was worried. He woke from a fitful slumber and sat up, looking back for the *Burning Sand*.

"No. Ahead." She pointed several points off the starboard bow.

He saw it then—a ship, large but not like the massive trade ships. He fumbled for the small spyglass they'd found in the skiff's supplies, lifted it, and studied the ship. It looked like a cutter. Large lateen sails gave it a look like a knife cutting through the sand. Its runners were long and sleek.

"That's a royal cutter," said Davud. "With the pennant of Sharakhai!"

She took the spyglass from him and looked while holding the tiller. "They're heading for Ishmantep. Maybe they know?"

"Or if not we could warn them! We may save them yet, Anila!"

Davud stood and waved. They both did. They shouted at the top of their lungs. Sound traveled uncannily well over the desert, but surely the ship's skis were making too much sound for them to be heard. And as distant as they were from the cutter, there was only a small chance someone on the ship had spotted them. Even if they had, they wouldn't bother with some skiff out in the desert, especially if they were off to do the Kings' will in Ishmantep.

"We need to go faster," Anila said.

Davud shrugged. "There's nothing left to do. We've jettisoned all we can."

"You could summon the wind again."

"I'll not risk it for this."

"You must! We need to warn them. We need to help!"

"And we will, as soon as we get there. We'll sail as quickly as we can."

Anila's face turned to stone. "You may be consigning them to death."

Davud motioned to the tiller. "Let me take a turn. You've been up all night."

She took a deep breath, held it, then released it in a huff and moved to where Davud had been sleeping. She lay down and fell asleep without another word.

He sailed onward, the cutter slowly but surely pulling away from them. Eventually it was lost altogether, and he wondered if he *had* consigned them to death. *It can't be helped. Blood magic isn't to be used frivolously.*

As the sun rose, he practiced the sigils in his mind. Fire. Water. Earth. Air. Command. Subsume. Exude. Destroy. He drew them over and over again, fixing them there, wondering what it was about blood that allowed them to take form. Why couldn't he do it without blood? Why couldn't Hamzakiir? The blood of the elder gods, Hamzakiir had said. There was power in it, but if that was so, and if it was true the first gods withheld their blood from Tulathan, Goezhen, and all the rest, then how was it *they* could perform the miracles they did?

Davud ate sparingly, but drank perhaps more than he should have. The working of magic had left him with a thirst he wasn't accustomed to. Indeed, after drinking, and still wanting more, he wondered if it was a thirst that would ever leave him.

"What did it feel like?" Anila asked.

He swung his gaze down to look at her. She looked almost peaceful, lying in the bottom of the boat. "What, calling the wind?"

She made a face. "No, pissing in the sand."

He tried to laugh, but all that came out was a sound a sick dog might make. "It *feels* as if we were very fortunate. It *feels* as if we could easily have died. Desperation drove me, or I might not have done it, but the experience could just as easily have torn *me* to pieces. Or you."

"But it didn't."

"You're treating it like some mundane implement, a scalpel to excise a cancer, a spear to be thrown against your enemies."

"It is. A *mighty* spear that many would kill to possess."

Gods, the way her eyes lit up when she spoke those words. *You would kill for it,* he thought, *that much is plain.* But Davud would do almost anything to give the power up. It gnawed at him even now, worse than at any time since leaving Ishmantep. "Anila, this power is nothing to trifle with. It is a desert asp. A barbed whip. A thing that would cut you as easily as your enemies."

Anila sat up and raised her hands to the sky and shook them in frustration. "But you *did* it! You mastered a spell!" Davud opened his mouth to speak, but she talked over him. "I'm no fool. I know it's not to be taken lightly. But whether the gods have shined upon you or cursed you, it is a power you now hold." She lowered her hands until they were fists shivering in her lap. He wasn't even sure she was aware of it. "We have enemies now. We have vengeance to deliver upon them. How better to do so than to use the very thing *he's* used against them, against *us?*"

"I'm no match for Hamzakiir."

"I'm not suggesting you stand against him directly. For now, we should take from him what he needs most, so that he is weakened, so that his other enemies may have him."

"Your thirst for blood is unbecoming, Anila."

"Your lack of *nerve* is unbecoming."

Her words stung, but also showed him Anila's nature. Bloodthirsty. Unwilling to search for peace. Again the vision of Tayyar, his skull caved in, superimposed over Anila's face. *Whatever did I see in you?* He was just about to tell her that he'd not allow himself to become a pawn in her thirst for revenge when he noticed something dark along the horizon ahead. Smoke, he realized. A thick column of it. Which could mean nothing good.

Anila followed his gaze. "Ishmantep," she breathed.

Indeed, as the smoke was drawn like a skein of wool higher into the blue sky, the walls of Ishmantep were revealed. The smoke issued forth in a steady stream from its center—the caravanserai itself, Davud judged.

"What's happened?" he breathed.

"We have to hurry," Anila said while holding out her arm, the same one Davud had pierced with the tip of his knife.

"Anila, I don't think that's a very good—"

"Hurry!" She shook her arm at him, pulling the sleeve higher. "They're all still there, waiting for us to save them."

"You don't know that."

"I *do*."

The column of black smoke widened. The fire was spreading. What might have happened, Davud had no idea, but Anila may be right. At the very least, they could arrive in time to rescue some of them. "We don't even know where they are."

"We'll find them, Davud."

She looked so fraught, so very hopeless, it approached comedy. Davud was conscious enough of his own emotions to recognize how dangerous it was to make decisions based on desperation, but he also knew he would regret it to his dying day if he didn't try everything he could to save his friends. As he pulled out his knife, Anila half smiled, half grimaced.

He pressed the knife into her arm and used the blood to draw a sigil on the palm of his right hand—the same one he'd used against the *Burning Sand*. He then drew it on his left palm as well. As he filled his mind with it, the desert came alive. He felt the wind whipping over the dunes, felt it whorl above him, felt it rush in a strong westward flow near the thin white clouds above.

He inserted himself into the wind that blew over the skiff, entered it like one might wade into a stream. It was so easy to feel it pass around him, to cup it in his hands, to form the currents anew. He almost laughed at the change, how difficult it had been with the *Burning Sand*, how easy it was now.

"Yes," Anila said. "Yes."

He spared one glance for her where she sat at the tiller. The wonder in her eyes . . . It made him uncomfortable, made him overly conscious of the flow he was now a part of.

Their skiff flew over the desert, coming closer and closer to Ishmantep. The smoke continued to thicken. It billowed like a pitch fire, writhing and angry and alive. He could hear bells ringing, cries of alarm, men and women shouting. They passed through the serai's gates, and all too soon the scale of the fire was revealed. The docks surrounding the caravanserai were aflame, as were the ships.

A line of men and women were hauling buckets from a well and trying to douse the flames along one of the distant piers. Another group of what looked to be a ship's crew was hauling an ancient caravel free from its place at dock, but the ship itself was fully aflame, fire licking along half the foredeck and creeping up the foremast's sails and rigging.

Along the dock, near what looked to be a Royal Sharakhani cutter, were a lone Silver Spear and a Blade Maiden wearing their typical black dress, turban, and veil. The Maiden dropped down to the sand in a head-over-heels leap, landing lightly and sprinting full tilt, but she skidded to a stop when she noticed their approaching skiff.

"By the gods," she said, staring at him. *"Davud?"*

He recognized her voice. "Çeda?"

As Anila dropped the sail and Davud snapped the rudder to one side to stop the skiff, Çeda removed the black veil covering her face and met them.

"What's happened?" Davud asked as he stepped out of the skiff.

"Just stay here."

She made to leave, but Davud rushed in front of her. "What's happened, Çeda? I can help."

She waved to the royal cutter. "Emre's in that ship. I have to get that water line moving." As she ran off, a Silver Spear in a dingy white uniform climbed down from the dock and headed for the cutter. Another Blade Maiden, a tall woman with what looked to be burn marks and holes in her black dress, followed. Both bore axes, which they used to hack against the hull, presumably to force their way in through the side of the ship. As powerfully as the Silver Spear was swinging his axe, the Blade Maiden matched him blow for blow. She hacked at the hull as if a newborn child lay dying within. But this was no mere caravan ship. It was a royal cutter, made of sterner stuff than a cargo ship. They'd not be getting in through the hull any time soon.

As three more Maidens dropped down to the sand, Anila tugged at Davud's sleeve and pointed to a stone archway that would lead them toward the interior of the caravanserai. "Come," she said.

Davud motioned to the ship. "We can't just leave them."

"We have our own friends to save!"

"You were in the forum the day of the attack." This came from one of the Blade Maidens, a warden by the insignia on the sleeve of her dress.

"We were," they said, bowing their heads in unison.

As she glanced at their skiff, a look of confusion came and went. There was a distinct note of sadness, or perhaps regret, as she said, "I've no idea how you escaped the fate of your fellow scholars, but you won't find them in there."

"What do you mean?" Anila asked.

"A short while ago the blood mage, Hamzakiir, escaped this caravanserai on two ships, and unless I'm sadly mistaken he took your fellow scholars with him."

"Took them where?"

"The gods only know. Now stand aside. There'll be time for us to speak when this is done."

Davud could see in the way Anila walked numbly away from the ship that she was crushed. She stared at the sand, then looked up to the caravanserai's arched gateway as if she were ready to walk into the desert, and keep walking until it claimed her for its own.

They'd failed. They'd risked so much, flown across the desert, and they'd failed. They'd missed their friends, those they'd vowed to help, by a *mere hour*. He'd had it in his power to see them here faster, but he'd withheld it until it was too late.

He knew he should feel every bit as crushed as Anila, but there was a part of him that felt only relief. To come face to face with Hamzakiir again so soon . . . It would have been their downfall. Or if not his—Hamzakiir had taken some strange liking to Davud, after all—then certainly Anila's. Had they come and thrown themselves against Hamzakiir and his men in hope of saving their fellow scholars, a task that seemed doomed from the start, Hamzakiir would have killed her, if only to give Davud another object lesson.

Grief warred with relief warred with worry as the thud from the axes and the shouting from within the ship entered his awareness once more. He stared up at the fire. As did Anila. Then they looked at each other, and without another word being spoken, Anila stepped toward him, baring her arm, while Davud drew his knife.

If they couldn't save their friends—the young men and women they'd learned with, cried with, rejoiced with—then by the gods they could save the people on this ship who might in turn help them gain their revenge. Davud pressed his knife once more into Anila's arm. He bled her more than their first time by the fire, more than the second time as the *Burning Sand* chased them down. Again he put his lips to the wound and partook of her blood. Perhaps it was because he was becoming used to it, perhaps it was because he was less scared, perhaps it was even Anila lowering her defenses, the two of them sharing in their sadness; whatever the case, this time was vastly different from the other two. The warmth of Anila's blood, of her body and soul, filled him. The slickness of it against her skin felt heady. It bordered on the erotic, to take this from a woman he'd lusted after and do so much with the lifeblood she'd given to him willingly. By Goezhen's sweet kiss the very taste was more delicious than anything he'd ever consumed.

Though he'd felt powerful when he'd managed to hold the fire in his hands that night alone with Anila, it had been nothing compared to the intoxicating violence of summoning the gale he'd driven against the *Burning Sand*. But neither could hold a candle to what he felt now. He felt invincible. A god in his own right.

He turned to face the fire. He didn't need the sigil drawn upon his palms or chest. He needed only blood and his own will. He spread his hands wide. He felt the kiss of fire against his skin, felt its contours as it licked the deck of the ship. As he'd done with the fire in the desert, he made it turn, made it spin like a gyre in the sea. It spun now, on an unseen axis of his own making.

The warden of the Blade Maidens turned to him. She called to him, eyes bright with worry. Another Maiden called his name. A woman he'd known when he was younger. He could no longer recall her name, for he was someone else now. He was some*where* else. There was only him, the fire, and Anila, standing in the cradle of the world.

As the fire continued to spin, he drew upon it. Like fresh clay on a wheel he pulled it upward, willing it away from the ship, commanding it to burn the sky instead of this ship that sailed the sands. And it obeyed. It did as he asked. But it left something in its wake. A cold the likes of which he'd never known. A cold that was wider than the desert sky, deep as night, and hungry. Gods, so very hungry. It clawed at him. Scratched. It *wanted*.

He scrabbled to control it, to force it away while compelling the fire to heed his will. He tried do both, but it only made it all the worse. Pain filled him. He was caught between pure cold and elemental fire. He wasn't ready for this. He should never have tried. And now that he was in the middle of it, he didn't know how to get out again.

They need you, came a voice, though who it was referring to he wasn't sure. So many depended on him. Lives were at stake.

Gods, how stupid he'd been. He should never have listened to Anila. He should have forced her to take the skiff to Sharakhai, not Ishmantep. And now they were both going to die because of his weakness.

You must choose.

But how could he? His fears were giving life to new fears, and those compounded further. They mixed with the growing pain, until he no longer knew who he was. Or where. Or *why* any of this was happening. It was so like those pain-filled days in the darkened pit when the change was upon him. He thought he'd returned there.

"Release me," he screamed. "Release me and I'll give you anything you want!"

But it didn't. It wouldn't. He was trapped.

He scrabbled away. He scratched and clawed. He heard himself scream. Or was that another?

Finally his world tilted. Something hard struck him from behind. In the sky, orange flame swirled, just as it had in the palm of his hand in the desert, but no sooner had this registered than the cloud above him burst. Flame spread outward like a convocation of starlings, thinning, thinning, until all that was left was a swath of dark black smoke that turned the sun a ruddy orange.

The sound of the world crumbling began to dim. He was returned to himself at last. Lifting his head, he saw others standing nearby. The Blade Maidens. Silver Spears. Others who lived . . . Gods, where was he? It came a moment later. Ishmantep.

He stood and saw the results of what he'd done. The cutter, while still smoking, was no longer aflame. He'd done it. He'd done it! And yet no one was looking at the ship. They were looking at something behind him.

With rapidly growing dread, he turned. Curled in a ball, several paces away, was the form of a woman.

"Anila?" Bakhi's bright hammer, *smoke* was rolling off her in waves. No, he realized as he dropped to his knees by her side, not smoke. It was a fog of cold. "Anila, can you hear me?"

Slowly, quivering like a newborn doe, she rolled toward him. Davud couldn't help it. He gasped. Her skin. It was puffy and blistered and black. Along the backs of her hands where the skin had split, blood slowly oozed. "Oh gods, what have I done?"

"Wuh . . . What . . . What happened, Davud?" He could barely understand her, so garbled were her words. "Did . . . Did we finish it?"

He touched her shoulder, hoping to console her, but he snatched his hand away when she grimaced and recoiled from his touch. "We did," he whispered to her. "We saved them all."

"That's good," she said weakly. Like a child lost in the wilderness, a child who'd given up all hope of ever being found, her body settled back into its previous position. "That's good."

As the fog continued to roll off her form, he knew with certainty she was going to die. She was going to die, and it was his fault.

Chapter 53

WHEN HE HEARD THE RATTLE of a wagon rolling up outside the
small room in Sharakhai's west end, Ramahd pulled a chunk of a
dark brown substance from a lacquered wooden box and set it into the bowl
of the shisha sitting beside him. The floor was layered in dark carpets. Pillows
surrounded the shisha. A lone lantern rested on a table in the corner, shrouded
in red veils, casting the entire room in a bleak, bloody pall.

Using a brand from a nearby brazier, Ramahd lit the contents of the bowl,
then blew on it. The dark substance lit, but not hungrily. It was a slow burn,
a subtly eager burn, as if it knew all too well the sort of night that lay ahead.
As the door opened at the top of the stairs, Ramahd drew a long breath from
one of the three shisha tubes. He tasted the bittersweet smoke, filled his lungs
with it, which in turn brought his memories of using lotus rushing back to
him. He hadn't lied when he'd told Lord Rasul he was no stranger to the kiss
of the black lotus. He'd used it more times than he cared to admit after Yasmine's and Rehann's deaths. There were times he yearned for it still, especially
when he felt he was no closer to avenging their deaths than he was when he'd
crawled back to Qaimir along with the other survivors of the Bloody Passage.

He would not have wished to do so now, but this was for Meryam and her plans. This was a necessary part of the story they were laying before Rasul lest he suspect something and bolt like a desert hare. It was necessary. But the touch of the black . . . It was so very, very lovely. An old friend come calling. *Well,* Ramahd thought, *a duplicitous friend, perhaps, but a welcome one this night, for there is dark business afoot.*

Two sets of footsteps descended the stairs. A form darkened the room's entryway at its base. Lord Rasul, grandson of King Kiral, stared about in confusion. He wore the same fine clothes as earlier that night at the Qaimiri embassy house. He wore no knife, no short sword, as some of the nobles seemed to be favoring of late.

"Welcome," Ramahd said, motioning Rasul closer. "Come. Sit."

Filtering down the stairwell from above came the sound of clopping hooves, the wheels of a wagon clattering away. As the sounds dwindled and were lost altogether, Rasul stepped into the room. Amaryllis, who had accompanied him down the stairs, stepped past the young lord of Sharakhai and made her way to the ring of pillows circling the shisha. She wore a fine purple dress, almost black in the red light. She was a sight, Ramahd had to admit, a loyal blade to the throne of Qaimir. Her unbound hair swept across one shoulder and down her chest as she sat and took up one of the three tubes snaking out from the shisha, not as if it were an *old* friend, but a friend she'd never left.

Rasul stared at the rising smoke as though it were a dead body. "Lord Amansir, what is the meaning of this?" He said the words with only a hint of anger. More noticeable by far were the notes of confusion and curiosity. *Promising,* Ramahd thought.

From the shisha, Amaryllis drew two short breaths then one long, all the while staring at Rasul with her dark, languid eyes.

"I asked for the meaning of this," Rasul said, his tone more biting. He tried to hold Ramahd's gaze, but his attention continued to drift sidelong toward Amaryllis.

Ramahd took another draw from his shisha pipe; it joined his first like a new voice in a rapidly growing choir. As he blew smoke into the air, the rattle of a chain came from the next room. A muffled call followed, as of someone gagged and calling for help. It sounded strangely distant, though, as if it were happening deep in the desert, not here in Sharakhai. The lotus, toying with him already, Ramahd knew.

Ramahd motioned calmly to the pillows. "Why don't you sit?"

Rasul stood his ground, but he swallowed. Licked his lips while glancing at the doorway over Ramahd's shoulder, the source of the sounds. *Here is a young man wholly out of his element.* Ramahd almost felt sorry for him.

"You have what we need, then?" Rasul asked, glancing toward the back of the room.

"We have not yet begun the questioning," Amaryllis said. As the rattle came again, she offered the mouthpiece of the shisha tube. "But we have time yet. Come, my lord."

Rasul ignored her, now wholly fixed on Ramahd, as if he knew that to even look at the shisha, or Amaryllis, would be his undoing. Ramahd held his gaze evenly as the muffled sounds came a third time. It was a sad moan, of a will nearly destroyed. Ramahd tilted his head back toward the doorway behind him. "If you must know, this is business I'm not yet ready to conduct." He drew another long breath, blew gray smoke toward the ceiling of the red room.

Colors began to shift. The edges of the table, the veil around the lantern, Rasul himself, took on a molten yellow glow, as if they'd been forged anew and borne down from the sun by Thaash himself. Ramahd turned, feeling the characteristic daze, like the feeling one has in a waterborne ship as the waves churn and the ship rocks. He poured three glasses of araq. Handed one to Amaryllis, who took a long swallow, eyes closed as if it were the sweetest taste in all the world. He poured another and placed it near the shisha where Rasul would sit if he so chose. A third he poured for himself, and drank. A syrupy liquid redolent of fire and smoke and leather, with a bright, coppery finish that tasted of anise and some unknown fruit the gods themselves would surely declare perfect.

He stared at the glass awhile, savoring the aftertaste. Exactly when Rasul had decided to join him he wasn't sure, but he was now sitting to Ramahd's left, taking the glass of araq in one hand and staring at it as if it were a woman, he an untested boy. It glinted blood red in the lantern light. Rasul downed it in one sudden swallow, then took up the shisha tube Amaryllis held for him. He stared into Amaryllis's eyes as he drew from it, a short breath first, and then a much longer one. His eyelids fluttered while Amaryllis watched, sharing with him the darkest of smiles, the lure of a demon in the night.

The three of them continued like this for some time. Ramahd poured araq. They drank. They smoked. Amaryllis moved around the table to sit next to Rasul. She leaned in to him, whispered words Ramahd couldn't hear. She ran fingers through his hair, kissed his neck. Rasul did not stop her.

When Ramahd finally noted the look in his eye—the one that told him he was now journeying to another place—he said, "Sharakhai is a wonder, is it not?"

Rasul, running his hand up Amaryllis's leg, swung his head slowly toward him. "It is."

"I weep," Ramahd continued, forcing himself to concentrate on what he needed lest he become as lost as Rasul, "when I see what the Moonless Host have done to it."

Rasul touched his forehead to Amaryllis's. He leaned in and kissed her on the lips. "As do I. I can only imagine what it must have been like."

"My lord?"

"The Bloody Passage."

The lotus was carrying Ramahd away. He'd nearly lost track of his purpose here, so bewitching was the symphony now playing within him. But those words . . . "What did you say?"

"The Bloody Passage," Rasul said. "It must have been terrible."

A woman sprinting across golden sand. An arrow taking her in the ribs as a line of desert men watch.

His wife, lost to the Moonless Host. To Macide. The vision of his wife's death—now seen in crystal clarity—drew him back to his purpose like reins on a willful horse.

"Those were difficult days," Ramahd said. "Days which have grown worse as the Host closes in."

"The Host does not *close in*. We will stop their every move."

Ramahd nodded, granting him the point though it was as foolish as the emperor from the children's rhymes who demands the wind stop blowing, the sea stop churning. When the sounds of struggle came again from the next room, it sounded like dozens had been caught and chained, ready for torture. The walls seemed to lean in and listen as Ramahd spoke again. "I'm most pleased Qaimir could help in some small way, my lord, before the caches had been compromised."

Amaryllis raked her fingers through Rasul's short hair, making furrows that quickly disappeared. "What caches?" she asked while planting kisses along his neck.

"The elixirs," Rasul replied breathily.

She drew his head into her hands, then kissed him on the lips, a long, sensuous thing. She pulled him away, stared deeply into his eyes. "Elixirs, my lord?"

"The draughts," he said. "Those that grant the Kings long life."

Amaryllis laughed, as if Rasul were but a boy who knew nothing of life in the desert. "My lord, it was the *gods* who granted them long life."

Rasul shook his head, leaning in for another kiss. "The gods granted Azad the ability to make elixirs. It's the *elixirs* that grant them their immortality."

Ramahd blinked slowly. He took in the contents of this ruddy, rusty room anew as a strange elation welled up from somewhere deep inside him.

Elixirs . . .

Elixirs that grant the Kings their immortality.

In a moment of crystalline clarity, he knew that this was what Juvaan had been searching for, what he hoped to feed to the Moonless Host, thereby weakening the Kings. And in turn, it was what the Kings wanted so desperately to hide. But . . .

"Why would the Host care?" he asked, forgetting in his lotus haze that Amaryllis was supposed to lead the questioning. "The Kings could simply make more."

"Not without Azad," Rasul said. "And Azad is dead, fallen to an assassin's blade."

The emotions that struck Ramahd were so fierce his eyes closed and his head reared back. Could it be? Another King, fallen?

Movement came from Ramahd's right. In the doorway stood Tiron's younger brother, Luken—the source of the false moaning, the rattling of unbound chains. Before him stood Meryam, wearing the raiment of a Qai-miri queen. Ramahd could only stare, so intent was she. Amaryllis, however, broke away from Rasul and backed away at Meryam's approach.

Meryam ignored them both, focusing solely on Rasul. "Azad is dead?"

Confusion plain on his face, Rasul looked from Ramahd to Amaryllis, then back at Meryam, who stood before him like a queen of the dead. "Yes." He seemed to know it was something he should not reveal, but Meryam was an unstoppable force.

"And now," she said, "three caches remain. Three stores of the elixirs that preserve the Kings like milk from Rhia's teat."

Rasul backed away from Meryam like a scuttling crab, as if he knew he should leave this place, knew that he'd made a terrible mistake by coming here. Luken stepped past them all and placed himself in the passageway leading to the stairs, cutting off Rasul's lone means of escape. Rasul watched him go, his look of fearful defiance crumbling to one of simple desperation. "Please. I'll do you no harm. We are allies!"

"How large are the caches?" Meryam asked, standing above him. When Rasul remained silent, Meryam stepped by his side and crouched, taking his jaw in a grip so fierce her knuckles turned white and Rasul's face pinched in pain. "How much *is* there?"

Rasul's throat convulsed. His breath came rabbit quick. He stared into Meryam's eyes, nostrils flaring, and then the look in his eyes hardened.

"Meryam!" Ramahd called.

Before anyone could react, Rasul had pulled a slim knife from his sleeve and slashed it across Meryam's body. Meryam warded off the blow with her arms, arching away from Rasul's swing. Even in the dim light Ramahd could see the depth of the cut Rasul had made across both forearms.

Luken was on him in a blink. Rasul tried the same move with him, but Luken was a fighter, through and through. He pulled back from Rasul's initial swing, timing his forward momentum to bring one hand against Rasul's wrist, holding the knife at bay, while the other went to his throat.

"Leave him unharmed!" Meryam called.

They all turned to her. Blood flowed from her wounds, a river that darkened the sleeves of her golden dress. She pulled at her wrists, ripping the buttons away, which clattered to the floor. Pulling the sleeve back, she examined the deep wound along her right forearm, then ran her tongue along the wound. Blood sizzled. Then she turned her attention to her left arm and did the same.

When she was done, her eyes were alive, black jewels in a sea of red. A grim smile lit her pallid face. She took Rasul by the coat and dragged him back to the pillows around the shisha. From the lacquered box she took a fresh hunk of lotus and set it in the shisha's bowl, and then, leaning close, she blew it a kiss. It flamed like a blossoming rose, petals unfurling, smoke rising, twisting, curling toward the ceiling like the vines of an ivy. She picked up the shisha tube and drew upon it, exhaling toward Rasul, who did nothing to stop it. "Leave us," she said, the chill of the Austral Sea captured in those two simple words.

Luken and Amaryllis immediately complied, heading for the stairs. Ramahd, however, remained. "Meryam—"

She held the mouthpiece out for Rasul to take. After the briefest of pauses, he took it, a look of cold resignation on his face. *Here is the grandson of a Sharakhani King,* Ramahd thought, *so different from the man who'd entered the room not so long ago.*

"I said leave us."

What could he say? This course had been laid out since the moment he'd poured his own blood down Tariq's throat. They needed to know what Rasul knew, and giving him back to the Kings was no longer an option. He supposed it never had been. He didn't wish to see Rasul tortured, or dead, but what would he do about it now?

"Could we not take him back to Qaimir? Use him as a hostage should things go poorly?"

Meryam swiveled her head toward him as Rasul took another draw from the shisha. "Your queen has told you to leave."

Ramahd held her gaze, but in the end couldn't maintain it. The hunger in them. The anger. "Of course," he said, then turned to the stairs.

Golden Rhia, a thin sliver above the city, trekked across the star-filled sky. Those few walking along this narrow, west end street gave little notice to the three of them, especially with Luken watching them like a hungry jackal. They passed Ramahd with the same sort of lotus glow as below in the cellar, but their edges were inked bright blue instead of gold. At first the city—the sound of it, the smell of it, its very corpus—felt as large as the whole of the world, but soon that sense reversed, and the world began to press in, crushing him bit by bit.

Amaryllis watched him silently, to Ramahd looking as though there was ill-intent in those beautiful dark eyes of hers. He knew her to be as loyal as

Luken and Tiron, but just then he couldn't shake the feeling that she was ready to pull a slim knife of her own and thrust it into his heart, so he sent her home to the place she kept near the western harbor. He felt nothing similar from Luken, but the man's breathing was like a ruddy forge, and Ramahd soon sent him back to the embassy house. He was alone with Sharakhai at last.

Nearby, a rooftop oud began a soulful song, other instruments across the neighborhood picking it up—a flute, a rebab, a tanbur. It quelled the feeling of unease in Ramahd, made him wonder what Meryam might be learning from Rasul. And that in turn made him wonder about Yasmine and Rehann. He'd begun this journey on a quest for revenge, but now that quest—and his promise to his wife and daughter—felt as distant as the stars above. His own quest was now tangled in Meryam's intricate web to the point that he would assassinate a young Sharakhani lord simply to gain information. Were Yasmine before him now, he didn't know if he could look her in the eye.

Have you found him, Ramahd? Have you found Macide?

My regrets, dear Yasmine, but I haven't even come close.

He sat with those thoughts burning inside his gut. At last the music faded. The sounds of the city quelled, became silent, a restless beast lying down for its slumber. An hour passed. Two. His mind cleared, at least enough to speak with Meryam. The sun would soon be brightening the east in any case. They'd have to leave Rasul's body in a nearby alley—one only a short walk from the most notorious drug den in the west end—before the city woke to witness it.

He took the stairs down to the cellar and its blood-red light to find Rasul lying on the pillows, eyes staring sightlessly at the ceiling, the shisha tube still twined between the fingers of his right hand. The haze of the lotus had dissipated, but the smell lingered. It made Ramahd's stomach turn, and yet such was the lotus's lure that it kindled within him a desire to sit and draw on the pipe once more.

Meryam leaned against the back wall, hands behind her back, looking more like a street tough from the Shallows than a queen from Qaimir. "We have a decision to make, Ramahd."

Ramahd came to a stop just outside the ring of pillows. Rasul lay halfway between them. "What have you learned?"

"Little more than what he told us before you left, but I'm convinced now he was telling the truth. Two Kings are dead, and with one of them their tie to immortality. Now the Moonless Host conspire to rob them of the dwindling remains of King Azad's work." She stared down at Rasul, her eyes sharp as broken glass. "We could take this to the Kings. We could give them this information and put a stop to the Moonless Host's plans. We could serve them Juvaan Xin-Lei on a spit, and likely exact concessions that would keep Qaimir safe for generations."

"Then why don't we?"

"Because such concessions would mean little if the slow decay of Sharakhai's power continues. Juvaan's queen positions herself. She sits at the edge of the desert like a mountain fox, waiting for the right time to pounce. Kundhun is too disorganized to consider a move for the desert, but we'd be fools not to think Malasan isn't doing the same as Mirea. I wonder if Queen Alansal knows something we do not, else why have Juvaan take such bold steps in the first place? Perhaps Sharakhai's fall is closer than we've ever guessed. And if that is true, it may not be wise to make bargains with the Kings."

"We'd be fools to think the Kings are powerless, waiting to be pounced upon by the likes of Queen Alansal."

In the corner, the lamp flame guttered for a moment, making the shadows sway nauseatingly about the room. "Perhaps there's a way to learn more."

"How?"

"Do we not have a friend in the Blade Maidens? One who might share what she's learned with us?"

"Çeda?"

"Just so."

At that moment, Ramahd could think of nothing but his pact with Guhldrathen, Çeda's life in forfeit should they fail to deliver Hamzakiir. *And my own blood used to seal the bargain, a thing the beast will surely call upon one day.* "What could a Maiden, freshly given her ebon blade, possibly know?"

Meryam chuckled, a sanguineous sound in the blood-red room. "There's only one way to find out, Ramahd."

Chapter 54

ÇEDA WATCHED AS TWO OF THE SPEARS, on Sümeya's orders, lifted the blackened form of Davud's friend, Anila, onto a makeshift stretcher. The poor woman moaned as they carried her away, but the sound was akin to a kitten mewling, weak-born and sure to die. Davud looked torn between following Anila and fleeing into the desert. There was still some blood at the corner of his mouth.

Davud, a blood mage . . .

How it had happened, she couldn't begin to guess, but now was not the time for that tale. "Go to her," she said to him. "Sit by her side. Comfort her if you can."

His gaze shifted to Çeda as though he hadn't realized she was standing there, as though he'd just remembered where he was and all that had happened. "Yes, of course."

She squeezed his arm. "We'll speak soon."

He nodded and walked away.

From the deck of the ship there came a crash, the splintering of wood. Melis and a Silver Spear had finally managed to open the magically bound door leading to the ship's interior. Crewmen came staggering onto deck, their eyes wide with sober relief.

After motioning Çeda to follow her, Sümeya headed for the ladder leading up to the pier. Together, they made their way onto the ship and below-decks. Sümeya stopped in the narrow passageway at the base of the stairs. Men were gathered around the captain's cabin. They made way for her and Çeda. Inside, Aziz lay on the floor, his eyes staring sightlessly at the beautifully worked wood of the cabin's ceiling. Emre was on his knees near his prone form, his expression one of shock and confusion. Melis—her black robes hopelessly dusted with golden sand—was leaning over Aziz, listening for breath, her fingers placed gently over the veins in his neck.

"What happened?" Çeda asked.

Emre stood slowly. "When the fire came he was ordered here to wait. He was sitting on the captain's chair"—he pointed uselessly at the chair, which was tipped over and lying in the corner of the cabin—"and he just . . . fell over. Straight onto the floor."

"He ate nothing?" Sümeya asked. "Drank nothing?"

"Not that I saw," Emre replied.

Sümeya looked to the Silver Spears, who shook their heads. "We saw nothing, Maiden," their captain said.

"Here," Melis called. She lifted Aziz's right hand and showed them a ring with a hinged lid. Within was a silver thorn with blood and some purple substance coating it. A poisoned ring. All Aziz would need to do was open it and drive the thorn into his skin. "He surely used it here," Melis said, pointing to a red mark on his palm.

It was in that moment, while everyone was staring at Aziz, that Çeda caught Emre looking at her. It was for a fraction of a second only, the blink of an eye, and no one but Çeda would even recognize it, but Emre was embarrassed. She'd seen the look on his face a hundred times. He'd got better at hiding it over the years, but she still knew.

He was lying. He knew how this had happened. Which could only mean one thing.

Emre had killed him.

———————— ←●→ ————————

They remained in Ishmantep for several days. At Sümeya's orders, the serai's shipwrights worked furiously to repair the *Javelin*. They might have taken another ship, but the ones that had survived the fire were even more damaged than the *Javelin*. A caravan came in on the second day—three massive ships, slow movers across the sand—and for a time Sümeya debated on commandeering one of them, but in the end she reckoned they'd be better off completing the work on the *Javelin* and making up the time on the journey.

Sümeya spent her waking hours sifting through Aziz's records. Melis, Çeda, and Yndris were ordered to search the temple, which was a foul exercise that taught them little they didn't already know: that Hamzakiir had occupied this place, and had performed grizzly experiments on the collegia scholars to turn them into those unnerving creatures.

"Do they know what's happened to them?" Yndris said one day as they were searching through the room of stained tables.

"Let us pray that the gods were kind," Melis said, leaving the rest unsaid.

Çeda *did* pray. To Bakhi, who may have come to take their souls as they'd changed, and to Thaash for them to find their vengeance if not.

Kameyl threw herself into her assignment: questioning the scarabs of the Moonless Host. She found, however, that they'd arrived only a few days before the *Javelin*, and that they'd been told little. After two solid days of interrogation, they revealed what Kameyl had already started to believe: that there was a rift in the Moonless Host. There was a power struggle between Macide Ishaq'ava and Hamzakiir over the direction of the Al'afwa Khadar.

Satisfied she'd gotten all she could from the men, Kameyl questioned those who lived in or near the caravanserai. Here too, she learned little, and became so overzealous in her search for anything of substance that Sümeya ordered Melis to replace her. In the end, they merely added to the story the old bookbinder had told them on the day of the attack, stories of Hamzakiir, disguised as Şaban, how he'd arrived, how afterward the pervading mood of industry in the serai had changed to one of uncertainty and fear.

By the time the repairs to the *Javelin* were complete, Sümeya felt confident they'd found all they were going to find, and she ordered their ship to set sail for Sharakhai; the Kings needed to know what had happened, before Hamzakiir could unleash his plans.

"The question is what Hamzakiir plans to do with them," Kameyl said that first night on the sands. She wore only her gray shift, which she'd pulled down over her shoulders so Melis, who was sitting on the same cot, could tend Kameyl's acid-burned skin. Kameyl grimaced as she applied a salve to the angry red flesh on her right arm, where she'd caught the worst of the shamblers' spray. The wounds were not life-threatening, but they were serious. The acid had burned not only her arm, but her right cheek and neck as well. The skin there was raw, and in the worst places was pocked and ridged like a barren landscape.

"If Emre's story is to be believed," Melis said, "they'll throw themselves against the aqueduct and try to tear them down." She shrugged. "Now that I've seen them with my own eyes, I can't say I doubt it."

"They could do that any time they wished," Kameyl replied, "far out in the desert where we'd never find them."

"But it isn't the destruction of the aqueduct they want," Çeda said, "not truly." All eyes turned to her. "They wish to strike fear into the hearts of those who love the Kings. They wish everyone to know that they are brave enough to stand against the might of Tauriyat. They wish to lure others to their cause by doing so. And they will if they succeed in their plans, but first, they need to be *seen*. They need to be *heard* by all in Sharakhai."

"Dear gods," Melis said softly, "where does it end?"

Kameyl immediately pulled away and stared scornfully at Melis. "When the Al'afwa Khadar and their sympathizers lie dead."

"Of course," Melis said, motioning for Kameyl to turn back. "It's only that I feel Sharakhai itself tiring of this fight."

Yndris lifted her head from her reading of the Kannan. "Find your nerve, woman."

"Mind your tongue," Sümeya snapped before Melis could respond. "She has as much nerve as you, young dove. As much as anyone in our order. She's proven it over and over again. The stories *you* have to tell, on the other hand, I can tick away on a single hand. Call her *woman* like that again and I'll let her take it out on your hide." Yndris stared with a cold expression, but then went back to her book, and Sümeya turned to Melis. "I feel it as well, the centuries of struggle, the weight on the people's shoulders, but there is nothing to do but fight. Give the enemy the smallest foothold and they strengthen their position. Give more and they will take the city."

Çeda nearly said it. *The desert cannot sustain your war forever. Speak with the Host. There must be a path to peace.* But it would be the height of foolishness with Yndris present. And Kameyl would never listen to her words.

Sümeya had surprised her, though. Çeda had never thought to see her bend. Then again, she'd never thought to see the First Warden lost in love.

Love breeds weakness, she could hear Yndris saying.

No, Çeda would say in return, *love breeds life.*

Melis continued her ministrations. Scars of every shape and size marked her body. A long, ragged gash across her ribs; three claw marks that ran like furrows down the back of one shoulder, several puckered kisses along her stomach and another in the meat of her right arm; a rounded lump on her elbow that looked as though something had grown beneath the skin. A dozen others, small and large, faded and fresh. They told Kameyl's stories—told them well—but so did the intricate tattoos over her arms, across her upper chest, across the entirety of her back. Intricate, scrolling designs and images that, along with the scars, told of a life filled with pain and will and passion that knew no bounds. *Where would the Kings be without their Maidens?*

Oddly, those born near Tauriyat laughed at the tales laid out on the skin of those who emigrated from the desert, considering them unworthy of the Amber Jewel. Those very same people would beam with pride when the first of their daughters' tattoos was inked on the back of their sword hand, and again as more tales were added. Kameyl's recorded the battles she'd fought, the enemies she'd sent to the grave. But they also spoke of her loves. A vine-like design that wrapped around her right arm, around her biceps and shoulder, was a poem Kameyl herself had written, a counterpoint to the hard life she led and an indicator to the gods the things she loved most so that they might choose an appropriate place for her in the farther fields.

"May I?" Çeda asked, motioning to Kameyl's arm as Melis began wrapping fresh bandages around her midriff.

Kameyl stared flatly into Çeda's eyes, but then nodded, twisting her arm this way and that to allow Çeda to see the words.

A girl who walks upon the shore,
A woman not yet grown;

She breathes the air of discontent,
Her life not yet her own.

She calls upon the river swell,
She wades into the flow;
Wondrous swift it bears her south,
A seed by wind is blown.

She lands upon a distant bank,
A place she does not know;
She looks upon her withered hands,
Nor maiden nor matron but crone.

"It's beautiful," Çeda said when she'd finished. Only months ago she'd found herself wondering when the river would come and take *her* to the places she wished to be—how long ago that seemed already—and now that it had, she wondered when it would stop, and where she would land when it did.

Kameyl stared into Çeda's eyes, perhaps weighing the truth in her words, but then she softened and gave Çeda one sharp nod.

"It will not be so bad as this once it heals," Melis said as she finished wrapping the bandages around her chest and shoulder.

"What care have I for that?" Kameyl had said.

She sat stoically as Melis applied more salve to the wounds on her neck. The only sign she was feeling anything at all was the reddening of her eyes and the occasional grinding of her teeth. She would soon recover, nostrils flaring as she took a deep breath and stared at the ship's hull as if she could bore into it by will alone. She was a severe woman, with sharp cheeks, an arrowhead chin, and eyes that pierced as deeply as spears, but for all that she was a beautiful woman in her own way. There were men who might want her—many men, in fact—but Kameyl would take none who would ask her to kneel.

In this, at least, she and Çeda could agree. Çeda would never take a man, have a child with him, and sit three steps behind as he ruled the house, but that didn't mean she need be alone, though. There had been days when she thought she would come to love Osman, the lord of the pits. He was skilled in the arts of sweat and skin and the sting of muscles pushed to the breaking point, but he'd always been so serious, his arms spread wide to encircle his holdings, haunted by the deep-rooted fear that someone, *anyone*, Çeda included, might put them at risk.

And then there was Emre. There had been many days in the House of Maidens when she dreamed of his stealing into her room and pulling her blanket from her bed. He would shush her when she tried to protest. Then he'd lay himself down on top of her. Kiss her how she liked—rough in all the right places, soft in the rest. There were days when her body ached for it. There were days when those dreams focused on another. The lord from Qaimir. He was gone now, returned to his homeland, perhaps never to return, and yet she had hoped to hear he'd come back to the embassy house. They were two of a kind, she and Ramahd, in a way that she and Emre were not. He knew the sorts of things she'd been through.

Her thoughts, as they had so often these past few days, drifted to Sümeya, the two of them lying on the sand, kissing, hands roaming. There were no two ways about it. Çeda had been using her. And yet her touch had been welcome all the same.

"What are you doing?" Yndris asked.

"What?" Çeda replied.

"You're sitting there like some moon-eyed calf."

Çeda shook her head. "Nothing." Then she stood and headed up to deck. She wanted to be alone, but how could she be on a ship choked with people? She moved to the ship's stern and sat along the gunwales. A short while later movement behind the ship caught her attention. Kerim, bounding across the dunes as the sun touched the horizon. She hadn't seen him since he'd launched himself into the dark tunnel after Hamzakiir. She'd thought him dead, but Kameyl had said he'd escaped and later fled to the desert. She hadn't been able to feel him then, and she could barely feel him now. He was masking his presence from her, she knew. She might have taken a petal and forced the issue, but what would be the point? She would leave him to grieve as he would.

The ship's captain called a halt well after the sun had set and true night had fallen. The crew ate quickly on the sands, and were preparing to return for their early morning departure when Çeda tugged at Emre's sleeve and motioned for him to walk with her. Sümeya watched the two of them, but said nothing as Emre stood and walked by her side, away from the ship.

"I thought you might wait until the middle of the night again," Emre said when they'd passed beyond the dune.

"The land becomes less rough in a day or two. I suspect Sümeya will start pushing for night sailing to reach Sharakhai as soon as she can."

"You're not worried she will see us speaking alone?"

"She knows we're close. She won't begrudge us a moonlit stroll. Besides, after what happened in Ishmantep, you've earned a bit of her trust." As they climbed the lee of the next dune, she debated on how to approach the subject, the reason she'd wanted to speak to him. In the end, she saw no reason to approach carefully. "Why didn't you tell me you were sent to kill Aziz?"

Emre glanced back. No one was following them, but he still waited until the ship and crew were once more out of sight before speaking. "What good would that have done?"

"We're in this together, Emre."

"I didn't even know if I would do it."

"But you did. You'd planned it all along. You aren't just gambling with your own life now. Mine's at stake as well."

"I know, Çeda. I'm sorry. He was a traitor. He had shifted his allegiance to Hamzakiir. He was feeding money and supplies to him and withholding it from Ishaq. If others felt they could do the same, it would cripple Ishaq's hold on the Host."

"If what Kameyl learned from the soldiers is true, it's *already* crippled."

"Exactly my point. We need to bring them back in line or Ishaq will lose control of the Host entirely."

Ishaq. Çeda's grandfather. And Macide, her uncle. It was a thing she'd still not fully digested. Her first instinct was to let it go, to wait to tell Emre until she'd had a chance to think on it more, but she'd just berated him for not sharing something she felt she had a right to know. "Emre, my mother was Ishaq's daughter."

That stopped Emre in his tracks. *"What?"* When she only stared, he asked, "Are you sure?"

She nodded. "Macide told me."

He stood there for a time, lost in thought. "Before the attack on Külaşan's palace," he said after a time, "Macide and I spoke. He said he knew Ahya, but didn't say how. It makes perfect sense now. He had that look in his eye, like the finch that filched Yerinde's secrets."

Çeda shook her head at the wonder of it all. "What a weave the threads of our lives do make."

Emre had half a smile on his face, a quip just there on his lips, but then his eyes seemed to stare inwardly. "I know what they're going to do," he finally said. "Macide and Hamid and the rest."

"What do you mean?"

"You were right. I shouldn't have hidden anything from you."

"What are they going to do, Emre?"

"While the Kings are at the aqueduct, they're going to attack the palaces. Three of them in particular."

"Which ones?"

"I don't know. They were waiting for that information when I left."

"Why, then? To kill the Kings?"

He shrugged. "I don't think so. I think they're hoping the Kings will be gone."

"Then why go at all?"

"I don't know. There's something hidden within the palaces. Gold, perhaps. Or something else they value."

"You must know more."

"Truly, Çeda, I . . ." He stopped, a look of horror stealing over him. He gripped her forearm and pulled her back.

She turned and saw it a moment later. She *felt* it as well. A presence lurking at the edge of her consciousness. She thought it was Kerim, but when she peered closer, she saw a glint of gold reflecting Rhia's light. It struck a memory of another night in Sharakhai, Beht Zha'ir, when she'd first met the King of the Thirteenth Tribe. This was he, Sehid-Alaz, but he didn't move, perhaps fearful of being seen from the ship, so Çeda stepped toward him, the sand piling around her boots as she took the slope down.

Once there she could see him at last, the sad king, the betrayed lord of the lost tribe. He rose up, crook-backed, eyes glinting. Emre approached as well, but remained a step behind her.

"Why have you come?" Çeda asked, though part of her was afraid of the answer.

All the old instincts, her fear of the asirim instilled in her from childhood, returned as he shuffled forward. The rattle of his breath made her cringe, but she pulled herself taller as Sehid-Alaz approached. *"I have come to open your eyes,"* he said, his words the rattle of windblown leaves. *"Much was hidden from you."*

"What? What was hidden from me?"

His only answer was to lift a finger and reach for her. All her instincts told her to pull away, but she stood still, waiting for his touch. The moment his finger brushed her forehead she felt herself falling as the world dissolved around her.

Chapter 55

With the twin moons Rhia and Tulathan hanging like lanterns over the desert, Çeda and Ahya's skiff sailed over the desert. Ahya steered while Saliah sat in the front. Çeda took the thwart between them, the knot in her stomach tightening like wet leather left to dry in the sun.

Çeda was sure Saliah was blind, and yet she turned her head this way and that, as if sensing the heat from a fire. She pointed with one long finger. "There," she said, and Ahya adjusted the course of the skiff. The moons were not quite full, thank the gods, so Beht Zha'ir was not yet upon them, but it was small comfort. Saliah was guiding them toward the dark patches that lay ahead—the blooming fields—and nothing could bode well from that.

They came to a stop well shy of the pitch-dark trees and exited the skiff. Saliah led the way, pressing the butt of her staff into the sand, then putting her ear to the head, as if she were listening to all that lay below. She did this several times, moving closer and closer to the trees, which looked to Çeda like a pack of black laughers huddled close, ready to charge the moment the three of them came near.

When Saliah approached, however, the branches began to part. Like a cloud of insects retreating from smoke, the thorny branches drew back, forming a tunnel to a clearing within the grove of twisted trees. The clearing was tear-shaped, and other spaces connected to it through arches or gaps between the trees, making it feel as though someone had crafted this place, planned it like some vast hedge maze.

Saliah led the way with Ahya and Çeda following hand in hand. No sooner had they passed beyond the bent trees than their branches rattled back into place. It sent a chill down Çeda's frame. She hadn't liked being near the trees in the first place, and she *hated* the idea of being trapped within them.

"Çeda should be the one to call to him," Saliah said, breaking the tense silence.

Ahya nodded, then knelt before Çeda and took her hands. "He is the one we spoke of, Çeda. His name is Sehid-Alaz, and he has lost his way."

The terror was rising in Çeda by the moment. "I want to go home, memma." The rattle of the adichara was all around her. "I want to go home."

Ahya squeezed her hands. "Don't be afraid. We only need you to call to him."

Saliah stared into the darkness of the trees. "Call to him, girl."

Nearby, the sand began to shift, to roll, as if a sand drake were lying beneath and twisting its body. She backed away. She knew very well it wasn't a drake. She knew what it was, but she didn't want to voice it. Doing so would only draw it nearer. "Home, memma! I want to go home!"

Her mother grabbed her moments before her foot caught on an exposed root. Çeda nearly fell into the adichara's thorns, but Ahya pulled her back and shook her. "Please be brave." She pointed down at the shifting sand. "Now call his name!"

Çeda didn't know why they needed him, the *father of their tribe*. She didn't know what her mother and Saliah expected her to do if she found him anyway. She only knew she had to leave. There must be a way out of here. She twisted away from her mother's grasp and ran through the nearest opening.

"Çeda!"

She kept running but slipped as the sand gave way beneath her. She screamed as her foot sunk into the sand, as something grabbed her ankle.

"Çeda! The thorns!"

She stumbled, pulling her foot free of the slip-sand, and kept running into another clearing, smaller than the last, then ducked down and crawled through a tunnel, hoping, praying it would lead beyond the trees to the open desert.

It did not.

Ahead was another large clearing. She searched desperately for a way out, but the trees surrounding it were ordered tightly, like rank upon rank of black-thorned soldiers. There were no more avenues of escape. "Memma!"

"Çeda, come back!"

She tried. She ran back the way she'd come, but stopped when the ground before her moved. An arm lifted up, clawing its way into the air. "Memma!"

She wanted to run past the asirim, but the thought of one of those things grabbing her kept her rooted to the spot. She backed away, stopping just short of the trees with their closed buds that looked like eyes on stalks. Had she not known how poisonous the trees were, she would have tried climbing them to escape, thorns and all, but she'd heard the stories of how painful the poison was, how quickly it killed.

Two arms lifted from the sand, a head lifted up and scanned the area. Çeda was shivering badly. Part of her wanted to scream, but she was too afraid that the black, paper-skinned creature would turn and come for her. The asirim were slow when waking—or so the legends said—but fierce and fast once they'd shaken off their slumber.

The memory of Leorah came to her, how calm she'd been, how uncaring of the world and its troubles. She remembered how, after Leorah had given her the piece of the petal, the vigor it had granted. It had given her too much at first, but then she had calmed. Quickly, she took out the kerchief from the small leather bag at her belt and unfolded it. Much of the petal had crumbled, bits and pieces falling away as she laid the remains out over her palm, but there was enough there to take. She picked up the largest piece and put it under her tongue, as Leorah had done, then took another.

An asir levered its angular body up from the sand, blocking the entrance to the small clearing. Another rose before Çeda, staring at her, bow-backed and sniffing like a dog emboldened by starvation. In the darkness of the grove, Çeda could see few of the asir's features. Lank hair. Emaciated limbs. Long, misshapen claws at the ends of its fingers. But the smell of it. Dear gods, it was the smell of sweetness and rot. It made Çeda gag even as saliva filled her mouth from the adichara petal.

The asir came closer as more rose behind it. "Çeda, come this way!" her mother called, but her words were cut off. Çeda heard a strangled sound, followed by a scuffle.

"Sehid-Alaz! Sehid-Alaz!" Çeda cried. "Please, I wish to see Sehid-Alaz!"

The asir before her crouched lower, put its face close to hers. A sound emanated from its throat, a bare rasp. Words, she guessed, but what it might be saying she had no idea. "I wish to see Sehid-Alaz," she said.

The asir snorted, then leaned forward and sniffed her neck. It shivered— whether in anger or excitement, Çeda couldn't guess—but then it turned and walked toward the center of the clearing while the other asirim cleared the way, leaving a rough circle of exposed sand. As the asir faced Çeda and beckoned her closer, it began to sink. First its feet were swallowed, then its ankles, then its shins. It beckoned again, and Çeda came closer, but she was deathly afraid of being drawn down into the earth.

When the asir spoke in a breathy whisper, another asir shoved her. The first grabbed Çeda's wrist even as its waist was lost to the grasping sand, and Çeda was pulled down as well. She hardly had time to scream—to claw at the sand, trying to break free of the asir's grasp—than she was drawn below the surface.

Stone scraped against her legs and hips, against her arms and shoulders. The earth pressed in, forcing the air from her lungs. And then, thank the gods who walk the earth, she was out and falling into darkness. Her ankle twisted as she landed, but the asir caught her, steadied her, then took her by the hand and led her through the darkness.

They wound this way, then that, walking for minutes on end, and all the while, the asir kept a tight grip on Çeda's wrist.

"Where are we going?" Çeda asked.

The asir said nothing. On and on they went, heading slowly downward. The air was cool in this place. They passed caverns filled with faint light emanating from unseen sources. Some were so large they made Çeda feel light-headed. How could such caverns exist?

When the way was dark she used her hand to feel along the tunnel walls. Sometimes it was hard, bare rock. Other times it was sharp. Other times still it was slick with moisture. Often she felt something rough and vine-like. Roots, she realized. She pulled at some when she felt them, and some of it broke away. They *were* roots. *From the adichara?* she wondered.

She lost track of time. She should be tired, especially after their long sail, but the energy of the petal carried her on. Eventually they came to a set of winding paths that led them even lower. Çeda heard dripping water. The petal must be wearing off, Çeda thought, because she had begun to shiver from the cold. Ahead, a soft violet glow lit the tunnel. It was distant yet. It looked like little more than a twinkling star, but it soon grew, and then Çeda could see the tunnel itself, which was almost perfectly round, as if one of Goezhen's wicked beasts had used its great claws to bore the passage. The roots were thick here, making the tunnel floor soft and spongy.

"What is this place?" Çeda asked.

But the asir ignored her. It held her wrist as if it feared she might run away. As if she could ever find her way back to the surface on her own. She would die before she found her way out again.

The tunnel ended in yet another cavern, and it made Çeda gasp. It was huge, the size of a cathedral, and shaped like a gemstone, narrow at the bottom where she and the asir stood, widening as it reached into the darkness. More roots entered this place through the cavern walls, making her wonder just how deep they ran. She might hack at them with a sword and find them ten feet deep. Twenty. Perhaps they reached to the darkest places of the earth where demons were said to dwell.

In the center of the space was a thing Çeda had to stare at to understand. From the ceiling came a clutch of roots that ended ten feet from the floor. The thick braid became thinner and thinner as it dropped from the darkened heights of this place, until all that was left was a thin strand. Along this length came moisture—water, Çeda supposed—dripping down onto a rock of sorts. The rock was translucent, like imperfect glass, and glowed from within with a brilliant violet light that after the darkness was almost too bright to look upon.

"What is it?" Çeda asked, squinting at it.

The asir ignored her. It released her hand and walked beyond the glowing stone. Çeda stepped to one side and saw there was another asir there, lying among the bed of roots. The asir that had led her here crept closer, caring and careful in the same breath, as though it wanted to help but regretted doing so in the past. The asir whispered—a wight in the night—while the other creature, longer, more frail, lifted its head, listening perhaps. It took some time, but it trained its eyes on Çeda, stared at her with rheumy eyes, the violet light casting its blackened skin the sickly purple of rotted eggplant. They remained this way for a time, the one asir whispering, the other looking Çeda over with an anger that Çeda guessed was only one small glimpse into a fount of hatred.

"Sehid-Alaz," Çeda said, for surely this was him, "I've been brought here by my mother, Ahyanesh Allad'ava, and the desert witch, Saliah Riverborn, to speak with you." Her throat caught. She swallowed before speaking again. "I was told you would know why."

The first, the one that had brought Çeda here, did something that shocked Çeda. She—Çeda could see her form better now and was certain she had once been a woman—reached out and touched Sehid-Alaz's cheek. For the first time, Çeda understood her words. *"Blood of our blood."*

It lessened neither the anger nor the despair that shone brightly in his eyes. If anything, it seemed to make them worse. The other asir spoke faster now. Sehid-Alaz's lips pulled back to reveal a sawtooth line of broken teeth. He struggled to pull himself up off the floor. He rolled, made his way slowly to his knees, then to his feet. He shuffled toward her with an unsteady gait, arms spread wide, head jutting forward as if he'd scented his next meal. He loped toward her. Then ran.

A bubbling terror rose up inside Çeda. She backed away, ready to turn and run, just as the other asir tackled him. The two of them scuffled over the ground. But Sehid-Alaz was undeniable, or the other was unwilling to fight. In the end, it amounted to the same thing. He tore at her skin with his claws. He lifted her and slammed her against the glowing stone. Over and over he struck her until black blood oozed from the back of her skull.

He allowed her to slip to the ground, unconscious or dead, then swung his gaze to Çeda, who turned and sprinted away as quickly as she could. With the petal driving her, she moved like a gazelle, and still she heard the huff of his breath coming closer and closer. She'd hardly made it beyond the mouth of the tunnel when he barreled into her.

They both fell onto the lattice of roots. He rolled her over roughly. His eyes pierced her. His nostrils flared as he leaned down and smelled her neck, her hair. He took her hand and licked the blood from a shallow cut she'd received when they'd fallen. *"Lies!"* he wheezed. *"Liiiieeeessss! Through her veins runs the blood of Kings! The blood of Kings!"*

"No!" she screamed back. "I am the daughter of Ahyanesh Allad'ava! I was given petals!" She ripped the small leather bag free from her belt and shook it beneath his nose. "Who but us would defy the Kings so?" Çeda didn't understand everything her mother did, but she knew enough to know that their defiance would mean death were the Kings to find out. She hoped Sehid-Alaz would understand and give up his terrible notion. *The blood of Kings!*

Sehid-Alaz reared back, his craggy face filled with surprise. He snatched the bag from her, brought it to his nose, and breathed deeply. He did so again, his hollow stomach hollowing even further. Then a third time. He swallowed, his chin quivering, and angled himself up on sticklike limbs to turn back toward the cavern. He walked back to the stone and the lifeless form of the asir who lay there, that creature who had once been a woman, then fell to his knees and picked up her hand. He stroked it with all the care a husband would show his wife. Bowing over his folded legs, still holding her hand, he cried. He pulled her to him and held her, and released an anguished lament that felt much larger than this place could hold, as though it would soon burst these cavern walls and shatter the desert sky.

Sehid-Alaz cried for a long while. So did Çeda. She was terrified of Sehid-Alaz, but she felt sorry for him as well, and the other asir he'd killed. When her tears ran dry at last, she approached him slowly. She kneeled and touched his shoulder, then ran her hand down his back. "She was loved," Çeda said softly, "and now she is free."

It was something she'd heard her mother say to Demal's younger sister at Hefhi's funeral. Hefhi had lain in a skiff, wrapped in white, ready to be given back to the desert. "He was loved," Ahya had said to her as Hefhi's skiff had sailed away, "and now he is free."

Sehid-Alaz lifted himself, his joints cracking. *"Freeee."*

"Yes."

"I will be free."

Çeda could hear the yearning in his voice, the deep desire. "One day, yes."

He kissed the dead asir on the forehead, then stood and took Çeda's hand. Without another word, he led her from the cavern and back the way they'd come. How he knew where to go, Çeda had no idea, but there was no hesitation when they came to splits in the tunnels. It took a long time, but eventually they came to a place of darkness. Roots wrapped around her, pulled her up and brought her into the light of dawn. She was among the adichara once more, but alone. Sehid-Alaz had not followed.

"Memma?" She wandered among them, looking for an exit. "Saliah Riverborn?" She came to the desert soon after.

Her mother was already running toward her. She swept Çeda up into her arms and hugged her close. "My sweet child, my sweet child, I'm so sorry. I should never have brought you here."

"You made no mistake bringing her here," said Saliah behind her. She strode toward them, her staff thumping against the sand. "We could not lose him to despair or madness."

Ahya said nothing in return, only held Çeda close as they returned to the skiff. She told them what had happened, and neither said a word. Neither, in fact, seemed surprised by much of it. Her mother, at least, paled when Çeda told her of the way Sehid-Alaz had killed the other asir, and how he'd attacked Çeda. "He said I was the blood of Kings, memma. Why would he think that?"

Ahya, sitting at the tiller, stared at Çeda in silence. She swallowed as the wind tugged at her tail of black hair, then looked to Saliah at the head of the skiff. "She cannot know. It's too soon."

Saliah, her eyes fixed stone-like on the horizon behind them, reached out and touched Çeda's shoulder. "You're sure?"

Ahya nodded.

"Very well," Saliah said as she stroked Çeda's hair. "Do you like to sail, child?"

Çeda shrugged, not understanding why she would ask. "I do."

"Do you sail often?"

"No," Çeda said, "but I have a zilij that I found. I skim over the sand with it."

"Tell me about it."

The sun was rising in the east, driving away the remains of the night. As the desert awakened and Çeda told her tale, Saliah continued to brush her hair, and the memories of her horrific night faded, lost like spindrift in the endless sands of the Great Shangazi.

Chapter 56

CEDA BLINKED. ABOVE HER, stars peered through the gauze of the desert night. Emre knelt by her side, holding her hand. He gave her a nervous smile as she rolled her head toward him. He reached out and wiped the tears from her eyes. "Why do you cry?" he asked.

"My mother." How could she explain it? "I saw her. She hid much from me."

A brief pause. "And you're surprised?"

"This is different. Saliah was there. She *robbed* me of my memories at my mother's request."

Emre stared at her, confused. She told him the story. All of it. From Hef-hi's death to Demal's hanging to seeing Leorah in the desert to her trip with her mother and Saliah. And then the journey beneath the sand, through the tunnels. Sehid-Alaz in his madness. "Where is he?" She looked around suddenly, worried that he'd gone.

"There." Emre pointed along the trough between the dunes.

She walked that way, Emre trailing behind her, and found Sehid-Alaz waiting around a bend. The ancient King of the Thirteenth Tribe . . . He looked so very small, even smaller than when she'd found him in that strange cavern. She knelt before him, silent, unsure what to say.

She took his hands and held them. His blackened skin felt smooth, dry, slick as sun-dried leather. After a time, he lifted his head and spoke in a rasp, *"You saved me that day."*

"I don't understand how."

"Our lives. Our existence." He stared at his hands in wonder, as if he still couldn't understand how all this had come to be. *"How it wears on the soul. Forbidden are we from taking our own lives, or the lives of our brothers and sisters. And yet in my madness I nearly took my own. And I ended the lives of two I had sworn to protect."* He drew a long, dry breath and looked Çeda in the eyes. *"You pulled me back from the abyss. Made me remember what I had yet to do. What we all must do. The false lords of Sharakhai were pleased with how far I'd fallen, but they would soon have come and ended my life had you not brought me back from the edge of the abyss."*

Çeda shivered, remembering the scene in the courtyard of Eventide, how Mesut had drawn a soul from his black gemstone—Havva's soul—and used it to chain her to another form. "You might have been given to another, remade to better serve him."

"It isn't enough for them to chain the soul anew. They force the old to consume the young."

The horror from that night was now mixing with rage at what Mesut and Cahil were doing and sorrow for the lives of those they required for such a foul sacrifice. "Why would Nalamae have made me forget you?"

"She was not Nalamae. Not then. She was still Saliah. And she knew too little. She had to tread with the greatest care, as is still true, which is why she could not come this night."

"She knows you've come?"

"She sent me. She knows of the coming conflict, but fears the attention of her sisters and brothers, who are as yet unaware of her new incarnation. She sends with me a message." He used his finger to draw in the sand, and when he was done, Rhia's light lit the angles of the old sign for *king*. The head of a jackal was drawn next to it. It was Mesut, the Jackal King, though he clearly didn't wish her to speak the name, or didn't trust himself to do so.

"What of him?" Çeda asked.

"You wish to invoke his bloody verse." His eyes took in both her and Emre. He'd heard them speaking, then, or had felt it in her heart.

"I do," she replied.

"Do not. The goddess and I beseech you."

For a moment, Çeda couldn't speak. "But . . . How could you ask me to stay my hand against *him*?"

"His gift from she of silver skin, his golden band . . . He has taken many souls in the years since Beht Ihman. All reside within that gem. It is an affront that echoes that terrible night. It is why I have sent others to take it from him. I have tried my best to prepare them, yet all have failed. Slaughtered for their treachery."

Çeda's mind was drawn to the room below the collegia tower where she and Amalos had sat, reading stories scratched into the bones of black laughers. "I read of one. A woman from Tribe Narazid."

Sehid-Alaz nodded slowly. *"Her name was Esmiya, and it was I who sent her."*

"How many others have tried?"

"Four. And all have perished, for they could not master the device the desert gods bestowed upon the King. The last was sniffed out by the King himself, and soon he had tied the deed to me. It was why he tortured me so before you found me as a child. It was the reason I was driven to near madness. So you see, I cannot risk you in such a way. I beseech you, leave him. Choose another."

"He will be allowed to live, then?"

"Never," he said sharply. *"We only need more time."*

Emre glanced nervously toward the ship. "Do you have more of the verses?"

Çeda nodded. "I have Beşir's, and he may be a good target, but I wonder if he will even be called to the harbor. He was not made for battle. The same can be said of Ihsan, Yusam, perhaps Zeheb as well. But Cahil . . . He will likely be called upon. He wouldn't miss it in any case. His thirst for blood is too great. And unlike the other Kings, he may be foolish enough to wade into battle without the protection of the Maidens by his side."

Sehid-Alaz's emaciated hand touched Çeda's. *"Take care that your hatred for his daughter does not cloud your judgment."*

"Yndris?" Emre asked.

Çeda nodded. "I will shed no tears for Yndris's loss," she said to Sehid-Alaz, "but neither will I let it affect me. I will make for Beşir if he is there, Cahil if not."

As she spoke, Sehid-Alaz squeezed her fingers, then stood and looked beyond her. Çeda could hear someone trudging over the sand. *"I was never able to thank you,"* came the whisper of his voice. Before her eyes, his hands began to dissipate, to fall away like sand. Indeed, he *was* sand. More and more of him fell, until the last was caught in a gust and Çeda felt something very like a kiss being placed upon her forehead.

With the footsteps nearly upon them, Çeda shoved Emre back onto the sand and lay on top of him. She slipped her hand around the back of his head, grabbed a fistful of hair, and drew him in for a deep kiss, a thing he immediately returned. For a few moments, their hands roamed—an act, only an act, but how it warmed her to feel his lips once more. And how fully he seemed to invest in this play staged for an audience of one.

"We leave early," came Sümeya's voice. She waited for Çeda to lift herself off of Emre. Çeda couldn't see her face well enough to read her, but her stance was stiff. "Return to the ship. Now." There was no question she'd meant that for Emre. He stood and bowed to them both, then left, trudging back toward the sandship. When the sound of his footsteps faded, Sümeya said, "We'll be returning to Sharakhai soon."

"Of course, First Warden."

"What happened before we reached Ishmantep. You and Yndris. You and I . . ." Sümeya was so rarely at a loss for words, but here she was, stumbling through this speech. Çeda wondered how long she'd thought about it before coming here. "There will be much to do, for you, for us. Hamzakiir and the Host are no threats to take lightly. Perhaps it would be best if I transfer you to another hand."

Çeda had had few enough lovers, and no relationship that had lasted any length of time beyond Osman, but she still recognized the note of loneliness in Sümeya's voice. The hope. She wanted Çeda to deny her. She wanted Çeda to fight to remain in her hand. But staying, if that was what Sümeya wanted it, would be a mistake. The time had come for Çeda to distance herself from Sümeya, and she was providing the perfect opportunity.

"Perhaps that would be best," Çeda finally replied.

Sümeya nodded once. "Very well," she said shortly, then turned and walked away, leaving a coldness in her wake—a coldness, Çeda was surprised to find, she very much regretted.

They reached Sharakhai seven days after leaving Ishmantep, a full twenty-one days since leaving the Amber City. As they were heading into the eastern harbor, clouds gathered, and a cool rain began to fall as they slid toward the dock. The heavy sand fouled the runners, making them crawl toward the berth the flagman was waving them toward. When they departed, the sun broke through, making the rain glow like drops of citrine against a field of sodden ash.

Emre remained on the ship. All had agreed, including Emre, that it would be best he not be seen. When night fell, he would be let out through the southern gates of Tauriyat with the understanding that he would return with news if he was able. Sümeya and Çeda and the rest of their hand were walking along the dock when Çeda saw Davud walking solemnly behind Anila, who was being carried on a stretcher toward the quay and a wagon that would take her to the House of Maidens, where she would be examined by the Matrons. The poor girl was wrapped from head to toe in bandages, to which had been applied a salve they hoped would help her frostbitten skin. They'd also given her the last of the black lotus stored on the ship. It was meant to help with severe pain, and who on the ship was in more pain than she?

"Davud?" Çeda called as rain pattered against her black veil and dress. He turned to her woodenly, as if his mind were with Anila and only Anila. "What will you do now?" she asked him.

Behind him, Anila moaned as she was lifted onto the wagon bed. He motioned absently, eyes distant and numb, full of regret. "I will see what can be done."

"The Matrons can work wonders, Davud. You'll see. But I meant *you*. What will *you* do?" They both knew she was talking about his newfound abilities.

"Hamzakiir told me to find someone in Sharakhai who can help me control it."

"And will you?"

He shrugged. "The Kings may never let me leave Tauriyat, Çeda. They may kill me rather than let me live in their city." He shrugged again. "The wind blows as it will." Without another word he walked away.

"Davud," she called, but he ignored her and hopped up onto the bed of the cart. As the cart rolled away, he watched Anila.

——————— ● —————————

High atop Tauriyat, in the lush garden of King Yusam's palace, Çeda stood by Sümeya's side as she told Yusam all that had happened since they'd sailed for Ishmantep. Ferns filled the space. Bowed trees masked the sky. A burbling spring fed Yusam's mere.

This was the very same place where Çeda had first met King Yusam, where he'd seen a violent vision in his depthless pool. Çeda had been fearful he'd kill her then and there and be done with her, but shortly after he'd said that not only would she be accepted into the Blade Maidens, but that Sümeya would take her into her own hand. Sümeya had come to the point where they'd discovered the grotesquely transformed collegia scholars. She was telling him how monstrous it had been to fight them, and it had been, certainly, but all Çeda could think about were the horrors the scholars had lived through, not just the ones who'd died in the temple, but those who still lived.

"Were they young or old?" Yusam asked.

"My Lord King?"

"On the day of the abduction, three scholars were counted among the missing. You may have had chance to know them. Süleiman, Taram, and Farid. Learned scholars all. Might any of the three unfortunate souls you saw in Ishmantep have been one of them?"

"How old were they?" Sümeya asked.

"I don't know precisely, but none were young. All three have surely seen fifty summers."

Sümeya shook her head. "As much as they'd changed, it's difficult to say, but no, I don't believe so."

"And you?" he asked Çeda.

"I agree," Çeda replied. "They both had the look of the young about them."

Yusam nodded to Sümeya. "Go on."

Sümeya did, finishing with the fires Hamzakiir had set, how Davud and Anila had saved the burning ship, and Anila's strange, ice-cold burning through Davud's clumsy use of blood magic. She went on to tell him of the repairs to the *Javelin* and their subsequent voyage to Sharakhai, but at that point Yusam seemed to lose interest. He paced along the balcony, arms crossed as he stroked his chin. His eyes were dark as his gaze flitted to and fro. No doubt he was comparing their story to his visions, trying to piece them together so that he could decide what to do.

It was a common enough look for the Jade-eyed King, but there was something different about him today, something Çeda had never seen in him, at least not to this degree. He was worried, she realized. Confused. He kept glancing at his mere, only paces away, as if he wished to go to it and see the future he and his fellow Kings were rushing toward. "First Warden, you may leave."

Sümeya glanced to Çeda, but then clasped her hands over her heart and bowed. "Excellence."

When her bootsteps had faded, Yusam motioned to the mere. "Do you recall my reaction when the two of us were last here?" He raised his hand. "Don't answer that. I imagine it would be hard to forget. Hardly a day has passed that I haven't considered that vision. All that I have done since has been in an attempt to avoid it."

"What was it, my King?"

"I saw the gods standing upon Tauriyat," he finally said. "A storm unlike the desert has ever seen troubled the sky. Goezhen raged, for what reason I cannot guess, but Tulathan stood next to him, trying to calm him. The other desert gods stood behind them. Thaash, Rhia, Yerinde, and Bakhi. Only Nalamae was absent. And Sharakhai itself was gone. Razed to the ground." He paced toward the mere, motioning for Çeda to follow. "It was not merely that image that made me rage so. I felt what it was like at that time. Whatever had happened, the gods themselves could barely withstand it. Something was threatening to tear them apart. To tear the *world* apart." He stopped and stared down into the depths of the black water. "Since then I've paid careful attention to my visions. Like a scent on the wind, I can tell which visions are connected to it. I can sift through them to find their common thread. They give me direction. Movement. And from there I can see where it will take us."

"The captain's journal. Finding King Aldouan's body in the desert."

Yusam nodded. "And you standing before a burning ship. They're leading somewhere, Çedamihn. The question is, where?"

Yusam's mere, and the notion that, no matter how careful she and others were, they could be unmasked with a glimpse from a dream while staring into that dark water, had always unnerved Çeda, but now the feeling had become so acute she felt her skin prickling with fear.

"Hamzakiir's plans?" she offered. "The attack on the aqueduct?"

"That"—Yusam shrugged—"is but one thread in the web, and not even the largest. There are many that are more important. The things we do now may lead to the death of Sharakhai. Perhaps the whole of the Shangazi."

"Surely you'll see the way."

At this Yusam laughed. "You disappoint me, Çedamihn. You speak like a storyteller in the west end, recounting tales of the mere and how it grants me anything I seek. So many, even some of the Kings, think there is nothing for me to do but act upon the visions once seen. But you should know better. There are shadows ahead. There is danger." He motioned to the mere. "Did you know that once I saw *you* here, looking into the depths of the mere?"

Çeda shook her head. Her heart was pounding, though she knew not why.

"You were caught in a vision, rapt. I wonder if that day was today."

Çeda could only stare, horrified, at the mere. She didn't wish to see her future. She was too afraid of what she would see. Too afraid of her own failure.

Yusam considered her, took in her garb, her desert boots, her black Maiden's dress, her turban. Then he stared deeply into her eyes, as if he'd found a second mere that might share more secrets with him. "No. Perhaps it wasn't." He motioned her back toward the palace. "Come, I've kept you here for a greater purpose."

They walked, and Çeda began to feel an itch at the nape of her neck. There was something different about Yusam, an intensity she hadn't seen in a long while. They entered the palace, where Yusam led them to a doorway with a winding set of stairs leading down. A servant was there, ready with a lantern that he passed to Yusam as he and Çeda entered the stairwell. Down they went, Yusam leading the way.

"Two days before your return," he said, "I happened upon a vision of a collegia master. Not the three we spoke of earlier, but another. In it, he was reading a story inscribed in copper leaf, as they do in the north."

At this, the itch along Çeda's neck crawled down her spine and slipped inside her chest. It felt like a cold hand reaching for her heart. *Please, Nalamae. Please not Amalos.* They came to a landing that revealed a hallway that ran straight as an arrow. At the far end, two Silver Spears stood guard on the opposite sides of an archway that beckoned like a reek dealer in a west end alley.

"I knew not its nature at the time," Yusam continued, his lantern throwing wild shadows over the amber stone as they marched in step, "but it seemed innocent enough, so I sent few Spears to investigate. With the groundskeeper's help, they searched the collegia for the room I'd seen in the vision. Small. No windows. A lone desk with several chairs and a simple set of shelves. More importantly, it housed a wealth of texts."

Yusam was so bloody calm, but Çeda was sure this was part of his test. *Remain calm. Breathe. Give nothing away.* "Not surprising, for a scholar to have texts piled on his desk?"

"No, but these were ancient texts, one and all. It smacked of a man looking into Sharakhai's past."

The implication was clear: it was not expressly forbidden by the Kannan, but all knew it was forbidden to look too closely into the origins of the Kings, and of Beht Ihman in particular.

They were nearing the archway now. The Spears bowed their heads, and Yusam and Çeda entered a room that was wide and long and made entirely of pristine white marble, including the four raised slabs situated in a square pattern at the center of the room. Three of the slabs were unoccupied. The fourth, however, held the naked body of an aged man with what looked to be three knife wounds in his stomach and another between his ribs.

Çeda had known the identity of this man from the moment Yusam had mentioned a collegia master.

Amalos.

The body was impeccably clean, as if Yusam had insisted his blood be drained lest it stain the white marble. He looked not peaceful, nor in pain, but instead slack, lifeless, as if he'd turned his back on this life in the moment of his death. When they came near, Çeda realized a patina-green leaf of beaten copper rested between his ankles. It had been hidden from their vantage near the archway, but now it filled her vision. There was writing on it. A record of some sort. Why would it have been brought here? Yusam, of all the Kings, wouldn't have done so without it having some great meaning.

Çeda composed herself before speaking, the shock of Amalos's death allowing her some distance from the feelings that would strike her when she was safely away from Yusam's palace. "What did the Spears find, my Lord King?"

Yusam moved to the opposite side of the slab, then set the lantern down. "His name is Master Amalos. They found him reading, exactly as I'd seen him." He picked up the copper leaf with the tiny words scratched onto its surface. "He'd been reading this. I thought it the key to a riddle, for it was bright, nearly blinding, in the vision I'd seen." Yusam held it above the lantern and began reading. "But now I'm not so sure, for I can't fathom how it relates to any of the other threads I've been tugging at.

Çeda desperately wished she could read it as well, but the angle of the light was to his benefit, not hers, so instead she read *him*. He stared, rapt, as if by reading it this one last time he could unlock its secrets. He didn't know, then. He hadn't learned what Amalos had been after, nor had he learned about Çeda's involvement. Or Zaïde's. But if he didn't know, how had Amalos died?

"Did they kill him out of hand?"

"Hmm?" Yusam looked up, his gaze momentarily lost.

"Did the Spears kill him?"

Yusam forced himself back to the present and stared at her soberly. "No. According to those men, our good master threw down a packet of some sort. It burst, filling the room with light and pounding their ears with sound. It stunned them, and by the time they had recovered sufficiently to give chase, Amalos had fled. They lost him in the tunnels, but found him hours later, not a hundred paces from the tunnel's entrance, bleeding from these wounds."

"I don't understand."

"Neither do we."

"He was murdered, but by whom?"

"Precisely, Çedamihn. Precisely."

Çeda thought for a moment he meant to indict *her* in some way, but she soon realized that wasn't it at all. However improbably, Yusam had come to trust her. Or rather, trust his mere, which of late had seen fit to show him visions that involved her. More than once he'd called her his divining rod, which had always made her supremely uncomfortable. Now, though, she realized she could use it to her advantage.

Though her instincts to always be careful around the Kings begged her not to, she held one hand out for the copper leaf. "May I see it, my Lord King?"

The bluntness of her question snapped him from his reverie. He looked down at the leaf, at her hand, and then an unreadable expression—hope?—crossed his face as he handed it to her.

She pulled the lantern nearer and read quickly lest Yusam change his mind. In the old script it told the tale of a woman who'd saved her family from a sand drake by offering herself to it. She'd walked, arms spread, toward the great beast. The drake had swayed this way, then that, aggressive in its movements at first. But as the mother came toward it, it quietened and lowered its head. The beast lay on the sand as she stroked the scales along its head. Then in a sudden flurry the drake lifted and drove beneath the surface, its wake furrowing the sand until it was gone altogether.

Why Amalos would have been reading it, and, more importantly, why the mere would have given it such prominence in Yusam's vision, Çeda had no idea. She handed the leaf back and shook her head, unsure what to say.

"There's one more piece of the vision I've withheld." Something dark scuttled inside Çeda's heart, but Yusam went on, "A white cowl pulled over a woman's head. The flash of a knife in the darkness. A dress stained red."

Çeda's mouth went dry. A Matron. A Matron had killed Amalos. By the gods who breathe, *Zaïde* had killed him. The moment the thought came, Çeda was certain it was true. It would have been all too natural for Amalos to go to her for aid. He would have confessed what had happened. Amalos hadn't known her as well as Çeda did, though. Her inclination was always to step carefully, lest they reveal themselves to the Kings.

And now that he *had* revealed himself, and brought his story to her, what would a woman like Zaïde do? She would protect herself. Protect her lifelong investment in the House of Maidens. She might even think she'd been protecting *Çeda*.

His body had been found hours later, Yusam had said. Çeda wondered if Zaïde would have gone to the others for advice, her allies in the House of Kings. She might even have gone to Ihsan, for Çeda was now certain Zaïde meant the Honey-tongued King when she'd said one of them might offer his protection. Had Ihsan condoned this? Had he ordered it?

Staring into Amalos's vacant eyes, she decided it didn't matter. Her thoughts strayed back to her conversation in Emre's cabin on the *Javelin*. *The enemy of my enemy,* Emre had said. *Is in the end no friend at all,* she'd replied. How true those words had been. Her soul was weary from the constant struggle to hide her nature, her heritage, the pain of her people. Indeed, to hide the very *existence* of her people. Ihsan might have become an ally, but never one she could trust. Better to make the Kings quarrel from within, to make them distrust one another, and see what came of it.

But how to do it? How to set Yusam onto Ihsan's scent?

Çeda feigned shock. "If a Matron is involved, my Lord King, it seems only logical that she would not be acting alone."

Yusam nodded. "Go on."

She put hesitation into her voice. "You would know better than I. The mere is a difficult device to read—"

"Speak, Çedamihn." His cat-like eyes were hungry.

"Tolovan ad jondu gonfahla . . ."

"What?"

"It's just . . . I cannot help but think of another betrayal the mere hinted at. On a ship in the desert, a ship you sent me to investigate. *Tolovan ad jondu gonfahla,* the first mate said." With crystal clarity, Çeda recalled how Yusam had looked when she'd said those words to him in his palace high atop Tauriyat. He'd frozen, realizing the purpose of the vision had been to deliver him those words. As then, his eyes were filled with confusion and worry, but unlike the last time, they were also brimming with calculation and intent.

As she had so often since entering Yusam's service, Çeda wondered at the mere. So many threads to draw upon, so many that crossed and recrossed, creating a weave so large it was impossible to comprehend. Here, though, she had shown Yusam a single thread that shone like a shooting star, a thing he could follow with ease to Ihsan's machinations. And once he found one betrayal, however small, it should be child's play to discover the rest.

Setting the leaf down beside Amalos's body, Yusam picked up the lantern and began walking away. "You have been a great service this day, daughter of Ahyanesh."

She turned to follow the Jade-eyed King, but gave Amalos one last look. *We've done this much, at least. Set the Kings to doubting one another, and that's no small thing.*

Chapter 57

K ING IHSAN HATED BEING LATE, and yet this day, the morning before
Beht Zha'ir, he hardly spared it a thought. Things had been going
well—with his plans, with Nayyan, with their child—that he thought just
this once the other Kings could wait on him. He entered the Sun Palace with
his vizir, Tolovan, by his side. Their footsteps echoed along the grand halls.

Despite his pleasant mood, a cloud hung over this place. It always had.
These meetings with the Kings were necessary, even vital to the health of
Sharakhai, but he'd always regretted that they'd decided to meet here. The
Sun Palace always reminded him of the days when this palace, the thirteenth
on Tauriyat, had been called something else, the days when another King had
ruled these halls.

He liked to tell himself he hadn't decided what to do with the other palaces once he and Nayyan ruled Sharakhai, but in his heart he knew the truth.
He would bring them down. All of them, Eventide as well. And then he
would build one anew using the very stones from those other palaces, one
that would dwarf them all high atop Tauriyat. It would be but one step in a
long list of steps meant to wipe away the taint the other Kings had lain over
the Amber City.

Winding through the palace, he and Tolovan made for the grand space where the Kings met each morning before Beht Zha'ir. The sound of conversation rose as they approached the domed room. It sounded rather soft. *Too* soft for a full meeting of the Kings.

Tolovan sensed it as well. He motioned to the scalloped archway a dozen paces ahead. "Strange, my Lord King."

When they came to the room, they found a sizable assemblage that included many Kings, their vizirs and viziras, and other trusted servants, but a number of key members were missing. That Onur, the King of Sloth, had chosen not to join them was of no consequence. What *was* of consequence was the fact that Kiral, along with Mesut, Cahil, and Sukru, were also missing. There had long been an informal alliance between those four, so it could be that they'd decided to take counsel with one another before joining the rest. If Husamettín weren't also absent, he might have thought little of it, but with so much conflict brewing, and Ihsan pulling many of the strings to make that happen, he worried.

Did they suspect that the Kings could not all be trusted? Were they trying to sway the King of Swords to their side? Ihsan had hoped he might still sway Husamettín to *his* side, but the man had always been as unyielding as the swords he wielded.

"Little matter," Ihsan said to Tolovan.

"Yes, my King."

As Tolovan broke away and went to speak with the other vizirs, Ihsan joined the Kings. He spoke with Zeheb and Azad first, but only long enough to ascertain if they knew what was happening. They did not. Beşir, the King of Coins, whose long, crag-lined face seemed especially severe, seemed to know little more. "I've enough troubles of my own," Beşir mumbled when Ihsan pressed, "without worrying about what the rest of you are doing."

"Of course," Ihsan replied, suppressing the urge to roll his eyes. The handling of Sharakhai's finances was no easy task, he readily admitted, but why did the man have to act as if it were the most burdensome thing in all the desert?

Külaşan's son, Alaşan, strode about in clothes that looked as ridiculous as they were expensive. Bright colors and piping and long sleeves. Bejeweled with garnets and citrine. He looked for all the world like a cock strutting among wolves, the false pride on his face trying to mask the nervousness within. Had this been Alaşan's first assembly, Ihsan might have attributed it to the pressure he was putting on himself to fill the shoes of his dead father. But Alaşan's callow unease had dwindled over the months since he'd taken up Külaşan's black morningstar. So what was he nervous about now?

The urge to speak with Alaşan was strong, but by this point it had become clear that Yusam was avoiding Ihsan. So instead of speaking with the young-ling King, he made straight for Yusam, stared into his piercing green eyes, and said, "Good day, my Lord King."

"Good day," Yusam replied with a cursory glance about the room.

"We seem to be rather light on Kings this morning."

"We do."

"Do you know why?"

He shook his head, and yet said, "There was some news."

"News?"

"It would be more proper if Kiral told you himself."

Ihsan made a show of looking around. "Were he here, I would most read-ily agree. But seeing that he isn't . . ."

Yusam blinked, then pulled himself taller. He said again, with more force this time, "It would be more proper if Kiral told you himself."

"Meaning that you, or more importantly, *he*, think it a matter for the King of Kings to decide."

"Meaning that it is sensitive."

"So much so that the other Kings are not to be granted counsel?"

Yusam stared Ihsan in the eyes, something he rarely did these days despite his occasionally biting tongue. "Such is the way in times of war, Ihsan."

"War?" Ihsan laughed, drawing the attention of the other Kings. "Are we at war?"

"If you don't know the answer to that question, then perhaps Kiral was right not to seek your counsel."

Well, well, Ihsan thought. *An interesting turn of events. Yusam, truculent.* Ihsan felt Zeheb and Azad watching. Zeheb even took a step toward them, perhaps to break the tension, but Ihsan waved him away. "I'm aware of our situation, my good King. My point is that we are at our best when we work together. Wouldn't you agree?"

At this, a bit of the old Yusam returned. The certainty in his eyes dwindled. He seemed to shrink before Ihsan's very eyes. "Yes, I would agree."

"Have you seen something?"

"I—" Yusam began, but he was interrupted by a number of figures entering the room from the far side.

"My apologies," came Kiral's booming voice. He made immediately for the thrones on the stone dais to one side of the room. "Please, let us begin. There is much to discuss."

Behind Kiral came Husamettín, Sukru, Mesut, and Cahil. Onur was not among them, but Layth, the burly Lord Commander of the Silver Spears, was. Ihsan had long wondered if he was ignoring an asset in that foul beast of a King, Onur. The man was not only distasteful to be in the same room with; he reminded Ihsan of everything he hated in himself. But he saw now the full extent of his folly. He should have brought Onur into the fold long ago, at least insomuch that he could control a man like Layth. Ihsan might be losing enough leverage with the other Kings that it could pay to have Onur by his side. He needn't call upon him often—neither Zeheb nor Azad could stomach his presence in any case—but there might come a day when he would need to rely not only on his ruthless nature, but his command of Sharakhai's only army, the Silver Spears, as well.

Ihsan had calmed his nerves by the time they were seated. Each King raised the glass of araq set before him and took a healthy swallow, though Ihsan noted the perfunctory manner in which Kiral did so, as if observances were the last thing he wished to deal with. "News has come of the Moonless Host and their plans. They have targeted the city's aqueduct, presumably to force a water shortage over winter and into spring. I've spoken with King Yusam, who has made great efforts trying to ascertain whether the coming spring will lead to a dry summer."

Yusam nodded. "Signs seem to point to a dry year, perhaps disastrously so."

"There are enough with the gift of sight in the Host," Kiral continued, "including Hamzakiir himself, that I believe they may have seen the same. Which makes targeting the aqueduct sensible from their point of view. It puts pressure on us all to show that we can withstand anything the Al'afwa Khadar choose to throw against our walls. If we fail, the scarabs will lift from the sands in droves to join their cause. If we succeed, we will still be portrayed as weak."

"So we stop the attack," Alaşan said.

The muscles beneath Kiral's pockmarked face worked. "When the time has come to offer your input, you will be informed, Külaşan'ava."

Face reddening, Alaşan stared at the King of Kings, then searched in vain for support from the others in the room.

Kiral ignored him entirely. "Sukru received word only hours ago of five locations where the Host would be gathering before the attack launches after moonrise tonight."

It had been a long while since Ihsan had felt his heart skip a beat. But it did now. Years, decades of planning had been leading up to this attack. If it failed—set aside the danger of it coming back to haunt him—it could take decades to align the stars properly once again. He *needed* the attack on the caches of the elixir to succeed. If Kiral made a move against the Host too early, it could ruin everything. "Are you quite sure the information is reliable?" he asked. "Has Yusam or Zeheb corroborated it?"

Sukru twisted his crooked body toward Ihsan. "It comes from a most reputable source."

Ihsan kept his focus squarely on Kiral. "Forgive me, my Kings, but we have been tricked before. Many times, in fact. It is why we agreed to speak to the full assemblage before taking any steps that would put us or our collective resources at risk."

Kiral took in his words with an ease that made Ihsan acutely uncomfortable. "There are times, as I'm sure you'll recall, when waiting became our worst enemy. The Host have become too adept at moving like water, slipping like snakes into the desert when we delay."

"And there are times when we have spilled our own blood by overextending. Need I remind you how closely our neighbors are watching Sharakhai? Zeheb told us only weeks ago how his spies in Malasan have reported an increase in their army's ranks. Why would that be when there is a long-standing peace accord to Malasan's east and impassable mountains to the north and south? They are staring *west*, and slavering at the thought of a weakened Sharakhai."

"The best way to deal with such a threat," Kiral countered, "is to show them that the swords in the desert are poised to strike."

"No doubt. And I agree in principle. I'm merely asking for a bit of prudence *before* we strike." What he was really asking for was a delay. He needed time to get word to the Host so they would be prepared.

But the look on Kiral's face, one of calm self-assurance, made the floor beneath Ihsan's feet feel like slip-sand. "You misunderstand me," he said with a smile. "I did not come here today to ask your permission. I have come to tell you what's already taken place. With the help of our Lord Commander of the Guard and twenty hands of Maidens, all five locations were attacked, and hundreds of the Host were found and put to the sword. Others were taken hostage for our good Cahil to attend to."

Ihsan felt the blood drain from his face. He wanted to scream. He wanted to strike that look of smugness from Kiral's face. But instead he calmed himself, sat deeper in his chair, as if he were relieved. "Praise be to the gods," he said. "Do we think, then, that disaster has been averted? Will there be no attack on the aqueduct?"

"It's too soon to tell," Kiral replied, easing back into his own chair and savoring a fresh pour from his glass that was very unlike the ritualistic sip of his drink earlier.

Does he know? Ihsan thought.

Doubtful. If he did, Ihsan would already be headed for Cahil's palace in chains. Kiral wasn't one for theater, but he *did* enjoy cowing the rest of them into submission, especially if he thought they were getting out of line, and he'd been hoping to force Ihsan back into line for some time now.

"With luck," Kiral went on, "they'll become desperate and attack as planned. If that is the case, we'll be waiting for them."

Ihsan lifted his glass to Kiral and drank as well, if only to avoid looking as furious and worried as he felt. "It seems brashness has paid dividends this time."

Kiral's smile widened. It was the sort a child gave when he knew he had the upper hand against his younger sibling. "My heart *rejoices* that these actions have met with your approval."

The rest of the meeting went about as expected. The four Kings who'd arranged for the attacks on the Host were lording it over the rest, Kiral giving orders for the night's preparations that Husamettín then expanded on. When it was done, Ihsan left without speaking to Zeheb or Azad. He was careful to avoid being seen with them too often, and today was a day for taking more care than usual.

"Is there anything I can do for you, my Lord King?" Tolovan asked as he joined Ihsan.

"There is," Ihsan said sharply. "Arrange a meeting with Juvaan Xin-Lei."

"My Lord, I know things seem dire, but be prudent. You've never met with him directly. Not about your plans."

"Prudence can fuck a goat and die in the desert for all I care. I need to speak with Juvaan now."

"Of course, my Lord." The look of worry on Tolovan's face withered and was replaced by one of cold purpose. It was the thing he liked most about his vizir. When the time for subtleties had ended, he was as ready to pick up a hammer as anyone.

Chapter 58

BY THE MORNING OF BEHT ZHA'IR, word had flooded the city. In the night, the King of Swords himself had led twenty hands of Maidens and several hundred Silver Spears in attacks on the safe houses where the Moonless Host had gathered for a massive assault against the Kings. So quick and violent was the attack that they'd slaughtered hundreds of soldiers, effectively foiling, or at the very least blunting, any attack that might be unleashed against the aqueducts.

After a debriefing from King Husamettín in the courtyard, a speech in which he addressed the full ranks of the Blade Maidens, they were dismissed to eat, to bathe, to pray to the gods before preparing for their mission that night. With Sümeya and Kameyl busy planning the disposition of forces, and Melis and Yndris called away on other duties, Çeda had a few hours to herself. She returned to the barracks and filled her mother's locket with freshly dried petals, she took out her book of poems and leafed through it. She wanted some perspective today—that there were bigger things at stake than her and her friends. She was terrified that Emre had been among the fallen, but there would be no knowing until the night had played itself out for better or worse.

She'd not been paging through the book for long when she noticed something flickering in the corner. On her desk. The stack of papers from Juvaan. One of them, improbably, had begun to burn a low blue color, hardly noticeable in the daylight. It had happened so quickly after she'd sat down she immediately looked out the window, wondering if someone had been watching, waiting for her. She saw only the courtyard, however. The stables beyond, the corner of the infirmary.

After glancing down the hall to make sure none of her sister Maidens were in sight, she moved to the stack of papers and pulled out the one that burned. It was charcoal gray, the flames licking the edges. It looked as if it would crumble at her touch, it *felt* that way too, but when she picked it up carefully by the edges, it held. On it, words were written in aquamarine flames.

If you would have news of your friend, meet me now on the roof of the Matron's building. Make sure you're not seen.

Juvaan. He wished to meet, and by Nalamae's grace he had news of Emre. She took up her pen, spilling ink in her haste, and wrote on the ashy surface.

I'll be there soon.

She waited, eyes flicking to her doorway, where sounds of a heated conversation were filtering in from the barracks courtyard. She didn't know what to do. Light it afire again? When she made to strike a flame to a candle, though, the paper flashed brighter and burned itself to nothing. The moment it was gone, she left her room.

She took the stairs down, headed out to the courtyard, and made her way steadily toward the Matron's building. She moved quickly and purposefully, head down, as if she were on an important errand. *And I am. Just not one the Maidens would approve of.* She reached an odd recess built into the northern face of the building. A fist of a rock stood there, a thing the builders clearly could have moved before setting the foundations of the building, but for some reason hadn't. With no windows facing the rock itself, it made for a blessedly easy, and more importantly *hidden*, climb. She gained the roof, a complicated landscape of peaks and jutting stone, but saw no one, so she took the time to explore it, crouched low. She stared out past the wall of Tauriyat, beyond the Wheel to the west end. She could see the tents of the bazaar. The buildings of Roseridge. The tenements of the Shallows. The curve of the Red Crescent. Places she'd run so often with Emre and Tariq and Hamid. *All divided from me by a wall of my own making.*

"One of the best views in the city, is it not?"

Çeda spun and found Juvaan Xin-Lei standing in the shadows of a stairwell, his alabaster hair pulled back into a tail. He strode toward her like a mountain puma, powerful but aloof. She looked for others—his guards, a Matron who'd led him here, but saw no one. "How did you get here?"

He shrugged. "The ambassador of Mirea might have reason to speak to the Matrons, even on a day like this. Perhaps *especially* on a day like this." He came to her side and stared out over Sharakhai. "I've come to cherish this city."

A curious way to begin the conversation. "Cherish or covet?"

With his cold ivory eyes, he stared at her in mild surprise. "I've done much to help the citizens of the desert in my time, accords and business arrangements that number in the hundreds, all of which helped to build the wealth of those who live here."

"As well as your queen's."

"What is a business arrangement if not mutually beneficial?" He turned to face her. "Speaking of arrangements, you once offered to help if ever I had need."

"I did."

"As you no doubt know by now, the Host lost a terrible number last night. Hundreds were slaughtered, crippling their position in the city. But I wonder, do you know *how* they were compromised?"

"King Yusam. King Zeheb. An informant. Who knows?"

Juvaan shook his head. "It was a betrayal from within the Host's ranks."

"A betrayal?" Çeda asked. "But who would—" She stopped, for she knew exactly who might do such a thing. "Hamzakiir."

Juvaan nodded. "I suspected he would do something like this in time, but when his ally, Lord Aziz, was assassinated in Ishmantep, he apparently decided sooner was preferable to later. It was a strategic mistake of grand proportions on Ishaq's part. Hamzakiir has used that show of strength as evidence that Ishaq cannot be trusted. He's won *more* to his side because of it." Juvaan paused and considered Çeda. "Now let's go a step further. Do you know why this attack is being waged?"

"To put pressure on the Kings."

"There is that, but their purpose goes much deeper. What I am about to tell you only a handful know outside the palaces of the Kings. The Host plan to use the coming battle as a diversion while other, separate attacks are launched.

Those attacks will be to find caches of elixirs, draughts that grant the Kings their long life, the remains of what was created by King Azad before he was killed."

Çeda began to pace. "Elixirs?" She could hardly speak. "Draughts that grant them long life?"

"That was Azad's gift."

Goezhen's sweet kiss, that's why she did it. That's why mother targeted Azad. Much of the mystery remained, like what Ahya had found and what role Ihsan had played in it, but this felt so very true. If Ihsan wanted to kill the other Kings, wouldn't a necessary first step be the death of Azad, thereby cutting off their tie to immortality?

"You look as if you're about to dig your own grave," Juvaan said.

"Forgive me, but much is starting to come clear." She continued to pace, working more of it through. "There are three of these caches, are there not?"

Juvaan's eyebrows rose in mild surprise. "My lady is well informed."

It's what Emre had told her, the palaces Macide had decided to attack. "And the caches hold all that remains of the elixirs?"

Juvaan shrugged. "Each King will have some set aside, no doubt, but these are the stockpiles that are closely guarded, closely inventoried. They have dwindled over the years, but the Host wishes to see them all destroyed, to bring about the destruction of the Kings in the decades ahead, even if all their other efforts fail. At least, those were *Ishaq's* plans, plans that now lay in tatters. With the support he's now gathered, Hamzakiir will attack, but he will not destroy the caches."

"He'll keep them for himself," Çeda said. "He hopes to remove the Kings but keep the elixirs."

"Just so, which would, as you can imagine, throw doubt on the age-old arrangements we discussed only moments ago."

"And what do you wish *me* to do?"

"Ishaq still wishes to destroy the caches. All of them. It is a chance that may never come again. But the forces loyal to him have been weakened terribly."

"There must be *some* in the city who can help."

"Some, yes, but not enough. The rest are poorly trained. Or are men and women no longer fit to lift a sword. They need proper soldiers."

"Then summon more from the desert."

"They would if there was time, but there is a cordon around the city now. The Kings have dispatched the Royal fleet. Dozens of ships patrol the desert, ready to inspect any that approach Sharakhai. If the attack were weeks away, there would be time to plan, to summon more scarabs. But there isn't. And by then the chance to win this prize will have vanished."

"I can't help that."

"No, but perhaps the son of Qaimir can."

"The son of . . ." It took her a moment to piece together what he was implying. "Ramahd? He's here?"

"He returned some weeks ago. He and his queen have influence in Sharakhai, perhaps enough to turn the tide against Hamzakiir and do what Ishaq wants."

"You would have Qaimir do this when you have as much or more influence in the city as they do?"

Juvaan shrugged. "I consider myself a shrewd businessman. Even you will admit that this venture has a low chance of returning its investment."

"Then why come to me now? Why risk brokering an arrangement with Qaimir at all?"

He laughed as if she were too young to understand the way of the world. "Because they very well may succeed! And if they do, that would be a rather *stunning* return for the effort put in."

"So you and your queen will sit like grinning jackals, waiting for the lions to make their kill? You'll not lift a finger when so much is at risk?"

"My dear, there's little enough at risk for Mirea. My queen is patient. As am I. If the Host fails then we wait."

"And if they succeed?"

"Well then, the landscape changes, does it not? And we'll be ready for that as well."

"You would pretend that you *helped* the Host?"

"Will this not help? If you're able to garner the support of Qaimir, would this conversation not be considered vital to the night's endeavors? Don't discount diplomacy, Çedamihn. Don't discount communication. You do so at your peril." He began backing away. "There's little time. Ramahd Amansir is in the embassy house now, and if the whispers I've heard are true, he's sent letters. Asking for an audience with *you*."

Çeda opened her mouth. Closed it again. *Why would he ask for me?* "I've heard nothing of this."

Juvaan made a flourish with both hands, a gesture that encompassed the whole of the House of Maidens. "As tense as things have become, I'm not surprised. As for the specifics, who can say? Go. Speak to him and his queen. Help your friends."

"Assuming they agree, how are they to find the Host?"

"There is one named Hamid. You know him, I believe."

Shy Hamid. Quiet Hamid. "Yes, I know him."

"He will be in Karakir Square when the sun sets." With an elegant bow, Juvaan turned and took to the stairs, leaving Çeda alone with a tempest of thoughts and emotions.

"The queen will see you now," the old servant woman said, and opened the doors to a sitting room in the Qaimiri embassy house.

As Çeda stepped inside the opulent room, the servant closed the doors behind her. A moment later, the doors to the right of the tall hearth were opened and in stepped Ramahd wearing the fine clothes of a Qaimiri nobleman. He was as handsome as she remembered, if a bit thinner. *Little wonder, if his harrowing tale of survival in the desert is true.* Behind him came a woman as gaunt as anyone Çeda could remember seeing.

"Queen Meryam," Çeda said, taking a knee and bowing her head.

Meryam moved to a chair near the tall fireplace. "Rise," she said, her voice rough as weatherworn leather. Çeda complied, at which point Ramahd smiled and waved her toward a couch opposite Meryam.

"I prefer to stand."

He looked as though he were ready to convince her otherwise, but then he quieted himself and took her in. "The Maiden's black suits you."

"Forgive me, my Lord Amansir. I'm in no mood to be mocked."

"It was no jest. You've changed since last I saw you. You look as though you're ready to take on the world."

"Yes, yes," Queen Meryam said. "I'm sure we're all very happy to reminisce, but I've a feeling our young Maiden came for a reason."

"Of course," Ramahd said, hardly glancing the queen's way. "What can we do for you?"

"I need your help. It's much to ask, but whatever your answer, I need to know that it will remain between us."

Meryam laughed. "You never told me how *very* sly she was, Ramahd. Rest assured, dear girl, it will go no farther than this room should we decline. Now tell your tale. I've much to do before the hounds come baying."

She meant the asirim, which made her wonder just how much the queen knew of the coming conflict. "Are you aware, your excellence, of what will happen tonight?"

Meryam looked her up and down. Her face was grim but her eyes were hungry. "Why don't you enlighten me?"

"The Host is set to attack the Kings."

"You seem strangely calm about it," Meryam shot back.

Çeda couldn't deny it. The realization that her mother hadn't died in vain had been a supremely freeing one. It had also put her in a fey mood. Besides, she'd reasoned that this was why Ramahd had wished to speak with her. As much as he and his queen's agents spied upon the Moonless Host, they must already know—or at least suspect—what was about to happen. "This is a chance I could never have hoped for, and now that it's here I'll do everything I can to make it happen."

"And you need my help."

"I do, though it will benefit any sovereign land that has come to feel that the Kings have amassed too much power."

"Is that so?"

"It is." She proceeded to tell them what she knew. Of King Azad, of the caches, of Hamzakiir's betrayal and Ishaq's wish that the elixirs were all destroyed. Ramahd seemed eminently unfazed by it all, so much so that she wondered if he'd played some part in its grand construction. Meryam, meanwhile, seemed more and more pleased by Çeda's tale. *No, not pleased. Eager, like a thief who'd been hoping for entry to the king's vault for years and had just found it both unlocked and unguarded.*

Çeda quickly came to the most difficult part. "I want you to gather your resources, everyone you can manage, and help me on this mission."

She'd implied it was for *her* benefit, but they all knew what she was asking. Ramahd's wife had been shot through with an arrow by the Moonless Host. His daughter had died when the survivors of that massacre had tried to reach safety. It had all been done at Macide's orders, and now here she stood, asking Ramahd to help his sworn enemy. The emotions she thought would play across his face didn't. Instead, he stared at her, unmoving, with something approaching wistfulness, or perhaps regret. She thought Meryam might answer for Qaimir, but she waited, deferring to Ramahd from some reason.

"Will you be joining them?" Ramahd asked.

"I will." She'd decided to the moment Juvaan had told her about the caches, the moment she knew why her mother had died to kill Azad. This would be the culmination of that night so long ago. This would see to it that her mother's death hadn't been for naught.

Ramahd considered, but not for long. "Very well," he said.

She waited for more, but nothing followed. "*Very well?* I will admit, my lord, that I rather thought there would be more resistance."

"You'd prefer that I decline?"

"I must know that you are sincere."

He nodded. "A fair enough request, and in reply I can only say this: that the needs of my country must come before my own. This is important to the security of Qaimir, and so I will go if my queen allows it."

She searched his eyes for something, anything, more. She turned to Meryam. "My queen, may I speak plainly?"

Meryam nodded.

"You'll forgive me, but I wonder if Lord Amansir would say the same were Macide Ishaq'ava to walk through that door. I know of the pain he went through. That you both went through."

Meryam swung her gaze to Ramahd. "She speaks truly, Ramahd."

In turn, Ramahd took a deep breath. "The desert changes every man. Isn't that what they say?"

"Yes," Çeda began, "but—"

"You don't know what happened to us out in the Shangazi. I won't bore you with the tale, but believe me when I say I've begun to regard those who tread *this* earth more than those who walk the farther fields."

There was a look of regret in his eyes. Had Ramahd *missed* her out there in the desert? Would a simple infatuation make him do this? Likely not. She believed his words, that he would do this if he thought it would further Qaimiran interests. But she thought, perhaps, it might be due to her as well, and for some reason that made her heart swell. It gave her some small hope that this night wouldn't turn out as foul as she thought it might.

"Very well, Ramahd." She held out her hand. "You have my thanks."

He looked down at her hand, and then, in the manner of the desert, took her forearm and shook it. His hand was warm against her skin. He smelled of tabbaq. Part of her didn't wish to let him go, but those were the thoughts of a lonely woman. *What need have we of men?* she remembered her mother saying. Hiding a smile, she pulled her hand away and bowed to Meryam. "Excellence."

Meryam nodded, her cold eyes boring into Çeda's. "Çedamihn."

"When the first moon rises," Çeda said to Ramahd, "meet me in Karakir Square. If you arrive before I do, ask for a man named Hamid." He nodded, and she left the embassy house.

With a cool wind beginning to blow, she wondered if she should have asked him more, made certain that his heart was pure, but there was little to do about it now if Ramahd wasn't willing to share. She returned to the House of Maidens and went to the apartments she shared with her hand. No one was there, so she left again, ready to head to the grand courtyard where most of the Maidens had been ordered to report an hour before nightfall. She would attend, listen to their plans for the night, and then, as soon as the sun went down, she'd slip out and return to Sharakhai. Explaining her absence would not be easy, but she had to take this chance. She left the barracks feeling more alive than she'd felt in months.

And heard the soft patter of sprinting footsteps too late.

She was just beginning to turn when bright pain burst across the back of her head. She staggered forward. Tried to run, to gain distance from her attacker. But the stone path ahead of her tilted. She heard footsteps, saw the black boots of a Maiden beside her. A knee pressed painfully into the small of her back. A hand clutched a fistful of her turban and angled her head awkwardly to one side.

A voice whispered harshly into her ear, "And what, by Bakhi's bright hammer, would a Maiden need from the Queen of Qaimir on a night like tonight?"

Yndris. By the gods, it was Yndris.

"I was—"

Before she could say more Yndris crashed her skull against the stone. "Don't answer that," Yndris said quietly. "My father will be most curious to hear your tale."

Çeda tried to fight, but it was no use. She was too dizzy. Too weak. Yndris lifted Çeda's head once more. Then came another crash, and her world went dark.

Chapter 59

CEDA DREAMED OF THE ASIRIM. They rested beneath the ground, co-cooned like insects. They waited, praying that this night would be their moment to emerge, to feast, to release the pain and rage that had been building like a suppurating wound. For some few, that call came. Like the toll of a distant bell, the Jackal King called to them. These lucky few squirmed. They clawed at the earth, emerging from their sandy graves beneath the twisted trees. They felt other forsaken entering the twilit night, but they thought no more of their brethren than this; they were fixed in their collective purpose, their minds chained, the shackles placed on them by the gods themselves.

An asir who had once been a man loped toward Sharakhai, summoned by the Reaping King and the crack of his whip. He bounded over the dunes, hoping that the feast might be over before he arrived, praying that it wouldn't end before he could slake his thirst. So it had been since Beht Ihman. So it would be until the gods decided he'd breathed enough of the desert's dry air. The two notions fought, creating a fire of confusion and hatred that drove him to simply *act* for the sake of doing something, anything, to quell the chaos in his mind.

His long, bounding strides brought him to the edge of the city. More of his kind joined him. They howled. They bayed. They smelled the fear of those huddling in the darkness of their homes. Sukru's whip brought them to the very center of the city. They searched each house for Sukru's sign—a hand, pressed in blood, lit by the twin moons and bright to their jaundiced eyes.

One by one the others found their marks, until he alone was left without one. He, Kerim Deniz'ava al Khiyanat, cousin to the King of the Thirteenth Tribe, stood paces from the door with the bloody print. He heard a man crying within, a child as well. Fear and sorrow poured from them, for they knew what stood beyond their threshold. *Tulathan, grant me this one small kindness. Let me leave the city no poorer for my efforts than when I'd arrived.*

His breath came through gritted teeth, the sound like stone abrading stone. His fingers flexed, summoning memories of how sublime it felt to rend the flesh of the living. And yet he found himself resisting the urge. His feet stayed rooted to the spot. He could do it. This one night, he could win.

And then he heard the lightning strike of Sukru's whip.

Kerim managed to turn, to look upon the Reaping King's bent form as he strode with the confidence of a god through the streets of the Amber City.

Please, Tulathan. But this once. I beg you.

In answer, the King swung his whip and struck the air above Kerim's head, so close he could feel its impact. It enveloped him, and all thoughts of defiance vanished like the storm clouds of spring giving way to the heat of summer. Kerim turned to the door. Approached it with halting steps. He drove his fist through it as if it were made of eggshells, then threw it aside and stepped within. He saw them, huddling in the corner, a father holding his son, praying to the gods.

He wondered, as he stalked forward, whether the gods would be kinder to these two souls than they had been to him. He didn't bother pleading with Tulathan for her kindness. He already knew what her answer would be.

An acrid smell drew Çeda from her well of nightmares. When she opened her eyes, she saw Yndris standing before her wearing her Maiden's black. Her turban was unwound and hanging around her shoulders like a Matron's cowl. Her dark blond hair brushed the black cloth. She was waving a tuft of wool beneath Çeda's nose. When Çeda recoiled from the bitter smell, she lowered her arm and stared at Çeda with a look eerily similar to the one Sukru had given Kerim before cracking the whip over his head.

Yndris stepped out of Çeda's field of vision. Her footsteps faded. A door opened and closed. Çeda's eyes grew heavy once more, as she slowly realized she was bound to a wooden frame. She drew a sharp breath and took in her situation anew. Leather straps held her arms, legs, and waist tightly in place. Strangely, the straps were spotless. Pristine. She could *smell* how fresh the leather was, as if the table had been built that very day. With growing alarm she tried pulling against the straps, but they were so stiff they hardly moved. Above her, a glass enclosure was set into the ceiling, a host of mirrors positioned there to catch the sun. They threw light about the room as the mirrors slowly turned, making Çeda feel dizzy all over again. From the brightness she guessed that two, perhaps three hours had passed since her return to the barracks.

Across from her, a short hallway led to a door, a different one than Yndris had used. River's Daughter leaned against the wall. It reminded Çeda what a hive of activity the House of Maidens had been. How could Yndris have brought her here without being seen? She must have had help, but who her allies had been, Çeda wasn't sure. There was no shortage of women who had reason to hate Çeda and would want to see the stain of her presence wiped from the House of Maidens. Any one of them might have aided her.

The door behind Çeda opened once more, sending a fresh jolt of fear through her body. Yndris took up a position across from Çeda against the wall, her gaze coming to rest on something over Çeda's shoulder. Another set of footsteps approached with a pace that spoke of leisure, a relaxed pace that felt distinctly twisted given Çeda's circumstances. Soon, King Cahil, wearing a simple but pristine kaftan, strode past her. He did not deign to look at her as he moved easily across the white marble floor. Instead, he seemed wholly intent on a table to Çeda's left. On the table's surface—and above it on various hooks and shelves—were sets of gleaming instruments, precisely ordered. Çeda was immediately reminded of the dank cellar to which Dardzada had taken her in hope of saving her from the adichara poison. That room, however, had been a grim place filled with grim instruments. This room was immaculate, as if it had been prepared for a surgeon but had never once been used. Nothing could be further from the truth. She could see it in the way Cahil's eyes gleamed, the casual way in which he picked up a brightly polished pair of pincers.

"I will admit," Cahil said as he examined the instrument's gleaming teeth, "I wasn't surprised when Yusam decided to allow you into the House of Maidens. He's a skittish shell of his former self. A feckless, flighty man who becomes more so by the year. But I was rather shocked when *Husamettín* granted you a blade. I thought him a man of good judgment, yet there he was, welcoming a thief who had made her way through the cracks in the walls and into the House of Kings like a scrabbling, scuttling cockroach." He rubbed his thumb over the spotless steel. He considered the pincers, working them for a moment, then set them down in the exact position they'd been before, choosing instead an awl with a handle made of a lustrous golden wood.

"But admit you he did, and granted you a place in a hand that should have been reserved for our finest young women." For the first time, he met Çeda's eyes, and all the stories of Cahil the Confessor King returned to her. Wild tales meant to scare her when she was younger, mythic in their power now. "And then he had the audacity to place *my* daughter in that same hand." Cahil strode toward Çeda. "An unforgivable sin, one the gods will surely make him pay for. Assuming they are just." He stopped by her side, inspecting the lines of the impeccably crafted awl. "Do you believe the gods to be just?"

Çeda worked her jaw before speaking. "I have found the gods to be as fickle as the Kings."

Cahil smiled as though he thought her comment particularly insightful. "At times, true. But in the quelling of the desert storm on Beht Ihman, and the granting of the Shangazi to the twelve true Kings of Sharakhai, they saw true." He stepped to her side and pressed the tip of the awl through the black cloth of her Maiden's dress, just over her right thigh. "Do you recall what I said I would do were you to assault my daughter again?"

"I didn't touch your daughter."

"But you did! You *have* assaulted her. You've assaulted us *all*." He looked her up and down, disgust clear on his young face. "Traipsing about the House of Maidens as if you were born in a palace, as if you had any right to set foot in it save as a woman prepared to be hung."

"I was tested by the adichara."

Cahil laughed. "The adichara? Only fools consider that ancient ritual a judge of any worth. The daughters of the Kings are innumerable. You're just another one of them, a seed lost in the mercurial winds of the desert, a weed that grew in whatever crack it happened to have been deposited." He pressed the awl so that she could feel its point, but no deeper. "And if I've come to learn anything about weeds, it's that they must be eradicated before they spread."

He pressed the tip of the awl deeper ever so slowly while staring at Çeda with dispassionate eyes, as if he wished to move on to more satisfying things but knew that this was the best way to go about it, to build fear not in leaps and bounds, but in cruel, subtle increments.

"Why did you go to the Qaimiri embassy house?"

"I wished to—"

A scream burst through her gritted teeth as a burning pain pierced her right thigh. His eyes filled with a deeper anger than Çeda would have guessed, Cahil drove the awl deeper.

"From the thousands upon thousands given into my care, I've learned that there are those who will spill the truth quickly, and those who gather their lies before speaking. You, Çedamihn, are certainly one of the latter. I can feel them inside you, writhing like worms ready to bore their way out through your skin." He drove the awl deeper still. "I bid you fight them. Let the truth free, and Yndris will be allowed to take her sword to your throat that much sooner."

Yndris watched, every bit as calm as Cahil had been moments ago. Was it this, Çeda wondered, the sort of hatred that had caused the Kings to sacrifice the thirteenth tribe? It had run thick in the time of Beht Ihman—how else might an entire tribe be sacrificed?—but it was still present now, an indifference carried down through time, veiled by the Twelve Kings and their vast collection of lies.

"Why did you go to the Qaimiri embassy house?" Cahil asked.

Spittle flew from Çeda's mouth as she fought the pain. Her breath came like a wounded dog's. She shivered from the effort of keeping it inside.

"Yndris said you were stubborn." A third time Cahil pressed the awl, this time until it pressed against bone. He smiled. "Believe me, I don't mind." He torqued the awl, twisting the muscles of her leg, the awl's tip scraping her bone. "I don't mind at all."

When he twisted it again, Çeda found herself screaming from the fount of pain that poured from the wound.

"I love him!" she cried, ashamed for having voiced even a single word.

The pain did not ease as Cahil leaned closer. "Lord Amansir?" He was so close now she could smell the citrus and sage of his perfume. "You *love* him?"

"She's lying," Yndris said. "They spoke of the aqueduct." Through the haze of pain, Çeda realized that Yndris had caught some of her conversation with Ramahd, but surely she hadn't heard all of it, or the interrogation would certainly have begun differently.

"Only to warn him away!" Çeda said. "I didn't wish him to get caught in the conflict!"

"Father, she's lying!"

Cahil raised a hand. "In due time, Yndris."

Finally, the pain in her thigh eased. Though the awl was still pressed deep into her flesh, she collapsed with relief. The leather restraints creaked as they took her weight.

A knock came at the door. Cahil acted as if he hadn't heard it. He stepped back and looked Çeda up and down, as though he'd just fashioned her from a block of wood. Then he walked back to the table. He spoke with his back to her as he perused the instruments before him. "Some people are like figs. But touch them and they split wide, spilling their secrets." He picked up a hammer and admired it. One side of its head narrowed to a vicious point, the other was flat with blunt spikes, the sort a cook might use to tenderize meat. "Others are like dragonfruit, prickly and difficult to open." He held the hammer in a shaft of sunlight and gave it a spin, making it glint like Goezhen's teeth beneath Tulathan's silver light. "Until you pound them with a hammer once or twice." He made his way back to her and lay the spiked head of the hammer against her left shin.

He brought the hammer back—

"You're going to have to decide which one you are, Çedamihn Ahyanesh'ala."

—then crashed it down against her leg.

A scream forced its way up her throat as the pain burst from her leg and through her entire being. Her mind expanded in that moment. She felt it reaching out as so often happened when she took the adichara petals. Her right hand ached. But it was an ache that buoyed her, an ache that touched on so many other things. It was in this moment that she felt *something*, or some*one*, in the distance.

Come, a voice called, so wraithlike Çeda had no idea if it was real or some remnant from her dreams. She felt a twinge in her right hand. A throbbing. Her tattoo. The poisoned wound. *Come.*

It was Sehid-Alaz, asking her to join him beneath the adichara. Could she? Could she escape this place? Could she shed this mortal coil and join him like a wight in a boneyard? She might, but there was a look in Cahil's eyes—so very pleased with himself, so self-assured. He'd given her that very same look in King's Harbor as he'd run his knife across Havva's throat. It made her wonder again if he'd taken his perfect, shining instruments to Çeda's mother, Ahya. With the return of that thought, the wish to know the truth became a burning desire. Maybe, here at the end, she could get Cahil to reveal himself. But even now she knew she couldn't speak of it. She might once have *demanded* to know more of her mother—what Cahil had done with her, who her father was—but what good would that do? She had more than herself to think about. She had an entire people to protect.

Sehid-Alaz beckoned once more. *Come.* He was trying to save her, but in so doing he put himself at risk. She was just about to tell him so when a knock came again at the door.

Again Cahil ignored it, his eyes lit with pleasure as he studied Çeda. "So"—the fingers of his right hand rolled across the hammer's rich, leather-wrapped handle, a caress she'd seen from many a dirt dog before a bout in the pits—"on the eve of a battle that might sway the very course of our city, you chose to speak with the queen of Qaimir and her lapdog. Again I ask, why?"

As Çeda struggled to breathe, to fight away the pain, gods help her, she thought about telling Cahil.

Do not ignore me! Sehid-Alaz pleaded. But where would he take her? Would he whisk her away to the desert? Yes. He meant to take her there, to turn her to sand as she'd seen *him* do in the desert.

I cannot! If Sehid-Alaz took her from this place, Cahil would know and Sehid-Alaz would be hunted down and killed. *My life is of no consequence. You must survive.*

No! You are wrong, my child. It is you who must survive.

Cahil seemed pleased by her silence. "Very well." But before he could do or say more, the knock came again, much louder this time. "My Lord King?" came an urgent, muffled voice.

Cahil's brow knitted, his look of pleasure fading. "Come," he answered sharply.

The door behind Çeda opened. The metallic rattle of armor filled the room. "Forgive me, my Lord King, but Kiral awaits. He has sent three messengers already. The last said that if Kiral is forced to send a fourth, he'll take heads when he arrives."

Cahil's face remained almost perfectly composed, but there was a tightening to his lips, a flaring of his nostrils. He regarded Çeda, then the hammer in his hand, then the soldier who'd spoken a moment ago. "Is my armor prepared?"

"It is, Excellence."

"Good. Go." He waved toward Çeda. "And speak of this to no one."

"Of course, my Lord King."

As the clank of armor receded, Cahil turned to his daughter with barely composed patience. He flipped the hammer and held it out to Yndris, handle first. "It is time for you to take matters into your own hands." When Yndris didn't take it, he added, "Assuming you're up to the task."

After a moment's pause, Yndris nodded. "I am, father." And took the hammer.

"Find me my answers, Yndris," Cahil said, and strode from the room.

The door clanked shut, and Yndris was left staring at Çeda with a look of indecision, as if she had no idea what to do now that she was alone in a room with a woman she'd hated from the moment they'd met. It was then that Çeda saw how very young she looked. She was a girl of seventeen, and though she likely thought herself as hardened as her father, it was clear she was anything but.

"Why did you go to speak to the Queen of Qaimir?" she asked.

"I went to speak with Ramahd."

She shook the head of the hammer at Çeda. "Don't prevaricate with me."

"I went to warn him away."

"And don't *hide* behind that story!" She struck Çeda's leg in the same place her father had.

A fresh scream erupted from Çeda. The pain in her leg was terrible, but her right hand burned as if she'd gripped a piece of the fallen sun. She reached out to Sehid-Alaz where he lay in the desert, desperate. She clasped hands with him, strengthening their bond, and felt him trying to draw her to him. But she resisted. *I will not come to you, Sehid-Alaz. You must come to me!*

There was hesitance, not because Sehid-Alaz didn't wish to come, but because of the chains that lay upon him. Çeda had felt the like before, had wondered if she could break them. She'd never tried, not truly, but she did so now, allowing the pain and anger over all the Kings had done to drive her.

A moment later, the walls between her and Sehid-Alaz fell, and Çeda felt the desert as never before. She felt like a stone in the dunes, breaking into smaller and smaller fragments as the sand slowly crushed her. The wind scattered the pieces across the desert, and with it came the feeling of helplessness, as if she were beholden to the Great Mother, and power, as if she could command the desert with but a wish.

As Yndris lifted the hammer again a breeze began to blow about the room. It gave Yndris pause. She stopped and turned. Saw a spinning whorl of dust behind her. The cloud grew. It was comprised now not merely of dust, but sand as well. It spun nearer to Yndris. Drew up along her frame.

"What are you doing?" she shouted, backing away, but the cloud followed her. "What are you doing?"

Çeda tightened her right fist. The pain it brought was nearly unbearable. An inhuman cry born of impotence and outrage burst from her, bringing strength to her limbs the likes of which she'd never felt, not even from the adichara petals. The leather split near her wrist, then broke asunder.

Yndris whipped the hammer at Çeda's head, but she ducked and it struck the wall and clattered to the floor. In a flash of black steel, Yndris drew her blade. She held it before her like a talisman that might protect her from the swirling sand. "Stop it!" she cried, waving the tip at Çeda. "Make it stop!"

After yanking the bloody awl free from the meat of her thigh and letting it drop to the floor, Çeda worked at the buckle on her left hand, but it was moving too slowly, so she ripped the leather free with an ease that surprised her. What was happening Çeda had no idea, but she wasn't about to question it. As the sand tightened along the axis of the spinning, undulating gyre before her, she strained at the thicker leather across her hips. It gave with a loud snap. The nails pinged off the stone wall somewhere to her right.

In that moment, the feeling she'd had of Sehid-Alaz vanished, leaving her feeling empty inside. She coughed as Yndris brought her shamshir down in a vicious, two-handed chop. Çeda ducked and the blade sunk into the bed of the table. Uprooting the last leather strap with one great heave, she dove to one side just as Yndris yanked her sword free.

Zaïde's training returned unbidden. Çeda slid wide as Yndris swung down, the sword passing so close it sliced the ends of Çeda's hair. Yndris tried to bring her blade back for another swing, but Çeda followed the movement, matching her hands with Yndris's. She drove forward, grabbed the wrist of Yndris's sword arm, and lifted high, using the arc of her movements against her. Body to body, Çeda placed her right leg just so and spun Yndris over her hip.

Yndris grunted as she crashed against the marble. Her sword went skittering away, but she twisted violently to free herself from Çeda's grip. Çeda saw her foot coming in too late. She took it across the cheek, twisting with the blow, using the momentum to roll away and grab Yndris's sword. As she kicked herself up to a stand she saw something bright flying toward her. Cahil's hammer caught her hard against the side of the head.

Disoriented for a moment, she saw Yndris, black-clothed, charging toward her. She struck out. Felt the sword sink into flesh. Saw blood as Yndris's fist came crashing against her jaw. Çeda shoved her back to gain space, then spun and delivered a compact back kick, sending Yndris flying, falling, flailing over the slick marble floor, blood streaking her path.

Yndris stood, favoring her left side where blood now darkened the black cloth. It glistened in the light shining down from above. She stared wide-eyed at her crimson-stained hands. With one last look at the sword in Çeda's hands, she turned and sprinted down the short hallway to burst through the door at the end.

As a rush of bright light lit the darkened hallway ahead, Çeda followed. Her limbs felt like fresh clay from the hammer blow, and her thigh burned brightly from where the awl had pierced muscle. She nearly tumbled, but managed to make it to the balcony where a brilliant view of the eastern desert was revealed.

Yndris was angling herself over the marble balustrade, spots of blood marking her path along the dull gray flagstones. She stared down at the sheer drop, then swallowed as she turned to Çeda.

Çeda had never felt sorry for Yndris, but she did now. They both knew she was going to die; it was just a question of which way. As Çeda advanced on her, she found her answer. Yndris looked down over the balustrade, and leapt.

Çeda rushed forward. King's Harbor, a massive hive of activity where crewmen prepared ships and hundreds of soldiers now gathered, was arrayed like a diorama below. Nearer to Çeda, directly below Cahil's palace, was a ravine, bushes and tall grasses coating its sides. And there, half hidden among the scrub trees, Çeda could see Yndris's form, arms and legs splayed like a forgotten wooden doll, her black Maiden's dress stark against the umber earth. The drop was extreme. Fifty feet or more. And yet Yndris still moved. Dear gods, how could she still be conscious? Çeda could see several broken branches on a nearby tree. She must have used it to break her fall.

Only now did the notion of what she had planned to do that evening strike her. She'd hoped to join Ramahd and, if the gods were kind, Emre to destroy the caches. But Yndris had ruined everything. One word from her or her father and Çeda would be uncloaked. Yndris would surely die. She'd already stopped moving. Likely she'd be dead in minutes from blood loss or the wounds she'd sustained on the fall. She'd probably never wake again, and even if she did, she'd never make it out of the ravine.

But what if she did?

Çeda was half tempted to find a path down and finish her off. But time was precious. The Kings were preparing for battle. Any hope of remaining a Blade Maiden and finishing what she'd started now lay in finding Cahil and killing *him* in the chaos of battle. Gods, if only she had understood the copper leaf Amalos had been reading, the one that had seemed so important to Yusam. She'd been working at the problem since reading it, the woman, the drake, saving her family, but she still didn't understand how it related to the Kings and her quest to kill them. But there was nothing for it now. If the gods had seen fit to keep the knowledge from her, she would have to be content with Cahil. If she were lucky and Beşir also braved the sands, she could try to kill him as well. But that meant leaving Yndris now.

Scraping together the sand and dust along the flagstones, Çeda gathered it up in her hand and lifted it to her lips. *I don't pray to you often, Bakhi, but I do this day. Please, take Yndris's hand. Deliver this foul girl to the farther fields.*

That done, she turned her back on the scene below. She had to get out of Cahil's palace, no easy task. She didn't know the layout. And while there might be only a few who knew of her presence, any of them might raise the alarm if she tried to leave through the palace proper.

Then she looked up. *Of course.*

Returning quickly to Cahil's pristine torture chamber, she picked up River's Daughter and cast Yndris's sword to the floor. She took what time she could afford to dress the worst of her wounds with strips cut from the white shift she wore beneath her dress. She couldn't risk passing out on the way back to the House of Maidens, and she couldn't very well return bleeding like a stuck pig.

That done, she went back to the balcony and, with no small amount of difficulty, gained the roof and made her way south over the angular landscape of the Confessor King's palace.

When she reached the House of Maidens near nightfall, a fierce, cold wind was starting to blow, laying a golden haze over the city. The Maidens stationed at the inner gates questioned her, but she gave them a tale of receiving a special mission before the night began and they let her through with little trouble. She was walking across the main courtyard, doing her best to hide her limp, when Sümeya spotted her. "Where have you been?" she said as she broke away from a dozen other Maidens in battle dress, all of them with the mark of wardens over their left breast.

"I was called away by King Cahil."

"Why? And why are you limping?"

"Forgive me, First Warden, but it's to do with the Moonless Host. He asked that I not reveal my purpose until he's had a chance to speak with the other Kings."

"Remove your veil."

She complied. There was no sense in hiding it. Sümeya grabbed Çeda's chin, turned her head from side to side, inspecting the place Yndris had driven her head down against the stones of the barracks, where Cahil's hammer had struck, where Yndris's foot had connected with her cheek. Çeda had stopped at a finger-thin stream on her way down from Tauriyat to wipe away as much of the blood as she could, but was certain she still looked terrible.

"Was Yndris with you?"

"No," Çeda said flatly.

She gripped Çeda's chin harder. "Was she *with* you?"

"No, First Warden. I swear it on my mother's life."

Sümeya continued to stare, clearly at war over how far to push this with the whole of the Blade Maidens ready to ride out to the desert. "You're a bloody mess," she said finally, releasing Çeda, "but we have need of you. Can you ride?"

Çeda nodded.

She glanced to the wardens, who were waiting for her. "Take an extra petal," she said while marching toward them. "Do it now so you're ready when the time comes."

"As you say," Çeda said, but Sümeya was already calling orders to another pair of wardens who had entered the courtyard.

Beyond Sümeya lay the gates to the city. As she had a dozen times on her way here, she thought of leaving, of fulfilling her promise to join Ramahd and destroy the caches. But she couldn't. She had to try to take Cahil before the other Kings learned of his suspicions.

Take an extra petal, Sümeya had said. She already *had* taken an extra. Two on the way here from Cahil's palace. Taking another might be dangerous, but the pain was still so great, so she opened her mother's locket, placed a third petal beneath her tongue, and limped toward the stables.

Chapter 60

A S NIGHT FELL OVER THE DESERT, the cold north wind intensified. Sand
drove against the line of Maidens riding out from the gates of King's
Harbor. To their left, the aqueduct loomed. It vaulted ahead, arch after arch
after arch, three levels tall, a dark ribbon occluding the stars like a roadway
to the heavens themselves. At the head of the issuing host, King Husamettín
led the way on Blackmane, a vicious akhala—one of the desert's gilded giants,
as they were called by the Mireans—with a shimmering golden coat that
darkened to a jet black mane and tail. The King wore an exquisite set of
armor: etched helm, gauntlets and greaves, vambraces, and a breastplate over
a shirt of fine chain, all made from a blue-black metal that was eerily silent.
Blackmane's barding had been forged of the same material, making the two
of them seem like demons sent by Goezhen to protect the city.

Sümeya, the First Warden, rode by the King's side on Whiteknife, the son
of Blackmane, a horse every bit as bellicose as his father. Kameyl and Melis
rode side by side behind them, and Çeda brought up the rear on her tall
mare, Brightlock. More Maidens followed, fifteen hands in all, seventy-five
warrior women, veiled and dressed in battle gear with ebon blades at their
sides, bows on their backs, and shields at the ready.

Behind them came two hundred Silver Spears on tall horses of their own. Their spears pointing skyward, they looked like an ivory serpent cutting its way over the soughing dunes. Hundreds more of the city guard had left earlier in the day, riding to their appointed spaces leagues out from Sharakhai. Among their number were scouts who would patrol and blow great horns carried on small, fast ships if they spotted the enemy. It allowed the Kings to cover dozens of leagues along the aqueduct.

Husamettín had chosen to station the bulk of their forces at four primary locations: the first and largest near Sharakhai, the other three at sections of the aqueduct that had fallen when a great earthquake had brought it down seventy years past. Each had been rebuilt, but none so grandly as before, resulting in three areas that might be damaged or destroyed more easily than the rest. Those, the Kings reasoned, were the places most likely to be attacked, and so were given the most protection. And if the Moonless Host attacked elsewhere, the shamblers might weaken the structure, but not before the scouts alerted everyone to the danger.

Each Blade Maiden had been given a special salve to rub over her entire body, even her hair. It smelled of goat fat and copper and eggs—foul, to be sure, but Husamettín's alchemysts said it would protect them from the caustic innards of the shamblers should they be caught as Kameyl had. There had been some left for the city guard, but only for a handful of their numbers, their elite. The asirim the Kings left unprotected. "There isn't enough," Sümeya had said when Melis had asked about it, "and who among us is willing to treat the asirim with the salve in any case? You, Melis? You, Hasenn?"

"Even if I were willing to touch their flesh," Hasenn, a broad woman with a wide face, had replied, "they wouldn't allow it."

"Just so, so keep your wits about you. We don't want to lose any if we can help it. Listen for the shamblers' screams. That will tell you when they're ready to burst. The asirim will no doubt be looking to avenge their sister who was lost in Ishmantep, so be ready. Force them away the moment you hear their screams. Or send them in quickly if others might be protected by doing so."

As they came to a rise, the wind threw biting sand against their skin. Tulathan had just risen over the eastern horizon as Rhia followed, rising from the depths of her distant grave. The two goddesses were reborn, returned to their power once more. This would be a rare holy night with the moons reaching their zenith simultaneously. It would be a night alive with blood and pain and passage to the farther fields. The very air brimmed with potential, as if the gods themselves watched, waiting to see which of the many paths that lay before the great city of Sharakhai would remain when all was said and done.

When Husamettín raised his right hand and stood in his saddle, their column halted. Each of the blade maidens took one of the adichara petals she'd been given earlier and placed it beneath her tongue. Çeda, however, disobeyed. Her wounds still pained her—especially where Cahil's hammer had struck her shin—but she'd already taken three. She would burst like one of Hamzakiir's shamblers if she dared take another.

Over the dunes ahead, forms loped toward them. The asirim, summoned by Mesut. They slowed as they neared the line of warhorses. It was now up to each Maiden to choose two, quickly and quietly and in concert with her fellow Maidens. Kerim stood out among them, his familiarity a flaming brand among candles. *Join me,* she said to him, *I beg you.* He had already been called by another Maiden, but Çeda exerted her will and Kerim bonded with Çeda instead. She chose another near him. *Your name?* Çeda asked, expecting a proud, defiant response, but she felt only bitter hatred, and it grew worse as she pressed for an answer.

Leave her! Kerim said. *She has been treated worse than most.*

Çeda relented. She cared only that the asir would obey, and this one was more than ready for blood. Çeda could feel it inside her, a thing that had been burning for the last four hundred years. For now, the simplicity of the asir's single-minded will would serve Çeda well.

Soon enough, all the asirim had taken their places, one to each side of their bonded Maiden's horse. Çeda had been in battle, but never at war. She felt the same sort of tension she felt before crossing blades, but the feeling that suffused the air now was much deeper, much broader. The tension threaded *through* her, spreading to all the other Maidens, all the other soldiers, even the King of Swords. As a group, they were grim, they were proud, they were confident, but they were nervous as well. They'd heard the stories from Ishmantep.

As the twin moons approached their zenith, silver Rhia catching up to golden Tulathan, the asirim began snuffing over the dunes like wolves hunting for a scent. The Maidens stood at the ready, spread in formation, each hand keeping their horses grouped in the shape of a five-pointed star. If the Maidens were restless—and Çeda could see it in the way they sat their horses, the way their eyes roamed over the landscape—Husamettín was alive with energy. The King drew Night's Kiss and rode Blackmane along the summit of a broad dune ahead, raising the arcing sword high in challenge. The blade shone black against the crystalline fabric of the heavens. His every move begged the Moonless Host to come. He was as eager to deal death as the asirim, perhaps more so. Or perhaps it was Night's Kiss. If legends were true, each night of the twin moons the great sword drove him to an animalistic rage. Some called it a curse of the gods, others a boon to Sharakhai. Only Husamettín and the gods themselves knew the truth of it, but Çeda found herself glad she wouldn't be facing him. Of all the Kings, he was the one she feared most.

Suddenly, Husamettín stopped and reined Blackmane over until he was facing east. He stared, standing tall in his saddle. Over the rushing wind, Çeda heard it, an almighty groan of pain and anguish, a cry that surely reached all the way to the empty halls of the old ones. Another came shortly after. And another. The sounds of pain rose sharply in pitch, as if it had all become too much, and then the first of the booming explosions fell across the desert. A second came a moment later, then a third. The shamblers, erupting. Even so far from it, Çeda could feel it beat against her chest and shoulders.

More cries filled the night, followed by a sudden upwelling of courage as the soldiers of Sharakhai moved to engage. The clash of steel came, then more explosions. This time the thunder was met immediately with howls of pain. Çeda couldn't help but picture the Silver Spears as the acid fell across them, melting their skin.

Husamettín rode back and forth, back and forth, adjusting his sword grip occasionally but doing nothing else in response to the misery befalling his soldiers to the east.

Sümeya spurred her horse nearer, even as renewed cries of pain rose higher in the night. "Shall we go to them, my King?"

Husamettín ignored her. He pulled Blackmane's reins and came to a halt, horse and rider both facing the sounds of battle. Çeda reckoned it raged only a league away, no more than two. They could be there in little time if they rode quickly, and yet Husamettín merely sat his horse, stone-still, studying the land below the aqueduct's grand arches.

"Eminence, we should—"

Husamettín's held up his left hand, the one holding Blackmane's reins, and cocked his head to one side. He pointed with the tip of his black blade to an area just short of the aqueduct. "There."

He'd no more than spurred Blackmane into action, the horse rearing for a moment before galloping down the dune, than the sand near the aqueduct shifted, sinking here, bulging there. A head appeared, sloughing golden dust from its bald pate as it lifted from beneath the surface of the sand. Fleshy arms with sausage fingers clawed ineffectually for a moment, but then the shambler's bulk was freed from the sucking sand. Others followed, each wading forward before gaining the sand's surface. Then they waddled toward the nearest of the aqueduct's stone supports.

It was difficult to tell but, by the light of the moons, the shamblers seemed to have a reddish tinge to them. And they were huge. Nearly half again the size of those unfortunate souls in Ishmantep. How they could even walk Çeda had no idea, but onward they went, plodding over the sand toward the aqueduct. These were the graduates, of course, transformed by a foul combination of alchemy and Hamzakiir's twisted imagination.

King Husamettín was already closing the distance with the shamblers. The Maidens were close behind, each calling out, trying to distract the lumbering forms, to stall them before they reached their goal. Çeda held her asirim back, though both Kerim and the nameless second strained at their bonds, clawing at the sand, twisting their heads about, snarling inhumanly as they tried to break free.

Not yet. I will have need of you both later.

Four asirim were allowed to join the Maidens' charge. They moved with incredible speed, easily keeping pace with the horses. It all seemed so very odd, though. The shamblers were too few. Only a dozen had risen from the sand. Where were the rest? Why would Hamzakiir have bothered to hide so few close to the harbor's gates unless this was another distraction?

As Brightlock galloped forward, Çeda scanned the way ahead. The sand.

The stone arches of the aqueduct. The rolling dunes beyond. The moons were directly overhead now, Rhia's golden face encompassed by Tulathan's, as if the silver goddess were protecting her smaller sister.

It was then, as Çeda thought of the moonlight shining down, that she realized. The aqueduct. The channel that carried the water. She scanned the water channel itself, especially where it entered the harbor's tall wall. She couldn't be sure, but she thought she saw movement there: dark shapes rising from the water.

The channel was easily wide enough for a man to hide in, wide enough for even the shamblers. It entered the harbor's great wall about three quarters of the way up, perhaps forty feet above the surface of the sand. Where channel met wall, iron grates prevented anyone from sneaking in, but if all the attention were drawn to the base of the aqueduct, it might be possible to move along the channel undetected and reach the very walls of the harbor.

As Çeda rode, she saw grapnel hooks being thrown from the channel to the top of the harbor walls. Men climbed, hand over hand, swift as snakes.

"An attack on the walls!" Çeda called, pointing with her ebon blade. Several of her sister Maidens had already seen, so it did the Moonless Host little harm if she called out a warning. The Silver Spears stationed on the wall cried out, but they were quickly overwhelmed by the attack.

Behind Çeda, two sharp whistles came from another Maiden. *Danger. Southwest.* Çeda turned that direction. She saw nothing amiss, but they'd just ridden down from the crest of the dune, so much was now hidden from them.

"Ships!" called Hasenn, warden of the hand behind Sümeya's. "Ships on the horizon!"

Husamettín slowed his pace and roared back, "Send the asirim to meet them!"

"There are many!"

"They'll not get past the harbor walls. Until they arrive, we concentrate on the danger before us."

Above, Çeda could see ropes being swung around the channel. Two scarabs had slipped down along the supporting column to wrap more ropes around the column beneath. Near the wall, meanwhile, the massive shamblers, each swathed in black cloth, were being hauled up to the top of the gates.

"There!" Husamettín called. "Fire arrows!"

The Maidens immediately sheathed their swords and drew short bows from their backs, including Çeda. Volley after volley were launched at the shamblers. They struck, over and over, the arrows driving deep. Dark liquid sprayed from the wounds; Çeda was not at all sure it was blood. As two of the monstrosities gained the wall, one of them fell, releasing a cry as it did so. For the first time, Çeda heard a word in their cries—"Nooooo!"—perhaps one lucid thought from a collegia student in the moments before he died. The body had no sooner thumped against the sand below than it burst in a massive explosion, sending a spray of stone and glistening ichor high into the air.

Despite the arrows flying, three more of the lumbering beasts gained the gates, then two more. One was caught in the channel, an arrow through its neck. As it cried out, trying to pull the arrow free, the men of the Host tried to push it over, for they knew what was about to happen. They'd just managed to lever it to the top of the channel when it exploded, sending men and a gout of water flying upward and outward. Parts of men and the exploded stones of the channel thumped to the ground in a broad circle, the sound of it rhythmic like the patter of a wide skin drum. The stout bottom of the channel held, but the sides had not. Water poured down in a thick stream, molten glass in the moonlight, before it dissolved and fell in a torrential rain to the sand below.

As the Blade Maidens and Silver Spears charged, a great moaning came from the inside the towering harbor gates. It was muffled, though. The shamblers had been positioned *inside* the harbor. Mournful cries and explosions followed. In four precise locations, sprays of liquid shot out from the gates like ghostly green fans.

The hinges, Çeda realized. They'd positioned the shamblers to release their viscera over the hinges. They were trying to weaken the gates. It wouldn't work, though. The gates were far too large. What good would weakening the hinges do with those monstrosities still standing upright?

Arrows began to fly against the men wrapping the rope around the upper spans of the aqueduct, but they were protected by shields held by others. The shamblers below reached the aqueduct's stone support, the very one the men above had tied ropes to. Like beggar children surrounding an unfortunate visitor to Sharakhai who'd been foolish enough to offer up a coin, the shamblers crowded the base of the stone column, directly beneath the men and the swinging ropes above. They locked elbows, pulling one another tightly against the column as a host of arrows sunk into their flesh.

"Leave the shamblers!" Husamettín called, pointing with his inky blade. "Take the men above!"

Çeda made sure to send her shots wide, but many of the Maidens' arrows, even loosed from horseback, struck home. The scarabs of the Moonless Host fell to the sands, landing with dull thuds. The two men wrapping the ropes around the column were slain with precise shots, but four more slipped down the ropes from above to take their place, and more after *those* men were shot down as well. Soon the stone of the channel had been wrapped tight.

Below, the shamblers began to moan in unison. Their bodies shivered from pain or ecstasy or who knew what?

Husamettín, instead of charging toward them, guided Blackmane toward the gap between the aqueduct's columns. He sheathed his sword and crouched upon his saddle. Timing his leap as Blackmane charged across the sand, he shot upward and grabbed the lip of the first stone span eighteen feet above. He lifted himself up and moved to the column to his right and began climbing hand over hand with powerful ease. He knew what the Host was trying to do and meant to cut the ropes before they could.

He'd no more reached the second span, though, when the shamblers burst. One by one, and then in a huge, collective explosion, their bodies erupted. A great bloom of sand and stone flew outward. The nearby dunes shivered from it, sand lifting and shifting in strange patterns. And then a rattle-clap thunder that sent sharp pain into both of Çeda's ears fell over the desert.

As the sound began to settle, Çeda heard a sizzling—the acid, she knew, eating away at whatever stone remained. Husamettín had hidden from the explosion inside the upper archway, but as soon as it died away, he leapt to the nearby column and resumed his climb toward the water channel.

The clearing of sand and dust revealed the damage to the base of the column. Much of it had been gouged away, as though insects had eaten it. The apple-core center still held, but more stone was sloughing off as the viscous shambler acid devoured it.

Husamettín reached the channel at last, where four or five of the

Moonless Host were trying to knock him free. He waited as they swung down at him, then timed one neat slice at the nearest man's neck.

Blood flowed.

As the swordsman tipped forward, his brethren grabbed him to keep him from falling. The moment they did, Husamettín clambered up, using the man as a handhold, blocking several hasty swings along the way and gaining the channel.

"Husamettín!" one of rebels called. "Husamettín has come!"

At these words, a host of scarabs, hidden until this moment, rose up from the channel on either side of Husamettín. There must have been three dozen of them. They charged the King of Swords, but Husamettín stood his ground. Night's Kiss arced through the air, creating a low hum like the buzz of a beetle's wings. It batted away swords ahead and behind, sliced arms and legs, slit neck and chest and belly, and all the while Husamettín crept steadily toward the spot where the ropes were tied.

The base of the column was beginning to crumble. The stones along the bottommost spans began to fracture and fall away. Husamettín fought to within a few scant yards from the ropes. He was going to reach it.

But then came a tall man with a short spear held in one hand. In his other was a glowing ball of orange flame. Hamzakiir. The soldiers made way for him, clearing a path to Husamettín. The King of Swords stood his ground, ready, waiting. Then he charged.

Hamzakiir released the ball of flame, and Husamettín brought Night's Kiss up in a vicious arc, splitting the flame with a low thrum. The flame was cut in two, the halves flying wide, twisting crazily through the night as Hamzakiir released another. Husamettín sliced that as well, then a third, then the two men were too close for anything but armed combat.

Hamzakiir's broad-bladed spear darted in, but was met time and again by Night's Kiss, which hummed as it blocked, as it riposted, as it came in from on high.

"Away! Away!" came a call from somewhere along the water channel.

At this, Hamzakiir sent a flurry of blows against Husamettín, then retreated as the column beneath him collapsed. The stone spans nearest the ground fell away completely. Then the second set of spans above that. Finally, the topmost arches—which supported the water channel itself—crumbled and fell, taking with it the massive section of stone held together by the ropes the men of the Moonless Host had tied around it.

A deluge of water rushed down through the freshly made gap in the channel, filling the desert with the sounds of a great and sudden tempest. The colossal stone weight of the aqueduct's roped section fell straight down, powered by the rush of falling water. It drew on the sets of rope, which were in turn tied to a thick cable, a hawser like those used to tow ships.

The hawser pulled taut, lifting a set of rigging with block and tackle. The other end of the rope was secured to the top of the harbor gates. Çeda was well aware how doubling or tripling sheaves in the blocks multiplied the strength being applied to the other end of the rope, and indeed, as the weight of the aqueduct's stones rushed down a massive groan came from the harbor gates—a sound like one of the old ones waking from his slumber, ready to walk the world and rend it in two for its many offenses. Metallic pinging sounds followed, and a creaking that made it seem like the whole of the House of Kings was slipping down along the slopes of Tauriyat.

But by Iri's black teeth, the gates still held. They held, and there was no way that the Host would breach the harbor, damaged gates or not.

Several of the Maidens had leapt from their horses and were climbing to aid their King. Above, Husamettín pressed forward, hoping to rout these lesser men from the top of the channel, but this was when the men on the opposite side of the divide began pulling together.

"Hup!" one of the scarabs called, and his men pulled.

"Ho!" And they pulled again.

"Hup! Ho!"

"Hup! Ho!"

As the air filled with a rain of arrows, the men pulled in unison, drawing on the rope, pulling the gates just a little bit farther. With so many, and with the gates' hinges already weakened, it was working. Slowly but surely the massive doors leaned farther outward.

Husamettín leapt the gap and continued his attack, but Hamzakiir was there to meet him. He blocked blow after blow from Night's Kiss. He was not nearly as gifted as Husamettín, but he didn't have to be. He was only buying time. He blocked and retreated, choosing his attacks with care. Other swordsmen helped, and still Husamettín crept closer to the men working the thick rope tied to the gates.

Hamzakiir had been pressed against the rearmost of those men when a great cacophony of splintering wood and shearing metal and men straining at the top of their lungs led to the fifty-foot-tall gates tipping to the point that nothing would hold them.

For a moment, all movement ceased.

The Maidens pulled up their horses. Husamettín's blade stilled in his hand. The men in the water channel stood stock-still, their eyes on the gates. Even the water seemed to freeze in midair.

All as the gates fell and crashed upon the desert floor like the doom of Sharakhai.

Chapter 61

ITWAS LATE AFTERNOON AS SUNLIGHT SPEARED through the dusty air in the upper reaches of the Qaimiri embassy house. Ramahd and thirteen of his men stood in a room that had once been the banquet hall but had since been transformed into a makeshift audience chamber. All but Meryam wore thawbs cut in the desert style, turbans that one might find among the wandering tribes, as well as armor beneath, some small protection for the night's endeavor.

Meryam stood before Luken, who held a bandage in his left hand. Meryam took his right and pressed the sharp tip of her thumb ring into it. "Know that tonight you do the will of your queen." Blood pooled in Luken's palm. "You are the swords I cannot lift, the knives I cannot thrust. Be sharp, children of Qaimir. Be quick. And return to me unharmed."

As one, all fourteen men replied, "Yes, my queen."

Speaking under her breath, Meryam touched her fingers to the blood and drew a sigil across Luken's brow. She did the same on both his cheeks, then his chin, and then, with the loving touch an artist has for her canvas, she brushed her fingers over Luken's skin. The blood smeared with her movements, but something else happened as well. His very skin changed—the color and the texture. The ridges over his eyes became less pronounced, his cheeks smoother, his chin more rounded. His nose widened. Even his beard changed. She ran her fingers through it, and it lengthened like thread being drawn from a skein of wool. After sliding her thumbs along his eyebrows, raising them slightly, she pinched his jaw between her thumb and forefinger, turning him this way, then that, inspecting him.

He looked a completely different man. Sharakhani, not Qaimiri. This was necessary, Meryam had said, and Ramahd had agreed. Should any of them die tonight, it was paramount that Qaimir be above suspicion.

"Go well," she said to Luken, then kissed him on both cheeks. After wrapping the bandage around his right hand, Luken bowed, then left the room to prepare the wagon they would take to meet Hamid and the men of the Moonless Host.

Tiron came next, and she did the same to him, pressing her ring into his palm, chanting ancient verses, using Tiron's own blood and the magic the gods had granted her to alter how he looked. She was done in little time—Tiron had a bit of Sharakhani blood in him already—but Ramahd could tell Meryam was already beginning to weaken. Her hands shook, and she was starting to breathe heavily. She was a gifted mage, but doing this, *altering* a man, was both complex and arduous. Most couldn't even attempt it, and those who could had to tread carefully lest they foul the ritual and cause permanent damage: scarring skin, blinding eyes, or turning bones to jelly.

But Ramahd had confidence in her. She had both the will and the power to see this through, so he let her continue. As Tiron wrapped the bandage around his hand, Meryam moved on to Cicio then Vrago then Gautiste, kissing each of them before they left. With each man, Meryam shook just a little bit more, so that by the time she came to Ramahd—the two of them now alone in the expanse of the room—her lungs were heaving as if she'd run from Sharakhai's west end to the top of Tauriyat. Nostrils flaring, she held Ramahd's hand. A count of ten heartbeats passed. Then twenty.

"I could go as I am," Ramahd said.

Meryam glared. "I only need a moment."

After a few more deep breaths, she pressed the ring into Ramahd's palm. The ring bit. Blood gathered. Meryam used it immediately, as if she were worried that even a moment's pause would lead to her surrendering to exhaustion. As her fingers brushed over his skin, he felt a twinge of pain. It spread quickly as she moved, pinching here, stretching there. It was uncomfortable, but little more than that.

He didn't mind the change in and of itself. If all went well they would return to their former selves in a day or so. But not if they died. That's what shook him to his core. If he passed to the farther fields, would Yasmine recognize him? Would Rehann? If not he would regret this forever but, as was so often the case, the needs of this life outweighed those of the next.

By the time she was done, Meryam shook from head to toe. Ramahd, however, had the good sense not to mention it. He was just glad he was the last.

"Go well," she said to him, but instead of a kiss on his forehead, she pulled him in for a kiss on the lips. Some small amount of the passion they'd shared in the desert returned, and then she was pulling away and motioning him toward the door. "Now send Amaryllis in. I will finish with her before you leave."

"She needn't come. We have enough."

"She's asked to go and I will allow it."

"Meryam—"

"My queen."

"My queen. There's no need for Amaryllis to—"

"She has long been an asset to me and Qaimir. She's earned the right. Now send her in. There's little time."

He bowed to her. "Of course, my queen."

He found Amaryllis waiting outside the room. She stared at him for a moment, but then her look hardened. "Do you think I'll hinder you, my lord?"

She wouldn't. She was in fine shape, and an agile climber. It would be hard to argue she wouldn't be an asset. "Take no offense. It's only . . . You're young, Amaryllis. You have much to live for. We may none of us see the sunrise."

The glint in her eyes was like a knife's edge now. "I am my own woman. I'm not afraid of dying, and our queen has already given her leave." She paused, daring him to speak. "Would you seek to deny her?"

He bowed and stepped aside, waving to the door. "Of course not."

When she'd entered, Ramahd made his way to the rear of the estate where a tall, windowless wagon awaited. He climbed into the dark, dank interior. Amaryllis soon joined them, rushing in and reaching for the door. She'd changed much in so little time. Her beauty stolen from her, her face was broader, longer than it had been. Her lips were wider. And her long black hair—all gone now, shorn close to her skin as if she'd just survived a bout with lice. Then she closed the door and the interior plunged into darkness, some small amount of light angling in through the gaps in the planks.

At a knock from Ramahd's boot on the floor, the wagon rumbled into motion. The smell of sweat and men's breath filled the tight space. The wagon shook them, leaning as it turned and slowed near the gates of Tauriyat. The driver spoke to the guards in muffled words. Even though they'd arranged this ahead of time and secured it with a healthy bribe, Ramahd worried that they would be inspected or stopped altogether, but soon they were off and into the city.

They clattered through the streets of Sharakhai. The wait felt interminable even though he knew they weren't going far. Finally the wagon came to a stop. Amaryllis opened the doors, and they all filed out. They were south of the collegia grounds, a busy enough place normally, but today it was practically deserted.

The wagon rumbled away as their group of fifteen made their way farther south toward Karakir Square. When they arrived, the city was still, nearing its slumber. The square was empty save for three young girls sitting at its center. When the girls saw them approach, one of them stood, stared at them with wide brown eyes, and sprinted down a narrow alley situated between a cooper and a chandler. In short order, a stout fellow wearing beaten but serviceable leather armor came striding out from the alley. He snapped his fingers at the remaining pair of girls and pointed down a side street. "You know better." The doe-eyed girl joined them, and the three of them ran, but not before sending interested glances back at Ramahd and the others.

From the alley came four more men, Çeda's friend, Emre, among them. The other three he'd never seen before, but one was a huge hulk of a man with a gritty look to him, the sort who looked for fights, the sort good at finishing what he started. All of them bore weapons: bows, swords, knives. The big one held a massive battle axe, the butt of it capped with a gleaming, steel spike. Çeda, however, wasn't among them. Ramahd wasn't sure whether to feel relieved or worried.

Before anyone could say a word, the sound of horse hooves pounded along a street somewhere to the west. Nearer and nearer they came, dozens of them, steel-shod hooves ringing against stone. A full company of Silver Spears, most like. Or Blade Maidens. All turned toward the sound, eyes wary, hands on weapons, but then, thank the gods, the sound began to fade.

"You're Hamid?" Ramahd asked.

The man with the sleepy eyes nodded. "Juvaan sent you?"

Ramahd nodded back.

Hamid looked over their group, then made a show of looking beyond them, as if more were coming. A dark laugh erupted from him a moment later. "*Fifteen* of you?"

"Fifteen finer you'll not find in Sharakhai," Ramahd replied, "but if you wish us to leave, you need but say so."

Hamid's laugh faded to a smile. "Let it never be said a Qaimiri places humility above pride."

Tiron bristled at this, but Ramahd held up his hand.

Emre stepped closer and whispered something to Hamid. "No," Hamid replied, loud enough that Ramahd could hear. "I know Ramahd Amansir."

"I am Ramahd Amansir," Ramahd cut in, "though not so long ago I wore a different face. All of us did." When Hamid stared doubtfully he went on. "Come, if you know Ramahd, as you say, then you also know the nature of his queen."

Cracking his knuckles absently, Hamid glanced over his shoulder to Emre. "You're sure it's his voice?" Emre nodded, a reluctant gesture if Ramahd had ever seen one. A pleasantly surprised look overcame Hamid as he took them in anew. In a flash, he'd drawn his shamshir. "By the gods who breathe, the Queen of Qaimir has stones so large she would send us the man who survived the Bloody Passage?" He took a step forward. "The Lord of the South? The man who has taken his sword to a dozen scarabs in search of our lord, Macide?"

Tiron, Luken, and Amaryllis all drew swords, at which point the men behind Hamid drew theirs. "Enough," Ramahd said, turning and spreading his arms, barring the advance of his men. "Sheathe your weapons." It took a moment, but they obeyed, only after which did Ramahd turn back to Hamid. "For this one night, our purposes align. I propose a truce."

"A truce?" Hamid said.

"A truce," Ramahd replied, "for this night only."

Hamid lowered his sword. "And what makes you think we'd accept?"

"Because the White Wolf herself came, at great personal risk, to beg my queen for our help." Ramahd stepped forward until he was within a sword swing of Hamid. "I understand the Kings have crippled the Host, slaughtering hundreds of scarabs. I understand as well they were not kind about it. I know your mission is grim, but if you would rather go alone, tell me now and we'll return to our homes and watch as the Kings crush the rest of you underfoot."

Hamid looked to Emre, giving him the chance to speak against Ramahd. Emre seemed to weigh Ramahd's words for a moment, but then half shrugged, half nodded. Not the endorsement Ramahd was hoping for, but at least he said nothing against him. With no small amount of wariness, Hamid drove his sword home into his scabbard and waved for the rest of his men to do the same. "Very well," he said, "though if we're going to leave, it's best we go now."

"Wait," Ramahd said. "Çeda said she would come. Have you had no word from her?"

Emre seemed dumbfounded by the news. "She told you this?"

Ramahd nodded. "She said she would meet us here if she could."

Emre didn't seem to know what to say, but Hamid looked up to the sky, perhaps weighing just how useful Çeda might be. "As much as I'd value an ebon sword by our side, time grows short." He turned to Ramahd. "Come, oh fearless fifteen. Let us stand side by side this night, and see what the gods have in store for us."

Ramahd nodded, and then they were off, jogging easily in two loose groups. Emre lagged behind, looking over his shoulder often as they headed through the city, but all too soon Karakir Square was lost and with it any hope of Çeda joining them.

They moved northeast, keeping wide of the garrison and the other holdings of the Silver Spears. They came after a short while to an expensive incense shop. They weren't able to see much of Tauriyat from ground level, but when Hamid led him up a winding set of stairs to an old belfry tower, the whole of the high hill opened up before them: the House of Kings, the House of Maidens, the great wall surrounding them, and the large manses of Goldenhill beneath.

Hamid pointed to the walls nearest their position. "We'll wait for our signal, then we'll position ourselves between those two towers, scale the wall, and head for Kiral's palace."

"And what of Zeheb's and Ihsan's? Are you planning on leaving their caches untouched?"

Hamid paused. "You're well-informed."

"My queen hates being left in the dark."

"So I've heard," Hamid said. "Fear not. There are others headed to the remaining two palaces. Our concern is Kiral's palace."

"And what's the signal?"

"We'll know when we hear it."

Ramahd hadn't been sure how he was going to react if he came across Macide, but he supposed Mighty Alu had shined on him this day. The leader of the Moonless Host wasn't here, which made it likely that he'd be heading to another of the three palaces.

Sunset came, and the city turned boneyard silent. Great lanterns lit one by one all along the Kings' wall, then the palaces above, making the mountain glow. Such things were unheard of on the holy night, but the Kings clearly thought whatever safety it might bring them worth the risk of angering the desert gods.

At one point, Hamid went down to speak to someone who'd arrived late. Emre joined Ramahd in the belfry tower a few minutes later. His time in the Moonless Host had tempered him. He looked different now. Less angry, more sure of himself.

Emre studied Ramahd's features, as if trying to find the man he remembered in the face that greeted him now. "Why did you come?" he said at last.

Ramahd knew what he was getting at. Why put himself or the interests of his queen at risk? It seemed foolish when viewed from afar, and indeed part of Ramahd hated being here. He was horrified by the thought of taking orders from Macide, either directly or indirectly, but when Çeda had come to him there had been no way he could deny her. She didn't know what he owed her, but *he* certainly did. The seed he'd planted when he'd agreed to Guhldrathen's demands might never actually bear its terrible fruit, but he would give her this: help when she'd asked for it, even if it meant setting aside old promises.

"It's not so difficult an equation to solve. I came because my queen has decided it's in her best interests."

Emre studied the eastern sky, where the moons were rising. "Just like that? Years of searching for revenge and your queen, your sister by marriage, a woman who's helped you kill our men and women since you returned from the Bloody Passage, decides to set it all aside and *help* her enemies?"

"You may find this hard to believe, but it's what kings and queens do. They find what's best for their country, and chart a course by that compass, no matter that it takes them to places they find distasteful."

A scolding laugh escaped Emre. "I'd never do what you're doing."

"No? Not even if Çeda asked you to?"

For the first time, Emre seemed unsure of himself. "Is that why you did it? For her?"

Yes. Absolutely. "I do it for my queen."

Emre weighed him, looking wholly unconvinced, then resumed his watch over the House of Kings. "I'm not surprised you've come to love her. She's abrasive as sandstone at times, but only because she's determined. Get beyond that, and you see her true self, and it's wondrous to behold."

Ramahd could hear the love in his words, his devotion to his friend. But then he wondered: *Have I truly seen Çeda? Because if that were so, I would never have agreed to Guhldrathen's demands.* "Let's just look to the task ahead, shall we?"

"As you say."

The moons continued to rise. The wailing of the asirim rose in the east, more of them than Ramahd had ever heard. It made his skin crawl. Just as Tulathan and Rhia were coming into alignment over Sharakhai, the sound of battle rose like a demon in the distance. Warriors shouted. There came a clash of steel and stone. Hamid rushed up the stairs and scanned the horizon.

"Now?" Ramahd asked.

Hamid shook his head. Soon after, though, several loud booms rose above the sounds of battle. Over and over they came, with shouting and screaming both preceding and following. Ramahd swore he could feel the impact in his bones. What in the wide great world could explode with such force?

"Be ready," Hamid whispered harshly down the stairs.

Moments later, there came a groaning sound, as if the desert were opening the doors to its heart. The look in Emre's eyes was one of fear, but not for himself. *A fear I know well, the sort one has for a loved one you're powerless to help.* A massive crash of thunder made each man in the belfry shiver. Clay pots rattled below. A pair of amberlarks Ramahd hadn't even realized were on the roof of the belfry tower took wing. Despite the call for silence on the Holy Night, Ramahd heard children begin to cry, heard their mothers and fathers shushing them.

As one, Ramahd, Hamid, and Emre spiraled down the stairs and rushed from the incense shop behind the rest of their men. They moved steadily northeast, wary of being seen, but they saw no one watching and their moves along the streets of Goldenhill went unchallenged. As they approached the walls of Tauriyat, a hand of Blade Maidens followed by two white-robed Matrons sprinted along the wall above. They were gone quickly, leaving the wall above them—as far as Ramahd could tell—undefended.

"Quickly now," Hamid said.

At this, Emre and the hulking brute with the battle axe unfurled ropes from around their waists. They flung grapnels up and over the edge of the wall, then the lot of them, twenty in all, scurried up to the top. With the nearest tower undefended, they rushed toward it and took the stairs within to ground level, secreting their ropes and grapnels at the base for use later in their escape.

If we ever make it back, Ramahd thought.

They could not see the battle, but they could hear it. It raged like the opening act to the ending of the world. Who knew how long it would last, though? Who knew how long it would be before the Kings' attention swung back to their palaces?

They ran with some speed now, though not *too* fast lest they exhaust themselves. The lower reaches of Tauriyat were relatively flat, but they were soon trekking uphill. Reasoning that few would be moving on Tauriyat, they took a gamble and followed the main road up toward the palaces. They were wary, though—prepared to run into the nearby brush if need be. On they hiked, ever upward, fear driving them as much as will. They passed fork after fork along the winding road, choosing the path that would take them to Eventide, the topmost palace.

When they were halfway up, they heard someone running toward them.

"Help!" cried a lone boy, who resolved from the darkness dressed in King Zeheb's livery. "Please, my lords! They've entered the palace of my Lord King Zeheb!"

"Who has, boy?" Hamid asked.

"The . . ." He stared, took them all in once more, then turned and sprinted pell-mell in the other direction. He was so winded, though, so hysterical with fright, it took little effort for Ramahd to catch up with him, grab a fistful of hair, and send him sprawling to the ground with a shove.

"Tie him," he said to Tiron, who worked quickly, tying and gagging the boy, then dragging him far off the road. With any luck, he'd be found in the morning but be no further trouble tonight.

On they went, higher and higher, twice running off the side of the road and lying in the manmade ditch as first a woman on a single horse and then a dozen Silver Spears on tall akhalas galloped past. At last they neared Eventide, the largest of all the palaces. In all his time in Sharakhai, Ramahd had never stepped foot within the palace. It was huge, with tall towers and walls along its southern face. It was not nestled into the mountain, as many of the other palaces were, but built on top of a promontory near the peak, as if it were surveying Tauriyat, the city below, and even the desert beyond.

"There," Hamid said, pointing to the left of the road, where a copse of fig trees stood.

Everyone was winded, but none were as bad off as Amaryllis. She'd trailed behind constantly, but had waved Ramahd off every time he'd tried to help. They had just made it into the deeper darkness of the trees when she fell to her knees and leaned against a trunk.

"We can't wait for her," Hamid said softly to Ramahd.

"Go on," Ramahd said to him. "I'll be along shortly."

He'd planned on commanding Amaryllis to wait, but she was already up. "I'm fine," she said, her words spilling out in a ragged groan between her sharp intakes of breath. She tried to walk past him, but Ramahd gripped her arm and stopped her. She tried to rip her arm free but Ramahd held her tight. "I'm *fine*," she repeated.

"Choose now," Hamid said. "Is she coming or going?"

The fire in Amaryllis's eyes was what convinced him. She might be tired, but she was ready to fight. That much he could see. "We're here now," he said to Hamid. "Let her come."

They caught up with others deeper into the grove. Ahead loomed a cliff, a dour face of stone. Atop it stood the walls of Eventide. Emre and the tall one called Frail Lemi crouched directly below a crook in the wall where a tower met the palace wall. Emre, their lone remaining coil of rope looped around one shoulder, a grapnel hanging from his belt, had one foot in Frail Lemi's interlaced fingers. With a lift so easy it made it seem like a game between father and son, Frail Lemi lifted Emre up. From there Emre was able to climb and launch a grapnel, which caught against the battlements above. As soon as he'd climbed the rope and gained the wall, the rest followed.

Frail Lemi had just reached the top when Ramahd heard the call of an amberlark coming from the darkness of the trees behind him. As Hamid whistled back, a form approached through the trees. Ramahd's heart started to pound. He wasn't even sure why, at first. But then, by the light of the twin moons, a tall man was revealed, a man with a forked beard, a black turban, a black thawb, and two shamshirs hanging from his belt.

By Iri's black teeth, it was Macide.

Chapter 62

WHEN THE GATES OF THE HARBOR FELL, a storm of wind spread from the point of impact. Çeda barely had time to rein Brightlock over before it struck. The unseen force of it threw her backward, off her saddle and onto the sand. She could only huddle there as the windblown sand scoured her. And even after the wind had died down, the impact continued to shake the very foundations of the desert. For several long moments, everyone stared, stunned by what had happened, but then many things happened at once.

The scarabs along the water channel began dropping on ropes hung to either side of the channel. Husamettín advanced on Hamzakiir with Night's Kiss held high over his head. Hamzakiir's arms were raised, but not in any sort of defense. His fingers looked as though they were drawing symbols in the air as Night's Kiss cut downward and cleaved him in two. As Hamzakiir fell, however, his form changed to that of a different man entirely. Hamzakiir himself was farther back along the water channel.

Husamettín saw and charged, the poor soul he'd cleaved falling over the edge of the channel and down to the sand. Husamettín cut down Hamzakiir once more, and again the blood mage traded bodies with another in the

Moonless Host. He was now close enough to the ropes that he grabbed one and slid down along it.

"Coward!" Husamettín called as two swordsmen tried to engage him. Seeing where Hamzakiir had gone, he backed away and leapt to the ground, landing in a spray of sand. He chased after Hamzakiir, but a dozen rebels blocked in his way as Hamzakiir sprinted over the fallen gates.

Somewhere inside the harbor, a horn sounded with a resonance Çeda felt in her bones. The Kings were calling everyone back to the harbor. Meanwhile, behind the Maidens, two ships crested the dunes, then two more, and more behind those, until a score of them were cutting through the sand, heading straight toward the fallen gates of King's Harbor.

Sümeya stood in her saddle, waving her sword high above her head. "To the breach, Maidens! To the breach!"

Brightlock had bolted, Çeda realized, but the horse returned when she whistled, weaving through the madness toward Çeda. Çeda swung up to the saddle in one smooth motion and urged Brightlock into a gallop. Together, they flew toward the harbor. Çeda kept her asirim near, but many others now gathered on the dunes to Çeda's left. Like a pack of wolves they chased down the nearest of the ships, a cutter with lateen sails. Two leapt upon the runners while three more scrabbled up the side of the ship. They climbed through the rigging, tearing at it, and in moments had cut the sails free to send them flapping away on the bitterly cold wind. One of the asir on the starboard runner brought both hands down against the support. Like a blow from a mighty maul, the support sheared in two. The ship listed and crashed against the dune in a plume of sand.

Another tall asirim charged ahead of a galleon. It was Sehid-Alaz. Çeda could see the glint of the crown upon his head. Çeda tried to reach out to him, to free him, heedless of what Mesut might do, but the ancient bonds upon him held true. The lord of the asirim, king of the lost tribe, arched his back, hands held high, then pushed as if he were plying his leverage against some great, unseen weight. Sand flew up before him, flying toward the galleon. Sand and stone and wind beat against the ship's hull and sails. A howling came from Sehid-Alaz himself, an outpouring of anger and frustration the likes of which Çeda had never heard. So hard did the sand blow against the galleon that its sails tore, then split lengthwise along a seam.

This did nothing to stop the ship's momentum, however. It continued to power forward. Sehid-Alaz waited, watching it come, then leaned one shoulder into the oncoming supports of the starboard runner. He was like a stone in the sand. The thick wooden beams that supported the ship burst into kindling as the ship's bulk flew past the long-forgotten king.

The ship tilted down and plowed into the dunes. Men fell from the rigging to the unforgiving sand, some crushed by the passing of the ship, which was gouging its way across the desert.

Several more ships were taken down, but many reached the harbor's entrance ahead of Çeda and the other Maidens. The ships crashed over the fallen doors, their runners hopelessly ruined, but the Host clearly thought it worth it to be that much closer to the harbor's entrance. From the sides of the ships, planks were lowered. Ropes uncoiled. Scores of scarabs, both men and women, disgorged from the ships, swarming over the fallen gates and charging into the harbor itself.

Sümeya whistled. *Rear two hands. Meet the enemy.*

Immediately, ten Maidens peeled away and joined the asirim as they met the approaching force. A company of fifty Silver Spears joined them. The other Maidens, plus their asirim and the bulk of the Spears, ran for the harbor's entrance.

Soon all was madness. Çeda rode into them, Kerim and the other asirim by her side, hoping to make it to the far side of the gathering line and lose herself in the confusion, but before she could go far an arrow caught Brightlock in the shoulder, sending the mare to the ground. Çeda threw herself free just in time to avoid being crushed. She rolled, losing River's Daughter in the process, then came to her knees slowly, ears ringing, pain blossoming along her ribs where she'd taken the brunt of the fall.

The world swam around her. She scrambled for her ebon blade, only just reaching it when a wall of enemy soldiers marched from the darkness like a fog descending on Sharakhai. Beyond them, the sails of the incoming ships were bright now that fires were being lit inside the harbor.

Çeda rose, sword in hand, as her two asirim howled and barreled into the oncoming warriors. They were vicious and feral, like maned wolves among a pack of dogs. The soldiers of the Host advanced, enveloping them and many others, hacking and slashing with curved shamshirs.

Despite her wounds, despite the chaos all around, Çeda felt those around her, heard the beating of their hearts. She fell into a rhythm, moving with them or against them as the intricate choreography of the fight progressed. The pattern complicated, then simplified, then complicated again. She blocked the swing of one soldier, sidestepped another as he tried to charge her. She dealt precise strokes to legs or arms, wounding but not killing, and made her way through the battle—past the ships, through the choke point at the gates and into the harbor proper.

Çeda fought for minutes on end, whirring, engaging, dropping the enemy before her, even while her asirim tore into them with a savagery that threatened to break Çeda's mastery of blade and body and bone and blood. All the while, she retreated toward the docks, toward the quay that hemmed three quarters of the great harbor in a sweeping arc. She had hoped that as she retreated the soldiers would leave her be, but they were crazed. They kept fighting well beyond what normal men and women would do. The effects of devil's trumpet were to blame, she knew, the serum Dardzada had made for Macide. The soldiers had taken it, and now they would not be deterred. They would die before they retreated.

More and more scarabs came, taking the place of those Çeda and her asirim felled. Soon Çeda was completely surrounded, leaving her and the asirim to fight a battle they could not win. Not in the long run.

When she tried to hack a path free of them, a sword nicked her leg, another blow landed along her shoulder, and she was forced to retreat. Those around her were mad with purpose. Çeda could see it in their moonlit eyes: kill one Maiden, and it would all be worth it.

Her asirim grew bolder, reaching into the enemy and grabbing an arm, lifting them and throwing them into the others. Çeda defended herself as well as she could, but the blows against her came more often now. There were too many to dodge, too many to parry.

That was when a gust of wind came so sudden and so fierce that Çeda was forced to shield her eyes. A dust devil, a tight, gyrating column of sand, swirled before her. It took a dozen of the soldiers, whipping them free of the sandy floor of the harbor and sending them flying.

As the scarabs turned, confused, something bowled into them from behind. Sehid-Alaz, Çeda realized. The king of the asirim had come to save her.

He rushed to Çeda's aid, his sickly sweet smell filling the air. He pushed Çeda toward the quay, then turned and met the remains of the Moonless Host. From that vantage, Çeda could see the battle writ large across the expanse of the harbor. The Kings had joined their soldiers. Sukru wielded his whip, sent it cracking forward, lopping off limbs, splitting shields. By the gods, he cut one man in two, all while cackling like a man every bit as deep in the throes of devil's trumpet as the soldiers of the Moonless Host.

Burly Zeheb wore a broad breastplate and thick chain-mail coat and helm. In his hands he gripped two madu shields, inlaid bucklers with a spike in the center and steel-tipped gazelle horns that spread like falcon wings from the sides. As he waded through the battle, blocking blows much more fluidly than his bulk would suggest, he punched the spike in the center of the bucklers through his enemies' armor, or stabbed at their throats with the longer gazelle horns.

Kiral was surrounded by a dozen of the Moonless Host. He held his two-handed shamshir, Sunshearer, in both hands, moving it with blinding speed, slipping among his enemies, dropping them even while more joined in, hoping to fell the King of Kings.

Moving in to protect Kiral's rear flank was Mesut, who wore bear claws—steel gauntlets with claws at the fingertips, spikes along the knuckles. He moved sinuously between his attackers, driving claws through armor as if it were wet paper.

From the vulture's nest high atop a nearby ship stood King Beşir, who loosed arrow after arrow into the enemy below. He held a dozen arrows in one hand, which he nocked and released, nocked and released, almost too fast for the eye to follow, replenishing his supply from the massive quivers on his belt. Standing near the prow of the ship, meeting any who thought to knock Beşir from his perch, was Azad, long knives held in either hand. His frame was spare, but he was a devil, blurring and twisting between the enemy as they came for him.

Beşir was a possible target. Assuming the bloody verse her mother had found was true, he was likely standing atop a ship for a reason: to cover his weakness beneath Rhia's watching eye. But Çeda desperately needed to find Cahil. She searched for him, wondering if he were lost somewhere on the far side of the growing battle.

She found him a moment later. He rode a black horse and bore a war hammer and a shield with his house crest, a hooded cobra on a black field. His armor was a gleaming set of fine chain, a spiked helm with a horsetail atop it that blew in the wind as his horse powered ahead. He swung his hammer to either side, felling scarabs. One he struck through the chest with the hammer's spiked end, then dragged the man across the sand before yanking it free.

Hide, Sehid-Alaz begged. *He will see you!*

She couldn't hide. With the other Kings occupied, she had a chance to kill Cahil. If it was all she managed to do after all her time in the Maidens, it would have been worth it. The line of scarabs near Çeda were pushing forward, but Çeda threw her asirim at them and then broke away. Facing Cahil, she pulled her veil free and waved her sword in the air. *"Hai! Hayah!"*

A moment later, Cahil spotted her. He stared as if he couldn't believe his eyes, then spurred his horse into motion. The horse broke through a group of Silver Spears locked in battle with the Host. Near Çeda, a fallen scarab lay dead, an arrow through his chest, a spear lying across his legs. Çeda stomped on the butt end of the spear, flipping it up. Grabbing the haft in midair, she took three long strides and launched it with all her might.

The spear flew through the night, the polished head catching the moonlight as it rotated lazily. It caught Cahil's horse dead in the chest. The horse screamed, throwing its head back, but in its frenzy it continued to charge. As Çeda was readying to roll out of the horse's path, it stumbled, then fell, throwing Cahil from his saddle.

He was up in a moment, well before she'd reached him. The two of them met, sword ringing against hammer as Cahil's rage was released. "Traitor child!" She could see the madness in his eyes as he swiped at her over and over. "What have you done with her? What have you done with Yndris?"

She met each of his blows, refusing to give ground. "Your daughter lies dead and broken in the ravine beneath your palace." She unleashed a fresh flurry of blows, blocking a kick with a raised shin along the way, sidestepping a hasty riposte, then charging forward and crashing her mailed fist into his jaw.

She brought River's Daughter down as she followed his movement, but he somehow held on to his hammer, used it to block as he rolled away and regained his feet. "I will make you suffer for what you've done."

"As you did my mother?"

"Who?"

"Ahyanesh, the woman whose forehead you carved with the sign of the thirteenth tribe."

He paused for only a moment. "You are her *daughter?*" And then he was on her again, raining blow after blow. "She was not with me long, child, but oh, how I made her suffer."

Cahil's words did not enrage her, as he'd hoped. They calmed her. For years Çeda had hoped to learn her mother's true fate. She'd guessed at what had happened after she'd entered the House of Maidens, but now she knew some small piece of it. And with that came a sense of something greater, as if her mother watched over her still.

Cahil was strong and he was fast, but Çeda could now feel the will of the asirim running through her. Not those here in the harbor—their reins were held too tightly by Mesut—but those in the blooming fields, those who'd refused Mesut's call or were too weak from their centuries of cruel existence. They buoyed her, gave her what strength they could.

It was enough. It was more than enough. She sliced Cahil's shoulder. She nicked his thigh. She sent his hammer high with an arcing uppercut swing from her sword. Then she kicked him full in the chest. Recovering quickly, he charged her, nearly maniacal in his rage, which only served to calm her further. She slipped past his downward stroke and sliced her ebon blade cleanly across his ribs. River's Daughter cut deep. Blood flowed like spilled wine, seeping into his fine surcoat.

She'd only just taken a step toward him, ready to finish him, when she caught something dark blurring in from her right. She rolled before the impact came, blocking one of Mesut's outstretched gauntlets. The other caught her across her ribs. The gauntlet's claws raked her and tore through her armored battle dress. Pain burned along her side as the battle roared around her. She kicked and rolled away, feeling deeper pain emanate from the wound.

"To touch a King without his consent," Mesut said in his hoarse voice as he advanced on her, "is cause for death. But this! You shall die more slowly than any other. Your family. Your friends. They will suffer by your side. You will hear their screams as they mingle with your own!"

Çeda retreated quickly, keeping him at bay with swipes from River's Daughter. She surveyed the field of battle, hoping to find a path to escape. She spotted it a moment later. A riderless horse. After slashing across Mesut's defenses once, twice, she turned and sprinted toward it. Mesut did not give chase. Instead he turned to a mounted Maiden and commanded her to attend him.

Çeda reached the copper-coated horse at the same time a Silver Spear was reaching for the reins. He saw her coming but thought her an ally, and so did nothing as she leapt and kicked him full in the chest. He flew backward, arms flailing, and Çeda swung up to the saddle. She was off in a moment, skirting one tight group of combat.

She heard a whistle ordering her to halt. She looked and found Sümeya on the far side of a bloody skirmish. Sümeya whistled again, her eyes confused, but Çeda kept riding as fast as the horse would carry her, out through the fallen gates, past the host of ships, and into the desert beyond. She glanced back, but saw no one following. Dear gods, where could she go? She'd fouled it all up. She hadn't been careful enough. And now she could never return. The Kings would want to make an example of her after she'd embedded herself so deeply in the weave of royal life. She'd be hunted to the ends of the desert.

And what had she achieved while here? Precious little. She'd gained some trust. She'd learned a few scraps of information. All her work, all those careful steps, what had they come to? She'd only killed one of the Twelve Kings—the sum total of her time in the House of Maidens.

As she drove her horse deeper into the desert, away from Sharakhai, it pulled to the right. She tried to correct course, but it only pulled harder. Then it stopped and reared, releasing a fearful scream. Çeda barely held on. Its hooves swiped at the air for a moment, and then it dropped and galloped to the left.

There was something ahead, she realized. A wisp of light, a gentle wave of luminescence the twin moons couldn't quite account for. Another coalesced to the right of the first, then another, and another. They were forms roughly the size and shape of a man, a woman, a child. More came, standing, waiting, as Çeda spurred the horse's flank. The horse charged, a beast trained for war, now resolved to run through the enemies arrayed before it.

The wights, these spectral ghosts, flew toward it. One raked an arm across the horse's chest. Another clawed the opposite side. The horse screamed and bucked as it ran, nearly losing its footing. A third wight arced across its path and swept its claws across the horse's throat. A wound appeared, deep and gushing blood. The horse pulled its head sharply to one side, veering, then toppling hard to the sand.

Çeda was ready, but the pains over her body—from Cahil, from Yndris, from Mesut and the battle—all flared to renewed life as she fell. She levered herself to her feet. Pulled River's Daughter as the wights circled around her. They hemmed her in, but did not attack.

She ran at them, screaming, "Fight!" as she swiped her sword at one, which vanished and appeared twenty feet farther away. "Fight me!"

At the sound of galloping hooves, she turned and saw a silver-white horse cantering toward her. Behind came another. She knew the riders well before the horses slowed and came to a stop. Mesut at the lead, Cahil behind, favoring one side, though not nearly as heavily as she would have hoped. The Kings slid off their horses and strode toward her with the sort of self-assurance given by centuries on their thrones.

"I will admit"—Mesut spread his arms wide, his gauntlets glinting dully in the moonlight—"here in the presence of the gods, that you had me fooled. You had us *all* fooled." The circle of ghosts parted for him, some fading to nothing, others sliding away. "Assassins have made their way into the House of Kings before, but none have bored so deep as you."

Cahil started to advance on Çeda, but Mesut held out a stalling hand and the Confessor King stopped. Mesut began to walk in a circle around her. Çeda held River's Daughter tightly, tighter than she should, and followed his movement while keeping an eye on Cahil as well.

"It was you, was it not, who killed Külaşan?" Mesut smiled. "I wonder at his words now. *You saved me.* Isn't that what he said?"

"He had come to hate his existence," Çeda said.

"Külaşan always had so many reservations. It's why he wandered as he did, always leaving Sharakhai. It's why he built his ridiculous palace in the desert, because he couldn't bear to be near us and our *eternal shame,* as he put it to me once. I suspect some of the others hide similar sentiments, but I will tell you, Çedamihn Ahyanesh'ala, *I* do not and never have. We were *granted* this desert. It is our *right*. And though there are some like you who think to take it from us, it will never happen. The Kings rule Sharakhai. The Kings rule the Great Shangazi. And it will always be so."

He lifted his hand and pointed to Çeda. The wights leaned toward her, floated closer. But as they did, the sand swirled beside Çeda. It lifted and took form, resolved a moment later into the lost king. He stood by Çeda's side, bent, frail, wheezing through gritted teeth. Çeda had never seen him with a weapon before, but he held a shamshir now, a thing pitted and nicked, bent near the middle. He held it with shaking hands, as if it pained him to merely touch it.

Sehid-Alaz lifted his arms and turned in an arc, palms facing the approaching wights. *"Not now, my children. Not here."* The lost king drew a breath, a thing that seemed to take great effort. *"Set aside your anger. Remember who you were."* Indeed, one by one the wights halted, held by Sehid-Alaz's will. *"You cannot have her,"* Sehid-Alaz said to the Kings. *"I deny you your prize."*

Cahil laughed. *"You* would think to deny us?" He pointed his hammer at the ghostly forms. "A man who failed to protect his people in every way?"

"I would, Cahil Thariis'ala al Salmük."

Cahil looked to Mesut. "Control your dog, my good King!"

To this, Mesut gave no answer. He was fighting a silent battle with Sehid-Alaz, hoping to regain control over him. Sehid-Alaz held him at bay, but it wouldn't last. Çeda had to help him, or she'd lose him to Mesut's will.

She charged Mesut, slashing with River's Daughter. Mesut blocked easily, but she felt his concentration slip. She dodged when he leaned in with a swipe of his gauntlets, then blocked another blow with a snap kick to his wrist. She engaged again and again, using all Zaïde had taught her, all Mesut had as well.

Sehid-Alaz began to moan. Already he was nearing the end of his limits. It was not merely the weight of Mesut's mind he was fighting, after all, but the will of the gods as well. Sand lifted around him, spun around his feet like a circling hound, but when Cahil came near, it quelled, as if the mere presence of a King weakened him.

Cahil engaged with Sehid-Alaz, who released a desperate cry that sounded like a building sandstorm. Cahil moving with maniacal energy, Sehid-Alaz backing away, wheezing as he blocked blow after blow. When Sehid-Alaz finally managed to sneak in a strike, Cahil blocked it and replied with a mighty downward swing of his hammer. It struck Sehid-Alaz square on the head.

Sehid-Alaz's form burst into a column of sand as the hammer drove into it. In an instant, he'd reformed behind Cahil. As the Confessor King turned to meet him, Sehid-Alaz's shamshir tore through the mail along Cahil's shoulder. Cahil fell, so forceful was the blow. He grunted in pain and tried to roll away, but Sehid-Alaz stepped on his shield, forcing Cahil to slip his arm out and leave the shield or be run through.

Çeda and Mesut continued to dance over the top of a dune. The sound of her ebon blade against his spiked gauntlets rang through the cold night air. The nervousness she'd felt earlier was gone. She was herself, her sword, and her movement. Nothing else. The power of the petals suffused her, pushed her on, but so did the beating of her heart, the beating of Mesut's heart, the two discordant rhythms somehow complementing one another.

"You're good, girl, I'll grant you that." Mesut blocked her blade, swiping at her. "But you cannot last forever."

She felt Mesut press on her more subtly and precisely than Zaïde had ever done. Her heart skipped a beat. She coughed and backed away. He pressed harder, and her heart began to flutter. The rhythm felt like the gallop of a horse ready to collapse from thirst and overexertion. It created a momentary lapse in her defenses.

That was all Mesut needed. He timed it perfectly, darting forward, blocking her blade to rake his claws across one thigh. She gritted her teeth, pushing down the pain, slipping back into herself. He wished to draw her away from Zaïde's teachings, his *own* teachings, but she would not allow it. She breathed deeply. Released it slowly, more in tune with the Shangazi than she had ever been. She felt the dunes. Felt the moonlight washing over it. She felt Sharakhai. Felt the great ring of the blooming fields. And she felt the roots of the adichara, reaching down, down, toward the heart of Sharakhai.

When Mesut came in again, her heart fluttered, but she let it. She felt him, his form, his movement, knowing how his body would flow, knowing how long it would be before she could take the gods' gift from him. She blocked twice and saw the slight overreach even as she lifted River's Daughter in an arc so sweet it comprised, over the course of its transit, her soul, her entire being.

His right hand, the one with the golden band and its black gem, was cut cleanly. It spun free. Mesut retreated, screaming from the pain, stumbling even before his gauntleted hand struck the sand. "Take her!" Gripping the stump of his right arm tightly, he regained his feet and ran. "Take her!"

Çeda felt something burn across her back. Felt another tight line flare across her right shoulder. The wights. They were flying in, reaching for her with ghostly hands. She swiped at them with River's Daughter and they backed away, avoiding the reach of her ebon steel, but there were so many!

She grabbed Mesut's golden band, which was slick with blood, and slipped it over her hand. Immediately the minds, the souls, of those around her crystallized. They became known to her and she became known to them. But their intent did not change. They were compelled to come for her at Mesut's bidding.

She swung River's Daughter, pleading with them. *You're free now. He no longer has the band.* Then aloud, "Slay your captor!"

But they didn't. Another reached in and ran a cold hand across the back of her neck before she could stop it. The fear was building inside her, but then she remembered.

Amalos's final act, the copper leaf and the story written upon it. The woman had saved her people by *offering* herself to the sand drake. It had hardly left her thoughts since she'd read it. Here, standing among these creatures being compelled to kill her, she finally understood. Amalos had found it because it offered the key to Mesut's bloody verse. Mesut had spoken of control. Always control. It was how he'd commanded the asirim since the night of Beht Ihman. But that wasn't how the golden band would be turned to her purpose.

Lowering her sword, she opened herself to the asirim. To Sehid-Alaz. To Kerim. To those assembled for war in the harbor and those that lay beneath the adichara. Most importantly, she gave herself to the lost souls gathered around her. She had never done anything more difficult, more personal. It was feeling love for the first time. It was the terror-filled moments of childhood when the ways of the world seemed so strange. It was so akin to the moments when her mother returned from Beht Zha'ir unharmed that tears came to her eyes. She was excited and terrified, more vulnerable than she'd ever been, but she refused to give in to the terror. She remained hopeful, an emotion she shared with the asirim, with the wights, any who would listen.

Soon she felt her own emotions echoing back to her from Kerim. She felt it from more of the asirim, and more still, until she stood as one with them. It was this—a bond to a life not chained by the gods—that sparked within those gathered souls a glimpse of their old lives. It allowed them to remember their freedom from so long ago. It allowed them to throw off the chains Mesut had placed on them.

Soon, the wights had slowed their advance. They lowered their arms. They waited and listened.

Çeda turned to Mesut. As one, the gathered souls did as well. She could feel Mesut trying to exert his will, but they would not be denied. Not any longer.

Lifting River's Daughter and pointing to Mesut, Çeda said, "Go. Slake your thirst."

Without hesitation they flew toward him, swooping like falcons. Mesut fought with his one hand, the battle claw raking across the ghostly forms. White lines appeared on their bodies. Attenuated screams filled the cold night air. Some even vanished from the wounds Mesut delivered with his god-given weapon. But there were so many, flying from all directions.

They delivered deep cuts along his legs. They sliced his arms. They tore at his ribs and his face, pulling his armor free, slashing his clothes from his body, until he was left naked on the sand, screaming, his flesh being rent from him as easily as his armor and clothes had been. With one last stroke across his throat, a spray of blood flying into the air, Mesut fell back and lay still. The wights circled him for a time, still slashing, cutting the Jackal King to ribbons.

Finally, as his form went still, so did the ghostly forms around him. Like trees after a storm, they gradually stilled. They dimmed, fading like dying candles until they were swallowed by the shadows of the night. Soon they were gone, and the desert was silent save for the drone of the raging battle in the distance.

Cahil stood ten paces away, blood darkening one shoulder and his right thigh. Sehid-Alaz was near him, one knee to the ground. They'd both been staring at Mesut, at the wights, but now Cahil burst into action. He ran not for Sehid-Alaz, or toward Çeda, but for the horses.

It was pure pain to move, but Çeda sprinted for them as well, hoping to cut him down before he could escape. Seeing that she was catching up, Cahil abandoned the chase and brought his hammer against her in a broad stroke. But she was ready. She dodged one blow, ducked beneath another, then delivered a perfect cut to Cahil's neck. He rolled away, but it still caught the chain mail that hung like a curtain from his helm, leaving a shallow wound.

He rolled over one shoulder, throwing a handful of sand at Çeda as he came up. Çeda shielded her eyes, ready to defend herself. But Cahil never came. He was running for the horses again. He climbed onto the nearest, grabbed the reins of the other, then spurred them both into a full gallop.

Reinforcements. He's going for reinforcements.

Çeda tried to summon the souls within Mesut's golden band. She felt nothing, however, nothing whatsoever, and knew her cause was lost. She either didn't know how to summon them or they'd been lost to this world, as Sehid-Alaz had feared.

As Cahil rode away, Sehid-Alaz collapsed to the sand. The pain of her wounds returning, she limped closer and lowered herself to the sand by his side. His breath came slowly, one hand on his chest. The hand over his heart moved to take hers. He gripped her hand feebly, his fingers like sticks, his skin like paper. But she could feel the love there, the tenderness.

"Thank you," she said to him.

Slowly, his eyes met hers. *"You must run, Çedamihn Ahyanesh'ala."*

She knew he was right. Cahil would tell the others of her treachery. There was no way for her to return to Sharakhai. "You must join me."

She made to lift him, but he gripped her wrists, stopping her. *"I cannot leave the others."* He squeezed her hand once more. The wind began to pick up, began to blow. *"But there is one last gift I can give."* Clouds of dust began to lift from the desert, began to blow across the dunes. *"It will not last long."*

As the wind tugged at her dress, she leaned down and kissed his forehead. "Thank you."

His eyes fluttered closed. His lips moved, but his words were lost to the sound of the growing wind. She leaned closer, listened carefully, but he'd gone still. The wind, however. The wind began to wail. It struck the dunes with a fury Çeda had rarely seen.

Hiding her face with her veil, she stood and made for the deeper desert. Like a child once lost, now returning to her mother, the sand embraced her.

Chapter 63

R AMAHD'S MOUTH WENT DRY AS HAMID went to speak with Macide. His ears rang with a high-pitched, disorienting chord. Within it he could hear Rehann's laugh, clear and bright and filled with sunshine. A time had never passed when it hadn't lifted his heart. *Mighty Alu, I'd nearly forgotten the sound.*

Suddenly he was there in the desert again, holding her in his arms as she stared at him, dying of thirst, eyes glazed and heavy-lidded, barely able to focus on him. He'd kissed her, felt her cracked lips against his before she'd breathed her final breath. "Go to memma, my darling. She'll be there, waiting. Give her a kiss for me."

She hadn't replied.

"I'll find you both soon. I promise you." She'd already gone, but it wasn't a promise to her living soul in any case. It was a vow that would follow her to the farther fields. He leaned in and whispered into her ear, "I'll kill the man who did this and then I will find you."

Just then Macide broke away from Hamid and headed straight for Ramahd. He came to an abrupt halt, however, when Ramahd drew his blade. From beside a nearby tree, Amaryllis waited with hungry eyes, tense and silent as she studied the two men. Hamid watched her warily, leaving his lord to his business.

"Is this what you wish?" Macide asked, left hand on the pommel of one blade.

Oh, how he wished to cross blades with him. How sweet the sound of steel would be. He could do it. There were too many swords at Ramahd's command for even Macide Ishaq'ava to escape alive. But Ramahd had agreed to this. Knowing full well what it might mean, he had allowed his shame over Çeda to override his desire to make this man suffer. "I've not come for you," Ramahd said, the words coming short and sharp, "only for Qaimir."

"I don't care why you've come," Macide shot back, "only that you finish what you've started. Let us go. Let us destroy those elixirs and weaken the Kings. What the gods have in store for us beyond that, who can tell?"

Ramahd couldn't move. He felt made of stone, trapped in a spell of his own making. From somewhere beyond the palace, rising up over the sounds of distant battle came a bellow that sounded like one of the elder gods readying to reforge this place anew. Macide took his hand from his sword and motioned toward the harbor. "The night wastes away, Lord Amansir, and our chances with it."

Damn me for the fool I am. He lowered the sword, then sheathed it. *Forgive me, Rehann.*

Macide nodded once. "Very well."

Things moved quickly after that. With two ropes at the ready, they were up to the top of the wall in short order. This time they left the ropes where they were, an avenue of escape should they need it. From the wall they took a set of stairs down to an empty courtyard. One side of it was open to a manicured yard with exquisite topiary and gravel paths. Hugging the interior of the wall was a glass-enclosed greenhouse, which they entered. After rushing between the rows of exotic plants, they passed through a walkway and entered the palace proper.

There they stood, wary, weapons drawn. A lofty hallway ran like an arrow for a hundred yards. Great brass lanterns on iron hooks bathed the entire length in golden light. A woman standing near a door holding a silver tray screamed. She dropped it and ran as the big one, Frail Lemi, began loping toward her, but she hadn't made it five strides before an arrow drove into her back. She fell in a heap against the fine blue carpet, one arm reaching use-lessly behind her for the arrow. Ramahd turned and saw Hamid nocking another arrow.

"Quickly," Macide said as he set off at a run, "before they can organize. And be ready for more than Kiral's men. Hamzakiir will have sent a detach-ment as well, and they'll not take kindly to our purpose here."

They all followed. Soon they heard footsteps, crisp against the stone floor-ing, but distant. They came to a set of wide stone stairs, one side leading higher into the palace, the other leading lower. As Macide led them down, they heard a scuffle. "Go, go!" someone whispered harshly. A moment later, the light along the landing below wavered and was doused, plunging the way ahead into darkness.

Macide pointed up the stairs. "Three lanterns," he said to Frail Lemi, who ran back up and returned bearing three of the large brass affairs. Frail Lemi's eyes were wide as the moons as he passed them out. "There are Blade Maidens coming," he said to Emre, completely ignoring Macide.

"How many?" Macide and Emre asked at the same time.

Frail Lemi immediately headed up the stairs, gripping the haft of his battle axe. "Two," he called over his shoulder.

Macide drew his twin shamshirs and followed, but he pointed Hamid down the stairs. "You know where to go."

Hamid nodded and motioned everyone else, including Ramahd and his men, to follow him. They swept down two more levels before reaching the bottom, where a darkened hallway ran straight ahead; another cut crosswise against their path. The air here was crisp. It smelled like a mountain spring, which felt distinctly wrong.

From above came the sound of swords clashing. Emre stopped in his tracks, clearly ready to run back up the stairs. "No, Emre!" Hamid hissed. "That isn't what matters, and you know it."

"He could die," Emre said softly.

Hamid grabbed him about the shoulders and shoved him forward, away from the stairs. "As could we all."

They continued ahead as the sounds of battle dwindled, then vanished altogether. After a short jog they came to a stone door with a round hole at its center. One of Hamid's men, a thin man with a wide jaw and goggly eyes, immediately knelt and took out a set of tools from a bag at his belt. As he put the picks into the keyhole, Emre held a lantern close, but the man waved him away. "Just back away, boy, so I can listen."

They gave him room, placing themselves between the door and the stairs. The sounds of battle resumed, but not from the stairwell leading up. It came from the righthand tunnel. Whether the battle had shifted to this lower level or echoed down from somewhere above, Ramahd couldn't tell.

Louder and louder it came. There were many swords, many men—and some women—shouting, releasing battle cries. Clearly it was no longer just Macide and Frail Lemi who were locked in battle; more had engaged, but whose side were they on?

Ramahd heard a click behind him. "It's done."

They could barely see him in the darkness, but he was pushing against the door. It groaned mightily as it swung inward. But then Hamid's man fell over as if he'd fainted. Ramahd heard something whizz by his ear. He turned and saw Amaryllis clutching her cheek. She plucked from her skin a small, red-feathered dart. Her eyes began to shake, as if she'd just woken and hadn't yet found her bearings.

"Ramahd," she said, staring at the dart. "Ramahd."

Ramahd caught her as she fell, lowering her carefully to the ground.

"Down there!" Ramahd said, pointing into the darkness. "We are not alone."

Hamid was already on the move, spinning and swinging his lantern and launching it far down the tunnel. It flew into the darkness, lighting the hall like a falling star, then burst beyond the vault door, spreading oil and flames.

What had once been darkness was lit like day. A dozen men were revealed beyond the flames, one of them with a blowpipe to his mouth. He took an arrow from Emre straight through the throat, a dart puffing from the end of his blowpipe and striking harmlessly against the wall as he clutched at the shaft of the arrow and tipped over.

The enemy were dressed in thawbs and turbans as well. Surely these were Hamzakiir's men, come to liberate the elixirs for their lord, but they were held off momentarily by the flames. Near them were two dark forms, low, hunkering to the ground, dog-like with blood-red skin that glistened in the firelight. They looked as if they'd been flayed until all that remained was muscle and sinew and odd, angular limbs. Each had a pair of horns that swept like scythes from the center of its forehead back. They had no eyes, but wide nostrils and gaping mouths that grinned with ranks of narrow teeth that might once have been sharp but were now broken and jagged, as if for too long they'd feasted only on bones.

"Into the vault," Hamid called, running and pushing the vault door open the rest of the way as Emre launched an arrow at one of the fell beasts.

The thing ducked sinuously, avoiding Emre's aim as if the arrow had been little more than a feather borne on a gentle wind. *Mighty Alu protect us. If these are the sorts of creatures Hamzakiir is willing to summon, I'll be glad to see the elixirs taken from his hands.*

Ramahd carried Amaryllis while Luken dragged the unconscious lockpick. They rushed into the vault, nearly a score of them in all. They'd just managed to push the door shut when something crashed into it from the opposite side. Every spare body threw themselves against the door, hoping to push the creature back, yet still it edged open. As Ramahd set Amaryllis down on the cold stone floor, one red arm reached inside. It twitched, insect-like, claws reaching. Poor Luken was at the door's very edge. The claws latched on to his left leg, dragged him down in a flash, and then the arm drew backward through the gap, taking Luken's leg with it.

One moment Luken was shouting in surprise and fear, hands scrabbling for purchase, and then next he was rolling away, his screams infinitely more urgent. The door boomed shut. All eyes turned to Luken. Blood gushed from his stump of a leg as if poured from a pitcher.

"Ramahd," Amaryllis whispered.

Ramahd ignored her. He could only stare at Luken's writhing. *The power of that creature . . . By the gods, we're all going to die.* But what about the elixirs? They could still finish what they'd set out to do, couldn't they? As he turned, looking for them, Amaryllis touched his arm. "Ramahd." When he looked down to her, she pointed to the fallen lockpick. "Give me his heart."

Luken's screams began to lose energy. Something thundered into the stone door, pushing it back once more. Dust sifted down through the air from the impact, gray against the golden light of the lanterns. The door inched inward, even with ten men pushing against it. A red hand reached in once more, Tiron tried to hack at it, but the thing grabbed his sword in one well-timed and inhumanly fast motion. Tiron's sword was ripped from his grasp and drawn through the gap just like Luken's leg.

I have to destroy the draughts. That's why we've come. He tried to rise, but Amaryllis held his wrist. "Ramahd, bring his heart to me."

He could only stare. *"What?"*

"Can you not see me?"

Such simple words, and yet they cast a spell on him. Amaryllis transformed before his very eyes. She became another. Whether a spell she'd put on them all before leaving the embassy house or an artifact of the way she'd changed her own features, it was no longer Amaryllis he saw lying before him, but Meryam.

He shook her shoulders. "You risk too much! How could you have come here?"

"I am responsible. It could not be left to others." He tried to speak, but she gripped his hand. "Make haste, Ramahd. Bring me his heart."

Ramahd looked to the man who lay so near, to the door that was pushing back further, the creatures' horns ramming into it again and again. When the creature reached in and took the head of one of Hamid's men, clawing away half his face in one quick swipe, Ramahd drew his knife and slid across the floor to kneel by *Luken's* side, not the lockpick's. If Meryam were going to devour a heart, he would not give her one that had been drugged. "Forgive me," he whispered to Luken, who had fallen silent at last. He drove it deep into his chest, then sawed at the man's sternum, wrenching it with all his might to cut through one rib, then two.

From the desperate huddle at the door, Tiron stared down at him, his face aghast. "What are you doing? My lord, let him be!"

But Ramahd kept sawing. Another rib was cut, and then he was slicing through skin and muscle, using his hands to rip away his ribs. Dear gods, dear gods, his heart still beat. He could see it, pumping slowly within his chest. "Forgive me, Luken."

"Leave him!" Tiron had abandoned his effort at the door and taken a step toward Ramahd when Emre charged into him, sending him sprawling to the floor.

Ramahd worked quickly, slicing Luken's heart free, and then holding it to Meryam's mouth. She took a bite from the warm, ruby-red flesh. She chewed, her half-lidded eyes fluttering. She took another bite as someone fell on Ramahd.

He was rolled roughly over. Tiron's face loomed large, half awash in golden light, the other half dark. "You dare despoil my brother's flesh?"

Something crashed harder than ever against the door. It swung inward. The head of one of the beasts poked in. Before a single sword could be brought against it the beast shouldered its way into the room.

Tiron rolled away from Ramahd. Both men gained their feet as the beast scratched its way across the blood-slicked floor toward them. It took a deep sword cut across its shoulder from an almighty swing from Cicio, but then the beast had him, a clawed hand grabbing his throat, too quick to follow. In a blink it had ripped the flesh of his throat free and was launching itself, horns lowered, toward Gautiste. Gautiste managed only a glancing blow off its horns before he was gored, one horn piercing his armor and hooking him. In one violent motion the creature twisted neck and body, flinging him away like a wolf with a hare.

The other demon was making its way into the golden-lit vault now. Some few of his own men, as well as Hamid, were still pushing at the door in a vain attempt at keeping it from the room, but it was a battle already lost.

The nearer creature clubbed Cicio, who had somehow managed to regain his feet and throw himself at the creature. As Cicio twisted into one corner and lay still, the beast, as if sensing a greater power in the room, swung its head toward Meryam. Its nostrils flared. It spread its arms wider, moved lower to the ground, as if it knew the threat she represented. Meryam had managed to lift herself off the floor. She was still chewing Luken's heart, blood coating her chin and neck. The hand that held the remains of the heart wore a glove of red. Her disguise was melting away, returning her to her own form as the blood ran through her, ceding Luken's power.

The fell beast ducked low. Then charged.

Ramahd tried to run into its path, but it was too swift. "No!" he cried.

And then it was on her. Meryam was standing, one hand held before her, ready to meet the creature's charge. As they met, Meryam's hand slipped beneath the demon's chin. The creature reared up. Its momentum stopped. It *lifted* off the floor as if it had struck a mighty wall of air. Ramahd thought she'd grabbed its neck, but it wasn't so. Meryam's right arm was shivering, fingers splayed, a whisper's breath from the red, glistening chest of the beast before her.

The demon's arms spread wide. It threw its head back, shivering, as if it had entered a state of rapture. Meryam took a step forward. She lifted the beast higher through a bond Ramahd could not see but could certainly feel, deep inside his chest. It was a hollow feeling, as if Meryam were drawing not only from Luken's blood, but from Ramahd's as well. Indeed, from every living man inside the room.

She lifted her arm high. The creature twisted in midair, chest tilting up, as if it were being laid upon a table. Then she brought her arm down and the demon with it. So ferocious was the motion that a web of cracks appeared along the stone slab. The room shook. Dust sifted down from the ceiling. The beast's chest was a ruin of skin and bone and blood. Its red, skinless arms clawed against the broken stone, leaving furrows, and then at last it fell still.

Meryam left it there. She turned to meet the second creature. The stone door was wide open now. Men with drawn swords were storming into the room. Ramahd met the nearest with his own blade, felling him quickly with a block and a slice across thigh, then throat. The second he downed as well, but there were more than they'd seen in the dark hallway earlier.

He fought off one, then another, backing away with Tiron on one side, Hamid and Emre on the other. But soon there were too many and his men became separated. Ramahd retreated deeper into the darkness, using little more than their silhouettes to fight them off.

Someone bulled into him. He managed a strike against their leg, but then he was down, grappling. The man had a kenshar, and used it to stab into Ramahd's side. His armor held, but he felt the knife's tip bite into his side. He raged, desperate as he fought the man for his weapon. But the enemy was on top of him now, knife gripped tightly in both hands. Its tip inched closer and closer to Ramahd's chest.

Ramahd released a primal scream, pushing with all his might, but it wasn't enough. The tip pressed into his clothes, pierced the light armor he wore beneath, sunk into the skin along the left side of his chest, over his heart.

Something dark blurred above Ramahd. The man straddling him spasmed, the knife driving momentarily deeper, but then he fell slack.

Ramahd rolled him away to find Macide standing over him. He shifted his two swords to his right hand, then held out his left for Ramahd to take. Ramahd did, grabbing his fallen sword, and Macide pulled him up.

He immediately returned to the battle. Frail Lemi was there, his battle axe gone. He was using a two-handed war cudgel, a decorated weapon made for a King. Even so, its utility was undeniable. He brought it down mercilessly against Hamzakiir's men, his face perfect with rage. Ramahd and Macide rejoined them. Tiron and Hamid and Emre were still there, pushing what few enemy remained into a corner.

Meryam was in the opposite corner, the lamplight just behind her, throwing strange shadows over the skinless beast. One hand was over its face, her thumb piercing the flesh beneath its chin. The other reached up and with strangely casual speed ripped his neck free. It fell to the floor, spasming.

Hamzakiir's men fought until their last, but soon they had all fallen beneath the onslaught that Macide and Ramahd and the rest were now able to bring to bear. Soon the only sound they could hear was the rasp of their own breathing, blood and bodies lying all around them. The survivors stood, chests heaving, grimacing from exertion or pain or both. All but Meryam. She stood before the beast, her own self now, the Queen of Qaimir, not a spy in her service. She breathed silently, nostrils flaring, unwilling or unable to take her eyes from the creature.

Macide looked to her, then to Ramahd. "We must move quickly."

Ramahd nodded. "Go." He turned to Tiron and Riccio, all that remained of his men, and pointed to Macide. "Go on."

Riccio bowed his head and followed Macide. Emre, who'd picked up one of the lanterns, walked by his side, deeper into the vault. Tiron stared at Ramahd a moment, his face unreadable, but then he glanced to Meryam, nodded, and followed the others.

Ramahd approached Meryam slowly. "Are you well, my queen?"

She didn't move a muscle, but Ramahd could feel the wonder in her. "The power in them, Ramahd."

"Hamzakiir."

"Yes." By the gods who breathe, she was *smiling*.

"Meryam, we must make haste."

It seemed to take forever for her to turn her head. "Yes, of course," and then she turned and walked deeper into the vault toward the light of the lantern as if nothing at all had happened.

When they caught up to the others, they were staring up at shelf after shelf of glass vials, each shedding a pale blue light. There were hundreds, thousands of them, a complex constellation glowing with the luster of moonlit adichara petals. This was what Hamzakiir had been after. This was what he'd hoped to steal from the Kings to fashion a King of himself, a new ruler of Sharakhai.

Everyone present was taken by the wonder of it. These very vials had, in part, secured the Kings' power for four hundred years. They had been granted to them through the power of King Azad. And now Azad was dead, and these were all that were left. These and the other caches that lay within the other two palaces—Zeheb's and Ihsan's. If the gods were kind, Macide's men had been as successful there as they were here.

Macide looked to Meryam, as if he weren't sure, after all that had happened, that she would allow it. He was right to worry, for Meryam was staring at the shelves as intently as she had the fell beast. But after a heartbeat, perhaps two, she nodded, turned, and walked away.

Macide nodded as well, and then they all set to, ruining shelf after shelf, vial after vial, until every single one had been destroyed.

Chapter 64

FROM A BALCONY HIGH UP IN HIS PALACE, King Ihsan listened to the dying battle in King's Harbor. From his vantage he could not see the harbor itself, but the sound carried surprisingly well. It had been going on for hours now.

The others would surely still be there. Kiral. Husamettín. Beşir and Mesut. That cretin, Sukru, and cruel Cahil. They would forgive Ihsan his absence. He had never been a fighter. Yusam would not have gone either. Azad, as agreed, had gone for appearance's sake, though Ihsan still wished he'd managed to find a way for him to bow out of the night's festivities while not losing so much face that it would harm their cause in the days ahead. They would be crucial days—the most difficult he had yet faced—so giving Azad over to danger for one night was a small enough price to pay for having suspicious eyes turn elsewhere. He knew already the Host's attack had succeeded in his own palace. And he was sure the same would be true of Zeheb's. They'd both had few enough Maidens at hand, and he'd made sure that their Spears were spread out in the wrong places to defend the caches.

Kiral's palace, however, would be a different tale. He looked up to Eventide, the bulk of the palace framed by a diaphanous veil of stars. He had no idea who had wound up victorious: Kiral's guard, Hamzakiir's men, or what remained of those loyal to Ishaq and Macide. Even if Kiral ended up with all his elixirs intact, though, the pressure of having so few remain would be enough to allow Ihsan to drive wedges between the King of Kings and those who kissed his feet.

His thoughts were interrupted by a carriage pulling up to the front of his palace. A footman ran out from the palace doors, but before he could reach it the wagon's door swung wide and King Yusam came forth. Behind him, squeezing his considerable bulk out from the cabin, came Onur.

"Well, well," Ihsan said softly. "How very interesting that Yusam thought he needed the Feasting King by his side."

As if he'd heard the words, Yusam swung his gaze up. His eyes met Ihsan's. The two of them stared at one another for a time, then Yusam headed purposefully toward the palace entrance.

Ihsan strode from his apartments. Halfway down the wide, carpeted stairs to the floor below, Tolovan met him, a concerned look on his face. "I know," Ihsan said.

"Why have they come?" Tolovan asked softly.

Ihsan walked past him. "We shall know soon enough."

Two great braziers lit the entrance hall. As Ihsan took the stairs down to meet the Kings, Yusam stared up, hands held calmly behind his back, his posture strangely formal. Onur, massive behind Yusam, watched with something approaching mild curiosity—this was a tale Yusam had told him, perhaps, that Onur wasn't ready to believe.

"I'm glad you've come," Ihsan said as he rushed down the stairs. "I've called for reinforcements, but with the battle—"

"Yusam says your cache was discovered," Onur broke in, "that everything in it was destroyed. Does he have the right of it?"

Ihsan bowed his head to Yusam, careful to keep a note of hysteria in his expression and in his voice. "If only the gods had granted the vision sooner. Yes, a force came and overwhelmed those here, they—"

"Take us to it," Onur said.

Yusam was strangely silent. In fact, he was now avoiding Ihsan's gaze, as if he didn't trust himself to speak, to be caught in the spell of Ihsan's voice.

"Very well," Ihsan said.

They went to the rear of the palace, then took the stairs to the lower levels. Down they went to the vault where Ihsan stored the elixir. The door stood open. A score of dead soldiers had been laid out for inspection. Ihsan had made excuses for them to remain—they required detailed inspection, he'd told his staff—before being taken away for proper handling. He'd needed them here to prove the bloodshed, to prevent any of the Kings from thinking Ihsan had allowed it.

Onur, waddling toward the vault's entrance, gave the fallen men little more than a passing glance. Yusam, however, stopped and inspected every single soldier, the two Blade Maidens, and each scarab of the Moonless Host who'd fallen. He spent the most time on a man with a grizzled face and a gaping wound along his lower back, the very place Ihsan had stabbed him.

"You killed him," Yusam said.

"I did," Ihsan replied, caught by Yusam's curiously emotionless words.

It had been absolutely necessary that Ihsan be near the bloodshed. He couldn't very well have allowed this night to pass without actually trying to defend the cache. Kiral might forgive a failed defense. He would never forgive cowardice.

Yusam stood from the body. "May I see the knife?"

"Of course." Ihsan pulled the curving, triple-bladed dagger from its sheath at his side, his gift from Tulathan on the night of Beht Ihman. He handed it to Yusam, who stared at it, his face a mask.

He turned and strode into the vault, dagger still in hand. He and Onur made their way to the broken glass, the remains of the elixirs still washing the floor in pale blue light.

"*You* killed him?" Yusam asked.

"I did." It had been a long while since Ihsan had killed anyone. It was not something he'd been proud of, but it had been necessary.

"And then you returned to your apartments." A statement. No question this time.

"By the time I had come, the damage was already done. Most escaped, but I took that man and returned to my apartments to send word to you and our fellow Kings."

"And who did you send, to deliver word?"

He knew, Ihsan realized. He hadn't yet sent anyone. He'd wanted more time to pass to ensure all was ready. Ihsan spread his hands wide, a disarming gesture. "Despite my best intentions, there has been too much to attend to. I was just about to call for them when you arrived."

Onur stared at Yusam. He was waiting. For what, though? Yusam's account of the events? And here with Yusam still holding Ihsan's knife, a convenient thing to have if they thought to take him with little trouble.

It was time—probably well *past* time—that Ihsan put his true talent to better use. "My lords," he said, drawing upon Tulathan's other gift.

But before he could say another word, Yusam nodded, and Onur charged forward.

"Halt!" Ihsan ordered.

But he'd always known his powers would be dulled against the other Kings, one of the many reasons he used them sparingly.

Onur plodded on, his massive fist powering into Ihsan's face and propelling him backward. He tried to catch himself, but his arms simply weren't working like they were supposed to. He stumbled, his legs like a plainsman's the first time dealing with the unpredictable swells of a sandship at speed. He came to a stop when his head crashed into the stone wall of the vault behind him and he slid down to the floor. His ears rang. Onur's trunk-like legs bore the King of Sloth ever closer.

"My Lord Kings—" Ihsan tried to say, but all that came out was a long slur.

Onur lifted him up, pressed him against the wall. Ihsan coughed. He closed his eyes, trying to blink away the stars. He swallowed in a vain attempt to clear the keen ringing sound. He tried to speak but Onur brought him back and powered him into the wall again, silencing him.

"Your counsel these many long years," Yusam said as he strode forward, still staring at Ihsan's knife. "Step by step, moment by moment, you played my fears against me." He came to a stop before Ihsan, his jade-green eyes piercing Ihsan's—an indictment, a declaration of truth that Ihsan knew he could never explain away, not when so much had been revealed to the King of Fate.

When Ihsan tried to speak again, Onur pulled him away from the wall, but Yusam forestalled him with a hand on Onur's meaty forearm. "Let him speak."

Ihsan laughed, spit blood to one side. He could see the humor in this, even if they couldn't—Ihsan's own actions acting like trail markers in a forest, leading Yusam bit by bit to this, his ignominious unveiling. "Your fears were so easy to play, my Lord King."

"You *meant* for this to happen." Yusam motioned to the immensity of the darkened vault, to the softly glowing floor behind him. In that moment, Ihsan saw something. A trick of the light. A trick of his own addled mind. He knew not which.

"I . . ." Ihsan paused as a wave of pain cause him to cringe and shut his eyes until it had passed. "I never meant for any of this to happen."

Yusam nodded to Onur, who took Ihsan in both his hands, lifted him, and drove him against the wall like a battering ram. Ihsan fell to the floor, Onur staring at him with porcine eyes, smiling. The ringing became more pronounced, so much so that he could no longer hear what Yusam was saying even though he could see his lips moving.

Yusam had just nodded to Onur again when something dark blurred in from his left. It retreated just as quickly, leaving a dark line across Yusam's throat.

Blood sprayed from the wound, coating Ihsan in time with Yusam's beating heart. Onur turned to look for the threat, and he'd just reached for Ihsan's knife in Yusam's quivering hands when a shadow cut across his forearm, leaving another line that began to flow with blood. Another came as a shadowy form appeared behind him. Onur shouted in rage and pain, turning once more, but the shadow slipped away like a cloud of vapor and appeared again behind him.

This time Ihsan saw an arm driving forward, a knife sinking deep into Onur's back.

Azad. It was Azad. His savior. Nayyan in disguise.

But Onur's bulk had always been deceptive. He lashed out with an elbow as Azad appeared again. It caught Azad across the head with a loud thump and she went flying, tripping over Ihsan's legs as Onur began to run, lumbering from the room, blood flowing from a half-dozen wounds, staining his skin and soaking his brown clothes black.

Nayyan, wearing Azad's skin, pushed herself off the floor. She reached for her two knives—the ones that had belonged to her father before she'd inherited them—but her hands couldn't seem to grip them. She stopped, simply breathed for a moment, then tried again. This time she managed to get her hand on one long knife, then the other.

She swiveled her head to look at him.

"A fine lot we are," Ihsan said.

She laughed with Azad's face, Azad's smile. But the eyes . . . The eyes were hers.

"He cannot escape this palace alive," he told her.

She nodded. "I know." Then she stood and loped from the room.

With the sun warming the horizon to the east, Ihsan watched as Yusam's carriage was rolled off the edge of the palace road below. The driver's throat had been slit. Both the driver and Yusam were in the carriage itself, unfortunate victims of this terrible night.

It would take a good deal of explaining, but simplicity in such circumstances always worked best. He and Onur had both come. Yusam had seen the attack in his mere, but had warned Ihsan too late for him to do anything about it. They'd inspected the vaults and then left together. What had happened after that Ihsan wouldn't learn until this morning, when the messengers who came to his palace would find the carriage and the bodies and inform *Ihsan* what had happened.

It would bring more independent witnesses. It would strengthen Ihsan's version of the tale. But only if Onur was found and dealt with as well.

Footsteps came into the room behind him. "Yes, Tolovan?"

"King Azad has returned."

"Send her in."

"Of course, my Lord King."

Tolovan said nothing of his slip of the tongue. He hadn't meant to call Azad *her*. He'd been so very careful since the night the assassin had killed her father. He'd have to redouble his efforts. Assuming, of course, he could manage to retain his foothold on this mountain.

Azad entered the room. The look on his face was answer enough, but he still asked, "What of Onur?"

"Gone. I tracked him to the edges of the palace grounds, but then found animal tracks."

"A panther?" Ihsan asked. It was Onur's favorite form.

"A cat's prints, to be sure. I followed the blood all along his trail until it neared the walls of Tauriyat, and then they simply vanished."

Ihsan shook his head. He should have been more prepared for Yusam. He should have had someone at hand to deal with Onur. But he'd never been one to dwell on the past. *Look ahead, look ahead. What's done is done.*

"What will we do?" Azad asked.

"Speak to Zeheb. Tell him the tale. All of it. See if he can find Onur. If we find him before he reaches the other Kings, we kill him. And even if he does return, there is little love for Onur in the House of Kings. We may yet use that against him."

Azad paused. "Are you sure it wouldn't be better to leave Sharakhai?"

Ihsan turned and stared directly into her eyes. "I would rather die." Azad's worries began to melt the longer Ihsan stared. "We'll see our way through."

Azad nodded and left, resolved if nothing else.

Ihsan, meanwhile, turned and strode back to his balcony and looked out over Sharakhai, wondering, as the sun's first rays began to steal over the city, what the days ahead would bring.

Chapter 65

CEDA LIMPED THROUGH THE DESERT, one hand pressed to the wounds along her ribs. The chill of the long night had finally been burned away by the morning sun. It was nearing midday, and she'd been walking since leaving the place where she'd left Mesut's body, where she'd left Sehid-Alaz to whatever fate awaited him. How long ago that seemed. The passing of an age. The dawn of a new world.

She turned and looked back along her path, wondering when the Kings would find her. Surely they would. It was only a matter of time. But she would not give in. She refused to stop now.

She had killed another King. Two lay dead at her hands. Another had been killed by her mother. If the gods were kind a fourth, Cahil, would die from the wounds she and Sehid-Alaz had inflicted.

Remembering how well Cahil had healed from the tip of her poisoned arrow, she laughed, the sound strangely deadened in the open desert. The gods were anything but kind. "They are cruel!" she shouted to the desert wind. She spread her arms wide and spun while staring at the clear blue sky. "Do you hear me? The gods are cruel!"

She waited for their response, but none came save the skitter of spindrift and the sigh of the sand.

She drew her sword. "Do you fear to face me, then?" She lifted it high and shouted at the top of her lungs, "Do you fear me?" She swung her sword down, slapping the sand with the flat of the blade. An amber spray lifted into the air, beautiful in its simplicity, then fell. "Come now! Face me! I am but a mortal!" For a long while she waited, but the desert only listened until her anger waned.

She resumed her pace, sword still in hand, feeling dizzy from lack of water. All her planning and she hadn't thought to bring any water. At least she had her mother's book. She felt for it.

And found the pouch missing.

She stopped, dropped her sword. Her hands felt along her belt, over her battle dress. Breath of the desert, it was gone. She looked back along her path, then ran over the dunes, searching, wondering whether it had been buried as the dunes shifted.

The hole inside her where her mother had once been widened. Threatened to consume her. She would let it. She would see her mother again.

She stared along the horizon. Toward Sharakhai. Gods how she wished to return and sit at Ibrahim's feet and listen to him tell the tale of the desert's birth. How she wished she could watch the Haddah flow while leaning over Bent Man Bridge. But that was her past, wasn't it? Like water beneath a bridge, she could return to that place no longer.

She turned, stared at the dune where her sword had fallen. It glinted dully, a gift of the Kings, a symbol of their rule, but like her, might it not become something different? Might not its *own* fate have passed it by? Might it not look forward to a new day?

She strode toward it, refusing to look back. When she reached the dark shamshir she held it before her, the dents and nicks that marked its length clear beneath the bright sun. "Together, then, yes?"

She sheathed it and limped on across the sand, feeling another wave of dizziness wash over her. She knew the signs well. She knew she needed water, but she'd been so desperate last night to escape that she hadn't paid attention to her path. She might turn north, head for the aqueduct. She might climb it and drink the clear mountain water, but the chance of being spotted by the Silver Spears or the Maidens was too great. She thought of stopping at the blooming fields, but those too were dangerous. Any of the asirim, willingly or not, might alert the Kings to her presence. Or even some of the Maidens were they attentive enough to sense it.

So she trekked on, hoping to find one of the small oases whose locations were drilled into every Maiden. It would have been an easy journey if not for her wounds. But the hammer wound from Cahil ached. As did the one on her head that Yndris had inflicted with the same weapon. A dozen other wounds she felt with every step, but the cuts from Mesut's gauntlets were the most troubling. Those wounds felt hot. A terrible sign, but one she couldn't focus on. Not yet. Find water, she told herself over and over, and *then* she could deal with possible infection or poison.

She came to a ridge, hoping for any sign of a water source, a bit of green, birds circling above. But there were none. Only a small, empty valley. She climbed down, slipped along the rock, struck her head as she slid toward the bottom.

She woke some hours later, woozier than she'd been earlier. From the fall. From thirst. From her wounds. She didn't entirely know. She levered herself up and walked onward as the sun began to set. She would welcome the cool night air, but she didn't wish to stop. She needed water, before she rested, or she might never get up again.

The world threatened to tilt with every step. The wind picked up, occluding her path. She wasn't even sure she was headed in the right direction anymore.

She collapsed to her hands and knees as the sun began to fail. She stood and fell again not ten paces later. She felt the wound on her shin, but only vaguely, much as she could sense the sun beyond a bank of fog. She felt the other wounds as well, but now they were little more than scratches.

The deeper wounds from Mesut, however. *Those* she still felt. They were reaching into her, deeper and deeper, inching toward her heart. She tried one last time to rise, but it was too painful. She rolled over to face the sky. "You did well, memma," she said, thinking of Azad and his death. "We can trade tales, yes? Of the Kings we killed?"

She fell asleep reaching for her mother's hand.

She woke to the sounds of shuffling, of sand shifting. Footsteps coming nearer, but hesitantly. A Maiden? A King? She rolled over and saw a dark form crawling over the sand. It scuttled like a scarab, its yellowed eyes haunted.

"Kerim," she whispered.

He came closer. He knelt and held her hand, put the back of it against the blackened skin of his cheek. She could feel the sorrow within him. For her death, perhaps. Or Sehid-Alaz's. Or maybe it was sorrow for their people.

She could feel the conflict within him as well. This was not easy, what he was doing—leaving the service of the Kings—but a bond had formed between him and Çeda. It gave him some small amount of freedom. Perhaps that was what he lamented, the fact that Çeda would soon be gone, and his freedom with it.

"I need water," she said.

Kerim stared into her eyes, then looked about, scanning the horizon. He shuffled away as sleep took her once more.

A snuffling sound pulled her back from the land of dreams. A moment later a small yip broke the silence of the desert. She felt something licking her side. It tickled at first, but then it touched the wound, which was either poisoned or infected or both, and the pain became bright white. It immediately began to feel better, however. She opened her eyes. Stared at the thin morning clouds high above, row after row of them, like furrows in a field plowed by the gods themselves.

She rolled her head and saw a furry face staring at hers. Large ears. Long nose. Tall legs spread wide to lower its head.

A maned wolf. A white maned wolf. The one she'd seen with Emre on their first trip to the blooming fields. The one that had saved her from the black laughers after Dardzada had tattooed her back.

"And where have you come from?" she asked weakly.

The wolf huffed, its eyes wide, waiting for something, though Çeda knew not what. Twenty paces away, Kerim crouched at the top of a dune, the same turmoil still roiling inside him. He watched her and the wolf, shifting this way and that on the sand, as if his body demanded he leave this place.

"Are you hungry?" Çeda said to the white wolf. "I'm afraid I've nothing for you this time."

It reached down and closed its mouth around her arm. No, her sleeve. It tugged, then yipped, almost as if it wanted to play, then it ran off, losing itself behind a dune.

She groaned as she tried to get up, but her wounds flared to life, and a fresh wave of dizziness and nausea overtook her.

The wolf returned, bounding toward her, huffing again as it reached her side. It waited still as a statue as she reached up, as she pulled herself up by its coat. She managed to reach her feet this time. Gods, how tall it had become. Its shoulders were even with her chest. Its head was higher than hers.

Together, they walked toward the top of the dune. There, lying in the early morning sun, were a dozen other maned wolves with brown coats, red manes, black ears. She didn't know if all of them were the same, but she recognized the massive one with the scars along its muzzle. When it saw them, the scarred one howled, and the wolves all stood.

Off they went in a line, southeast.

Çeda and the white wolf followed. And Kerim came behind.

Acknowledgments

This book marks my sixth published novel and my ninth book written (ignoring those few false starts quite a few years ago). I was told it was going to get easier at some point. I'm still wondering when that's going to happen, because so far, each book seems every bit as hard as the last one, if not harder. *With Blood Upon the Sand* was certainly no exception. This was an ambitious novel. There was a lot of pressure for the second book in the series to move things forward in a strong and positive way. It was also a challenge to expand on the many threads that were introduced in *Twelve Kings in Sharakhai*. I'm proud of the result, and I hope you enjoyed it, but I certainly didn't do it alone. There are a lot of people to thank for helping me along the way.

First and foremost, I need to thank my wife, Joanne, and my two wonderful kids for carving out time for me to pursue this career. They sacrifice constantly for me, and I'm eternally grateful.

I'd like to put out a special shout-out to three people that put in a lot of time helping me to steer the ship. Paul Genesse, your help, as always, was crucial in finding the heart of the story, staying true to it, and accentuating it wherever I could. Rob Ziegler, thanks for the help overall in critiquing and plot bashing, but especially for your advice on the book's opening chapter. It was an addition that created shockwaves that were felt throughout the entire novel. And Justin Landon, thanks for your thoughts on the first third of the book in particular. Your feedback really made me strip the story down to its essentials to keep things moving.

Others read the book at various stages and provided valuable feedback. To Sarah Chorn, Tracy Erickson, Chè Adventure, and Femke Giesolf, thank you so much for reading this not-very-short manuscript and providing your thoughts on it. I truly appreciate it.

The entire team at DAW Books deserves a healthy round of applause for helping me with so many things along the way, from Betsy Wollheim providing not only editing, but art direction, publishing advice, and so many other things, to my copy editor, Marylou Capes-Platt, always kicking my proverbial arse to write better, to the endless efforts of the production staff, proof readers, marketing and sales, and others who helped with endless tasks that go along with bringing a book to market. Likewise, the Gollancz team have been terribly helpful, not only my UK editor, Gillian Redfearn, but the wonderful staff who help to get the books into the hands of readers; thank you so much for all your unsung efforts.

To my agent, Russ Galen, thank you for tending my career, bringing me along as I grow into this new profession. And thanks to Danny and Heather Baror for bringing the series to a wider audience worldwide. The very thought that my books are being read in multiple countries in multiple languages is a constant thrill for me.

Lastly, thank you to the fans, who have embraced Çeda and the larger tale of Sharakhai. Your support has been tremendous already. I can't wait to see where we take this series.